Honors for the first books of
LEGENDS OF THE GUARDIAN-KING

The Light of Eidon

Booklist
Top 10 Christian Novels 2004

ForeWord Magazine
*2003 Book of the Year—Silver
Science Fiction*

Christian Fiction Review
Best of 2003

Christy Award—2004
Fantasy

The Shadow Within

Borders
*Best of 2004
Religion and Spirituality*

Romantic Times
*Best of 2004 Finalist
Inspirational*

Christian Fiction Review
Best of 2004

Christy Award—2005
Visionary

Books by Karen Hancock

Arena

LEGENDS OF THE GUARDIAN-KING
The Light of Eidon
The Shadow Within
Shadow Over Kiriath

LEGENDS OF THE GUARDIAN-KING

KAREN HANCOCK

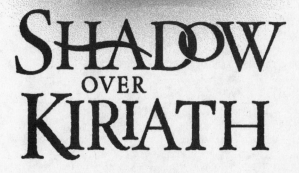

SHADOW
OVER
KIRIATH

BETHANYHOUSE
MINNEAPOLIS, MINNESOTA

Published by Bethany House Publishers
11400 Hampshire Avenue South
Bloomington, Minnesota 55438

Bethany House Publishers is a division of
Baker Publishing Group, Grand Rapids, Michigan.

Printed in the United States of America

Library of Congress Cataloging-in-Publication Data

Hancock, Karen.
    Shadow over Kiriath / Karen Hancock.
       p.   cm. — (Legends of the guardian-king ; 3)
    Summary: "Abramm's coronation is still underway, and rival leaders are plotting their return to power. Will Abramm hold onto victory, or will his enemies succeed in destroying his beloved realm?"—Provided by publisher.
    ISBN 0-7642-2796-3 (pbk.)
    1. Kings and rulers—Fiction. 2. Power (Social sciences)—Fiction.
3. Coronations—Fiction. I.Title. II. Series.
    PS3608.A698S537   2005
    813'.6—dc22   2005020515

KAREN HANCOCK has won Christy Awards for each of her first three novels—*Arena* and the first two books in this series, *The Light of Eidon* and *The Shadow Within*. She graduated from the University of Arizona with bachelor's degrees in biology and wildlife biology. Along with writing, she is a semi-professional watercolorist and has exhibited her work in a number of national juried shows. She and her family reside in Arizona.

For discussion and further information, Karen invites you to visit her Web site at *www.kmhancock.com*.

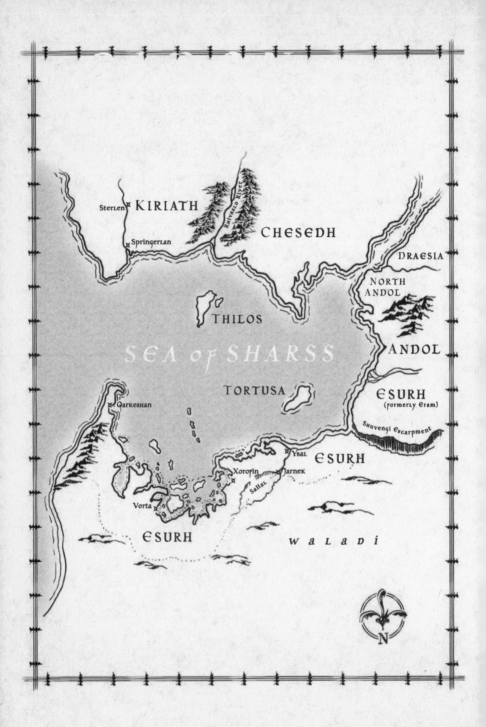

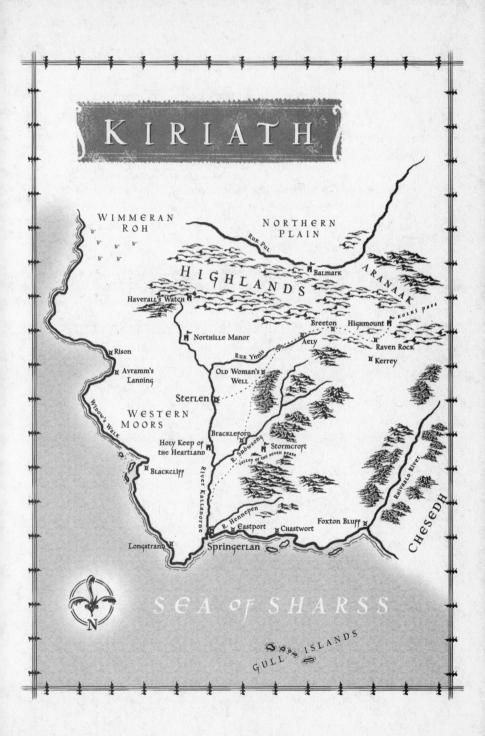

Do not fear the suffering that is to come. For some of you are about to be cast into prison by the Adversary, so that you may be tried. See it through for the time appointed, steadfast unto death, and I will grant you a crown of life. . . .

—From the *Second Word of Revelation*
Second Scroll of Parthas

PRELUDE

"ABRAMM KALLADORNE *will fall, Vesprit.*" The rhu'eman warhast Hazmul did not speak the thought aloud, but the breath of
his host body fogged the window glass before him anyway, blur-
ring his view of the snow-dusted Grand Fountain courtyard
below. In the gray light of the foggy early-spring morning, a
lengthening line of gleaming carriages queued up at Whitehill's
front entrance to his left, preparing for the coronation procession. *"If all goes as planned, that fall will begin today."* He sipped
from his porcelain teacup, then added, *"All is going as planned, I
trust?"*

Though his rhu'eman underling, Vesprit, stood behind him,
Hazmul didn't need to see him to sense the pleased confidence
rippling through the underwarhast's essence. *"It is, sir,"* Vesprit
replied.

"You've cracked the stone and awakened the miniol?"

"A couple of hours ago now."

Servants' voices drifted from the sitting room of Hazmul's
apartments. He ignored them. Human ears could not discern his
conversation with Vesprit any more than human eyes could discern their bodies. The servants would see only the fleshly host in
which Hazmul dwelt, standing at the window of his sumptuous
east-wing bedchamber sipping morning tea. Underwarhast

Vesprit would be a faint amber glow, unnoticed in the lamplight.

As the underwarhast began a recitation of all that had been attended to in preparation for this momentous day, Hazmul continued to sip his tea and watch the coaches gather, the end of their line soon disappearing into the fog. Down in the valley, the University clock tolled the half hour in a single deep tone. Hardly had it struck when the palace doors flew open and a party of nobles cloaked in furs and dark woolens emerged. They glided down the snow-dusted steps to the first carriage, head of the procession that would soon wind down to the Hall of Kings at Avramm's Mount. As its doors slammed shut and the vehicle sped away, the next one rolled immediately into its place.

A momentous day this was indeed, the culmination of weeks of preparation among friends and foes alike. Today Abramm Kalladorne, whom some called king of Light and others deemed servant of Shadow, would be officially and ceremonially crowned the thirty-sixth king of Kiriath. Today he would move among his people as he had not in all the six months since he had slain the morwhol, would stand before them arrayed in the full splendor of the royal regalia and receive the crown in all the solemn ritual and majesty Kiriathan tradition could muster. And in so doing, would either convince the masses he was indeed Eidon's choice or bitterly disappoint them with the proof that he was not.

It was Hazmul's intent that bitter disappointment soundly edge out any thrills or encouragement—a goal he had worked toward for six months now. With four thousand years of experience, he was well versed in the ways of destroying a man and took particular pride in his ability to neutralize those servants of the Enemy who crossed into the battlefield of their so-called destiny.

It was a great and intricate dance, an effort that took time, patience, cunning, ruthlessness . . . and the ability to exploit a man's weaknesses, day by day grinding away at his confidence. As king, Abramm had provided him many areas to exploit, but the richest had been the damage wrought by the morwhol. The day after its claws ripped through Abramm's face and arm, Hazmul had teased to life the latent spore it had left behind. Before long, Abramm's nearly-closed wounds had suppurated viciously, his natural spore-intolerance erupting into a raging defense that left him fevered and bedridden for almost a week. When it was over, his left arm was twisted with red, ropy scars, and the marks on his face were far from being the thin white lines his physician had predicted.

Now, after six months of living in denial, Abramm would face the reality of what he had become. Last night Hazmul had ignited his growing frustration with his arm into a confrontation with the one man able to really hurt him: his longtime friend and ally, Trap Meridon. Asked outright, Meridon had admitted he believed Abramm's arm to be irredeemably crippled, an assessment Abramm had not received with good grace.

Today he would see the rest of what had been done to him— the facial scarring he pretended was inconsequential. Already struggling to escape the mental morass of bitterness and self-pity into which Meridon's revelation had plunged him, Abramm's shock at seeing his new face should push him in so deep he would be helpless against the attack Hazmul had planned for the final act of today's little drama.

"*His aura this morning has been consistently blue-black and murky,*" Vesprit reported now, "*and the frequency of coruscation has fallen off dramatically. I don't see him recovering before the ceremony.*"

Hazmul turned his attention briefly to the tendril he'd had on the king since early last evening, confirming Vesprit's report. Abramm was still being dressed in the royal bedchamber. And while Hazmul could not read his thoughts at this distance—not an easy task even in the same room—Abramm's emotional state came through clearly in the low, throbbing tones of despair.

"*Probably not,*" he agreed, "*but I don't want to take any chances. He's surprised us too many times before.*" Below him the noblemen and their ladies flowed from the palace in an almost continuous stream to board their carriages and wheel away. "*What of Madeleine? Were you able to plant the images I suggested?*"

"*Her guardian put up a strong fight, but we prevailed.*" The frequency of Vesprit's essence intensified with admiration and approval. "*You called it perfectly, sir. We tapped something so strong it shocked her right out of the dream."* A trill of amusement whirled through Vesprit's vibrations as he added, *"Her aura was blue-white when she awakened, then immediately turned to scarlet."*

"Did she tell anyone what she'd dreamt?"

"Not a word. But she sat there in the bed for at least twenty minutes, her face in her hands, before the color returned to normal."

"Weeping?" Hazmul sipped again from his cup.

"No. She was more horrified and confused. And still aroused, despite it all. . . . She seemed unable to settle that part down." Vesprit paused. *"How did you guess her feelings for him were so strong, sir? We've all noted their attraction to one another but . . . we had no idea hers was that powerful. She had to have been hiding it even from herself."*

Hazmul allowed himself a small smile. *"I've had a lot of experience with these creatures."* He checked the tendril on Abramm again: still no change. *"You're sure she'll have no contact with the king this morning?"*

"She may not even attend the ceremony, sir. When I left, she was still in bed, her maid worried she'd taken ill."

"Good. Even a chance meeting in the hall could be disastrous. Her influence on him is too great."

"Don't worry, sir. We've got the double rank of guards on her as ordered, and her brother, that idiot Leyton, is on his way to her chambers as we speak. Though, truly, sir, I doubt she'll be able to look Abramm in the eye for days—let alone speak to him. She is as rattled as I've ever seen her. It was a masterful blow."

Again Hazmul nodded. *"Sounds like she'll be no help to him during the ceremony, either, which is what I'd hoped. . . . What about the miniol? Has anyone noticed it yet?"*

"No, sir. But even if they sensed something, it would never occur to them to inspect the stone."

Captured by Alaric the Bold six hundred years ago, the border stone had been set beneath the coronation chair to symbolize Kiriathan authority over the borderlands. A benign participant in countless Kiriathan coronations, no one had any reason to suspect it harbored an ancient evil that might one day rise to take its revenge. . . .

Hazmul asked a few more questions, gave Vesprit his final

instructions, then dismissed him. Below, the carriages continued to emerge from the fog to his right as others rolled away from the palace stairs to his left. About now they should be hitching up the king's vehicle, unaware that an illicit nighttime jaunt across the Royal Preserve in the hands of two witless stable boys had cracked its front axle—a crack that would be made manifest to all in about an hour or so.

Hazmul smiled at the moving carriages. It never hurt to put redundancies into one's plans.

He touched the tendril again and went alert with the change he sensed in it: sharp fear alternating with self-condemnation. The question of uncovering the bedchamber mirror had finally been asked. *Excellent. Are you going to look at them, Abramm?* he thought wryly. *Or are you too much of a coward?*

He waited, but nothing happened.

"Sir?" The human voice, startlingly loud, intruded upon his mental surveillance. He turned to find his manservant standing in the bedchamber doorway holding a heavy overcloak. "It's time," the man said.

With a sigh, Hazmul set his teacup on an end table and strode toward the servant. *Well, you rarely get everything to go as you wish, no matter how brilliant and well executed the plan.*

But just as the servant placed the cloak upon his master's shoulders, a shock of dismay and anguish leaped through Hazmul's connection with Abramm, the emotions so strong they made the rhu'ema's borrowed body shudder in sympathetic vibration. And brought a smile to his lips. *Then again, sometimes you do.*

THE
HALL
OF
KINGS

PART ONE

1

Earlier, as Hazmul had lingered in his east-wing apartment monitoring the king's emotional state, the king himself stood in the royal bedchamber, gritting his teeth against the pain and bitter humiliation of having his left arm tugged like a sausage through the sleeve of his diamond-crusted doublet. Though his valets had had to work with the stiff and withered limb for almost six months now, and Abramm was well accustomed to the pain that accompanied the way they had to bend and stretch it to get it into his sleeves, it all seemed worse today. Partly because his doublet's stiffness and tight cut made it especially difficult to don, and partly because the whole operation kept bringing to mind the bitter knowledge that his arm would never get any better. That he really *was* a cripple.

The garment settled onto his shoulders, its diamonds sparkling around him as Haldon tugged the front edges together and set to fastening the long line of buttons that held it close about Abramm's torso. Barely had he begun when, behind the ring of older servants, young Jared cried out and began stomping the life from yet another of the many staffid that had come after the king that morning. As he picked up the smashed carcass and went to throw it in the fire, a page hurried into the bedchamber, stopping in the spot Jared had vacated and dropping a quick bow.

"They said Lady Madeleine has not come by yet, sir," the blond lad reported breathlessly, speaking of the men on guard in the apartment's anteroom.

"Thank you, Harry." The intensity of his disappointment surprised him. After all, Maddie hadn't said she was coming, and he had no reason to expect her, busy as she had to be on this coronation day. But he'd grown accustomed to her checking in with him each morning, and though she could still annoy him to distraction, he found her presence buoying. And today he felt keenly the need to be buoyed.

In the half year since his triumph over the morwhol at the Valley of the Seven Peaks, nothing had gone right: the Mataio remained a threat, Gillard's supporters remained elusive, and every project Abramm had initiated to prepare for the coming Esurhite invasion was plagued with problems. While his nobles resented and sought to stymie his attempts to wrest aid from the Chesedhans on the one hand, fires, epidemics, food shortages, insane military commanders, shipyard accidents, and freak storms frustrated his efforts to build up Kiriathan defenses on the other.

Naturally, it hadn't taken the Mataio long to capitalize on the situation. Borne by anonymous pamphlets, its leaders' views flowed into Springerlan's streets and taverns, continually rehashing his many problems as they denounced him as a fraud, attacked his motives and his character, and gave specific voice to the doubt on everyone's mind these days: if Abramm *was* Eidon's choice, why had his reign been so obviously cursed?

Today's coronation was supposed to resolve the matter, the conferring of the regalia being a sign of divine anointing. Tradition required the ceremony be cleanly executed, however. Accidents, delays, embarrassing missteps, or bad weather would all be counted as ill omens. So would any fumbling with the regalia when they were bestowed, and Abramm had already dropped the practice Orb of Tersius several times during rehearsals. Those who wished him ill were predicting he would do it again today and thus provide "unequivocal proof" that Eidon's hand was against him.

In addition, Abramm's advisors believed Bonafil meant to denounce him openly during the ceremony itself, and all the Terstans on his cabinet were convinced he would come under direct rhu'ema attack, as well. To face all that, he must be strong and confident in the Light. But after the barrage of difficulties that had assaulted him in the last day or so, he was about as deep into the Shadow's grip as he'd ever been.

Yesterday had begun as this one had: without Lady Madeleine's morning appearance. That was followed by a nasty argument with his uncle over the Chesedhan treaty, then yet another practice wherein he dropped the orb, not once but three times. He'd spent the midday meal brooding over it all, fighting to break free of the Shadow's increasingly protracted holds on him.

Then, as if timed to arrive precisely when it would do the most damage, a copy of the latest pamphlet was delivered to his hands. The most vitriolic yet, it pointed out that not only had Eidon failed to bless Abramm's projects, he'd also declined to heal him of his wounds, leaving him hideously scarred and maimed for life. *Why,* the writer had asked, *would this be so when Eidon's own Words of Revelation demand that his servants be without flaw?*

Even before Abramm finished reading, he knew who had authored it: rhu'ema. Yes, the elusive Darak Prittleman was doubtless the human vector, but this was far too close to the mark to have come from anyone but the rhu'ema—both in the words and in the timing. Even knowing that, he'd been knocked solidly into the Shadow's control, from which he'd initiated that misbegotten conversation with Trap Meridon and come face-to-face with a reality he'd long suspected but been unable to consider until now: that he was, indeed, permanently crippled. The thought still made his stomach churn and brought cold sweat to his brow.

Haldon finished buttoning the doublet, adjusted the cravat, then pulled sharply at the cuffs of Abramm's underblouse while Smyth fastened the five golden chains of Abramm's kingly rank across his chest and Durstan belted on the empty sword harness. As they laid the red velvet cloak across his shoulders, a staffid that had infiltrated its folds scurried down his arm. Haldon immediately knocked the vermin away, and this time young Harry had the honor of stomping it to death as Abramm's valets stood by looking pale, chagrinned, and frustrated. They had searched his bedchamber numerous times this morning but failed to find nest or sack. Bowls of onions had been placed throughout Abramm's apartments, yet still the things came, as if materializing from the air itself.

"It's all right," Abramm said, wrist tingling with the spawn's proximity. "We'll solve this mystery later. For now, let's proceed."

And so they did, Haldon tying the cloak across Abramm's chest as the others pulled and straightened the garment's train around his feet. When all was properly arranged and no more staffid had appeared, they stepped back to assess the results of their efforts, studying him with silent, grave expressions.

Finally, he frowned at his grand chamberlain. "That bad, is it?"

Haldon gave a start, then a ghost of a smile. "Hardly, sir. You look magnificent." He gestured to the full-length mirror draped in heavy white linen. "Would you like to see for yourself?"

Every man in the room gasped, gazes flying to the chamberlain in alarm, while Haldon himself paled and gulped with astonishment as if he, too, couldn't believe what he'd said. It was only then that Abramm acknowledged the mirror had been covered for months and he'd never once commented on it. Nor had he told anyone to uncover it.

"Was it your idea to drape the mirror, Hal?" he asked, nodding at it.

A red flush replaced the pallor in Haldon's weathered cheeks.

" 'Twas Count Blackwell's idea, sir," Smyth volunteered, when Haldon couldn't find his tongue. "Though we all agreed he was right in not wanting to add to your distress. We planned to wait until you asked." He flicked a glance at the chamberlain, whose gaze was now fixed upon a point beyond Abramm's shoulder.

"But I didn't ask, did I?" Abramm said.

Haldon's Adam's apple bobbed. "No, sir. I don't know what I was thinking to suggest we unveil it now."

And after Trap's revelation last night, I certainly don't need to have my nose rubbed in any more of my losses. My mood is foul enough as it is.

Good advice, and he almost took it. Until he realized what a coward he must look to these men—afraid even to look at his own face!—and ordered it uncovered after all.

Haldon's eyes darted to his own, his long, wrinkled face frowning. But he only said, "Yes, sir," before grasping a fold of the linen and stepping back. The pale fabric rippled free to reveal the wooden-framed reflection of a tall, blond, straight-backed man dressed in white, his diamond-covered doublet glittering in the lamplight beneath the crimson robe flowing from his shoulders. The diamonds and velvet and golden chains of rank, the powerful shoulders and commanding stance, the stern brow and determined set of the jaw all hit him in a half-heartbeat of time, bearing a sense of strength and regality that hardly registered as his eyes focused on the face and horrified shock swept away all else.

Twin tracks of shiny red scar tissue, the inner one thicker and more ragged than the outer, slashed the familiar features from brow to jaw, in no way "barely noticeable." Discomfort writhed within him, pressing him to turn away. Disbelief held him steady as his left hand lifted to awkwardly stroke the scars, fingertips rough along their tight and tender length.

"They're so wide," he murmured, "and red." *I never should have let them shave the beard. At least I'd have something to mask them with, even if Maddie doesn't think the wild mountain look appropriate. Better that than this.*

"It's only been six months, sir," Haldon said quietly.

"They'll draw every eye like filings to a lodestone. The Mataio will have the happiest day of its history." His arm fell back to his side.

No wonder they're saying I can't be Eidon's. . . . And when I go out there today, when they all finally see me for themselves, they'll be more convinced than ever the lies are true.

He found himself struggling to breathe, hands trembling, knees weak and wobbling. Anguish wailed through him. *Why have you done this, my Lord? I trusted you!*

A thumping of footfalls preceded the arrival of Shale Channon, captain of Abramm's Royal Guard. He burst into the bedchamber full of trouble to report, but the moment he saw Abramm standing among his valets he stopped to stare, wide-eyed and slack-jawed. Another wave of painful self-consciousness seared through Abramm's soul. Then he took hold of himself, the effort sharpening his voice as he asked Channon why he was there.

The captain drew himself upright. "Sir, the front axle o' yer carriage has broken. It canna be fixed, and so—"

"Broken? Didn't you inspect it just yesterday?"

"Aye, sir. The master o' coachmen is guessin' a crack, sir. Prob'ly got wet when the coach was washed yesterday an' didna dry completely. When the temperature dropped last night with this storm, it froze and split the wood. 'Tis Eidon's mercy alone the thing slid off the lane comin' up from the coach house. Otherwise it surely would've snapped when ye hit th' drop goin' into Talwether Square. And what a mess that would be."

A mess and a mishap of gargantuan proportion. A sure sign of Eidon's displeasure with Kiriath's newest king. Not that anyone would need additional confirmation after one look at his face. Chagrin piled upon chagrin. Maybe he should just cancel this whole thing, abdicate as half the realm wanted him to, and leave the rule to Gillard. Even if he was lying unconscious in the Chancellor's Tower.

"With all th' carriages in use," Channon went on, "Princess Carissa has offered ye hers. She'll take Prince Leyton's, who'll move with Lady Madeleine t' Duke Simon's, who'll take either Duke Oswain's or th' one we've reserved for Cap'n Meridon after the ceremony. They're working it out now."

Which would cause a dreadful delay and birth a host of bruised egos and hard feelings. . . . Again he thought of turning his back on it all.

And wouldn't your enemies love that? asked a dry, familiar voice at the back of his mind. *They win the final confrontation by default. But, then, you know as well as anyone that the best way to win a war is not to have to fight it at all—or have you forgotten that you are fighting a war here?* An invisible war, of course, fought against the unseen rhu'eman enemies who were unquestionably responsible for all that had befallen him of late. The broken carriage would be laughably obvious, if not for the serious repercussions it carried.

Jared had been whispering into Haldon's ear, and now the white-haired chamberlain straightened from their conversation and cleared his throat. "Perhaps His Majesty could dispense with the carriage altogether," he said when the captain looked at him, "and ride Warbanner, instead."

Channon's eyes widened. "Warbanner's been in the pasture all week, m' lord. He'll be muddy and shaggy and—"

"Apparently not." Haldon glanced down at Jared, who squared his shoulders under the combined gazes of captain and king.

"We brought him in yesterday, sir," the young man said to Abramm. "Gave him a bath and a trim, combed out his mane and tail, and left him in a clean box stall in the Green stable."

"We?" Abramm asked.

"Philip Meridon and me, sir. And Lady Madeleine. It was her idea, in fact. Said it wouldn't hurt to have him ready in case something went wrong."

Madeleine. That explained how they'd handled Banner. Maddie had an uncanny touch with the horse. And an uncanny ability to anticipate Abramm's needs—though he doubted her actions yesterday were solely about that. More likely she was trying to escape her brother, Prince Leyton, with whom she'd fought that morning. And it would be just like Maddie to spend the day before the most important social event of the year down in the stables washing a horse. The thought almost made him smile.

"I do na think it'd be proper for ye to ride to yer coronation on a war-horse, sir," said Captain Channon, frowning. " 'Twill be called an ill omen."

"And my broken carriage will not?" Abramm shook his head. "No. War-banner is clearly the better solution. And frankly, I'd rather ride than sit in a carriage."

"I'll see to it, then, sir."

Channon took his leave, and with him went the brief respite Abramm had enjoyed in his presence, even if he had brought news of trouble. At least the carriage hadn't broken on the way to the Hall of Kings. And Maddie's fore-sight in preparing Warbanner was a welcome development indeed. A thread of hope wove through his despair. Maybe things wouldn't turn out as badly as he feared.

He noted the mirror looming to his right, its reflected figure tauntingly vague at the edge of his vision. Maybe the scars weren't as bad as he'd first thought them, either. Maybe the shock of seeing them for the first time had made them seem wider and redder than they really were. Maybe another look would be more objective, give him reassurance.

It did not. Confronting that face in the mirror again only showed the scars as raw and savage as ever. Again they knocked his thoughts reeling and made him want to crawl out of his own skin. Whatever relief he'd enjoyed through the distraction of the carriage incident and his amused affection for Maddie's ministrations was lost in a renewed storm of bitter despair. *That cannot be me. Surely that is not me.*

"Sir, truly they are not as bad as you think," Haldon said quietly. "We all have become so accustomed to them we hardly see them anymore, and . . . they're nothing to be ashamed of, anyway."

"Eidon does not scar and maim his servants, Hal."

"That passage refers to a different time and mode of service, as I am sure you are aware, sir. In truth, Eidon has dealt quite a few hurts to his servants, all in the name of their blessing and his glory."

"I see very little of either in this situation," Abramm retorted. "And when I go out there in the next few moments, everyone will see the Mataians and the pamphleteer are right. For how can I be Eidon's and look like this?"

Haldon looked at him very directly, swallowed once, then jerked up his chin and said, "No, sir. The question is how you can be Eidon's and *think* like this!"

Abramm stared at him, shocked by the stern challenge in his voice as the other servants gaped in astonishment. Then his anger flared. He was about to erupt when the dry mental voice said, *Why don't you save that energy for your real enemies and pay attention to what this man is saying? Or do you really mean to give it over to them without a fight? Whining and mewing like a babe, simply because you're not as pretty as you once were.*

That's not it!

Then why are you making such a fuss?

Abramm's gaze switched from Haldon to the image of himself in the mirror.

You said once that you would accept whatever Eidon made of you, observed the voice in his head. *That you would give up everything you had for his sake. Apparently you didn't really mean it.*

I did mean it! I just . . . didn't think he would do this.

And that was the sticking point. Deep down, he had not believed Eidon would cripple him. So long as he maintained his devotion to the Light and the Words and worked very hard, he'd counted on being rewarded with a full recovery. When the time came to go before his people to be crowned, he'd expected to be whole and well, astonishing everyone with the power of his God.

Instead his arm was truly crippled and his face forever scarred, and Eidon had let it happen. *For my blessing and his glory. . . .*

He stared at his lean, hawkish countenance, at the twin tracks of scarlet that slashed it, struggling to comprehend how this could be for his blessing, struggling to find even a vapor of comfort in the thought. But he found only bitterness and fear, rising by the moment as he realized he would soon have to go before his people and show them what Eidon had made of his "servant."

He closed his eyes, blotting out the scarred face, the surrounding servants with their pitying expressions, the velvet brocade drapes and the mahogany sideboard.

Down in the valley, the University clock began to toll the hour as across the room the door opened and closed. Soft footfalls approached, a whispered exchange ensued, and after a moment Haldon cleared his throat.

"Sir?" he said quietly. "They're ready for you now."

2

With the strains of Mandeville's *Second Concerto* ringing in the air around her, Lady Madeleine Abigail Clarice Donavan, Second Daughter of the Chesedhan King Hadrich, finally reached the bottom of the Hall of Kings' sloping central aisle and turned right. Heart thumping against her ribs, she angled across the open forestage in time to the music, her brother, Crown Prince Leyton, at her side. Together they headed for the royal box beside the granite outcropping that was the hall's stage. In the eastern alcove beside them, an audience glared down at them, just like the larger audience now at her back had glared as she and Leyton had come down the aisle. At least no one had thrown anything or shouted insults. Yet.

Leyton led the way up a short stair into the velvet-swagged box and along the front row to Simon Kalladorne's side, where he pivoted to face forward. Maddie followed suit, leaving the chair immediately to her left the only one in the box still waiting to be claimed. A raft of the highest nobles in the land stood on the risers behind her, their hostile gazes beating against the back of her neck. Few of them liked her much, anyway, and seeing her standing as her sister's substitute in the place of highest honor beside Kiriath's own crown princess only made things worse.

Leyton Donavan had arrived three days before the coronation with the news that his father, King Hadrich, had agreed to the marriage alliance Abramm had proposed. Seeing as the prospective bride would not arrive for at least another month, everyone believed they'd be discussing the matter for weeks. Instead, not twenty-four hours after Leyton's arrival, Abramm had shocked them all by putting his own signature to the treaty. His privy counselors—and everyone else, for that matter—were still reeling from the speed of it all.

Even Maddie had been surprised.

Surprised. *There* was an understatement.

The thought knotted her stomach and stirred dangerous memories of last night's dream—the kind you wanted to forget the moment you woke up and realized it *was* a dream, because you would never do the things you had done in it. In fact, it was hard for Maddie to accept the fact she'd even *dreamt* of doing them. And yet the very passion that had made the thing so scandalizing had also burned its images indelibly into her mind. . . .

He stood before her in the practice hall, holding her hands and gazing into her eyes. Even though Briellen stood nearby chatting with the courtiers, Maddie could not make herself look away, not even when his hand slid about her waist and pulled her to him—

Oh plagues! Think of something else.

Grimly, she focused on the rough granite stage below, the High Table of the Regalia to her right and the tall-backed Coronation Chair directly before her. To her left, just beyond where the granite sheared down to meet the carpeted forestage, stood the Receiving Throne on its five-stepped dais. Beyond it, a sea of faces flowed up the natural amphitheater along which the Hall of Kings had been built. Vertical white banners bearing Abramm's dragon-and-shield coat of arms dangled above the restless crowd. At the height of the slope, a drapery-lined passageway beneath temporary wooden balconies led in from the front anteroom. Kiriath's crown princess was just now emerging from its opening to start down the aisle. Once she had taken her place in the royal box, Abramm would begin his own procession.

The thought quickened Maddie's pulse and sent warmth flooding through her again. . . .

Leyton leaned against her to murmur something, and she flinched, embarrassment flaming her face. Thankfully, he was looking toward the back of the stage, and she could gather her scattered thoughts without having to field questions about what was wrong with her.

Then she saw what he was looking at and realized she needn't have worried: the regalia. Or, more specifically, the Crown of State, looming above the other implements on the white silk cloth. To hear Leyton talk about the crown, you'd think the thing had been sent by Eidon himself, when it was clearly just an ostentatious monstrosity designed by men to impress other men. Its heavy gold base and transverse arches were cluttered with jewels of all shapes and sizes—its maker obviously ascribing to the "more is better" aesthetic. But Leyton was obsessed with it and oblivious to the way his constant talk of it only increased the paranoia of a court that had already openly suggested he'd come to steal it. She'd tried to warn him, but as always, he'd waved her off.

Disgusted, she returned her attention to Carissa, who was now halfway down the aisle. Behind her, blue-tunicked royal guardsmen lined up in double ranks along the first quarter of the aisle in preparation for the king's arrival, while on the narrow balconies in the side walls overlooking the crowd, trumpeters moved into position, their brass instruments flashing against all the gray. Very soon, assuming the disaster of the broken carriage had truly been absorbed and accounted for, the trumpeters would blare out a fanfare and Abramm himself would appear up there where the guardsmen were now.

As her heart stuttered into double time again, she took herself to task. *He's got a coronation to worry about. He's not going to be paying attention to you, so how could he possibly learn about that ridiculous dream? You're being silly.*

Unless it wasn't just nerves and embarrassment she was feeling. Unless the dream revealed more about her true desires than she wanted to admit, and some of this was actually—

It was just a dream, she told herself firmly.

So why did you dream it? Where did it come from?

I don't know. Maybe Leyton's harangue from yesterday morning set it off. He'd run afoul of the rumors that she'd been one of Abramm's paramours and had taken her to task for three long hours, undeterred by her repeated and fervent denials. *Or maybe . . . maybe the rhu'ema put it in my head.*

Why would they do that?

I don't know. But they must've. Because it wasn't me.

You've been attracted to him since the day you laid on eyes on him.

Only because he was the White Pretender. And the killer of the kraggin—

And strong and smart and honorable, and not too bad looking, either.

No, not bad looking at all . . . but so what? I'm not some Lovesick Sessily looking for her man. I don't even want a man. Least of all a king. Which is precisely why this dream couldn't have come from me. It was all out of character. Where would I even get the material for it? I've hardly ever been kissed, let alone—

Plagues! Her thought veered away from yet another all-too-available memory as embarrassment choked her. *Why do you keep thinking about this?*

It was only a dream and it means nothing. Put it out of your mind and leave it there!

The wooden planks of the temporary box shook under her feet as Carissa climbed the outer stair and stepped into the royal box to claim the last velvet-cushioned chair. The musicians reached the end of their selection, and everyone looked up at the trumpeters. But the men did not move, and after a brief hesitation the orchestra launched into yet another piece.

Carissa sat down, and everyone else followed her lead in a great rustling of satin and silk. As the music spilled into the vast hall, the princess leaned against Maddie's left shoulder and asked quietly, "How did you know the axle would break?"

Maddie turned to her. "I didn't."

"They're saying you did."

"And I suppose they think I caused it, too."

"Well, it was extraordinarily prescient of you to have gotten that horse ready."

"After everything that's been going wrong, it only made sense to have a backup. And I had the time to do it." She said this last quietly, lest Leyton hear her. He had been furious at his inability to track her down yesterday after his morning harangue—naturally it hadn't occurred to him to look in the work stable for her.

Carissa cocked a brow. "Every other noblewoman in the land is about to gasp herself into a fainting fit with the pressure of preparing for this day and you had time to bathe a horse." She shook her head. "It's a good thing you're the *Second* Daughter and not the First. You wouldn't last one day as queen."

Maddie snorted and turned her gaze to the rank of stone statues across the stage from them. "I wouldn't even try." Her sister, Briellen, was the one who had been groomed for that position, and Maddie well remembered all the lessons on language and diplomacy and deportment. She remembered the restrictions as well: princesses who would be queen did not climb the masts, or swing out of the stable loft on a rope, or play in the mud by the catfish stream. Certainly they must never ride a horse bareback and astride, nor milk a cow, nor clean up manure. Princesses were not to speak their minds, must not read too much, or talk too much, or be too silent. Singing in public was unacceptable, and the making of songs was beneath them. Above all else they must be obedient. Or else learn how to manipulate those in authority over them so they might look as if they were obeying.

"You dreamt of Abramm last night, didn't you?" Carissa said, breaking into her thoughts.

Maddie had no idea how she managed not to flinch. *Oh, Eidon, please. She didn't share it, did she? I will die of shame. I will absolutely die.*

Shortly after Abramm had slain the morwhol, the two women had discovered their mutual connection to his dreams. Maddie had not thought this was one of them, and now she felt about to choke on the fear she'd been wrong.

"After what Meridon told him yesterday," Carissa went on blithely, "it's hardly surprising he'd dream of fencing. Even that bizarre contest for your sister's hand makes sense."

Horror prickled across Maddie's skin, for her own dream had involved her sister and the fencing practice room, too.

"What did Meridon tell him?" Maddie asked warily.

Carissa was frowning at the white-robed Mataians seated in the front row of the main audience and now turned back to Maddie with raised brows. "You didn't see Abramm this morning?"

"I barely made it to the palace entryway in time for the procession. You would not believe the troubles I had this morning." *Troubles facing my maid, troubles getting out of bed, troubles looking at myself in the mirror, troubles being here at all. . . .* "What happened?"

Before Carissa could answer, a muffled boom that sounded as if it had come from up in the anteroom drew their attention. It was apparently nothing, most likely a door slamming or some partition falling over. But long after Maddie had made that deduction, the crown princess continued to stare toward the main hall. Just as Maddie was about to ask her what was so interesting, she turned back and finally answered Maddie's question.

"Last night after practice Abramm made Captain Meridon tell him what he really thought about him getting back use of his arm."

Maddie gaped in horror. She knew very well what Meridon thought about Abramm's chances of a full recovery.

"Abramm asked him outright," Carissa said. "It wasn't like he had a choice."

"Certainly he had a choice. He knows the future no more than Abramm does. And neither he nor Channon are even remotely objective about it. They act like he's made of glass." She shook her head, trying to calm the fury that gripped her. Of all the stupid, arrogant, impossible things to say! How could he have done such a thing? Bad enough to think it, but to actually—

She groaned aloud as a new thought hit her. Abramm had probably seen the scars on his face this morning, too, which would only make it worse.

Guilt at not having checked in with him assailed her with bitter force.

"They're just afraid he's going to get sick again," Carissa murmured.

"Well, it's ridiculous. His illness was spawn-induced. He's over it now. Why don't they back off and let him be who he is?"

"It was hard seeing him so close to death, Mad."

Maddie kept her eyes fixed upon the coronation chair below, its dark Hasmal'uk stone peeping out from the shelf beneath the cushioned seat. She knew far too well how hard it had been to see him like that. Harder still having no one to share her terror with.

"I think it shocked them to realize how close we were to losing him," Carissa said. "And then to find he'd lost so much. . . ." She glanced back toward the Mataians again.

"Well, locking him in a closet is hardly going to change anything." Maddie frowned and craned her head around Carissa's form. "What are you looking at over there?"

The princess sat back sheepishly. She hesitated, then let out her breath and said, "That man there at the end of the row of Mataians—the big one sitting all hunched over. Does he look . . . odd to you?"

"No more so than any of them. Except perhaps for his bold and flawless posture." Sarcasm sharpened her tone.

Carissa snorted agreement.

"Why do you ask?" Maddie pressed.

"I think he's watching me."

"I doubt he can even see you from where he's sitting. Besides, his face is hidden in that cowl, so how would you know?" Maddie glanced again at the big man, who was, she realized now, sitting directly aligned with Carissa, his line of sight unobstructed by the royal box. But why would he be watching her? Just to unnerve her?

In point of fact, High Father Bonafil's young apprentice, Brother Eudace, *was* watching them, his weird blue eyes driving a chill up her spine. Big and luminous, they reminded her of fish eyes, cold and almost inhuman.

Her thoughts returned suddenly to something Carissa had said earlier—about expecting Maddie to have gone to Abramm this morning to repair the damage Trap had done. The truth was, even if she'd known about it, she wouldn't have gone. Because of the dream.

Meridon had no doubt cursed his loose lips all night, for it was truly not the sort of thing he was given to saying. And it was unusual for Abramm to have pressed him so insistently. Abramm knew how important it was that he himself go into this coronation with confidence and courage.

Her breath hissed softly over her teeth. *I knew that dream didn't originate with me. It* was *the rhu'ema.* They wanted her flustered and off balance so she *couldn't* go to Abramm this morning. . . .

They're manipulating all of us to get to him, she realized. *He* is *going to be attacked today. Somehow, someway, in this place.*

She glanced again at the Mataians, most of whom were apparently praying now, amulets glowering at their throats. She knew what sort of beings lived in those amulets. Her eye flicked up to the hammerbeam ceiling. Were more of them swirling around up there?

Suddenly another part of all this came clear to her, another reason why she'd been assaulted with that dream. It wasn't simply her visits with Abramm in the morning that distinguished her relationship with him. There was also the link through Eidon's Light they shared, something stronger even than the dream connection he shared with Carissa.

But . . . *Oh, Eidon! How can I possibly reach out to him today?* She didn't think she'd even be able to look at him without thinking things she had no business thinking. And to get that close . . . *Oh, please. Don't make me do that.*

At that moment the musicians completed their air and paused again. Conversation melted away, and as the last notes faded to silence, a roar arose from the square outside. She glanced again at the ceiling and shivered with foreboding.

Then on the balconies above the crowd, the trumpeters snapped to attention, their long brass horns held lengthwise before their bodies. The roar grew louder and her heart flew into her throat.

He's here!

3

As Abramm rode into the people-packed square outside the ancient Hall of Kings at the northwest end of the Mall of Government, the crowd's roar buffeted him like a flock of birds, wings beating at him from all sides. The moist low-hanging clouds reflected their cheers so loudly his ears rang and his insides quivered. Warbanner pranced and sidled beneath him, shaking his head and snorting at the fluttering hats and kerchiefs and homemade shield-and-dragon banners. A roped cordon had kept spectators at bay until now, but here the crowd had squeezed passage down to the bare minimum.

A coach would have kept them back and eliminated the worry of someone being injured by the temperamental warhorse, but Abramm wouldn't have changed it for anything. Riding Warbanner was the best thing he could have done. His left arm might not be able to button a doublet or clasp an orb, or even hold a dagger firm against the incoming thrust of a sword, but he could still ride, could still control the fiery young stallion with ease. That, coming after Haldon's challenge and the words of the dry mental voice whose origin he wasn't quite sure of, had done much to right his thinking and restore his confidence—if not in himself, then at least in Eidon. For Eidon was the one who had brought him to this day, and he knew that, whether anyone else did or not.

He followed the path through the surging crowd, winding around a central statue clogged with onlookers and on to the bank of stairs ascending to the portico of the Hall of Kings. There he dismounted, bemused to find himself wishing he could ride into the building and all the way to the stage. *As if a dumb beast can help me where the sovereign God of creation cannot. . . .*

Once inside he stopped midway across the Hall's narrow antechamber so his attendants could remove his fur-lined outer cloak and pull out the train of scarlet velvet that had been pinned up for his ride, the whisper of their movements echoing in the well of its empty, high-ceilinged space. Directly ahead of him stood the velvet-hung corridor beneath the temporary balconies, framing a glimpse of the Hall itself. The audience there would receive him far more critically than the one he'd just passed through, many of them still angry about the marriage treaty.

His train in place, Abramm's attendants stepped back and the men at the door looked to him expectantly. Dread shivered through him. Then, drawing a deep breath, he straightened his shoulders, lifted his chin, and strode forward. The men ahead turned to signal others, and as he stepped through the opening at the end of the balcony passway, the trumpets blared and the entire audience in that vast hall stood and turned toward him.

A sea of wide-eyed faces stared at him beneath descending ranks of long white banners, and suddenly he could hardly breathe. The steeply sloping central aisle seemed half a league long, the Receiving Throne on its stepped pyramidal dais at the end of it shrunken with distance. Having to march with agonizing slowness to keep time with the orchestra's majestic processional, he saw over and over the dropped jaws and the widened eyes of surprise, and with every step grew increasingly aware of his uneven gait and the way his arm kept curling up at his side. His scars burned so fiercely he thought they must be glowing.

It was daunting and suffocating and overwhelming . . . and yet there were moments when his awareness shifted off of himself and the people reacting to him and onto the hall in which he walked and the fact he was here to be crowned king of the land in the full glory of Kiriathan tradition. Something as unthinkable as this had seemed impossible not even a year ago. Eidon had brought him here, no question of that.

Finally the end of the long aisle drew near, white-robed Mataians on his right in the front row, Trap Meridon in the aisle seat across from them: the place of honor for a man who had stood by his king through betrayal, slavery, and civil war, and would for that service be elevated to the peerage today. He met Abramm's glance evenly, no sign of guilt or wavering, despite the rift between them. But that had always been Trap's way.

Abramm angled past the Receiving Throne and on toward the granite mount, noting the Mataians' glares as he passed them. That they were present and so openly hostile gave credence to his fear Bonafil meant to challenge him today. Might as well prepare himself to meet it, for all the ugly marring of this ceremony that would produce.

With the royal box looming ahead to his right, he climbed the short stair and stepped onto the ancient granite stage. The moment he did, he felt the unmistakable sense of unseen, malevolent eyes opening in grim welcome. His Terstan advisors were right: it wasn't only the Orb and Bonafil he'd have to deal with today. . . .

At the mount's edge, he turned back to face the great hall, his gaze flicking up to the shadowy network of beams overhead as the chief herald's voice boomed through the heights, announcing his arrival and asking if the people would accept him.

They were supposed to burst out with a cheer of acclamation at this point. Instead, the herald's voice faded into an accusatory silence that instantly returned Abramm's attention to the crowd. The Mataians stood in the first rank across the forestage from him, closed-mouthed and smirking, their arms crossed upon their chests. His gaze drifted to the people beyond them, shock stealing his breath. Would they refuse to accept him? Would this crowning be over before it even started?

Then a single voice rang out: "I accept him." A few echoed it, then more, the numbers gradually increasing until the majority of those present had approved. But it was a lukewarm acclamation, more dutiful than heartfelt, and it left him profoundly shaken. He turned to cross the granite toward the Robing Station just below the royal box, where the Keeper of the Regalia and his deputies waited. His train hissed loudly in the silence, and hostility pressed at him from every quarter, so that his stomach churned and his scars burned hotter than ever.

As he drew up before the Keeper of the Regalia, Lord Fortesque, the two deputies came round behind him to remove his scarlet cloak. Fortesque held a stiff floor-length garment supposed to represent Eidon's Light, though it looked more like the wire mesh garment Abramm had suffered through the rehearsals with this last week. His cloak removed, Abramm turned toward the Robing Chair, seeing peripherally the nobles still standing in the royal box behind it. Muffled coughs and low creaks occasionally broke the silence as Fortesque slid the robe's stiff sleeves up Abramm's left arm first, then his right. At last it settled onto his shoulders, suddenly fluid and supple as if it were made of heavy silk. Startled and a little irked they'd made him use the awkward and uncomfortable practice garment, he turned his back to the chair and saw all three of the officials staring at the robe in open-mouthed

And somehow the rod came to lie along Abramm's arm, right where it was supposed to.

The Fortesque ghost disappeared, then wavered back into view carrying a thick clot of shadow. The orb! It must be the Orb of Tersius. The orb Abramm was going to drop the moment Fortesque laid it in his hand. That would roll off his palm and shatter on the granite beneath his feet.

Fortesque held out the clot. The buzzing increased and the shadow coils tightened further, so that Abramm's breath came now in small pantings. Bizarre images flooded his mind—glowing spheres hanging in darkness, trees big as towers, strange, monstrous creatures walking among them. He felt the frenzied eagerness of the thing in the rock poised to invade his flesh and told himself that was not possible. The Words promised he could not be taken with the Light living inside him. . . .

Somehow through all the confusion, he saw his left hand extend, palm up as if nothing were amiss, felt something cool and slick and heavy settle into it. And stay there.

It began to dawn on him that Eidon *was* working here. That what he was doing, he did regardless of rhu'eman distractions and threats—and Abramm's own failure to withstand them. . . . And rightly so. Neither his life nor his service had ever been about his own ability and strength. Whatever his failures, they'd all been dealt with on that Hill of Reckoning outside Xorofin, and Eidon was never the one who accused and condemned. Only his enemies did that. The rhu'ema. The Shadow within him. Eidon already knew what he was and had long since forgiven him.

As Abramm's frame of thinking shifted, it was as if scales fell from his eyes. The clot of darkness dissolved, revealing the smooth milk-crystal sphere that was the orb lying in his palm. As he stared at it, its surface brightened steadily until it became a globe of brilliant white. *A kelistar?* he thought, squinting at it. *Why confer upon me a kelistar? And why is it so heavy?*

He looked up. Fortesque had been replaced by a lean sober-faced man with close-cropped white hair and a face scarred even worse than Abramm's. Abramm hardly noticed the scars, however, caught by the man's eyes, which were dark as the night sky and every bit as deep. Familiar eyes. *My Lord Tersius?*

He should not be sitting here, staring dumbfounded. He should be out of this chair and falling on his face. But he could not move—even though, he realized suddenly, the thing in the rock had released him, retracting its black

surprise. Only then did he realize the wire practice robe really had borne a close approximation to the original. Until today.

He sat in the simple wooden chair and the robe swirled like water around him, sending a chill of wonder up his spine. Meanwhile those in the royal gallery sat down in a symphony of creaking and rustling, followed by the rest of the audience in a vast, extended susurration. Abramm did not think that any in the audience, save perhaps those nobles closest to the front of the box, had noticed the robe's change.

He eyed the white gold weave draped over his thighs. What did it mean? Would he have Eidon's special protection today?

Laughter erupted in his skull, high-pitched and mocking. *Eidon's protection! How naïve. . . . How presumptuous. . . .*

The voice drew his eye to the tall, narrow Coronation Chair, now forward of his position on the stage. On a shelf beneath the velvet-cushioned seat lay the slate-colored stone of the border lords, placed there to symbolize the crowned king's authority over those lands as well as Kiriath. The chair's solid wooden sides and back hid it from the main audience, but he could see it clearly. And the moment he focused upon it, a blue light chased across its surface, then coalesced into a fuzzy glow at the stone's heart, alternately revealed and obscured by shifting veils of darkness. His chest constricted with shock: a rhu'ema lived in the Hasmal'uk stone!

How could no one have noticed that? True, the chair's shelf had lain empty during rehearsals, the stone brought out from the Jewel House only this morning. But since then, at least a dozen of the Terstans who were part of his royal guard had been down here securing the place. How could they all have overlooked such a menace?

And menace it was, waiting for him to sink right into its lap.

Light's grace! I can't sit on that thing!

But to refuse would make it appear as though he had been chased off, the very sign his enemies had predicted. . . .

My Lord, what do I do?

The ceremony marched onward without regard for his concerns. Fortesque brought him the Coronation Ring, anointed him with the oil, and finally laid the jeweled sword upon his open, outstretched hands, none of which evidenced anything close to the change that had been wrought in the robe. By then fear had gained a hold again, churning like a restless serpent in his belly. He was so rattled he hardly heard Fortesque's charging of the duties of the sword and uttered his own avowal purely by rote before sliding the sword straight into his empty sheath. Shocked faces betrayed the hideous breech of protocol—he was supposed to have handed the sword back immediately after his avowal. Suddenly it no longer mattered.

Whatever disasters he had envisioned for this day, none were as potentially devastating as this. And there was no way out, for now he must approach the Coronation Chair and take his seat to be crowned. Protocol already in shambles, Abramm risked a glance toward the audience. The white-robed Mataians sat stiffly along the front row, leaning toward him, eyes ablaze with the same baleful scarlet as their amulets. Above them darkness congealed in the intricate weavings of the ceiling beams. And in the stone beneath the Coronation Chair the blue fire burned brightly.

Reluctantly he crossed the stage to the chair, pausing before it to stare at the tall, dark-wood back with its carved images of Alaric's coronation, its heavy side-pieces, its red velvet cushion, all gilt with the blue light. The rhu'ema laughed in his mind. *I have you! I have you!* it squealed like some vicious child at play.

You have to sit down, he told himself. *Surely the change in the robe is Eidon's promise of protection.*

Just as he protected you from the morwhol? He cut off the bitter question at once, uncertain whether it had originated with him or elsewhere.

A mutter swept the audience. No doubt Bonafil was on the verge of calling out his denunciation. A quick glance showed the lowering darkness had obliterated the ceiling above the dangling banners, boiling out of itself and flickering with multicolored ribbons of light.

Abramm made himself turn around, his back to the audience now, an uncontrollable tremor in his gut. Silence gripped the chamber.

I'm not ready for this, he told himself. He could feel the people's growing concern, the rhu'ema's cackling triumph. The desire to flee swept over him— a wild, unthinking compulsion riding the memory of the morwhol's claw dragging through his face when he'd trusted. He'd *trusted*! And what had it gotten him?

You have to sit down, Abramm. You have no other choice.

And so he sat. And the darkness took him, as he'd feared it would. The great chamber dimmed to near invisibility as old terrors arose from the grave of his memory: being pinned to the stable floor by Gillard's friends, helpless to stop them from smearing him with horses' dung; standing enchained and naked on the Qarkeshan beach, helpless to stop himself from being sold into slavery; helpless to stop the morwhol's claws from tearing through his cheek,

or Shettai from bleeding out her life on that Xorofin ledge. . . . How could he protect a kingdom when he couldn't even protect the woman he'd loved? When he couldn't even protect himself?

A dark mist coiled around him, pinning his arms, squeezing his chest. Spangles of light twitched at the edges of his vision. Someone—it had to be Fortesque—loomed up before him, his form pulsating with the pale white glow of Terstan Light. The Keeper of the Regalia was Terstan? Abramm hadn't known. . . . Could Fortesque sense what was happening? Could he help? And where was Maddie? Surely she must know what was happening. Why didn't she help him?

The dark coils squeezed him tighter, leeching his strength so that he sat weak and shaking, fearful he would be unable to hold even the scepter in what was normally his strong right hand, while his ruined left quivered with the agony of reignited spawn spore. Bonafil and Prittleman were right. He really wasn't Eidon's choice, after all. What people would ever want a scarred and crippled weakling as their king? Or one as flawed in soul and spirit as he?

Despite all your attempts at devotion, you still can't make yourself submit to him, can you? Still can't make yourself really trust him.

Distantly Fortesque intoned the litany for presenting the Scepter of Rule, a long thin rod now floating in front of Abramm, one end occluded by a lump of darkness.

You let the Shadow have you constantly, the condemning inner voice went on. *You have no strength of will. No wonder your wounds festered. No wonder everything's gone wrong. Why should he bless you when you're so faithless? After all the time you've spent poring over his words, you should be strong in the Light. But look at you. You're a disgrace and an embarrassment.*

Shame twisted within him. It was true. He failed constantly, was failing now, in fact, and surely after all this time he shouldn't—

Fortesque laid the scepter into his weak and shaking hands, which somehow Abramm had raised from the chair's armrests unaware. He stared at the official's shimmering figure as disembodied voices buzzed in his ears. The cool rod thrummed against his palms, reminding him that he was supposed to transfer it to rest along his right arm. But the voices were strong upon him, deriding him, urging him to lower his fingers just enough to let the implement fall, for surely he was not worthy of carrying it.

Behind him he sensed a flare of triumph and a sudden hardening of decision. Bonafil was about to stand. . . .

coils down into the stone, where it huddled in abject terror, hoping to avoid notice.

Tersius vanished, and here was Fortesque again, holding the crown aloft between them as he intoned the litany of the crowning ritual. Light gleamed on its golden base and arches, reflected softly from the gigantic pearl at its top, and flickered in the myriad of precious stones. Abramm had seen his father crowned with this artifact and was now, incredibly, about to be crowned with it himself. His breath caught and his heart fluttered as Fortesque concluded his litany and called upon Abramm to take the Oath of Rule. Once he'd done so, Fortesque spoke the ritual's final words:

"Remember always from whom you receive this crown: the King of kings and Lord of lords who grants all earthly power. You are but his hand. And you answer always to him. To whom much is given, from him shall much be expected."

Abramm watched Fortesque's arms lower toward him, felt the crown settle onto his head, pressing heavily into his brow. Suddenly the chair shuddered beneath him and a loud crack rent the silence. With a cry of rage, blue fire corkscrewed around him as the creature that had lived in the stone fled upward toward the shadowed ceiling. Fortesque stepped back, startled, and in the gallery spectators looked upward, murmuring in surprise, though Abramm doubted any had seen it as fully as he had.

And here was Tersius again, standing before him as Fortesque retreated to the back of the stage. Abramm felt the Light within him now, strong and warm and clear, though apparently none of the spectators could see that, either. He frowned. *If I truly am your choice, Lord, why won't you make that clear to the people I'm supposed to rule?*

"And why are you ever seeking to make your business that which is not your business?"

Abramm felt the blood rush to his face. *Forgive me, Lord.*

"You're supposed to stand and face them all now."

Thoroughly befuddled, Abramm did so, dropping neither staff nor orb, though the crown bore heavily upon his brow. Leaving the chair, he strode around it to the front of the stage where for the first time all those in the audience would see their king crowned. The herald was supposed to announce his name and the multitude cheer their new king, but no one moved and the herald said nothing.

Behind him, Tersius spoke again. *"You have entered into the function of your destiny, Abramm. Are you willing to go forward from here? To be conformed to my image and so become a true witness of my Father's power and grace?"*

Of course I am, my Lord.

"Consider well. The road ahead will be more difficult than anything you have yet faced, though its blessings are beyond anything you can imagine. Is this what you want?"

Abramm hesitated. *More difficult than what I've already experienced?*

"And gloriously better. But the choice is yours."

And if I choose not to go forward?

"Then, for a time things will go easier for you."

Abramm looked over the hall filled with people staring back at him, at Trap in the front row, Philip beside him, then their father and mother. Across the aisle from Trap, the Mataians glared more fiercely than ever, the fire from their amulets lighting up eyes clogged with the curd of the sarotis. *Sarotis? How can they have sarotis? They are not Terstan!* But the thought was lost as he saw straight through their skulls to brains entwined and squeezed by ropes of scarlet fire. He felt their pain, their bondage, their misery . . . and their rock-hard resolution to fight him, no matter what.

His gaze lifted to the people in the stairstepping ranks of pews behind them. His people. His calling. His realm.

My Lord, I owe you everything. I am nothing without you, as you have shown me yet again. Whatever you will for me, that is what I want.

"Very well, then."

At that moment, as if he had realized his chance was slipping away, High Father Bonafil leaped to his feet, jabbed an arm at Abramm, and shouted out his denunciation. He had not even finished speaking when the Light rushed through Abramm in a great storm of power. Every piece of the regalia blazed with it, and all around him men flinched back in awe. Except in that front row, where Bonafil's Mataian brethren had leaped up beside their leader, originally to support him in his denunciation but now to flee screaming up the long aisle.

As they disappeared beneath the balcony, the orb swelled in Abramm's hand, brightening to an unendurable brilliance that exploded in a firework of white sparks. They sailed out in every direction, drifting down over the vast audience: tiny stars of life for those who saw and knew and wanted. . . .

Their light grew brighter, filling all his vision and expanding his awareness. Multiple images assailed him: a great army beneath the combined banners of Chesedh and Kiriath; a woman veiled in white, facing him, the Light flowing strongly through their clasped hands; a dark cave filled with the rush of churning waves and a pungent salt-seaweed aroma; a pair of Esurhite galleys moored in the cove below Graymeer's Fortress, dark-tunicked soldiers racing out of the opening at the cliff base to board them as shouts rang out from the ramparts above; more galleys streamed away from a cluster of fog-veiled islands to the south; while to the north, a great dark cloud alive with baleful flickerings hung low over the borderlands and crept slowly southward. . . .

He focused on the woman but could not see her face through the veil. Then a shadow passing over them drew his gaze upward to where soared a massive dragon so huge it seemed impossible the thing could hold itself in the air. Its golden eye fixed upon him as it wheeled majestically against a fog-bound sky, and he shuddered with the cold dispassion of its regard. Perhaps one day it would come for him, if he became troublesome enough. . . . But not today.

At the end of its circuit, it veered away, long wings flapping languidly as it disappeared into the southern distance.

The vision faded, and he stood again in the Hall of Kings, upon the very granite where his namesake Avramm had been crowned. He stared at the people before him, all of whom were on their feet. Their eyes were wide, their mouths agape. He could see the Light reflecting in their faces and off the gold Receiving Throne atop its dais before him, and even off the struts of a ceiling suddenly free of shadows. It was Eidon's own Light, and it was coming only from Abramm, from the regalia that he wore.

And as he watched in wonder, all the hundreds in that vast audience dropped to their knees before him.

4

As the brilliance of the Light dimmed, Captain Eltrap Meridon stared up in wonder at his king, chills zinging over his body. The robe shimmered like water around Abramm's tall, straight form, the crown afire on his brow, its light bleaching the scars on his face so they almost disappeared. His lips were firm, his jaw resolute as his gaze swept the crowd of stunned onlookers.

Eidon had revealed his choice. Whatever doubts people had regarding Abramm's kingship earlier, they were gone. The Mataians' empty bench stood in powerful refutation of their vicious claims, and Trap would forever cherish the memory of them fleeing up the aisle in screaming disarray. He loved knowing that after all the rhu'ema had done to make this day a disaster, they had been chased off as ignominiously as their human puppets.

As for himself, he could only laugh at his foolishness for indulging in that torment of guilt and worry last night over his dire words to Abramm. Foolish words they were, for he did not know if they were even true, and it would have been better never to have uttered them, but hindsight always trumped foresight.

The crown continued to dim, gradually revealing its changed shape. Only a few charred strips remained of the ermine-trimmed cap, while the heavy gold base with its two transverse arches had been reduced to sagging silver filigree. The massive pearl listed dully atop them, the gemstones faded and opaque, rendered insignificant against the plaited circlet—the original crown, perhaps?—shimmering beneath the ruined base.

At last the herald recalled his job. With a gasp, he stiffened his spine, threw back his shoulders, and let his clarion voice ring out in the silence, formally introducing Abramm as the thirty-sixth king of Kiriath, "confirmed before us this day by Eidon's own hand."

As if to make up for their former reluctance, the people bounded to their feet, shouting acclamation in a tumult of sound that drowned both trumpets and choir. Numerous calls of "Long live King Abramm!" raised themselves above the din, and Abramm stood there, letting it all roll over him, a half smile touching his lips.

Philip leaned against Trap and shouted into his ear, "You still think that arm won't come back, brother?"

He'd been furious with Trap for telling Abramm he was crippled, vigorously taking his older brother to task for making predictions he had no business making.

Now Trap could only smile and shrug in reply. Whether Abramm recovered use of his arm or not was up to Eidon. But if he didn't, it wouldn't matter, for his true strength had always lain with Eidon. This just made it more obvious.

The cheering went on and on until Abramm gave up waiting for it to stop. Indeed, the cries intensified as he strode to the side of the stage and down the stair, then back across the forestage to climb the five-step dais of the receiving throne. His limp was barely noticeable, his shoulders straight, chin high, just as a king's should be.

As he settled onto the throne, Trap's eye caught on sudden activity in the royal box beyond him. In the second row, Lords Foxton and Whitethorne were discreetly hauling a dazed and disheveled Byron Blackwell back to his feet. Nor was he the only one. Several of the ladies farther up in the box were also being fanned back to consciousness, and even Lady Madeleine, standing in the front row with her brother, seemed to have succumbed. Knowing her link with Abramm through the Light, Trap wasn't too surprised. She did not, however, seem terribly debilitated, pushing away from Prince Leyton's supporting arm as Simon now stepped past them to begin the offering of public fealty.

As the others in the box jostled into line at his back, Simon descended the stair to the forestage, where he was the first to kneel at the foot of the Receiving Throne dais and offer his public oath of fealty. Then he returned to his seat in the box as one by one the others did likewise, a process that took almost two hours to complete.

Then it was time for the ceremonies of elevation. As the first name rang out, Trap's stomach twisted itself into a hard and breathless knot. Suddenly he recalled just why he was sitting in this honored first space of the first bench, his brother and parents beside him, and all four of his sisters with their husbands on the bench behind: today the swordmaster's son would be made a duke.

He had not believed it would actually happen, despite the fact he had known Abramm's intentions for months and had rehearsed this part of the ceremony for days. For one, he'd not been sure Abramm would make it through his coronation without disaster. For another, it was one of those unthinkable developments only Eidon could conceive and Trap himself had never quite been able to get his mind around. Even the act of arguing that it was far too high a rank to bestow on a commoner—and Trap had argued that—had seemed surreal.

Now as the first man knelt on the upper levels of the receiving dais, Trap thought of the oath he'd sworn to Raynen more than six years ago to go with Abramm into exile. He'd believed it a death sentence for both of them. Instead, here they were, Abramm a king and Trap about to be elevated to the highest hereditary rank in the peerage. Not only was it unbelievable, he wasn't sure he even wanted it.

He watched as Abramm parceled out to his own men the lands he had confiscated from Gillard and his supporters. Then, before Trap knew it, the herald was calling his name and he was kneeling before his sovereign.

What happened after that passed in a haze, blurred by the sudden intense self-consciousness Trap experienced at being the focus of hundreds of pairs of eyes. Abramm was thorough in enumerating his reasons for granting this exceptional degree of elevation, relating all the story of their journey together, and finally coming to the end.

"If it weren't for this man's devotion, I would not be here today. If anyone deserves this highest accolade, it is Eltrap Meridon, son of Larrick, defender of Raynen, Captain of the King's Guard, the White Pretender's Infidel, the Dorsaddi's Lord Deliverer, and henceforth, by my hand and sword"—he touched the tip of the Sword of State first to Trap's right shoulder, then to his left—"Duke of Northille."

The sword tip touched the top of Trap's head and released a burst of Light, its warmth shooting down through his bent knee and the soles of his feet.

Only as it faded away and the sword's touch withdrew did he breathe again. And then he was offering his own sworn oath of fealty, already given once in the stern cabin of *Wanderer* en route to Kiriath some nine months ago, now offered publicly, the oath of a duke and not a simple armsman. After that he stood, and the Officers of Ceremony came to lay across his chest the red ribbon and gold chains of his new rank. Then, at last, he turned to face the audience behind him as the herald called out his new name to the assembled multitude, and chills washed over his body yet again.

I am a lord. I am a duke. . . . I am a swordmaster's son, for pity's sake!

Philip was grinning up at him, looking ready to burst. His father was worse and his mother's cheeks were wet. Behind them, in the second row, his sisters and their husbands sat gape-mouthed, for they had never believed he would amount to anything—he was still unmarried, was he not?

After standing for what seemed far too long, he turned back to the king to drop a deep bow, then back-stepped to his seat. As he sat down, Philip punched his arm and Father reached across to take his hand and squeeze it, tears glittering in his eyes.

Abramm retired briefly to a side chamber and reemerged in the long, purple Robe of State. He was supposed to have replaced the heavy Crown of State with the lighter Crown of Rule, but had apparently chosen to retain the original. Stripped of the ruined arches, base, and jewels, its pale plaiting still shimmered against his brow with its own light, echoes of its earlier fire. He'd also retained the jewel-hilted Sword of State, as well as scepter and orb, though in the case of the latter two, he was supposed to.

As the musicians played a majestic recessional and all the audience stood again, Abramm strode up the center aisle toward the top of the hall. Trap turned with the others to watch him go, glimpsing now for the first time the many cravats lying untied about their owners' necks, doublets and shirts unbuttoned to reveal the golden shields that only hours ago had been burnished into the chests beneath. Tens of them. Maybe even hundreds. Just like had happened at the Valley of the Seven Peaks after Abramm had slain the morwhol.

As the king passed beneath the temporary balcony and out of sight, Carissa exited the royal box to start the recessional. Leyton and Madeleine, Simon and Oswain Nott—the other two of Kiriath's three dukes—followed after her, keeping a respectful distance between themselves. Trap waited until the gray-wigged Nott had ascended halfway, then stepped out behind him and joined the recessional himself, walking a gauntlet of cheering onlookers and enjoying, for the first time in his life, the privileges that came with being the Duke of Northille.

Outside, bright, warm sunlight poured from a cloudless midday sky, the slushy morning snow long since melted and evaporated, leaving the streets dry beneath the feet of those who crowded them. *This will be a good omen,* he thought as he descended the stairway toward the carriage waiting to bring him to the palace and the coronation banquet still to come. Then he smiled. *Though after what you've done today, my Lord, I can't think why anyone would still be looking for omens.*

He was nearly to the carriage when he realized the footman holding its door open was his brother, Philip.

"What are you doing here?" he asked, pausing before the open door. "I thought you were coming out with Mother and Father."

"Channon pulled me out right after the king left, my lord *duke*," Philip said, emphasizing the last word with a smile like to break his jaw. "Seems I've got some prisoners to interrogate." He gestured toward the carriage seat as he glanced back at the door where the new Count of Strafford, Lord Foxton, and his wife would soon emerge from the hall to board their own carriage now waiting in line behind Trap's.

With a schedule to keep and no time to dally, Trap climbed reluctantly into the carriage. "Why are *you* interrogating prisoners?" he growled. "And why now?"

"Esurhites tried to take Graymeer's this morning," his brother replied, shutting the door with a snap.

Trap's head whipped around in horror.

"It was only a pair of scouting galleys," Philip hurried to assure him. "And all aboard both were caught. Duke Simon was notified when the news first came, during the giving of the fealty. He made the decision to hold off telling the king until he changed into the Robe of State."

Trap nodded approval. If the action had already concluded and the threat was neutralized, no need to cause unnecessary disruption of the coronation. "But why are *you* interrogating the Esurhites?" he demanded.

Philip shrugged and his grin returned. "I'm the only one who speaks the Tahg."

"I speak it better than you by a long shot. And I have more experience questioning prisoners."

"Aye, but you're a duke now, brother," Philip reminded him with a thump on the door. "You have more important things to do." He stepped back with a salute, and before Trap could say any more, the carriage lurched forward. Thus the new Duke of Northille also experienced for the first time the limitations of his new station.

More important things to do, he groused inwardly. *Like what? Ride in this carriage and wave at people? Receive the insincere congratulations of a flock of two-faced courtiers who, truth be told, would rather send me off to exile again?* He'd not missed the glare Oswain Nott had given him as he'd passed by in the recessional. *More important things to do, indeed! What could be more important than finding out how the Esurhites attacked and why?* It could be no accident they had chosen today to do it. Not only had Graymeer's stood vulnerable with a quarter of its usual force to defend it, this was the coronation day of the White Pretender, the man hated above all others by the new Supreme Commander of the advancing Armies of the Black Moon.

But no, Trap was a duke now, and that meant, apparently, that all he was allowed to do was sit around and look aristocratic. *I knew I should never have accepted this position!*

At the palace, the door guards welcomed him with broad grins. Which made the cool and sudden silence of his reception inside the already crowded entry atrium all the more startling. Many of the courtiers had raced away from the Hall of Kings in advance of Abramm's departure so as to provide a welcome for him here. Now, as Trap stopped in the entry to strip off his gloves and let the servants take his cloak, all conversation ceased and every eye turned his way, few of them friendly.

Abramm, of course, was not present, having gone immediately to his chambers to change out of his coronation clothes. After that, if Trap knew him at all, he'd be calling an emergency meeting of his war cabinet, something a captain of the king's guard might have had the privilege of attending, but another thing denied to a duke. Or at least to this duke, though he supposed he could force his way into it if he wanted. . . .

Simon was not in the atrium, either, nor surprisingly, was the Chesedhan crown prince, Leyton Donavan. But Oswain Nott was, happily in conversation with Princess Carissa, who had her back to the door and didn't see Trap's entrance. Nott did, however, his hard, narrow eyes fixing coldly on Trap the moment he entered. As the only other duke in the room, Nott should have hastened to congratulate him. Instead he stood staring, and Trap could see his conflict—the desire to turn away and shun his new rival warred against not wanting to offend his king. Before either position could win out, Carissa turned to see what had captured everyone's attention and, breaking into a grin, came at once to greet him. Nott was left standing there, and Trap did not miss the flash of rage that darkened the man's long face.

"Welcome to Whitehill, my lord duke," Carissa said to Trap as she dropped a deep and respectful curtsey before him. Blood rushed hotly into his face.

"Oh, look, Princess," said Lady Madeleine, who had tagged along at Carissa's elbow and seemed none the worse for her earlier fainting spell. "You've embarrassed him. Not used to being a duke, I guess, are you, sir?"

Carissa beamed at him. "Well, he'd better hurry up if he's going to—" She broke off as Madeleine's elbow jabbed her ribs.

"If I'm going to what?" he asked, trying to ignore the fact that they were still the center of everyone's attention and that the onlookers had begun to whisper among themselves as they watched.

"Did you hear about the birds?" Madeleine countered, oblivious to their audience.

It took a moment for the word to register with him. "Birds?" Had *they* attacked along with the Esurhites? A new skill among the disciples of the Shadow? Or was it merely feyna, misidentified again?

He noted Arik Foxton come in behind him about that time, noted the servant who spoke into the new count's ear and sent him hurrying away up the east hall. Summoned to that War Cabinet meeting, no doubt.

Carissa had taken up the story of the birds. "When Abramm stepped out of the Hall of Kings they say a whole raft of white pigeons erupted from the eaves—all on their own." Her face was flushed, her startling blue eyes alight with an excitement he sensed wasn't wholly related to her story, but which, he thought, made her more beautiful than ever.

"Pigeons," he repeated, as his mind finally caught up with her words. Not feyna. Not even at Graymeer's.

"There were no baskets," Carissa went on, "no handlers, no one who had anything to do with it. It was a miracle. Another sign."

"Aye, and there's more," Madeleine added. "People have been healed all through the city today—the blind and deaf and crippled made whole. Right about the time the crown was placed on Abramm's head."

"I'll wager your brother is excited about that," he said dryly.

She grimaced as he glanced around, looking for Leyton again. Trap was about to ask where he was when he noticed Nott headed his way, an insincere smile pasted on his long lugubrious face. Apparently the man's desire not to offend the king had won out. A longtime wearer of Eidon's shield and recently come to his position upon his father's death, Nott was the man Abramm was expected to appoint as First Minister of his cabinet in the next day or two.

Before he reached them, however, a servant stepped up and bowed. Assuming the man was bowing to Carissa, Trap ignored him. Until he said, "My lord duke, the king requires your presence."

"The king?" Trap repeated blankly. From the corner of his eye he saw Nott stop in his tracks as, again, total silence gripped the room and all the courtiers looked Trap's way. It was a vapid remark, to be sure, but hardly enough to warrant the degree of shock with which they were now regarding him. And why did Nott look as if he'd just eaten a mouthful of bad roe? More than that, why was Carissa smiling in that *I-know-something-you-don't* sort of way?

The servant gestured toward the east wing. "My lord?"

And why was he gesturing to the east wing? The king's chambers were to the west. As Trap followed the man out of the atrium and down the mirrored corridor, he realized it must be the war council. Abramm's war room was in the east wing, and Trap did have some experience fighting the Esurhites. He felt a stab of chagrin to think he'd believed Abramm would really leave him out of things. . . .

Sure enough, he was shortly ushered into the familiar second-floor chamber, the rank of tall windows lining its eastern wall flooding the room with light. A long gleaming table lined with high-backed chairs paralleled them. Closer to the main door a number of damask-upholstered chairs and divans stood in clusters on a green and gold Sorian rug, and a blaze crackled in the marble fireplace.

Though Abramm had not yet arrived, several men were already present: Grand Marshall Simon Kalladorne, the bulldoggish Grand Admiral Walter Hamilton, and their respective assistants, as well as the commanders of Kildar and Graymeer's fortresses, and Seth Tarker, head of the king's intelligence network. Shale Channon, in full dress uniform, was also present, as were Arik Foxton and Leyton Donavan. With the exception of the latter, Trap had come to know all of them well in the last six months.

Now all conversations cut off as he entered, and every man within turned toward him. Simon was the first to offer congratulations, clasping his hand and clapping his shoulder. "No question you deserve this, son. And of all the men I know, you're one of the few who can probably handle it."

Trap looked at the older man in surprise, for he knew Simon had been among those who argued against giving him the dukedom. He seemed wholly sincere now as he added, "It won't be easy, though. There are many who opposed this and will continue to do so."

"I'm sure they will, sir," Trap responded, thinking wryly of Nott's sour look.

"If you need any help at all—advice on servants, accountants, where to get a good deal on breeding stock—don't hesitate to ask."

"I won't, sir. And thank you."

Admiral Hamilton made the same offer, and soon the rest of the men were clustered about him, offering congratulations, seeming genuinely pleased by his promotion, particularly Captain Channon.

Brannock Whitethorne entered in the midst of it all and added his congratulations, and just as conversation was turning to the reason they'd been called here, Mason Crull, the small, bespectacled assistant to Royal Secretary Blackwell, burst into the room, breathless and pale as mist.

"It's Prince Gillard!" he said with quiet intensity once the door was safely shut behind him. His gaze tracked from face to face. "He roused this morning! Right about the time the other healings happened. Cried out and sat up in his bed. First time he's moved at all in six months, much less spoken."

The fire crackled and popped as the men digested this. Then Simon asked in his gravelly voice, "You're saying Gillard's conscious?"

"No. He fell back into his stupor almost immediately and remains as senseless as ever. His guards have been locked up in the suite with him until the king decides what to do about it."

"The king's been told, then?" Shale Channon asked.

"When he changed to the Robe of State. I've just come from interviewing Gillard's attendants, in fact."

Simon scowled. "When his supporters learn of this we'll have yet another spate of harebrained rescue plots to waste our time with. As if we have any to waste—especially after what's happened today."

"Well, hopefully we'll keep it quiet and they'll never know," Crull said.

"Unless," Simon began, "it turns out he's finally coming out of—"

He was interrupted as the door opened at the back of the room and the doorman entered. "Gentlemen . . . the king."

And Abramm stepped into the room. He had exchanged his white coronation suit for a doublet of burgundy brocade and black trousers but still wore the jewel-hilted sword and the ancient crown of Avramm. Without its blazing light to overshadow them or the beard to hide behind, his scars seemed startlingly vivid again, giving his hawkish face a fierceness Trap had not noticed before. Indeed, as Abramm stopped beside the high-backed chair at the table's head and raked the gathering with his gaze, Trap felt the tension ratchet up in the men around him. And coming on top of that display of power in the Hall of Kings today, Trap could well understand if they were no longer sure who he was, nor what to do in his presence.

The king's blue eyes fixed upon Crull and he frowned. "Where's Blackwell?"

"Ill, sir," Crull said, bowing. "H-he suffered another one of his fits during the ceremony, sir." Ever since his encounter with a tree branch the morning Abramm faced the morwhol, Blackwell had been prone to such fits, particularly when he became excited. "It left him—" the small man grimaced— "quite unable to function. They had to carry him back to his chambers."

"Will he be all right?" Abramm asked.

"I believe so, sir."

Abramm regarded him steadily for a moment, then nodded and indicated that everyone should take their places at the table. In the past, Trap would have stood somewhere on the room's wainscoted sidelines as Captain Channon and the high officers' assistants were doing. Now he had his own seat, the place of highest honor, in fact, directly to Abramm's left. Crull, serving in Blackwell's stead, sat to Trap's left, then Foxton, Seth Tarker, and the commander of Kildar. Simon, Whitethorne, Admiral Hamilton, and the commander of Graymeer's sat across from him, with the blond, ruddy-faced Leyton seated at the end.

Sitting at the same table with a foreign crown prince, a duke, a high admiral, a count, an earl, and the king himself did not feel at all real. But Trap had little time to contemplate, for as soon as they were settled, Abramm got down to business.

The Esurhites had rowed a pair of scout galleys in on a still sea under cover of the morning fog and moored at the old sea entrance on the west side of the cliff where Graymeer's sat. Each boat carried a thirty-man crew— twenty to row, ten to fight—and between the two had sent twenty men ashore. Before they could accomplish their still-unknown goals, a wind had sprung up to blow away the fog, and the lookouts spied the boats. Stones dropped from the fortress's ramparts had inflicted sufficient damage that, even though the galleys escaped the landing, one of the Chesedhan warships Prince Leyton had brought with him had chased them down.

Meanwhile, the fortress defenders had surprised the invaders in the tunnels on their way up from the sea and captured all of them. The prisoners had arrived at Wetherslea Prison in Springerlan shortly before the coronation proceedings had concluded. Kildar's commander confirmed there'd only been the two galleys, no larger attack force waiting out in the fog. Hopefully Philip Meridon would find out just what they'd intended to accomplish.

"The thing that troubles me most," said Abramm, "is how they got here. We've had no sightings, so it's unlikely they came up the coast. That casts suspicion on the Gull Islands, no matter how barren and unnavigable we believe them to be." He glanced at Admiral Hamilton. "As does the continued absence of your scout ships."

The ships had been sent out almost three weeks ago, and even accounting for the storm that had blown in the day after they'd left, if they'd found nothing they should have been back several days ago.

"They say the Gulls are Shadow-bound," Leyton remarked blandly, speaking for the first time during the meeting. "Perhaps the barrier of mist that protects them has extended farther out than you counted on. Without wind, ships cannot sail."

Abramm frowned at him, but agreed that could cause things to take longer than anticipated and decided to wait a few more days before sending out a fleet of search vessels. That decided, he informed the commander of Graymeer's he intended to visit the fortress tomorrow to have a look at things himself. "But I want no special preparations made."

Commander Weston's militarily stiff bearing somehow stiffened even more. "No preparations, sir?"

"You and Brookes are the only ones who are to know I'm coming."

Trap leaned forward, suddenly uneasy. "What are you thinking, sir? That we didn't get them all?"

Abramm glanced at him grimly. "I'm thinking we're dealing with Esurhites—sent by the son of our good friend Katahn ul Manus, who trained him well in the tactics of the games. It may be there's nothing for us to find— but I'd like to preserve our advantage of surprise as long as possible. I'll know more after Lieutenant Meridon finishes."

"Sir," Channon said, stepping away from the wall, "if you really think there might be a trap waiting up there—"

"I don't. But rest assured I wouldn't think of going without your protection, Captain. We'll simply do so as returning soldiers rather than the king and his escort." He glanced at Trap again. "I hope you'll consider coming along, as well, Duke Eltrap."

"Of course, sir."

The door opened at that point, and a servant slipped in with a message for the king's ear alone. At Abramm's nod, he hurried out and was immediately replaced by Ethan Laramor, who also spoke to the king privately. Except that *his* whispered message caused Abramm's eyes to widen as he turned to look full at the border lord who now straightened. "Gold, you say?"

"Yes, sir."

"And you say it's solid?"

"As near as we can tell without breaking it all apart. Do you want me to have it brought up?"

Abramm glanced around at his counselors, who watched him with unveiled curiosity. He said nothing to them, however, and finally turned back to Laramor. "Bring it up to the banqueting hall, when we're finished eating."

After he left, Abramm grinned at them and said, "This is definitely turning out to be a day filled with extraordinary events." He paused, letting their curiosity deepen. Then the smile vanished and he returned to the matter of Graymeer's, finished up a few last details concerning tomorrow's expedition, then dismissed the fortress commanders, their assistants, and finally Leyton Donavan. Only then did he listen to Crull's report on his visit with Gillard's attendants and make arrangements to visit his brother's bedside later that night with Simon and Trap.

Then, when it seemed to Trap that there could be nothing left to discuss, he leaned back in his chair, steepling his fingers before him, and tracked his gaze across his advisors, a smile pulling at his lips. "So, gentlemen, have you considered my suggestion of a candidate for First Minister?"

As all eyes immediately darted to Trap, he felt the hairs on the back of his neck lift with a horrible sense of portent.

"We have considered your suggestion, sir," Simon said neutrally. "We all agree the man is reliable, trustworthy, experienced, and intelligent. Except for the matters of social standing, which we've already discussed, I believe he is well suited to the position."

"And you would fully support his appointment?"

Simon's eyes fixed upon Trap. "I would, sir."

"As would I, sir," said Hamilton.

Foxton and Whitethorne voiced their approval, as did Crull, adding, "The count gives his blessing, too. And a poll taken of the members of the Privy Council at large has resulted in approval by an overwhelming majority."

Pox and plagues, Abramm! Trap thought, looking full at his king. *You wouldn't . . .*

"Thank you, gentlemen," said Abramm. "You are dismissed." His shrewd blue eyes fixed upon Trap. "Save for you, Duke Eltrap."

The others trooped out, exchanging sly looks and suppressed smiles. Trap's sense of foreboding intensified. As the door snicked shut, Abramm clasped his hands on the gleaming table before him and looked at his friend soberly.

Trap's stomach began to churn, and when Abramm said nothing, he finally broke the silence himself. "What is this, sir?"

"I'm sure you've already guessed, my friend." The blue eyes held his own. "I want you to be my First Minister."

For a moment Trap had a sensation of falling, of the room twisting around him while his stomach lurched and his ears rang. His teeth came together with an audible click and his chest seemed to have squeezed all the air from his lungs.

The king's First Minister held the highest position of governmental rank, second to the king himself in power and rivaled only by the office of Royal Secretary when it came to access.

"You are not pleased," Abramm said quietly.

Trap scowled at him. "You'd make me a poxed politician? When you know how much I loathe politics? And how unsuited I am to the eeling and subterfuge that goes with it?"

Abramm bore the outburst placidly. "I neither want nor expect you to *eel*. I need men with integrity to help me run this government. Men who are competent and trustworthy." He paused. "There is no one I trust more than you, Trap."

Directly across the table a wood-colored staffid suddenly folded its body lengthwise along the table's edge and skittered toward Abramm. Barely had Trap noted its presence before a thin white thread of Light leaped from Abramm's clasped hands to impale it. The creature flinched, clung briefly to the table edge, then fell away. He heard the small clicks of its legs and carapace on the chair, but soon those, too, faded.

Abramm had never taken his eyes from Trap's face, waiting for his answer. Beyond him, outside the window, the trees' newly budding branches waved gently in the breeze, their tops glinting with the warm late-afternoon light, the bottom two-thirds of them already steeped in shadow.

Trap exhaled sharply. "I appreciate the honor that you've given me, the regard in which you hold me . . . but, sir, I know nothing about being First Minister."

Abramm's brows arched with amusement as he leaned back in his chair. "You know more than you think, my friend. You understand men. And all of this . . . *politics*, I'm finding, is not so very different from the battles we waged with our blades in the gaming theaters. At the hilt of every blade there's always a man. . . ." Abramm glanced down at his finger tracing the outline of the wood's grain in the table's polished surface. "Your reaction now and your words to me last night—those are precisely the reasons I want you." He looked up again. "Who else is going to tell me to my face what they really think, Trap? Especially when they have reason to believe I'm not going to like it. You saw the way they looked at me when I came in earlier—as if I'm some sort of avenging god."

"Well, you did put on quite a show today."

"It's not been just today."

Trap met his gaze for a long moment, and the sight of his king's resolve sent the first wave of terror sweeping through him. "Light's grace, Abramm! I'm a swordmaster's son! They're having a hard enough time accepting me as a duke. Who would ever accept me as First Minister?"

"My cabinet, for one." He paused. "And you've been more than a sword-master's son for some time." Again Abramm watched his finger trace the lines of the wood's grain. "However, if you really can't abide it, Oswain Nott will be happy to take up the slack."

Trap snorted, surprised by the strong aversion that rose up in him. "That's not fair. You know what I think of Nott!"

Abramm kept his gaze on his fingers, the scars bright and vicious along his face. "He's the only other duke we have. Indeed, since he inherited his position, he should have precedence. . . . I just don't happen to think that makes him the hands-down expert in affairs of state he seems to think he is."

"You're twisting my arm here, Abramm."

And now his king looked up at him, eyes twinkling. "Merely stating the facts, my lord duke."

"Is that why you've made me a duke?"

The twinkle left at once, and Abramm's expression sobered. "I've made you a duke because I wanted to express my gratitude for all you've done. I offer you this position on my cabinet because I've always had you to guard my back, and I need you more than ever."

"*Guard my back.*" He would have to use those words. *And it was no acci-dent that he did, was it, my Lord Eidon? How can I refuse him now? Or you, for that matter?* Trap pushed himself back from the table with a sigh of resigna-tion. "Oh, very well, I'll do as you ask. As much as I'm able. I just don't think I'm very well suited to this."

Abramm grinned as he, too, sat back in his chair, blue eyes twinkling again. "I guess we'll find out, won't we?" Trap's doubtful expression only made his grin widen and he stood up. "I don't know about you, Duke Eltrap, but I'm starving. Let's go eat."

5

When Abramm entered the banquet hall with Trap in his wake, he was greeted by the creak and rustle of one hundred and six chairs pushed back across the carpeted floor as his guests sprang up to receive him. Four linen-clad tables ran the hall's grand length, while a fifth sat on a raised dais at the head of and perpendicular to the others. All chairs at that high table were occupied save the center two, reserved for Abramm and Trap. Madeleine, he noted happily, stood on the dais immediately to the right of the central chair, and he wanted nothing more than to stride up there at once to begin grilling her about the vision he'd seen during the ceremony. Instead, he bowed to the constraints of his office, taking his time to speak to those who stood along his path, many of them new-made Terstans as of today.

It was an odd thing to have urbane statesmen twice his age, hard-faced border lords, world-savvy merchants, and wealthy freeman landholders acting as overawed in his presence as young princelings. They approached him as if they expected the Light to flare again before their eyes, and many struggled to articulate their words of greeting.

"Eidon's grace be upon you, Your Majesty."

"May your reign be long and prosperous, sir."

Some would hardly look him in the eye. And yet, as acutely uncomfortable as their awe made him, the pragmatic part of him knew he would be wise to tolerate it. For surely it would make them more amenable to approving the tax and conscription orders he would soon put before them.

The men and women at the high table were less intimidated than those on the floor, but even here he sensed a new stiffness. Everitt Kesrin, Ethan

Laramor, Temas Darnley, Arik Foxton, Oswain Nott—even Uncle Simon—all seemed to regard him from behind some invisible barrier, the gap between him and them wider now than ever. Even Carissa, though she had beamed at him from the moment he'd stepped onto the dais, lost her smile as he stopped before her. Staring up at him wide-eyed and solemn, she dropped him a curtsey as reverently as if he were a stranger, and when she lifted her face to his again, her eyes gleamed with tears.

Unnerved, he stepped past her to his own place at the table, Trap's empty chair to one side, Lady Madeleine and her brother, Crown Prince Leyton, standing on the other.

Madeleine's curtsey was even more perfunctory and distracted than usual, and Leyton seemed to find the whole affair secretly amusing. But then, he always looked as if he thought life were a vast joke, the details of which only he perceived. He'd sat through the War Council meeting with the same expression he wore now, in fact.

A big man, he was several years older than Abramm and firstborn of the Chesedhan king's brood. His weathered features were a coarser, stronger version of Maddie's, his pronounced freckling testifying to his preference for the out-of-doors over palace halls. Shrewd, gray-blue eyes crouched beneath bushy, blond brows, watching Abramm with a keen light of appraisal and the ever-present amusement.

After receiving Leyton's respects, Abramm stepped into the space between his chair and the silver- and crystal-decked table before him, the last to come to the table. Before and below him stretched the hall with its massive paintings and blazing chandeliers, the ranks of servants waiting along the wainscoted sides, and the bejeweled and satin-clad guests who filled it. To his surprise those guests now spontaneously burst into cheers and applause. *Quite a contrast to all that fuming over the treaty yesterday*, he thought wryly. And yet the outburst moved him deeply.

He let the applause continue for a few moments, then held out his hands for silence. After thanking them for coming, he offered a brief summary of what had happened at Graymeer's that morning, stressing that the small group of invaders had been apprehended and that, for now, all was well.

"Eidon has delivered us with a stiff wind of impeccable timing, alert and courageous guards stationed on the fortress walls, and the much appreciated action of the vessels our Chesedhan friends have so graciously supplied us." He gave a nod to Leyton and Madeleine as he said this last. Then, as was his custom, he asked Eidon to bless the food and the remainder of the day's proceedings, and sat down. Everyone else followed suit, and the servants at last bustled into action.

As one of them reached past his left shoulder to set down a goblet of wine, he pulled his napkin into his lap and glanced at Maddie, happy to have her sitting on his right side where she couldn't see his scars. And then he wondered at himself, since, of all people, Maddie must certainly have grown accustomed to them by now.

"Well," he said conversationally, "this has been quite a day."

Though she flashed a smile at him and agreed it had, he saw that something was amiss. She looked nervous, almost guilty, her gaze meeting his for only half a heartbeat before darting back to the crowd again. And when a servant reached past her to set her wine goblet on the table, she picked it up at once and sipped.

A horrible thought struck him. *She isn't caught up in this new awe of me, too, is she?* He couldn't believe *she* would be intimidated by what Eidon had done. And yet, hadn't Simon mentioned earlier that she'd been among those who had fainted during the coronation? He frowned and was on the verge of asking her about it when a plate of ruffled leaf lettuce dressed with oil and vinegar was set before him. The interruption gave him just enough time to realize her fainting would not be a good topic of conversation.

He stole a glance at her and decided it wasn't awe that was affecting her. Just sitting here he felt the radiation of her discomfort. Granted, he knew she detested this sort of thing, and it had to be an added burden that she was serving as stand-in for her sister, Briellen, his bride-to-be. But this was more than that. Perhaps she and Leyton had had another argument.

He thought to put her at ease with conversation, but everything he could think to talk about he did not want to discuss in front of Leyton. Thus he settled for making bland commentary on the coronation soloist: Madeleine had written the words to the song, after all. Unfortunately, he could hardly recall it, having been distracted by everything else that had been going on, and his words made her no less tense.

Finally he gave up and turned his attention to Prince Leyton, sitting on her far side. "You and your ships have arrived just in time, sir. Already we are in your debt, and the treaty barely signed."

Leyton accepted his thanks with a nod and a half smile. "Truly sir, it was not our ships, but the wind you conjured to drive off that mist. A brilliant ploy, if I may say so. All of it. You have effectively allayed all doubts regarding your right to the crown. Though your foreknowledge surprises me. How did you know the Esurhites would be attacking?"

Abramm let his surprise show. "I can assure you, Prince Leyton, had I known they meant to attack Graymeer's, I'd not have left it standing there with a quarter of its usual manpower. That the wind came when it did was solely Eidon's doing."

Leyton smiled in that ironic way of his and cocked his head. "At just about the same time you were receiving the regalia, I understand. Which makes for a remarkable coincidence, I'd say." His eyes flicked away to the table as he picked up his wine goblet and lifted it as if in toast. "Almost makes one believe there might be something to those tales that say your regalia have special powers."

Abramm grew suddenly wary. Beyond the treaty negotiations, he had paid little attention to Leyton Donavan in the three days since he'd arrived, preoccupied with his own troubles. He did know his courtiers widely held that Donavan had come here to steal Kiriath's regalia. Long believing the artifacts possessed supernatural powers that could be harnessed and used by their bearer, the Chesedhans had, over the centuries, repeatedly sought to take them for their own. If that was truly Leyton's ambition, today's manifestations could only have intensified his desire.

"The scepter, they say, can command the winds, after all," Leyton remarked.

"And yet in all our six hundred years of history, it has never done so."

"There are legends that indicate Avramm used the regalia against the Shadow. And Alaric did, as well."

"Your legends. Not ours." Abramm glanced down at his plate to spear another forkful of lettuce. "There's nothing in our historical records to support any of those wild claims."

"Perhaps your histories have been altered."

"Perhaps your legends have been concocted, exaggerations based on a kernel of truth."

"Rather like your own tale of having faced a morwhol."

Abramm lowered his fork with its uneaten mouthful back to his plate and turned to his Chesedhan guest, regarding him steadily for a long moment. Madeleine sat motionless between them, her gaze fixed upon her salad. Abramm was trying hard not to admit he disliked this man—he was about to marry his sister, after all, a decision the Chesedhan banners he'd seen in that Light-given vision had confirmed. But Leyton reminded him far too much of Gillard: the condescension in his tone, the half-lidded manner he had of looking at a man, the way he always seemed to be playing some mental game.

Unable to decide if Leyton truly believed he had made up the tale of the morwhol or was just trying to bait him, Abramm decided to let it go and kept to the subject at hand. "Your people have long held our regalia to be more than they are, I fear," he said quietly.

Leyton's bushy blond brows shot up. "How can you even say that, sir? When everything that's happened today has only proven you have no idea what you have. Did any of you expect the regalia to manifest as they did? You didn't even know what your crown really was, hidden beneath the gold and jewels your ancestors laid over top of it! How can you accuse us of making your artifacts more than they are when you obviously have no idea *what* they are to begin with?"

Abramm's irritation spiked, fueled as much by Leyton's audacity as from the humbling recognition that he was right. Abramm had had no idea the orb was a purveyor of kelistars, hadn't known the true crown was the simple plaiting he now wore—hadn't known that all of it would produce a grand vision he still did not know how to interpret. That he'd *seen* the Esurhites heading into Graymeer's just about the time they'd actually done it still astonished him. And at the same time did not help him understand the rest of what he'd seen, since save for the stream of galleys leaving what looked like the Gull Islands, none clearly unfolded in present time. He wondered again if Maddie had participated in any of it, if she might be able to help him figure it out, and then—suddenly and stunningly—he considered whether she might have told Leyton what she'd seen.

Something in Abramm's expression must've communicated his displeasure, for Leyton looked suddenly chagrined. "Your pardon, sir," he murmured, the intensity leaking out of his manner. "I fear I have been overbold."

"Indeed," Abramm agreed. He thought of asking the man flat out if he'd come to steal the regalia—just to get his reaction—then decided there'd be no point in deliberately provoking him.

"I get excited when I think about the possibilities," the prince said.

"Perhaps, then, you would do well not to think in that vein," Abramm advised. "Whatever they are meant to do or be, they belong to Kiriath, not Chesedh, to be used by Eidon to confirm the man he chooses as king. Which he has done."

For a moment the amused light in Leyton's eye flickered out, replaced by a flat expression impossible to read. Irritation? A grudging respect where none had been before? Or a cool calculation that was not at all friendly?

Abruptly Leyton's half smile returned. "Well, Your Majesty, there's certainly no question he's demonstrated your place here." And, bushy brows lifting in concert with his arm, he raised his goblet in toast, then took a second, longer draught from the vessel.

Abramm turned his attention to his food as Leyton did likewise, utensils clinking against the fine porcelain. He hadn't accused the Chesedhan of coveting outright, but he thought Leyton had gotten the message. Abramm truly hoped this treaty wasn't a sham. Kiriath sorely needed the Chesedhans' help. And if Chesedh was truly facing Belthre'gar and his armies, as rumors indicated, King Hadrich would be insane to make an enemy of his neighbor to the west.

Abramm grew aware of Maddie beside him, pushing the lettuce about on her plate but eating none of it. Did *she* know what Leyton was up to? Was that the reason for this uncharacteristic skittishness? She had come to Kiriath determined to protect her country's interests, after all, and it had to be obvious stealing Kiriath's regalia would not be in those best interests. But if she considered Leyton's plans a bad idea, he thought she'd more likely be formulating plans to stop him, not sitting here quivering and pale.

He exchanged a few more benign words with her but, with Leyton listening closely at her shoulder, got no further than he had before. Deciding he'd spent enough time with his difficult guests, he rewarded himself by turning his attention to his newest duke, expressing the pleasure he'd taken earlier in watching the elder Meridon's reaction to seeing his son made a nobleman. Swordmaster Meridon and his wife were in attendance at this banquet right now, as were Trap's four sisters and their husbands, all recovered from the shock that had turned them into wax statues during the elevation ceremony. "I suppose now they'll be wanting to visit you in your manor out at Northille," Abramm remarked. "At least you'll have plenty of room to escape them if need be."

"And with this new job you've given me," Trap added wryly, "plenty of things to give me excuse. Maybe it won't be so bad after all."

Abramm grinned at him. "There'll be others, too," he teased. "You'll be amazed at the relatives you suddenly discover you have."

Trap glanced at him sourly. "Is that supposed to make me feel better?"

Abramm's grin widened.

It was not until the main course of roast bullock and golden potatoes was served that Leyton was finally drawn into a conversation with Simon seated at his far right and Abramm had a chance to speak to Maddie unmonitored.

Leaning toward her, he murmured, "Are you feeling poorly tonight, my lady?"

She flinched but did not look at him. "I'm fine, sir."

"Because you're not eating. And you seem . . . tense."

She stared at her plate as she moved the meat about with increasing agitation. A furious flush stained her cheeks. "You know how much I detest these courtly doings."

Aye, he knew. But he also knew he had never seen her this cowed. Was Leyton's influence over her this powerful? Unlikely as it seemed, he really had little idea what their relationship was like. Beyond the fact it didn't appear to be amicable.

And already—*a pox on it!*—Leyton had noted their conversation and was turning from Simon to interject, "Detests them? Now, *there's* an understatement!" His eyes met Abramm's over her bowed head. "She should've been born a milkmaid, not a king's daughter." He chuckled at his witticism, seeming unaware—or not caring—that he was the only one to do so.

Abramm expected Maddie to parry with a sharp retort, even heard her take a breath to do so. But in the end she only sat mute and red-faced, rapidly tumbling a piece of meat about on her plate.

Well, whatever is going on with you, my lady, he thought at her, by now thoroughly perplexed, *I see I'll not find out now.* This evening, perhaps during the fireworks or the ball, he would seek her out apart from her nosy brother and get the truth.

Maddie cut a tiny piece off one of the already-cut morsels of beef on her plate and put it in her mouth, chewing slowly and swallowing. Then she glanced at him, offered a quick smile. "See? I'm fine." But she couldn't hold his gaze for long and soon returned to studying her plate.

They proceeded through the meal's various courses, and eventually an innocent question from Abramm spurred Leyton into a recitation of his hunting experiences. Maddie had warned earlier against bringing this subject up, but Abramm had forgotten. And paid the price. What he didn't expect was the way Leyton suddenly related his own experiences to Abramm's recent encounter with the morwhol. Incredibly, he truly did seem to believe it had actually been a bear and that Abramm was allowing the exaggerated tale to circulate unrefuted for the sake of winning his people's support.

"Bruin are fearsome enough predators in their own right, as I well know," Donavan said. "Myself, I think I might *rather* face a morwhol than the big boar that just about nailed me up in the Laagernath five years ago."

And now, Prince, another big bore is about to nail me, right here in my very own banquet hall. . . .

"Grizzle-backed, head large as wine keg, paws like dinner plates . . ."

He waxed enthusiastically in the telling of his tale, as beside him, Madeleine loosed a quiet sigh of resignation. It wasn't a bad story—save for wondering how much of it was true—until, incredibly, the man had the gall to suggest that had Abramm used the techniques just described he'd have escaped the grievous injuries he had sustained in his own battle.

Leyton's eyes darted briefly to the scars on Abramm's face as he said this, and it took the king a moment to recover his poise enough to speak. "I'll have to remember that the next time I find myself facing a bruin of that size, sir."

Between them, Madeleine was cutting another thin slice of meat, her expression grim, teeth clenched.

"I think you will find it most helpful," Leyton said smoothly. He paused to finish up his last bite of beef, then embarked on a new and even more tactless subject. "I understand you were quite the swordsman before your accident, sir."

Maddie's fork twisted from her fingers and fell to her plate with a loud clank as she looked round at her brother in apparent astonishment—Abramm couldn't see her face, only the tension in her shoulders.

As always, Leyton seemed unaware of the clumsiness of his conversation and the offense it had given. "A pity," he continued, shaking his head sadly. "I was hoping to cross blades with you sometime. When a man reaches a certain level of expertise, as I'm sure you know, it becomes difficult to find an opponent who can give you any kind of a contest at all."

Abramm shrugged. "Well, I haven't given it up entirely. I'm sure a match could be arranged."

"Oh no, sir. I wouldn't want to—" Leyton broke off.

You wouldn't want to embarrass me? "I practice daily, sir. It would be no problem. Besides, how could I let such a challenge pass unmet?"

"Well, then . . . excellent! Perhaps I can even be of help in your rehabilitation. Whenever you wish to set it up, I'll be happy to oblige."

Between them, Maddie loosed another sigh and picked up her fork.

They were just finishing dessert when Ethan Laramor led a cadre of armsmen into the room—those in the lead carrying sturdy trestles, the six bringing up the rear bearing a platform with a large, lumpy burden covered with a linen sheet. Once the trestles were set up and the platform slid onto them, Abramm stood and the room fell into silence.

He turned to the small group of border lords clustered at the front of the table farthest to his left, lamenting anew that more of their fellows weren't in attendance. With the passes still closed, he'd known most would be unable to leave the highlands for his coronation, but in the end he'd traded the need to get it done before the Esurhites attacked against the need to bind the border lords to him. Now he half wished he'd waited. It would have been good if more of them could experience the coming revelation personally.

"It has come to my attention," he announced, "that when the workmen removed the Hasmal'uk stone from the Coronation Chair to transport it back to the vault after the ceremony, they found it had undergone a transformation." He returned his gaze to the border lord. "Lord Ethan?"

Laramor tugged the sheeting aside to reveal the familiar lozenge-shaped stone lying like a fattened hog on the platform. It had been cracked down the middle, the two sides gaping about a hand's width apart at the top. A thin shell of darkened rock, which appeared to have once encased it, was broken now into shards as if it had been popped right off the inner surface. An inner surface comprised of pure gold.

As those nearest leaped to their feet with cries of astonishment, Abramm stared at it with amazement of his own. Though Laramor had already informed him of the stone's change, it was another thing entirely to actually see it.

One of the border lords called out from his place at the closer end of the leftward-most table. "Sire, may we have leave to examine it?"

"You may, sir. But keep it orderly." Abramm glanced at Captain Channon, whom he'd already instructed regarding his guests' viewing of the stone.

As Channon sprang to see to it, Trap turned to Abramm with a cocked brow. "You're turning granite to gold now?"

"The Light did it," Abramm replied with a grimace. "Maybe when it drove the rhu'ema away. I only know that I had nothing to do with it."

But he could feel Prince Leyton's eyes upon him and knew this revelation would not help convince the man the regalia were not the talismans of mystical powers Chesedhan legend made them out to be.

Now Simon leaned around the crown prince and said, with some excitement, "Melt it down for sovereigns, sir. Think of the supplies it'll buy. And the armsmen it'll support."

Abramm saw at once that he was right, a chill of wonder crawling over him.

"It seems Eidon favors you yet again," Leyton said quietly. But Abramm liked neither the tone of his voice nor the look in his eye.

FIRST

FURY WRITHED WITHIN the man's body—more, truly, than human flesh should be able to stand. Hazmul made no effort to curb it. What, in his unveiled form, would have manifested in lurid, blinding explosions and searing heat, was forced to channel itself through the body he had taken on. Muscles contracted to rigidity, then exploded in violent motion; tooth ground upon tooth; the heart drummed frenetically against the chest cavity, forcing blood and adrenaline through dangerously distended arteries and veins. In the delicate capillaries of the brain, a tiny vessel swelled on the verge of rupture. . . .

Hazmul knew it, even through his rage. Knew if he did not control himself, the vessel would burst and the body become useless to him.

He didn't care. He almost wanted the silly thing to die, weak bag of water that it was.

We almost had him. He should have been ours! He was ours!

Hazmul still could hardly believe what had happened. He'd been in close contact with Terstans for centuries and prided himself on his toughness, his ability to endure a multitude of manifestations of Light without the slightest flicker of unease. He was a warhast, after all.

But this . . . this *searing* had taken him completely by surprise. Just as he'd been about to help the miniol strengthen its hold on its target, the Light had burst upon him, spearing through the buffering flesh of his host. . . . The next thing he knew, he was lying here in this darkened room, brought here from the coronation because he'd *"had another spell."*

Another wave of fury swept through him. He could hear the air exiting the trachea of his borrowed body in deep, ragged grunts. It brought no comfort to know the others had been overbowled just as brutally, nor that all the unfleshed host gathered in that hall to witness what was to have been Hazmul's great victory had fled screaming. *He* was a warhast, and warhasts did not collapse when faced with manifestations of the Light. Particularly not when they came from within a mere man. When he found out who among his organization was the cause of this debacle, he would see them damped. He would *not* tolerate incompetents.

Already he'd had to endure a rhu'eman inquiry regarding the incident with the morwhol last fall, when the boom of Abramm's passage into his destiny had been heard all the way down to the Throne. Whatever had happened in that coronation hall today would have been heard, as well. There would be a full investigation this time.

The little cadre of inspectors would probably arrive tonight, questioning him in their sly, smarmy tones, auras sparkling with presumed superiority. Hazmul swore harshly and felt his host's limbs thrash. The vessel began to vibrate alarmingly. He teetered on the verge of letting it rip, letting the useless blob of pudding destroy itself.

But to give in to that urge was exactly what Hazmul despised in his inferiors, and so, finally, he curbed his wrath. The pressure eased. The racing heart slowed; the breathing deepened; the fists unclenched. Abruptly he realized he was drooling.

Disgust welled in him. So weak these creatures were. And this body in particular.

He brushed away the spittle, startled to note that the hand he used was blistered and burned. With that awareness came the perception of smoke burning his eyes and nose. He looked around at the splintered, blackened furniture, some of it still smoldering. White shards of porcelain littered the wine-colored carpet. The velvet drapes hung in scorched shreds beside the window.

He felt another surge of disgust, this time with himself. The mess would have to be cleaned up and the room redecorated without arousing suspicion—an inconvenience he could ill afford at present. He should have exercised more self-control. And if he wanted to stay in control of this situation, he'd better calm down right now and start thinking again.

Not long after Hazmul regained his composure, Underwarhast Vesprit slithered through the crack under the bedchamber door, arriving as a saffron ribbon of light wreathed in veils of shadow. Seeing Hazmul up and alert, the underwarhast immediately shifted phase to present his formal persona and bowed in salute.

Like all Bright Ones, Vesprit was beautiful, his high-cheekboned face set off by a mane of long, glossy black hair briefly tamed by the silver circlet on his brow. His smooth skin gleamed with the subtle amber glow of his characteristic essence, and there were times looking at him made Hazmul resent having to hide within the clumsy ugliness of his current host. On the other hand, he would not be able to accomplish nearly as much were he not so shielded, and thus he must bear it for the short time needed to carry out his plans.

He saw the beautiful dark eyes flick around the room, noting the devastation, saw the brief darkening of uneasiness that shivered across his essence.

"*So tell me what happened, Underwarhast,*" Hazmul said. "*Abramm was reeling when I left the palace. Devastated by the sight of his scars and securely in the grasp of his Shadow. . . . How could he have recovered in time to facilitate a manifestation like that?*"

"*I'm not sure, sir.*" Vesprit did his best to suppress the vibration of his doubts, but it was a skill he had yet to master, one he would have to if he expected to advance higher than underwarhast. Indeed, if he had a superior officer less compassionate than Hazmul, he would have been sent to the *ghahera* on the spot, for such doubts were highly insulting. Fortunately, Hazmul was sensitive enough that he also perceived the harmonic of Vesprit's accompanying admiration for him, and so he let it go.

"You're afraid of him, aren't you, Underwarhast?"

Vesprit's form suffused with the muddy ochre of embarrassment. *"Sir . . . he is strong in the Light."*

"Of course he is," Hazmul cut in dryly. *"We wouldn't bother with him if he wasn't. But even with the Light, he is hardly more intelligent than a cockroach. Moreover, the Shadow lives within him, waiting to do our bidding. How can you think we won't defeat him?"*

"I . . . I suppose I didn't think it through, sir."

"No. You did not. Now, what happened after I left the palace this morning?"

"Well, sir, there was Lady Madeleine's preparation of the horse. The krator on duty said learning of it produced a definite lightening in Abramm's aura. And his man Haldon said—"

"Give me the memories."

"Yes, sir." And Vesprit opened his mind to release the recollections of the two kratori assigned to monitor Abramm and Lady Madeleine.

An instant later, Hazmul swore aloud. *"How was I not made aware of this? She spent half the day at it!"*

"Sir, it didn't— We didn't think it would make any difference. She was just trying to escape her brother. Who could have guessed Abramm would choose to ride the horse? It's against tradition. His clothes weren't right for it. The horse is hard to handle and unaccustomed to close crowds. . . ."

"And the old man? Haldon. He should never have been given the opportunity to speak."

"We had no idea he would challenge him like that, sir. The words were out before anyone had any inkling he was going to say them."

"Who was on duty?"

Vesprit told him.

"See that he's disciplined for inattention. There is always some indication of these things; he simply did not draw the right conclusions. Most likely because he made too many assumptions. Haldon may only be a chamberlain, but he, too, carries the Light and, worse, has become as fanatical about living in it as the king. Such men are always a danger."

Vesprit murmured his assent as Hazmul fell into silence, already compiling the information he'd received. A nasty Light plague would emerge from all this, but such things happened to everyone now and then. Of greater concern was the regalia's manifestation.

"How was it Abramm was able to trigger the regalia? I sensed him when he arrived, and he seemed nowhere near strong enough to have done that."

"No, sir." Vesprit hesitated. *"The consensus is that He over-ruled."*

Hazmul stared at his underling, fear ghosting through him for the first time. He squelched it immediately lest it be transferred to his host's aura and Vesprit note it. *"Lodge an official protest, then. That is against the rules. I'll file another when the investigative team arrives. If it's true, no one can fault us for this."*

He paused, aware of the sick suspicion that this situation might be more complicated than he'd thought. All the theatrics that went on today would very likely provoke Abramm's curiosity as to what he had in the regalia and could lead him into an investigation that could be very troublesome. Not only with regard to the regalia but also concerning the other things that were part of his royal inheritance—things so far Abramm had no idea about; things that, if Hazmul had his way, the king would continue to be ignorant of indefinitely. Better set some distractions in motion right away.

"Initiate containment measures on the plague at once," he said to Vesprit. *"And get our boy Prittleman fired up. I expect he already is, but don't let his passion wane. I want a new pamphlet. Give him some extra protection and get as many copies out as you can. How receptive is he to suggestion?"*

"Given the right sort, sir, very."

"Good." Hazmul went on to detail the sorts of things he wanted the pamphlet to say.

When he was finished, Vesprit's essence was vibrating with an unmodulated concern that bordered on alarm. Hazmul kept his own irritation tightly controlled. *"You have an objection to these instructions, Underwarhast?"*

Vesprit sparked with surprise and chagrin, immediately tempering the frequency of his reactions. Then he straightened his shoulders and said firmly, *"Sir, if you have Prittleman write these things, Abramm will take strong measures. Someone will surely give him up."*

"Let me handle that." Hazmul took satisfaction in noting how his own confidence worked to settle Vesprit. He went on. *"That Terstan group that broke off from Kesrin under the cobbler—they were disgruntled with Abramm's toleration of the Mataio, so I'm sure they'll be happy to hear how Bonafil and his boys were driven from the coronation. I want you to see that they are ecstatic."*

"Yes, sir."

"Very good, then."

It was not a direct dismissal, but one Vesprit should have read as such. Still he stayed, concern flickering through his essence.

"What is it now, Underwarhast?"

"What about Abramm himself, sir? Shall we continue our work on him at the same pace or intensify?"

Hazmul snorted. *"Of course not! What have you been doing for the last four thousand years?"*

The warm lemon of surprise flared across Vesprit's form. *"I've spent all of it in the deep south, sir. There haven't been too many with the Light. And I thought the rule was that whenever they have a success we're to immediately pound them with a counterattack."*

"That is only one of several relevant guidelines, all of which must be considered together: flexibility, variability, and target awareness are also in view here. If we become so predictable he knows what we're doing, we've lost our advantage. He's on to us now, ready for another attack. So we'll let him think he's won for a time, while we turn our efforts in other directions."

Vesprit's saffron glow deepened with understanding and approval. *"I see, sir."*

"I'm thinking it would be profitable to play on Lady Madeleine's feelings for him. She'll try to ignore them, of course, but we won't let that happen. In fact . . . if we can tease his to the fore, as well . . . why, that would be perfect."

"Perfect, sir? I thought she was a danger to us. That she made him too strong."

"That was before the coronation. Now she is merely her sister's

rival for his attentions. . . . If she can win him, and we can provoke him to act upon his feelings . . ."

"Oh yes. I see, sir. It's brilliant!" Vesprit's sudden flush of awe was so profoundly stimulating, Hazmul had to struggle for a few moments to keep his host's aura placid. At length he gave a brief nod, as if Vesprit's reverence made no difference. *"You may go then, Underwarhast."*

As Vesprit shifted phase and flew off, Hazmul turned to the other Bright One who had come in during their conversation and waited quietly in the sidelines. *"Now, about the king's brother . . ."*

6

At dusk, just after the banquet ended, everyone went out on the terrace and balconies to view the fireworks shot off over the bay. Then Abramm started the coronation ball by dancing a solo round with Lady Madeleine, again serving as stand-in for his absent bride-to-be. She was as stiff and cool as she'd been at dinner, hardly looking at him, hardly talking, hardly even touching him. As soon as her duty was done, she made herself part of the crowd and, throughout the remainder of the evening, managed to elude him every time he tried to seek her out—though occasionally he did catch her looking at him from across the room. Eventually she disappeared altogether, and though he feared at first that she'd retired for the night, on further consideration, he decided she had more likely escaped to the royal gardens, lit up tonight in concert with the ball.

Hoping to catch her there, he set out on a stroll with Trap Meridon, ostensibly to discuss the day—the ball had been afire with talk of all that had happened in connection with his coronation—and his plan to visit Graymeer's tomorrow. They hadn't gone far before Channon quietly reported that Maddie was in the tea garden, giving direction to Abramm's strolling.

As they came out on the uppermost terrace of the multileveled tea garden, an armsman stepped from the concealing shadows and directed Abramm's eye to the cloaked figure standing below them at one of the garden's mid-level overlooks. Lights glimmered in the surrounding foliage and lit the overlook's railing. Below her, nestled at the garden's midst, stood the teahouse, aglow with its garland of kelistars. With a sudden squall of nerves, Abramm ended his conversation with Trap and went on alone, hearing his friend's voice, low and indignant behind him: "What the plague, Captain! You're encouraging them?"

Out of earshot before he heard Channon's reply, Abramm grimaced with annoyance. Where had Trap gotten the idea there was a *them* to encourage? All Abramm wanted to do was talk to her without that insufferable Leyton listening in, and without all the court getting the wrong idea.

Wrapped and hooded in her cloak, Madeleine stood at the rail of the overlook, staring over an array of terraces lit with swirls of tiny orblights. She must have heard the grit of his feet on the gravel, for she turned toward him while he was still some yards off. Seeing him, her eyes widened and her body stiffened.

"Ah, Lady Madeleine," he said, drawing up before her. "I hoped I might find you out here."

"Your majesty." She dropped him a curtsey.

"I trust I'm not intruding."

"Of course not." But it was obvious from her tone and manner that he was. She straightened, her eyes darting up to his and down again so quickly he wondered anew if his scars, stark and shocking now on his newly clean-shaven face, were putting her off.

An awkward silence ensued, and after a moment she turned back to the rail. Distant strains of music warbled, overlain by the crackling of his men's booted feet on the ground cover as they ranged out around him, their protective net unusually close tonight on account of this morning's attack.

Finally Abramm murmured, "Shaving the beard was *your* idea, you know."

Her chin came primly up, only the front lines of her profile visible beyond her cloak's hood. "And a good idea, too," she said, still facing the garden. "You looked very handsome today."

He snorted. "Please, my lady. You needn't lie to me. I know what I look like."

She continued to stare at the garden for a moment, then sighed and watched her gloved hand stroke the marble balustrade before her. "No, sir, I don't think you do."

"I've seen my face, Maddie. This morning, when I bid them to uncover the mirror."

"You didn't see your face. All you saw were the scars."

He gave a bitter chuckle. "It's hardly possible to see anything else."

Now, finally, she turned toward him, staring up at him from out of the cowl's shadows. He watched her eyes, wide and dark, rove across his face, touching the scars only briefly before meeting his gaze. Her expression softened and she shook her head. "Oh no, Abramm, it's very possible not to see them at all." And for a moment she reminded him of Shettai standing on that Xorofin balcony, staring up at him with a tearstained face. Except that Madeleine wasn't crying.

He frowned. "Well, then, why have you been so standoffish today? Why do you act like it hurts to look at me?"

Her breath caught and the softening vanished as she turned back to the garden. "You just signed a treaty agreeing to marry my sister. What do you want me to do? Throw myself at you like Lady Leona does?"

"Of course not!" He laid a gloved hand on the balustrade, leaning so he could see her face around the edge of the concealing cowl. "I just want you to be normal again."

"Well, I can't be normal. Not with everything that's happened."

"You mean the ceremony?"

She was silent for a long time. "My troubles are hardly your concern, sir. Just believe me when I say it's been a . . . a very hard day." And with this last, her voice trembled and she turned her face away from him, hiding behind that wretched cowl.

He frowned at her, more befuddled than ever. Before he could pursue the matter, however, she pushed off the rail and stepped away from him. "I'm getting cold. Do you mind if we walk a bit?"

"Of course not." *It must be Leyton haranguing her about all those rumors.* She'd not cared about them before, but with her brother's coming and Abramm's signing of the treaty, the courtiers' antipathy toward her had intensified. With half his nobles still outraged at his "inexplicably rash" decision, she was the natural focus for their anger. And Leyton's fixation with the regalia hadn't helped.

They strolled along the winding path through sculpted topiaries, the thin strains of violin wafting through the darkness around them. The early spring night was cold, the air heavy with the scent of damp leaves. Terstan orblights sat along the path and rested in various holders along the way, while overhead the trees stretched their bud-swollen branches against a brittle, star-filled sky.

"Was there something you wished to speak to me about?" she asked finally, her voice resuming its normal pitch and stability.

Was there anything else he wanted to talk about besides her inexplicable behavior toward him today? Ah, yes . . . the manifestation. "I was wondering if you saw any of what I saw while the Light was on me this morning. The galleys moored at Graymeer's. More of them coming out of fog-bound islands. The northland in shadow. . . . A great army beneath our combined banners. . . ."

An arched footbridge rose up before them to span a chuckling streamlet, their footsteps echoing hollowly as they crossed it. She said she remembered nothing but the Light, blazing out of him, then added, "You really saw the galleys at Graymeer's?"

He nodded. "At the same time they were actually there, I think. I saw a great red dragon, too, flying overhead."

"A red dragon?" she breathed, her surprise evident. Of course she'd made the connection at once: he wore a red dragon on his arm.

"I have no idea whether it's real or symbolic. Maybe both. It seemed to mock me."

They walked on for a bit before she said, "I saw nothing like that."

He frowned. "So what did you see?"

She shrugged.

"Well, you must've seen something. What made you faint?"

"How did you know I fainted?" she burst out, stepping around to face him and bringing them both to a halt. "Did Leyton—"

"Simon told me."

"Oh." She looked at her feet, the cloak's cowl dropping forward to hide her face. "Well . . . it wasn't a real faint," she said to the ground.

Abramm felt his brows fly up. "You were *pretending* to faint? You? My lady, I must say—"

"Not pretending!" Her head came up sharply and she glowered at him. "I was just . . . unsteady on my feet." With that she turned away and started down the path again.

He hurried after her, asking as he came abreast, "Why? What did you see?"

"Blackwell passed out entirely, though. Had to be carried from the hall and was taken to his rooms."

"I know."

"Had another one of his fits, they said."

"Yes, I know that, too."

"It's a pity what happened to him that day at Seven Peaks."

"Aye. It is." He frowned at her. "But I don't want to talk about Blackwell right now, my lady. I want to know what made you 'unsteady on your feet.'"

Again the tension thickened between them. She wrapped her arms about herself beneath her cloak and walked on without speaking. Then, "You don't want to know, Abramm. It means nothing. And it would only—" She stopped. Swallowed. "It would only make things worse."

"What things? How?"

At that point she reached the last straw of patience, whipping round on him and snapping out, "Didn't you learn your lesson with Trap last night?! Some things it's just better not to know."

"Why are you angry with me, my lady?" he protested helplessly, feeling as if they were playing a game of snap the whip and he was on the end of the whip. "What have I done?"

"Nothing! I'm not angry with *you*." And now she had her back to him again. "I'm angry with myself."

This conversation was growing more opaque by the minute, and every way he tried to make it clearer only made things worse. He lifted a hand to touch her arm, thought better of it, and pulled back. "Maddie, what's wrong?" he said finally. "I don't understand."

"No . . . You don't." And she started on again.

"Well, then—"

"Abramm, please! Just grant me my privacy on this and don't ask any more."

And so he did as she bade him, and they walked down the serpentine paths, crossing streamlets and planted glens until at last they came to the bottom of the garden, where a clipped green surrounded the narrow, white-marble, octagonal building that was the teahouse. Tall, glass-paned doors and windows stood in every wall, and kelistars rimmed the eaves of its cupola. A warm red glow inside betrayed the central brazier of coals set into an empty water basin to provide warmth for chilled garden walkers like themselves.

They climbed the three stairs up into the house, where garlands of tiny orblights hung from the high ceiling, casting a pale light over the interior. Narrow stuccoed walls decorated with leafy scrollwork interspersed the glass, and beneath the central brazier, the marble floor was tiled in a starburst pattern. Dried camellia blossoms strewed the entranceway, unrolling into staffid the moment the couple stepped onto the floor proper. Abramm killed one with a burst of Light as from the corner of his eye he saw a second skitter toward his companion—who impaled it with her own tendril of Light.

Maddie proceeded to the brazier while Abramm circled the room, glancing out the tall windows. His habit of continually taking stock of his sur-

roundings had been beaten into him years ago in Katahn's training compound, and he retained it here, despite the dark figures of his armsmen now
positioning themselves in the foliage at the green's edge.

Save for the staffid, the interior offered no obvious threat. It was dark
enough that courtier spies could not see clearly what went on between
them—yet not so dark they could imagine things that weren't happening.
Not that that had ever stopped them.

Killing two more staffid before he'd completed his round, Abramm finally
stopped at the brazier beside Lady Madeleine, who had stuck her gloved
hands between the front edges of her cloak to warm them over the coals.
Appreciating the warmth on his face, he held out his own hands and took the
opportunity to study her profile. Even lit by the warm glow of the coals, her
skin looked pale beneath the scattering of freckles, and shadows cupped her
eyes. She was tired and hurting, and he had no idea how to fix her.

Suddenly it dawned on him that her problems today, whatever they were,
hadn't originated with Leyton, though Abramm had no doubt he'd been
used. Maddie was a servant of Eidon, just as Abramm was. A valuable supporter, one he trusted and relied upon more than he wanted to admit. For his
unseen enemies to succeed in their attack on him, they had to neutralize
Madeleine just as they had Trap.

"The rhu'ema were after you this morning, weren't they?" he asked quietly. "Trying to make sure you couldn't help me during the ceremony."

For a moment she ceased to move. Then she drew her hands back inside
her cloak and sighed. "They were." She turned slightly toward him, her cloak
brushing his own as she looked at him over her shoulder. "I'm sorry I didn't
come to you this morning. I was just . . ." She trailed off awkwardly, eyes
dropping blindly to his chest.

He smiled at her. "Too busy seeing to my horse?"

"No!" Her eyes darted up again, flashing indignantly. "If you think I had
time to go out to the stable—"

"I'm teasing, my lady. Truth be told, learning Warbanner was ready to ride
in the midst of the crisis this morning was welcome news indeed. He pulled
me out of my black mood." He shook his head. "Your foresight continually
amazes me."

She shrugged and turned her attention to the coals. "I was really just trying to get away from Leyton."

He smiled down at her, full of gratitude and affection, thinking how complex and unpredictable she was, how quick-witted and, sometimes, like

tonight, undeniably attractive. The way her eyes flashed with that indignation, the endearing tilt of her chin when she sought to be firm—and the tendril of fawn-colored hair that always found a way to dangle in a long curl
beside her face and offset it all. Over and over she astonished him with her
ability to predict and accommodate his needs. Sometimes he thought she
knew him better than he knew himself. "Well," he said softly, "it made the
day."

A moment she was silent. Then, "No, sir, 'twas *you* who made the day."
She turned to him, her eyes locking upon his own, and she spoke even more
softly than he had. "Every inch a king you were. Even before the Light was
on you."

Her face, tilted up toward his own, glowed in the dim warm light of the
kelistars, her pupils like deep, dark pools. And as he looked down into them,
it was as if some imperceptible wind blew through him and everything
changed. He felt a dangerous slippage, a stirring of some deep and powerful
feeling within him, a sense of something monumentally disastrous about to
happen. His heart pounded frantically against his ribs. . . .

Her face darkened as if she were blushing, and she stepped sharply away,
turning her shoulder to him again, arms once more folded across her chest
beneath her cloak. "I think it's time for me to go, sir."

Her words startled the breath out of him and brought the blood rushing
inexplicably to his own face. His heart still galloped in his chest, his mind
churning with confusion. What had happened just now?

It took him a moment to find his tongue, and he spoke lightly, striving to
cover his discomfiture. "So you *are* feeling poorly, then."

"What. . . ? No. I mean . . ." When her voice came again it was weak and
trembling. "I mean, I think it is time for me to leave Kiriath altogether."

At first the words didn't register, as if they'd been spoken in a foreign
tongue. Then, "Leave Kiriath? Why?"

"It's just . . . It's time. There's really nothing more for me to do here."

The teahouse floor sagged beneath his feet. "But what about your
research? What about the songs? What about the *wedding*?"

She muttered something he could not distinguish, then snorted softly and
turned to face him. "Oh, come, Abramm, you've never cared a fig about any
of my songs. Truth be told, you'd rather they not be written, and don't think
I don't know that."

"That's not . . . entirely true." He felt his face burn anew.

"Well, getting away will help break this block I've had with them, if nothing else."

"But your research on our history and the fortresses—"

"There are any number of men imminently qualified to assist you in that, and who would be euphoric to do so."

"If I wanted them, Maddie, I'd have gone to them in the first place," he said sternly, frowning at her. "I want *you*."

She stared at him, startled, lips parted, face chalk-pale.

"*I want* you." His own words echoed in his ear as he realized how that might have sounded and flushed with embarrassment again. But surely she understood how he'd meant that. . . . He was sworn to marry her sister, after all.

"I'm sorry, sir," she said. "I don't believe I can be of help to you anymore." With that, she pushed away from the brazier and left him there, listening to the sound of her hurried footsteps as they faded into silence.

———

Maddie fled the teahouse in a state of total discombobulation. She could hardly think, could hardly breathe, could hardly even see, as was proven when she ran smack into someone coming down the path into the teahouse grotto. She never saw his face, just bounced off of him, muttered an apology, and raced on without looking up, desperate to get away before everything came flying apart. She thought it might have been Simon Kalladorne, probably the worst person who could have happened upon that little scene. . . .

But what difference did it make now? She was leaving. She had told Abramm her intent, and it was final. Soon it wouldn't matter what anyone thought.

Oh, Father Eidon! What was I doing? What was I thinking to look at him like that and say those things. . . ? She had spent most of her adult life seeking to avoid the amorous attentions of men. On those few occasions where her usual off-putting persona failed, she had even resorted to physical persuasion, having once shoved a hapless suitor so hard the man had fallen down the bank of stairs at his heels. And while some she minded less than others, she could not recall ever thinking she might like a man to hold her in his arms. . . . Until tonight when she had stood there in that teahouse looking up at Abramm, her heart leaping at the change that had swept across his face and the sudden possibility that he might do a good deal more than take her in his arms.

He's going to marry your sister! What is wrong with you?

She was tempted to blame it on the dream, but after a day of trying to do that—to say nothing of that cursed vision!—she knew it was useless. The rhu'ema had only pulled up what was already there. If she dared to be honest with herself, she had to admit she'd been in love with Abramm Kalladorne since the day he'd come ashore from the battered *Wanderer* nine months ago. He'd been filthy, disheveled, exhausted, and reeking of kraggin. Yet when he'd stopped to greet Kesrin and his gaze had briefly met her own, her soul had come alight as if she'd waited for him all her life.

But that's all romantic nonsense. And even if there is one chosen soul mate for each of us, he can't be yours because he's already chosen Briellen. You'd best just get out of Springerlan before you humiliate yourself entirely.

At least that little scene they'd just played out in the teahouse had taken place where no one but he could see. And she took comfort in knowing he would find the possibility she was in love with him to be so ludicrous, it would never enter his mind.

And yet . . . there at the end . . . *"I want you,"* he'd said fiercely, and the look in his eye . . . *Don't think of it. It was only your imagination. Like the vision . . . your own desires and nothing more. Light's grace, Mad! You don't seriously believe the man could ever love you, do you?*

And if he could, that would only make things worse.

Why didn't you just let him think you were ill? It would have stopped the questions, at least, and you wouldn't have been such a babbling fool.

Not wanting to run into anyone, she went up to her east-wing, third-floor apartments by way of the service stair, wiping away the tears as she went. Her maid, Liza, took her cloak and gloves in the darkened sitting chamber, where a single lamp and the hearth fire provided the only illumination. Though it was well after midnight, she was too cold and agitated to seek her bed, and so stood by the fire, glad of its warmth upon her face and fingers, content to be safely alone at last. She stared blindly into the dancing tongues of amber, listening to them hiss and snap. From down in the valley, the University clock tolled the half hour, its deep tone mingled a heartbeat later with the closer, louder chime of the mantel clock. She breathed a sigh of release.

"Well," came a low, familiar voice. "I was beginning to wonder if I would have to wait until morning for your return."

She whipped around, aghast to find her brother seated in one of the chairs clustered behind her, sufficiently cloaked in shadow that she hadn't noticed him.

"Leyton!" she cried. "What are you doing here?"

He stared up at her, the firelight gilding his bushy blond brows and casting a ruddy glow across his weathered face. "You told me you were retiring for the night. I wished to speak with you privately, so I stopped by hoping to catch you before you'd gone to bed. Instead, I found you weren't even here." He paused, his gaze not leaving hers. "I've waited almost two hours, Madeleine."

She frowned at him, suddenly and intensely irritated. "Well, if I'd known your intention I surely would've made the effort to accommodate you." *If he finds out I was with Abramm there'll be another lecture. Oh, Father Eidon, where have you been this day? I can't take another grilling from Leyton. Have mercy on me and get rid of him!*

"So where were you?"

"Walking in the royal garden. I enjoy the lights." She turned back to the fire to continue warming her hands.

"Sharing a lover's tryst, were you?"

She stifled an angry reply, stood there a moment to gather her patience, then let out a long sigh. "I thought we'd settled this."

"So did I. Yet barely twenty-four hours later you're wandering the gardens alone at night. Although I don't think it ended alone." He paused and the chair creaked as he rose and came to stand beside her, resting one hand on the mantel. "Were you with the king tonight, Madeleine?"

She sighed again, realizing he would find out anyway. And who knew what the story would have swollen into by morning. "He came upon me in the garden. We walked to the teahouse, where we spoke briefly, and then I left."

He pushed away from the mantel, muttering something inappropriate for a lady's ear. Madeleine turned to watch him. "We were there five minutes at the most. It was nothing."

"Well, that's not how the court's going to perceive it. Even if you care nothing for your own reputation, why don't you show a little concern for your sister? Do you know what they've been saying about you today?"

"You think I went out there looking for him?"

"Did you?"

"No! I went out there to get away from—" *Him.* But she couldn't say that. "From you for one. From conversations like this. And frankly, I couldn't care less what they're saying about me."

"Hagin's beard, girl! After that little vomiting incident this morning—"

"Vomiting incident?"

"—and your apparent swoon during the coronation—"

"There was no vomiting incident!"

"—the current consensus is you're carrying Abramm's bastard." He finished as if she'd not spoken.

She stood there, mouth open to speak, no words coming out. For a moment she couldn't breathe. Then a tide of heat suffused her face, though not for the reason Leyton supposed. Or, at least, not solely.

He nodded, believing he'd scored his point. "Perhaps you begin to see the value of discretion. You and I may know the tale's not true, and I'm sure eventually it will be manifest. . . . But plagues, Maddie, in the meantime it's downright embarrassing!" He pressed his lips together. "Already people are laughing at Briellen. While others wonder if she might be used goods, as well."

She gave a snort. "Once she arrives you know no one will even care. As for me, you can relax. There'll be no more embarrassing indiscretions because I'll be leaving as soon as I can arrange passage. I told the king tonight."

And that set him back. Rather more soundly than she'd expected. He stared at her for a long moment, mouth half open. Then his bushy brows drew down. "You can't just leave."

"Of course I can. I'm Second Daughter. I can do as I wish. . . . And I wasn't vomiting this morning!" She stepped to the chair he'd just vacated and dropped into it.

"But . . . if you leave now, they'll be sure you're with child."

She rolled her eyes. "I'll be gone, Leyt. I won't care. And Bree will walk into nasty rumors whether I stay or go."

"But you've been living with these people. You know them. I thought you'd want to help her get settled, introduce her around. Try to make this thing work."

Maddie stared at him in sudden suspicion. "We both know that Bree will have no need—or desire—of *my* help settling in." She frowned at him. "She *is* coming, isn't she?"

"Of course. Why would you think otherwise?"

"Oh, only the small matter of our ancestors' repeated attempts to steal Kiriath's regalia . . . and your own far too obvious obsession with them. You weren't exactly subtle at dinner tonight, brother."

"I'm not here to steal them."

"So then, were you simply trying to annoy the man?"

"I was trying to figure out if he had any idea what he has."

"How could he not after what happened today?"

"I don't know, but it seems he doesn't!" And she saw the passion rise in him with almost physical force, sparking in his eyes and tightening every muscle into eager alertness. He dropped onto the chair beside her and leaned over its arm. "By the prophets, Mad! They proved more than half the legends true today—the wind clearing off the clouds, the Esurhites discovered, the healings . . . all those conversions. Even the transformation of the Hasmal'uk stone. I could hardly contain myself."

"Yes, that was obvious."

"And yet, he spoke as if it was all Eidon's doing, a one-time event, not something he can control and wield against our enemies."

"Well, he *was* the one at the center of it all. I'd be inclined to give him some credit for knowing who was doing what."

Leyton shook his head. "He's only been changed four years, Mad. It's completely reasonable to think he's as ignorant and undiscerning as he seems." He sagged against the chair's back, eyes drifting to the flames. "All that power . . . all that promise . . . It's like giving a finely balanced rapier to a child." His eyes came back to her. "And you— You at least *know* the tales. I'd expected you would have been studying them, hoped you might have stumbled onto something already. Instead he's got you wasting your time on old fortresses."

"Ophiran guardstars are a known entity. He's seen one of them in action. I'd hardly call it a waste of—"

"The regalia may well be the key to the survival of both Kiriath *and* Chesedh!" he interrupted sharply. "Something that can be used offensively against the Shadow's hordes. Something that can drive them back and utterly destroy them!"

But she hardly heard the end of his outburst, her focus honing in on what he'd said at the first. *Key to Kiriath and Chesedh's survival?* She realized then that his passion sprang from more than the simple excitement of seeing long-held beliefs coming true. His tone held an undeniable note of desperation. And that was most unlike Leyton.

Abruptly it all fell into place. "You brought those ships to Kiriath because they're useless to Chesedh now, aren't they?"

He went very still, his gaze fixed on the fire, big hands clenching the chair's arms.

"I knew things had to be desperate for Father to give Briellen to the Kiriathans," Maddie whispered.

Leyton sighed. "Not exactly desperate. But not good, either." He spoke quietly. "North Andol has fallen, and Draesia surrendered without a peep. Shadow holds all the southern regions of the strait and is moving into the eastern portions. The winds are all but gone. To take any sort of offensive action, we must have galleys ourselves—we've been frantically building them for months now. At least our wind-driven vessels can be used here. And preserved if things go badly at home."

Cold to the core, Maddie sagged back in her chair.

"There've been no emissaries yet," he went on, "but they'll come, offering the same deal they offered the Draesians: surrender and they spare both land and people, allowing us to go on with our lives as usual—save for the governors Belthre'gar would set over us, and the black-tunicked soldiers garrisoned among us, and the forfeiture of a reasonable tribute. . . ."

"And all who wear the shield forced to renounce it in favor of allegiance to Khrell," Maddie said grimly.

"That was not part of the negotiations, of course."

"Of course." But they both knew it would come. Had to come. Shield bearers hindered the power of the Shadow.

As if he read her mind, Leyton said, "Shadow's already closed our eastern borders. We've had our trade lines cut off, treaties with Draesia and both Andols changed by fiat. Our supply of iron has been eliminated. We've made a few agreements with the barbarians to the north but they're not much help, besides being untrustworthy. Much as it galls to admit it, we *need* Kiriathan wheat and iron and men. We need cannon and shot and powder, and the Western Isles are now our only source."

They sat in silence for a time. Then she roused. "And you've told Abramm none of this?"

He smiled wryly. "When negotiating a treaty, little sister, it doesn't do to let the other party know how desperate you are. . . ." The smile faded. "There's more."

She regarded him soberly.

"Belthre'gar took all three daughters of the king of North Andol for his harem—after having the king's sons killed before their father's eyes. It was the last thing the old man saw before being blinded. Payment for their resistance, Belthre'gar said." He watched his fingers pick at the fibers on the chair's padded arm. "That, I think, was what pushed Father to sign Abramm's treaty. Better a Kiriathan than that Shadow-loving savage. Bree'll be here within two weeks."

Two weeks! The coldness in her belly spread up to her shoulders and arms. What for so long they had dreaded was practically on their doorstep. "Abramm needs to know, Leyton. Especially this last. Belthre'gar really does have a personal grudge against him. Finding out Father's sent Bree to him . . . will only make things worse."

"He's already threatening to kill us and take our lands, Mad. How could things be any worse? Besides, I won't risk Abramm getting cold feet. Bad enough all this talk of the treaty and wedding being a trick to get the regalia."

"For which you have mostly yourself to blame."

He made a face. "I'll not deny my fascination with them. Nor even that I've given thought to what we could do with them back home. . . ."

"Most likely a big fat nothing. They obviously belong to him."

"And he, just as obviously, has no idea what he's got in them."

"He knows more than you think."

"But not nearly enough, I fear. Someone needs to instruct him as to the nature of what he's inherited."

"Is that what you were trying to do at dinner? Instruct him?"

Leyton's gaze returned to her, speculative now. "Actually, I was hoping you might be the one to enlighten both of us."

Suddenly she could hardly breathe, distraught by the quick, hot, heart-leaping eagerness to burrow herself back into Abramm's life; the opposing dread of soon seeing him with Briellen and knowing he would always be off-limits. The fear that if she stayed, her feelings would be discovered, that she might, in another cascade of mindless impulses, reveal them to him.

But against all that was a firm, resolute voice asking how she could put such petty, personal concerns before the fate of their two realms.

"Why did you faint today, anyway?" Leyton asked, his question intruding into her thoughts. "If you're not ill. Did you feel their power?"

And again she felt as if a giant hand squeezed her chest. What could she say that wouldn't give everything away? "I felt the Light," she said finally, choosing her words with care. "I don't know if it came from Abramm or the regalia or Eidon himself. After that . . ." *I only know there was a wedding . . . and a coming storm, and mingled armies . . . and, according to Abramm, a great red dragon circling overhead.*

Oh, Father Eidon, what does it all mean? And what do you want me to do?

Down in the valley the University clock tolled the first hour of the new day, followed a heartbeat later by the chime of the mantel clock.

"So will you stay?" Leyton said. "Will you help us?"

She sighed deeply. "I—I'll think about it."

7

Abramm stood motionless in the teahouse, reeling in the wake of Maddie's abrupt departure. *"I'm sorry, sir. I don't believe I can be of help to you anymore."*

How could she say such a thing? Even if she didn't know how much he relied upon her, surely that determination was up to him to make. He wanted to command his servants to bring her back, wanted to order her to stay. He could do it. He was king, and as long as she was in his realm, his commands held sway over her.

Except . . . she was no longer the Second Daughter here alone. She could appeal to her brother, the Crown Prince of Chesedh. The treaty would be destroyed and Kiriath would lose Chesedh's much-needed protection against their Esurhite enemies. And in light of the attack on Graymeer's this morning, Abramm knew the day of reckoning was fast approaching.

Besides, if she was unhappy here, how could he think of forcing her to stay? He'd chalked her restless moodiness up to her troubles with the song of the morwhol, promised for the coronation. But six months of working had left her nothing to show for it, and now he realized that something had been deeply amiss even before Leyton's arrival. Today's events had merely brought it all to a head.

The grit of leather soles on gravel drew his eyes to the walkway leading up to the teahouse where a tall silver-bearded figure approached, cloak flaring out behind him: Simon, come to find him for their trip to Gillard's bedside tonight. He couldn't have missed Maddie's departure.

Abramm met him at the doorway. "Your timing is excellent, Simon. I was just about to leave."

"Is Lady Madeleine all right?"

"She's had a difficult day."

"So I've heard." Simon fell into step beside him as they crunched back along the graveled walk. "First thing out of bed she was vomiting, then that fainting spell at the coronation. The courtiers are calling it—"

"Morning sickness. I know." Abramm kept his voice even, though his anger was already simmering. "Except she wasn't vomiting."

"You're certain of this information."

"Yes."

They walked in silence for a bit, then Abramm said, "I despise all this gossiping."

"Perhaps you should consider avoiding her, then, sir. Evening meetings like this one, however innocent, do nothing but fan the flames. And I'll tell you now, the way she looked as she ran by me—ran into me, truth be told—made it look anything but innocent. Whatever you said to her distressed her a great deal."

It wasn't I who said it. It was she. And if it was so distressing, why did she say it?

But he had nothing to say to Simon's suggestion, reflecting unhappily that she'd apparently already solved the problem herself. Perhaps that was the very reason she wanted to leave. It couldn't be pleasant to be continually accused of being the king's mistress.

They climbed the graveled path up through the garden, and when Abramm said nothing more, Simon introduced a new subject: "I suppose you heard Donavan's talk tonight about the regalia's supposed powers: that the scepter can control the winds, the jeweled sword has killed a thousand men in a day, and he who wears the crown can see a hundred leagues. . . ." He trailed off, glancing sidelong at the crown Abramm still wore.

Abramm smiled at him. "I cannot see a hundred leagues, Uncle. But I doubt he would believe me."

"He wants them, though. He was practically drooling over them this morning before the ceremony. And afterward?" He shook his head. "I'll admit that for all I fought you on it, I'm daily seeing more and more need for this alliance you've made us. But I still don't trust the man. What if this whole thing really is a sham to get at our treasures?"

"The Esurhites have already attacked us, Uncle. And the Chesedhans helped catch them. Maybe even kept them from launching a larger force against us. If it is a sham, we've already reaped significant benefits." He thought back to his conversation with Leyton at dinner, which seemed even odder in retrospect than it had at the time. "And if the news we've just received about the fall of North Andol and Draesia is true, the Chesedhans will need our help and goodwill as much if not more than we need theirs. I can't believe he'd risk destroying that with another attempt to steal them. And if that truly is his intent, surely he wouldn't be so obvious about his interest."

"Maybe he can't help himself. Like a man in love with a woman he can never have. . . ." He glanced at Abramm sidelong, but when the latter only stared at him blankly, he went on. "He asked me today when the facsimile he believed you to be wearing this evening was made."

Abramm snorted. "What did you tell him?"

"That it wasn't a facsimile. Though I think he already knew that." He fell silent, the crunch of their feet upon the gravel mingling with the chuckle of the streamlet beside them. "He has no regard for you at all, you know. Laughs at the tales of your exploits, scoffs at the idea you were the White Pretender, all of it especially galling given the wild stories he tells about himself."

"Maybe that's why he doesn't believe mine: because he knows his own are false."

Simon snorted agreement. "In any case, I submit he needs to be watched."

"I'll talk to Seth about it. It wouldn't hurt to focus on him a little more."

Trap and Channon met them at the top of the gardens, and the four men strode on in silence, going round to the coach house, where a closed carriage awaited to bring them to the Chancellor's Tower and Gillard. Abramm's thoughts shifted now from the problem of Leyton and the regalia to the problem of his brother, who had lain shrunken and insensate for the last six months in the tower's top suite. He had no reason to think the tale of Gillard's brief awakening was untrue, nor did he expect to learn anything new on this visit, but he felt compelled to look into it personally, nonetheless. The man was his only remaining brother, after all, and had suffered a dreadful loss. More than that, Abramm half hoped his own presence might somehow stir Gillard back to wakefulness, though why he would want that, he could not say.

Trap made a small kelistar to put in the sling that hung from the coach's ceiling so they wouldn't have to ride in darkness, and the two dukes sat facing their king. Trap spent a few moments relating some of the things he had gleaned from the conversations he'd participated in or overheard this night—confirming to Abramm's secret delight the rightness of appointing the man his First Minister—while Simon sat silently beside him, his features growing more and more stern the closer they got to the tower.

The University clock was striking the first hour of a new day as they alit from the coach at the ramp leading up to the great square tower. Though Abramm was heavily cloaked and hooded, the cold moist air of the riverfront crept in around his newly bared cheeks and neck, raising gooseflesh in its wake. He glanced left toward the front of the coach, the horses' pluming breaths obscuring the darkened tower yard beyond. Soldiers on the night watch marched their short beats in slow cadence at various points along the fence, while out on the river a barge clanged its warning bell.

The tower's heavy wooden door stood open, flanked by four guards. Abramm strode quickly up the ramp and into a chill, musty anteroom where a tallow dip guttered on a small corner table. Captain Channon awaited him there, along with the old man Abramm recognized as the head of Gillard's three attendant-keepers.

The old man dropped Abramm a bow. "Welcome, sir."

As Simon and Trap stepped in behind him and the heavy door squealed shut, Abramm said, "Master Gregory, isn't it?"

"Yes, sir." The man bowed again, almost compulsively, and now Abramm saw the awe in his eyes. "If you'll come this way, sir?"

He led them up a short stair into the tower's large first-floor room, stone floor covered with a braided rug. Rough-hewn tables and chairs sat empty before the fire.

"I understand you were with him when the event occurred?" Abramm asked of Gregory as they crossed the room to the tower's single stairwell.

The man turned and gave him an abbreviated bow, avoiding his eyes. "Aye, Your M-Majesty."

"Tell me what happened."

Gregory led the way into the ancient spiraling stairwell, so narrow its walls brushed Abramm's shoulders. "I was sweeping out the hearth when a wind rushed through the room," the man said, "though the windows was closed and locked. I leaped up an' he cried out. Arched up in the bed, a bright light on his chest. His eyes was open, but he saw nothin'. 'Twas frightenin' weird, sir."

"When he cried out, what did he say?"

"If 'twas words, I couldn't make 'em out. More like a moan. He was sittin' all the way up by then, eyes right on me, but blank an' dead. Then the light went out and he fell back."

They climbed a few moments without speaking, the shuffle of their footsteps and the rasp of their breathing echoing around them.

"And that's all?" Abramm asked presently.

"Been layin' there ever since, sir. Just like he's laid there these last six months."

They spoke no more, for by then the effort of climbing made it too difficult. They passed five successive locked doorways on five successive landings before reaching the last one, six floors above the street. Gregory produced an iron ring of keys and fumbled out the one he needed. It clanked into the lock, the tumblers' grinding loud in the small stone-enclosed space. Then the door creaked inward, and Abramm stepped into the first chamber of the crown prince's sumptuous two-room prison suite. A large rectangular sitting room was furnished with satin-upholstered chairs and divans, elegantly finished end tables, and in the opposite wall, a marble fireplace. Paintings and tapestries provided decoration, and a dining table attended by two chairs stood before a draperied window on the right. Another curtained window faced it from the left, the only illumination coming from the small hearth blaze and three tallow dips placed randomly about the room.

The other two of Gillard's attendants waited straight-backed in the gloom. One had apparently donned trousers and jerkin just in time, his tardiness betrayed by the hem of his nightshirt dangling from under his jerkin. Both bowed as deeply to the king as their master had, and Abramm sensed again an awe that bordered on fear. Both scrupulously kept their eyes from meeting his. He studied them a moment, then asked, "Did either of you witness the prince's awakening?"

"No, sir," said the more appropriately attired of the two, fixing his gaze upon a point somewhere in front of Abramm's polished shoes. "Though I did hear a cry coming from the room that was much too deep for Master Gregory, sir."

"And . . . have you told anyone of this?"

"No, sir. We've been locked in ever since." Resentment tinged his voice.

Abramm turned to Gregory. "What of you, sir? Who have you told?"

Gregory bobbed and waved a hand at his companions. "Well, these two, o' course. And the man I sent to inform you."

"No one else?"

"That Lord Crull who came t' question me later. But that's all, sir."

Abramm told them to see it stayed that way, adding, "I'll see him now."

Gregory fumbled again with his key ring, unlocking the chamber's inner door and stepping back for Abramm and his party to enter.

The suite's second chamber was much smaller than the first and sported but one window—also hidden by drapes—in the center of the far wall. A canopied bed stood to the right, a hulking wardrobe to the left, facing the bed's foot.

Again the only light came from the coals on the inner-wall hearth to the left, and a night candle on the bedside table. Abramm could easily have conjured a kelistar to improve things, but found himself unwilling to do so. He strode to the bed, Simon at his side, Trap moving to the other side as the door closed discreetly behind them. Channon stood guard on the inside, while Will Ames and Ian Crocker took up posts in the outer room.

Every time Abramm came up here to look in on his brother, the shock hit him anew, like a kick to the stomach. Gillard, once so tall and strong, now lay pale and waiflike, hardly bigger than Jared. In fact, one might take him for a boy were it not for his thick beard and long pale hair. His white bed shirt gapped open at the neckline, revealing a bony chest bereft of its former musculature and furred with a pale blond pelt. The hawkish face was narrower, the bone structure almost delicate—all but a measure of what the morwhol had done to his entire frame.

Simon glanced at Gillard, then strode to the window on the outer wall and cast back the drapes, his back to the room as he gazed on the darkened city beyond the window's iron bars. Abramm noted the action peripherally, his attention commanded by the frail form before him and the tangled emotions roiling within him.

How are you even alive, brother? he wondered, not for the first time. *You've neither eaten nor drunk anything for six months. You should be dead by now. . . .*

Whatever the morwhol had done to Gillard's great physique, it had also worked a magical sleep on him, letting him waste away even as it bound him to this world—until today, when the Light had briefly awakened him.

For what purpose? Was the end near and Eidon giving him another chance?

"He might be pretending," Simon said from the window, his gravelly voice harsh in the silence. "Perhaps one of us should pierce his arm to make sure."

Abramm frowned at him, repelled.

He and Gillard had a shared history, a shared parentage, a shared knowledge of what it was to be male and royal and Kalladorne. Even beyond that, he sensed they were in many ways alike. Having lost all his blood kin but

Simon, Carissa, and Gillard, Abramm could not help hoping someday he might share with his only surviving brother the closeness of family ties neither of them had ever known. But even as he hoped, he gave uneasy acknowledgment to the Words' warning that a man's enemies were often members of his own house.

"Why have you hated me so much, brother?" he murmured. "You were always stronger. Faster. Better. Everyone admired you. . . ."

Or did they? Was your confidence all an act? And your hatred directed more toward yourself than me? He was struck with a sudden pang of insight. He'd always believed Gillard had never felt inadequate as he himself had—never felt he didn't measure up, never felt the pressure to perform. But that was not true. Abramm had been condemned as worthless from the start and never really tasted approval. But Gillard had—and must've known deep down how easily it could be lost.

Gillard had been no better off than Abramm, enslaved to the ever-present fear of failing. Looking at him now, Abramm felt a sudden depth of compassion for the man. A Star of Life bloomed at the end of his fingertip, surprising him at first, for he had not consciously thought to make one. Surely the Light had already visited Gillard today and been rebuffed, so why did he now offer again?

And then Abramm understood.

He drew a breath and prayed aloud, "My Lord Eidon, Sovereign Father . . . please, don't take him yet. Give him another chance, as you gave me. All those times I slapped your hand away, yet you persisted. . . . Surely you can persist a little longer with him."

His brother slumbered on, unmoving save for the slight rise and fall of his chest.

Then his uncle's familiar gravelly voice sounded out of the darkness, sharp with bitterness and closer now as he had come to stand at the foot of Gillard's bed. "Why are you praying over him? You should execute him."

Abramm arched his brows. "Isn't it enough he lies here weak and helpless, wasting away before our eyes? He can't last much longer."

Simon stared down at the younger Kalladorne. "So long as he does, sir, he remains a danger to you. If your enemies steal him away, they could use him as a figurehead indefinitely, claiming him to be alive when he is not. In fact, after what happened in the Hall of Kings this morning, I'd say your Mataian friends will be desperate to get him and do just that."

Abramm glanced aside at him sharply. *After what happened this morning?*

Has Eidon finally gotten your attention, as well, Simon? His uncle hadn't been among the multitudes who'd received the mark of the shield today, but perhaps there had been a softening.

Nevertheless, he was right about the Mataio.

"If they get him, they can say anything, and who could prove them wrong?" Simon went on. "Probably claim to heal him right off. Then get some stooge to be his stand-in."

"I thought you loved him, Simon," Abramm said softly.

His uncle shifted uneasily beside him and did not answer at first. Abramm could hear his breathing, interposed with Gillard's faint, regular snores. Then the older man let out a long breath and said, "He's a traitor. Tried to kill you, tried to take the Crown for his own gain. And in the end he sided with the Mataio. Whatever I felt for him has long since died. And so should he."

His words faded to silence. The fire popped. Gillard slumbered on.

Abramm sighed and shook his head. "I can't just kill him. Not like this. Look at him, Uncle. He's a shell of what he was. And after what Eidon has done on my behalf today, what reason have I to be needlessly cruel? If he were awake, could look into my eyes and spit in my face, maybe then. But not like this." He bent and placed the Star on the table beside Gillard's bed, watched as it rolled slowly over the uneven surface and came up against the base of the candlestick. Simon frowned at him darkly, but said no more.

Abramm glanced again at Gillard, at Trap, then strode for the door.

A low, distant boom echoed through Gillard's darkness, followed by jangling keys and the grating of a lock. He opened his eyes, but still the darkness enshrouded him, soft, deep folds of it cradling his body from beneath and pressing down upon him from the top. He opened his eyes wider, turned them all around, seeking something besides the darkness. There was a faint gray glow to his left, but the darkness kept his head from turning to see its source.

He blinked and stared at what must be the ceiling, seeing folds and streaks of greater darkness in the shadow above him.

Where am I?

He recalled awakening earlier to a blinding light that hovered directly in front of him as he sat upright. Then the darkness had swooped upon him again, a thick, woolly presence that blotted out all sound. Or almost all sound.

He'd heard voices briefly. Men speaking from somewhere above him, one to his left, the other somewhere down by his feet. One he'd recognized as Uncle Simon. He couldn't recall the words, but the pleasure he'd felt at knowing his uncle still cared warmed him now as he recalled it.

The other man's voice had been familiar, too, deep and strong with a lilt of foreign accent. He thought of it in recall, trying to match it with various names and faces, none the right fit until at last—

His breath caught. *Abramm lives!*

The realization unleashed a tumble of memory—the battle between them; the trap Gillard had set for his brother at the Temple of Dragons; the feel of the morwhol's bloodlust as it loped inexorably toward them; the euphoric anticipation of his coming victory: Abramm vanquished by the beast Gillard would slay to take his brother's place as the heroic killer of monsters. But the thing had turned on Gillard instead, closing a twenty-foot gap in a single leap and toppling him backward to the stone. Its teeth had sunk into his shoulder, and he felt himself being pulled into it. . . .

He stared at the folds of shadow, trying to recall more and finding only darkness. The creature had intended to consume him, revealing that intention only at the last. Was he inside it now? Feeling like a man, but really a beast?

A shudder swept through him, setting his limbs jittering against the bed of darkness upon which he lay face up, arms at his sides, legs out straight. A beast could not lie like this. . . .

Am I even still alive?

New fear gripped him. Then he heard a distant bang, and men talking amongst themselves, excited but not afraid. He smelled a whiff of smoke as from a fireplace, and when he pressed his hands against the surface upon which he lay, it felt for all the world like a feather-stuffed mattress. He was lying in a bed, then.

But how did I get here? And what happened to the beast? Perhaps it only thought me dead and turned to Abramm before it finished. Perhaps it killed him, and they've brought me back to Stormcroft, the only surviving heir to the throne.

But no . . . the voice had been Abramm's.

Horror seized his heart and for a moment he thought he might suffocate with the power of it. *Pox and plagues! He must've won! Somehow, some way he must have killed it. I must be his prisoner.*

Urgency set his heart slamming against his chest. He stared around, eyes open as wide as they would go, as if that might somehow enable him to see his surroundings. The shadows overhead were the draped fabric of a canopy.

On the wall to his left, beyond the door, he saw the red glow from the hearth fire, probably burned down to coals from the look of the light and the silence. And that faint gray glow at his side was probably a night candle. His fingers gripped and twisted the linen sheets upon which he rested. *Yes, it was a bed, all right.*

Then he heard the low familiar tolling of the University clock in Springerlan marking the second hour of the morning and went completely rigid. *He's put me in the tower.* Yes, he recognized it now. The suite at the top, the same one in which he himself had imprisoned their brother Raynen.

Panic exploded in him and he tried to sit up but couldn't move. *Am I tied down? Shackled?* He could feel nothing binding either arms or legs and concluded he must have been drugged. Abramm had learned that sort of thing during his years as a Mataian. *Fire and Torment! I can't believe he won!* He heard strange grunting sounds and felt his teeth grinding together. *I have to get out of here.*

He strained mightily to move just one arm until sparkles of white glittered at the edges of his awareness and the darkness overtook him again.

When he regained consciousness, the room no longer seemed as dark, the light from the night candle on his bedside table casting a pale glow across the quilt that covered his body. He tried to turn his head enough to see the candle, his breath soon coming in loud desperate gasps as slowly, a hairsbreadth at a time, he managed to tip his head to the left. . . .

And stared with incomprehension. The night candle had burned itself down to a nub and gone out. But on the table at its base stood a perfect sphere, no larger around than his thumb tip, and it was from this that the light emanated: a pure white incandescence that hurt his eyes to look at it.

So he turned them away, frowning fiercely at the canopy. This was a Terstan thing! Raynen had conjured one for him once, promising it would burn a shield on his chest just as it had in Raynen's. He recalled the day as if it were yesterday—the horror he'd felt to know Raynen was truly one of *them*, and the difficulty of refusing him without offending when every fiber of his being wanted to howl with outrage and revulsion. That moment was overlaid by another: Raynen as he had been at the end, eyes occluded with the white curd, jabbering his madness as they had locked him into this very suite. And now someone . . . *Abramm!* sought to bring all that to Gillard.

Outrage blasted through him in a red heat of energy, enough that his arm twitched violently on the bed beside him. He tried again, wanting nothing so much as to knock that hideous orb out of his sight . . . but the blackness overtook him first.

The jangle of keys awakened him in time to hear the door creaking inward. Light stabbed his eyes so brightly he could only perceive his visitor by squinting. The man was cloaked and cowled. Gillard caught only a glimpse of his form before the door swung shut again. And now an irrational terror swept over him. It was Abramm come to murder him in his bed—just recompense for all the evil Gillard had done against him.

His visitor swept up to his bedside as silent as a spirit. The light of the Terstan orb illumined the rough weave of the cowl—but not the face. And then the man bent toward the table and made a sharp movement, and the light winked out.

Which for some reason only added to Gillard's terror. He opened his mouth, felt his tongue move and his throat flex, and somehow managed to croak, "Please!"

The man's hand pressed against his arm, and he felt its coldness even through blanket and sleeve. "Fear not, my lord," came a low musical voice. "I am a friend."

A friend? Why don't I recognize your voice? Gillard swallowed nervously, but a thread of hope tempered his fear. He opened his mouth to speak again, but the hand tightened on his arm. "No, Your Highness. Let them think you sleep on. You must regain your strength before we can move you." The hand patted his arm. "Take courage, sir. And wait."

8

The next day, sunlight finally broke through the early morning fog to flood the hills across which Lady Madeleine and Princess Carissa rode, igniting the muted gray landscape to vibrant emerald. Against the green flared new-blooming patches of brilliant white summersnow, while thickets of lavender gullberry shimmered along the road; their sweet scent gilding the freshening breeze. Here and there rafts of yellow daffodils nodded amid stiff green leaves, and out on the hillsides, newborn lambs gamboled under the watchful eyes of their mothers. Overhead, white-and-gray gulls soared on the updrafts against ever-widening patches of blue.

It was as if all the world had suddenly awakened, amazing Maddie by how much a simple change of lighting and the feel of the sun's warmth seeping through her woolen garments could lift her spirits.

Maybe things weren't as bad as she had thought.

She'd passed another night plagued by unsettling dreams that, this time, had obviously originated from Leyton's grim report on the state of her homeland. Finally driven from her bed, she'd stoked up the fire and pulled one of the overstuffed chairs into the corona of its warmth, where she'd huddled under a throw, reading the Words of Revelation and praying for guidance until dawn.

Carissa had arrived that morning during breakfast, sliding into the chair across the table from Maddie to declare without preamble, "It *was* him. At the coronation, at the banquet, and again last night after the ball. I'm sure of it."

Maddie set down her teacup and regarded her friend with concern.

"Rennalf, you mean. Here. In Springerlan."

Carissa claimed to have seen her ex-husband—Abramm had granted her a divorce six months ago—three times while they'd been in Stormcroft waiting for Abramm to heal, then twice within two weeks shortly after they'd returned to Springerlan. Unfortunately, no one but Carissa had seen him, and with no other evidence to support her story, some feared the sightings were no more than the product of terrible memories and the lingering fears that he would yet return to abuse her. No one had come out and said as much to her face, but it was clear Carissa knew she was not wholly believed.

"It was him, Mad," she repeated fiercely. "He was in the little alcove with the flying horse on the way back to my chambers, and he *wanted* me to see him. Stepped out of the shadows right when I'd get the best look. He's shaved his beard and pulled back his hair, but it was him." She paused, then added, "Hogart saw him, too. I told Captain Meri . . . er, Duke Eltrap, last night, and he said he'd tell Abramm . . . but I've had no word yet."

Maddie picked up her teacup again and sipped. "Hogart saw him?"

"Running away. He can't say it was Renn for sure, but he'll confirm someone was there. Maybe I should just go rouse Abramm and tell him myself." Carissa sagged back in the chair, winding a ringlet of golden hair around her index finger.

It was at that point a messenger from Carissa's apartments arrived with a large hand-inked invitation card for the princess. She untied the lacing and opened the flaps to scan the contents. Her expression soured. "Oh, mercy," she murmured. "A breakfast invitation from Oswain Nott. What a way to start one's day."

"He certainly does have his eye on you."

"I don't want to offend him—especially not on the heels of Abramm passing him over for First Minister. . . . You want to come?"

"I very much doubt Nott would appreciate my presence. Besides, I'm about to leave for a morning ride out to Treasure Cove."

Carissa's eyes brightened. "What a splendid idea! I'll come with you."

Not exactly what Maddie'd intended, but how could she refuse the crown princess?

Thus she now found herself riding in the early morning beside the king's sister—across the southeastern leg of the royal preserve, then along the eastern headland toward the cove—heading in a direction directly opposite Graymeer's. Hogart and several of Abramm's armsmen attended them.

At first Carissa was driven to talk out her anxieties, speculating as to how

Rennalf had gotten to Springerlan with the passes still snowed in, why he'd come at all, and what he'd been doing in Mataian robes at the coronation yesterday. Of the three, only the first had a likely answer: Rennalf had reopened the etherworld corridor Abramm had shut down in Graymeer's six months ago.

The more she talked, the more certain she became this was the case. But when she suggested they return to the palace to insist Abramm go up to Graymeer's and make sure, Maddie pointed out that Abramm was certainly already up there.

"Already up there?" Carissa protested. "But he has that foreign dignitaries' tribute—"

"Not until two. Plenty of time to ride out and back, especially if he set out early."

Carissa's eyes narrowed. "Is this what you two talked about in the garden last night?"

"No."

"Then how did you—"

"I know him, Carissa. So do you. After what happened yesterday, is there any doubt he would go out there first chance he got?" *Especially having seen those galleys moored at the base of the Graymeer's outcropping in his vision. . . .*

Her thoughts caught on the realization that he'd seen them in actual time. Maybe it hadn't been a vision at all. Leyton's tales of the regalia claimed the crown gave a man the ability to see for leagues. Abramm had claimed no unusual ability to see a long way, but what if it wasn't straight distance? What if, like the corridors that took you to distant places in the blink of an eye, it enabled him to see places that were leagues away as if they were right in front of him?

Her heart constricted. He'd also seen Esurhite galleys streaming out of a bank of fog he thought might hide the Gull Islands. If that was present time, too, it would not only support Leyton's story about the dire situation in Chesedh but give weight to his theories about the regalia, as well. And reinforce the need to unlock their secrets as soon as possible.

Oh, Father Eidon! I don't want to stay here. Surely it would be better for everyone if I left.

Carissa had fallen into her own musings, and now, inevitably, thoughts of Abramm's coronation triggered memories of what Maddie herself had seen. A vision sufficiently similar to what Abramm had described that she couldn't think she had made it up wholly.

She had soared on the winds above a fortress by the sea where a wedding ceremony was being performed on the uppermost ramparts. Spectators filled the tops of the wallwalks as well as both inner and outer wards: men and women dressed in silken finery, yet bearing with them the banners and weapons of war.

She'd spiraled downward toward the bridal couple, who faced one another with joined hands. The groom was tall and blond, his face marred by two red scars, and the bride seemed inexplicably unfamiliar, though it had to be Briellen. Maddie had circled closer as Kesrin looped the long white ribbon of Chesedhan wedding tradition around the couple's joined hands. The bride's veil lifted from her face, and she still did not look like Briellen for all Maddie tried to make it so. Then, as she passed behind Abramm's broadshouldered form, she realized it was not her sister at all, but Maddie herself.

The realization had catapulted her into the very body she had just recognized, so that now she stood looking up into Abramm's smiling blue eyes as the ribbon twirled round and round their joined hands, binding them in law and custom and fact for the rest of their lives. . . . It was then, as comprehension dawned and disbelief was chased by sudden, howling protest, that all grew hazy, colors and shadows bleaching out into a strong white light.

The next thing she knew she was pushing herself off Leyton's shoulder, aware of his arm pressed against her back, his hand gripping her waist as he held her upright on wobbly knees. She remembered Simon coming around him, the old duke's hawkish features narrowed into a frown, his blue eyes fixing upon her sharply as she strove to regain her senses and her poise.

A terrible fear had gripped her as she realized what she'd seen. Such a thing could only come to pass if Briellen had died, for she was First Daughter and given already to the king in treaty. For a moment her agitation grew so intense she thought she might become ill. Then rationality reasserted itself. No sense leaping to horrid conclusions with so little real evidence. Indeed, her own vision might even be the proof of Briellen's survival. Since Maddie had served as stand-in for her sister in the coronation ceremony, the vision could simply have been a reflection of that role. Her middle had finally unclenched, and her breathing eased as the fear fell away . . . leaving sorrow of a different stripe in its wake. . . .

"Are you all right, Mad?" Carissa's low query now broke into her thoughts. "You look even wearier than you did yesterday."

"I'm fine." They were coming down over the eastern headland, heading for the beach, a great column of gulls circling ahead of them against a sky of tattered clouds.

"I noticed you didn't eat much this morning, either," Carissa persisted.

Maddie exhaled a long breath and looked at her companion evenly. "But not because I'm sick." She snorted, recalling Leyton's suggestion. "Or with child."

"Of course *I* know you're not with child!" Carissa frowned at her. "Plagues, Mad! I nearly came to blows with Leona last night defending you! You weren't the only one to faint during that ceremony, after all."

"Well, for that I thank you."

They rode on in silence, watching the gulls dive and circle up ahead. Then Carissa said, "You didn't answer my question. And ever since your brother arrived with that treaty, you've been particularly out of sorts."

"Leyton has a way of doing that."

"I was thinking more of the treaty."

Suddenly Maddie could hardly breathe. She kept her gaze fixed upon the rutted road before them but felt Carissa's eyes upon her.

"You're not jealous, are you?" the princess asked.

Madeleine barked a short laugh and spoke in words that sounded strained even to her own ears. "Jealous? Why would you think that?"

Carissa held silence for a long moment as the horses' plodding hoofbeats rose up around them and the distant squawks of the gulls drifted to them on the wind. Finally she said quietly, "You've fallen for him, haven't you?"

Surprise and renewed alarm whipped Maddie's head around, denial poised on the tip of her tongue. But the moment she saw her companion's grave and vaguely sympathetic expression, she knew it would be pointless. She looked away, catching her lower lip between her teeth as she found herself fighting back tears, and disgusted anew by the emotional wreck she had become these last few days. "Is it that obvious?"

Carissa chuckled softly. "The way you look at him? I'm afraid so."

Maddie winced and turned her eyes to a pair of long-winged kytes floating among the gulls over the green slope ahead. A puff of gullberry-scented breeze caressed her face. Then she groaned. "I can't believe I'm humiliating myself like this. Especially knowing he doesn't care a whit."

"Oh, I wouldn't say that. . . . He's just worked harder at not seeing it than you have."

It took a moment for Carissa's words to register. Then Maddie looked around at her in surprise, and the princess met her gaze with a rueful smile.

"*I want you!*" Abramm's words rang in her memory as vividly as when he had spoken them, and they still had the power to make her hope that somehow, some way, he had meant more by them than just his concern for her research. She quashed it grimly. "That is not a possibility I have any business considering, Riss."

"Why not? You'd rather let him lock himself into a loveless marriage? To your own sister?"

"It has to be this way. Our countries need this treaty." *Especially if things are as bad as Leyton says.*

"We may need the treaty, but we don't need it to be sealed with a marriage."

They came over a gentle rise, hearing the sound of the breakers now as they got their first glimpse of the sea, visible beyond the grass-covered rise ahead of them. Out beyond the surf line, vegetation-crowned sentinel rocks stood amidst pulsing fountains of white spray, encircled by rafts of squawking gulls.

"I don't think it's a wonderful idea," Maddie said. "But it is what it is. No matter how much you rail against it, they're still going to do it. And frankly, I doubt Abramm will mind at all. My sister is everything I'm not: beautiful, charming, stylish. Men fall in love with her the moment they meet her. You'll see."

"If he's already attracted to you, Mad, it's highly unlikely he'll be interested in a woman who's everything you're not."

Maddie frowned at her, suddenly exasperated. "Why are you doing this, Carissa? It can't work between us. Even if Bree wasn't part of the picture—I don't want to be a queen. And even if I did, I'm not at all suited to it."

"Nonsense."

"You said it yourself yesterday."

"Before I realized how truly brilliant it was for you to have readied Warbanner. Before the ceremony unfolded and the Light came on him and you fainted in the middle of it all. I remembered the day he faced the morwhol and how weird you were when we were fleeing down the Bright Falls canyon. All blank-faced and deaf, like you were somewhere else. And then after that boom, suddenly you were back and certain he was alive." She paused, pulling a strand of windblown hair from across her face as she looked intently at Maddie. "I know you share his dreams. But there's more to it than that, isn't there? You saw something yesterday during that ceremony. While he saw the Esurhites breaking into Graymeer's, you were seeing something, too."

Maddie fixed her gaze on the road again, now a sandy track through thick patches of wind-stirred beach grass. Her heart beat rapidly as the sudden desire to spill it all welled up in her. She was so sick of bearing this alone, having no one to share her heartache with, no one to seek for counsel. Carissa had become a good friend these last six months, and Maddie knew her to be a devoted student of Eidon and his Words. Why not tell her? She'd already guessed the worst and hadn't laughed. If nothing else, just hearing herself tell it would give Maddie new perspective.

She glanced over her shoulder. The men followed at a respectful distance but were still too close to risk speaking.

Coming over the second rise, they found the beach stretched out beside white ranks of breakers. Wreckage strewed the shore, remnants still floating in from the ferocious storm two weeks ago—bits of wooden planking, scraps of canvas and rope, lanterns, flags, what looked to be part of the ship's hull, and possibly even a piece of mast—lay scattered up the sand before them, festooned with mounds and ribbons of seaweed. Out beyond the surf line, the great cloud of gulls soared and dipped in a great writhing mass that was focused on one spot in the water—apparently the birds were feeding on a school of fish that had risen to the surface.

As they rode down the rocky bluff to the beach, Maddie suggested they go beachcombing. When Carissa frowned at her, she smiled and glanced meaningfully at the men now clustering around them. "I love walking the beach barefoot—feeling the sand beneath my feet, the surf on my legs."

Carissa regarded her for a long moment, her expression as inscrutable as any of Abramm's. Then she, too, glanced back at the men and finally agreed.

They dismounted, stripped off shoes and stockings, and left their horses in the care of one of the men as they set off together, skirts tied up at their waists. As one of the men rode along the bluff to keep a watch, Hogart and another followed out of earshot behind them.

They walked silently for a bit, stopping to examine the shard of hull that jutted up out of the sand, picking up a few shells and a small carved box. Then, as they left the ship's hull and started toward the mast, Maddie spoke: "I saw Abramm's wedding."

Carissa drew closer, watching her intently.

"It was held on the wallwalk at Graymeer's." She swallowed. "Except his bride wasn't Briellen." She stopped again, and Carissa guessed the rest:

"It was you."

Maddie flushed and fixed her gaze on the sand before them as she nodded. "The dream I had the night before the coronation wasn't the same as yours. Or his, I think." She flushed again at the memory.

Again Carissa picked up the part she hadn't shared: "So *that's* why you turned so red when I mentioned it."

Maddie turned her face to the sea, the wind blowing her hair back out of her eyes. "I know the rhu'ema did it—pulled out feelings I'd been denying, made them so vivid and strong I couldn't ignore them. Or help him when they attacked. I understood all that soon enough. So when I had the vision, or whatever it was, I thought it was more of the same."

"The Light was on you, Mad. It couldn't have been rhu'ema."

"No. But it could've been my own desires laid over what he was seeing. Anyway, after that I knew I had to leave. I told him so last night in the tea garden." She snorted bitterly. "He lamented the loss of his prized researcher."

"You probably shocked him silly and it was the only thing he could think to say," Carissa said dryly. "You really have no idea how much he relies on you, do you? And I don't mean for research."

Maddie watched her fingers toy with the white shell she still held. Then she sighed. "I only know it seems like a death sentence never to be able to see him again. The only thing worse would be seeing him with my sister. . . ."

She fell silent, and they walked on, a particularly high wave washing around their calves, eating away the sand beneath their feet. Sea gulls flapped and squawked around them as they came even with the great feeding column out beyond the surf.

"I don't think leaving's the answer," Carissa said presently.

Maddie sighed her frustration. "Maybe not. I was so sure it was the right thing to do when I told him, but then Leyton cornered me in my suite." She paused, glanced aside at her friend. "You have to promise you'll tell no one what I'm going to say next."

Carissa promised.

Maddie turned her gaze forward again, toward the piece of topmast lying on the sand in a curl of canvas ahead of them. Three sea gulls stood perched upon it, pecking at seaweed. "He said things are much worse back home than he's let on, and he thinks the regalia have special powers Abramm could use to defeat the Armies of the Black Moon. He wants me to stay and help figure out what they are and how to use them. And Abramm's had me searching for information on the fortresses and the guardstars, and I'm just now starting to have some success, and . . . I don't know what to do. On the one hand I want to leave, but on the other I think if I could help defeat the southlanders

I should put my personal feelings aside and stay."

"I agree."

"But if I stay, I'm afraid he'll find out how I feel . . . and I can see no good coming of such a thing. Worse, I don't know if I can bear to watch him marry my sister."

"You don't know it will happen that way."

"How could it not?" Maddie looked at her soberly. "The only way to break the treaty now is if Bree were to die, and that would be hideous. Besides, your claims to the contrary, I don't think Abramm has the slightest interest in me—at least, not like that. So the whole thing is ridiculous. Ridiculous I should feel like this and ridiculous that I should have to think of leaving at all. And yet . . ." She wrapped her hands about her chest. "I prayed all night . . . but nothing seems any clearer."

A sea gull landed on the glistening beach ahead of them, a small red shell in its beak. It walked along before them, back and forth, studying them with its bright yellow eyes.

After a time Carissa sighed. "Well, if it's not clear, it seems to me you must wait until it is. The only thing you know for sure is that there's much of value to be discovered and you've been asked to help do so. That's something you know you can do. So do it. One day at a time. Bury yourself in your books, and avoid him entirely if you have to."

"Avoid him? How? I have to report whatever I find."

"You write out your reports anyway. Just hire an assistant and let him deliver them."

Ahead of them, the sea gull dropped its shell on the sand, bent its head to peck at it again, then ran on ahead of them, leaving its treasure behind. Maddie shook her head. "I'm not sure I can trust myself to stay away. Last night I nearly spilled it all to him. With no intent of doing so . . . yet there I was." She stopped and closed her eyes. "I really think it would be better if I just left."

"But if it's Eidon's intent that you stay . . ."

"How could it be? I'm in love with a man who's essentially married."

Another big wave flooded around them. Ribbons of seaweed tickled Maddie's legs, then wrapped around them as the wave receded. She stepped free of them and walked on, noting that the gull's bright red shell lay before her on the dark and shining sand. And now that she was closer, it did not look like a shell at all.

She was only a stride away from it when the next wave flowed around her feet, picking up the object and floating it toward shore, then bringing it back on the outflow. Scooping it up as it went by, Maddie straightened to examine it more closely, Carissa peering over her shoulder. As she realized what it was, a chill spread from spine to back and shoulders, neck and arms. For on her flattened palm stood a tiny dragon, carved of red stone, its wings outstretched, tail hooking out behind, pinhead crystalline eyes glittering in the sun.

The world shifted about her and she felt as if she'd been kicked in the chest. A red dragon. Flying.

"Oh," Carissa said. "That's an Esurhite fetish. Soldiers carry them for protection."

Maddie looked at her blankly.

"And it couldn't have floated all the way from Esurh because the currents are wrong." She plucked it off Maddie's palm and turned it over in her fingers. "In fact, it might not have floated at all—that bird could have brought it straight here on the wing."

"You're saying Abramm's fears are correct and there are Esurhites on the Gull Islands?"

"Well, I doubt this will convince Admiral Hamilton and his cronies, but that's as reasonable an explanation for this thing being here as any."

If Carissa was right, the danger was here, too, not just in Chesedh. Time was every bit as short as Abramm feared. Could it possibly be Eidon's intent for her to leave now, when she might be able to help unlock the secrets of both the regalia and the fortresses? Secrets that, as Leyton suggested, might mean the difference between life and death for them all?

"I don't think it's a coincidence you were the one to find it, either," the princess said, holding the tiny dragon out for Maddie to take back. She smiled thinly. "Looks like you've got your answer, my dear: you're supposed to stay."

Carissa dropped the figurine into Maddie's outstretched palm, and Maddie stared at it, feeling destiny swirl around her, yet unable still to see it clearly. Then, before she could wrestle her thoughts into any kind of coherent order, one of the men cried out behind them, "That's no school of fish. That's a body!"

She turned with Carissa to see all three men racing out through the incoming breakers toward the pale mound that floated beneath the column of gulls—a mound she saw now was very obviously not a mass of fish but something far more gruesome.

Madeleine had still been sitting by her fire studying the Words of Revelation when Abramm and his party, dressed in the gray tunics and woolen mantles of rank and file armsmen, joined the corps of soldiers awaiting them west of the King's Bridge. Notified beforehand that a group would be meeting up with him that morning, the commanding officer accepted them without comment and without apparent recognition.

The trip was made without incident, and by the time they were climbing the fortress switchbacks, the sun was up and Abramm nursed a rising tension. Philip and his commanding officer had finished their interrogation of the Esurhite captives not too long before Abramm left the palace. As hoped, they had come away with more than the southlanders intended to give them, concluding that the Esurhites had indeed intended to take the fortress, though not alone and not immediately. They also suspected there might be some who'd not been caught and were hiding in Graymeer's tunnels. And almost certainly they would seek to set up an etherworld corridor to connect the place with their homeland so they could funnel through enough men to eventually take and hold the fortress. This was particularly troublesome news coming on the heels of Trap's report that Carissa claimed to have seen Rennalf yesterday. Not once, but three times.

Reaching the top of the switchbacks, they rode through the sequence of newly installed gates in the repaired barbican and main outer wall. After six months of work, Graymeer's was no longer a collection of crumbling, roofless, griiswurm-infested structures. The interior buildings now included a new barracks, stables, and granary in the inner ward, while the officers' quarters on the third terrace had been reroofed and fully refitted, becoming habitable almost three months ago. And the work continued apace. Scaffoldings stood everywhere, along with pieces of construction equipment and diminishing piles of rubble.

The maze of tunnels beneath them, unfortunately, was another story. Though the upper levels had been scoured of spawn by the blast of Light Abramm had released when he destroyed the first corridor six months ago, those below remained infested. It was a constant battle to hold ground gained, and no one knew how far the tunnels descended. Still, they had been holding it, and given Graymeer's history, things were going well.

Once the officers' quarters had been completed, Abramm had stayed overnight once a week, as much to supervise the work as to reassure the men that it was safe. Only in the last fortnight, when coronation preparations had kept him way, had the rumors sprung up again—tales of ghostly voices, of malevolent pools of darkness, and most recently, of a barbarian warrior who walked the deep dark passages with the green eye of the ancient hill god, Hasmal, glaring from his forehead.

Now, as the returning soldiers disembarked from their wagons near the gate, Channon led the king's group up to the inner ward, where Graymeer's second in command, Lieutenant Brookes, awaited them at the stables. After they had dismounted, Brookes saluted Channon, bowed to Duke Eltrap and Lord Ethan, and in keeping with Abramm's instructions, entirely ignored the rest of them as he introduced the three armsmen who had been first to surprise the Esurhites in the tunnels yesterday.

Then he led them around the back of the stables to a doorway in the middle west tower and down a narrow winding stair with Abramm safely sandwiched in the middle of the entourage. Kelistars tucked into niches along the outer wall lit the spiraling stairwell and the corridor it emptied into. Lasting about twelve hours from the time of creation, kelistars made a welcome substitute for candles and torches and, some believed, helped to keep the corridors free of spawn.

The door-lined corridor led to another stairway, this one switchbacking, narrow and very steep, its walls and ceiling finished with quarried stone. Connecting the fortress with the cove below, the upper part of this ancient passway had emerged relatively unscathed from the barbarian occupation. Only as it approached the bottom of the outcropping did the arcanely carved tunnels intersect it, and then only in four places. A heavy, iron-bound wooden door had been installed between that compromised portion below and the fortress itself, a door the Esurhites were breaking through when Graymeer's defenders had confronted them.

It was to the small chamber that preceded this doorway that Brookes led them, where three armsmen were wrestling a new door into position under the watchful eyes of a fourth. All four looked up in surprise, and then the three with the door laid down their burden and hastily saluted.

Brookes motioned them back against the chamber wall, and Trap and Ethan stepped forward to examine the door. Two bright blond planks lay between the age-darkened boards of the original, the latter bearing the black scoring indicative of Esurhite Shadow magic.

Trap noted as much in his comments and questioning of Brookes, who agreed with his assessments. Abramm listened with only half an ear. The moment he had entered this chamber, a cold creepiness had crept over him, icy fingers of wrongness dancing up the back of his neck. His eyes kept returning to the fourth armsman standing in the darkened lower corridor below where the steel door hinges protruded from the wall. The armsman had stood to attention like the rest when Abramm's party arrived and, like them, now watched Trap and Ethan—particularly Ethan—as they examined the walls and questioned the men Brookes had brought with them. But Abramm noted a subtle tension in his stance, as if he were on the verge of fleeing. Or attacking.

He was a big man, clean-shaven, his frizzy blond hair drawn back into a tail at his nape. Though he stood in the shadows, Abramm could see his face quite clearly. The features were rugged and weathered, the hard mouth bracketed by deep, harsh lines, the eyes radiating crow's-feet. There was something about him, though, that made Abramm think he was not an arms-man at all. He carried himself wrong. And despite his bland expression, his jaw was tight, his shoulders tense, and his hands poised on the sword belt at his hip.

Most perplexing of all, he looked familiar. . . .

When Ethan stepped over the door and passed directly in front of Abramm, the big man turned as if watching him closely. Abramm must've gasped or flinched when he saw a glint of emerald light flash at the base of the armsman's throat because immediately the man's eyes shifted from Ethan to Abramm himself, and the moment they did they narrowed and flicked to the scars on his face. They widened a hair, his brows twitched up—but then his gaze returned to Ethan, apparently unconcerned.

"And you say they tried to use the fearspell and their fireballs upon you, Sergeant?" Trap said, directing his question to one of the armsmen Brookes had brought with them.

"Yes, sir," the sergeant replied. He went on to describe the encounter, but already Abramm was returning his attention to the man in the shadowed corridor.

Who had vanished.

"Plagues!" he cried, leaping across the door to follow.

"Sir! Wait! Where are you going?" That was Channon, alarm ringing in his tone.

Abramm heard the hiss of steel on steel behind him as his men followed after him. His own blade was already out as he raced down the corridor, sur-prised at the way the light carried so far from the chamber. He could see the weathered stones, the twists and turns and bumps in the floor as clearly as if he still stood surrounded by kelistars. And up ahead, he could even see his quarry, turning out of sight.

He's gone into one of the rhu'ema-made tunnels.

Trap was on Abramm's heels now as he raced for the junction and turned into a passage hewn through solid obsidian. He heard footsteps ahead and recalled the last time he'd been down this deep, drawn then by receding footsteps, as well. . . .

"My lord, please," Trap cried behind him. "I can't see a blasted thing."

What in the world is he talking about? Abramm wondered. The corridor was dim and shadowy, but still light enough to see from the kelistars behind them. Besides, with the way the man ahead of them glowed with green fire, what more did he need?

A little caution might be wise.

But that man isn't an Esurhite. He looked more like a barbarian. . . . What would a barbarian be doing this far south? What would he be doing in my fortress? The thoughts flew through his mind as he raced down a steep ramp.

Not a barbarian. But how about Rennalf of Balmark?

The ramp spit him into a circular chamber in time to see Balmark disappear down one of several openings. Abramm dashed in pursuit, around a curving corridor, up a short stair, and through a doorway into a long, low-ceilinged chamber at the midpoint of which his quarry was now drawing to a stop.

As the man turned back, Abramm heard Trap's muttered oath from close behind him, and several things registered. That the man before him was unarmed yet smiling, while on either side of him, dark-featured men in dark tunics stood frozen in various positions of rising and sitting, all of them staring in open astonishment at the three men who had so suddenly burst into their midst.

Now the border lord made a hurling motion at Abramm, who conjured his Light shield instinctively. But there was nothing to ward, only a strong gust of wind that caught the front of his cowl—already pushed back on his head from his run—and hurled it onto his shoulders, revealing his blond hair and telltale scars to all the men in the chamber.

And somewhere off to his right a low, astonished voice called out in the Tahg, "It's the Pretender!"

9

Everyone jolted into action simultaneously. Swords grated from scabbards as shouts echoed through the chamber, and Abramm's own men flooded around him into the room. In a moment they had closed with the enemy, their swords alight with Terstan fire, leaving Abramm standing there in the midst of them with no one to face. He saw the big border lord cuff one of the Esurhites across the side of the head and crumple him to the floor before disappearing into the back of the chamber.

Racing after him, Abramm found a narrow, twisting slit that spilled him into yet another slag-walled corridor. Sensing movement to his right, he turned to meet it, twisting aside as he brought up his rapier—only to realize that Balmark waited on his weaker left side. As the border lord's blade drove up toward Abramm's chest, he thought to bat it aside with his gloved left hand, but the stiffened limb had barely twitched into movement when the steel plunged into his side.

He felt nothing at first, twisting back and off the blade as his own rapier deflected the border lord's auxiliary dagger. Rattled, he backed another step to break contact and regroup, part of him shocked the man had bested him so easily, another part recognizing the desperate need to maintain concentration.

Balmark grinned at him. "Not quite the dangerous, invincible warrior ye thought ye was, eh? Lost a bit more than ye imagined, I guess."

He raised the rapier, and Abramm brought up his own blade, refusing to entertain the self-recriminations already gathering at the edges of his mind.

Balmark continued to leer at him. "Ye think ye can take m' wife from me, melt down our sacred stone fer yer sovereigns, and not pay fer it?"

He straightened a bit from his crouch, his expression hardening as the amulet at his throat flared. *"Drop the blade."*

He said it quietly, but Abramm felt the power of Command wrap about his arm, weighing it down, pulling at his fingers. He stepped back again, letting the rapier's tip fall, feeling the sword's hilt shift in his loosened grip, his eyes never leaving Balmark's. The other man noted the changes and his lips twitched with satisfaction. He let his own blade tip drop as he stepped toward Abramm, radiating menace and intimidation. *"Drop the blade."*

Abramm let the rapier tip fall farther, nearly touching the rough-hewn floor. Balmark stepped toward him again, the power of his aura crowding in on Abramm's awareness. Then, just as he came into range, Abramm whipped the blade up, slashing diagonally at the man's face. The border lord lurched back, the cut in his brow gushing dark streams of blood into his eye and down his cheek. He wiped quickly at the eye with the back of his left hand, blinking furiously, and barely managed to deflect Abramm's follow-up attack.

Abramm stepped back and around with his left leg to present only his right side and sword arm toward his opponent, increasing his reach even as he brought his useless left arm out of the action and reduced the size of the target he made.

Balmark came at him with a furious barrage of strokes, rapier alternating with dagger, forcing Abramm inexorably backward down the dark, curving passage, the emerald glow of Balmark's amulet reflecting eerily off rough-hewn obsidian walls. Abramm suspected the border lord was maneuvering him into a trap—anything from an arcane menace to a backward tumble down an unexpected flight of stairs. Worse, he was being pressed farther and farther from his comrades and ever deeper into the Shadow-held warrens. Soon he felt the familiar warding aura of griiswurm, and not long after that glimpsed their tentacled forms clinging to the walls and ceiling around him. But try as he might, he couldn't find the right combination of strokes and footwork to turn the momentum in his favor.

A fetid, stomach-turning smell wrapped around him, coupled with an inexplicably familiar buzzing, like a hive of honeybees . . . and yet . . . not.

More griiswurm tangled across the walls, and the passage widened as the stench grew thicker. The buzzing writhed across his skin like the prickling that filled the air during a violent lightning storm. Balmark's amulet flared, reflecting eerily in the man's eyes, so that the rhu'ema that lived in it seemed to be looking directly at Abramm. He felt its hatred and its desire to destroy him. But he also felt its fear.

Something brushed the back of his neck, and he flinched, glancing up and around. In that moment of distraction, Balmark lunged. Abramm parried clumsily, lunged in a counterthrust that was blocked by the other's dagger, and suddenly the border lord's rapier speared Abramm's forward-bent thigh. Shock jolted him, again not from the pain but from dismay that his defenses had been breeched. The second time in ten minutes. It was like being back in Katahn's compound, a neophyte, constantly punished by pain for his failings. Balmark was right: he had lost more than he'd guessed.

Again the border lord attacked, forcing him backward. He twisted off balance on his bad hip, then stumbled into a veil of tough, sticky cobweb that stopped the momentum of his fall even as it clung to shoulders, head, and back. He froze, realizing instantly that he had been driven into a nightsprol's lair, where struggling would only bind him tighter.

Balmark grinned and straightened out of his crouch, well out of the reach of Abramm's rapier. The buzzing was louder here, the prickly sense of power coursing wildly over his flesh. To his left, green light reflected off streamers of webbing.

Both men panted heavily now. The border lord wiped his eye again, his face covered in the blood that had flowed from the cut on his brow. His grin widened. "Ye've provoked the wrath o' the Great Ones with yer blasphemies. Now ye'll pay fer it."

The little twinges and shivers that had been vibrating through the webbing told Abramm the lair wasn't abandoned. Now the nightsprol approached, albeit cautiously. Perhaps it could sense the Light in him. Or maybe Balmark was holding it at bay, forcing it to wait while he killed Abramm with his own hand, then left his body for it to dispose of.

Abramm's fingers tightened on the rapier's hilt.

Suddenly a shout echoed up the corridor behind the border lord, drawing him around as Abramm recognized Trap's voice and shouted back. Instantly Balmark whirled to Abramm and charged. Having his right arm free of the webbing, Abramm parried crisply, sliding his blade under the incoming thrust and into the muscle along the bottom of the man's forearm. The border lord recoiled, then charged again to strike with his dagger, forcing Abramm to twist back and away, thus miring himself more deeply in the nightsprol's binding silk. His target missed, Balmark staggered forward, and the thick web seized his dagger. Cursing, he flung himself backward before his arm could be caught, leaving the weapon behind.

More shouts echoed up the corridor and Abramm responded, desperate they should get there before the man eluded them. He held up his rapier again, but Balmark wouldn't take the bait. Instead he plunged straight into the nightsprol's sticky lair. Abramm turned his head to watch him and saw now the passageway that led through the shrouds of silk, ablaze with the bright green light that emanated from somewhere deep within the web.

Understanding struck him with the force of a blow: it was an etherworld corridor! Protected by its location in Graymeer's Shadow-cloaked, uncleared depths, and the nightsprol and its lair.

He felt a surge in the power crawling across his flesh and, howling his frustration, sought to free himself from the trap, trying to maneuver his rapier to cut the webbing that held him and losing hold of the blade in the process. As it clanked to the floor he flung himself forward in a desperate attempt to break free. But that only enwebbed him so firmly, his feet no longer touched the floor.

Finally, exhausted and frustrated, he made himself stop. As his own gasping breaths subsided, he sought to hear the approach of his men and thought bitterly of the humiliation of being found like this—how they would stop in the doorway, how their eyes would widen with horror at the sight of him, then go quickly to pity. They'd hurry forward in concern, asking if he were all right.

Of course he wasn't all right! How could he possibly be all right? He'd just been bested at swordplay by a poxed barbarian, stabbed twice and wrapped up like a fly for the man's beast! Everything he thought he'd gained these last six months had in a few moments' time been revealed as nothing more than delusion. He was an idiot not to have realized Balmark would come at him from his weak side, a fool to have barged into the corridor without even stopping to look. Now, as he went back through the sequence of the fight, looking at every mistake, he saw clearly how it all came from thinking he was more than he was. And so he had paid the price.

The great killer of kraggin and morwhol, hung up in a nightsprol's web, waiting for someone to come cut him down. Nausea crawled up into his throat.

Where are they? he wondered. *Why don't they hurry up and get it over with?* His breathing was quieting enough now that he should hear voices echoing down the corridor and the slap of hurried footfalls. Maybe they were gathered in the darkness out there, laughing amongst themselves at his predicament, enjoying the sight of the great White Pretender reduced to this.

The web convulsed violently, snapping him up and down as it snapped him out of the self-contempt into sudden fear and the recollection that Balmark hadn't left him here alone. Now the nightsprol chittered not far behind him, its fetid smell strong enough to choke. Pain had bloomed along his left side, while his right thigh felt as if the blade were still sticking in it. He'd be hard-pressed to defend himself even if he wasn't hanging here like a side of bullock.

The web bobbed and shivered as if the creature were skittering a little ways forward, then stopping to look before skittering even closer.

Where were his men?

"Ye've provoked the wrath o' the Great Ones with yer blasphemies," Balmark had told him. *"Now ye'll pay fer it."*

There were probably rhu'ema here, unseen but watching, savoring all of this. Waiting with eager anticipation for the beast to arrive and inject its poison into him.

That is your Shadow thinking, he told himself.

But that only launched a new round of self-recriminations. Not only was he a failure as a swordsman and king, not only was he an unqualified idiot to blunder into this predicament at all, but here he was again, letting the Shadow rule him, despite everything that had happened, all that he knew, everything Eidon had done for him. Here he was supposedly mature enough in the Light as to have entered his destiny, and he couldn't keep himself in it for any length of time at all. Even if he could, what good would it do him? He had no idea how to wield it against such as this nightsprol, no idea how to destroy the corridor behind him, no idea how to make the regalia work, assuming they even did. . . .

But I do. Eidon's words stopped the enumeration of his lacks but did not dispel the resentment.

So what am I supposed to do? Abramm asked. *Hang here and let you do everything?*

No, you are free to go ahead and keep trying for yourself.

But I've failed. All I do is fail. You've taken away the only strong thing about me. So what's left? I'm scarred and crippled and worthless.

Hardly worthless, my son. But definitely helpless. And spending far too much time contemplating your situation and your failings. I put that shield on your chest for a reason, if you'll recall.

To mark him indelibly as Eidon's own. A brand of ownership, yes. But also a promise of security and blessing. There was no way to remove it, as there was no way to sever the relationship between them, even should Abramm desire it. Eidon was his father now. Forever. And as a father, he had promised never to abandon his children. The resentment shriveled into chagrin.

I'm insulting you. Again.

Yes.

He heard the nightsprol's triumphant squeakings as the web shivered violently. He imagined the spawn lurking above him, dark fangs poised to sink into his neck. He kept a tight lid on the Shadow within him, even now seeking to flood his soul with fear. *Why do you always have to let these things get so close?*

It is part of conforming you. . . .

He was panting now, sweat beading his brow, his heart thumping a rapid staccato against his chest wall. Any moment now the Light would surely blast it away. Any moment—

He felt the wind of the creature's movement an instant before it dropped upon him, dark legs piercing his arms and hips and legs, fangs sinking into the side of his neck. Its poison burned out from them across his shoulder and down his back and twisted left arm, awakening the residualized spore that dwelt in his flesh and reigniting the firestorm of doubts and accusations that had only just subsided.

Then something slammed into him from the front, and a blade of white fire plunged deep into the beast on his back. He felt its shock and agony as his own, the Shadow shuddering within him, overwhelmed by the sudden explosion of the Light. Like a drowning man who sees his deliverance, he seized that Light and clung, letting it race through him, forcing the Shadow within him back into captivity and burning away the newly injected spore along with the reawakened old.

And then his perception shifted. He saw the room, filled with black strands of webbing, two men, the bulbous, multilegged corpse of the nightsprol lying beside them, and beyond, the irritating emerald green of the etherworld corridor. His sight shifted again, so that for a moment he saw all the fortress at the same time—the Esurhites captured by Abramm's men in the adjoining chamber, the men on the ramparts above, the miles of dark tunnels around him and far below, crawling with rhu'ema spawn, and here and there, the bright ribbons of the rhu'ema themselves, mostly glimmering in the lowest, darkest reaches, but also, as he'd guessed, in the same room with the two men and that hideous corridor, burning oddly as if it were in the side of his chest. For a moment, it seemed, he had, in some inexplicable way, become the fortress itself.

The corridor could not be tolerated. He sensed the evil that created it, the evil to which it was connected. Through it, more darkness would come, more spawn, more enemies. It was an abomination. It *must* be destroyed.

The Light exploded out of him and into the corridor. He sped across fields and mountains and rivers he knew to be in his own realm, at the same time glimpsing a cascade of images—objects and people, creatures that shouldn't be—all rushing through his mind in one brief, overwhelming onslaught.

Then it was gone. As the Light faded from his eyes, he heard a strange peeping behind him, its frequency dropping off rapidly until it stopped altogether. Blinking away the afterimages, he found himself back in the underground chamber. An acrid stench burned his nostrils, and he sneezed, realizing then that, while the web still clung to him, it no longer bound him. He turned in its suddenly fragile grasp, watching in wonder as the motion rippled through layered curtains of silvery strands, collapsing them into dust as it passed. The pale, sparkling powder drifted downward, dusting the night-sprol's dark, bulbous shape where it lay still in the chamber's far corner. Not far from it stood a blackened, smoking depression in the stone, remnants of the destroyed corridor.

The man beside him sneezed, drawing Abramm's attention. He already knew it was Trap and that he had come alone. Channon must have searched the opposite leg of the corridor when they'd left the slit. Though he had confidence Channon would be as tight-lipped as Trap when it came to speaking of the particulars of the incident, there was some deep part of Abramm that cringed at the thought of the other man seeing him enmeshed in that web. Bad enough Trap had seen it.

At least it was over. He was still alive and the corridor was destroyed. As relief cascaded over him, whatever had kept the pain of his wounds from registering in his awareness suddenly ceased to do so. He gasped with the sudden surge of agony, causing Trap to leap up, his brows drawing down with sudden suspicion.

"Are you all right, sir?"

"Not really." Abramm staggered toward the nearest wall, hardly able to put any weight on his leg. "I ran into Balmark, as I'm sure you've guessed. He got past my guard. Twice."

"He stuck you?" Trap's brown eyes widened in alarm, then roved swiftly over Abramm's torso. "Where?"

"Once in the leg. Once—" Abramm gestured vaguely at his left side where a small, red-stained slit in his tunic marked the sword's entrance point—"around here somewhere."

"Plagues!" Trap stepped to the doorway to shout for Shale.

———

Not long after that, Abramm was topside again, resting in the commander's own bed, his wounds cleaned and dressed. Though the fortress physician had recommended he reschedule the foreign dignitaries' tribute and spend the night in Graymeer's resting, he had refused. It wasn't like he'd never been stuck before, and he didn't want to make the incident bigger than it was already sure to be by canceling all his commitments and going to bed. Pain was a familiar companion to him, and anyway, what difference was there between lying in bed and sitting in a chair?

The reports had all been made and the day's incident discussed with his men while the physician had tended him. He'd given his orders for them to continue mapping and filling the warrens as best they could, then sent Laramor off to the north to keep a better eye on Balmark. The men, except for Trap, had left to see to their respective duties, and finally it was all winding down.

Waiting now for the commander's carriage to be prepared, he lay propped on a mound of pillows, watching the sea gulls fighting to land on the large rock beside Commander Weston's new quarters and offices. The rock had so long been a roosting spot for the gulls—at the moment crowding every inch of its surface—that it was covered with their guano. It didn't seem a restful spot, for few birds ever got to roost very long, pushed off by the sheer numbers of the others that perpetually crowded in, knocking others from their footholds, or sometimes outright attacking them.

How different is that, he wondered wryly, *from the way men act about their own areas of power? An endless cycle of comings and goings, thrown off gradually or suddenly, always having to be ready to defend their ground. . . .*

Not so different at all, he supposed. And he was grateful for the knowledge that his own position was ultimately not his to defend. Eidon had put him here. Eidon would remove him, if that was his will. . . . But that didn't take the edge off what had happened today.

The ease with which he'd been overcome still shocked and humbled him.

And, oh, it did gall to have to admit that the barbarian border lord had stuck him, not just once but twice. An inferno of raging self-condemnation yawned on one side of him, a swamp of self-pity on the other, while he clung grimly to the narrow path of knowledge that Eidon had allowed this for a reason. Part of the conforming process he'd mentioned during the coronation ceremony, and again just lately in the warrens.

Tersius had lost everything—even his life—before he'd finally won. Could the one who would follow him expect any less? He would die, too—to his old life, his old ways. Reliance on his fleshly strengths had to be stripped away, and it was not a pleasant process.

Abramm glanced at his new duke. "You've been holding back with me, haven't you? In practice. You and the others."

Trap had been watching the constant, mesmerizing shifting of the gulls on the rock, as well, and now Abramm's words started him out of his trance. Immediately his expression drooped with chagrin. "Maybe a little."

"Or maybe a lot?"

Trap shrugged and turned back to the multipaned window. "We didn't see any reason to push it. You had enough to deal with. Besides, it's not like you have to do that sort of thing anymore. That's why you have a king's guard."

Stripped.

I liked being the White Pretender, Lord.

You would rather be the Pretender than the king?

The question made him realize how silly he was being, how much less stimulating and comfortable it had been to actually *be* the Pretender than it was to think about having been him.

No, Lord. You've made me what you want me to be. I will be content with that.

He sighed, then said to Trap, "Now I understand why you were so displeased by my acceptance of Leyton's challenge match. He'll probably wipe up the floor with me."

Meridon turned to look at him, his expression sour. "Aye. He probably will." He paused. "Are you changing your mind about that, then?"

"No. Just bringing my expectations down to reality."

———

Besides taking far too long, the ride back to Springerlan was neither pleasant nor restful. Abramm sent messengers ahead to delay the start of the trib-

ute, and still arrived with barely enough time to change. Because he knew
he'd be unable to climb any steps at all, he had them bring him round to the
west wing's ground-level entrance, where Haldon awaited to escort him to a
nearby suite where he could prepare for the ceremony. He'd barely stepped
into the hallway when the problems began alighting on him, rather like those
sea gulls on their rock at Graymeer's.

Admiral Hamilton was there to report the discovery the princess and
Lady Madeleine had made at Treasure Cove that morning—the wrecked vessel and the remains of one of its crew identified definitely as one of those
deployed to explore the Gull Islands. The source of the ship's demise
remained unclear, however. And there was still no word from the vessels that
had gone out with her.

As Abramm reached the suite he was to use, Hamilton was replaced by
Byron Blackwell, making perfunctory inquiries as to His Majesty's injuries
while clutching a wrinkled typeset pamphlet that was clearly the focus of his
attention. Indeed, as soon as the dictates of protocol were satisfied, Blackwell
erupted with outrage over the new depths to which Prittleman had sunk,
rattling off the man's latest accusations as Abramm stripped off his gloves and
a servant removed his cloak.

"I know you're hurting, sir, but you've got to put a stop to this," Blackwell
concluded, muscles ticking at the corner of his left eye behind his spectacles.
Like the fainting fits, he'd had the tick ever since he'd run himself into the
tree branch the day Abramm faced the morwhol. Gray hairs threaded his
lank brown locks, still shoulder length despite the growing trend among the
courtiers to follow Abramm's lead with shorter hair. "You can't go on toler-
ating this increasingly outrageous criticism," he added. "People will see you
as weak."

Abramm listened to him calmly, refusing to let his emotions rise to the
outrage Blackwell seemed intent on kindling in him even as he refused the
wrinkled pamphlet the count so obviously wanted him to take. Instead he
handed his gloves over to Haldon and expressed his pleasure over Blackwell's
recovery from his fainting fit yesterday, a comment that caused the count's
pasty face to suffuse with red.

"Couldn't be better, sir. Although it would do much for my peace of mind
if we could lay this matter of the pamphlets to rest."

And so, finally, Abramm accepted the paper and skimmed it, finding it
every bit as noxious as Blackwell claimed. The king was a servant of Shadow,
its writer declared, and Gillard was the one who'd *really* slain the morwhol,

credit denied him because he was unable to defend himself. This was proven by Abramm's refusal to execute him for treason—because he knew Gillard had saved his life that day.

Abramm quit at that point and handed the paper to Jared to burn. "Draw up a proclamation," he said to Blackwell. "Any tavern, inn, or other establishment in which these pamphlets or any like them are found will be shut down indefinitely. Any person found handing them out will be arrested for treason."

He turned to Channon. "I want Prittleman found today. If he's moving around, people will have seen him." He addressed Blackwell again. "Add to the proclamation the assurance there'll be no prosecution for any who give up information regarding him today, even if they've sheltered him in the past. . . ." He paused. "But only today. All who henceforth willfully give him aid—or contribute to the spread of his lies—will be prosecuted as traitors to the fullest extent of our laws."

"Yes, sir."

The king turned again to Captain Channon, considering his next words carefully. "I want you to start by searching the Keep."

Shocked as he obviously was by these orders, Channon offered only a "Yes, sir" and departed. Then Abramm turned again to Blackwell, who seemed no less surprised.

"Well, you did recommend I be tough with them, Count." Abramm zapped a staffid as it skittered out from under the nearest chair.

As it flexed backward in its death throes, Blackwell closed his mouth and drew himself more upright. "Indeed, sir, but . . . to search the Keep . . ."

"Makes perfect sense." Abramm snorted. "Prittleman's been hand in glove with Bonafil for years. The only reason I've held off searching it this long is to avoid giving the perception of deliberate persecution. Pritt's probably been there from the start."

"But the repercussions—"

"Will not be as bad today as they would have been before my coronation."

Byron frowned out the window toward the Keep. "Bonafil will protest, sir."

"Indeed," Abramm said grimly. "I'm counting on it."

10

"I know these things are basic for many of you," Everitt Kesrin said to the crowd gathered in Whitehill's Blue Theatre that night for Terstmeet, "but if you think you already know them, think again."

Trap winced inwardly at the rebuke and resolved to pay attention to the kohal's message for longer than a minute at a time. He sat in the king's box at the left front of the audience at large—an audience big enough to fill the room for the first time since Kesrin began teaching months ago. Forward and right of Trap sat the king, bent over his writing table, rapidly penciling notes by the light of the great chandelier hanging over the audience at his back. Trap could see the hunch of fatigue and pain creeping into his shoulders—hardly surprising, given the fact he'd not rested since they'd returned from Graymeer's.

The low stage at the room's front stood in shadow, allowing Kesrin's Light-created images to show up brightly at his side, and just now a soldier, fully armed and armored, glowed in vibrant golden lines to his left. Tonight the kohal had interrupted his study in progress to give the sudden glut of newcomers—many of them newly marked—an overview of what those new marks meant. Familiar material to Trap, who'd received the shield when he was six and knew the Words backward and forward. Who also knew that no matter how many years one studied, nor how basic the truths being taught, there was always something to learn.

But knowing didn't guarantee doing, and tonight Trap's head was so full of the day's events—and tomorrow's potential troubles—the basics couldn't hold him. If Abramm had taken risks this morning in Graymeer's, it was nothing compared to what he'd done this afternoon. Ordering the Keep searched had taken as much courage as chasing a known enemy through the fortress's tunnels. And it had ignited a political firestorm that was still spreading.

Bonafil had burst into the throne room to protest that very afternoon, interrupting the foreign dignitaries' tribute already in progress. With his gray-and-white robes fluttering like wings, the Mataian High Father had stalked across the marble floor as if he were the king himself. Pushing aside the Thilosian ambassador at the foot of the throne, he'd glared up at Abramm and cried, "You *dare* to send your men into the consecrated portions of the Keep? Profaning our most holy of places?!"

The amulet at his throat had pulsed with a ruby light echoed by the scarlet sparks in his eyes. Threat radiated out of him, and no one spoke nor moved. Trap wondered if anyone could.

Abramm must have felt the man's power, for it was directed primarily at him, yet he met the fiery gaze as if it were nothing. "Give me Darak Prittleman, Father," he said at length, "and I will instruct my men to depart."

But of course Bonafil would never admit to sheltering the man and launched into the denunciation he'd apparently intended to deliver at Abramm's coronation: a rapid-fire expulsion of vitriol that Abramm soon cut off with a barked demand for silence.

His words dammed up in his throat, the High Father gaped like a fish, eyes bulging with disbelief. Knowing the Mataio still held the hearts of the majority of Kiriathans, he must have thought Abramm would not defy him in a face-to-face confrontation. But the icy calm with which Abramm regarded him had sent chills running down even Trap's spine.

"Your words are treasonous, Father Bonafil," said the king, deep voice echoing in the stone-still room. "Spoken to my own face before these forty witnesses. Surely you cannot think I will allow that?"

The High Father's eyes narrowed as his mouth closed and his brows drew down. "Come against me, Pretender," he grated, "and Eidon will repay you double measure."

At which point Abramm had turned to Shale Channon. "Escort the High Father to Wetherslea, Captain. Secure him in one of the top-floor suites and see that his needs are met, but grant him no visitors."

Again the holy man's mouth had fallen open, but he was hauled away before he could regain himself. Only as the throne-room doors closed behind him did they hear his screams of outrage.

The tribute resumed as if nothing had happened, but outside the story spread like wildfire. Reactions ranged from euphoric bravado over Abramm's firm stand against Mataian intimidation to outraged declarations that he had grossly exceeded his authority. If ever there was a good time for Abramm to have done this, Trap knew it was now, with the coronation miracles fresh in people's minds. Even with all the recent conversions, Mataians remained the majority among Kiriath's citizens. Should they come to believe their Terstan king and his friends meant to force them to abandon their beliefs, they *would* resist. A fact some of the king's alleged friends seemed to have forgotten.

All through the post-tribute reception and banquet and even in the halls outside the theatre prior to Terstmeet, Trap had listened to a stream of idiotic bluster and threat—inflammatory words that could easily spark a riot. Abramm was far too preoccupied to notice it, and in fact, much of the talk was not expressed in his presence anyway, since he'd already castigated one man for suggesting the Mataians be rounded up and whipped.

But out of his hearing, numerous high-ranking officers and nobles—men who should know better; not all of them even Terstan—talked and laughed without regard for the effect their words might have on the realm at large. It frustrated Trap keenly, and he feared before the evening ended he would be called upon to confront it. Hardly how he'd hoped to begin his service as First Minister.

"You wear that shield because you're his!" Kesrin's voice, suddenly loud and forceful, intruded upon Trap's worries. He blinked, chagrined to realize he'd wandered off again. A golden shield shone against the shadows beside the podium now. "It is his sign of ownership, a visible reminder of his calling on your life. A calling you will never be able to fulfill if you do not pay attention in Terstmeet."

And again Trap grimaced under the rebuke. Worse he'd lost his last chance to make it right, for the kohal was starting his closing prayer. Profoundly annoyed with himself, Trap bowed his head with everyone else and acknowledged his failure.

Usually, the moment Kesrin started praying, Abramm left the theatre, exiting with his guards through the left front side door so as to draw as little attention as possible. Tonight, of all nights, Trap expected him to make a hasty departure, for he couldn't last much longer. Thus he was surprised— and chagrined—to hear no sounds of movement during the prayer and, when it was done, to find the king still seated at his desk. At first he feared Abramm had reached the end of his strength and was unable to stand. But just as he started to stand himself, he realized the king was staring at a woman who stood by the front side door: Lady Madeleine.

Apparently she had slipped in during the lesson, for she had not been there at the start of it. In fact she'd been impossible to find since she and Carissa returned this afternoon from their discovery of the shipwreck in Treasure Cove. Her brother had suggested she was ill when she'd not accompanied him to the tribute and banquet, but when Abramm had sent servants to her apartments, she was not there. Now she stood looking wide-eyed at Abramm, clutching a black leather folio and a bound copy of the Words to her chest.

At Trap's back, the audience, having risen immediately upon the conclusion of Kesrin's prayer, now noticed the king's continued presence. People lingered in the nearest rows, and Trap heard them commenting nervously among themselves, wondering why Abramm was still here, if his wounds were paining him, if they dared speak to him.

Below him, Madeleine's attention shifted from Abramm to Leyton, heading toward her down the side aisle. Immediately her lips tightened and she turned to hurry out the door. Half a heartbeat later, Carissa stepped into the aisle, blocking Leyton's path and forcing him to stop and answer her greeting, a pleasantry he carried out with patent frustration. Meanwhile, Abramm left Jared gathering up the pens and papers and stepped awkwardly out of the box to follow Madeleine.

Driven by years of habit, Trap started after him, then aborted the motion as he saw Channon and Philip attending to that duty. *You're a duke now,* he told himself. *And you have no reason to follow.* But it was difficult to watch the other men go off with him, knowing their charge might collapse at any moment. At least tonight there would be no webs for Abramm to blunder into, unless one counted the web of attraction Madeleine so obviously held for him.

He then perceived the sudden silence around him and realized he was not the only one who'd watched the king disappear through that doorway. Nor to have seen whom he was following.

"Not exactly subtle, is he?" Byron Blackwell said dryly, standing now at his elbow.

Trap shrugged, irritated at Blackwell's criticism. "What need has one of subtlety when there is nothing to hide?"

Blackwell snorted.

"He's done nothing improper, Byron."

"Nothing besides meeting her unchaperoned at all these odd times and places and thus fueling the gossip as high as it will burn. I don't think the First Daughter will be quite as understanding of such behavior as we are. . . ." He paused, light flashing off the disks of his spectacles as he glanced again at the side door. "Makes me wonder how much he really wants this treaty after all."

Trap had nothing to say to that, though it troubled him in a way he could not articulate, and he was glad when, after a moment, Byron hailed Arik Foxton and left Trap standing there alone. He glanced again at the door through which Abramm had departed and considered going after him regardless of propriety. If only he could think of a reasonable pretext for doing so.

"I see it's going to take you some time to get used to *not* shadowing him everywhere he goes." Carissa's voice broke into his thoughts and drew his gaze around to where she stood behind him.

He smiled sheepishly. "Your eyes are far too discerning for comfort, my lady." He glanced around. "Where's Prince Leyton?"

"Off to harangue his sister, no doubt."

He nodded. "Where was she today, anyway?"

"I don't know." Carissa glanced toward the raucous laughter erupting behind him. "I suspect one of the libraries."

"Abramm sent men to both. She wasn't there."

"Well, if Madeleine doesn't want to be found, it's not likely she will be."

He frowned at her. "Why would she not want to be found?"

The crown princess shrugged and fixed her gaze on something behind him. "Most likely because she didn't want to be interrupted in whatever she was doing."

He thought about asking what that might be, but he knew Carissa well enough to realize she'd have volunteered the information if she wanted to share it. Maddie had been the one to find the Esurhite dragon fetish—which no one besides her and Carissa had yet seen because Channon hadn't thought to ask for it and no one expected her to disappear. Not that anyone really needed to see it. Its significance lay in its use as indication the Esurhites had taken the Gull Islands, though with the recent storms it really could have come from anywhere.

"You wore that same suit last night, didn't you?" Carissa's question broke into his thoughts, so at odds with them it took him a moment to figure out what she was talking about.

He glanced down at his gray doublet and breeches. "Yes, I believe I did."

"A man who is a duke and a First Minister really needs to have more than one suit in his wardrobe. You're going to have to get your tailor working harder."

He felt his eyes widen at her. "My *tailor*?"

"I can recommend a good one if you like." She smiled.

My tailor?

"Or perhaps you would like me to simply give the name to your secretary."

"I don't have a secretary."

"Well, you're going to need one of those, too." She was plainly enjoying herself.

He was still trying to get his mind around the notion that he should have a tailor. Before the conversation progressed further, however, they were interrupted.

"Your Highness," came a low, familiar voice from Trap's right. "Your devotion to the Words is an inspiration. Despite all your troubles of this long day and past night, here you are. Lovely as ever." Duke Oswain Nott followed his words with a courtly bow.

Carissa blushed furiously, while Trap's stomach tied itself into a knot of distaste.

"I trust you are fully recovered from your scare last night?"

The princess looked startled at the question. Nott didn't seem to notice, shaking his head sympathetically. "How gratifying, at least, to have had your claims borne out today."

Carissa's mouth was tightening, her brows drawing downward in an expression that reminded Trap eerily of her brother. "I presume you are speaking of Rennalf of Balmark, sir, and I assure you I would prefer my claims not to have been borne out and him still trapped behind snow-locked passes."

"I understand completely. I am surprised, though, that Abramm hasn't assigned you a special protective detail. With that leg injury and all the furor over Bonafil, it must've slipped his mind." He paused, smiled, and added, "I'd be happy to escort you safely to your door, though."

I'm sure you would, Trap thought sourly, marveling at the rapidity with which his dislike for this man was growing.

"Why, Duke Oswain," Carissa asked, "whatever would I need a special detail for? I have my own men with me, and—"

"With Rennalf still at large, my lady, your men may not be sufficient to protect you, wily warlock that he is."

Trap's irritation finally got the best of him. "Rennalf is not at large," he said. "He escaped through the corridor before Abramm destroyed it."

Nott turned to look down his long nose, gray brows arching upward as if he could not believe Trap had actually spoken to him without first being addressed. "Ah, the new Duke of Northille." He gave Trap a nod that was at best cursory, then said, "Just knowing a man went through a corridor doesn't tell you where he ended up."

"The king is convinced he's in Balmark."

"Ah." Nott chuckled. "That must be where he is, then." But he couldn't quite keep the condescension out of his tone. "I do understand why you might be concerned, though. Don't your lands butt right up against his?"

"No, my lord duke." Trap allowed himself a small smile. "Balmark borders the Ruk Pul, far to the north. My land is just south and west of the Highlands, bounded by the River Kalladorne on the west and the Goodsprings Valley on the east. . . . The only holding it directly abuts is Amberton."

Nott grimaced and waved a dismissive hand. "Northille, Amberton, Goodsprings . . . I can't keep all those little fiefdoms straight." His own holdings extended east of Springerlan across most of the Keharnen Plain, including its accompanying seacoast, providing him vast tracts of farmland, a bustling fishing industry, and a lock on the proceeds of the salt flats at Chastwort. He added, "The only thing I know for sure is that they're a breeding ground for Mataian heretics." He flicked Trap another smile. "Perhaps with you running things, Northille, we can make some inroads there." He paused. "There haven't been Mataians on any Nott holding for over a decade now."

"I'm not sure that's a distinction I'd be bragging about today," Trap said dryly, feeling his ire rise.

Nott blinked at him, surprise opening his long, furrowed face.

"The Mataians are still in the majority, sir," Trap pointed out when the man seemed not to understand. "And though Abramm holds the Crown by inheritance and human law, he does so in defiance of Mataian standards. People are already resenting Bonafil's arrest, even when all agree Abramm had no choice. If they think he means to deny them their faith . . . we could have another war on our hands."

By now Nott's surprise had turned to incredulity. "You presume to lecture *me* on matters of politics and religion, Northille? When you have been a member of the peerage less than forty-eight hours? I suggest you curb your hubris, sir."

Trap had expected Nott would react like this, just not so soon into the conversation. Nor with such sharp and blatant disdain. It shocked his brain to blankness and momentarily robbed him of his ability to speak. Nott smiled down at him smugly, as he realized uneasily they had now become the center of attention. Anger and frustration roiled up in him, and in that moment he wanted nothing so much as to pull out his sword and start lunging. Which, of course, would never do.

Seeing he had rendered his opponent speechless, Nott turned very deliberately to one of his companions and said, "Not for ten years have Mataians dwelt on my lands, nor will they again, so long as I'm duke. If we don't start cleaning our own houses, Eidon will soon be doing it for us."

"I hear there's talk in the river districts of storming the Keep tonight," said one of the men beside him.

"Perhaps we should go and join them," Nott said. "Cloak ourselves in robes and cowls as the Gadrielites used to do and give them a taste of their own medicine."

And where before he was speechless, now, even knowing he was being baited, Trap couldn't keep his mouth shut: "Do that," he said, "and you'll likely find yourself with a suite next to Bonafil come morning."

Nott stared at him rigidly, his features suddenly seeming like ragged slashes carved out of rock. His dark eyes narrowed. "Are you threatening me, sir?"

"Merely advising caution, my lord duke."

And still Nott stared at him, eerily expressionless while the aggression swelled between them until it seemed ready to burst into hideous disaster— the shouting of words that should never be spoken, the leveling of untenable threats, even the potential for violence. But in the end Nott held his temper, perhaps because he realized Trap had spoken truth. Finally he smiled tightly and said, " 'Twas only jest, sir. You can't think we would really do such a thing."

And around him the others tittered nervously.

Trap turned away without comment. He'd made his point. Perhaps not in the best way possible, but made, nonetheless. And he had not humiliated himself utterly, nor been turned into a blustering fool by his own temper. It helped that, as he made his way up the aisle toward the main doors, a number of men stopped to offer their appreciation for what he'd said and even expressed surprise he'd had the courage to beard Nott, new as he was to the peerage. But of course, none were peers themselves.

Just before he reached the open double doors he found himself again face-to-face with Carissa, who had watched the entire interchange and whom he thought had been behind him. Now she smiled as if nothing untoward had occurred and said, "I was wondering if you might walk me back to my chambers, Duke Eltrap."

He frowned. "Surely you're not concerned about Rennalf, my lady?"

"Not at all, sir. I just wanted to enjoy the company of a friend . . . and avoid that of those I find distasteful." Her gaze flicked to something over his shoulder as simultaneously Nott's voice rose sharply above the mutter of conversation.

Trap grasped her intent immediately and frowned. "Don't you think I've irritated him enough tonight?"

She snorted. "You are First Minister, Duke Eltrap. And the king's favorite. *Nott* is the one who should be wary of giving offense. Though I fear he may be incapable of understanding that."

"He's a powerful man, ma'am. He could make a lot of trouble for Abramm. For me, as well."

She eyed him speculatively. "I've never thought you the sort of man to be timid of trouble, sir."

"Only of stirring it up for no good reason."

She cocked a brow at him. "And keeping company with me is not a good reason?"

He felt the blood rush to his face. "It is an excellent reason, Your Highness," he said.

"Well, then . . ." Her eyes laughed at him, for she knew that she had won.

They left the theatre and started up the switchbacking stairway that led to the palace's main level, the smack of his boots upon the polished marble intermixing with the rasping rustle of her wide skirt and petticoats. As the voices of those lingering outside the theatre receded behind them, she said, "Well, sir, I'd say you've had a splendid first day. In addition to standing up to Nott's arrogance as well as anyone I've ever seen, for a while now you've actually stopped being a king's guard. Which proves there's hope for you yet."

He knew she meant him no malice, but her words stirred up all his doubts regarding his suitability for his new station, and prevented him from coming up with a suitable response. After they had walked in silence for a few more strides, she said, "You are displeased with your promotion?"

He could not answer her at first, and when he did, he chose his words carefully. "To be honest, my lady, I don't know what I think about it. I have

SHADOW OVER KIRIATH | 133

no knack for flattery, nor for hiding my thoughts—as has just been made obvious. Being a politician is a position to which I have never aspired. Truth be told, I almost feel as if your brother's sold me out."

She shrugged. "If you don't like to think of yourself as a politician, then think of yourself as a statesman . . . for surely it is an honorable position. Or do you think the task of governing to be so unimportant it should be left only to the weak and dishonest to carry it out?"

The advice rendered him silent for a time afterward, for he had never thought of it in that light. She didn't allow him to withdraw into his own musing for too long, though. As they reached the top of the stairway and continued along the hall there, she thanked him for walking with her. "I don't know what is going on with Nott, but lately, I can hardly go anywhere without running into him. He actually asked me to breakfast with him this morning!"

"Did you accept?"

She smiled. "Why do you think I went with Madeleine on her ride?" She shook her head. "It's almost like he's wanting to court me or something."

"Perhaps he is."

"Why would he do that?"

Trap shook his head. "I don't know. Maybe it's because you're the crown princess. Or perhaps it's your wealth. Or the fact that you are a stunningly beautiful woman. . . ."

"Ah, there, see?" She smiled at him. "You do have a knack for flattery."

"It wasn't flattery, my lady. It was simple truth."

"Simple truth, indeed. Look at me. I am an old woman."

"Aye. You're positively ancient."

"Used up. Damaged goods, as they say."

"A wreck. Nothing left at all. I can't imagine any man wanting you."

She cocked a brow at him. "Are you mocking me, sir?"

"Well, you know what the Words say: Answer a fool as his folly deserves. Or, in this case, her folly."

"And now you're calling me a fool?"

He couldn't quite keep the smile off his face. "No flattery, my lady. Just truth."

She gaped at him. "Why, Duke Eltrap, I do believe your new position has gone to your head."

And now his smile became an open grin as she shook her head and after a moment responded with a grin of her own. Not long after that they drew up to her door, which the footman was already opening.

"Here you are, Highness," Trap said. "Delivered safe and sound to your quarters, with not a warlock in sight."

"Thank you, sir." She gave him a courtly nod, but then, rather than sweeping into her room, she laid a hand on his arm, looking up at him with those piercing Kalladorne eyes. "I do not think my brother made a mistake, sir," she said quietly. "I believe you are fully deserving of your new title and that you will be a most able First Minister."

11

Abramm followed the narrow service passage behind the theatre's side door out onto the midpoint of the ramp leading down to the south gallery. Just as he stepped out onto it, he saw someone moving into the gallery at its lower end. Guessing it was Madeleine, he sent Philip to get her, then turned to Channon and held out his hand for the cane the man had carried all afternoon and evening.

Abramm knew he shouldn't be here. He'd pushed his body far past reasonable already. Sitting upright for the last hour had been difficult, and he'd been on the verge of capitulating to his advisors' continual suggestions that he rest, when he'd seen Lady Madeleine. After fearing all afternoon that she'd left for the Western Isles upon her return from Treasure Cove, he couldn't let this opportunity slip away without talking to her.

White-stuccoed walls loomed around him now in a downsloping hall lit by kelistars resting on candlesticks and wall-sconce brackets. Ranks of wall hangings alternated with night-darkened windows on one side and their corresponding mirrors along the other. A thick Sorian rug of royal blue and gold served as runner down the long corridor, empty and silent but for him and Channon— until some ten strides behind them he heard a door close, followed by approaching footsteps. "Whoever it is," he told Channon, "get rid of them."

His captain turned away and Abramm continued down the ramp, leaning heavily on his cane now, gritting his teeth against the pain. Already he was feeling light-headed and faintly nauseated, ruefully acknowledging the likelihood he'd have to be carried back to his apartments. Behind him low voices echoed, their words indiscernible but the irritation in their tones clear. He thought he recognized Leyton Donavan's voice but did not turn around to see lest he encourage the man to hail him.

More than halfway down the ramp, prudence finally won over curiosity, and he abandoned his plan of meeting Madeleine in the gallery. Balancing with the cane, he sank awkwardly onto one of the many padded benches lining the long hall. His side was no worse than a throbbing ache, but it was a fiery agony to bend his leg at all. Dropping his back against the wall, he waited, knowing he had felt worse pain and berating himself for going soft.

Best think of something else.

He had sat there for what seemed a considerable amount of time, sifting through the day's events and the many repercussions that were sure to come from them, when doubled footfalls approached up the ramp, signaling the return of Philip with Lady Madeleine. Hearing them, he opened his eyes and sat forward, seeing that Maddie still carried her bound copy of the Words and her folio of notes. He also noted she had apparently not bothered to change out of her riding apparel all day, for she still wore the blue wool jacket and split skirt that was her favorite.

When she reached him, she dropped him a curtsey and came up frowning. "You look like death itself, sir!" she blurted with her usual direct approach. "Why are you not returning to your chambers to rest?"

He smiled and shook his head. "Because these ill-advised clandestine meetings we keep having seem to be the only way I'm able to talk to you of late."

She flushed, the color spreading up to her hair and down to the scooped neckline of her gown. "You could've summoned me."

"I tried. No one knew where you were." He gestured now at the padded bench beside him. "Please sit with me awhile."

Her frown deepened, but she sat—perched upon the bench's edge as if ready to flee at a moment's notice. "I was at the University library," she said.

"Ah. That explains everything, then."

Her chin came up. "I can't help it if your people are inept," she said tartly, and he found himself rejoicing to see what appeared to be the return of the old Maddie.

"Unless, of course, you influenced their not finding you." As adept as she was at making speaking cloaks, he wouldn't be surprised if she could work one to baffle the eye as well as the ear. Indeed, her face positively flamed.

"I was reading," she said. "I didn't want to be disturbed."

"And naturally forgot all about the ceremonies of today and your part in them—"

"I'm through with those ceremonies. It only stirs things up and"—her gaze dropped to her hands, clasped tightly upon the book and folio—"makes things worse for you."

He regarded her wordlessly, waiting for her to go on. But now she watched her fingers pick at a crack in her folio, having gone back to that frustrating nervousness that had characterized his last two encounters with her. He grew aware again of the scars running tightly down his cheek and wondered if they were putting her off more than she wanted to admit.

She stilled her hands with a sigh and laid book and folio flat upon her lap. Then she lifted her face. "Briellen received a double portion not only of beauty but of the social graces I lack. She'll have your courtiers eating out of her hands in a day, whereas I only seem to put them off more and more. The less they see of me, I figure, the easier it will be for both of you."

His heart fell at the implication of her words.

"And anyway," she finished awkwardly, "I had no idea you'd want to speak to me."

"No idea? After what you found today?"

"What could I tell you that the others couldn't?"

"Well, for one, I'd like a look at the dragon fetish you found. Dragons do have special interest for me these days."

"Yes, I know." Her gaze returned to the books in her lap. "But you were busy today, and . . ." She trailed off.

"Back there in the theatre, I had the distinct impression you were waiting to talk to me."

"I was. But when I saw you, I knew this wasn't the time." She looked up at him. "Truly, sir, you do look awful. You should be—"

"Resting. I know. And I will happily oblige you once you satisfy my curiosity." He paused. "And what *were* you doing just now in the gallery?"

She flushed and her chin jerked up. "I was looking for a painting. But really, sir, it can wait." She must've seen the annoyance in his expression, for she added quickly, "It was just some things I learned in the history of the Western Isles I was reading today."

History of the Western Isles? His heart sank even further. *She really does mean to go.*

"Did you know they were colonized by the old Ophiran Empire?" she asked.

"Yes."

"And that the Ophirans protected their borders and far-flung fortresses with guardstars?" He nodded and she continued. "There was a guild of Ter-stans that created and installed them. . . ."

"Yes. I learned that in Hur."

"Ah. Of course." Her brief burst of excitement died back to the awkward tension he was coming to despise. Why wouldn't she tell him what was wrong? What had happened to that refreshing directness that had so long both befuddled and beguiled him? And why was she so set on leaving just when he needed her most? It made no sense at all.

Before he even realized what he intended, he burst out, "Light's grace, Maddie! I don't know what's gone wrong between us, but I don't want you to leave!" She looked up at him in surprise and he barreled on. "I need your eyes and your wit and your spirit. It would be like losing—" He scrambled to find an appropriate comparison. "Like losing Warbanner."

And that, he saw from the souring of her expression, was not the thing to say at all.

"Yes," she said coolly, "I imagine he would be a great loss."

"He would be . . . but . . . but you would be a greater one." *Oh, Eidon, I am making a mess of this.* "I know I have plenty of capable researchers. But none that can . . ." And here he trailed off, partly from the embarrassment of recalling what he'd said to her last night at this point, partly because he had just come up against something he couldn't articulate.

Her face could not have been more expressionless. "That can what?"

"See things the way you do," he said helplessly.

She looked down at her hands, apparently unmoved by his appeal. And why not? He'd done little more than beg her to stay. And could think of no more to add. "Can't you stay a little longer, at least?"

And still she looked at her hands, clasped together, motionless atop the Book of the Words. She sat there, silently, and he felt the moments ticking by, timed by the beat of his heart.

At length, she let out a long, shuddering breath and said, "Briellen is not going to understand the rumors that have sprung up around us, sir. If I stay, it would be best if we had nothing to do with each other." And now, finally, she glanced up at him. "Which shouldn't be that difficult. I'll simply put all my comments in writing and have my assistant make the verbal reports to you."

He frowned at her, not at all pleased with such an arrangement but seeing no good reason to refuse it. It was certainly better than the alternative. "Very well. If that's what you wish."

Her eyes dropped back to her hands, now more clenched than clasped. "It is," she whispered.

When she didn't move and seemed disinclined to say more, he returned to their earlier subject: "So then, what painting were you looking for?"

"The one of Avramm's coronation." Her eyes came up again as she seemed to seize upon this opportunity to discuss something relatively benign. "I was reading an account of the event this afternoon and recalled there was a painting depicting it. I wanted to see how the two compared."

He cocked a bemused brow. "And you just had to rush down here to see it now, though the place is deserted and the light bad?"

Her fingers began to pick at the folio crack again. "I have my own light. And I was down here anyway, so why not?"

"You were hiding, weren't you?"

A grimace twitched her lips. "Oh, very well, yes. I saw Leyton coming down the ramp and just didn't feel like facing him tonight." She looked around as if in sudden realization. "I can't think why he's not here now."

"I sent him away."

Dismay flooded her face and he could almost hear her groan.

"He can hardly hold you accountable, my lady. You were obviously trying to escape me."

"That's not the way he'll see it," she muttered. She sat silent a moment, then sighed. "I really was interested in the painting, though."

"Well, I can help you there. You ran right by it. It's not a painting, you see. It's a wall hanging." He gestured toward one of the pieces down the left wall not far from where they sat.

Her eyes sparked with interest and she leaped up, then remembered herself. "May I have your leave, sir?"

"Of course." As she hurried down the ramp toward the object of her interest, he drove himself to his feet, trying not to wince and gasp as he did, and giving thanks Channon had provided him with a very stout cane. Right now it was bearing almost all his weight. The first few steps were the worst.

The ancient tapestry hung from ceiling to floor and was nearly as wide as it was high. Its colors were muted and dark, its lines blurred with age, its style the rough, clumsy technique of the ancients. A man wearing a robe of fur knelt on a square rock amidst a grove of tall dark trees. Another man held a stylized crown over his head as a group of nobles looked on.

She shook her head. "That's not at all like what was described. Is this the only one?"

"The only one I know of." He stepped closer, frowning at it. "It's awfully dirty, though. Maybe if all that mold were removed it would look different."

"Mold?"

"Or mildew. Whatever it is." He reached past her to scratch at the dark gray fibers clinging to the work. The moment he touched them, a green spangle shivered across the weaving's surface and he saw that it had been enspelled. From her gasp, he knew Maddie had seen it, too. They glanced at each other, then stepped closer to the hanging and began to strip off the network of fibers that covered it—neither mildew nor mold but something of the Shadow. Abramm soon discovered that little currents of Light set into it coalesced the fibers into stiff, integrated patches that lifted free from the tapestry beneath to be more easily pulled off.

Slowly, patch by patch, they uncovered the work that lay hidden beneath— one like nothing in all the collections of the palace, the University, or even the archives in the Hall of Kings. Fine deeply colored threads had been worked into a tableau of exquisite detail and nuance. Scarlets, blues, a wealth of greens interspersed with rich browns and luminous blacks, the whole accented by shining silvers and golds. It reminded Abramm strongly of the Robe of Light, and the more they revealed of it, the more convinced he became it was no ordinary weaving of wool or linen, but very possibly a work of the Light itself.

Once they had pulled away most of the obscuring veil, they stood back to regard a completely new scene: Avramm didn't kneel at all, but stood on a much lower stone, presumably at the base of the natural amphitheater upon which the Hall of Kings was built. The first few rows of onlookers' backs had been rendered in the foreground, gathered around the king as he was crowned. Beyond swooped the valley, cut through by the River Kalladorne and bounded on the far side by the western headland. The sky, no longer cloudy, was light blue, with puffs of white cloud.

As for Avramm, he was a small, dark-haired man who already wore the real crown upon his head—the same plaited skeins of light Abramm had worn yesterday. The ancient Avramm also wore the Robe of Light, and held the scepter in one hand, the orb in the other, just as Abramm had. A plume cloud of tiny stars extended from the orb toward the onlookers, some of whom reached out toward it.

"It's just like what happened with you," Maddie breathed while Abramm gaped in astonishment.

She moved back to the tapestry again, holding up her kelistar for a better view, finally pulling over one of the benches so she could climb up and peer at the area of her interest: something on the horizon at the far left edge of the work. A moment she stared at it, then glanced over her shoulder at him. "I think this is Graymeer's . . . shown fully built here, at the same time as he's being crowned. Which makes it unquestionably Ophiran. And this gold and silver thing here . . . must be the guardstar."

He stepped closer, not needing to climb onto the bench, and saw that it was indeed his fortress. And that she could be right about the guardstar. Wonder flooded him. The Heart had been left intact but buried in its platform in Hur. What if Graymeer's still had its heart buried somewhere? If they could find it and ignite it . . .

"It would solve all the problem with the warrens and the possibility of more corridors being opened," he murmured. To say nothing of the protection it would give them from the Esurhites. With such a wonder in place . . . he might not even need the Chesedhans.

She had left the matter of the guardstar and was now peering at another part of the scene not too far away from the fortress. He heard a faint, "Oh!" and then, after a moment, "It's your dragon, again." She glanced back at him as she pointed to something in the sky floating not too far from the fortress. He stepped closer still.

It looked exactly like the dragon in his vision.

Chills crawled madly across his flesh. He stared at it, reliving his coronation vision and feeling again the suffocating power of this creature's evil.

"Sir?" Byron Blackwell's voice broke into his thoughts and drew him around. His secretary hurried down the ramp toward him, the look on his face presaging he had yet another crisis to report. "They've found the—" His voice choked off as his eyes fixed upon the tapestry hanging at Abramm's back. "Why. . . ? Where. . . ?" His eyes tracked to Maddie and back to Abramm.

"It was cloaked," Abramm said. "All these years, and we didn't even know it." He glanced at the hangings across the hall from him and added, "Who knows how many more are hidden in the same manner." *And what kinds of things we might learn from them.* He drew his thoughts back to the moment. "What did they find, Byron?"

Blackwell gave a start and cleared his throat. "The printing press, sir—in the bowels of the Keep, as you expected. No Prittleman, though. And trouble's brewing down in Southdock. A mob's come together, threatening to storm the Holy Keep. Two squadrons of royal troops have already been sent to quash it."

Abramm nodded. "I don't suppose I need to go down until it's over."

"No, sir. Probably be better if you waited."

"Well, see that I'm kept informed."

Blackwell frowned at him. "You should be in bed, sir. You look on the verge of collapse."

As soon as he said it, Abramm was swept with a wave of wooziness. He staggered for a moment, then shook it off. "I'll be going there very soon," he told his secretary. "Don't worry."

Blackwell continued to frown at him. "Yes, sir." He stepped away, glanced at Madeleine, then at the tapestry again before hurrying off.

It was almost as if he had taken all of Abramm's energy with him, for no sooner had he departed than the wooziness was back, stronger than ever. Maddie said something once Blackwell was out of earshot, but her voice sounded blurred and distant. When Abramm turned to ask her to repeat herself, he set the entire hall spinning around himself, as at the same moment his legs turned to water. He collapsed on the bench, grunting as fire flashed up his leg.

He heard Maddie say something, her voice high-pitched, her words coming far too fast to understand. Then Captain Channon was bending over him and Abramm gripped the man's arm. "I think I'm going to need that chair you were talking about earlier, Captain."

"Yes, sir. Philip's bringing it right now."

Gillard passed the day dozing in and out of wakefulness, his thoughts focused on the dilemma of how he was going to gather his strength. His supporters would rescue him as soon as he was strong enough. But he wasn't going to make much progress without food and water. How they thought he would be able to get any of either so long as he must convince his keepers he was still asleep remained a mystery. And he was beginning to grow rather miserably thirsty.

It took all his willpower not to open his eyes and ask for water when his attendants came in to check on him that afternoon. If not for his interest in their talk he might have given himself away. But he was fascinated to hear that Prittleman had apparently been writing pamphlets critical of the king, which had finally pushed Abramm into having the Holy Keep searched. Of course High Father Bonafil had to protest, and naturally Abramm had to arrest him. It made him want to laugh even as it made him angry.

He could understand the laughter . . . but why was he angry? He had no liking for Bonafil nor for the Mataio, and Prittleman was a stiff pain in the lower regions. He'd intended both men to die beneath the morwhol's claws, though obviously they had not. *Was I the only one the beast got?*

No. He knew for sure it had killed Rhiad. And from the men's talk, he gathered Abramm had not escaped unscathed, either, for they spoke of his crippling and the hideous scars on his face—news that filled Gillard with intense satisfaction. He wished now he'd opened his eyes the night before so that he could have seen the damage for himself. How crippled was crippled? Had the king's retainers brought him in on a chair? He didn't know, but it amused him to think of his hated sibling being carried everywhere by lackeys.

At last the men left him, and he was freed from the temptation to ask for a drink. Once the door lock grated again and all sounds faded, he finally opened his eyes. Late-afternoon light poured through the window to his right, striped with the shadows of the window bars. He was indeed imprisoned in the suite at the top of the Chancellor's Tower. Would his new friend come again tonight? The man had promised it would be soon. . . .

He awoke later to the deep gong of the University clock echoing over the city. An orange glow flickered across the bed canopy's gray folds as if someone had stoked the fire too high. He managed to lift his head enough to see past his toes and the footboard to the hearth in the wall on his left: nothing there but a bed of coals. His eyes returned to the canopy, then to the window in the eastern wall. The curtains gapped open, their edges flickering with the orange illumination.

The fire was outside.

A great boom shook the glass and the bed and the organs in his chest, and he clutched the sheets beneath his hands, fear washing over him in a great cold wave. What dreadful turn of events now? Just when he thought he would be rescued.

Another boom. Then another, smaller but closer, perhaps at the base of this very tower. A voice called sharply from the chamber adjoining his. A door squealed open—not his own but apparently the one leading out to the stairwell. The voice echoed again, calling a name, then burst into a torrent of profanity. The door slammed shut, the key jangled, and everything started happening at once. Shouts, bangs, screams. Now a grating in his own lock, the door flying open, searing lantern light slicing through his velvet shadows. Cowled men stood along his bedside. One of them bent over him, assuring him they were friends. . . .

The voice was familiar again, though he couldn't see the man's face for the glare of the lantern behind him. The men at the foot of his bed had been doing something with the bedding, and now the one who had spoken did likewise at the top. At his word Gillard felt himself lifted off the bed in a makeshift stretcher. As quickly as that he was carried from the suite, noting the bodies of his guards sprawled unmoving upon table and carpet in the adjoining chamber. Then they were out on the landing and moving down the stairs, around and around and around.

No one said anything. Out the door they went, then across the tower's cobbled yard, surprisingly devoid of soldiers. Those who were on guard clustered at the railed north fence watching the great conflagration leaping against the dark sky. Smoke swirled thick and acrid on the air, pieces of ash and debris floating down on every hand.

Gillard's carriers bore him swiftly through the iron gate in the riverside fence to a small dock, where awaited a lightless barge of the kind used for carrying bales of wool downstream from the heartland, then restocked with a variety of goods for its return trip. Gillard's handlers passed him off to men waiting in the barge, and within moments he had been tucked among the casks and kegs.

Shortly after that he felt the barge move, carried upstream for now on the incoming tide, gaining all the distance it could before its crew must resort to sail or pole or mules pulling from along the riverbank. Soon after that the man who had spoken to him in the tower returned to offer him a single cup of water and no more.

"Your innards have to get used to working again. Too much and you'll be in more pain than you can imagine."

The man left, taking the light with him, and Gillard felt waves of weakness flood over him. He heard a couple more vigorous explosions as sleep overtook him. Later he awakened to a lighted lantern and a new keeper: a bald, narrow-eyed string of a man dressed in a Guardian acolyte's robe. The stranger gave him two cups of water this time, promising warm fish broth soon.

As he dozed off again, he heard the University clock toll, so faint in the distance now he could barely hear it. One . . . two . . . three . . . four strikes. Almost dawn now.

And no one had caught up with them yet. . . .

HIDDEN
TREASURE

PART TWO

12

It was over a week before Abramm was finally able to make the trip out to Graymeer's to search for its guardstar. For two days following his collapse outside the gallery, he had lain in bed so stupefied with laudanum he had little awareness of the storm that raged through Springerlan. On the third day he decided he wanted his wits back and refused to take any more, but its effects took another day to wear off, so it was almost four days after the fact that he learned of all that had transpired as a result of his decision to search the Holy Keep.

On the night following the arrest of High Father Bonafil, a Terstan mob had ransacked the place, burning and bashing everything in the ground-level buildings before blowing up the Sanctum itself. Royal troops had intervened, arrests were made, and men—mostly Terstan—were tried and punished. Which displeased the city's Terstans almost as much as the destruction of their Keep had displeased the Mataians.

To make matters worse, in the midst of all the chaos, Gillard had been spirited away from the Chancellor's Tower. Trap, who as First Minister was charged with acting in Abramm's stead, ordered the city closed down the moment he was told of the disappearance, initiating a house-to-house search. But those actions failed to turn up the prince and only increased the tension between the two groups.

The rumor mill spun out wild tales of royal troops dragging off hapless Mataian families to be tortured for their faith, and of the veritable warren of Shadow-filled passages discovered beneath the Sanctum. People grumbled at the soldiers and the restrictions, called each other liars, and incited ridiculous concerns over what the future held. Finally a group of hysterical Mataians staged a small riot down by the docks. Seeing the situation spiraling out of control, Trap reopened the city before even a fifth of it had been searched, precipitating the immediate exodus of fearful Mataians and destroying any chance of keeping the escaped prince close.

Emboldened by the First Minister's concessions, the Mataians further demanded he release High Father Bonafil, but by then Abramm was sufficiently clearheaded to take back the reins of rule and refused. He did promise to consider providing the displaced Mataians with assistance in building a new Keep—but that would be contingent on their abiding by the laws of the land. He further assured everyone that the Duke of Northille had done precisely what Abramm himself would have done had he been able, and that he was very pleased with his First Minister's actions.

He did, however, personally interview some of the soldiers who had been on duty in the tower yard the night Gillard was taken and from that concluded his brother's escape had been carried out by means of the Shadow's powers of deceit: every man he spoke with insisted that even had he not noticed the kidnappers going in, he surely would have seen them carrying out a man as incapacitated as Gillard was. That they had not, meant they'd either been Commanded to forget or the perpetrators had been cloaked in Shadow.

He also made a personal inspection of the network of tunnels found beneath the Keep—riding down to the ruins in his coach and submitting to the indignity of being carried in an open sedan chair to the point of interest, then limping about with the help of his cane. He did it not so much to see the tunnels—of which he already had intimate knowledge—but to draw renewed attention to their existence. He made no proclamations about them but did make a point of wondering out loud how there could be such things of obvious evil beneath the Flames that were supposed to drive it all off.

Finally, nine days after he and Maddie had uncovered the amazing images of Avramm's coronation on the tapestry, the crisis had quieted enough that Abramm was able to return his attention to the problem of his fortress's vulnerabilities—and the tantalizing possibility that its guardstar might still be on site.

He began his investigation by concentrating his efforts on the peculiar mound of bird guano that stood on the inner ward's upper terrace adjacent Commander Weston's offices. Roughly the size and shape of the platform that had supported the Heart of Hur, Graymeer's mysterious mound had over the years been believed variously to be—under its coating of guano—a rocky outcrop, an ancient rubble pile, and even nothing more than a massive accumulation of droppings, petrified over the centuries. Targeted briefly for removal when workers had leveled the upper terrace to rebuild the commander's quarters, it had turned out to be much harder than anticipated and the project had been abandoned.

Since they'd gone at it from the sides without success on the original attempt, Abramm suggested this time they start digging down from the top and that they soak it with water beforehand to soften it.

The men brought out ladders, buckets, shovels, and picks and set to work while the displaced sea gulls swirled around them, squawking in protest. In fact, the birds couldn't have made the work go harder if they'd been trying, repeatedly landing on the mound, getting in the way, pecking and biting those who sought to chase them off, and sometimes diving at the men in defense of their territory. Finally the supervisor deployed several men with clubs to drive them off. Forced to abandon their prized perch, they circled above the work site, congregated along nearby walls and roofs, and walked restlessly about on the ground some distance away, filling the air with their raucous calls.

After an hour of minimal progress, Abramm departed from overseeing the operation directly and toured the wallwalks before climbing the main lookout tower. Disappointment weighed on him as he realized he wasn't likely to get the answers he'd hoped for in the time he had allotted to be here. Given the current political climate, he did not want to be away from the palace more than half a day. Besides that, he had to face the combined Tables this afternoon, hoping to persuade them to approve his request for both a war tax and a conscription order. Not a happy prospect with all the Mataian lords still angry with him.

He followed Channon up the spiraling staircase, Trap, Philip, and Jared on his heels. By the time they reached the tower parapet, his right leg was reminding him sharply that it had hardly begun to heal from Balmark's sword thrust. At least he'd made the climb on his own power, something he could not have done only a few days ago.

The tower floor had been repaired and the crumbling parapet finished off months ago, but the project of extending the walls back to their original height had been postponed so as to devote manpower and materiel to more urgent needs. With the fog lurking perpetually upon the southern seas these days, added height would not extend their range of view.

From this vantage Abramm could see the morning fog already shredding over the land, burned off by the sun's clear rays. The tang of the salt air was a welcome reprieve from the stench of the bird dung below, and up here the sea gulls' calls were not so much enraged as sullenly resigned. He turned to the sea, where the mist still hung thick, shrouding the lines of a Chesedhan frigate as it glided slowly away from them past the mouth of Kalladorne Bay. Kildar Fortress on the opposite headland lay completely hidden and would likely remain so throughout the day. Having swathed the southern shoreline for weeks now, the fog had everyone spooked. The other day there'd been an alleged sighting of several galley ships off the coast of Chastwort. The subsequent discovery of a small fleet of long, narrow Thilosian fishing vessels, blown off course by the recent storm, had relieved the coastlanders' rising panic. But the fact remained—anything could be out there.

He watched the frigate move into the mist until all but its topsails were lost to sight. The Esurhites had to know about the morwhol by now, and that the White Pretender had become king of Kiriath. They would know, too, that they had best strike before he readied his people to defend themselves.

Restlessness drove him back across the landing to look down into the inner ward. Two men stood atop the mound, flailing away with the spike ends of their picks. The iron was at least biting into the guano's pale surface, though with penetrations of only an inch or so at a time, they stood little chance of uncovering anything worthwhile today. *And what if there's nothing there at all? Then I've wasted their time and effort, and drawn them away from more productive pursuits.*

"I don't know, my lord," Trap said from his side, as always seeming to read his mind. "The platform and stanchions in Hur were not encased like this. Why would this heart be so encrusted and the other not? And, as I've asked before, why didn't it reveal itself to you when you cleared the fortress of spawn six months ago? Or when you were crowned? Or when you destroyed the latest corridor last week?"

Abramm had had the newly reclaimed tapestry brought up to his apartments the very night he and Maddie had found it, so Trap had seen it many times by now. He'd conceded Abramm's hopes had merit. But they knew so little about these hearts—or guardstars, as Maddie said they'd been called—he'd been unable to embrace those hopes as his own yet.

"Maybe it did reveal itself," Abramm said. "Under all that guano, who would see it?"

He felt Trap's eyes upon him. "Do you have any other reason besides size and shape to think there's something there, sir?"

"Size and shape seem fairly compelling indicators."

"Well, if you really think the barbarians hid it from us in plain sight . . . maybe it would help to shoot it with the Light. See if that might help break it up easier."

"Good idea," Abramm said. "Jared, run and tell Lieutenant Brookes to try using the Light on that thing. And tell him— Wait a minute." His eye caught on the party of three riders coming through the main gate, and his heart leaped as he recognized one of them even from a distance: Madeleine.

"What is *she* doing here?" Trap muttered, glancing at Abramm accusingly.

"I didn't invite her, if that's what you mean."

Trap frowned at him. "Then why is she here?"

"Well, let's find out." Abramm turned back to Jared. "After you talk to Lieutenant Brookes, fetch Lady Madeleine up here for me."

"Yes, sir."

Trap was scowling at him outright now, Channon's expression of disapproval only slightly less obvious. "I thought you and she had decided to avoid each other," the Duke of Northille muttered.

Abramm shook his head in exasperation. "I can't believe you two! Of all people, you who know me best and are with me most, you know there've been no trysts."

"I've seen the way she looks at you, Abramm." Trap glanced at Channon, who wasn't quite bold enough to nod his agreement but managed to show it anyway. "More than that, I've seen the way you look at her."

"The way I look at her? I haven't even seen her since the night we found the tapestry. And as for how she looks at me—in case you haven't noticed, she stares primarily at the floor whenever she's in my presence."

"Exactly."

Abramm stared at him in befuddlement.

Meridon rolled his eyes. "It just seems more than coincidental that the first time you're away from the palace in over a week, here she is."

"She's the one who suggested we keep away from each other in the first place, Trap. If she wanted to see me, all she had to do was ask for an audience." Not that she'd *ever* done that. "I hardly think she'd follow me all the way out here to do it."

Trap did not argue his point, his gaze focused now on Madeleine's party, glimpses of which could be seen between the buildings as they ascended through the inner ward toward the terrace and the work on the mound.

Abramm was surprised by the degree of pleasant anticipation he felt at the prospect of seeing Maddie again. He'd not liked the new arrangement from the moment she'd suggested it, and the last nine days had only increased his dislike of her plan. Her assistant, Jemson, a weedy little man with thin, perpetually windblown hair and a sparse beard, had delivered to Abramm her written reports every couple of days. Unfortunately, he was never able to answer any of Abramm's questions, forcing the king to write them down and send them back with him. She always answered promptly, but her answers always demanded further correspondence, so that in the end—though not in person—they had their dialogues anyway. It was just infernally inconvenient now, and he longed for the days when he'd been able to thrash such things out face-to-face.

He watched now with his men as her group came into full view in the yard below them and dismounted. Maddie was greeted by Lieutenant Brookes, who immediately gestured toward the watchtower, presumably calling her attention to Abramm's own presence. From a distance he thought she seemed to stiffen as she turned her face up toward him, hand shading her eyes. He lifted his hand in greeting, and she responded in kind. Then she turned her attention back to the mound atop which two workers now stood directing tendrils of Light into it. When the effort seemed to have no effect, they gave up and the laborers returned with their picks. But now it seemed to Abramm they were loosening much larger clods of guano than previously.

The rapidly approaching patter of feet on the tower stair preceded Maddie's arrival, and as she ascended into view he turned, startled by how pretty she looked. Flushed from the ride and the crisp morning air, the high color of her cheeks brightened the blue of her eyes and imparted a glow of life and energy he wasn't accustomed to seeing in the courtiers who surrounded him. Her fawn-colored hair was pulled into the long braid she preferred for riding, tendrils of it teased free by the wind to float beguilingly around her face. She stopped before him, breathless from her ascent of the stairs, and her eyes came up to his, held there for a moment, then darted away as she dropped him a short curtsey. "Your Majesty."

And for some reason—most likely Trap's ridiculous accusations combined with the fact both men were staring hard at him—Abramm felt acutely self-conscious. *"I've seen the way you look at her,"* Trap had said. Whatever that meant. Now he felt as if he couldn't look at her at all, could hardly even talk to her without them seeing hidden signs of desire. Thankfully, she didn't look at him again after that one brief glance. He hoped his companions were alert enough to take note of it.

"My lady, how pleasant to have you join us. If I'd known you were interested, I would have invited you to come with us."

"Oh. That wouldn't have been . . . I mean . . ." Her eyes flicked up to his again, and her color deepened with embarrassment. "I'm sorry, sir, but I didn't—" And then, thankfully, she gave up trying to be diplomatic and just blurted it out: "I didn't know you'd be here, sir. I was told you would be resting in preparation for your address to the Table of Lords this afternoon, that Duke Eltrap would be supervising the excavation of the mound."

Abramm grimaced. "Yes, well, if some of my advisors had their way, I'd be resting for the rest of my life. And my address was prepared days ago." He turned back to the parapet and focused again on the workers at the mound, feeling a jab of disappointment at knowing she'd only come because she thought he'd be in Springerlan.

"Who told you he wouldn't be here?" Trap asked her now.

"My assistant, Jemson. I believe he got the information from Count Blackwell. Or maybe it was Mason Crull. Of course, Jemson could well have misheard. His strengths do not reside in verbal communication."

"So I've noticed," Abramm said sourly.

She came up on his right, glanced over the edge of the parapet, and gasped, drawing his startled attention. She stood frozen, eyes wide, gloved hands pressed hard against the stone ledge, face dead white beneath its scattering of freckles. He looked downward, seeking whatever had unnerved her, but found nothing—just the wallwalk with its cannon and its bored guards on patrol.

"What's wrong?" he asked, turning toward her as she pushed off the stone and turned her back to it, eyes closed, face still far too white.

"What did you see, my lady?" he asked, looking down yet again.

"Nothing," she said, opening her eyes and giving him a small smile that tried to convey embarrassment and couldn't quite divest itself of the fear. She lifted her chin and fixed her gaze upon the mist-cloaked sea. "I guess I didn't realize how high we were."

Abramm frowned at her. She'd told him that in her youth she'd taken special pleasure in climbing the masts of her father's ships and had spent hours up there alone avoiding her tutors and chaperones, so he found this hard to believe. Yet her fear was obvious.

"Perhaps you would be more comfortable if you went back down," Trap suggested.

"I'm fine," she said to Trap, then made good on her claim by shaking off her discomfiture and turning to Abramm.

She began rattling off all she'd learned of the guardstars, even though much of it she'd already given to him. How Avramm had been drawn to the guardstar at Avramm's Landing when he first came ashore, though accounts differed as to whether it was lit or not. The books in which they were recorded had disappeared, however. . . .

As she chattered on, he was surprised by how much pleasure he found in listening to her. He missed her excited recitations, even if he often couldn't follow them. They almost always led somewhere intriguing.

"It's almost like they're hidden." She paused, her eyes darting up to his and then away. Gazing over the inner ward, she pulled a strand of windblown hair from across her face and said, "Rather like the tapestry. And the crown. And even the way the regalia manifested after being lost to you all these years. That can't have been an accident." She turned to him then and said, "You don't happen to know where I might find the original architectural plans for the palace, do you?"

He shook his head. "Newer ones, yes, but I know all the oldest plans are gone. I looked when we were trying to map out all the secret passageways to get them blocked off."

"So. Another thing lost," she said. "Or hidden."

The gull came out of nowhere, causing them all to duck as its claws caught on Madeleine's hair, pulling out two loose loops above the braid. Then it was gone, leaving them all to straighten in astonishment, staring at the moving dome of gray-and-white birds soaring and flapping around them. Where earlier Abramm had assumed they were circling by rote, their attention focused on the mound, now he saw a malevolence in their dark glittering eyes and an intelligence the birds themselves did not possess.

He turned to Maddie. "Are you all right?"

She nodded, fingering the loops of hair the gull's claws had pulled loose, eyes on the circling birds.

Trap said, "Sir, perhaps it is time to see how they are progressing with the mound."

Abramm offered no argument, and they descended from both tower and wallwalk. As they entered the inner ward's top terrace, Abramm was gladdened to see the workmen had finally broken through the hard outer crust of guano and were now shoveling out mounds of soft dark earth even more odiferous than the moistened guano.

"Smells like they used it for a latrine," Brookes commented beside him.

Abramm wouldn't have been be surprised if they had, knowing the hatred rhu'ema and their servants nursed for things of the Light.

As the workmen dug deeper, it became apparent that the mound had an outer stonework wall with three heavy iron struts emerging from the stone and bending downward toward the center of the structure. The men had dug down about four feet and had removed almost all the earth when they found bones laid out across the hole's hard-packed floor: six human skeletons whose crushed rib cages all bore the golden shields of Terstans glittering in the sternums.

They brought the bones out and laid them along the mound's outer slope, and for a while work ceased as everyone stood and stared at them.

"Odd that they didn't take the gold," Maddie murmured.

It had long been the custom of Eidon's enemies to rip out the sternums of the vanquished and burn them to melt out the gold.

"I think they wanted to make a statement," Abramm responded, suddenly and acutely aware of just how deeply the mark upon his chest penetrated his body.

In addition to the skeletons, they found the remains of several long-dead griiswurm still clinging to the stone walls, and a cache of gold medallions and silver jewelry. But no guardstar.

"This certainly looks like one of the platforms, though," said Trap, standing back as the workers chipped away the softened guano from the exterior.

"Maybe someone moved it," Maddie suggested.

"With all those passages below," said Trap, "there's certainly a wealth of hiding places."

"Or maybe they just destroyed it," Abramm said. "We don't know they can't be destroyed, do we?"

"We don't know they can, either," said Maddie.

Abramm walked around the mound again, the vague recollection of a dark muggy chamber tugging at the edges of his mind. Finally, for lack of a better idea, he climbed the rough-cut steps and jumped down into the shoulder-high hole that had been dug out, then walked the perimeter of the excavation, the hole about as twice as wide as he was tall. The iron struts had been pressed down and sideways against the stonework walls, running along their circumference amidst the petrified branches of an ancient vine. Soot painted the walls and hard-packed floor, but there was neither sign nor sense of a guardstar's presence. He sent a flickering of the Light toward the ground but felt no answering flicker from below.

A scrabbling sound mingled with the gasps of expended effort marked Trap's arrival at the hole's edge, Maddie right behind him.

"The accounts say it was roughly the size of a cannonball," she supplied.

"I know what one looks like, my lady. And they're bigger than cannonballs."

He stopped in his circuit and stood, hands on his hips, staring at the ground. *Where is it, my Lord? Is it even here at all?*

An image floated up in his mind, an underground grotto lit by the bluish glow of filtered daylight coming in through an underwater opening. Low rocky ledges stood exposed by the tide, gleaming with moisture and pocked with dark pools. Near one of the pools, nine leathery orbs lay split like halved melons, each thick dark rind cradling a tiny tentacled kraggin no more than a hand's breadth in length. A tenth, uncloven, stood apart from the others, perfectly round with a pebbled, leathery skin that was black-veined rather than mottled.

He looked up at her. "Remember when we found those kraggin eggs a few months—"

He broke off, his gaze drawn to the mass of sea gulls that appeared to be diving straight toward her. Twenty of them, at least. The threat was so unexpected—so hard to even see as a threat—that he stood there gaping a moment too long. Trap, apparently alerted by Abramm's sudden fixation, was already turning to face the birds as the first of them hit, striking Maddie about the head and shoulders in a frenzy of claws and beaks and beating wings. Trying to evade them, she stumbled forward, slipped on the edge of the hole, and tumbled into Abramm's arms. Her shoulder thudded into his chest as he caught her, pulled her close, and twisted round, putting his back to a feathery barrage of squawking birds. Wings and claws and beaks beat at his back as he hugged her to him, instinctively conjuring a shield of Light around them. He felt the strong, close sense of her mental presence mingled with his own, and the shield redoubled its strength. The gulls screamed. Distantly he heard Trap and other men shouting.

Then the birds were gone. The men still shouted somewhere as he stood there with Lady Madeleine hugged so tightly against his chest he could feel the rapid beat of her heart, feel the soft touch of her hair against his chin and smell her clean lemongrass scent. One of her arms clutched round his back, and the other rested across his chest, her hand gripping his biceps. For a moment he stood there, acutely aware of her softness and her womanly curves and her scent as his fear for her dwindled away and something else took its place. Something hot and tingly and not altogether unfamiliar.

She seemed to sense it even as he did, for they released each other and stepped sharply back at the same time. She didn't look at him, but her face was as red as he'd ever seen it, and from the feel of his own he could only give thanks Trap and Channon were off chasing gulls. For a moment they stood there awkwardly. Then she turned to scramble back out of the hole. After a moment's hesitation he stepped to catch her about the waist and boost her up, even that small contact accelerating his heartbeat, and stirring up feelings he desperately did not want stirred. Will Ames was coming up the stair by then and hurried to help her onto the edge. Abramm pulled himself up after her and stood stiffly beside her. *It was only embarrassment,* he assured himself. *The embarrassment of finding her in my arms like that . . . nothing more.*

Thankfully, Maddie immediately started down the chipped-out stairway, and after a moment, he followed her, careful to keep his distance. Trap and Channon converged upon them from different directions, having chased away the gulls on opposing fronts. Or rather, moved their landing places back from the mound. They could do little against those that still circled overhead, and Trap, as usual, was eager to get Abramm out of harm's way.

The king raised a dubious brow. "You think I should run from sea gulls now?"

"When they stop behaving normally? Yes."

"They've been attacking people all day." He scowled at the rows of birds lining the roof peaks and tower eaves, all of which seemed to be looking down at him smugly. Almost as if they'd known what knocking Madeleine into his arms would do to him. *But how could they know what I didn't know myself? And what did it do, anyway?* "Even if their behavior is questionable, I'm not about to let them keep me from finding the guardstar."

"You don't even know it's here, sir. If it has been hidden, you know how long it might take to find it. Especially if we have to search all the passages down in the warrens. It's probably cloaked and . . . pox! For all we know, whoever took it could have thrown it into the sea. In fact, now that I think about it, that would be the most logical thing for someone to do who was trying to get rid of it."

Abramm frowned at him, opened his mouth to offer what even he knew to be a lame justification for his stance and froze as his thoughts caught on what Trap had just said. The sea. Right before the gulls had knocked Madeleine into his arms he'd been thinking about something to do with the sea . . . and a blue-lit chamber. . . . It was a grotto. Down by the boat dock . . . and there'd been—

"Eggs!" he said triumphantly. "The day we found the kraggin eggs in that grotto by the sea—remember? Nine of them we clove but the tenth we couldn't." They'd burned the cloven ones, but the tenth—they'd guessed it was a cannonball put in with the netted eggs to hold them beneath the water's surface, coated by some sort of algae—had been brought up to Weston's office as a curiosity and doorstop.

Abramm had only to make the request, and shortly Commander Weston arrived, lugging the thing himself. Its skin, dried and hardened in the months since they'd found it, was now as hard as any rock. At Abramm's direction Weston set the orb down in the midst of the dug-out mound, then climbed back up the side of the hole to stand beside the king, the duke, and the Second Daughter of Chesedh, all of them staring down at it in hopes it would do something.

"It only lit up in Hur when all those Dorsaddi took stars," Trap said after a few minutes of nothing happening.

"Lots of people took stars last week at the coronation," Maddie pointed out.

"More than there were Dorsaddi, that's certain," Abramm put in. "So if that's the trigger, it's not worked. . . ."

"Maybe it's a percentage," Trap suggested.

Abramm glanced at him skeptically.

"Maybe there's something in the tunnels below that's influencing it," Maddie said. "Some kind of spawn or other Shadow invention."

"Hur was full of spawn and Shadow," Abramm told her, "and the Heart still lit." He paused, looking down at the black-streaked globe again, disappointment sharpening. "It's more likely this really is a cannonball—or just an odd rock—and we're making fools of ourselves. It really doesn't look much like the one we had to light at Hur."

"We could try to melt it down, sir," said Commander Weston. "That would show us if it was common iron, at least."

Abramm glanced at Maddie, who stood on the other side of Trap. "Would a guardstar melt?"

She shrugged. "I have no idea. But your crown seemed to be able to withstand higher heat than gold or diamonds."

He stared down at the thing, considering.

"Maybe if the struts were pulled up and the ball set atop them?" Trap suggested.

Abramm frowned at him. "Didn't the one at Hur straighten out its own struts when it came alive?"

"I don't remember. But . . . it can't hurt, can it?"

It seemed like an awful lot of effort for something that could very well be nothing more than a doorstop, an odd rock, or a cannonball.

He was still dithering when the distant boom of Kildar's noon-hour cannon echoed across the compound. *Pox and plagues!* Noon was the very latest he could leave and get back to the palace in time for this afternoon's meeting with the Tables.

He heaved a sigh. "Very well, why don't you see if you can melt it down or burn off the covering . . . and bend up the struts. Might as well do it all."

As Weston left the mound to comply, Abramm turned to Maddie, intending to invite her to ride in the carriage with him back to Springerlan, as protocol dictated he should. But before he could speak, she asked if she could stay behind and observe the proceedings, an offer he accepted with considerable ambivalence. He was happy on the one hand to have her keen eyes and wit still involved in the project, but disappointed to leave her behind. In fact, it was only then he realized just how much he had been looking forward to that carriage ride. And not just for the conversation.

It was a realization as startling as it was disturbing.

13

Maddie rode back to Springerlan late that afternoon, having spent the time since Abramm left sketching the newly revealed platform, then lunching with Commander Weston in his dining room while the men removed the struts from the sidewalls and took them off to the forge to be straightened.

By the time she left, they'd freed two, and the team assigned to burn the orb had only made the covering harder in the process of heating it, as if it had been made out of mud rather than algae. She'd expected it would be something like that. While the structure Abramm had uncovered did support the tapestry record of a guardstar having been here, it seemed little more than a glorified candlestick. Her real reason for staying behind had been to avoid riding back with Abramm. Then she'd lingered further to avoid riding back alone with her thoughts.

Just the few hours she'd spent with him that morning—to say nothing of the inadvertent tumble into his arms—had reignited all the feelings she'd been stamping down to embers over the last nine days. Indeed, the plan to avoid the king by distracting herself with her research and making her reports through Jemson had worked so well she had at times gone for several hours without thinking of him at all. As she'd ridden out to Graymeer's that morning, she believed herself well on the road to being rid of this illicit, illogical, impossible infatuation.

When she'd entered the yard on the fortress's upper terrace and saw Jared standing there with Lieutenant Brookes beside the excavation, she'd gotten her first inkling that things were not as she thought them. Then Brookes had greeted her with the news that the king was up in the watchtower, and even seeing him from afar her heart had rammed itself up into her throat while her mind skittered frantically for an excuse to leave.

Then Jared was presenting her with the king's invitation to join him in the tower, and what could she do but obey? When she'd emerged onto the parapet platform to stand before him and he'd looked down at her, broad-shouldered and regal, the wind tousling his golden hair over those level brows, she'd been aghast at the intensity of her response. His blue eyes took her breath away every time she looked into them, and even with the scars raking down his cheek, she still thought him the handsomest man she had ever seen.

Somehow she'd managed to pull her eyes away, but that had only started her mouth going, and the next thing she knew she was babbling about Jemson and not having expected Abramm to be here. A fine thing to say to the king of the land. Then she'd glanced over the parapet and found the very images of her dream wedding staring her in the face, and all her wits had left. She couldn't breathe, couldn't think, and believed she might faint right there. Somehow she had pulled herself together, offering him an excuse she couldn't recall before launching into another of her frantic monologues, hoping it didn't sound as hysterical to him as it did to her.

But none of that compared to what had happened when the gulls knocked her into his arms, and he'd held her tight against his chest, and the Light had flowed between them. She'd stood frozen and breathless, not wanting the moment to end, even as she sensed he was as startled and aware as she was. She'd felt the sudden acceleration of his heartbeat, then a flash of heat whose origin she couldn't identify, and they'd broken apart as if governed by one mind.

But then, after a brief moment of awkwardness, he had gone on as if nothing had happened, arguing with Trap about the sea gulls, recalling the eggs, having the strange orb brought out . . . while she'd stood there trying to regain her poise, trying to pay attention to what they were saying, trying to stop being so exquisitely aware of him.

On the ride back, she returned to the arguments that had bolstered her during her nine-day confinement: that he didn't care, that he only wanted her here for her "wit" and her "eye," that she meant no more to him than his horse. . . .

And yet, each time the memory of being in his arms resurfaced, she felt it all again—the same rush of heat, the same desperate longing, the same intensity of emotion that took her breath away. Over and over and over, all the way back to Springerlan, despite her determination not to think about it, despite being horrified to discover she was not as in control of her feelings as she thought and was, in her own way, as silly and vulnerable and mindless as any of the most foolish girls she'd ever known, the thoughts kept returning. And what was she going to do when Briellen arrived?

Maybe she should leave, after all. Maybe she'd misread Eidon's will and let her own desires dictate her course of action. Basing a life decision upon the finding of an Esurhite fetish? How much sense did that make? The red dragon was not something associated with Eidon, after all.

But it is associated with Abramm.

Maybe the rhu'ema had worked that sea gull, making him drop the thing so Maddie would find it and think she was supposed to stay. Maybe it wasn't Eidon's will at all. What had she really accomplished by staying? They still knew almost nothing about the regalia. Or the guardstar . . .

Oh, Father Eidon . . . I'm so confused. I know you have a special place for me, my own destiny. Show me where you want me to go. . . .

An image of Graymeer's wallwalk, seen from the tower, floated into her mind, populated with the people from her dream, the bride and groom standing with the Chesedhan wedding ribbon woven about their joined hands.

Something close to terror shivered through her, and she blotted the image from her mind, turning her thoughts immediately elsewhere, searching for something—anything—to distract her from that unproductive, maddeningly tempting line of thought.

Like the fact she'd been tricked into coming out here at all. Like the fact that someone had given Jemson the wrong information about Abramm's activities today. Though her new assistant was notoriously unreliable when it came to recalling casual comments, she did not believe this was one of those times. He knew she was interested in the excavation and knew that she would not go out if the king was there. He wouldn't have made a mistake about something like that.

And anyway, now that she thought about it, it was ludicrous to think Abramm would have sent Trap out to dig the mound alone. If she'd had half a brain she'd have realized it right away. Unfortunately, when it came to Abramm, she seemed to lose all capacity for rational thinking. Still, she would ask Jemson where he had gotten the information. . . . Carissa had told her yesterday the court gossips were all abuzz with the fact that Maddie and Abramm had not seen each other in over a week and that some were wagering how long it would be before their next "meeting."

Was today someone's idea of ensuring his wager won?

She got a good idea of the answer to that question shortly after she returned to the palace, when Lady Leona and her friends waylaid her at the foot of the west-wing staircase.

"Back from your trip to Graymeer's, I see," Leona said with a wicked smile. "I hope you weren't attacked by any more sea gulls!"

"I wasn't. But how did you know I went to Graymeer's, Lady Leona? Or that I was attacked by sea gulls at all?"

And all her ladies tittered in their obnoxious we-know-something-you-don't manner.

"Well, those big loops of your hair pulled up from your braid are something of a giveaway," Leona answered with a nasty smile. "Besides that, the king's men gave us a full report."

A full report, did they? Maddie sighed. Even when she tried to be discreet it didn't work. Why couldn't people mind their own business?

"Knocked you straight into the pit they'd dug, the men say, though you don't appear to be injured. Except for your hair, of course."

Leona's ladies tittered again and exchanged knowing glances.

"I wasn't injured, my lady."

"I guess you have the king to thank for that, eh? Or perhaps your own quick thinking." Leona smiled prettily while her eyes remained hard and cold. She leaned closer and lowered her voice. "You don't really think any of us believe for one moment it was an *accident*, do you? Falling right into his arms? Please, Madeleine, what do you take us for?"

A flock of circling, squawking sea gulls, but with less brains?

"Besides, were any of us to find ourselves in a similar situation, I can assure you we'd have done exactly the same thing. I just wish you'd be a little more friendly and share with the rest of us poor deprived ladies what it felt like."

Maddie stared at her blankly, silenced as much by her shock at Leona's blunt suggestion as she was by the flood of her own memories. And then, by the heat that rose in her face.

"Oh, look," said Lady Amelia, "she's blushing!"

"I don't know, Madeleine," Leona said with another wicked smile. "You're going to have to cover yourself better than this. What is your poor sister going to say?"

Maddie pressed her lips together, decided she'd had quite enough of this, and started past them.

Leona said, "Word came this morning that she's just crossed over the Rhivaald at Foxton Bluff. Should arrive within the week, they're saying."

Madeleine refused to stop moving, refused to give them any more material for their fun. If Leona detested her, Maddie took comfort in observing that the feeling was mutual.

"Just thought you'd like to know, dear. . . ." Leona purred.

"I'm told that toast and tea are good for morning ailments. . . ." Lady Melissa called after her.

Maddie left the tittering behind and hurried along the crowded hallway toward her chambers, stepping in quickly and closing the door with a great sense of relief. She walked across the empty sitting room and on into the adjoining bedchamber, where Liza was picking wilted buds off one of the flower arrangements.

Ignoring the girl, Maddie's eye caught on her reflection in the vanity mirror. Stopping, she stared at the freckled face with dismay. No great beauty there, that was certain. Her hair all flyaway, two big loops of it bobbling off her crown, her nose and cheekbones as red as a crofter's girl. No, like that milkmaid Leyton was always saying she should have been. *I wish I had been born a milkmaid. At least those cows wouldn't talk back!*

A sense of profound inadequacy swept her. She hated the way she looked. Hated that she couldn't seem to make herself adopt the customs of the other women with regard to dress and adornment, even as she tormented herself for her differences. What was that she'd said to Abramm last fall? How you had to accept your differences and leave others to their own opinions, living in who and what Eidon had made you to be? Yet here she was, fretting again at how pathetically plain and unattractive she was. It made her thoughts about Abramm even more absurd and painful.

Especially in light of the fact that Briellen would be here in only a week or so.

She turned from the mirror with a grimace, realizing Briellen was the reason for this sudden pique of self-condemnation. For all she'd anticipated her sister's arrival as the cure for her infatuation with Abramm, now that it was actually coming to pass, she dreaded it. Dreaded the old smothering, soul-killing sense of inferiority that was sure to overtake her. That was already overtaking her.

She left the mirror, went over to her desk, and dropped into the chair with a sigh. Then she frowned, leaned forward, and lifted the leaf of inked parchment where it lay beside her pen and inkpot. "Liza . . . did you notice the book I had out here?"

"Yes, milady. And I was sure not to disturb it, either."

"You didn't move it?"

"O' course not, milady. I know better 'n that!" Her eyes flicked to the desk and widened. "It's not there?"

"No. Who was in here today?"

Of course there had been no one save Jemson, whom Maddie summoned at once. But he knew nothing about it. Which gave Maddie a moment of doubt: he'd been the one to send her to the fortress on the pretext of Abramm not being there, after all. Maybe it wasn't Leona who had given him the wrong information. . . .

But no, she couldn't really believe that of the man.

A few moments of searching and recalling brought her to the realization that they had taken not only the book but the map she'd begun drawing, as well. Which said to her as strongly as anything that the book held a treasure someone did not want her to find.

She'd discovered the volume three days ago, slipped in among a row of thick tomes, completely out of the cataloguing order. It was the journal of the architect who had planned and designed one of the early additions to the palace—a volume she'd inquired after ever since she'd learned of the other missing books. If they weren't in the University library, and they weren't in the royal library, nor in the king's private collection . . . then there must be another room, hidden somewhere on the grounds. Uncovering Avramm's tapestry had made her more certain than ever there was a secret library somewhere, similarly masked. But it would take her a century to go through each inch of the palace searching for it, and even then she might miss it. The best way would be to start with the original floor plans.

Unfortunately, she'd been unable to find anything less recent than a hundred years ago. When she'd found the journal she'd been thrilled. Though it had not held actual schematics, it had offered detailed descriptions. From those, she'd begun to compile her own drawings. Now both book and drawings were gone.

"Not entirely, miss," said Jemson as she lamented this fact to him. "There is the copy you had me make of your most recent work last night."

"That's right!" she cried. "Are you sure you still have it?"

He did, and delivered it over to her along with a sheaf of architectural plans. "These came from the king earlier," he said. "The servant said you'd asked for them."

She studied them eagerly for a few minutes, then slumped back in her chair. "These are contemporary," she said. "I wanted older plans." But Abramm had said he didn't have any. She sighed in disappointment, her eyes wandering over the lines on Jemson's copy of her drawing. After a moment she frowned and sat forward, pulling closer the top leaf of the stack Abramm had sent over. Absently she told Jemson he could go, continuing to compare, line by line, the two maps.

A few minutes later she sat back with a gasp and a cry of dismay. There did indeed appear to be a hidden room, concealed right in front of everyone's eyes for centuries, it would seem. Unfortunately, it was also right in the middle of the royal apartments.

But how could she possibly investigate that? And how could she send word? She didn't really trust Jemson. And anyway, though he was a Terstan, he wasn't strong in the Light and probably wouldn't be able to even find the illusion that cloaked the entrance, let alone walk through it.

Beyond that, there was the fact that someone didn't want her to find it. If he knew she already had, and if the missing books were in it, what was to stop him from removing them before she could get there?

An audacious idea came to her, and at first she discounted it, laughing at herself for even considering it. But when it wouldn't leave her alone, she began to consider it more seriously. Yes, it was bold, but its very boldness argued for its success. People saw what they expected to see. It was a principle she'd used repeatedly. Indeed, the only person she would definitely have to worry about was Abramm. He might not see past her disguises any better than the others—certainly his record was poor—but she didn't think she could be with him and keep her wits about her. She'd have to figure out a time to do it when he wasn't there. Sometime soon, before the book thief could guess the truth. Perhaps in the morning while the king went out to ride.

14

Gillard awoke to the sounds of trickling water and the distant braying of an ass. He lay in a real bed again, in a small stone-walled room. Sunlight flooded through a narrow glassed window to his left, pooling on the patterned rug in a vivid splash of scarlet against what was otherwise a tableau of grayness. He couldn't see well through the glass, but it looked like dark, snow-patched hills rose outside against a blue sky.

He'd long since lost track of the days, recalling only that he'd been transferred from barge to carriage to barge again, then finally to a shaded wagon when they'd left the river for good. Drifting in and out of consciousness, he had noted numerous times when his bed tilted sharply as the wagon labored up some mountainous road. That, in addition to the air's increasing coldness, indicated they were in the northernmost regions of the realm, most likely in or crossing the estates of Northille and Carnwarth.

He recalled arriving here last night, borne on a litter from the wagon through frigid darkness into the warm, smoky haven of an old keep's great room. Cloaked men had clustered around him, blocking his view of anything save the heavy-beamed ceiling high above him, and speaking to each other as if he were not there. He would've reprimanded them for this lapse if he could've made his tongue work. Next thing he knew they were transferring him to this very bed, a broad wooden-framed affair with a down-stuffed mattress and silken sheets. Which seemed an odd thing to find in such a rough and barren chamber so far from civilization.

The tightness that constricted his chest last night had vanished along with the oppressive weakness, replaced by a deep aching in his legs and arms. He was, however, able finally to lift his hand to scratch his face—and was startled to find he'd grown a beard. He let his fingers play over the long whiskers, feeling as off-balance as if he'd suddenly been tossed from the bed. He distinctly recalled being shaved by his valet the morning he had gone out to face Abramm . . . and while it was clear he'd been captured and imprisoned for some time, it didn't seem long enough for his whiskers to have grown this much.

His exploration continued to his hair, increasing his dismay: the long, pale locks extended halfway down his chest. Then he saw his hand and the sense of disorientation became so strong the bed seemed to spin around. His hands were large and powerful, heavy boned, thickly tendoned . . . but this thing . . . it looked hardly more than a skeleton, the fingers weirdly long, the width of the palm thinner by half than what he recalled. And with those long, curved nails, it looked almost . . . womanish.

A chill of horror spread through him, and again he felt the pressure on his chest. This couldn't be his hand! And yet there it was at the end of his arm, its spidery fingers opening and closing as he bade them. . . . The other was just like it. And now, holding both aloft before his eyes, he saw that the arms were also shrunken—not just the depletion of skin and muscle . . . the bones were smaller, looking delicate and weak. Indeed, he was already shaking from the effort of holding them up.

"Torments take you, Abramm!" he hissed, letting them fall to his sides. "What have you done to me?"

The approach of footfalls outside preceded the door's opening, and in stepped the same thin, shaven-headed acolyte who had attended him since shortly after his journey had begun. Shutting the door with his heel, the man carried a tray on which sat a steaming, red-glazed bowl alongside a tin cup and a crust of dark bread. He looked near middle age despite his acolyte's robe, and his pate was several shades lighter than the skin on his weathered face, as if it had only recently lost its covering of hair. His nose was round and red, his mouth too wide for the narrow face and eyes. Seeing at once that Gillard was watching him, he broke into a smile so tight it seemed painful.

"Ah, you are awake, my prince. Splendid. Ready to eat, I trust?" He came around the bed to set the tray on the small table at Gillard's left.

"Where am I?" Gillard growled. "Who are you? What's happened to me?"

The man, whose stiff posture hinted of a military background, bowed. "You are at Haverall's Watch, sir. Safe and sound. As you will remain so far as we have life to protect you." His voice was dry, nasal, and prissy.

"Haverall's Watch?" Gillard frowned. "That's a Mataian place."

"Indeed it is, sir." His visitor stood beside the bed. "And as such it will shield you from the eyes of the evil ones. . . . Now, if you'd like to sit up, I'd be honored to assist you." Without waiting for agreement, he lifted Gillard's shoulder a bit to pull out the pillows and plump them up. Then he hooked his hands under the prince's armpits and gently shifted him upward, propping him in a half sit against the pillows. It was an operation that left Gillard breathless. And sitting just halfway up made the room spin.

Meanwhile, his visitor pulled a chair from near the fire around to the side of the bed where he'd left the tray, then sat upon its front edge so straight-backed he might have had a metal rod for a spine. "Now we can put the tray in your lap," he said, doing just that. Gillard noticed then that the man's right thumb was stuck permanently in an extended position, unable to press toward the palm and rendering the hand virtually useless. A substantial, clean-lined scar—the kind one got from a blade—ran across the base of it into the palm.

His visitor picked up the spoon with his left hand, clearly not his hand of choice, and began awkwardly feeding his charge the thick, beany porridge he'd brought. It was an unpleasant affair, for he kept dropping the spoon, sometimes into the bowl, sometimes onto the tray, sometimes onto the napkin he'd spread across Gillard's chest. And every trip the utensil made to Gillard's mouth, it trailed gravy, so that, if it weren't bad enough having his face covered with a nest of whiskers, now he must suffer the indignity of having gravy all over them. Gillard wanted to snatch the spoon away and feed himself, except that his own limp, aching arms were unlikely to do a better job.

As he ate, his gaze flicked repeatedly to the man's narrow, weathered face with its tight lips and dark, too-close eyes, thinking again that he looked familiar. It was the first time he'd actually looked at him with anything approaching a clear mind, and memory stirred. A gray cloak. A small red flame . . . those last days before his showdown with Abramm, the hideous march up to the Valley of Seven Peaks, dogged incessantly by the cowards Abramm had sent to torment him. Slipping in and out again, they'd cut ropes, loosed horses, damaged wagons and tents and tack, appearing like spirits only to melt into the darkness should anyone confront them. What kind of fighting was that? The coward's way, that's what.

But what did it have to do with the man now feeding him? Gillard had brought no Mataians with him. Or wait . . . maybe he had. The paleness of the man's pate and the glaze of brown stubble pricking through it indicated he was a recent convert. So he wouldn't have been bald and robed before Seven Peaks. Was it Matheson, maybe? He studied the face as he accepted another spoonful of porridge, allowed his bearded chin to be wiped and gave up. "You only answered one of my questions," he said.

"Indeed, sir. That is so." His attendant sat back in the chair, bird-bright eyes fixed upon Gillard's face. "You still don't know me, do you?"

"You look familiar. I feel I should, but I can't seem to call it up."

"Mmm . . . well, it doesn't surprise me after what was done to you." The acolyte leaned primly forward, plucked up the bread crust, and broke a piece off. "Once I was Darak Prittleman. Lord of Lathby, First Secretary of the Nunn, and Headman in the Laity Order of Gadriel. Now I am merely Brother Honarille."

The moment he said his name, Gillard stiffened with both recognition and revulsion. Prittleman! So it was Abramm who'd ruined his thumb. How odd that observation should be so pleasing.

"A recent change of name and status, I gather?" asked Gillard.

Prittleman's thin lips tightened and he gave a single nod. "I am a wanted man, sir."

The former Gadrielite dipped the chunk of bread he had been holding for some moments now into the bean porridge and offered it to Gillard. When the prince had finished chewing the morsel and swallowed it, he was offered a sip of watered wine. Then, as his acolyte attendant took up the spoon again, Gillard asked quietly, "What was it that was done to me?"

Prittleman's fingers tightened on the spoon. "You were enspelled, Highness. After you killed the morwhol and saved your brother's wretched life, he thanked you by working a deathsleep over you. So he could take the credit for himself. While you have lain like one dead these last six months, he has basked in his stolen glory, making himself at home in the palace, claiming Eidon's favor, even while allowing all manner of wickedness and atrocities to be committed against his true servants. . . ."

He rambled on, but shock had closed Gillard's ears. *Six months! I've been bedridden and senseless for six* months? *No wonder my hair and beard are long as a hermit's. No wonder I feel so weak . . . and* Abramm *did this?* He found that hard to believe. Abramm was a Terstan, which of course Prittleman saw as a great evil. But Gillard had known Raynen, and his father, and a handful of others who wore the shield, and none had the ability to cast a spell of sleep over anyone. In fact, he had never known them to cast any sort of spell at all.

"Thanks to the unceasing petitions of the handful of faithful who have remained here," Prittleman said, "the spell has been broken, my prince, and you are freed."

Gillard received this declaration uneasily. "*I* killed the morwhol, you say?"

The beady eyes narrowed. "You don't remember?"

"I remember it attacked me . . . bit me in the shoulder." He frowned as the memory resurfaced, as vivid as if he'd experienced it yesterday: pinned helpless to the ground by the beast's great weight, gagging on the stench of its breath and bloodied coat, its vicious laughter echoing in his head as it sucked away his strength and breath . . . and life?

It had betrayed him. He thought it would kill Abramm, and then he himself would kill it and get the glory for doing so. Only at the last moment had he understood it meant to kill them both, drawing his life energy into itself first so as to be strong enough to kill Abramm.

He shuddered, then reminded himself that it had failed. He still lived and it, apparently, was dead, though he did not recall how it had died.

"It had you," Prittleman explained, "but then Eidon was persuaded by the fervent entreaties of his holy ones and provided you the strength to prevail."

The holy ones and Eidon, again. I see where this is going.

"You killed it with your bare hands, my prince."

"My bare hands?" His glance fell upon those hands now, thin and bony beneath skin as translucent as silk. They reminded him of his long-dead grandmother, all angles and bones. It was hard to imagine lifting a cup to his lips these days, let alone killing a morwhol.

The former Gadrielite seemed to read his mind: "It must have been his spell that took your memory of it, my prince," he said.

Ah. That made sense. Except . . . why leave me alive at all? Why not simply kill me? "And you were there? You saw all that?"

"They should be calling *you* Morwhol Slayer, my prince," Prittleman declared. "Not him. The danger was past, you had saved yourself and him, but you were still weak and drained from your efforts when he pounced, spinning his evil upon you so that he might take your place and seduce away your people. And so he has. And all of us who supported you, who gave allegiance to the true Flames, we have been cast down. Our lands and titles taken, our reputations destroyed, our very lives in danger. Many have fled to Chesedh and the Western Isles, others are imprisoned—he had the gall to lock up High Father Bonafil! Can you imagine?"

Gillard didn't think that was supposed to please him, but it did, even if it was Abramm who'd done it.

Prittleman was off and running again, words spilling out of him willy-nilly, making his story hard to follow.

"I thought hatred was a sin, brother," Gillard interrupted finally. "I thought it diminished the Flames."

"Not when it is directed at that which is evil. In fact, we are commanded to hate the Shadow and all associated with it. And your brother is consumed with Shadow, spreading his darkness over the people he has deceived."

The bowl emptied, Prittleman removed the tray and set it on the bedside table. "I am only grateful Eidon has seen fit to deliver me so that I may continue to serve. The creator sees all that has gone on, and he will neither forget nor overlook. I am confident that in time he will restore me to my former position. As he will you, sir, should you seek recompense from him."

Gillard smiled grimly. "Your faith is admirable, brother, but I prefer to seek my recompense from Abramm." He scratched the beard again. "I don't suppose in the meantime you could arrange for someone to serve as my valet."

"I am sorry, sir, but no. As you can imagine, your brother is searching desperately for you. For me, as well, for I have not been kind to him these last six months. As secretive as we made your arrival, it has still raised a few brows among the brethren here. If you were to have a valet . . . well, that would ignite far too many questions. If the beard is bothersome, it would be my honor to shave you."

Gillard looked at him in mild alarm, noting again the cuts and nicks and missed spots of whiskers on that weathered face. Prittleman frowned and put a hand up to his chin. "I know my hand is not the steadiest, but I've not yet slit my throat." He had an odd, wheezing laugh.

Gillard shuddered. "That's all right. I'll do it myself."

"Sir, I very much doubt—"

"When I'm able, of course. Until then I'll live with it."

"As you wish, sir."

———————

The morning after his address to the Tables, Abramm rose early, spent some time in prayer and meditation, and then went out for his morning ride. Barely had he reached the stable when Jared caught up with him, breathlessly informing him that Master Belmir had arrived at his apartments to request a private audience. "Lord Haldon bid him wait, sir," Jared said, "to see if I could catch you before you left on your ride." He paused. "He came in a common robe, without attendants, sir, and we got the sense he doesn't wish to be widely seen."

Abramm hesitated only a moment. That Belmir had come surreptitiously implied he sought to talk rather than accuse and denounce. And after Abramm's less than successful attempt yesterday to persuade the Table of Lords of the need for another tax and conscription writ—thanks largely to Mataian opposition—he would take every opportunity to change things.

He returned to his apartments by the back stairway, where Haldon was waiting for him. "I'm sorry if I overstepped, sir," the chamberlain said, closing the door behind him. "But I thought—"

"No. You did right, Hal." Abramm unfastened the ties of his cloak.

"He's in the sitting chamber," Haldon said. "And quite restless."

"Is he?"

The chamberlain stepped around behind him to lift the cloak from his shoulders as Abramm stripped off his gloves. "I brought him some orange juice and twistbreads," said Haldon. "Would you like some, as well?"

"Just some juice." He handed over the gloves and strode down the short hall past Haldon's tiny quarters into his own bedchamber, then through the study beyond it and into the royal sitting chamber.

Master Belmir sat in one of the blue-and-white-striped divans arranged around a table before the marble fireplace. Sipping a glass of orange juice, he stared up at the huge painting of the Battle of the Hollyhock on the wall beside the hearth without seeming to see it. He looked smaller than Abramm remembered, more wizened, his long braid thin and more than half white. Looking around as Abramm entered, he leaped to his feet.

"Your Majesty," he murmured, giving Abramm a short bow. "Thank you for seeing me."

"Please, sit down, Master," Abramm said, taking the divan facing Belmir.

After Abramm had settled, Belmir sat himself, still holding on to the juice glass and staring down at it through his wire spectacles as if he didn't quite know what to do with it.

The last time Abramm had seen this man, he had been riding at Gillard's side, appearing out of the mist to block Abramm's attempt to meet the mor-whol outside the Temple of Dragons. According to what Abramm had learned, when Belmir had seen Gillard go after Abramm, and Prittleman had run for the valley, he'd ridden on into the pass himself, leading his holy men with their pan of flames in a futile attempt to stop the beast. There hadn't even been a confrontation. The morwhol was so focused on Abramm it had blasted by them, killing most of them incidentally before it sucked up their tiny flame and ran on. Belmir was one of the few who survived. He'd been brought back to the Holy Keep without fanfare and there had all but closeted himself these last months, healing from injuries reputed to be more than physical.

Because of this, plus the fact that few had even noticed Belmir at Gillard's side that day—along with blatant sentimentality—Abramm had declined to pursue him for his treasonous stand with Gillard. The man had been his discipler for eight years, after all, and Abramm had grown to love and respect him in ways he could hardly articulate. Nor was he the only man who'd supported Gillard that Abramm had pardoned.

"Well, Master," Abramm said, "what brings you out of seclusion so unexpectedly? And at such an early hour?"

The holy man looked up, his eyes magnified by the lenses of his spectacles as they flicked to the scars raking Abramm's face, then down to the juice glass again. He turned it once in his hands, then set it on the table between them and sighed. "I've come to plead for the High Father's release."

"Ah." *Plead, he said, not demand. That's promising.*

"Though not in an official capacity, of course," Belmir added. "Few, in fact, know I've come. And many would be irked if they did. But I felt I might offer a perspective you have not yet heard."

"I'm listening."

The old man's eyes went again to Abramm's scars, held there a moment, then dropped to the shieldmark on his chest, glittering between the open-neck edges of his blouse and jerkin. Abramm did not wear the mark exposed when he was formally dressed anymore—but when working or relaxing he made no effort to hide it, and now his former discipler's gray eyes fixed upon it for some time before rising again to meet his own. "You must know the kind of tensions his imprisonment is breeding. It's certainly not the way to make yourself friends among us."

As Haldon arrived with his juice, Abramm cocked a brow at his guest. "I didn't think making friends with Mataians was even possible for me."

Belmir grimaced. "Perhaps 'friends' is too strong a term. Let me just say there are those among us who do not support this radical element that is taking hold of our faith. We believe the Words command us to respect and obey the civil leaders Eidon has placed over us."

Abramm sipped the cold, tart juice, giving himself a moment to cover his surprise and the sudden strong surge of hope his former mentor's words had provoked. He set the glass on the table, too, then looked up at Belmir.

"Yet you've come to plead for the release of a man—your superior, in fact—who obviously does not agree with you."

Belmir frowned. "The people are afraid, sir. Rumors are running rampant. And with your obvious preferences for Terstan advisors, your impending marriage to a Chesedhan, the closing down of the city, the search, the High Father's arrest, and the destruction of the Keep . . . no one is sure what you'll do next. Many fear persecution and seizures. There is talk you've already executed Bonafil and that you mean to use the tax and conscript writs you asked for to build an army that will purge the realm of your enemies. They believe you mean to abolish the Mataio. Even the leaders who would not oppose you hesitate to speak out."

"There will be no purge," Abramm said firmly. "No persecution, no seizures, no legal sanctions nor fines. Each man answers to Eidon for his choice of faith, and I have no intention of interfering with that."

"But the people . . . do not know you well enough to rest in that, sir. Especially when you continue to hold their spiritual leader unheard from and unseen . . . and even if your intent is otherwise, you know there will still be persecution. There are Terstans who will take it upon themselves to drive out the heretics or avenge themselves for past wrongs."

"And the persecutors will be punished. Which has already happened, I note."

"Yes, sir. That's true. You have been . . . quite fair." Belmir's eyes dropped to the mark on Abramm's chest again, held there a moment, then dropped further to his own hands now folded in his lap. He sat there for some time, and when he lifted his head again, he looked deeply grieved.

"I don't understand," he murmured. "You were the most worthy novice I ever discipled. After you disappeared, I prayed for years for your deliverance, rejoiced when you returned last fall to think my prayers had been answered. Only to find you had . . ." He glanced again at Abramm's shieldmark, then returned his gaze to Abramm's, his brow furrowed with bewilderment. "What happened to you, son? How could you have been so strong and been turned so thoroughly?"

For a moment Abramm hardly knew what to say. In the first place because of his surprise at the sudden radical turn the conversation had taken. In the second because it was the first time any of his Mataian brethren had asked him why he had changed. And in the third, how could he possibly express it all in a way Belmir would understand, and even more important, accept? If he told him the first and strongest reason: that a former High Father had actually been possessed by a rhu'ema, one of the very creatures the Flames were supposed to ward, the man's ears would close immediately and the conversation degenerate into cries of "Blasphemy!" and "How dare you!"

Better to emphasize the positive—the reality that Abramm had found at the end of all the lies and illusions.

He sighed and rested his elbows on the chair arms, clasping his hands before him. "I suppose, if you boiled it all down, it was because from the first it was Eidon I sought, not the Mataio. I wanted with all my heart to know Eidon. And in the end I came to see that he wasn't in the Flames."

The old man frowned at his fingers as they traced the grooving on the chair's wooden arm. "And you think you've seen where he really is?" Belmir couldn't quite keep the dryness out of his voice.

Abramm smiled. "I know I have. He lives in me. He speaks to me—"

His words sent a jolt through the other man, who looked up wide-eyed. "You claim the divine lives within your own flesh! Sweet Elspeth have mercy, sire! Do you hear what you are saying?"

"Blasphemy to you, I know." He smiled again, ruefully now to think for all his care he'd provoked the cries of blasphemy anyway. "I thought the same thing at first. But I know differently now. There is no way to come to know Eidon on our own terms. Shadow cannot wipe away Shadow, not with soap and water and not with endless sacrifices of wooden slats." He looked down at his fingers and was surprised when a Star of Life took form on them, hardening as he caught it between thumb and forefinger. "It was a long and painful road," he said. "On which everything I'd ever thought was presentable and righteous about me had to be stripped away before I would admit the truth. But in the end I did, and it was the wisest decision I have ever made."

He rolled the Star between his thumb and forefinger, then leaned forward to set it on the table beside the empty juice glasses.

Belmir stared at it, pale-faced. Then his eyes darted up to Abramm, and the look on his face was one of disapproval and utter disappointment.

"I see I have made you uncomfortable," Abramm said. "Forgive me. Some find it repellent. Others see but a dull and harmless pebble. I hoped you might see at least a glimpse of what it really is." He reached forward again and took it back, closing his fingers about it and feeling it dissolve into his palm. "I came back changed because I found him, old friend. These scars are but the testimony of that fact . . . for they remind me that it was his Light that slew the beast that made them." He paused, and then his brows lifted in sudden understanding. "You saw the morwhol suck up your holy flames that day, didn't you? Saw them make it stronger when they should have driven it away. Maybe you even felt the pulse of Light that destroyed it. That's why you've closeted yourself all these months, isn't it?"

His former discipler's wrinkled face had become cool and hard. "You see things as you wish it, son, not as they are. It was the *Flames* that delivered me that day. And how the morwhol could have—"

The man's frown deepened as his eyes focused on something at Abramm's back, even as the sense and flicker of movement at the corner of Abramm's own visual field drew him around. To his amazement a cleaning girl had just entered the room and was now busily dusting the sideboard. *What the plague? Haldon knows better than to let cleaning staff wander in while I'm receiving guests!* He frowned at her and said sharply, "Miss, you may leave us now."

The girl gave a start, half turned in his direction and bobbed a curtsey. With her face turned toward the carpet, she mumbled, "Aye, sir," and fled into the adjoining study. Leaving him stunned and breathless with recognition. *What is she doing here? And dressed as a servant again! Does she have no sense at all?*

But this was not the time to unravel that mystery. He turned back to Belmir, who unfortunately used the interruption to return his focus to the matter of the High Father's imprisonment.

"Bonafil is the High Father, sir," he said as if the other conversation had never occurred. "So long as you continue to detain him, the people will grow increasingly fearful. If you release him, however, or even allow him visitors who might testify of his well-being, it would go a long way toward allaying the people's concerns."

Abramm had to bite his tongue, tempering his disappointment with the observation that the other topic had likely run its course anyway and was just as well left as is. Still, it was hard to let it go.

"If you just allow him to be seen at his window, it would help," Belmir went on. "I think most people, in their hearts, will acknowledge he was wrong to confront you as he did. . . . But after a reasonable time of punishment . . ."

"It was always my intent to release him eventually. When the time is right. Whether that be sooner or later, I cannot say yet. Though I am far from convinced that having him returned to his place of authority would have the kind of calming effect you suggest. Nevertheless, I will take your counsel under advisement."

"Thank you, sir."

Abramm stood. "If that is all, then?"

"Yes, sir, I believe it is."

15

As soon as Belmir left, Abramm turned his attention to Lady Madeleine. He expected that, having been discovered, she'd have taken her cue to escape down the back stair, but when he stepped into the study to make sure, she was waiting for him.

"My lady, have you lost your mind?" he asked as he shut the door behind him. "What are you doing here—and pretending to be a servant no less?!"

"I didn't want anyone to see me come in. I've cloaked myself. No one recognized me—"

"*I* recognized you."

"But only because you were angry that I interrupted your discussion with Master Belmir. And you know me well." She turned back to the small wooden table she had been in the process of pulling out of its niche, the marble figure of a water nymph playing with dolphins set aside on the floor. "Did you conjure a Star for him?"

He refused to let her sidetrack him. "The others know you well, too."

"Yes, but they don't look at me like you do."

"Like I do?" Alarm sharpened his voice. "What's that supposed to mean?"

"I mean you actually look at me. The others don't."

He felt his brows rise. "You expect me to believe that I'm the only one who actually looks at you?"

She rolled her eyes. "No. But you're the king. You see me. The others—they just see a high lady. If I'm not wearing the right clothes they can't make the shift because, you see, you're either a high lady or nothing, and the noth-ings are never allowed to look closely enough at the high ladies to actually *see* them, nor are the high ones allowed to look—"

"Yes, yes, I'm aware of how that works," he interrupted, relieved to know it wasn't more of Trap's *"I've seen the way you look at her"* nonsense. "That still doesn't explain—"

"I *had* to do it." She seemed barely able to contain her excitement. Her hair floated in wisps around a face that was flushed and eyes that fairly glowed with energy.

"You *had* to."

The story tumbled out of her: how she'd found the book tucked between the shelves, brought it back to her apartments to make her map, only to have book and map both stolen while she was at Graymeer's yesterday.

"Thankfully, I'd had Jemson make a copy of my work in progress, and once I had the newer plans you sent over, I saw where it had to be and came up here to confirm."

Dressed as a servant, she said, to avoid inciting new gossip. "Though . . . I thought you would be out riding, sir."

"And when you saw that I wasn't, it didn't occur to you to back out, I suppose."

She frowned. "Well, no. Actually, it didn't."

"So someone stole your book and map because he didn't want you to find something, yet you continued your search for it and told no one."

"Of course." She tossed her head. "He might just as well have said 'You're on the right track, keep at it.' I certainly wasn't going to back down then."

He shook his head, aghast at her audacity and knowing it would do no good to reprimand her for it. "And so what is it you believe you have found?"

"A hidden library. Just like with the pictures in the gallery."

He stared at her, uncomprehending.

"You know how I've been telling you there are supposed to be records? Journals, histories, memoirs, and such in the royal library that I cannot find? Yet the librarian there tells me they were sent to the University. And when I go to the University they swear they never received them and suggest they were moved to a private library on palace grounds. I seemed to be getting nowhere. Well, that book showed me they were right. There is a private library. Yours. It's just that there's more of it than we've realized. See?" She gestured toward the niche between bookshelves that she'd uncovered by moving the table. "You can see the spell quite clearly if you put your mind to it," she said, stepping toward it.

He turned as she did and watched her disappear into the wall with openmouthed astonishment. Moments later he followed her, stepping through the cold-lard sensation of illusion into a narrow chamber lined with books and lit by the weak daylight filtering through the window embrasure at the room's end. As in the main study, the stacks soared past his head, accessed by a narrow ladder whose top end ran along a rail fastened to the upper shelf. Years of dust covered the floor, the drapes, the books, the single table and chair at the room's midst, the benches of the window embrasure, and even the windows themselves. Its scent mingled with that of mildew and aged books, tickling his nose.

He gazed around avidly, his mind seizing at once on an oddity he'd long noticed without consciously remarking on it: how the outer study's narrow L-shape embraced a mysterious rectangular space that had no entrances—not even in the adjoining bedchamber. It had been there all along, and no one ever noticed.

Maddie stood beside him as one stunned, even though she'd been the one to theorize the room's existence in the first place. "It really is here!" she breathed.

"I'm amazed it could be hidden all this time and no one realized it." Abramm stepped farther into the room. "That window's not even boarded up."

"Of course not. Someone would have noticed that." She turned her attention to the dusty shelves. "But look at all the books!" She started for the wall in front of them, then stopped, turned back, and flicked her fingers. Abramm heard the faint chiming sounds of a cloaking spell. Then she bloomed a kelistar to life and began to brush the dust off the ranks of book spines, tilting her head to read their titles.

No sooner had she begun than she let out a squeak and pulled a volume from the shelf. "It's *The Histories of the Hollyhock*! So Master Dewes was right all along. It was here."

If she'd barely contained her jubilation before, now she gave up trying, hopping up and down, turning to squeeze his arm with both hands in her excitement, then turning back to the book. "I believe this will see a lot of your questions answered!" She blew the dust from its cover and opened it, paging gingerly through the age-yellowed leaves. "Look at all this—firsthand accounts!"

As he started toward the table for a look, the sole of his shoe crunched something on the floor, drawing his attention downward to a pile of curling shreds of parchment. Squatting, he made a kelistar and saw at once that it wasn't parchment but the desiccated remains of the bags in which staffid had been planted.

"So this is where all the staffid were coming from," he muttered. Haldon and the others would be glad to know the infestation wasn't due to any failures of housekeeping.

She squatted across from him to give his find a closer look. After a moment she looked up at him gravely. "That means someone else knows about this place."

"Likely whoever took your book."

"And it's someone who has access to your quarters. Plagues, Abramm! If he could plant *these* . . ."

"It could have been one of my servants under Command."

"But they all wear shields now."

"Not all of them. And just wearing a shield is no guarantee of immunity anyway." A fact he knew from hard experience. "Just as there are those without one who can resist."

She frowned at him.

"I am king, Maddie. If I only let those with shields serve me, it will cause people to seek them for the wrong reasons and breed resentment."

"So you'll take the chance of letting the rhu'ema that possessed Saeral get close to you?"

"I'd like to think I'd recognize him, no matter what form he takes this time."

She made a face. "He's already deceived you once. Why think he won't again?" Her eyes strayed past his shoulder to the stacks behind him and widened. "Light's grace!" she whispered, rising to step around him. "Here it is!"

And she pulled yet another volume from the dusty shelves. "Do you know how *long* I've been looking for this?!" She laid the book reverently on the table beside the others. Abramm bloomed a new kelistar into the air and bent to read the title over her shoulder: *The Records and Forthtellings of the Kings of Light*.

"This will tell you about the regalia, I bet." She opened the book, flipped past the title pages, then stopped and murmured, "Oh dear, this first part's written in the Old Tongue. It'll take me a good while to decipher. . . ."

And he found himself positively delighted, thanking Eidon for his foresight in arranging this complication, because from the tone of her voice he was pretty sure she wouldn't be leaving anytime soon.

She made another kelistar, set it on the books she'd already stacked on the table, and paged rapidly through the age-yellowed leaves, muttering to herself and pointing out pictures or lines of text. "Oh yes . . . look at this. It must be Avramm when he first came ashore. And I'll bet this is Alaric the First leading the Gundians. *Utharn* . . . Yes, that would be right. Oh, and look here! It's a drawing of the first crown."

He leaned over her shoulder again to see it, but as had happened with all the other things she'd pointed out, she flipped to the next page before he could even register what she was showing him. "There's question as to whether it was actually made here in Kiriath or brought from Ophir," she said. "They didn't really have crowns in Ophir, from what I've studied, at least not like we know them. More simple weavings of grass or vines, which your crown certainly looks like, so . . . Avramm must've had a man skilled in Lightcraft."

"Lightcraft?"

"You know, the wielding of the Light to form actual objects." She kept her eyes on the book as she paged.

"I thought that was a myth."

"Well, I don't know anyone who can do it, but considering everything else we didn't know, maybe it's more a transformation—ooh!" Her eyes widened. "This must be Merennis II in prison. There has been argument whether King Oswain had done it. . . ." She went on, popping here and there, as was her way, dropping this name and that, rattling on in a continuous monologue he found difficult to follow, as much for its disconnectedness as for the fact it had been too long since he'd studied Kiriathan history. What he recalled was only the broadest of outlines—which didn't match up with some of what she was saying. It only seemed to him that the more she looked at it, the more excited she got, until finally she set it aside and went back to the shelves to search for more. Her exuberance continued to mount as she discovered volume after volume of apparent significance.

He wasn't sure when it happened, but sometime in the middle of it all, he stopped seeing the books and the pictures and the possibilities and started seeing her. Seeing her in a way he never had before. How full of life and passion she was. How real and true, honest as few dared to be. Her eyes especially intrigued him, deep blue-gray of the open sea, just now sparkling with her intense enthusiasm for this project, and her pleasure at finally having solved the mystery and hopefully providing him soon the answers he sought. They were truly windows to her soul, the glass clear and clean, drapes fully pulled aside so that the light inside blazed out, all her being revealed for anyone to see. . . .

"You have beautiful eyes." The words were out before he realized he'd actually spoken them.

She stopped midsentence. Blinked at him as if he'd spoken in some other language. "What did you say?"

He felt the blood rush hotly into his face as his tongue clove in horror to the roof of his mouth. *Plagues! How could I have said that?*

Thankfully, she must not have actually discerned his words, for now she grimaced and said, "You weren't listening, were you?"

His blush grew hotter. "I'm afraid you left me behind some time ago, my lady. You have much more context for all of this than I do."

"I'm sorry. I let my enthusiasm get the best of me, I guess. It's just—" She glanced down at the ancient tome lying open in her hands. "I'm sure we'll find the answers to so many of our questions. If we could get the guardstar working at Graymeer's you might not even need this marriage—" She broke off with a look of dismay and caught her lower lip between her teeth, then turned from him to close the book and set it atop one of the three stacks she was now building. "I'm sorry . . . I shouldn't have said that."

He sighed. "So you think the marriage is a mistake, too, do you?"

"I didn't say that, sir."

"But you do."

She looked down at the book upon which her hand still rested, fingers tracing the gold-imprinted leafing on its cover. "It's not my place to say."

"I'm asking you to say. And if I ask you, it is your place."

And still she watched her finger tracing out the golden patterns. Then, "I know our peoples need each other now more than ever. Maybe it wouldn't take a marriage to unite us. . . ." She pulled her hand away from the book and clasped it in the other, fingers intertwined. "But I don't think my father would ever see it that way. As much as your people distrust mine, so mine begrudge yours. Your marrying her and siring sons through her would give us a stake in this land we never had before."

"Exactly what my advisors fear."

"But that is the point, is it not? To become united."

"To become allies. Not one large realm."

She frowned.

"*Is* that what they're about? To win our lands for theirs?"

"I think they're only about surviving, Abramm."

"So it is bad, then." And when she did not respond, he added, "I asked Leyton. He was very politic, admitting nothing. Yet that in itself gave me my answer. I've heard from others that Chesedh's southern coasts are completely bound in Shadow."

He watched her closely, reading the conflict of loyalties within her, knowing that her answer would tell him much about her own priorities. Her fingers worked back and forth in that way that betrayed her agitation, then stilled as she reached her decision. She lifted her eyes to his, held his glance for a long moment. "Not Chesedh's. But the entire southern half of the Strait."

"So the ships he brought are useless."

"To my father, yes. But not yet to you. Perhaps not ever to you."

He cocked a brow.

"If the scepter can stir the winds and drive away the Shadow, your ships will carry the day."

"Is that what Leyton's here for, then? The regalia?"

She exhaled a breath of almost exasperation. "Why must you always think the worst? You know the Words command us otherwise. Kesrin was just talking about—"

"I remember the message, my lady. And have also taken note that you've avoided my question."

Anger sparked in those lovely eyes. Then she set her lips and turned away, frustration making the movement sharp and jerky. "I don't know," she said, beginning now to go through one of the piles of books she'd gathered, parceling out the individual volumes in some categorical order apparent only to her. "If he's really after the regalia, he has not admitted it to me." She paused, the soft thumps of the books filling the musty silence for a moment. Then she reached the bottom of her pile and stopped, fingertips resting lightly on the table as she stared at the last pile. "I really don't think he'd do that. You *have* agreed to marry our sister, after all."

She *would* have to remind him of that. He grimaced and turned away from her. "Which no one thinks I should do. Including you. And if Leyton had the regalia, Chesedh might not need this union at all."

"Except that no one knows how they work, including Leyt," Maddie said behind him. "And we don't have time to ignore other options while we try to find out. It may be they'll only work for you—the theory *I* happen to ascribe to."

He went to the window and stared out through the dust-filmed glass, realizing for the first time he had half hoped this *was* all about stealing the regalia. That Briellen was not really on her way and never would be. But if what Maddie said was true . . . He thought again of his vision of the combined Kiriathan and Chesedhan banners and felt a sense of inevitability in it all. If he'd been destined to become king of this land, it also seemed he was destined to marry the daughter of the Chesedhan king . . . whether he wanted to or not.

"Will I like her, Mad?" he asked softly. "Will she like me?"

He could almost feel her eyes upon him, startled, he imagined. Then he heard her snort. "What does it matter? You're going to marry her regardless, aren't you?"

"Yes. But it would . . . make things easier."

She was silent for a time, while he watched the gardeners down below. Then he heard her sigh. "She's absolutely beautiful. And charming. Every man who lays eyes on her seems to fall instantly in love with her, so I can't see you having any problems there."

That was hardly an answer that cheered him. He couldn't help but think of Shettai's talk of men as goats, desiring women for no reason other than their beauty. . . . And anyway, that wasn't really what concerned him. In fact, great beauty could be a source of trouble. "But will she be good for Kiriath?" he murmured to the glass. "Will she be a good queen?"

Maddie made a strange sound, as if she were snorting or laughing . . . maybe choking. He turned back, but she still stood calmly beside the library table, lit by the soft light from the window. Her chin came up as his gaze met hers. "I think she'll make a good counterpart to you, my lord, because in so many ways she's what you're not. She loves the social scene, the clothes, the parties—all the spectacle of royalty." Things Maddie herself detested, he knew. "It will be a good balance for all the austerity you've imposed."

He felt his brow lift. "You think I've been austere?"

"Of necessity, I understand, but yes, that is how you are perceived."

Out in the sitting room the mantel clock began to strike the hour, its tinny chimes followed a beat later by the deep low tones of the University clock in the valley below.

"We've been in here an hour already? Plagues!" He started for the door. "Hal and Byron are probably beside themselves trying to figure out where I've gone to."

"Sir—" She stopped him with a hand on his arm. "I think it would be best if we kept this discovery a secret for now. I don't want to have to track these books down again. And it may be they wouldn't even move them this time, just destroy them outright."

"If they were willing to do that, they'd have done it in the first place," he said. "And anyway, once whoever put the staffid in here returns, he'll know someone's been in here."

"Yes, but he may not return soon. I'm not saying keep it secret indefinitely, just . . . until I have the chance to go through some of it."

"Well, I'm putting a guard on it, regardless."

Before she could answer, Haldon's familiar voice intruded from somewhere nearby, but sounding as if it were smothered in wool. "What is *this* doing here?" And then, louder: "Jared?! Did you move this?"

"Well, so much for keeping it secret," Abramm murmured. He strode back through the spell and nearly gave his grand chamberlain a heart seizure.

The older man leaped back with a cry that was swiftly stifled as he recognized his king. "Your Majesty!" he gasped. Then his eyes darted to the wall at Abramm's back. "What in the—"

"It's the rest of the library, apparently. Cloaked so no one would find the books it contains. I'd like to keep it that way for the moment."

"Of course, sir." Hal's eyes came back to him, and Abramm saw his train of thought shift. "Sir, we've been looking for you for over an hour." He paused. "The Princess Briellen has arrived."

Abramm frowned at him. "Briellen?"

"Aye, sir."

"She's here? Now?"

"Aye, sir."

At that moment Jared appeared in the doorway between study and bedchamber. He looked surprised to see Abramm but turned his attention to Haldon. "You called me, sir?"

"Run and tell Count Blackwell I've found the king. Right here in his own study."

As Jared hurried across the study and into the sitting chamber, Abramm said, "How could Briellen be here so soon? She just crossed over the Rhivaald."

"That was the party of her attendants, sir. Led by a decoy to draw off potential kidnappers. The real princess came in secret ahead of her. She arrived nearly an hour ago, and they made her stand on the front step before admitting her because no one believed it was her. Prince Leyton has gone out riding somewhere, so he can't vouch for her, and Madeleine has disappeared, as well. Then, of course, we couldn't find you, either. Count Blackwell had them put her in the Ivory Apartments, even though nothing was ready—" He broke off as his eyes shifted to something behind Abramm and widened. "Lady *Madeleine*?"

"Did you just say my sister has arrived?" Madeleine demanded, her freckles standing out sharply on her pale face.

"Yes, my lady." The chamberlain's eyes flicked to Abramm almost reproachfully, for it couldn't have escaped his notice they'd been alone in a room neither Haldon nor most anyone else knew about. Hardly an appropriate situation for a man to be in on the day he was to meet his bride.

"You are not to tell anyone about this room, Haldon," Abramm said calmly. "You do understand that?"

"Well, yes, sir. Of course."

"Nor that Lady Madeleine was here this morning."

"But . . . they've been looking all over for her, sir. Someone needs to attend the princess—"

"And so she shall," Abramm said.

"I spent the morning in a new study cubicle at the University library," Madeleine said as Haldon's eyes went doubtfully to the maid's clothing she was wearing. "Since I've had a problem with being harassed—yesterday someone even stole some of my materials—I'm trying to keep a low profile."

He didn't look convinced but claimed he understood.

"I'll go to her at once." She started to pass in front of Abramm, then stopped to lay a hand on his arm. "You will put a guard on this room?"

"I said I would," he murmured.

"I mean right now. In all the confusion, it would be easy for someone—"

"Don't worry about it, milady. Now, you'd better go before Jared gets back here with Blackwell."

She continued to look up at him, and as he met her gaze he felt a cold weight descend upon his heart. *I didn't think it would be so soon.*

"Neither did I," she whispered, startling him with the realization that once again he'd spoken his thoughts without meaning to. But then she was striding past him, heading for the bedchamber door. Barely had she disappeared through it when Jared did indeed return, Blackwell on his heels.

16

Maddie hurried up the long marble stair to the Ivory Apartments in the west wing where her sister, Briellen, had been quartered. Already courtiers cluttered the stairway, chattering excitedly about the new arrival, noticing Maddie only after she had pressed by them. She had taken the back way from the royal apartments to her own rooms, where she'd exchanged her servant's outfit for the gown she now wore.

The corridor at the head of the stair was packed with people. She felt their eyes upon her as she hurried between them, and heard their snide comments, but for once they barely registered. She was still reeling from the shock of learning Briellen was actually here.

Haldon's announcement had hit her like a blow to the chest. Her ears had started roaring and she'd sagged against the library table, finally slithering into the chair beside it. As Abramm's voice rumbled at the edge of her perception, she'd urged herself to stand and go out there while it was only Haldon. Bree would need to see a friendly face at the end of her long and anxious journey, and Maddie knew as well as anyone how hostile this court could be. With Leyton gone missing that duty fell to her.

But at first all she had wanted was to crawl into some hole until she could feel her body again.

"Will I like her, Mad?"

How could he ask her that? How could he?! *Because he has no idea how you feel, that's how, and you should be thankful.*

But still it had been hard to answer. Her throat had swelled up and she'd struggled to get out the words . . . *"Everyone likes Briellen . . ."*

And she'd been right: it wouldn't matter one way or the other. He would marry her because he had to. Because they needed the treaty. Briellen's secret journey said that more convincingly than ever.

And so at last she'd pulled herself together and stepped through the enspelled doorway to stand at Abramm's side and face Haldon's inevitable shock and evil suspicions. At least she had confidence in his ability to keep his mouth shut and could hope the story wouldn't be all over the palace before she even reached her own quarters.

The Ivory Apartments' tall paneled door was opened for her by Will Ames, he of Abramm's personal guard, allowing her to slip into a lofty sitting chamber beyond, while the courtiers outside strained for a glimpse inside.

Gold-gilt ivory wallpaper swirled across walls behind large gold-framed portraits of Kiriathan queens. A rug of pink-rose motif against gray and mauve stretched beneath a scattering of chairs and divans, also in mauve. Two servants were lugging a small trunk into the bedchamber, from which she heard Briellen's voice, sharp with that imperious edge it got when she was tired and things weren't going well. As she instructed them where to place it, Maddie almost turned and fled, certain that the moment Briellen glanced at her, she would guess Maddie's awful secret. Her older sister might tend toward self-absorption, but that very flaw produced in her a hypersensitivity to the actions, words, and expressions of others. Particularly as they affected her own situation. And while it was one thing to laugh about ridiculous rumors, it would be quite another to learn they might have some basis in truth.

But she hadn't come here just to run away, and she'd had to deal with Briellen all her life. A few more minutes weren't going to make a difference, and there was no reason to think Briellen would read her that easily. It was guilt that made her feel so exposed. Drawing a deep breath, she strode on.

Briellen Donavan stood in the midst of the bedchamber, cautioning the servants to have care as they lowered the trunk to the floor. Bags and boxes littered the floor around her, and a mingle of cast-off garments—cloaks, hats, blankets—piled the bed behind her. She wore a gown of fine tan-colored wool slashed with panels of forest green silk. Her golden hair was piled atop her head in a billowing cloud, looser than she liked it and frayed around the edges from her travels, the strain of which showed in the dullness of her porcelain pale skin and the dark smudges beneath her startling sky-blue eyes.

As Maddie stopped inside the door, Briellen waved a hand at her and told her to see that water be heated for a bath, then broke off to reprimand one of the servants who had, despite her instructions, dropped the trunk. Midstream, she broke off that, too, and turned again to Maddie, her eyes widening. "Madeleine? Good heavens, girl! I thought you were one of the servants. We're going to have to deal with your wardrobe, I see. . . ." She opened wide her arms. "Come and give me a hug. It's good to finally see a friendly face around here."

Reluctantly Maddie came forward to embrace her sister. "I'm sorry I didn't come sooner. I just learned you were here."

"Just learned?" Briellen drew back from her. "I've been here over an hour! And where is Leyton?"

"I don't know. But we just heard yesterday that you'd crossed the Rhivaald. No one expected you to be here this soon."

"But I sent *word*. Last night just after we set up camp. A special rider."

Camp? Briellen was camping? That more than anything attested to the urgency and the importance of Briellen's mission.

"So far as I know he never arrived," Maddie said.

"Or if he did, his message wasn't brought to the right places." Briellen rolled her eyes. "Right. What am I thinking? I'm in Kiriath, after all. Someone probably *wanted* to embarrass me." She turned to one of her servants and sent the girl out for bath water.

"Well, not anyone associated with the king," Maddie assured her.

A slight frown creased her sister's brow. "I suppose not. If it weren't for Count Byron I might still be standing on the front step." The frown deepened. "Where were you, anyway? They said you couldn't be found, but I can't see how that is possible."

"You know I've always been good at slipping away when I want to."

Briellen frowned at her. "Why would you need to slip away here?"

Maddie told her about her research and the problem with someone taking her notes.

"So you were at the University," Briellen said. "In the library. Not with Abramm."

Maddie hoped her flinch of surprise didn't show. "Why would I have been with Abramm?"

Briellen flung up a hand. "Well, I don't know. They say you two have become quite close, and he was apparently missing, too. Supposed to have gone riding this morning, then changed his mind at the last minute and returned to his apartments. Not long after that they couldn't find him." She stepped aside as a pair of servants came in with pails of bath water, passing between the two women and on into the adjoining, tile-walled bath chamber. When her gaze came back to Maddie, it was sharp with something that looked very much like suspicion. "I also overheard the servants talking. Apparently you were seen both entering and exiting his apartments during the same time period. Disguised as a servant, they said."

There was no way Maddie could stop the blood from draining out of her face, nor her mouth from falling open. She had been right to fear the tale would spread fast, it seemed. But who was responsible? Not Haldon, certainly. Nor the members of Abramm's guard. . . . So it must have been someone in the antechamber she'd passed through in hopes of going unnoticed in the stream of other menials serving the royal residence.

She realized suddenly that Briellen's sharp expression had turned to one of gray-faced shock. "It's *true*?"

Too late to deny it now. Anyway, she preferred not to lie. "I was there, yes, but—"

"Hagin's beard, Maddie!" Bree jerked away from her, only to whirl sharply back. "Have you lost your mind? Seducing your own sister's fiancé?"

"I wasn't—"

"They said you've been seeing him for months." Her voice began to rise. "That you had near free rein of his apartments. They even said you may be carrying his bastard!"

"I'm *not*! Plagues, Bree, calm down. You of all people should know how vicious the gossips can be. They hate me precisely *because* I've been standing in for you, and many of them think Abramm should marry one of their own." She lowered her voice. "There are women in this court who would like nothing more than to see this treaty destroyed."

Briellen had her arms folded across her chest. "You just admitted to being in his chambers, Madeleine."

"Yes, but not for that. I told you, I'm researching Kiriathan history. I only went there because I needed some materials from his library and, as you yourself pointed out, he was supposed to be out riding."

"And you had to dress up as a servant to do this?"

"I was hoping to *deflect* the gossip, not fuel it. I didn't think anyone would notice me." But someone had. The one who'd stolen her book and map, perhaps? The one who already knew of the hidden library?

Briellen still looked unconvinced.

"I swear to you, Bree. There is nothing like that between us."

"So you don't have feelings for him?"

Maddie drew a deep breath and let it out. "We're friends." *Certainly that's the case as far as he's concerned.*

The crease was back between Briellen's brows, and Maddie feared that her attempt to evade the question had only succeeded in answering it. She sighed. "Oh, Bree . . . what difference does it make? Even aside from the immorality of what is being suggested—do you really think I would do such a thing to you? To Papa and Leyton? To all of Chesedh?"

Briellen only stared at her, that half frown on her face, suspicion simmering in her eyes.

Maddie exhaled in exasperation. "You can't seriously be regarding me as your competition, can you? I swear, all I am to him is a researcher. One he often finds pushy, intrusive, and irritating."

That finally seemed to break the ice. Briellen snorted ironically. "Well, I, of all people, know how irritating you can be."

Maddie refrained from saying she often had similar thoughts about Briellen and shook her head again. "The moment he sees you, Bree, I've no doubt he'll be smitten like all the others."

At this, the last vestiges of hurt and suspicion vanished, and a smile twitched her sister's perfect lips. "You think so?"

Maddie rolled her eyes. "You don't?"

The smile gave way to a relieved sigh, followed by an impulsive, repentant hug. "I'm sorry for doubting you, Mad. It was just . . . to be hit with it first thing." She spun away chuckling. "I have to admit, I did find the notion of you as a king's paramour hard to imagine. And now that I think about it, this whole misadventure is so typical." She shook her head. "Will you ever grow up, girl? You know when you're royalty you can't do anything in a palace without someone seeing you. Even the mice watch and whisper."

Maddie didn't bother to inform her that for most of her life she'd done plenty of things people hadn't seen, even when she did them in plain sight. It was only her ties to Abramm and Briellen that drew the attention to her now. Ties that very soon now—hopefully today—would be broken, leaving her free to retire to the solitude of her library cubicle and her books, where she would lose herself in unraveling the workings of the guardstars and the regalia.

The mantel clock struck the half hour, drawing Briellen around with a sudden new concern. "Where *is* Leyton?"

"He must've gone out riding," Maddie said. But she, too, was growing restless. She'd planned to stay only long enough for Leyton to take her place.

Having narrowly escaped one disaster, she wanted to be gone before Briellen dragged her into this afternoon's proceedings. With most of her ladies apparently still on the road, she seemed to have almost no attendants, which made Maddie very uneasy. The last place in the world she wanted to be was at Briellen's side when Abramm got his first look at her.

"Can't they send someone out for him?" Briellen asked.

"I could go, if you like."

Briellen waved a pale hand. "Don't be silly. I need you here. I'm set to meet the king at four o'clock, which doesn't give us much time."

"Us?"

Briellen ignored the question, turning to the two gowns her maids had just laid out on the bed, one silver, one burgundy and lace. "I haven't decided which dress I should wear and I was counting on his advice." She gestured at the gowns. "What do you think? Should it be the silver or the burgundy?" She picked up the latter and pressed it to her body, holding the bodice up to her neck. "I'd like to wear the burgundy, but I fear it might be too frivolous for the occasion."

Indeed, it was a frothy thing. "Why do you ask me?" Maddie demanded crankily. "You know I pay little attention to that sort of thing."

"Yes, but . . ."

"It's got to be the silver, my dear," said a familiar male voice. "If he is the king of Light, you must be the radiant queen."

They turned to find their brother standing just inside the door, handing his gloves off to one of the servants as another took his cloak.

"Leyton!" Briellen flew across the room into his arms, and he spun her around, just as he had done since they were children.

She immediately launched into a running stream of all that had befallen her since the moment she'd left Salmanca, words tumbling over one another as she unloaded all her adventures and trials and worries upon her always attentive big brother. When she'd finally run down and they parted, Leyton turned stern eyes upon Maddie. "What's this I hear about you being seen in the king's apartments this morning?"

"We've already resolved that, Leyton," Briellen said. "She was after some books. Now . . . you're sure about the silver?"

"Absolutely."

Briellen nodded and turned to Maddie. "That means you can wear the burgundy, then."

Maddie scowled at her. "Why would I want to wear your dress?"

"Because, knowing you, I'm sure none of yours would be acceptable for a formal presentation."

Maddie's mouth fell open. "Wait a minute, Bree. I'm not—"

"Yes you are, and don't argue with me. Don't pretend to be surprised, either. You have to have realized that with all my ladies still on the road, I have no other attendants."

"But . . ." Maddie could hardly breathe. "I can't . . ."

"Nonsense. This dress is the height of fashion. Even you will look lovely in it."

"Not that that matters," said Leyton, "since no one will be looking at you anyway."

"He's right," Briellen assured her with a smile. "You'll be hardly more than a dress."

"Then grab one of your maids and put her in it. I have other things to do besides be a dress."

Briellen rolled her eyes. "A maid as my attendant? The first time I'm presented to my bridegroom? Don't be absurd."

"Though it might not be a bad idea," Leyton muttered, "given Maddie's record."

Briellen ignored him, looking at the gown, then at Maddie. "It is going to have to be taken out. You seem to have put on a bit of weight since I saw you last." Briellen turned to her maids. "Nelisa, start ripping out the bodice seams. You can fit her while I have my bath." She turned to Maddie. "That way you can tell me all about Abramm. I want every little detail so as to make the best possible impression." She smiled sweetly.

Maddie stared at her in shock, words of utter and absolute refusal poised on her tongue. She must've been wrong in her earlier conclusion that Briellen had guessed her true feelings. Not even Briellen could be this cruel.

Oh, please, Father . . . don't make me do this. . . .

But despite her plea, no deliverance came. Knowing that if she made too much of a fuss she would only resurrect Bree's suspicions and get her all out of sorts, she acquiesced, resolving to bear it as best she could. Eidon would get her through this.

And so he did. But it was hard. Hard to endure the subtle put-downs Briellen shot at her all afternoon, hard to endure the tedium of being fitted and dressed and fussed over all the while feeling like the proverbial sow's ear that could never become a silk purse. Seeing Briellen's beauty so closely beside her own plainness made her more painfully self-conscious than she'd felt in years.

Her siblings were right when they had insisted no one would notice her. When finally they stepped out of the Ivory Apartments to make the progression to the throne room, she was so completely lost in the corona of Briellen's radiance she doubted the few people who looked at her even recognized her.

The courtiers were awestruck by Briellen's glittering presence, her grace, her beauty, her gracious way with them. No cool ice princess, she stopped to speak to people along the way, received their adoring comments with thanksgiving and flashed her winning smile repeatedly, leaving behind a swath of star-struck aristocrats.

As always, the men could hardly keep their jaws off the floor, their eyes darting from her plunging décolletage to the sweet innocence of her perfect features and luminous blue eyes. And though in some foolish and irrational part of Maddie's mind she had clung to the belief that Abramm would be different, he wasn't. Sitting there on his throne in all his glory, he stared at her glaze-eyed like all the rest. In fact, he was probably worse.

She recalled little of the remainder of the ceremony, and dinner passed in an increasingly painful blur. Being Second Daughter she had to sit directly right of Briellen and the king, close enough she could hear their conversation. Could hear her sister utter the very comments and questions Maddie herself had fed her that very afternoon, which often provoked his laughter and almost always a gratifying response. She reflected on what an odd thing it was to keep her gaze deliberately averted from the man yet have all her attention riveted upon him just the same. He fairly glowed with Light and power at the edge of her field of vision, the essence of him filling all her soul, her awareness of his presence so acute she could hardly bear it.

Briellen, of course, ignored her, as did Abramm. Which left only Count Blackwell, seated on Maddie's right, to distract her. And he was almost worse than no distraction at all. He kept looking at her with a bright, invasive intensity and asking if she was all right—for she didn't look well—until she wanted to scream at him to shut up, that she wasn't all right and there was a good chance she might never be all right again. When he wasn't pestering her about her health, he drooled over Briellen, marveling at her beauty and her charm and remarking repeatedly at what a wonderful queen she would make. His conversation couldn't have been more distressing if he'd deliberately tried to make it so. When he began to speculate as to how soon an heir might come along, she had to turn away and concentrate on eating her dessert, beseeching

Eidon to draw his attention away from her.

Terstmeet was somewhat better, for it gave her something else to think about and to her relief wasn't a diatribe on jealousy and self-pity, though she thought perhaps she needed one. Even better, Briellen nodded off midway through the message, which wasn't something Maddie should rejoice about but did anyway—for she knew Abramm would not be impressed by it. Then she confessed her judgmental attitude and reminded herself that it would make no difference whether he was impressed or not, he would still marry her. Besides, the poor girl had had a very long day, at the end of a long and difficult journey, in addition to having a very short attention span and no experience with the Kiriathan Terstans' way of worshipping.

After the message, people lingered around the new couple, commenting on how good they looked together. They were a study in opposites, all his strength and sternness of feature setting off Briellen's soft, girlish radiance. Or perhaps it was Briellen's insubstantiality that made him resonate with such masculine strength and power. Whatever it was, even Maddie had to admit they made a stunning couple.

But she didn't have to dwell on it. Nor did she have to stay and listen any longer; she had fulfilled her duty. But she did have to speak to Abramm about the library and thought it better she do so here, in plain sight, rather than risk another firestorm of gossipy exaggerations.

It took some doing, but eventually she got him alone, Briellen momentarily cornered by a pack of drooling male courtiers—not something she appeared to mind at all.

"You were right," Abramm said, watching his fiancée with a relieved smile, "she is charming. And I'm astonished at how well everyone's responded to her."

Having had enough of such talk to last a lifetime, Maddie went straight to her business. "What of the library?" she asked quietly.

"It's under guard, as I promised." He turned his gaze back to her, his expression mild and detached. "We'll be having a general reception in the morning from nine until noon. You should be able to get some work done then."

She frowned. "I don't think I should go back there. Gossip's already spread that I was seen entering and exiting your apartments this morning in a servant's smock."

His brows drew down but his eyes twinkled. "I don't know why you thought that would work in the first place."

"Well, it was the first thing Briellen confronted me with, so I don't think working out of your apartments will be a good thing."

"No . . . probably not. I'll have the books sent to you. The ones you stacked on the table. I'll send Philip Meridon with them as a guard. For you and for them. We can set up a study room with a lock, as well, if you'd like. Beyond that, I suppose we'll just have to trust Eidon to keep them safe."

"Yes. I suppose so." The conversation was over, but she couldn't seem to say the words to steer it in that direction, couldn't seem to find her tongue at all now as she stared up at him, helpless to stop herself. He stood there meeting her gaze, possibly uncertain what to say next, though she couldn't tell. Indeed, for the first time in months she found his expression impossible to read. Abruptly he stepped back with a nod, murmuring the words of disengagement, and she watched him walk away, aware now of the glances that flicked her way and the people whispering to one another around her.

Desperately she took command of herself—though far too late—and headed for the door.

———

Shortly after his initial interview with Darak Prittleman, Gillard had fallen asleep again. The next time he awoke he rested higher on his pillows than before, wore a clean shirt, and found his hair tied back into a queue. He also found, to his dismay, that the long beard that had sprouted from his jaw over these last six months had been shaven away, despite his having turned down Prittleman's offer to do so.

Prittleman himself sat at his bedside, a small smile on his face as he watched Gillard stroke his barren chin. A tray bearing a bowl of steaming porridge and cup of tea rested on the bedside table by his knee. Seeing Gillard was awake, he asked him how he felt. "Better" was all he could say. Neither said anything about the beard, Gillard preferring to think Prittleman had gotten some other Guardian to do it rather than consider the prospect of his clumsy hands coming anywhere near his face or throat with a razor.

As before, Prittleman fed him messily and told him again what had befallen him, assuring him that plans were being put in place to rectify the injustices done.

"Has he released the High Father yet?" Gillard asked when he seemed to have run down.

Prittleman said he had not, and gained a second wind as he rattled on about some other Guardian having gone to plead his case, only to be arrested for his impertinence. "They're going to have to choose a new Father," Prittleman said gravely. "Abramm won't let Master Bonafil talk to anyone. My guess is he's already dead."

As the days passed, Gillard slept less, ate more, and soon was able to feed and shave himself. Unfortunately, even though he could complete such simple tasks without mishap, they always drained him of energy, so that he fell back onto his bed weak and exhausted, where he would sleep for hours. Thus, it was more than a week before he felt strong enough to stand, though Prittleman warned it was too soon and stood by to catch him, frowning grimly.

Indeed, just swinging his legs over the side of the bed made him so woozy he had to sit for several moments, eyes closed, before the world settled. Then, ever so slowly, with Prittleman holding his arm, he eased onto his feet. His legs wobbled like noodles as a pins-and-needles prickling shot up and down them. Gradually, though, the muscles recalled what they were to do and his stance grew firmer.

He looked up at Prittleman with a smile. "There! That wasn't so bad."

Prittleman smiled back now, his expression looking pained as always. "Wonderful, sir! Wonderful!"

But despite his words, something suddenly seemed very wrong, though Gillard could not figure out what it was.

"Shall I help you back into your bed now, sir?" Prittleman suggested after a moment.

"I want to walk to the window."

"Are you sure that's wise?"

"Either help me, Prittleman, or get out of my way."

Grim-faced and reluctant, Prittleman helped him shuffle across the scarlet rug to the narrow window, on whose ledge he propped himself, breathless but triumphant. Gazing at the newly greened hills outside, he sighed. "What I wouldn't give to take a ride just now!"

"Oh, my lord!" Prittleman exclaimed in alarm. "Even if you were fully well, that would be impossible. The king's men are searching everywhere for you."

Gillard scowled up at him, only to be hit again with that disconcerting jolt of *wrongness*. Again he sought to understand the cause . . . and finally it hit him: he was looking *up* at Prittleman. They stood toe-to-toe and he was looking up at the man, when previously he'd been the taller by nearly a head. More than that, Prittleman seemed broader across the chest, thicker of bone and muscle than Gillard had remembered him. How was it possible a man his age could have grown so much? Or was it. . . ?

Gillard looked down at his hands—narrow, skeletal, revoltingly feminine. He examined the rest of his body and found an echoing shrinkage—not just of height but of bones and muscle, too.

"Pox and plagues!" he choked in horror. "How is this possible?"

"Abramm did it, as I've told you," Prittleman said. "With his evil Terstan power."

Gillard stared at his hands and feet, at his thin, bony legs. *No. This cannot be.*

Suddenly, all his strength left him, and his legs, wobbling wildly, gave way as a great purple-and-black cloud billowed up around him. He was vaguely aware of Prittleman catching him and carrying him back to bed, and then a dry, nasal whisper: "Remember, my prince—as Eidon has delivered you, he can also restore you. You have only to ask. . . ."

17

More than two weeks had passed since Briellen's arrival. With his wedding a mere twelve days away, Abramm stood alone on the balcony of his apartments, savoring the fresh sea scent and quiet solitude of the early, fog-bound morning. Sparrows chirped in the gnarled oak nearby, its barren branches glimmering with the bright green buds of new growth. Occasionally one of last season's few remaining dead leaves came loose, fluttering down to the black-and-white terrace below, where a servant was attempting to sweep the tiles clean.

Beyond the terrace a row of cedars spired against the mist-blurred backdrop of the city and its river, a broad silver ribbon running down to the bay. Barges and small craft already cluttered its surface, the common folk having begun their day hours ago. Most of the bay lay cloaked in fog, the tall-masted ships riding at anchor barely visible through the veil, which muted even the bells and shouts down at the docks.

He pulled a bare hand along the water-beaded balustrade, clearing away the condensation before bracing folded forearms on the damp marble. Leaning over them, he stared thoughtfully southeastward in the direction of the Gull Islands out there far beyond the fog, but near enough a galley could reach Springerlan in three days if the seas were calm. As they were today, and had been for the last week.

But not because the Shadow holds my shores. At least, not yet.

He could feel it gathering, though, and reports said it now held most of the Sea of Sharss. Every morning he came out here to watch the mist, to check the moisture, to reassure himself it was not yet here. But he knew the time was coming. The darkness was inexorably approaching, and with it the invading armies. Would Kiriath be ready? And was this Chesedhan alliance he'd worked so hard to make what Kiriath truly needed to repel them after all?

He remembered vividly the night he'd met his bride. How he'd watched her come up the red runner in his throne room, as astonished by her beauty as everyone else. Indeed, the eyes of every man in the room had been fixed upon her, and he had sensed their admiration and desire—and their vicarious satisfaction that it was their king who'd won her. Yet even in his astonishment Abramm himself had felt a curious flatness. Amazing as Briellen's beauty was, it seemed brittle and evanescent, a thin shroud of ice, easily shattered. And so it was.

As she came out of her curtsey and lifted her gaze to his, her eyes had fixed in startled horror upon his scars and she'd stiffened in obvious revulsion. Though it had to have been only a moment before she'd regained her poise and her calmness of expression, the damage was done. He had spoken the formal exchange of greetings by rote, the words hardly registering as he sought to wrestle down his panic and pain, and he thought perhaps she'd done the same.

To her credit, though she'd obviously not been prepared for his disfigurement, she'd adjusted to it quickly. Not once for the rest of the evening did she give any sign she found the scars disturbing. She'd been warm, witty, pleasant, interesting, and sweetly flattering. Everyone loved her, and he heard no more objections to his coming union with a Chesedhan princess, neither that night nor in the days to follow. The misgivings were now completely his own.

In the nearby oak, the sparrows erupted in a furious cacophony of chirping, drawing his eye to where they fluttered and jumped about a black, heron-shaped bird he recognized immediately as a feyna. Ignoring the sparrows, it flew out of the oak to the balustrade some ten strides down the balcony from him and stabbed its needlelike beak into one of the railing's marble carvings. Which turned out to be a staffid's carapace. Still sluggish from the cold, the staffid writhed in slow motion, its color shifting from ivory to its natural gray and blue. The feyna shook its head, then flipped its prize into the air to catch and swallow it whole, extending its slim, dark neck as it worked the resulting bulge downward.

Grimacing, Abramm returned his gaze to the terrace below him, and his thoughts to the mounting restlessness that had plagued him of late. Although he had tried hard to please and entertain his bride-to-be, as the days passed she had grown increasingly discontent. There was always something wrong: the entertainment was shoddily done, her seat was lumpy, the chamber drafty, the décor old-fashioned, the food bland, the servants rude. . . . She wanted to have a dance when they had a reception, a night of game playing when they had a dance, a symphony when the Table of Lords was to meet.

Worst of all, though she'd not yet said it to Abramm's face, he'd heard she was growing increasingly frustrated with his "fanatical" insistence on attending Terstmeet every night—particularly one she didn't even consider a proper Terstmeet. After the second day she had refused to continue attending until she was offered services to her liking. She wanted the glass paintings, the golden plates and sticks to hold the stars and sparklers, the incense, the multiple choirs, and all the other accoutrements typical of Chesedhan services. Since Kesrin had no intention of catering to her, Abramm either had to let her go unsatisfied, replace Kesrin with someone more amenable to her desires, or provide for her a separate service.

It had all blown up a few days ago when she had insisted he take her out to Two Hats Island, a trip he considered unacceptable on account of the fog and recent galley sightings. But when he'd refused, she'd only conspired with Darnley and Nott to arrange a voyage anyway. He'd stopped them—forcibly—right before they embarked. For two days afterward, she'd all but refused to speak to him, while at the same time flirting outrageously with the other men.

And then, in her volatile way, she changed, having either forgiven him or simply grown bored of being angry. Or maybe it was the picnic in the palace orchid house yesterday that had placated her. Or the evening performance of Maddie's White Pretender song put to stylized actions which had amused her very much. Whatever the reason, suddenly she was all smiles again, plying him with flattery and shameless flirtations. All of which was much more pleasant than her earlier behavior, but made him uneasy, nevertheless. As much as he wanted to believe her affection was genuine, he sensed otherwise.

Now, with the wedding hardly more than a week away, he found himself battling an increasing aversion to marrying her.

The feyna had been walking toward him down the balustrade for some moments now. As Abramm watched it from the corner of his eye, it stopped within arm's reach and turned its head to eye his left arm, angled to the right in front of him. The ovoid scar on his wrist, much smaller than in the days after he'd first received it, gleamed beyond the cuff of his shirt. The creature eased forward, and he felt the Shadow part of him stir with interest.

Suddenly the feyna drew back its head and jabbed its beak downward, only to be impaled by the spear of white light that leaped from Abramm's hand. The spawn jerked backward, wings flapping wildly as it staggered on stilt legs, then toppled out of sight toward the fog-shrouded terrace below.

"Would that all your problems were dispatched so easily," said a familiar voice from behind.

Abramm turned. Trap Meridon leaned against the doorframe, holding a cup of tea. "Too bad you can't use that offense on your Chesedhan friend this morning," he said with a lift of his cup.

He took a sip as Abramm turned back to the balustrade, frowning at the reminder that he'd be facing off with Leyton Donavan in fencing practice a couple of hours hence. The match was the direct result of the challenge issued and accepted the night of Abramm's coronation—another burr among the irritations his betrothed had brought him. After Rennalf had rudely awakened him to the sorry state of his fencing skills during their face-off at Graymeer's, Abramm had put off setting a date for his contest with Leyton. Every day he delayed, after all, meant one more day's worth of improvement. But the Chesedhan had badgered him relentlessly, and when the man began to hint Abramm might be afraid to face him, pride had taken over and the meeting was scheduled. Even then Abramm had assumed it would be no more than a quick bout in the practice hall with only his trainers and regular fencing partners as audience.

Leyton had other plans, inviting all Briellen's Chesedhan entourage, guards and ladies both, which had finally arrived last week. Even Briellen claimed an interest in the match. With so many Chesedhans planning to attend, Abramm's nobles decided he would need supporters of his own, whereupon Blackwell suggested they might need a bigger venue. But Abramm did not want to confer on the affair more significance than it deserved—which a bigger venue would do. More than that, the likelihood was great he'd be humiliated, and that would be hard enough to swallow without having the whole city on hand to watch it.

Which raised the question of why Leyton was so intent upon it in the first place—and especially that so many of his countrymen see it. They'd both acknowledged Abramm's skills had been lost to injury and that he was still in the process of regaining them. Both expected him to lose . . . so . . . did the prince desire only to discomfit him, then? And for what purpose?

Unless *they* didn't want the treaty to occur, either . . . but then, why even go to all the trouble of coming here?

He didn't much like the answer that came so quickly to his mind: *They didn't come for the treaty. They came for the regalia.* Still, even that didn't answer why Leyton would desire to deliberately humiliate him.

"I heard you had word from Ethan," said Trap, drifting forward to stand at the balustrade and gaze off over the fogbound docks.

"Aye. The pigeon came in just at dusk last night."

"And?"

"Not good. The barbarian warlord Aistulf visited Balmark Manor at least four times. And now Rennalf's openly talking rebellion, using his outrage over what I did to the Hasmal'uk stone as his excuse. I doubt he'd be so bold if he hadn't made some kind of an alliance."

"At least we know he's back north."

"For however long that will last." Abramm sighed. The barbarians, splintered by intertribal rivalries and warfare, were not a serious threat in themselves, particularly not when combined with the geography of the Kiriathan northland, whose passes had long been guarded by the border lords. It had always been as much for their own protection as for Kiriath's. But if they had switched sides, it would not be a good thing.

"I was hoping they'd have sense enough to see they'd be better off aligned with me, but apparently not," Abramm said.

"Oh, I don't know. Ethan said most of them still favor you."

"He said that before the business with the stone. And Balmark's not the only one who's irked with me for that. I probably shouldn't have had it made into sovereigns."

"You needed the money," Trap said flatly. "And anyway, you couldn't have turned it into sovereigns if you hadn't turned it into gold first. The transformation works as much on your behalf as it does against you. Maybe more." He paused and sipped his tea. "Eidon still has his hand on things, my lord."

"That is my only comfort," Abramm said grimly. "But this news does make me all the more eager to get this Chesedhan treaty finalized." He sighed. "Even as I dread the final step."

His friend made a face. "I tried to suggest an alternative to Leyton the other day, but he seems quite incapable of believing any man would not want to marry his sister. King Hadrich's 'most precious jewel,' he called her."

"Spoiled as she is," Abramm said dryly, "I can believe that."

"I feel sorry for her."

Abramm looked at him sharply. "Don't tell me *you're* smitten, too?"

Trap smiled and shook his head. "Hardly. But if you look at it from Briellen's point of view, it can hardly be easy. She's had a rough month. Rousted out of her comfortable palace life to travel at top speed over mountain roads for days when she's obviously not accustomed to that sort of thing. Worrying all the while that kidnappers might strike and spirit her away to Belthre'gar's harem. And even if they don't, at the end of the road waits a man she has to marry whether he's to her taste or not. Or whether she's to his . . ." Trap hesitated. "Which it's obvious she's not, I might add."

Abramm grimaced his frustration. "You know I've done everything I can think to make her happy. If there's something else—"

"Oh, you've been very proper, very polite. And as difficult as you are to read, most people probably have no idea you're not utterly enchanted. But she knows."

Abramm frowned into his friend's eyes for a moment, feeling twinges of guilt mingled with irritation. Finally he returned to the view with another grimace. "Aye, well . . . the lack of feeling is certainly mutual."

"True." After a moment Trap loosed a long sigh. "Are you *sure* you want to go through with this, Abramm?"

"Not at all. I just don't see that I have much choice."

Trap had no response to that, and not long after, Philip Meridon joined them, a stack of books balanced up one arm.

"Lady Madeleine sent these over for you, sir." He pulled a medium-sized, burgundy-colored book from the top of the stack and handed it to Abramm. "She's put a note in this one and said you should read it before this morning's match."

Abramm took the book with a pang of disappointment, wishing more strongly than ever that she'd come herself, even as he understood why she hadn't. Whatever was going wrong between him and Briellen, Maddie's presence wouldn't help. Still, he was getting very tired of this enforced separation. He wanted to *talk* to her, not read her notes.

Now he glanced at the book's title—*Traditions of the Hill People*—then pulled the folded and wax-sealed paper from its leaves. "Do you know what this is about, Phil?"

"No, sir. She just now gave it to me as I was leaving to bring these other books back."

Abramm gave him a nod and a dismissal, then opened the note and scanned its contents.

If there's any way you can pull it off, you need to beat him today, she'd written. Meaning Leyton, of course. *He'll never respect you if you don't. See the paragraphs I've marked in the book. Already, he's been boasting of how quickly he plans to disarm you. The members of Briellen's escort even have bets going as to how long it will take.*

He smiled down at the paper. *Trying to fire up my ego here, are you, my lady?*

He's very good, the missive continued. *And he knows you can't hold a dagger in that left hand, so he'll work that to his advantage.*

"What's it say?" Trap asked.

Abramm handed it over as he turned to where she'd placed a ribbon to mark the relevant passage. She hadn't marked the specific paragraphs, but he found them easily enough: a description of a custom among the Chesedhan hill folk involving a trial by combat to determine a man's worthiness as a bridegroom. In it, the suitor faced the potential bride's brother or father in nonmortal combat wherein each would seek to disarm the other. If the suitor succeeded, he was counted worthy of the young lady's hand and free to make her his wife.

"Well," he said, handing over the book. "Apparently she thinks Leyton is out to use this match to demonstrate my worthiness to marry his sister. . . ."

"What?" Trap scanned the passages himself, then looked up with a frown. "You think he'll want to cancel the treaty if you fail?"

"I have no idea. Maddie seems to think my winning is important, though."

Trap handed back both note and book. "Well, then, I guess you'd better hang on to your blade."

18

When Abramm arrived at the Hall of Fence that afternoon, he was unpleasantly surprised to find the high-ceilinged main hall set up to accommodate his match, rather than the smaller, more private side chamber he'd requested. In fact, he was quietly furious, for it constituted a direct disobedience of his orders.

Tiered seating had been set up on three sides of the long oval ring—two short banks, one long—the opposite long side lined with tall windows opened to let in both breeze and light. More tiered platforms stood outside against a backdrop of birches sparkling with new spring growth. Over an hour before the match was to start, spectators already filled the benches.

But to make a scene now by demanding the venue be moved to a smaller facility would only compromise the dignity of his office and disappoint his courtiers. He would find out who was responsible for this later—he already had a good idea—and have it out with him in private. Thus he slipped into his changing room without comment, trading cloak and doublet for his white fencing breeches and loose, long-sleeved shirt. Then he started through his warm-up exercises.

When he finally reemerged, supporters lined his path to the ring, offering encouragement and affirmations of their confidence in him, seeming to have forgotten he'd recently been wounded in the fight with Rennalf of Balmark, not to mention the still-lingering damage done by the morwhol. The Chesedhans struggled not to laugh at what they saw as Kiriathan hubris, while Abramm's supporters scorned them as ignorant fools. It all reminded him ironically of his days in the Games when the fierce rivalry between fighters' supporters often carried a political subtext.

You need to beat him today, Maddie had written. *He'll never respect you if you don't.* Why did it matter if Leyton respected him as a swordsman or not? As Trap had pointed out a few weeks ago, there was much more to being king than waving a sword around. And he couldn't believe the Chesedhan truly put stock in such superstitious ways of divining a man's worth as that contest described in Maddie's book.

Leyton awaited him in the ring, dressed in slim-cut fencing breeches and a leather jerkin slit low at the neckline to reveal his Terstan shieldmark. To Abramm's surprise, Briellen stood beside him, a folded square of pink cloth resting upon her palms. As Abramm joined them, she dropped him a curtsey.

"Your Highness," he said. "I'm honored you have come to watch our little practice match."

"It is my honor to support you, sir," she replied, bowing her head again before coming out of her curtsey.

Around them people settled swiftly into silence. When the only sounds were the faint rustlings of their incidental movements and the occasional creaking of the platform boards beneath their feet, Briellen straightened her shoulders. Lifting her chin, she pitched her voice loud enough for all to hear and said:

"In ages past, the Princess Ildana, daughter of the great King Morane, was loved by the valiant Barragon, one of her father's mightiest men. She in turn loved him, to the dismay of the sorcerer Namoni, trusted advisor to the king, who wanted her love for himself. Seeing at last that nothing save death would break the bond between Ildana and her warrior, Namoni raised up a neighboring kingdom to wage war against Morane. Many died, and the situation became grave. Namoni told the king that to prevail he must have the protection of the fabled Orb of Fire, guarded by the dragon that lived in the high passes of the Aranaak.

"As Namoni had known he would, Barragon volunteered to retrieve the precious orb. On the morning he was to leave, Ildana came to him with her token—a scarf woven of Eidon's Light. Imbued with her love for him, it would protect him and grant him success. And so it did, for though his battle with the dragon was fierce, the scarf brought him back to her unharmed, and they were wed. So it was that ever after a lady gives to her beloved a similar token before he goes into battle . . . that he might be strengthened by her love and come back to her whole.

"Thus I present to you, my betrothed, a token of *my* love and respect, that you might have success in battle today and return to me whole." She held out the folded square of pink, then turned her hand, holding on to a pinch of it so that the long swath of silk slithered almost to the ground. It shimmered with a translucent, light-glazed opalescence, edged all round with fine lace.

He took it reluctantly, his nape crawling. What *was* this about? Briellen's story was far too grandiose for this proceeding and didn't seem to fit with Maddie's trial of worthiness by combat scenario, either.

Not knowing what else to do, he gave her a short bow. "Thank you, my lady. I shall do my best to be worthy of it."

She dropped him another curtsey and then, as the audience applauded, made her way into the royal box set up for her and her ladies. Abramm stood motionless, wondering what to do with her token. He'd stuffed Maddie's into his jerkin, but that hardly seemed appropriate here. Nor did setting it on the bench. Finally he decided to tie it around his waist. It was long enough he could almost wrap it three times round, but he settled for twice, tying it off and tucking in the ends so they wouldn't get in the way.

Then, at last, the contest began.

The combatants donned the padded canvas vests they always wore for practice matches, then moved to the center of the ring, where they gave each other a perfunctory bow and assumed their ready positions. Abramm brought his rapier up to meet Leyton's, his heart pounding like a novice's. The blades were dull, of course, the tips blunted, but they were still long, narrow rods of steel capable of delivering significant injury. He remained unsure of Leyton's purpose in this, and that little presentation about wars and dragons and scarves of protection hardly eased his mind.

Still, what could the Chesedhan prince hope to gain by killing the king of Kiriath in front of more than half his court? He'd be killed himself on the spot and the two countries set at war in a heartbeat. So it couldn't be that.

In any case, at least Trap had taken to working him harder of late, so maybe he wouldn't humiliate himself as badly as he might have earlier.

His opponent began to circle. Warily, Abramm followed his lead. Leyton Donavan had a solid well-built frame, a little on the bulky side, but he moved with the strength and grace of a natural athlete. The façade of social pleas-antry he had worn since he'd arrived had vanished, and while the man might be a bore, he was without doubt also a warrior. His rugged features had hard-ened, his eyes glittering with ferocious purpose.

They continued to circle, Abramm content to stay out of the line of attack, giving himself time to calm down. Behind Leyton's half-crouched form, the long wall of windows with their backdrop of sunlit trees gave way to the tiered spectators' gallery at the ovoid arena's end. It, in turn, gave way to the longer stretch of gallery opposite the windows and then the other shorter bank of seats and faces beneath a large chandelier. And now, here came the windows again, the pattern repeating as he continued to turn: short gallery, long one, short one, windows . . .

Leyton lunged, the movement sharp and clean, a quick dart in and out. Abramm parried easily and countered with a lunge of his own, diverted just as easily. The tips of their blades wove small circles as the men returned to their slow circling.

Abramm attacked first this time, Leyton blocking and counterthrusting, and they parted again. Circled, clashed, parted again. And again, as the match warmed and they shed their initial tentativeness. Thrusts and counterthrusts came quickly, forcefully, and it wasn't long before Abramm noted he had adopted the sideways stance again, almost instinctively, knowing his crippled left hand had little use here. Leyton was too good. And Abramm was just good enough to hold him at bay with right hand and long blade alone.

"Weakening already, sir?" Leyton purred. "When we've hardly begun?"

Abramm blinked in surprise, barely managing to parry the incoming thrust.

His opponent smiled. "I knew this was going to be easy. I just didn't expect it to be over this quickly."

So the Chesedhan was a goader. Well, that was hardly a surprise.

His future brother-in-law rushed him, forcing him backward with a quick barrage of strokes that ended as suddenly as it had begun. Once more they circled. Leyton smiled and spoke again, but Abramm hardly heard him, having long ago learned not to react to empty talk—Beltha'adi himself had tried it and failed. Around and around went the windows and spectators and chandelier. His left hip ached, while the muscles in his recently healed right thigh quivered with the fatigue of repeated lunges, already beginning to cramp.

He thrust quickly, found his blade caught by the other's dagger, and then here came the counterthrust. His own short blade caught it, and he gripped the haft hard to keep hold of it, but the pain shot up his arm anyway. Then his hand went numb and the dagger spun free. He twisted sideways, out of range, and contact ended.

He heard the gasps of the spectators around him, felt their chagrin and their pity. Across from him, Leyton smiled, dark eyes mocking. Abramm only shrugged inwardly—he'd expected to lose the dagger eventually—and kept his concentration fixed on the task at hand.

Donavan struck again and again, seeming to grow frustrated after a while with only the narrow profile of Abramm's form as a target combined with a blade that darted every which direction, catching him in whatever he sought to do. Thus, for a time Abramm held his own. But eventually fatigue wore him down.

Finally Leyton lunged and, when Abramm parried, turned his blade to slide the tip through the woven metal basket protecting Abramm's hand. Pain lanced across Abramm's knuckles but did not loosen his grip, and when Leyton tried to flip his blade away, Abramm yielded with the movement as he twisted his wrist to catch the Chesedhan's basket with his own sword tip. Once the two blades were locked, he jerked his arm up and out, swinging his body back to avoid the other man's dagger, and they slid apart. Leyton attacked at once, coming around with the dagger. Abramm caught it, and realized his mistake instantly, too late to correct. The dulled point of the Chesedhan's long blade pressed into the canvas over his heart, and he froze.

Leyton grinned at him, his face running with sweat. Abramm glanced down at his chest, then lifted his arms out and away, blade up and stepped back out of contact. "Congratulations, sir," he panted. "You've beaten me." *But at least you didn't disarm me.* For the first time he felt the sweat dripping alongside his own face, felt the soaked fabric of his fencing shirt clinging to his chest under the canvas vest and the wicked throbbing of his hip and leg.

Donavan, panting just as hard, lowered his own blades and received his congratulations with a nod. His rugged face was flushed, his blond hair plastered to his skull, but there was a light in his eye that said he would have crowed aloud if he'd beaten anyone other than the king. "You certainly didn't make it easy for me, sir," he offered by way of condolence.

Abramm received the words with a half smile, lowering his rapier to his side. "I thank you for the workout, sir." With that he bowed and strode to the side of the arena, where Headmaster Tedron handed him a towel to wipe his face and servants unfastened the canvas vest. There was no way to ignore the silent shock of the crowd as it watched him.

Well, he'd had a good idea how this would end, and they had, too, for all they'd tried not to believe it. The White Pretender was only mortal, and he'd done the best he could. But it was still embarrassing, and shame still clawed at the back of his throat. He knew all too well that no matter what your past accomplishments in the ring, you were remembered by the last thing you did in it. If that was lose, well . . . *I probably shouldn't have let myself get talked into this . . . or at least not gone ahead with it in front of everyone after I'd given express orders to use one of the smaller rooms.*

His anger rekindled at that thought. He stopped beside one of the servants. "Tell Count Blackwell I'll see him in my apartments in an hour."

As the man slipped off to obey, Abramm glanced at Briellen, sitting in her box at the bottom middle of the long gallery of spectators. She was looking at her brother, so it was another's eye he caught—Maddie's. His heart leaped at the sight of her, for he hadn't expected she would be here. Standing in the box with her sister and her sister's ladies, she was the only one who had turned away from Leyton to watch Abramm leave and did not look nearly as disappointed as he thought she should. Indeed, the approval in her expression did much to take the sting out of his own disappointment. He considered going over to her, but even as he did, she turned and slipped behind Briellen, her determination to avoid him obvious. Which generated a new and completely different sense of disappointment.

With a cabinet meeting to prepare for and no further reason to linger, he bathed quickly, changed back into his court clothing, and returned to the royal apartments well within the hour he had given himself. While he waited for Blackwell, he stood in his study, fingering the fine lace and silken weave of Briellen's scarf and admiring the way the light rippled across it.

He'd brought the token back personally, in case she might find it insulting were he to leave it behind with his sweat-soaked fencing apparel—though the scarf was sweat-soaked, as well. As he studied it now, he recalled all that production before the match. He was still no wiser as to what it was about than he'd been at the start, but he didn't believe for a moment Briellen had given him this for love.

For love. The phrase stimulated memory of another young woman, this one with a freckled nose and captivating eyes. Cloaked in dark wool, she'd stood in the shadows of the early morning and pushed folds of fine white linen into his gloved hands. *"So take it for love, then,"* she'd murmured.

A chill washed up his back, across his arms, and up his neck.

"Sir?" He turned at Haldon's voice. "This young lady is from Princess Briellen's entourage. She would like to know if the lady may have her token back now that you have survived the match."

Abramm turned his eyes to the girl, who was looking steadily at the floor. "Was I supposed to give it back?"

From the way she blushed, he thought maybe not. "I'll have it sent back as soon as it's laundered," he promised her, handing it to Haldon. With a short dipping curtsey, she hurried away. He stood staring at the doorway through which she'd exited, thinking that Maddie had never asked for her scarf back. . . . Or had she and he just didn't know it?

He turned and strode to the sitting chamber doorway. "Hal, do we still have that white scarf I had when I faced the morwhol?"

Haldon turned from where he was conferring with the servants. "Yes, sir. Cleaned, pressed, and packed away."

"Where?"

"The big trunk in your bedchamber. Shall I get it for you?"

"No, that's not necessary. I just wondered if she'd taken it back." He grimaced. *Briellen's probably just insulted me and is having a good laugh over the fact I don't even realize it.*

"Sir?" It was Haldon again. "Count Blackwell is here."

————

Madeleine left the Hall of Fence as quickly and unobtrusively as she could, afraid all the way back to the royal library that she would be stopped by a servant and commanded to attend her sister. Or Leyton. Both had been surprised to see her, for she'd kept herself in near seclusion since Briellen had arrived. Briellen had already grilled her about where she'd been all this time and had given Maddie a number of suspicious looks throughout the brief time they were together.

As for Leyton, she had no idea what he was up to, but that little performance on the practice floor angered her. Was he *trying* to humiliate the king? Did he *want* to break the treaty? Seeing his crowing triumph, she'd considered giving him a piece of her mind immediately afterward but decided that would bring her too close to the point of exposing feelings she did not want exposed. Especially to her brother. He probably wouldn't tell her what she wanted to know anyway. Certainly he wouldn't take her advice.

Thus she retreated to her library refuge without comment and left them to their conniving. If she could figure out the regalia's secrets, what her brother and sister were scheming wouldn't matter. Besides, Abramm had acquitted himself quite well in the match.

But best not to think of that too much.

She'd known it would be a risk to let herself see him today, and she'd thought long and hard about it, knowing she could in moments undo all the progress she'd made these two weeks. But curiosity—and concern for him—

won out. She wanted to know what Leyton was up to and, now more than ever, was convinced it had nothing to do with the upcoming wedding. She was very thankful Abramm hadn't been disarmed. . . .

But again, best not to think too closely about the match itself.

As it turned out, her summons came later that afternoon in the form of an "invitation" to share tea with Briellen in the Salmanca Room. Already irked that she had to disrupt her routine and abandon the evening ride she'd planned, her state of mind was not helped by the sly glances and furtive whispers her passage through the palace generated among the courtiers. Even worse was finding that Leyton had apparently been invited to tea, also.

She heard the two of them arguing all the way from the Hall of the Warriors as she made her way to the sunny Salmanca room at its end. For all Briellen's talk of the walls watching and hearing, she seemed unconcerned about it now. Interposed with Leyton's nearly inaudible tones, her voice was loud and shrill.

"You told me if he lost, I wouldn't have to marry him," Briellen said petulantly.

"I said nothing of the kind. The marriage was never at issue."

"Then why did you make me do all of that with the token? Now I look like a fool."

Maddie slowed as she approached the doorway, hoping Leyton would answer before she had to interrupt. She heard him sigh. Then with his typical evasiveness he ignored the query altogether.

"You have no choice in this, Bree. Father sent you here to marry the man for the good of our realm. You've known it from the start, so I don't understand where all this contrariness you've manifested lately has come from."

"I just don't think he likes me very much."

"You don't think he *likes* you?" Leyton's voice rose with incredulity. "How in the world can you think such a thing?"

"I don't know. He's just . . . so reserved."

"That's the way he is. All those years of Mataian celibacy, no doubt. Though I must say with all the fault-finding you've done lately, the prevailing theory around the court these days is that you're the one who doesn't like him."

And now having stood there much too long, Maddie cleared her throat and stepped into the room. Surprised by her sudden entry, they broke off their discussion and turned to greet her.

"Madeleine," Briellen said, after only a moment's awkwardness. "You're finally here."

Leyton, by contrast, glowered. "I suppose you heard all that."

"Me and half the palace," Maddie said. She frowned back at him. "I couldn't help but notice, too, that you didn't answer her question about the token. Why *did* you have her do that?"

Leyton's glower intensified. "It's a Chesedhan tradition. I thought it would add interest to the match and honor him at the same time."

"You knew he couldn't win."

"He's supposed to be the White Pretender. I thought he'd find a way. Or at least he'd use the Light."

"Use the Light? It was just a simple practice match."

"Tradition says *Eidon* will give the victory to the man who is worthy," Briellen put in.

"Surely his worthiness to marry you was decided before the treaty was signed," Maddie said dryly.

Briellen frowned, but Leyton only stared with that flat expression that told Maddie she was getting close to something he didn't want her to know. She opened her mouth to pursue it—

And then wanted to shout in frustration when the servants chose that moment to enter with the cakes, tea breads, and pot of hot water, and Leyton glanced round at the clock. "Oh! Look at the time. I've got an appointment downtown. You'll have to excuse me, ladies. Enjoy your tea, now."

He gave them a bow and left before anyone could say a word to stop him.

"Well," said Briellen, "it's good to see you out and about." She smiled. "Although it looks to me as though you're working much too hard—eyes all red, shadows below them. Are you going to sit down?"

Maddie sat across the small table from her.

"Really, dear, you look positively haggard," Briellen went on. "And don't think people aren't noticing. Don't think they aren't talking."

"Bree, they've been making up things about me since the day I arrived. I stopped catering to them long ago."

"Well, then perhaps you could cater to me. Because some are actually suggesting I'm jealous and have forbidden you to come round." Her chuckle had a strange edge to it. "Others wonder if you're finally beginning to show and have begun your lying in." She patted her hand against her waist to demonstrate an expanding womb, as if she feared her reference had been too oblique.

Maddie rolled her eyes. "If I were, I wouldn't be 'lying in.' I'd be leaving. In fact, I would have left long ago."

"Yes. I suppose that *would* be the best solution."

Maddie looked at her sharply. "Do you want me to leave, Briellen?"

"Of course not. Why would I want that?" She motioned for the servants to pour the tea.

Once the cups had been filled and the cakes chosen, Briellen wielded her considerable talent for making small talk by asking Maddie benign questions about her reading, followed by a recounting of some amusing events that had occurred last week in the palace. Then, out of the blue, she pounced:

"I thought we agreed you wouldn't be visiting him in his apartments anymore."

It took Maddie a moment to realize Briellen's "him" referred to Abramm. Though she recalled no such specific agreement, she knew better than to say so. Nor to protest that if the king summoned her she'd have no choice but to obey. Instead she simply said, "I haven't been there since the day you arrived, Bree. I make all my reports in writing, and Lieutenant Meridon has been ferrying books back and forth for me."

Briellen regarded her in silence, her gaze sharp and suspicious. "So you're saying you've not been to his apartments," she said finally.

"That's what I'm saying." She knew Briellen didn't believe her but gave thanks when her sister dropped the matter and returned to less threatening subjects. It was the first time Maddie had ever been on the receiving end of Briellen's social graces, and as the hour progressed she began to understand why people loved her. She had an uncanny ability to make you think she truly liked you—even for someone like Maddie, who knew otherwise.

The conversation wandered from the amusing and whimsical to the reflective, including the unwelcome observation that Abramm must have been a very handsome man before his face was ruined with those scars, whereupon Maddie had to bite her tongue to keep from saying she thought he still was. Thankfully Briellen noticed nothing, prattling on about the orchid collection and the strange Terstmeets they had here, and then she fell into a lengthy defense of why she was sure Abramm was pursuing another woman. She raised Leona as a possible competitor, confessing it hard to believe because Leona's brother, Byron, had been so sweet and helpful to her.

"He was the first one to greet me the day I arrived, you know. And even now, if I need anything, I have only to go to him. He's really quite extraordinary, so it would surprise me if his sister is the one."

"I can say with almost total certainty," Maddie assured her, "that you have nothing to worry about as far as Leona is concerned."

"You don't think she's after him? Because I do."

"Oh, she's after him. She just doesn't have a chance of capturing him. He's committed to marrying you, Bree, and he's not the sort of man to keep a mistress . . . or even to indulge in the occasional extramarital affair."

"Thanks to all those years of being a Mataian, I guess. . . ."

Maddie smiled at her obtuseness. "He's yours, Bree. You needn't worry about that."

"Well, thank you for that comfort, little sister. And I suppose you do know him well enough that your opinion has merit, hmm?" She smiled sweetly.

And again Maddie was smacked with sudden wariness. It was not helped by the way Briellen now launched into a recitation of all the men who'd caught her eye in court, rattling on about her flirtatious encounters, even with married men like poor Arik Foxton and Brannock Whitethorne's son Geoffrey, and speculating that so-and-so liked her, and Lord Such and Such was obviously smitten. Which didn't seem at all the proper sort of conversation for a woman who was to be married in little more than a week. But every time Maddie tried to steer her away from the topic, she came right back.

The clock just finished striking five and Madeleine was rising to leave when her sister blindsided her one last time: "Stay away from him, Mad. I mean it. I'll take you at your word when you say there's nothing between you two, but I'm tired of being embarrassed. Stop hiding out, and stop visiting his rooms."

"Bree—" But she broke off, knowing it was useless to protest further. She'd already declared her innocence over and over, and it had fallen on deaf ears. Why think anything would change? But it was frustrating that after all her efforts to stay away and be discreet and give no fuel to the gossips, they'd found something anyway. And worse, that Briellen believed it.

"Do you understand me, Madeleine?" she said sternly. And there was something in her eyes that gave Maddie a sudden chill.

"I do."

"Good." And she flicked her hand as if to dismiss a servant. "You may go now."

Unnerved and uneasy, Maddie took her leave, passing the *"extraordinary"* Count Blackwell on his way in with a book in his hand and a servant bearing a beribboned velvet box in his wake. Seeing Maddie, he stopped and said,

"Oh, good. They said I'd find you here. The king asked me to give you this." He held out the book. "We found it on the table of the Cabinet meeting room this afternoon. No one had any idea where it came from, but Abramm thinks it might be the one you lost."

Stolen, actually, Maddie thought as she saw the title. Blackwell held the book for a moment as she took hold of it, smiling at her. "He thought you might want to put it back with the others."

"Yes, sir. Thank you. I'll do that." As he released the book, she caught a glimpse of Briellen's suspicious glare and added, "I have a special locked room now, where I keep them while I'm working on them."

"Ah." Blackwell then turned from her and proceeded toward the First Daughter. "Your Highness, the king sends his compliments and thought, in light of your support of him in his match this afternoon, you would appreciate this token of his esteem. It is an old family heirloom, a bracelet his mother once wore."

Maddie took her leave quickly lest Briellen decide to call her back so she could help her admire the gift. Indeed, she was surprised at how much Abramm's generosity bothered her.

In retrospect, the entire conversation bothered her. Briellen, volatile as she was, had seemed unnaturally so today. The dark intensity of her paranoia interspersed with the deceptive pleasantry of her small talk had been particularly unsettling. And all those stories of her flirtation were just plain weird. Something wasn't right.

Then again, it couldn't be easy to have to marry someone you didn't like. It was one of the reasons Maddie herself had always given thanks she'd been born Second Daughter. Briellen had been prepared for this, though, had known it was her sacrifice to make for her people. Maddie had long thought it was a sacrifice she valued, but maybe things looked different when the prospect of actually making that sacrifice was staring you in the face.

There was something else, too. She glanced down at the book Byron had returned to her. The rhu'ema who had come against Abramm at his coronation were still here, still working. She had no doubt they did not want this treaty ratified. And Briellen was not only a pivotal figure in the affair, but one that could be easily manipulated.

SECOND

HAZMUL STOOD ON the darkened balcony of the royal gallery that evening overlooking the crowded King's Court below him. He was letting his host do most of the talking tonight, something he often did of late, as the man's thoughts had become more and more one with Hazmul's. So often now he said and did exactly what the rhu'eman warhast would have directed him to do, the actual direction was not even needed.

It had been a masterful stroke to use this particular man. Hazmul had made the change four years ago, when the former High Father Saeral's body had become useless—as much because hosting Hazmul's powerful essence had worn it out as because the position it held had become functionally irrelevant. With Gillard on the throne and Abramm no longer a player, he'd wanted to be closer to the hand that held the reins of Kiriathan power. When Abramm returned, it had been an easy matter to manipulate his host into a position of influence.

He watched the vivacious First Daughter below, cutting a swath of light and life through the star-struck courtiers, promising so many, so much. . . .

"I see she's wearing the bracelet we prepared," he said to Vesprit, who lurked in the deeper shadows at the back of the gallery. *"Has anyone commented on it?"*

"No, sir."

He smiled down at the young woman and shook his head. It had taken almost nothing to steer her onto this track. She was so ripe, so easily worked: emotional, self-absorbed, filled with gossamer dreams that had no chance of ever coming to fruition. And so very weak in the Light. She reminded him of Raynen in many ways.

It helped, too, that she and Abramm were so fundamentally incompatible. And that Abramm was in love with someone else.

His smile broadened. It was so amusing to insert one weak person on the verge of fragmenting into the midst of his enemies and watch them all go to pieces around her. He'd seen it happen over and over, just as it was happening now.

"The bracelet should do its job well," he said. "Next will be to move the king and Madeleine back together."

"She's been adamant about avoiding him, sir."

"Of course she has. He, on the other hand, is growing quite impatient. It won't take much of a nudge to get him to break the 'rules' and summon her. When he does, be ready. I want them alone together long enough for them to act on all this heat they're generating."

"And then send in one of my people?"

"Yes, but keep it subtle. This is a very sensitive part of the plan. If they become suspicious it could ruin everything."

"I understand, sir."

Hazmul had no doubt Vesprit did, but he was still inexperienced in dealing with humans who carried the Light. It would probably be best if Hazmul took a more personal hand in things over the next few days. Just to be sure everything was managed as it should be.

19

Gillard did not want to wake up. At least, not into the nightmare in which he'd recently been living, shrunken by whatever power Abramm had brought to bear on him. It was too horrible, too impossible to believe. He didn't want to believe it. Wouldn't believe it. But he kept waking up and finding himself trapped in this unfamiliar body. Even the face wasn't right. He'd insisted Prittleman—*No. It's Brother Honarille. Must remember to call him Honarille*— bring him a piece of polished metal last night, certain that some sort of switch had occurred and he inhabited a body not his own while his own flesh was in turn inhabited by whoever owned this one. His first sight of the narrow face in that metal mirror had set his heart soaring.

It wasn't him. He still had hope. He had only to find his own body and make them give it back. Make Abramm give it back. Or the Mataians, or whoever had stolen it. He'd dreamed of doing just that. . . .

But now he was waking up again, feeling the bed around him and loath to come back to consciousness where he realized the face he'd seen last night had been but a thinner, frailer version of the one to which he was accus-tomed.

Voices muttered nearby, pitched low as if they did not want to be heard.

"So can you help him?" said one. It sounded like Prittleman—*No! Honarille.*

Silence ensued, during which he heard the bird cries outside, the drip of water, the distant hollow clunk of buckets being dropped, and closer the crack and pop of a fire.

"Nay," said the second voice, deeper and rougher than the first, but also vaguely familiar. . . . "He was bound t' the beast. What it took from him, it took fer good."

"So you're saying . . . he'll be like this for the rest of his life?"

"Unless yer Eidon has powers I dunno about." Irony sharpened the rough brogue.

Gillard considered whether he should open his eyes and reveal that he had heard them . . . but didn't. For fear he might start pleading. Already he was feeling ill again.

"We should leave before he wakes," Honarille said.

"Afraid he'll learn the truth 'fore ye can ply him with yer empty promises?"

"They are not empty, sir."

"Well, time'll tell, I wager."

Gillard heard the rustle of their clothing and the clink of spurs—unlikely apparel for a Mataian—and opened his eyes a slit as they were turning away. Honarille's companion was a tall, heavily muscled man in border-lord fur and leather with a mane of blond frizzy hair falling halfway down his back. He wore it brushed back from his forehead, mostly loose except for a braid at each temple. His jaw was covered with a dark blond grizzle, sprinkled with gray, and like his voice, his form rang bells of familiarity.

Gillard waited for the door to close, for the latch to fasten, for the sounds of their footsteps to descend out of earshot, then sat up and shoved back the blanket. The room whirled momentarily. When it settled, he swung his legs over the bedside and stood up, waited for another wave of dizziness to subside, then shuffled to the window. Only the fear of falling and being unable to get up restrained his steps. As it was, he reached the opening barely in time to see the mysterious visitor riding away on a large bay horse.

Horsemen, likewise in furs and leathers, awaited him in the fringe of a leafless wood beyond the bridge, and they all galloped away together, their horses' breaths steaming in a cloud around them. Border lords. Now he knew who his visitor was: Rennalf of Balmark.

Gillard stared at the gray skeletons of the trees into which the men had disappeared, grinding his teeth as something close to panic rose within him.

Not long after that the door opened and Honarille stepped in with a tray of porridge and tea. As Gillard turned from the window, he stopped. "Oh. You're up." He did not look pleased.

"That was Rennalf of Balmark, wasn't it?"

Honarille's expression became guarded. "Who?"

Gillard made a face at him. "I heard you talking. I know who he is."

Honarille came around the bed to set his tray on the table. "I asked him to come because he has knowledge of the dark ways. I thought he might be of help, but I was wrong."

"He said I was bound to the beast, that it was responsible for my condition, not Abramm."

A crease formed on Honarille's brow beneath his stubbled pate. "In truth no one knows save you and Abramm. And from what you said, you don't recall either way. There's a tale that it sucked Master Rhiad right into itself, though, so I thought, maybe . . ." He trailed off.

"I do remember it biting me," Gillard said, staring blindly at the green hills. "I remember it sucking away my strength. . . ." He fell briefly into the memory, then pulled out of it with a shudder. "He said I'll be like this for the rest of my life."

Honarille stepped up behind him. "He knows nothing of Eidon, as he admitted."

Gillard snorted. "Eidon. Right." He felt as if he teetered on a gulf of despair. To be like this for the rest of his life . . . *Oh, can't it be a dream? A nightmare? Surely it's too impossible to be true. People don't just shrink.*

Honarille came around to face him beside the window, his narrow face grave. "Truly, sir, all is not lost."

"Yes it is."

"Eidon *can* restore you. You must believe that."

"Well, I do *not* believe it, Prittleman!" He glared at the other man, slamming the window embrasure with his fist for emphasis—then gasped as he both heard and felt the bones in his hand snap like dry sticks. He gasped again as the pain took him, sharp and nauseating, bending him over the window ledge as Prittleman fluttered behind him, tormenting him further with alarmed and repeated inquiries as to what was wrong.

———

Nine days before their wedding, Abramm took his midday meal alone with Briellen on the terrace. At least as alone as a king and princess could be with bodyguards and servants on every hand and a quartet of musicians playing back by the orange trees near the palace doors.

The idea had been Blackwell's, whom he'd come a breath from dismissing permanently as Royal Secretary after the fencing-match debacle. That he hadn't was testament to his memory of how the man had stood by him when he'd first come to Kiriath and his conviction that Byron had truly thought he was doing what was best the other day, even if he had disobeyed a direct order. Which of them was right remained undetermined.

In any case, the next day Byron had gathered his courage and approached him regarding the matter of Briellen. "I would suggest you spend some time alone with her, sir. Try to establish at least some measure of rapport with her before your . . . well . . . before you have to face each other on your wedding night."

The thought filled Abramm with such cold panic he knew his secretary was right.

The day was bright, mild, and beautiful. He had ordered the linen-covered table to be set up at the terrace's edge where the view was best, the indigo bay with its scattering of white sails framed between the opposing stands of dark green cedars. She, fearing a breeze might disturb her coiffure or give her a chill—not unreasonable considering the depth of her décolletage—had requested the table be moved back to a more sheltered, though less pleasing, aspect.

As always, she was an easy conversationalist, chattering away quite charmingly. He had only to smile and nod and interject an "uh-huh" or an "mmm" here and there. Unfortunately, not having to work for something to talk about left his mind free to wander, and wander it did—to the most inappropriate subject possible: Madeleine. She had Briellen's same way of bouncing from subject to subject when she was excited, although Maddie's conversation was enormously more interesting to him than Briellen's. There were other differences, as well.

Briellen sat before him perfectly coifed, and Abramm did not think he'd ever seen Maddie without that errant tendril dangling against her cheek. Briellen's porcelain-white complexion made him think fondly of the freckles that spattered Maddie's, often over a flush raised by wind or cold. Briellen's pink satin gown could not contrast more with the muted tapestry weaves and sturdy blue-gray woolens Maddie preferred. As Briellen smiled and batted her lashes, Abramm saw Maddie's solemn intensity, eyes flaring with the strength of her will or flashing with the quickness of her wit, all of it lit by the warm steady glow of Eidon's Light dwelling within her heart.

Then Briellen would say something requiring an answer and break him from the spell to wonder what in Eidon's wide world was wrong with him. He was supposed to be getting to know his bride better, putting all his focus upon her. Supposed to be probing beneath that veneer of sparkling beauty to see who she really was, what her dreams and fears were, what mattered most to her. . . .

Not thinking about her sister. Who never intended to marry at all. And certainly not a Kiriathan. Nor a king. He almost smiled, thinking of the way she'd said that to him so primly the night they'd first met. Almost the first thing out of her mouth. . . .

He caught himself again, and finally forced himself to take greater part in Briellen's conversation, questioning her more actively on the details of her discourse, why she preferred this fabric to that one, where she thought the best lace could be found, who was her favorite composer, what was her favorite ballad. . . .

It seemed she was not a lot deeper than what she appeared. A person consumed with entertainment, with the stimulation of social life, with herself and her appearance, with the gossip regarding the doings of other people. She lived one day at a time for no more than that, apparently, and he got the impression that, under the charm, she harbored no more feeling for him than he did for her.

At one point he brought up Eidon, asking when she'd first taken the Star. She couldn't recall and showed little interest in pursuing that line of conversation, save as it applied to her demands for her own chapel. Which he told her he was still arranging and which she informed him now would not be acceptable. "The East Salon is simply not large enough," she said.

He frowned, holding his temper and counseling himself to make an effort to understand. "My lady, truly, I wish I could accommodate you. But . . . we are preparing for war and have neither the time nor resources to start new building projects. Tell me why your chapel *has* to have all the things you've requested right now."

She looked at him as if he were a simpleton. "Because that's how Eidon wants it."

"And why do you believe that?"

"Because . . . What do you mean, why do I believe that?" She frowned at him. "That's the way it's done."

"Says who?"

She stared at him. "Why, the kohali, of course!"

"Well, here it is the Mataian brethren who would most agree with you."

She frowned uneasily for a moment, then her brow cleared and she shrugged. "Well, just because they do doesn't make me wrong."

"I'm not saying it does. I'm only saying that, nice as those things are, in the end it's the Words themselves that matter most. They tell us so themselves. And even logic supports it, since they are the only clear means we have of knowing who Eidon is and what he wants of us. Should we not then set ourselves to study them as we have never studied anything else in life?"

She sniffed. "I don't think it's like that at all. I think we know him through our hearts. And the sparklers and the songs and the beauty . . . The Words teach that, too."

"True. But beauty is only superficial. I can look at your face and see great beauty. But that is not all of who you are. And beauty can be lost—*will* be lost if you live long enough." She frowned at him, and seeing he trod on dangerous ground, he hurried on. "To know you, I have to know your actions, your words, your thoughts. I have to know the things that matter most to you."

She stared at him for a long moment, as if she didn't quite grasp what he was talking about.

"So it is with Eidon."

Her face grew blanker still. Then, "You talk as if he is a person. Like me."

"He *is* a person."

Her delicate brows flew up in surprise, then drew down again. "He is the almighty creator. He is Father Eidon over all."

"And he is Tersius, the son, who became a man to walk among us and take our punishments upon himself. Though he was perfect and deserved none for himself."

Her eyes were glazing. A moment more she stared at him. Then she huffed a half laugh. "You weary my head with such talk, sir, speaking as one of the kohali. What does that have to do with my request? I ask only what I need so that Eidon may be worshipped properly."

Recognizing the futility of continuing, Abramm abandoned his cause and turned to the much less prickly subject of the loveliness of her gown.

After the meal he placed her hand on his arm and they strolled the East Terrace together, enjoying the warm midday sun and the embroidery-like swirls of newly planted orange and yellow flowers. For a time she was blessedly silent, and he listened thankfully to the rustle of her gown, the crunch of the gravel beneath their feet, and the distant calls of the seabirds.

Presently he roused himself and asked her about the story she had told as prelude to his fencing match with her brother, specifically about the dragon she had mentioned.

"Are there many dragon stories in your tales?"

"A few. The older ones. My granny says they used to live up in the Aranaak. She thinks they might live there still. . . . Most people say that's only legend. Though the southern races have dragon tales, I've heard. Great sand dragons that come out of the Waladi." She paused. "They say it is a vast desert of sand with not a drop of water for hundreds of leagues—no trees, no plants, nothing but sand." She chuckled. "But really, it seems quite impossible to me that such a place could exist, so I suspect those stories are untrue, as well."

"Actually it does exist," he said casually. "Though how far it stretches I cannot say, for I've only been a few leagues into it. But it is every bit as bare as they say."

She laughed delightedly. "Oh, come, sir, you jest with me."

"Not at all. And while I have heard of sand demons, I've not heard of sand *dragons*. Though the words are similar."

"Words?"

"In the Tahg. The word for demon and the word for dragon are similar: *shemayah, chenaga*. I could see one being corrupted into the other, particularly by foreign speakers. The question is, which was it originally, demon or dragon? Or are they both the same thing?"

She frowned but said nothing, and he took his cue to move on to something of more interest to her. As they returned up the seaward side of the terrace, he saw that a group of courtiers had gathered to watch them from the landings of both stairways.

To his surprise and immediate concern, he saw Simon, Trap, and Walter Hamilton among them. Not wanting to alarm the ladies nor mar the rapport he'd built with Briellen today, he walked past them with a nod and escorted her to the palace doors. There he delivered her into the embrace of the gathered courtiers and with a sense of relief watched them sweep her away up the vast corridor beyond the doors. He'd finished his assignment, though in truth he felt further from her than ever. *In time*, he assured himself. *When we get to know one another. Surely there is something we can share. . . .*

Then, shaking her from his mind, he turned to greet those few courtiers who had lingered around him, paused briefly to listen to the personal concerns several hoped he would address, and finally returned to the landing outside where the three highest-ranking members of his war council awaited him.

"There've been two more galley sightings," Simon told him without preamble. "Two vessels yesterday by a fisherman returning to port at Tidewall and one this morning by a shepherdess off Dolphin Point."

"Drawing steadily nearer Springerlan," Abramm observed.

"Aye, sir." There was a note of undeniable satisfaction in his uncle's voice. Simon was convinced that if the rumors were true that Belthre'gar had demanded Briellen to wife in exchange for sparing Chesedh, there could be little doubt he would be furious to learn Hadrich had given her to Abramm instead. It was thus reasonable to think he might attack on the day they were to be wed. The Esurhites had already tried to ruin Abramm's coronation. Why not his wedding, as well? Especially when they might even succeed in stealing the bride.

"It's never more than two or three, though," Abramm said.

"No doubt to put us off, keeping the rest hidden in the mist so we won't know their full strength."

"He's got to know I'd have a good idea of his strength. If they could hide some, why not all? Why tip their hand and give up the advantage of surprise?"

"Maybe he wishes to get us rattled before he comes," Hamilton said. "A tactic you have used to advantage yourself."

"Yes." Abramm stared out across the blue sea to the cloud bank lowering on the horizon. "Make the enemy think you're far when you're near, near when you're far. Make him think you're large when you're small. . . ." He hesitated, then brought his eyes back to the men beside him. "And small when you're large."

Simon nodded. "Exactly, sir."

"What, then, is your recommendation, gentlemen?"

They exchanged glances and Simon said, "Implement your plan to defend against an imminent attack, sir."

In any other circumstances Abramm would have agreed without hesitation. But with preparations for the royal wedding fully underway, and the city's population swelling daily with arriving attendees, a false alarm would cost much in both substance and inconvenience. Worse, it would reduce the people's willingness to react as quickly the next time. He guessed from the glances his advisors had shared just now that they had the same reservations. Yet they still recommended going forward.

A moment more he hesitated, then, "See to it."

Simon and Admiral Hamilton hurried off, but Trap lingered.

"You're thinking about the guardstar, aren't you?" Abramm asked him.

His friend nodded. "Have you been back up there at all since the day we dug out the mound?"

"No. Truth be told, I don't have much hope for that thing. I suspect it is just a cannonball. But even if it isn't, I still have no idea how to ignite it."

"Wouldn't hurt to give it another look, though."

"You want to come with me?"

"I'd be honored, sir."

They decided to go the next morning, and in light of Byron's suggestion that his sudden, complete avoidance of Lady Madeleine was provoking as much suspicion as his meetings with her ever had, Abramm summoned her to audience later that afternoon, asking her to bring any relevant information on the guardstars she might have discovered. Then he turned to the matter of implementing his plans for defense.

He returned to his apartments around four o'clock, disappointed when Maddie wasn't there. Nor had anyone received word from her, though he was assured the message had been delivered to her apartments. As he entered his study and approached his desk to go through the sheaf of documents he'd brought with him, he noticed a large, loosely folded square of white linen lying on one corner. Maddie's token. Haldon must have gotten it out for him despite his claim it wasn't necessary. He set down the documents and smiled, feeling a burst of tender affection as he picked up the scarf. At least *she* hadn't asked for hers back. Not that she ever could have used it again, since it still bore the faint brown blotches of his blood.

It was not nearly as fine as the scarf Briellen had given him, its weave coarser, its rough-spun threads bulging with slubs and burrs, and it was odd how only one of its long edges had been hemmed, the other three left ragged and unraveling. As if they had been torn. Which seemed a peculiar way of making a scarf.

As he fingered those raveled edges, he recalled the fine lace that edged Briellen's token. This fabric had more in kind with that from which undergarments were sewn. Or bedgowns. An image came to him from that last night when he'd met Maddie in the hallway, still in her bedgown. One made of a fabric very like that which draped in his hands. He frowned as sudden understanding crowded aside the tender feelings. This was no Chesedhan heirloom! No wonder she hadn't asked for it back.

He shook his head, feeling silly and chagrinned—then smiled again. Who but Maddie would be so disregarding of propriety to do such a thing? To have the gall to—

Haldon appeared in the study doorway. "Sir, the Lady Madel—"

But she was already pushing past him, her face flushed, eyes flashing with excitement. "I've just come from talking with Kohal Kesrin," she burst out, "and he says the Words most definitely make reference to your regalia! Although not as you might think. I've also come across three instances where the guardstars do seem to be lit by a triggering event, like the Dorsaddi conversions. Though there are other cases where it seems to do so spontaneously . . . whether because there are enough in the land who have taken the shield or not, I can't tell. . . ." She rattled on, but he hardly heard her for the sheer delight he took in having her doing it. It was like the sun returning after weeks of fog, and he was astonished by the way her presence energized him.

She stopped midsentence as her eyes fixed upon the length of fabric in his hands and widened. She glanced up at him, full of wariness. "You still have that?"

He looked down at it. "Briellen asked for hers back. But you didn't. I've been wondering which of you had broken with the tradition."

"Both of us. I had no idea you'd keep it, bloody and torn as it must've been."

Behind her, Haldon withdrew into the sitting room.

Abramm looked down at the scarf and rubbed its folds together between finger and thumb. "Well, it was kind of a memento. I thought it might even have special meaning, though now that I've been looking at it more closely, I'm not so sure. The way only this one long edge is hemmed"—he held it up so she could see—"while the others are unraveled and rough perplexed me. Then I realized—" He looked up at her. "This is the bottom of your bedgown, isn't it?"

Her face flushed bright red, and he laughed outright. "You gave me the bottom of your bedgown as a token to take into battle?"

"I had nothing else at the time. Here, give it back if you find it so offensive." She reached for it.

"Oh no!" He snatched it away. "I'm not giving this up, for I'm sure I'll never get another one."

"Come on, Abramm, give it back." She lunged again and caught his hand, not letting go as he swung it around, laughing, the fabric fluttering like a banner around them.

"You must put this in the song," he said. "How the Second Daughter of Chesedh presented the beleaguered King of Kiriath with the bottom of her bedgown as preparation for his great battle with the monster."

"Now you're being cruel." She had both her hands on his, working to pry his fingers free.

"Cruel? Not at all. It saved my life, remember."

She looked up at him, startled, and though his voice had been light and teasing, the words unexpectedly rocked even him. They had never spoken of what had happened that day when he had faced the morwhol, when Madeleine had called him back from his inner darkness with the fervency of her prayers and the depth of her love for him. Now they stood frozen, their tug-of-war arrested, her hands clamped on the fingers of his right hand, her left shoulder pressed against his chest. Her eyes were fixed upon him over the tousled curtain of long, loose hair that splayed across his chest and sleeve, long locks of it caught on the buttons of his doublet. Suddenly and intensely aware of the fact that she was once again in his arms, he could hardly breathe, wondering if she could feel his heart hammering at the walls of his chest against her shoulder.

He thought she must, for at that moment she let go his hand and pivoted sharply away, the movement halted by the strands of hair still caught on his doublet buttons. Grimacing, she stepped close again only to find she couldn't turn her head enough to see what her fingers were doing. And so Abramm had to work the silken locks free himself, his fingers suddenly clumsier than ever.

When he was done, he smoothed the strands back into place long after they needed smoothing, and she stood there letting him do it, her hand trembling upon his chest. Then, almost as if it had a mind of its own, his hand left the silken hair and trailed along her jaw to lift her chin so that her eyes met his. They were wide as saucers, blue as the ocean depths. Her lips were parted, her breath coming in shallow little draughts.

He drew the backs of his fingers up the rounded curve of her cheek, traced their tips across the endearing scatter of freckles, then downward to touch the parted lips, so close now to his own. "Why did you have to be born Second Daughter?" he breathed.

The rattle of the servants' back door closing in the adjacent hall and a mutter of approaching conversation broke through the heat rising within him, and he stepped back sharply, stunned to realize what he'd been about to do. She jerked back likewise, looking like a deer caught in a huntsman's torchlight. The scarf, which had come to wind itself around them in the scuffle, hindered their efforts to escape until she grabbed it and looped it over her head. Pressing it into his hands, she turned and fled out the back way, much like she had the morning she'd first given it to him.

And, also as on that first morning, he stood in her wake, reeling, not with surprise anymore, but with the power of what he felt for her and the fact it was undeniably reciprocated.

20

The next morning Abramm stood at the base of the excavated mound in the inner ward at Graymeer's and stared up at the orb resting atop the trio of now-straightened struts. It looked no different than the last time he'd seen it: pebbled, gray skin streaked with black, the uppermost portions of it starting to shrivel. After the incident with the bedgown scarf yesterday, he'd not expected to hear any more from Maddie, but she'd surprised him by sending Philip over with her thoughts on the guardstar. It was a dry and academic missive and not very helpful. She also suggested he visit the royal gallery again, and so he had.

But though he'd examined closely the original picture of Avramm's coronation, he'd gleaned nothing new. Several other works had been uncovered by the search team Abramm had assigned to go through the gallery after his initial discovery, and while they made it clear that at one time there had been a guardstar here—as well as at Avramm's Landing, and even Sterlen—none indicated how they might be activated. Nor did a record of what once was provide any reassurance that the guardstars might remain in any of the three locations.

"Well," said Trap, standing at his side, "maybe if you went up there and struck it with the Light."

Abramm frowned at the orb silhouetted against the foggy sky. He had worn Avramm's crown today, hoping it might enable him to see something he'd missed before, but so far it had not. Now he shrugged. "Worth trying, I guess." Especially since he had no other ideas. With a wary glance round for attacking sea gulls, he climbed the stair to the top of the mount.

After the day the birds knocked Maddie into Abramm's arms, Commander Weston had gone on a campaign to eradicate them, stationing men around the mound with clubs to chase them away, assigning others to net and kill those who persisted in roosting there at night, and finally setting out poisoned fish when they grew too wary to roost. As a result there was only a handful of them here today, the most, Weston said, they'd seen in over a week. Which Abramm considered as significant as their aggressive presence had been the day he'd had the mound dug out. They circled him closely now, and he thought perhaps the crown was what made him know they watched him with more than just birds' eyes and brains.

Dropping into the dug out hollow beneath the orb, he held up his hand and directed a flow of Light at the artifact. When that had no effect, he pulled himself lightly back onto the wall, then leaned out along one of the struts to physically touch the orb so the Light could flow directly into it.

And that time he felt something. Not a stirring exactly, but a sense of hollow darkness that sucked the Light into it and would not let it out. Which had to be a lie, for he knew without doubt that the Shadow was not stronger than the Light and could not hold it captive. It had only consumed Tersius because he had agreed to allow it to, and in the end he had overcome it.

So maybe this orb is allowing the darkness to hold it. But why? And how can I change its mind?

He tried it again, with the same results.

And then the distant, flat boom of a cannon echoed across the compound, bringing him to rigid attention. He looked over his shoulder. "What the plague was that?"

"Probably Kildar running ranging exercises," Trap said.

"I thought they'd be moving up the ammo all morning." Abramm slid off the strut and jogged down the mound's stairway.

"Maybe they're ahead of schedule," Trap said. "I know Simon's gone out there, so maybe he's gotten them moving faster than usual."

Weston was nodding. "We'll be ready to start our own practices here, right soon." He paused. "It could also be one of the Chesedhan vessels at practice."

"Without telling us?" Abramm asked. "They'd have to be—"

He was cut off by another boom, followed by a bellow from the ramparts, confirming that the men at Kildar were indeed firing upon something.

Despite his gimpy hip, Abramm was first up to the wallwalk, though only because the others had held back out of respect. Weston handed his own telescope to Abramm and took that of the sentry. Two flashes lit the morning mist still veiling Kildar as the fortress guns went off again—but several moments passed before they heard the paired booms of their firing.

Abramm aimed his scope south of the muzzle flashes, searching for a target, or even one of the five Chesedhan vessels on patrol out there, but only gray mist filled the telescope's circle of view.

A sudden high-pitched scream drew his gaze around and up to a bright, smoke-spewing streak now hurtling skyward from the fortress. He stared at it in shock, watching it blossom into a fountain of white sparks against the tattered sky. It was a signal rocket, alerting Kildar's sister fortress and the ships in the harbor that Kalladorne Bay was under attack.

At his side, Weston began bawling out orders. In moments the wallwalk swarmed with activity as the cannon crews raced up the stairs to jockey their guns into position, as the bores were cleaned, the charges placed, the balls rolled in. In the yard below Abramm heard the oven fired up to prepare the hot shot. Then it was back to tight, tense waiting as the mists floated desultorily between them and Kildar. . . .

Before long the civilian vessels that had been called to action drifted into position, a ragged line stretching from headland to headland composed of everything from three-masted merchant vessels to rowboats. Armed mostly with pikes and gaffs and whaling harpoons, they constituted little more than a physical barrier, but it was better than nothing.

Once more they saw muzzle flashes at the fortress, heard the delayed reports of their firing. Then out in the mist, another gun flashed and boomed. Three more rounds followed from the same vicinity, and finally Abramm glimpsed the topgallants of one of the Chesedhan vessels. Men's voices carried eerily across the water, bellowing orders. More flashes preceded more booms. And still no sign of the enemy. *Are they so spooked they're firing on themselves?* Abramm wondered.

He had his spyglass focused on the point where he'd last seen the topsails when Weston loosed an oath. "There they be, boys!"

Abramm lowered the telescope and saw them—three black, long-necked vessels, riding low in the water, each with two square sails and ranks of shining oars along both sides. They glided easily through the still seas, evading the bigger, wind-dependent vessels as if they were no more than dangerous shoals. "Hold your fire," Weston commanded. He'd wait, Abramm knew, until they were well within range, making use of the fact that Graymeer's wasn't supposed to be an active fortress yet.

Kildar fired again, the ball splashing not far off the most distant galley's starboard oars. Now came the Chesedhans sailing slowly after, with not a prayer of catching up. The galleys drew up together in the mouth of the bay, languid oarstrokes stopping altogether, both banks trailing in the water to bring the vessels to a stop, still far enough from the line of civilian vessels to gain ramming speed if needed.

"What are they doing?" Weston growled.

As if in answer, the lead-most galley unfurled a banner down its forward sail, a white background emblazoned with a red dragon rampant.

And again Weston expressed his shock and displeasure. "That's Belthre'gar's personal device, sir!"

"Yes."

"Why are they just waiting? Chesedhans'll catch them for sure like this."

Abramm squinted through his telescope at the men standing on the deck of the lead galley, the one flying the red dragon rampant. They were dark-skinned, dark-haired, dark-tunicked men, the leader of whom was made obvious by the gold threads in his purple tunic. But there was more that caught his eye than golden threads. For though the face was too small to be distinguished clearly, it still had a sharp, hatchet cast that was familiar, as was the short, broad-shouldered frame and silvery hair pulled back tightly into a warrior's knot on the nape of the man's neck. The figure of a man Abramm knew well.

Beside him Trap said in surprise, "Why, isn't that—"

Abramm was already pushing off the parapet, heading for Weston, now some ten strides down the wallwalk directing the aiming of the nearest cannon.

"I want you to fire well over and in front of them," Abramm told him. "And see that a boat is prepared. With my coat of arms hung from the mast so the device can be clearly seen."

Weston frowned only slightly. "A boat, sir." His inflection didn't quite make it a question.

"I know the dock's been repaired," said Abramm, "and I thought you'd been equipped with a couple of officer's skiffs."

"Well . . . yes, sir, we have been . . ." Weston frowned a moment more, then turned and gave the order.

As the underling scurried off, Trap joined them, telescoping his spyglass back to its smallest size. During all of this, Captain Channon had been staring from Abramm to the galleys and back again. Now he said to the king, "You're going out to meet them."

"I am. As is Duke Eltrap. And I'll expect you to accompany us, Captain Channon."

Channon blanched. "Of course, sir."

With the soldiers looking on in astonishment, they left the wallwalk and shortly were bobbing out across the gentle swells of the calm morning sea to meet the galleys. Which, Abramm thought as they approached, looked much larger now than they'd appeared from Graymeer's ramparts. He felt a sudden squall of concern that he'd made a mistake when none of the stern, dark faces looking down at him from the galley's railing were familiar. Then he realized they were standing stiffly, as if at attention, and he relaxed.

Sure enough, when he swung over the gunwale after Channon and Trap, he found himself awaited by two short rows of dark-tunicked men: the Esurhite equivalent of an honor guard. And standing at the end of that aisle was his former master and present friend, Katahn ul Manus. The estranged father of Belthre'gar himself, Katahn wore his Terstan shield displayed defiantly between the unbuttoned neck edges of his tunic.

Trap and Channon had parted as soon as they reached the deck, and they now flanked Abramm as he walked the honor guard stone-faced, determined to maintain as much kingly dignity as possible. Katahn welcomed him with a similar expressionless mien, until Abramm drew closer and the stoicism turned to surprise as the man's eyes traveled slowly up Abramm's form to fix upon his face, lingering on the scars before meeting his eyes.

Abramm stopped before him, and for a moment neither of them said anything. Then . . .

"So the tales are true," Katahn said in the Tahg. "You did, indeed, slay the Shadow dog. Though why I should be surprised, I do not know." His eyes ran down Abramm's form one more time, snagging now on his left arm, not hanging quite straight at his side. "And I see it was not without cost."

"No, not without cost," Abramm agreed in the same tongue.

"And now you are King of Kiriath." He paused, then added soberly, "Soon the great tales of the Games will be enacted for real, it seems."

"But not with the ending envisioned by the Game Masters, I hope," Abramm said, just as soberly.

And then, as quick as that, they grinned and embraced Dorsaddi style. Afterward, Katahn turned to accord Trap similar honors while Channon stood by, looking profoundly uneasy. The greetings concluded, Abramm instructed his captain to take the skiff over to the leader of the harbor defense line and tell them to stand down.

Channon left without protest, though it appeared to take all his strength of will to do so.

Abramm turned again to Katahn, relief and joy expressing themselves in exasperation: "Are you mad, sir? Coming in here bold as gulls when you must have known we'd see your ships as hostile?"

Katahn's teeth flashed in his dark face. "A Gamer's luck, Pretender."

"A Gamer's audacity, more like. Especially when you unfurled that banner!"

"It was my device before it was Regar's. I have every right to sail under it."

"Every right, perhaps, but it's only by Eidon's grace you weren't all sunk."

"On a day as still as this?" He glanced skyward as he gestured toward the sea. "We had the undeniable advantage. Though you surprised me with the shots from Graymeer's. I hadn't heard you'd gotten it operational yet." Now he grinned. "In any case, I thought you might welcome the demonstration, just in case your people still aren't convinced of the deadliness of our 'primitive rowboats.'"

Abramm nodded. "And for that I thank you. It has been a most effective lesson."

By now Channon had reached the lead vessel of the harbor defense line—a bulky fishing trawler with booms extending on both sides. Through Katahn's spyglass, Abramm watched him argue with the trawler's brawny, bearded captain, finally turning to gesture back at the lead galley where Abramm's own banner had been unfurled beside Katahn's red dragon.

Katahn, it turned out, had come up from Thilos along the coast, staying mostly in the mists to avoid just such a welcome as he'd received. They assumed at first his fleet had accounted for the recent sightings—until they compared locations and found that not all of them matched. On the other hand, he'd been well out from the shore and had seen no sign of any larger force, though he wouldn't rule out its existence solely on the basis of that. And when Abramm related his reasons for fearing an attack might be launched on his wedding day and his suspicions about the Gull Islands, Katahn nodded in grim agreement.

"The winds have died almost completely across the gap from Qarkeshan," he said. "And if the stories of a secret channel leading to the largest of the islands is true, you could have a big problem on your hands. Especially if they've got a corridor operating there."

"This is not good news you bring me, old friend."

Katahn grinned at him. "You are the White Pretender, sir. I'm sure you'll figure a way. And fortunately, you are also a friend of the great Katahn ul Manus, who is a few weeks late for your coronation but brings you gifts that may aid you in your struggle."

And so he did: four large chests of gold, a dozen fine Dorsaddi ponies, and six Esurhite galleys loaded with Andolen silk, Draesian wheat, wine, olive oil, citrus, and a variety of armaments. There was gunpowder, which he'd gotten at a fraction of the normal cost, shields, pikes, several cannon, and three large catapults. He'd also brought several ancient Terstan books "rescued" from the Andolen royal library before Belthre'gar burned it.

And, most important of all, he brought fresh news of the war, which was not going well for those in opposition to the Armies of the Black Moon. "Though the word of your victories over the Shadow and your ascension to the throne have spread far and wide."

"To good or bad effect?"

"Belthre'gar is more determined than ever to see you destroyed. His Broho boast daily of what they mean to do to you when finally they face you. But the rank and file . . ." He grinned. "They are not so sure. . . ."

But Abramm found that to be little consolation after the demonstration Katahn had put on today. As much as they'd prepared, it seemed they were still sitting here with the front door wide open.

A crowd had gathered on the dock when they arrived, its numbers steadily increasing as they headed up to the palace. Katahn enjoyed himself immensely, looking around with bright interest. When he stepped through the double front doors, however, and found himself face-to-face with the entry banner bearing Abramm's coat of arms, he stopped and pointed a finger at it. "I noticed this earlier . . . and wondered why in the world you would incorporate the mark of slavery that brands your arm into the device that symbolizes your kingship."

Abramm shook his head. "This was created for me before I was born. The man who designed it is ten years dead, in fact. I never even met him."

At that the old Gamer seemed startled, his eyes narrowing upon Abramm, an unreadable expression coming over his dark, hatchet-like face.

But before Abramm could ask what he was thinking, Simon Kalladorne burst through the front door behind them, just returned from Kildar, where

he'd overseen the Kiriathans' disastrous first engagement with Esurhite galleys. He did not look happy, and now, seeing Abramm standing there with
Katahn and his subordinates, he stopped in a surprise of his own.

"Ah, Uncle," Abramm said. "This is my former master, the infamous
Katahn ul Manus. Recently departed from Andol by way of Thilos."

Katahn sketched a sharp bow. "My lord duke," he said in his flawless
Kiriathan.

Simon stepped forward, glance flicking down to the shieldmark glittering
in the deep V of the Esurhite's unbuttoned tunic, then over to Abramm.
"You welcome the man who enslaved you?"

"Gillard was the one who enslaved me. This man made me into the White
Pretender." He glanced at Katahn with a grin. "He also helped me slay the
great Beltha'adi."

"No, Pretender," Katahn demurred, "it was Eidon's hand in both cases."

"Well, Eidon's hand used yours." He turned again to Simon. "And he
brings us news from the front. As well as six fine galleys."

"Well, after that little demonstration today," Simon said sourly, "I'll admit
we could surely use them. Though how we would train our men to handle
them in time, I do not know."

"I give you the crews, as well, Simon Kalladorne," Katahn said.

"All slaves?"

The Gamer gave a single dignified nod.

Simon's scowl deepened. "We don't hold with slavery here."

"True, but they don't have to know that." The dark eyes glittered with
amusement. "At least . . . not right away."

Simon flashed a look at Abramm, who shrugged. "Not much difference
between slaves and conscripts that I can see. And at the moment we need
them. At least until we can train our own men." He turned again to Katahn,
gesturing toward Haldon, who had been standing there awaiting his cue since
they'd entered. "Take a couple of hours to get yourself settled here, look
around, eat . . . relax a bit. We'll talk more tonight."

Movement at the corner of his eye drew his attention then to a tawny-
haired woman in a modest gown of dark blue emerging from the small group
of courtiers and servants gathered at the west end of the Hall of Mirrors.
Immediate recognition triggered both pleasure and a current of mild alarm.
He'd thought she'd left with Briellen and some of the other courtiers last
night. Having worked themselves into a panic over the recent galley sightings,
they'd decided to evacuate north. Given the possibility the Esurhites would

try to snatch Briellen, he'd approved it and had assumed Maddie would go with her.

Now, in the wake of their encounter in his study yesterday, he wasn't eager to find himself back in her presence so soon, seeing as he'd not yet figured out how to diffuse his growing feelings for her.

Fortunately for him, her attention was fixed entirely upon Katahn. Belatedly glancing at Abramm, she dropped him a hasty curtsey, then said, "Is this really him?"

And in spite of his discomfiture, Abramm grinned. Pure Maddie, of course. What else could he have expected? "Katahn ul Manus, in the flesh, my lady," he said with a short bow and a lifting of his hand. He turned to Katahn and introduced him to the Second Daughter of Chesedh, bracing himself for the inevitable onslaught of questions and surprised when she only stared at the Esurhite as if she had no idea what to say.

Katahn greeted her with a courtly nod and his excellent Kiriathan, and that jolted her from her spell. Her face went pink as she begged his forgiveness for her stare. "It's just an amazing thing to meet a legend," she said.

Katahn snorted. "My lady, you have already met the true legend among us. And, if I am any judge, are on familiar terms with him, as well."

Abramm flinched, while Maddie's blush turned bright red. He saw the Gamer's brows lift, saw the dark eyes dart questioningly to Trap. Desperate to squelch this flurry of unspoken communication, Abramm asked her why she was not with Leyton and Briellen. Only Briellen had gone north, Maddie told him, her voice steady, even if she wouldn't look at him. Leyton had elected to stay behind and help with the defenses, she added, though she had no idea where he was at the moment.

I should send someone to check the Jewel House to make sure the regalia are still there, Abramm thought dryly. *At least I know where the crown is.*

Maddie's attention reverted to Katahn. "I understand your galleys had quite a run this morning, evading our Chesedhan vessels with ease."

Katahn grinned at her. "It was a windless morning, my lady. We had the advantage."

"Plus, you must have known the reach of the fortress cannon. What is the average speed of your vessels?"

Abramm cleared his throat and, drawing her attention back to himself, glanced significantly at Haldon and the waiting servants.

She colored again. "I'm sorry, sir," she said to Katahn. "There is much I'd like to ask you." And then to Abramm: "I assume you'll be holding a reception for him tonight?"

A reception? Tonight? He hadn't thought of that, more interested in the galleys and in prying out of his old friend whatever information he had that could help them in the coming conflict.

"Everyone will want to meet him, after all," Maddie went on. "And it will help distract folks from the scare and inconvenience they've had to deal with today. Though, granted, it won't give them much time to get all their feathers back in order."

"Their feathers?" Katahn echoed.

"Peacocks spend much time preening, you know," Maddie said. "So that all their adornment is in proper array when it's time to be displayed."

Trap was scowling, but Simon had to look away, trying to suppress a smile. Katahn just looked puzzled. Abramm steered him around toward the servants.

"I'm afraid that in some respects your Games were a little more accurate than I wanted to admit," he said in the Tahg. "Which you will see for yourself presently. For now, please, take your ease. We'll talk when we've all been refreshed."

With a nod, Katahn allowed himself to be escorted away, but not before he'd taken one more reflective look at Abramm's coat of arms.

As soon as he'd departed, Simon and Trap closed around Abramm in a maneuver that appeared almost coordinated to cut him off from Lady Madeleine. If it was, he didn't protest, allowing them to walk him along the nearly empty Hall of Mirrors, as Simon conceded Abramm's assessment of the dangers posed by Esurhite vessels was far more correct than even he could have guessed. "What do you suppose their average speed is?"

"For short distances?" Abramm asked. "Faster than a horse can gallop, I'd say."

Simon shook his head. "We're all going to have to reevaluate our defense plans—both harbor and on land. . . . At least we've got a little breathing room."

How much remained to be seen. And he was already dreading the complaining that would fill these halls once the courtiers had returned from a flight they hadn't needed to take.

He thought perhaps Maddie was right—that an informal reception would be just the thing. With the infamous Esurhite Gamer on display, they would at least have something else to talk about.

21

As one of the highest-ranking nobles in the land and Katahn's friend—as well as being one of the few who spoke the Tahg—Duke Eltrap was assigned to escort him to the informal reception held for him that evening in the Crimson Reception Hall. They met at the Esurhite's palace rooms and walked down together.

Katahn was suitably appreciative, remarking at various architectural details and saying over and over how glad he was to get off that galley. "I thought we would row around in the fog forever," he exclaimed.

And when they reached the reception hall, he stopped and looked around in astonishment, then turned to Trap and said in the Tahg, "Now, this is especially nice."

Trap grinned at him. "I thought it would appeal to your southlander tastes."

The Crimson Reception Hall was one of Abramm's mother's redecorating projects, taken up shortly after Trap had come into Raynen's service. Her choice of vivid scarlet wallpaper had initially shocked the court. *"Eye-searing!"* one elderly countess had branded it—behind the queen's back, of course. Other descriptors included garish, hideous, and nauseating. Time and familiarity had made it more appealing, especially at the end of Kiriath's long dreary winters. White-lacquered wainscoting, marble fireplaces, and tall windows curtained in gold modulated the red walls, as did the expanse of ivory carpeting with its delicate tendrils of gold and green. Three huge chandeliers set with hundreds of kelistars illuminated the room, where already quite a few courtiers and uniformed officers stood in knots of conversation. As a string quartet played in the next room, servants circulated freely among the guests with trays of food and drink.

"This is quite a crowd," Katahn said beside him. "I thought you Kiriathans were at war."

"Preparing for war. Though to most of these people that means packing their things and fleeing upriver. But you're right, this is quite a crowd. I'd guess many of them didn't finish packing before they learned no attack was coming, after all."

And even then they were disgruntled at the inconvenience. Those who *had* managed to get out of Springerlan quickly were even more upset. They had begun to trickle in this afternoon—fatigued, frazzled, and furious. *"All that trouble and it's a false alarm?"* he'd heard one woman say. *"How could he have done this to us so close to the wedding!"*

As if it were just some heedless bungle the king had made as he went about his day. As if the need for someone's gown to fit properly could in any way be called a problem when compared with the possibility of being invaded. The worst of it was, Abramm had not even told anyone to leave. If they'd panicked and rushed off before they even knew for sure there was a hostile fleet out there, was that not their own doing?

Fortunately, as Maddie had suggested, Katahn's presence had taken the edge off their displeasure. What a novelty to have real Esurhite galleys moored in the harbor! And an honest-to-goodness Esurhite Gamer visiting the palace! Moments after he and Trap had entered the room, they were crowding around him, fascinated by his person, intrigued by his violent past, astonished by how well he spoke Kiriathan.

Trap dreaded the moment Briellen returned, however, for she was not likely to be so impressed, and Abramm had personally approved her plan to leave. She was sure to be furious beyond anything she'd yet displayed, and her temper had already become well-known among Whitehill's denizens. Indeed, he half hoped she wouldn't make it tonight, just so the rest of them could enjoy this evening—even if missing it would increase her ire tenfold.

They'd just visited one of the side tables for a bite of meat pasty when the music changed, conversation broke off, and everyone turned toward the doorway as the Crown Princess of Kiriath arrived, Lady Madeleine a forest-green shadow in her wake. He noticed Madeleine almost as an afterthought, and part of his brain made the dry observation that, while neither of those ladies had fled the city with the other courtiers, Prince Leyton, who had claimed all on his own that he would stay, apparently had, for he was still nowhere to be seen.

But those were minor thoughts, swiftly swallowed up by his overwhelming awareness of the crown princess as she glided across the carpet toward them. She wore a gown of deep plum, its tight, deeply scooped bodice trimmed with silver against a billowing skirt paneled with silver trelliswork. Her golden hair was piled in curls and narrow braids upon her head, a single long curl set loose to lay provocatively across the pale skin of not-quite-bared shoulders. Tonight her delicately hawkish features were coldly beautiful, even intimidating, particularly as those sharp blue eyes fixed upon the Esurhite at Trap's side, then flicked down to the shield glinting between the open edges of his tunic. Her gaze came back up to his with a slight frown. Whereupon he bowed and said, "Your Highness."

She nodded to him, then turned deliberately to Trap and said warmly, "My lord duke. It is good to see you whole and well."

He cocked a brow at her. "You had reason to think I would not be?"

She shrugged. "This morning was a time of great uncertainty." A smile touched her lips. "I have learned again the wisdom of Eidon's Words when they command us to put away vain imaginings. . . . All the fear I caused myself turns out to have been for nothing. Again."

She feared for me? "Well, all is secure for the moment," he said.

"Aye," agreed a dry, irritating voice from just behind his right shoulder. "But now when we really do have to run, how many of us actually will?" It was Oswain Nott. What a surprise. "And of those who do, how many will do it with alacrity?" The man stepped abreast of Trap and bowed to the princess. "My lady, your loveliness exceeds itself each time I see you."

The remark would have nettled Trap even more than it did if he hadn't seen Lady Madeleine, still at Carissa's side, all but roll her eyes in response to it. Nott, of course, failed to notice—it was questionable whether he knew Madeleine was even there.

Carissa maintained her icy poise. "Surely you are not presuming to second-guess my brother's judgment, are you, Oswain?"

Oswain? When did it become Oswain?

"Not at all, Your Highness. Abramm did what he thought best under the circumstances." He paused, then turned to Katahn with a smile. "Whoever could have guessed all these ominous sightings of enemy galleys would turn out to be the vessels of a friend bearing gifts? Galleys, slaves, ponies, gold . . . He has brought the king a genuine trove of treasure."

Carissa's expression did not soften. Instead she turned her eyes to Katahn and said, "If gift is truly what it is."

"Your Highness!" Katahn protested. "You cut me to the quick. I swear to you by the power of the Light—all I have done has been only to aid him."

"You have yet to convince me, sir."

"Oh, come, madam," Madeleine interjected. "Lord Katahn risked his life to help Abramm kill Beltha'adi. And gave up his place as ruler of the Armies of the Black Moon for the Light. He is a loyal friend." She turned to him herself. "Is it true you've brought some ancient Ophiran books, as well?"

"Ah, a damsel coming to my aid," Katahn said with a grin. "How unexpected." He gave Maddie a short bow. "Princess Madeleine, is it now?"

"Just lady, sir." And she curtsied to him rather prettily. Indeed her face was flushed with excitement, her eyes asparkle, and Trap could see why Abramm might find her attractive. He could also see the questions crowding up against one another in her mind, ready to spill out of her mouth, and decided he'd better head her off before she got started.

"Where is your brother, my lady? I've not seen him all day."

"My brother?" She blinked, thrown from the current of her thoughts into a momentary eddy. "Oh, I just learned he left this morning to catch up with Briellen."

"He left this *morning*?" Trap asked in mild alarm. *Before or after the action took place?* he wondered. But he but did not think it politic to ask. Especially not with Oswain Nott pressing against his elbow. If he were still Captain Meridon, however, he'd be heading down to the Jewel House right now. But he wasn't Captain Meridon, he was the Duke of Northille . . . and the duke had to stay and make polite conversation.

Madeleine had already dropped the subject of her brother to hone in on Katahn again. "I am amazed at your Kiriathan, sir. You speak it wholly without accent, so far as I can tell. I understand now why Abramm thought you were his friend when he went with you from the villa in Qarkeshan."

"You know about that, do you?" He grinned, obviously pleased with himself.

At Maddie's side, Carissa's frown deepened and her chin came up, the gesture a replica of Abramm's. "You needn't act so proud of it, sir."

Katahn turned wide eyes upon her. "Why not, my lady? Had it not been for my lack of an accent, Abramm never would have gone with me. Had he not gone with me, he'd never have become the White Pretender. Had he not—"

"Yes, I know the progression. But it was duplicitous all the same, and I can't see anything to admire in one's ability to deceive. Certainly not one who claims to live in the Light."

Katahn glanced at Trap and murmured in the Tahg, "I see she has not forgiven me."

"Well, you did use her rather cruelly," Trap replied in the same tongue.

"As you continue to enjoy doing, apparently," Carissa said witheringly, reminding them both that she, too, understood the Tahg. Her blue eyes narrowed upon Trap. "You especially disappoint me, Duke Eltrap, for you've become nearly as boorish as your backward friend. Good eve to both of you."

And, straight-spined, she turned and glided away. Madeleine watched her go with patent dismay, hesitating as if giving thought to launching her barrage of questions right now. One look at Trap made up her mind for her, however, and she turned to follow her friend. As they moved off, he overheard her ask the princess, "What were they saying, my lady?"

Nott's voice prevented him from hearing more. "Well, I guess she's put the both of you in your places." He looked at Trap with that supercilious expression that was so infuriating. "I'm surprised at you, Northille. I thought you had courting on your mind, but apparently I was wrong."

Courting?! While Trap reeled at that unexpected and outrageous accusation, Nott directed his remaining comments to Katahn before finally excusing himself and drifting away toward the food table. At least he was not so obvious as to drift in the direction of the princess.

In the lull that followed his departure, Katahn said, "Courting?"

"It's Nott who's courting," Trap said. "Not me."

"Yet he clearly sees you as a threat."

Trap gaped at him. "She's the Crown Princess of Kiriath and I'm just a—"

"Duke?" Katahn supplied.

Trap frowned. "Swordmaster's son. Duke or not, I'm still a swordmaster's son and hardly fit for the likes of her."

"From what I understand, she's a divorced woman. Surely that—"

"Means nothing whatsoever," Trap said sharply.

Katahn's brows flew up in surprise. He changed the subject at once. "Well, it's nice to see she's reconciled with Abramm, anyway."

Realizing how strongly he'd just reacted, Trap felt suddenly foolish and wondered at himself for his sudden prickliness. Probably fatigue. He had been up since before dawn, after all. "She's taken the Star, as well."

"That is welcome news. And explains, I would guess, her remark about duplicity." He grinned. "What about the other one? That Lady Madeleine—"

"Ah, beware of her, my friend."

"So she *is* on familiar standing with the king."

Trap glanced at him uneasily, chagrined his friend's thoughts would go in that direction. "You could say that," he said warily.

"Yet you all looked so uncomfortable earlier when I made that very obser- vation." Katahn paused, dark eyes fixing upon him. "Rather like you do now."

Trap loosed a long, weary breath. "Lady Madeleine is . . . a problem."

"She seems a bright young woman." Katahn turned to look at the object of his commentary, who stood across the room with Carissa and Kohal Kesrin. "Inquisitive, alert . . . not intimidated by social convention."

Trap loosed a dry chuckle. "No, not intimidated at all!"

"I know they look nothing alike, but she reminds me of Shettai."

"Exactly."

Katahn flashed him a puzzled, penetrating look. Then, after a moment, he nodded. "The Kiriathan prejudice toward Chesedhans jeopardizes this union, doesn't it?"

"There is more acceptance of it than you might think. That's not the problem." He hesitated. "She's not the one he's marrying."

Katahn stared at him. "But . . . did I not hear her introduced as the daugh- ter of the Chesedhan king?"

"The Second Daughter . . . the one given to Eidon and through whom Chesedhan lines of inheritance do not pass." He fell silent, watching the object of his discourse. "It's the *First* Daughter Abramm is bound to marry."

At that moment the musicians burst into the piece that heralded the king's arrival, and shortly the doorman's deep voice announced his presence. After a brief flurry of greetings, Abramm made his way around the room to the dais that had been set up at the room's far end, Trap and Katahn follow- ing. There he and his guest settled into the two high-backed chairs that had been placed there, and the three of them soon fell into a lively discussion regarding the possibility of an Esurhite stronghold on the Gull Islands.

An hour or so into the event, Katahn was formally introduced, stories were exchanged, and then they sat down to enjoy a performance of the Ballad of the White Pretender. Arranged and performed as a duet, the song's normal singers had both fled with the others yesterday and had not yet returned. Thus, to Trap's surprise, Madeleine had agreed to sing the piece herself. She had changed into a traditional balladeer's costume and now wore a white, short-sleeved peasant's smock with a wide, scooped, ruffle-edged neckline and a blue tunic over top, its bodice tightly cinched to a slim waistline that completely belied the gossips' insinuations of pregnancy. Her hair was arranged in the looser peasant style of plaited and unplaited locks looped on her head, tendrils of it trailing down beside her face and onto her neck. She sat on a chair atop a small platform that had been set up at the midst of the space before the king, her lirret in her lap.

The lights were put out save for the cluster of kelistars netted and hung from the ceiling above her. As everyone found their places, she sat utterly still, hands on the lirret's gold frame, head bent as if she were gathering her nerve. Or praying. Or, most likely, both.

After a moment she drew a deep breath, lifted her head, and placed her fingers on the lirret's many strings. The audience fell silent, and now Trap found himself praying, as well, uneasy at the prospect of listening to an amateur and reluctant to see the woman embarrassed. Her fingers danced over the strings in an opening glissando and she began, astonishing Trap and everyone else in the room with her clear, sweet soprano voice. In fact, her rendition of the song was the most moving he had ever heard, calling up feelings he had known himself during his own times in the southland. She sang of the longing for freedom and home and the love that waited there as if she had experienced it herself.

And her voice was incredible, holding notes of pure tone that seemed at times more like light than sound. Little sparkles—miniscule kelistars—danced from her fingers as they moved across her harp, and the Light glowed in her face. Though she started the song with her eyes focused downward, halfway through he noticed they'd come up to fix upon the king and did not leave his face thereafter. All the fear and longing and mythic heroism of the Pretender's journey was there, and yet she sang it like a love song, as if he were the only one in the room. And the yearning that threaded it tore even at Trap's heart.

Abramm sat utterly spellbound.

When she finished, no one moved nor said a word for a long, long moment. Then the king gave her a single grave nod of approval, and his courtiers burst into enthusiastic applause. Within moments she was mobbed, everyone talking at once, astonished that so entrancing a voice could reside in the body of such a plain-looking woman.

Trap kept his own gaze on his king, who sat quietly on his throne, lost in thought, looking almost as sad as Madeleine had sounded.

Then, before the courtiers' enthusiasm had even begun to wane, the doorman was calling out in his loudest voice the arrival of Princess Briellen. And barely had his words been spoken when she swept into the room, trailed by Lady Leona, both of them haggard and travel weary. As silence clamped down on the gathering, she strode to face the king upon his dais.

"So it was a false alarm?" she burst out before he could say a thing. "You did not wait to be sure? Our wedding means so little to you that you couldn't even give it a thought?"

He frowned. "The wedding is over a week off."

"You could have waited. You didn't have to ruin everything."

He glanced around the room, stone silent now, no one moving, every eye fixed on the two of them. "You are clearly tired, my lady," he said calmly. "We'll discuss this in the morning."

She stamped her foot. "Do not put me off, sir! We'll discuss this now. I demand an apology. You had no right to do this to me! Do you realize what you've just put me through? Do you realize what everyone is going to think? Don't you care at all? Of course you don't!" She feigned a brittle, high-pitched laugh. "Why would I think that? You've never cared about me from the start! And don't think I don't know why!"

By now her brows had drawn down into a grimace, her fists were clenched at her sides, and her voice was escalating into hysteria. Words tumbled out in a chaotic stream, a pastiche of wild accusations combined with viciously personal attacks of the sort that shouldn't even be spoken in the back rooms, much less screamed in the face of the king of the land. Maddie and Carissa gaped from the edge of the crowd beyond her. And they weren't the only ones. In fact, Trap had never seen a woman so . . . unhinged.

When she finally ran down, he could only thank Eidon for the blessing of silence and pray it would last.

She stood there panting and rigid as her audience divided its attention between her and the king, waiting breathlessly to see which of them would speak next.

Abramm appeared entirely unfazed, looking down at her in the same bland way he had looked at Rhiad that day aboard the ruined *Wanderer* when the holy man had accused him of being a heretic. Only when it became apparent she would say no more did he finally speak.

"My dear, you are clearly overwrought. Exhausted, I'm sure, from the stresses of the last few days. Forgive me for having put you through it all. Please, do not think you need do anything save recover your strength this night. Duke Eltrap will escort you to your apartments so you may rest and refresh yourself after your ordeal."

Briellen's eyes bulged with astonishment. The high color that had drained from her pale features now rushed into them again.

Reluctant, but determined, Trap stepped quickly to her side and said quietly, "If you'll come with me, Your Highness?"

She ignored him, glaring now at Abramm, while Trap marveled that a woman so beautiful could become so thoroughly repulsive in but a few moments. Then, instead of erupting into more fireworks, Briellen's anger crumpled into dismay. Her lips trembled and her eyes filled with tears as the harridan transformed into a crushed little girl. She turned away without ever looking at Trap, jerking her elbow out of his reach as if she expected he might clasp it to help her on her way, and strode for the door.

He followed, exchanging the briefest of glances with Madeleine as he strode past her. The princess walked briskly down the gleaming corridors, and he had to strain to keep up with her, glimpsing courtiers and servants hiding behind columns and in window embrasures, and ducking out of sight into side corridors. The only sounds were that of her skirts hissing, her heels snapping across the marble, and the counter rhythm of his own boots.

Then to his everlasting gratitude, he heard the clatter of footsteps behind him, rapidly catching up. Maddie came abreast of him, then stepped ahead to place herself between him and the First Daughter. Wordlessly they trooped up the stairs to the Ivory Apartments on the second floor of the east wing.

Trap left them at the door, breathing a quiet sigh of relief as he turned back and headed down the stairs. Prince Leyton passed him on his way up. The Chesedhan flashed him a tight look that could have been inquiry or anger, but was definitely awkward. They might have spoken had not that screaming shrew voice, muffled by at least one door, suddenly echoed again through the marbled hall.

———

Maddie had never been happier to see her brother walk through the door in all her life, for immediately, Briellen shifted her ire from her sister to him.

"Where have you been?" she screamed. "This has been the most horrible day of my life and where *were* you?"

Maddie had never seen her so upset. She alternated between hysterical crying and fomenting rage, going on and on about Abramm and what a heartless monster he was. "How could he have done this to me? Bad enough I have to marry him. At least the wedding could have been special. Now he's ruined it. For nothing."

She threw herself into a chair and buried her face in her hands. "I will never be able to show my face in court again."

"Oh, Bree, come now." He knelt beside her and wrapped his arm about her shoulders. "It's not as bad as all that."

"It is. We should just leave. He hates me! He must, to have humiliated me like this!" Then the tears gave way to fury again, her back stiffening as she pulled away and turned to glare at him. "You must put things to right. He cannot be allowed to talk to me like that!"

"Oh," Maddie said dryly, "but you can shriek at him like a madwoman with all his courtiers looking on? He arrested Father Bonafil for much less."

"I wasn't shrieking. I never shriek. I was being forceful."

But Maddie had turned to address their brother. "She was completely out of control, Leyton. If you ask me, Abramm showed remarkable restraint."

"Restraint!" Briellen squeaked.

"You called him a hideous monster. Screamed at him to his face. Struck at his most vulnerable spots without the least bit of remorse and certainly no idea of how hurtful you were being."

"How hurtful *I* was being?"

"Those words will not be easily forgotten. By anyone, least of all him."

"I'm sure he's forgotten them already. It's obvious he cares nothing for me."

Maddie frowned at her, trying to understand what had set all this off. It couldn't be the simple inconvenience of having left the city to flee a possible invasion . . . she'd made that choice herself and packed lightly. The wedding was barely affected. Perhaps it was getting near the time for her monthly bleeding. She had always been especially difficult right before that. Maddie drew a deep breath. "Well, even if you have no respect for him as a man—"

"I don't and I never will!"

"—you should at least respect his office. And be thankful he called it exhaustion and took half the blame."

"He should have taken all of it. And to dismiss me like that is inexcusable!"

Leyton looked from one to the other, and from the expression on his face, Maddie knew he must have heard other reports before he'd come. Now he frowned at Briellen. "I'm sorry this has happened, but if Abramm has credited your behavior to exhaustion, I believe he is right."

"I will not leave this go, Leyt."

He frowned at her. "What is wrong with you? Are you *trying* to destroy this treaty?"

Briellen flashed a nasty glance at Madeleine. "Perhaps you should ask *her*."

"Bree, she is not responsible for those rumors."

"No? Why don't you ask her about how she gave him her token before he faced the morwhol? Why don't you ask her when's the last time she's been to his study? The last time she's found herself in his arms?" She glared at Maddie. "Maybe only yesterday?"

Maddie stared in blank-minded shock. *How did she know? There was no one there!* But there must have been. Because obviously she did know.

Leyton rolled his eyes in exasperation. "As well as ask you about the love letters you're exchanging with Lord Geoffrey. It's all nonsense. Abramm is not a bad man. From what I've seen, he has treated you kindly and with respect."

"He's cold and stuffy and lacks all sense of humor. More than that, he's hideous! Those scars! How do you expect me to fulfill my marital duties when I can hardly bear to look at him, let alone have him touch me?"

"You're being ridiculous."

"And *you're* giving me a death sentence by forcing me to marry him."

"Well, we all sacrifice as we have opportunity for the good of the realm. Isn't that what you wanted? And we need this alliance."

"You said we only needed the regalia—"

"I did *not* say that. I said we might be able to use them."

She turned away from him. "Oh, just go, both of you!"

But before either of them could move, she whirled on Maddie again. "I know what you're doing. On the road today, Leona told me everything."

"Briellen, please—"

"What? Are you going to deny it all again? Tell me that you still haven't been to his study since I arrived?" Briellen shook her head with a look of disgust. "You're a terrible liar, Mad."

"Eidon's mercy, Bree. I've done *nothing*."

"Nothing? You've made him fall in love with you, and you call it nothing?"

Maddie gaped at her, shocked out of the ability to find her tongue.

"Oh, and there you stand looking stunned, as if you haven't the faintest notion what I'm talking about." Briellen's expression turned abruptly feral. "Get out of my sight, you little slut! I never want to see you again!" With that she turned away and flung herself back onto the chair.

22

Maddie returned to her own rooms by the back route, too upset to risk meeting anyone who might speak to her. Her emotions felt as if they'd been riding on a ship caught in ferocious seas, first climbing high to balance on a pinnacle of wonder, then dropping fast and deep into a dark trough of looming disaster.

"You've made him fall in love with you."

Her first inkling of his true feelings had come with that incident in his chambers yesterday, when she'd stood there in his arms, breathless and light-headed as he'd stroked her hair; when she'd let him tip her face up to meet his searing blue eyes. His fingers had sparked little tingles of Light as they traveled up her cheek and across her nose, while she'd wondered if she'd fallen into another dream.

And then he'd wished she'd not been born Second Daughter. She thought he was going to kiss her, and she'd wanted him to, even as another part of her shrieked for her to flee before all was lost.

As if it weren't already.

They'd been interrupted, of course, and she had fled, though obviously not in time. Fled out to a leafy bower in the tea garden where she could sit unseen to touch her face where he had touched it and dream of his lips upon hers . . . even as she remonstrated with herself for indulging in such insanity. What could possibly come of such a thing but disaster and heartache? Was she ready to cast all her integrity aside and take the roll of mistress? In direct violation of Eidon's very clear commands? More than that, was he? No. Never.

She knew him that well, at least.

But it took her a long while to talk herself out of her craziness, vowing never to let herself get into a situation like that with him again. Then the warning of a possible Esurhite attack had come and she'd actually felt relief, knowing he would be occupied and she'd have no reason to interact with him. Except there'd been no Esurhite attack, it had been Katahn ul Manus, whom she'd heard about and read about for years. Here, in the flesh, the former owner of the White Pretender.

She'd fought with herself over going to meet him, for surely it meant an encounter with the king. But it was in public, and she'd had good reason to ignore Abramm as she focused on Katahn, so it had not gone badly. But then came the disastrous reception, which she was now kicking herself for suggesting. Blackwell had claimed the king wanted the ballad of the White Pretender to be performed in Katahn's honor, but no one was in town who could do it. In retrospect she could not imagine what she'd been thinking when she'd agreed. Was it a desire to see the Gamer's response? To please the king? To prove to herself she was completely composed and able to do whatever duty required? Or was there something deeper and more powerful at work—a hidden, perverse desire to elaborate on the song the two of them had begun the day before in his study with the bedgown token.

Whatever the reason, she had agreed, then got such a case of stage fright she feared she'd be unable to sing at all. But when the song began, when the melody had caught her and the story unfolded and she'd given herself over to it, she had inadvertently tapped into her own deepest longing. In so doing, she'd bared her soul to all of them, and worse, to him. Before she knew it, her eyes had come up and she saw only Abramm, who stared back at her as one enspelled.

The degree to which the courtiers had responded afterward surprised her almost as much as Abramm's impassivity. Receiving from him naught but that one expressionless nod of commendation, she might have thought he'd hated it—if she hadn't known him as well as she did. That degree of stoicism usually meant he'd been deeply stirred.

Which was perhaps why Briellen's accusation had hit her so hard.

"You've made him fall in love with you."

She grew aware of the familiar surroundings of her quarters as if awakening from unconsciousness. One moment she had been hurrying down a dark, narrow stair and the next standing in the middle of her sitting room. Liza hovered nearby, watching her warily, and when at last Maddie looked up, dared to ask, "Are you well, milady?"

"No, Liza. I'm really not."

"But I heard about yer singin' fer the court and all. Heard it was wonderful. Like the luima themselves, they're sayin'."

Maddie stared at her, hearing the words but not really registering them. *She's talking about that blasted song. How does she know? She wasn't there. Does all the world know?*

"Ever'one's talkin' of it, milady," Liza went on as if she'd heard her question. "Of what a sweet voice ye have. Touched by the Light, they're sayin'. Wonderin' why ye haven't sung more."

With an inward groan Maddie walked from the sitting room toward her small bedchamber. Before she got there her attention was snagged by the book sitting on her desk. It was the one Byron Blackwell had returned to her after her ill-fated tea with Bree. She frowned now and touched her fingers to its title. *I thought I put this back with the others. . . .* Or had she brought it back up as part of the packing she'd started yesterday for possible evacuation? Surely not. For though she had planned to bring some of the books if she went, she wouldn't have picked this one. Having discovered the hidden library, she no longer needed it. And in any case, she'd already had Philip take all those books back to the royal library.

Still frowning, she picked it up. Things must not have been as she remembered, though, or it wouldn't be here. *I should put it back with the others.* But that would mean a trip through the palace, and she'd have to pass by the Crimson Reception Hall to get there. *Though I could take the back way.* Still there was no reason to return it right now. Better to wait until morning, then slip down before people were awake.

On the other hand, going now would give her a good excuse to be gone. She could take it back and maybe even stay to get in a few more hours of work. Already she was feeling the restless urge to flee, birthed by the expectation of hearing Leyton's knock on her door at any moment. She'd put him off right after Briellen had banished them from her quarters, too upset to answer his questions just then. He was probably counting the minutes, waiting for her to calm down before he approached her again.

Decision crystallized and she turned back to Liza. "Bring me your cloak."

Her maid stared at her in surprise, then hurried to her tiny room for her gray woolen cloak. As Maddie swirled it over her own shoulders, Liza's eyes widened. "Ye be wearin' it, milady?"

"Aye, and you're not to speak a word of this to anyone. I'll be back later.

If Leyton comes, tell him you haven't seen me."

"Aye, miss."

Maddie pulled the cowl over her head, picked up the book, and slipped out the door, hoping that if the palace "eyes" could mistake Philip Meridon for herself, perhaps the reverse would be true, as well.

She was halfway to the royal library when it dawned on her that if Leyton didn't find her in her quarters, he'd guess immediately where she'd go. Suddenly certain he was already there, she slowed to a stop. He'd probably arrived at her quarters shortly after she'd left. She looked down at the book, trying to think what to do next and knowing she was more rattled than she wanted to admit. *Maybe I should just go back to my rooms and go to bed.*

She turned abruptly and yelped in surprise as she nearly ran into Byron Blackwell, who lurched backward with a cry of his own. Then his eyes widened. "Lady *Madeleine?*"

She felt her face grow hot. "I'm just returning this book." She held it up, realizing as she did that she was now going in the wrong direction.

"Ah . . ." His lips quirked as light flashed off his spectacles. "Well, I suppose I can understand why you might be wearing that cloak *tonight. . . .*"

Her flush deepened. "I . . ." But all she could think was how foolish she must appear, a notion reinforced by his openly curious regard.

Then he smiled. "That was a magnificent performance you gave tonight, my lady. I have to admit, when I asked you to do it, I thought the king had lost his mind." The smile deepened. "Obviously he knew what the rest of us did not."

She stared at him, embarrassed by his praise and uneasy with the dual meaning that could be derived from his words.

"I'm surprised you haven't performed more often," he added.

"It is not fitting for members of the royal family to perform in public in Chesedh."

"Well, that is not the case here in Kiriath. I hope we'll be hearing more from you." With that he gave her a nod and continued on his way.

Shortly thereafter she was hurrying past the back stair to the royal apartments when it occurred to her that she could drop the book off in the hidden library. That she could, in fact, even stay awhile. So far as she knew, only she, Abramm, Haldon, and Philip knew of its existence. There was sure to be no one up there now, for Abramm would still be involved with his reception and, if she knew him at all, would be up late into the night plying Katahn ul Manus with questions. And even when he did return, he'd have no reason to enter the library tonight. These days Philip was the only one who used it. She could slip in and no one would know she was there. Leyton wouldn't be able to find her and perhaps she would have peace enough to think all this turmoil through.

Part of her was aghast that she would even consider this. *You cannot go into his chambers tonight. Are you insane? Do you want to ruin the treaty?* If she was caught *this* time, Briellen would never forgive her. Or Abramm.

But the voice of protest was weak before her growing desire to hide there.

She turned and went back to stand at the foot of the stair. *There's sure to be a guard, though. How will I get past him?* She looked at the book in her hand. It would be dark in that back hall. Phil had been coming and going regularly and at odd hours. . . . So long as she kept her face in the shadow . . . why wouldn't he think she was Philip?

Crazy as it was, the more she thought about it, the more she liked it. And as it turned out, when she eased the door open, the guard was gone. A dim light shone out of the servants' wait room down the short hall, washing over the man's form where he stood in that doorway, listening to the excited conversation of those within. She heard Haldon's rumble and Jared's higher tones intermingled with the unfamiliar voice of the one who had brought the gossip. She heard her name, Abramm's . . . and then Briellen's and felt her face flush again as her middle squirmed. The voices lowered, drawing the guard farther into the wait room, and she seized her chance, slipping into the hall and quietly closing the door behind her. Then she darted for the bedchamber.

The voices grew louder and abruptly clearer. "He said Briellen thinks the king's really in love with Lady Madeleine!"

"Well, she's not the only one to think that," Haldon said dryly.

Ears burning, Maddie hurried through the dark bedchamber into the study. The niche table and statuette had been replaced with a tapestry which she now lifted aside as she stepped through the wall behind. The cold-lard sensation of the illusion gave way to the dusty book-lined room she'd found weeks ago. Moonlight filtered through the tall windows at its far end, the weak light insufficient to penetrate very far into the shadows. It smelled mustier than she recalled, and there were no longer any books on the table, but her suspicion that the room had remained largely undisturbed since its discovery seemed accurate.

Unwilling to make a kelistar for fear of being discovered, she made her way slowly and carefully toward the window. And as her excitement waned, she was struck with an almost overwhelming sense of Abramm's presence. It was so intoxicating she wondered if perhaps, beneath all her other rationales, that was the real reason she'd talked herself into coming here. To be near him in the only way she could now.

She sank down on the window seat, staring at the river with its nine bridges, chains of red-gold light arching across the dark surface, the barges drifting up and down between them. The wind rushed against the window and whined in the eaves, and from somewhere out of sight behind the palace, moonlight illuminated thin fingers of cloud spun out by the wind over the city.

How can everything have gone so bad, so fast? How could Briellen believe those things?

Because she heard your song tonight, perhaps? Because she saw the way he looked at you while you sang? The memory of that took her by storm, rolling sharp and vivid into her mind. She put her hands to her face, overwhelmed with the rush of emotion it evoked. In those moments it seemed he had seen her soul as she saw his, the two of them resonating together as if part of the same chord.

A deep, aching sense of need and longing crept over her, tightening over her heart and chest until finally she bent over her lap and put her face in her hands, giving voice to her misery.

"Oh, Father Eidon, sometimes I think I won't be able to live another day if I can't see his face and hear his voice, and I know that is wrong because he's only a man and it's you I should love more than all others, but . . . but I want him, my Lord. More than I have ever wanted anything."

She fell silent, and although her voice had been barely above a whisper, she felt suddenly aghast and embarrassed at how helpless she was before her own desires. *But why does it feel so much in every way that he is the one you have made me for . . . when everything is against us ever being together? Am I just deluded?*

For a moment she sat there, listening to the wind outside, frustration like a hard lump in her throat. Then a new and startling thought formed in her mind: *Do you want him so much, then, my daughter, that you'd give up your freedom to become his queen?*

She lifted her head, stunned. Was that an answer? Was that the choice she must make?

Heart pounding, she stared blindly at the streamers of moonlit clouds drifting over the city.

Of course it was the choice. What did she think? Even if somehow Abramm did not marry Briellen, he was still a king . . . in every sense of the word. Whoever he married, she would have to be his queen.

The thought drove into her heart like a poniard of ice, and she hugged herself miserably, letting the tears come.

––––––––––

Those in the Crimson Reception Hall remained in a state of frozen silence for what seemed a full minute after Briellen had stalked out with Trap on her heels. Then Maddie hurried after both of them, and people began to move again. Abramm sat on his throne, watching them blindly, wondering when he was going to start feeling something. That she had shocked him was an understatement. That she had hurt him . . . undeniable. To be told by a woman to your face, in front of more than half your courtiers, that the sight of you made her shiver with revulsion could hardly do less than hurt. And yet he felt nothing. In fact, if anything he felt a sense of satisfaction. Of rightness.

Once they began to move, the courtiers began to talk, uttering quiet exclamations of astonishment, disbelief, and dismay. Those first drops swiftly became a torrent, as astonishment turned to indignation and indignation to outrage. Everyone had his rendition of what was said, his opinion of what was meant, and soon the room resounded with a roar of sound that Abramm finally silenced, offering to them his own view on the matter, which ultimately was the only one that mattered.

"The Words command us to bear the burdens of others and forgive," he said, his voice echoing over the crowd. "None of us knows what the princess has endured this day. Nor in the days preceding her arrival here, but it can't have been easy nor pleasant. We are also commanded not to gossip and malign, and I will expect you to hold to that where this matter is concerned."

With that he decreed the party should continue, received a goodly number more of his courtiers in audience before finally taking leave of the group in the company of his closest advisors. Once alone in the gleaming halls, Simon sputtered with outrage of his own. "Forgiveness is all well and good, as is refraining from gossip. But plagues, Abramm, you cannot ignore a draft horse when it is standing in your sitting chamber. She had no right to—"

"What? Would you have me imprison her as I did Father Bonafil?"

"Perhaps it would drive some sense into her vacuous little mind! I cannot believe you intend to marry this woman. Nor am I the only one."

He ranted on and Abramm let him go, for it was not unexpected and

Simon didn't understand. He finally left in a fit of helpless exasperation.

After that Abramm returned to his apartments with Trap and Katahn, who presented him with the two Ophiran books he'd brought, and further information about Esurh. They sat in the sitting room until the wee hours, drinking brandy and talking until Abramm finally noticed the older man's fatigue and had mercy. But as soon as he was gone, Abramm understood at least part of why he'd been so indefatigable in his questions and suppositions. With Katahn out of the room, he was left alone with Trap. And Trap had been far too quiet and watchful this night.

Indeed, they weren't alone more than a handful of breaths before his friend said, "Well, that was quite a diatribe your betrothed let loose tonight."

Abramm studied his brandy snifter and frowned.

"I have to say, though," Meridon went on, "your reaction has surprised me. I'd have expected you to be more shocked and hurt than you seem."

"I *am* shocked."

"But not hurt."

Abramm looked up testily. "What is this? I'm not upset enough for your taste, so you're trying to stoke the fire a bit? Why should I be hurt? I'm well aware she dislikes me."

Trap grimaced. "I suppose you have a point." He paused, fingering his own snifter, then said, "I thought Maddie did an astonishing work with that song. She does her music no service by giving it to others to perform."

Which took Abramm so completely by surprise there was no way he could stop the blood from rushing into his face. "Yes," he said tightly, "it was beautiful."

Beautiful. Haunting. Intimate. The song and voice had tapped into powerful, deeply buried feelings—felt first in Esurh as the White Pretender and felt now as King of Kiriath: alone, trapped, and yearning with all his soul for that which he could not have. Home and freedom and the joy of true love. With that peculiar propensity of hers, she had once more invaded his soul, finding all the right strings to pluck, playing his heart as expertly as she'd played her lirret until everything in him resonated with the piece.

Nor had he failed to notice how fetching she looked in that peasant girl's costume, with its low, wide neckline and the tightly cinched bodice.

Across from him, Trap sighed and said quietly, "What kind of game are you playing here, Abramm?"

Abramm turned to him sharply, frowning. "I'm not playing any kind of game!"

But Trap only met his gaze evenly for a long, breathless moment. Then he snorted and looked away. "That's what I was afraid of."

Abramm's frown deepened. "I have no idea what you're talking about, and frankly it's been too long a day for this."

"Indeed it has, my lord. I shall take my leave, then, if you wish."

"Do that, sir. I will see you tomorrow when the cabinet meets."

But then he was left alone with his thoughts, and that was even worse. Hal helped him remove the doublet and cravat and put them away. Finally, stripped down to breeches and shirt, he sat and looked through the books, trying hard to keep his mind off all the events of this very full day and most particularly off Maddie and her song.

"And I dream of the meadows, green gold 'neath the sun, sweet with the dew of the morn. . . ."

After pacing awhile, he decided he should see the books safely ensconced in the library before he retired, and went to do that. Stepping through the illusion-cloaked doorway into the quiet mustiness of this hidden place was like a balm. There was a sense of peace here that wrapped around him like a warm blanket. Even the mustiness appealed. Maybe he would never reveal its presence. . . .

Smiling at the thought, he laid the books on the nearest desk, and then, instead of turning round and stepping back into his study, he moved toward the window.

He stood before it, staring at the city, the river with its scattering of barge lights and the nine bridges arching over it. Moving rafts of clouds hung low overhead, blown in on the wind since sundown, shifting and shredding against the full moon now high in the sky. The same wind whistled through the eaves and beat against the window glass, the trees tossing before it in a dark, crawling sea of movement below.

Something seemed to unwind in him, leaving him feeling bruised and battered. It wasn't true that Briellen's outburst hadn't hurt. It had, probably more than he realized right now. But it had come at a time when it didn't . . . matter.

He touched the scars on his face, stroking the slick, raised length of them, thinking of the woman who called them badges of honor, who said they spoke of his courage and his pain. . . . The melody from Maddie's ballad rang through his mind, carried by her sweet, haunting voice. *"And I long for the green and the sun on my face and my true love who waits for me there. . . ."*

The words she sang seemed to have come straight from her heart . . . a communication she dared not make any other way. She loved him. Deep down, he'd known it since the day he'd faced the morwhol, but yesterday's incident with the bedgown scarf had made him acknowledge it as he had refused to do before. And in acknowledging that, he had to acknowledge the other part of it: her love was not unreturned.

Was that why Briellen had been so vicious tonight? Had she seen some of that performance? Or had it happened before, and she'd seen what Trap and Carissa and Channon and Eidon alone knew who else had seen for months now? That her husband-to-be cared nothing for her and everything for her sister?

He stepped closer to the window and bumped into what he'd thought was a pile of fabric spilling off the bench. Barely visible in the shadow, he'd taken it for a furniture covering cast aside when they had first discovered this place, but the moment he made contact with it, he knew his mistake. He jumped backward and sideways even as it lurched up with a small cry, and then the person—for he saw it was a person—cringed back against the embrasure as if fearful he meant to attack.

The form, the scent, the voice, the distinctive pattern of Chesedhan braiding—even with only the moonlight he recognized them instantly. "Maddie!" But recognition unloosed such a flood of emotion in him that he could do no more than speak her name and after that stood frozen, staring at her.

He had moved somewhat to his right in his jump backward and crouched now at an angle, facing her where she sat on the bench opposite him, moonlight flooding through the window at her side. It spun silver glints into her tawny hair and reflected provocatively off the pale expanse of neck and bosom above the swooping ruffled neckline of her peasant's blouse. The costume's tightly laced bodice accentuated her fine full figure, and her eyes on him were deep and dark from the dim light. She had never looked more beautiful.

When the emotion had subsided enough for his mind to start working again, his first thought was that he should turn and walk away immediately. The realization that he was standing there ready to tear her limb from limb was his second.

He straightened out of his crouch and lowered his hands to his sides. "It's long after midnight, my lady! What are you doing here?"

She leaped up from the bench, words tumbling out of her. "I just came to return a book and did not mean to stay. It was only to be for a moment.

But then I didn't want to go back to my chambers. I was afraid Leyton would be there wanting to talk, and I've just had enough of my siblings for one day. There's such a sense of peace here. And I guess I needed a place to think and pray. But I certainly didn't intend to fall asleep, and—" She blinked at him. "What are *you* doing here, my lord?"

He couldn't help but smile. "Well, it is *my* library, my lady. In *my* chambers."

"Oh. Right."

"I wanted to see the books Katahn brought me were safely stowed before I retired for the night." And now that he'd done that, he should leave. They were alone here, without fear of interruption, and the desire to touch her— and be touched by her—was growing more unmanageable by the moment. Best to leave. Best to say his good-nights right now and turn away.

"So you've brought them," she said, apparently trying to sound natural, and failing.

"Yes," he said. "Would you like to see them?"

"I would."

But neither of them moved to act on this suggestion. Instead his hand once more betrayed him, drawn up to what looked like the dried track of tear running down her cheek. Her lips parted at his touch, and she trembled visibly as his fingertips trailed down the tear track to her jawline. "It's been a difficult evening," he murmured.

"Aye, it has." She stared up at him, not the slightest bit confused by his sudden change of subject.

"But your song was beautiful. . . . I felt as if you sang it just for me."

"I did," she whispered, and he saw in her eyes the same yearning that had so infused her sweet voice as she'd sung. A yearning he could no longer deny that he shared. *"I want you,"* he'd told her in the teahouse, thinking at the time he meant only her wit and her research, believing later it was just stress and natural physical needs prompting him, and forced now to admit that what he wanted was far more than any of that.

She stood less than a forearm's length away from him, though he had no recollection of either of them closing the gap that had been between them. Having followed the tear track to its end, his fingers wandered off on their own, exploring the contours of her face—brows, temple, cheekbone, nose, lips, jawline, neck . . . She closed her eyes, reveling in his touch, her face tipped up, her chest rising and falling erratically. A moment more he hesitated, the voice of conscience telling him again that he should leave. Then he bent his head and laid his lips on hers. . . .

And was forever changed.

Night became day, and darkness, light. What had been by comparison only faint stirrings in his heart now exploded into knee-weakening passion. Her arms came up around his neck as he crushed her to him. It was as if she had sometime in the past been ripped forcibly from his flesh and was now being drawn back just as forcibly. The Light flashed and flared within them, binding them together as it never had before.

A book-laden table standing beside the embrasure tipped over with a crash. That, followed by the sudden strong sense of being watched brought him sharply and stunningly to his senses. He pulled his mouth free of hers and straightened, staring down at her in horror. *Oh, my Lord . . . what have I done?*

She looked up at him dazedly, hands resting on his shoulders. Desire rose in him again and very nearly mastered him. For a moment he didn't care that someone was coming. Didn't care that they would be found. That they were intended to be found.

He shook it off, staring down at her, stricken. "Forgive me, my lady," he whispered. "That never should have happened."

With that he turned and fled, blundering out through the cold wall of the enspelled doorway—and stopping dead to find Byron Blackwell standing right there, holding a night candle and looking away through the study door into the sitting chamber. He turned back, saw Abramm, and started violently. "My lord! I didn't realize you were here!" His gaze flicked around the room, a puzzled crease between his brows.

"What are *you* doing here, Blackwell?"

The man had a very odd look on his face. Abramm could not help but think of the tendril he'd come to know as Saeral's touch and wonder . . . but the thought was swept away before it could be completed.

"I came to bring you this." Blackwell held out a book, peering around the king as he did to look at the niche through which Abramm had just emerged. "Didn't there used to be something else here? A table, perhaps?"

"You'll have to ask Haldon," Abramm said, a trifle louder than he needed, hoping Maddie heard him and would have wit enough to keep herself hidden in the library till Blackwell was gone. "He has charge of such matters."

"I do think he's changed it."

"It's well after three in the morning, Byron. Why are you discussing the furniture with me?"

"Sorry, sir." Blackwell's spectacles glittered in the dim light. "Are you well, my lord? You look . . . a bit flushed."

How the plague can he tell I'm flushed in the dark?

But again the suspicion was washed away and he was left only with the question of his wellness. "I've had a difficult night, Count Blackwell. And I'm very tired."

"Yes, that Briellen does seem to be quite a handful. Marrying her will take a true act of courage, I believe."

"If that is all you have to say to me, sir," Abramm said irritably, "then I bid you good-night."

But it seemed to him that he saw on Byron's face, just as he turned away, a small smile of satisfaction.

CHAPTER

23

Sleep was slow in coming to the king that night. Despite his protestations of fatigue to Blackwell, once the man had departed, Abramm stepped into his sitting chamber and went out onto the balcony for a while, hoping Maddie would take her cue to slip out the back entrance. Standing beneath the shifting clouds, he welcomed the chill, damp air for its cooling effect on his overheated mind and body, while he castigated himself for his loss of control. Why hadn't he listened to that little voice of conscience and left the moment he realized she was there? Because he thought he was strong enough to wrestle down the urges struggling inside of him. And for that arrogance, came far too close to committing the same sin with Maddie as he had with Shettai.

The thought made him shudder anew.

I'll just have to keep away from her, he told himself. *We'll have to reveal the library and move the books. Go back to using Jemson as the go-between.* Yes, it would be an obvious departure from his recent behavior, and yes, the courtiers would talk and no doubt rightly surmise why he was doing it. But what choice did he have?

You could marry Madeleine instead of Briellen. . . . After that outburst tonight, Leyton just might find a way to accept it.

But he dismissed the thought at once, knowing it could never be, and shoved himself away from the balustrade to pace beside it. He paced and prayed, and reproached himself until the clouds had obscured the sky, and the moon had been reduced to a faint light shining through them halfway to the unseen horizon in the west.

Finally, thinking Maddie surely must have left by now, he reentered his apartments, thoroughly chilled, and fell asleep in his under blouse and breeches across the foot of the bed, the strains of her haunting voice drifting through his dreams.

His sleep was fitful, plagued with erotic dreams that culminated in a sequence where he met her in the library again. This time desire won over conscience, driving his dream self to take from her what only a wedded husband had the right to—right there on the bench of the window embrasure. It was as wonderful as he had imagined and he did it without a pang of guilt. Then, in the way of dreams, the scene shifted and he found himself not on the window seat, but on the ledge outside Xorofin, lying in a pool of blood, Maddie dead in his arms.

He jumped up with a great shout of "No!" and his anguish was so piercing, so overwhelming, it tore him from the nightmare. He found himself sitting up in his canopied bed in the shadows surrounding the small kelistar gleaming on its nightstick beside the bed. No ledge, no Maddie, no blood. . . . But as soon as his wits returned, he recalled the real incident in his library only hours ago and his gut cramped. Lurching up from the bed, he snatched the washbasin from atop the side cabinet and vomited into it.

When he was done, he found Haldon at his side, offering a glass of water.

He took it without meeting the other man's gaze, aware of Jared standing wide-eyed just inside the back bedchamber door. Durstan and Smyth stood behind the boy in the shadowy back hall. Abramm said nothing to any of them as he rinsed out his mouth and wiped his lips with a trembling hand. He rinsed again and handed the glass back. Then he stood staring at the floor, forcing himself to take deep, slow breaths as he grimly pushed back the terror.

"Is it spore, my lord?" Haldon said in a low voice.

"No."

"Something you ate, then?"

"Leave me alone, Hal."

The chamberlain departed like a wraith, leaving the king to step onto his balcony again, where dawn was just beginning to lighten the cloud-bound sky. He felt like a rag, soaked and wrung out again, twisted and trembling and weak. If he'd had the strength he might have gone down to the lake for a row. As it was he contented himself with pacing until gradually he began to feel himself again. And knew what he must do. He stopped and stood staring out over the city and the pewter ribbon of the River Kalladorne, dull and muted in the growing light of a gray day. Rain scent hung in the air.

Oh, my Lord . . . he wailed inwardly. *If there is any other way . . .*

But there was not. His dream had made that clear. The next time . . . . But there must not *be* a next time. He had only to figure out the details of his plan . . . and then maintain the nerve and strength of will to carry it out.

It would be the hardest thing he had ever done in his life.

———

Maddie had indeed waited until she heard Blackwell's footfalls recede, and then Abramm's after him. The protracted silence that ensued assured her he was waiting for her to depart, and finally she peered through the enspelled doorway into the deserted study. The servants' wait room still flickered with one dim light, but she slipped out without being discovered and returned to her chambers without seeing a soul.

If she thought her emotions on a wild sea before, it was nothing compared to now. The highs were glorious, so lofty, so powerfully exultant her flesh could hardly contain them. She sat on her bed, alone, and recalled the shock of seeing him standing in the library before her, followed by the warm rush of excitement as she'd realized he wasn't going to walk away like she expected. Recalled the rapture of feeling his fingers on her face and then his lips covering her own, his arms around her, her body turned to fire. Better than she had dreamed, by far. . . .

She soared on a crest of joy for what she had seen in his eyes: that her love was not one-sided. That, against all reason, he felt as she did. It was not delusion. It was real.

Then, even as she reveled in the wonder of that realization, touching her lips where his had touched them, trying to hold on to the magical memory . . . the other would intrude. The crashing table, the cold tendril of triumphed discovery that had wrenched them apart, the look of horrified realization on his face as he'd backed away.

"Forgive me, my lady. That never should have happened."

Perhaps it shouldn't have, but it had. And she could not regret it. Briellen had been monstrous to him ever since she'd arrived, but no less than this night. How could he marry her now?

But the question only started an entire chain of reasoning as to why he couldn't and why he could, and . . . the fact was, he felt that kiss never should have happened.

Which brought her to the lowest trough of her stormy emotional seas. For if he thought thus, he would have to act thus. Which meant he intended to go through with the marriage, cementing the treaty, sacrificing himself—and her—for the sake of his realm.

Sometime around dawn she fell asleep and didn't awake until Liza's voice intruded into her dreams. "My lady, please. Ye must wake up. The king has called for ye."

The king . . .

She woke at once, filled with dread, staring at her maid blankly.

"He's called ye to audience in half an hour, milady."

Maddie glanced at the mantel: almost ten o'clock. "Where?" she said, pushing back the cover and swinging her legs over the bedside. "In the throne room?"

"Nay. 'Tis informal. How could it not be, with him givin' ye only half an hour?"

Informal? Is that good or bad? Wondrous possibilities soared in her heart, matched with disturbing alternatives. But sitting here wondering wasn't going to answer questions.

Half an hour later she arrived at the king's apartments, entering through the front doors for a change, and was immediately shown into the sitting chamber. A moment later Admiral Hamilton emerged from the study, map case in hand. He gave her a bow, then continued on to the anteroom as her attention shifted to Abramm, who entered in his wake.

The king looked as if he had slept no more than she, for his face was pale and haggard, and shadows cupped his eyes. Even so, just being in the same room with him made her pulse race and heightened her every sense to an exquisite level of awareness.

They exchanged the pleasantries protocol demanded with an awkward correctness. Then he got to the point: "There's a guardstar in the fortress at Avramm's Landing, I'm told. I'd like you to go up there and look into it. There may be some books in their library, as well."

"Go up to Avramm's Landing?"

"As soon as possible. It's important that we figure out how to get that thing lit. If nothing else, Katahn's little demonstration showed me that. I was hoping perhaps you might be able to leave today, in fact." He smiled stiffly. "We have no time to lose. And I've got a vessel ready to move out this afternoon. I'm hoping you'll consent to be on it."

He looked right at her, his face that schooled mask of nothingness that could mean anything. "You did say you wanted to leave. This way you can satisfy us both. And it would probably be best for Briellen, as well."

By now the room was fluttering around her and her heart thundered in her chest. She glanced over her shoulder at the servants standing just inside the door, hesitated with a moment's uncertainty, then conjured a speaking cloak and took a step forward. He stared down at her with that maddeningly bland expression.

"So last night meant nothing, then?" she said finally, her voice tight and low.

His face did not change in the slightest. "I told you it never should have happened," he murmured, turning to the fire.

"But it did happen."

He nodded. "And because it must not happen again, I think it's best that you go."

She stared at him, feeling strangely hollow. "So you're really not interested in Avramm's Landing," she said finally. "I could just as well go on to the Western Isles."

"If that is your desire." He spoke quietly and continued to stare into the flames, their light flickering across his face, turning the scars red.

Anguish twisted in her chest. "I should have left weeks ago," she muttered. "And I should never have performed that song. That's what's made it all unravel."

"It would have unraveled anyway." He paused, still staring into the fire, then murmured, "Your song I will remember for the rest of my life."

And at that a sharp pain lodged itself in her throat and she found herself blinking back tears. From the first moment she'd realized she loved him, she'd known it would end like this. Even if it turned out he might actually love her, she'd known nothing would be changed. Kiriath needed the treaty, and Briellen was the only way to get it. It was just a horrible, impossible situation that had finally reached its inevitable and heartbreaking conclusion. And there was nothing she could do about it.

She swallowed the lump, then drew a deep breath to calm her quivering flesh and lifted her chin. "Very well," she said sturdily, amazed that her voice could come out so calm and even. "What time does the ship leave?"

He turned then to look down at her, surprise flickering across the unreadable mask. It was gone in an instant, everything turned to stone again— except for the tiny bunch of muscles that rippled at the corner of his jaw. After an interminable moment, he gave a nod, as if some deal had been closed, and turned again to the fire. "Four o'clock this afternoon," he said flatly.

By now she could scarcely hear for the roaring in her ears. But somehow her mouth was telling him she would pack her things at once. Dimly she heard him say he would send someone up with all the information, and also an escort to take her to the boat. She told him an escort would not be necessary, though she appreciated the kindness offered. Then, in the same mindless way as her mouth had spoken, her body curtseyed and walked her out of the room, through the antechamber and into the upper gallery, filled now with courtiers and supplicants eager to place their petitions before the king. *Don't you dare lose it here, Mad. You can't let them see your pain. They'll be laughing over it for years.*

Thus, she walked among them calmly, though she knew she must look dazed because she saw the eyes darting her way, saw the heads leaning toward one another, the quiet commentary exchanged. She heard none of it. Even the greetings made directly to her she perceived as meaningless babble, answering them by rote and moving on.

In this state she crossed the King's Court and climbed the stair to the west wing, until at long last she reached the safety of her own apartments. And there, the very moment she closed the door behind her, the world melted around her and she collapsed onto one of the green patterned divans. With her ears ringing and her head spinning, she put her hands to her face, and for the first time realized tears were streaming down her cheeks. *Oh, Eidon!* she thought, horrified. *Not in front of all of them!*

But then again, what difference would it make? She was leaving. Abramm was sending her away. He'd chosen Briellen. But she wondered why—when she'd always known he must—the reality could still hurt this much.

"Maddie?" Carissa's voice.

Oh, please, Father Eidon, send her away. I cannot face her.

But Eidon did not listen, and Carissa dropped onto the couch beside her to wrap an arm around her shoulders. "Maddie? What's wrong? What did he say to you?"

But she couldn't speak. For she knew that if she tried she would make a scene, and she desperately did not want to do that. Bad enough she had to leave. Bad enough she'd shown him her heart and he'd spurned it.

"Maddie, please. What has happened?"

And despite all intention to the contrary, Maddie found herself choking out the story.

———

After his cabinet meeting, Abramm changed into plain shirt and breeches, shrugged into a leather jerkin, and went down to row around the lake. It was cool beneath the low-hanging clouds, which were just starting to spit rain. He took only one bodyguard—today it was Philip—and set off to row the circuit, guaranteed, for the most part, of not being interrupted until he was done. Precious few of his courtiers had the desire or ability to row out and join him, and Trap said few would have the nerve anyway. It had become an aphorism around the court that if the king was rowing, you knew he was troubled.

Usually he had the stimulation of cabinet meetings and courtier petitions to keep his mind off things he'd rather not think about. Today, they'd only irritated him. Today, he'd had a hard time paying attention to anything, and he reflected grimly that his inattention had not gone unnoticed. No one had said anything openly, of course, but he seemed to be asking his people to repeat a lot, and guessed there'd been a number of times things had been repeated even when he hadn't asked.

Now he fell into the familiar, comfortable rhythm, his boat leaping forward—backward from his perspective—in eager response to the strength of his pulling. His left hand could not grip the oar well enough to keep hold of it, so he had had a special leather sleeve made for the handle that was attached to a glove with a leather wrist thong. In essence the contraption tied his hand to the oar so he could work it.

Knowing the lake well enough by now—he could row with his back to the direction of his progress and still navigate perfectly—he skirted the west bank without noticing. The creak of the oars in the locks, the drip of water from the oar blades, the faint groaning of the vessel's wooden hull as it moved through the water—these were welcome sounds after the chaotic chatter of the cabinet meeting and the palace halls. No one asking him anything, no one expecting a decision, no one here but Philip, who knew to pretend he was not here.

Abramm's interview with Maddie kept cycling through his mind, shriveling his heart with every repetition. The way he'd been so cool and businesslike, wincing at the pain in her voice even as she'd tried to hide it. He'd known she would challenge him about last night, that she knew him too well to ever believe it had been nothing. But they had to behave as if it were—especially him. Her mention of the song had rattled him, but it was the moment when she'd acquiesced that had nearly done him in. Of course she would understand, of course there would not be hysterics and pleading and rivers of tears. Of course she would jerk up that chin and agree . . . and in that moment the words to stop it all had been at the tip of his tongue.

It was only the vision of her dead in his arms that gave him the power to go on. The vision and the certain knowledge that she was meant for someone else, because he was meant for no one.

Still, there were moments he could hardly believe he was doing this, for it didn't seem possible life could go on without her. Moments when the desire to put an end to the whole mad plan nearly overwhelmed him.

Just a few more hours now. If he could hold on a few more hours it would be done . . . and this constant nagging of guilt and desire would finally be silenced. There would be no more action he could take. She would be gone and he would be free of her. Free to concentrate on his wedding. On his regalia. On his fortresses.

"Sir?" Philip's quiet voice broke into his thoughts. "Princess Carissa is standing out on the north dock. Looks like she might be waiting for you."

Abramm glanced over his shoulder and almost swore aloud. He had no illusions as to what she might want to talk about. But avoiding her would serve nothing. He knew she would simply ride to the other side of the lake and await him when he finished. She would have her say. He might as well get it over with.

Thus he rowed silently up to the dock, excused Philip from further service, and Carissa took the young man's place. She did not sit at the boat's prow as Philip had, however, but came to sit on the thwart at its stern so she didn't have to talk to Abramm's back. They exchanged a minimal greeting, then he rowed off again.

When they were well away from the dock, Carissa said quietly, "I've spoken with Maddie."

Abramm kept rowing and said nothing.

She frowned at him, but he fixed his gaze on the mist-veiled trees at her back. Finally, seeing he wasn't going to cooperate, she huffed her irritation and burst out, "What the plague are you doing, Abramm? And don't waste your breath telling *me* you care nothing for her. She told me what you did in the library last night."

Abramm gritted his teeth and felt the blood rush into his face, felt his stomach knotting even more tightly than it already was. Coming to the end of his stroke, he lifted the oars enough to tuck the right briefly under his left hand so he could conjure a cloaking spell with his right. Voices carried far too well across the water on a day as still as this. As the faint chiming settled around them, he returned both hands to the oars and finally looked her in the eye. "Last night was a brief aberration that by Eidon's grace alone did not develop into outright disaster."

Her brows drew together. "Last night was something that's been building to a head for months, Abramm. Don't talk to *me* of brief aberrations."

Now it was Abramm's turn to scowl, feeling his irritation rise at this sudden bout of big-sisterly bossiness. "Well, whatever it was, it doesn't matter. I said I'd marry Briellen, and that's what I'm going to do."

The oars squealed in the locks as he began to row again.

"Briellen loathes you. Which she's stupidly revealed to the entire court and in the process lost whatever friends she's made herself."

"We're not required to love one another."

"Well, I don't see that you're required to *marry* one another, either. Rewrite the stupid treaty without that part. And if Hadrich fears his daughter falling into Belthre'gar's hands, tell him she'd be better off not married to you anyway, since Regar would want her for that reason alone. If he knows you don't love her, he won't even bother with her."

"She's the First Daughter of Chesedh, Carissa. She has worth to him from that standpoint, too."

"So you'll cast out the woman you love to protect that vicious harridan from Belthre'gar? What sense does that make? If you're going to protect someone, shouldn't it be Maddie?"

I am protecting her, he thought. But Carissa wouldn't understand, and he wasn't about to explain it. And so he said, "This isn't about protection."

"You just said it was. That you were marrying Bree to protect her."

"No, *you* said that. I'm marrying Briellen because I said I would."

"That's an even stupider reason."

He rowed on in silence.

After a few strokes she pressed him. "Leyton's heard the gossip by now and no doubt senses the turning of the court's attitude toward her. If he has a brain at all, he's rightfully worrying she's soured the whole deal. Give him an offer, and he'll probably fall over backwards trying to accommodate you."

"Perhaps he would."

For a time the only sounds were the creaks and the squeaks and the rhythmic dripping of the water. Carissa waited expectantly, her eyes continuously darting over his shoulder toward the southern dock, which he knew from the lay of the land and the character of the foliage was rapidly approaching at his back.

Finally seeing he was not going to answer her, she burst out, "Why are you doing this, Abramm? It's like you're trying to punish yourself. What man in his right mind would bind himself to a woman who's publicly declared she despises him? It's insane."

"That may be, but it's not really your concern, now, is it?" he said, looking her straight in the eye.

Her face tightened and her eyes flashed. As he lifted the oars, letting the boat's momentum carry them on toward the dock, she uttered a cry of frustration. "You're every bit as muleheaded as Father was! Well, fine, then. Destroy your life if you're so set on it. But know that you'll destroy Maddie's in the process. And likely Briellen's, too."

He unwrapped the wrist strap and drew his left hand from its glove as she spoke, then drew both oars from their locks and laid them alongside the gunwale. As the boat bumped up against the dock, he turned to cast up the rope to the men waiting there, one of whom was Trap. As the rope was snugged to a piling, he released the cloaking spell and turned to help Carissa up the ladder, but she knocked away his hands and climbed it herself. He swung up after her without comment.

Trap clearly hoped to speak to him, too, but Abramm pushed past him as if he weren't there, stopping a little farther on so the servant could lay his cloak about his shoulders. But then he strode away up the graveled path toward the palace before the others could catch up.

Later that afternoon, he went down to the wharf to watch Maddie leave. By then it was raining steadily, but he took no shelter, watching from a distance as she boarded the longboat that would bear her out to the merchantman he'd booked her passage on. He'd thought he couldn't feel much worse than he had this morning when he'd asked her to go, but he did. As he stood watching her, it seemed as if something vital were being torn out of him, inch by inch, in a long, slow torture. He kept wanting to call out and stop her.

But every time he came close to faltering, he remembered the image of her lying dead in his arms in the pool of her own blood. That would be the price she'd pay for loving him. He'd done it to one woman. He wasn't doing it to another.

Once aboard the longboat, she sat in the stern looking back over her shoulder, cowl cast back, hair darkened by the rain and plastered to her skull. She was weeping, though how he knew that he could not answer. Any tears would surely be carried away by the water sheeting down her face, and she was too far away for him to see her expression.

Even so, as the boat slid away from the dock, he felt as if she were staring right at him. It was almost as if she recognized him, though he knew that was not possible. He'd been careful to disguise himself in commoner's clothing, wrapped in a cloak of dark wool, his face hidden beneath its cowl. For the same reason, he stood alone in the rain, his guards hidden from her sight. Because it wouldn't help her to know he stood here. Wouldn't help her at all to know how much he loved her and that he did this thing because of that love.

He stood there until the boat had reached the merchantman, watching as she and her maid and the two retainers she'd contracted to escort her were all borne up to the deck, along with their gear. Then, as the longboat headed back to shore, he saw the activity aboard the bigger ship increase as men climbed the masts to adjust the sails. He heard the call to weigh anchor, then the rhythmic clanking as it was drawn up. Finally the ship began to move. He imagined he saw a dark-robed figure standing at its stern staring back at him, though that was, of course, ridiculous.

But still he stood there, waiting in the rain, his cloak long since soaked through, the clothing beneath it drenched. Stood there until the vessel disappeared at last around the western headland and she was gone.

THIRD

WARM AND DRY IN his coach where it stood parked on the lowest landing of the Avenue of the Keep, Hazmul had watched the two of them from the time they'd come down to the dock until the *Starchaser* slid out of sight behind Graymeer's Point.

Only then did the tall, dark-cloaked figure that had come to stand at the end of the pier turn and head back to his own coach, hidden behind the buildings on the main dock. His bodyguards, nearly as soaked as he, emerged from their hiding places and hurried along in his wake, revealing the truth of who he was to those who had eyes to see. Which, on this gray, rainy afternoon, were few indeed.

Smiling, Hazmul pulled down the wooden shade and blocked out the rainy tableau. Then he knocked on the wall beside him to signal his driver. As he pulled his lap blanket up around his shoulders, he heard the clunk of the brake being released, then the slap of the reins and the muted call to the team to "get up." The coach lurched into motion.

Well, that was far easier than I thought it would be . . . though it really was too bad we couldn't have caught them in the act. That would have been such fun.

Their discovery was not essential in the bigger picture, however. Once Abramm found out how badly he'd been betrayed by the woman for whom he'd just given up everything, he'd be devastated. The treaty would be ruined beyond rescue, and the chance of him uniting with the woman he truly loved all but nonexistent. Indeed, if events progressed as Hazmul hoped, it would very soon *be* nonexistent, for she would be dead.

He smiled. Yes, it had been a decent bit of work. The next few days would be quite amusing. And the wedding . . . Well, he very much doubted there would be a wedding.

THE
GULL
ISLANDS

PART THREE

24

At long last Gillard had been allowed to venture out of his second-floor chamber to walk around the ancient stone-walled keep. With Prittleman— Brother Honarille—hovering at his side, he had carefully descended the winding stairway, crossed through a deserted great room and stepped into the Watch's cloister garden.

Most of the brothers and acolytes were out of the keep itself, working the Watch's larger summer garden situated down the hill. The extensive plot being the source of much of their food for the year, every hand was expected to contribute to the effort, leaving Gillard free to walk inside for a bit without worry of being seen.

Not that anyone would recognize me, if they did, he thought bitterly.

The cloister garden was bounded on three sides by two stories of living and meditation cubicles beneath a sloping slate roof. Within its sheltered confines, the old elm and apple trees outpaced their wilder cousins, branches already budding with new growth. On the ground, the green tips of crocus and daffodil had already poked through the ancient mulch, bright accents against a gray tumble of rambling woody stems. He heard the distant cackle of the Watch's chickens, smelled the pungent odor of the milk goats. Overhead, silhouetted among a network of skeletal branches against a clear blue sky, a mockingbird sang its rambling song.

With Honarille at his side, Gillard shuffled along the circular garden path. Its stone pavers, buckled by age and rising tree roots, were treacherous enough he was bitterly hesitant to chase Honarille off. Another fall could be disastrous.

His right hand was now bound to a board that held it flat. Fortunately, only the last two fingers and the corresponding long bones in his palm had broken, although in several places. The limb would not be totally crippled, but there would be a significant reduction of usage.

He tried not to think about that, for it made him feel like a bit of flotsam carried along by a mighty current that did not care whether it shattered him against the rocks, flung him off a cliff, or pulled him under to be drowned. Never had he felt so helpless—betrayed by his own flesh, which every day revealed some additional frailty.

Brother Honarille suspected all Gillard's bones to be equally brittle, their substance drained away along with muscle and skin. "You'll have to be careful. Something as simple as coming down wrong off a step could break your leg."

Gillard wasn't sure he believed that, but neither did he want to test it. Nor did he express any lament at this new revelation, knowing it would only elicit another declaration of Eidon's restorative powers and renewed pressure for Gillard to take formal vows in his service.

Now, as they walked, Honarille chattered brightly, relating some of the ridiculous stories that had been coming up from Springerlan about Abramm. That at his coronation the regalia had manifested and driven away the mist around Graymeer's to reveal an Esurhite invasion attempt. That there'd been healings . . . That the border lords' revered Hasmal'uk stone had been turned to gold. Worst of all—and this one he knew was likely true—the Chesedhan princess Abramm was to marry had arrived and was said to be even more beautiful than her reputation claimed. Which, of course, had to be a result of her Chesedhan witchcraft. "They say she's completely captivated the court," Honarille told him. "He's supposed to marry her in three days."

Perhaps Honarille understood what that statement would do to him, but Gillard was entirely unprepared for the consuming rage. It was so unfair that he should be hiding up here, shrunken and fragile, while Abramm received the realm's accolades and married the most beautiful woman in the land. For a moment Gillard wished he really believed Eidon did exist just so he could vent some of this fury at him.

It took him a while to calm down. As they looped back to the place they'd entered the garden, he saw a man dressed in Guardian gray seated on the stone bench beside the door to the Great Room. He was old, of medium height and stringy build, with a long, fat, frizzy gray braid and a receding hairline. Gillard supposed him to be communing with his god.

But as they approached, the man glanced up and stood to meet them. Only when they stopped and Honarille bowed his head and murmured a respectful "Master" did Gillard realize this was Master Amicus, head of the Watch. The man had visited him in his room a couple of times, and now he recognized the bold forehead and freckled, age-spotted face. Small blue eyes crouched between red rims, glistening with tears that arose not from sentiment but from some ailment that caused his eyes to water constantly.

Wonder why Eidon hasn't healed him, Gillard thought irreverently.

"Master Amicus," Gillard said, giving him a nod.

"Welcome t' Haverall's Watch, Gillard."

His greeting took Gillard aback. No "my prince" or "my lord." Not even a "sir." Just "Gillard." He could hardly remember when he'd last been called by his given name unadorned. Even Uncle Simon had not presumed such an air of familiarity save when he was sorely disturbed.

If Amicus noticed Gillard's surprise, he gave no indication of it, proceeding with the usual opening conversational gambits of asking about his health and how his quarters suited him. Eventually, though, he came round to his agenda.

"The king's men're coming. Prob'ly be here in the next day or two. Searchin' every house an' barn an' sheepcote in the valley. Even the wells do na escape their eye. Word says they're going through the keeps top to bottom, broom closet to pantry to privy chamber, na even respectin' the sanctity of the prayer rooms."

"Well, seeing as their master has cast your own High Father into prison, that's hardly surprising," Gillard remarked.

Amicus bowed his head. "Ye see our problem, then."

"With keeping me here, I presume."

"Aye." He paused. "If ye was to take a place among us, however . . ."

Take a place among them? Am I not already among them. . . ? Oh. "You mean as an acolyte," he said aloud.

"Aye."

Gillard flung an irritated glance at Honarille, then smiled at Amicus. "Not in a thousand years."

"An acolyte is na vow bound, save t' the eight years of service he's promised. At the end of that time, ye'd be free t' go yer way. . . . And in the meantime stay safely anonymous among us."

"Even eight months would be too long for me." Gillard looked again at Honarille. "I can't believe you thought I'd even consider this."

"They'll be comin' here," said Amicus, "and they will find ye."

"So I'll ride out into the woods while they're here."

"Ye dare not risk ridin', son." The old man's watery eyes dipped to Gillard's board-bound hand. "And anyway, they'd just find ye easier that way. Surely ye've seen we haven't much in the way o' woods around here."

"Hide me in your wine cellar, then, or . . . Wait, you don't have one of those, do you?"

"Even if we did, it wouldna serve ye, son. They're searchin' ever'where." He paused. "The best solution is to lose yerself among us."

The best solution for me? Or for you, Master Amicus? It had just dawned on Gillard that Amicus wasn't concerned simply with protecting him. In fact, that was undoubtedly the lesser of the Master's interests. He feared what would befall him and his keep should Gillard be discovered here. As Gillard himself had just pointed out, if Abramm had the gall to imprison the highest man in their organization, he wasn't likely to balk at punishing some lowly Guardian Master.

"I can't imagine how I would fit in, Master Amicus," Gillard said finally. "I'm hardly acolyte material."

"P'rhaps not inwardly, but outwardly, ye'd fit in quite well." Again he paused. "I'm na sure you're aware just how greatly yer travails have altered yer appearance."

Gillard grimaced, displeased by this reminder of a subject he preferred not to contemplate. "If I'm that changed, why bother at all? I'll just lie in my bed and you can tell them I've got the grippe. Or the plague, if you like."

"They're lookin' especially fer a man abed."

"Well, then, I guess I'll have to find help elsewhere, for I have no interest in taking vows of any kind. Save perhaps to have my kingdom back and get revenge upon the one who stole it from me."

Amicus's watery eyes fixed upon him shrewdly. "Not even if the one may enable ye t' fulfill the other?"

Gillard frowned at him. "I don't think you understand, Master. I don't believe in your Flames, or your purpose. I don't even believe in Eidon."

Amicus regarded him soberly. "Would it help if I suggested that belief is na a prerequisite fer the taking o' the vows?"

"How can I swear to serve a god I don't believe exists?"

"In truth or in pretense, ye still serve."

Gillard felt his eyebrows rise.

"The Heartland is Mataian country. Right now, they trust ye no more than they do Abramm. If ye were t' do this . . . they'd rally round ye by the hundreds."

"I thought I was supposed to be in hiding. I thought that was the whole purpose of your suggestion in the first place. If word gets out I've come and taken vows here, the king's men will surely come, so what would be the point?"

"I didna mean to suggest we'd reveal yer presence now, o' course. But in due time the truth *will* get out, passed quietly from supporter t' supporter. A secret knowledge. A secret hope. To the king it'd be no more than a rumor he surely expects will arise. And all the time ye spend serving as humble acolyte without it being common knowledge will only accredit yer cause the more."

"So you want me to take a vow to a god I don't believe in, abase myself to become his acolyte and spend the next eight years living a lie?"

Amicus smiled. "P'rhaps 'twill turn out t' be more truth than lie."

Gillard snorted. "I wouldn't hold my breath." He shook his head. "I've always believed you holy men were a duplicitous bunch. I just didn't think you were so deliberate about it."

"What'er the Flames require . . . sir." Amicus allowed himself a small, amused smile. "I will await yer answer. And remind ye that the sooner it comes, the better fer all of us."

———

As tears once more blurred the print before her, Lady Madeleine dropped her head back against the wooden side of the window seat in *Starchaser*'s large stern cabin and gave up trying to read. They were five days out of Springerlan, and even when she could actually see the words, she couldn't concentrate on them. But no matter how many times she berated herself for her lack of discipline and swore she would not allow herself to think of Abramm any further, each succeeding phrase just sent her back to him. It was as if he had filled all her mind, had so pervaded her soul she could do nothing without it reminding her in some way of him. His smile, his level brows, his broad shoulders, those blue, blue eyes, his strong, beautiful hands . . . his voice . . . his mind . . . his lips upon hers.

She closed her eyes, feeling the ache rise in her again, trying to head it off with reason—*you could never be queen of the realm and don't want that anyway*—trying to find the Light before the grief took her . . . and failing, as always. It was like sliding down an ice-coated hill, swooping into a misery that only gained intensity with the fall. Once she'd started down it, there was no stopping until it left her numb and gasping at the bottom. Where guilt would flail her for putting herself at the mercy of feelings that weren't remotely rational—again.

At least she'd managed to keep from weeping aloud. And the spells were not lasting so long anymore.

When this one passed, she took a deep, hiccuping breath and wiped her face with her hands, annoyed with herself but reminded anew that she wasn't nearly so strong as she'd thought she was. She glanced at the book in her lap and decided she'd be better off with the Words and her notes from Terstmeet.

A little later, she was just settling back on the padded bench with book and notes when her eye caught on something outside the wide, multipaned stern window. The day had been misty, raining off and on, the sea a dull gray in the late afternoon. A dark runner of coastline crouched to her left, and out in the distance loomed the black shapes of the rocky islands and monoliths through which they had just come, veiled like everything else with a thin curtain of mist. Set against them, almost in line with the white furrow of *Starchaser*'s wake, hung a thicker bit of cloud, probably a squall, from the look of it.

Rain began to fall again, obliterating the view as it drummed on the deck overhead and pocked the surrounding sea, a curtain of silvery streaks that triggered the unwelcome memory of the man on the dock the day she'd left Springerlan. The one who'd stood at the end of the pier alone in the rain, watching as the longboat had borne her out to *Starchaser*. She'd had no reason to think he was Abramm, but even so, as the gap of gray water had widened between them, she'd wept unrestrainedly. Once aboard the merchantman, she'd refused her servants' urgings to take shelter and had gone to the vessel's stern to find him still on the pier; she had stared at him until she could see him no more.

Only when she finally turned away had the pain hit her—so intense it took her breath away, so deep she thought it would kill her then and there. She must have cried out, for Liza and Peter were beside her in moments, urging her again to come out of the rain.

In the captain's spacious stern cabin, which he'd vacated for her comfort, she'd stood like a sleepwalker as Liza stripped off her drenched garments and clothed her in a warmed bedgown of soft, thick silk. After a supper of hot broth and soft bread, of which she ate very little, her maid put her to bed. She did not waken for twenty-four hours.

When she did, she'd only wanted to go back to sleep and never wake again. On the second day, she'd not left her bed, and it wasn't until the morning of their third day at sea that she'd taken herself to task and demanded she stop all this woe-mongering. She had lost many things in her life, seen many hopes die, and never had she been one to lie weeping in a puddle of self-pity. That she did it now for love of a man she could never have was abhorrent to her, and she refused to let herself continue in it any longer. Not only was it a total violation of the person she prided herself on being, it was an insult to Eidon, who surely could have stopped all this had it been his will.

And anyway, she really and truly did not want to marry a king. The responsibility of that position combined with the loss of freedom would make it a jail sentence. Indeed, she'd probably bring down the nation with her missteps and blunt ways; certainly she'd make many enemies. Abramm sending her away had been a blessing for both of them, and it was time to put all that behind her and move on.

So she'd arisen and washed, dressed, eaten, taken a walk about the deck, talked cheerfully with the captain at some length about the ship and the shore and the weather, and then had gone below to crack open the books on the Western Isles she'd brought to prepare herself for her new life.

Days later she was still reading the same introductory pages without comprehending one word that she read. The only things that could hold her interest were the Words of Eidon, and even that didn't always work.

Now she stared blindly out the small, rain-pecked panes at the rain-swept afternoon. *Face it: he is not the man for you, nor is that the life Eidon has chosen for you. And you know very well, whenever Eidon says no to something, it's because he has something better.*

Something better. That was what she must hang on to. To keep recalling, over and over, that he had control of her life, that he loved her, that none of this was surprising to him and all was working out as it should. This brief bit of pain, mostly the result of her own headstrong desire to have her will rather than embrace his, would in the end work out for her benefit. Just like Abramm, she had a destiny. What it was, she did not know, but sooner or later Eidon would show it to her. And when he did, when she finally walked into it, the Words promised her that it would make all this turmoil worthwhile. She just had to be patient and keep on living in the Light.

She drew a deep breath, feeling a semblance of peace again and taking comfort in the realization that these moments were coming more often of late . . . that it wouldn't be long before this was over. As soon as she arrived in Avramm's Landing, she planned to book passage to the Western Isles, hopefully leaving within the week. A two-month voyage would be just the thing to close out this unfortunate chapter in her—

She frowned and sat forward, peering through the glass. The rain had stopped, and with its passing she saw that the clot of mist still swirled in *Starchaser*'s wake. Had, in fact, gained on them. Moreover, she thought she'd seen something in it. At first she supposed it was a rock, but on further reflection realized *Starchaser* would have sailed close by it not long ago, and she'd seen nothing of the kind.

Though you weren't exactly paying attention, she told herself dryly.

Still, the more she watched it, the more inexplicably threatened she felt. Finally she went up to the quarterdeck for a different view of it, figuring at the least the captain could assure her it was indeed a rock.

Instead Captain Windemere told her they typically gave the rocks wide berth. "But let us put the spyglass to this mystery."

Surprisingly willing to accommodate her vague suspicion, he peered at the mist clot with his telescope for some time before handing the glass to her with a regretful shake of his head. She studied the mist even longer than he had, but nothing untoward revealed itself. Finally her aching arms could lift the glass no longer, and she gave up.

"Sorry for the false alarm," she said, embarrassed as she handed the glass tube back to him. He took it soberly, slid it shut, and told her " 'twas no trouble at all. I appreciate the extra eyes."

It was his smile that made her realize he, like Liza, was simply happy to see her up and showing interest in something besides her troubles. When she asked what else it might have been if not rock, he was diplomatic enough not to say imagination and speculated it could have been a whale or small fishing boat. At which point he eyed the cloud again. "Though I must admit, it is odd how it's hung together so long. . . ."

She turned to look again herself. "And the way it's following us."

He frowned but faced his ship again, glancing up at the rigging, where the sails swelled before the afternoon breeze.

She asked him then of the fortress at Avramm's Landing, and he happily shared his knowledge, though much of what he told her she already knew. Avramm, a captain in the Ophiran emperor's personal guard, and a devout Terstan, had been at sea heading for Hasmal'uk when he was hit by the great Cataclysm unleashed by the sinking of the Ophiran Heartland. The massive wave had shattered his four ships to flotsam and hurled him and a handful of his crew ashore near an old imperial fortress with a guardstar that was slowly dying. Avramm had re-ignited it, casting back the darkness that had gripped the region for centuries, and as a result eventually became king of Hasmul'uk. The guardstar had gone out again sometime during the Middle Years of Kiriathan history, but no one knew why. Nor how to relight it.

In the midst of Windemere's enthusiastic recitation of this history, his first mate approached from the taffrail and stood at his side, waiting to be acknowledged. Maddie noticed that he kept glancing backward, but she refrained from doing so herself until the captain finally wound down and turned to his subordinate. "What is it, Mr. White?"

"Cap'n . . . that cloud you and the lady was looking at earlier? I think there's something in it." He paused, looking uncomfortable. "More than that, sir. I been watching it for over an hour and I believe it's following us."

"Something in it?" Windemere asked. "You mean like a vessel of some sort?"

"Yes, sir."

The captain frowned. "How could it make the cloud stay around it as it follows us, mister?"

"I don't know, sir."

"I do," said Maddie soberly.

The men turned to her in question.

"Esurhites," she said.

They exchanged a quick glance; then Windemere looked up at the sails. And in the fading light of the late afternoon, Maddie could see the breeze was faltering.

25

Two days before the royal wedding, the Duke of Northille stood in the second-floor bedchamber of his new house in the prestigious Bayview district of Springerlan, threading his arms into the sleeves of the short-waisted jacket his valet held up behind him. In front of him, his tailor carefully folded into its linen wrapper his new suit in progress, which he had just tried on for its last fitting. Arms now in the jacket's sleeves, Trap started to shrug the garment up over his shoulders, then stopped as he remembered to let the valet do it for him.

"I'll have it ready for you by eight tomorrow morning, sir," said the tailor.

"Excellent," Trap replied. He left the man gathering his pincushions, chalk, and tape measures into a satchel and stepped into the hall outside, bemused. *I have a tailor. When, in all my life, would I ever have imagined I'd have a tailor?*

And more than a tailor. He had a personal secretary, an accountant, a couple of lawyers, a handful of personal servants, more than a handful of domestic servants, grooms, stableboys, several fine horses, a burgeoning wardrobe, and a home in a district populated by the richest men in Springerlan. His own home, not leased. And this was only a temporary residence.

The stair he descended was carpeted with a fine Sorian runner, the walls beside it richly paneled, and the spacious antechamber below dominated by an expensive crystal chandelier. At the foot of the stair he stepped aside as a pair of movers came through the open front door with the fine bedstead he'd just purchased and began jockeying it up the stairs. He had slept on a pallet last night, as much for the pleasure of sleeping in his own house as to get away from the king's foul temper, increasing now in inverse proportion to the number of days left before his wedding. Tonight it would be the feather bed.

"Sir?"

He turned to his doorman, who stood holding a basket of fruit. "This just came from your sister. Her servant's asking when would be a good time for her and her husband to come over."

Trap grimaced. His older sister had been content to ignore him for almost all his thirty-two years of life. Now that he was a duke, however, she'd become suddenly friendly, barraging him with unwanted gifts, cards, and invitations. Two days ago, mere hours after his secretary had closed the deal on this house, she'd waylaid him in the palace, lamenting that she and her husband could not afford the rent where they were staying. Might he know of more suitable lodgings?

He'd offered his new home, of course, and then his other sister had found out and sent him her own notice—not request, but notice—that they'd be arriving on the eve of the wedding. So now, in addition to having his father, mother, and Philip on hand for the many gatherings he had slated for the next week, he would also have to contend with his two sisters and their children. At least his other two sisters were likely to remain in the Heartland, where they lived with their very large families. Should they somehow manage to arrive for the wedding, he would certainly have a houseful.

Which both irritated him and pummeled him with guilt for not feeling more generous about it all. It wasn't as if he deserved any of what he had, so why shouldn't he share it with them, his blood relatives? They were sisters to a duke now, and from the look of things, they were reveling in his change of station even more than he was.

He gave a time to the doorman, then went into the dining room to eat his breakfast. He was nearly finished when his secretary poked his head around the dining room door. "The Princess Carissa is here, sir. She was out and about and decided to drop by with a housewarming gift. Vernault has taken her to the drawing room."

A housewarming gift?

Carissa had, in fact, been the one to find him this house. Simon had helped him with recommendations of secretary and accountant, both of whom had seen to the rest. Within two weeks of his being elevated to the peerage, he'd acquired a veritable retinue of employees and he'd hardly had to do a thing.

She stood in the sparsely furnished drawing room supervising the unwrapping of the very large painting she had brought. Though he'd only moved in yesterday, already the still-uncarpeted room held two divans, three chairs, a sideboard, and a small table. Lace sheers hung at tall, eight-paned windows in the front and side walls, the trees that surrounded his house showing as dark ghostly forms through the fabric. A clock already stood on the elaborately carved mantel above the fireplace, where the servants had kindled a blaze for his unexpected guest.

She turned to him the moment he entered, lighting up his day with her smile. "Ah, Duke Eltrap. Good morning to you, sir."

At least Trap was getting used to that moniker and no longer felt the urge to turn and look for someone standing behind him. "Good morning, Your Highness."

"Don't worry. I know about your meeting with the Heartlanders from your duchy this morning, so I'll not keep you long."

He cocked a brow at her. "You are certainly following my affairs with a close eye, Highness."

She smiled. "Have to keep track of our up-and-coming young statesman. And you are quite the talk of the town these days, you know. Even Oswain Nott managed to parcel you a grudging bit of praise for your diplomatic ways."

Trap grunted and turned his attention to the huge canvas emerging from its wrappings. He felt his eyebrows lift with surprise. It was a storm-swept scene of two armies faced off in a field by the sea. "*Prelude to the Hollyhock*," he said, looking up at her in astonishment.

Her smiled broadened. "I've watched you eyeing it for months."

"But it was hanging in your own drawing room—"

"I've already put up its replacement. Young Nash has finished the consignment piece I ordered. Did a fabulous job, too."

"But . . . you said you loved this one."

"Aye, and I expect you to hang it over your mantel so I can see it every time I come to visit." Her eyes twinkled.

"Well, then, by all means, that's where it will hang." He gestured for the servants to see to it, then said, "You didn't have to deliver this personally, Your Highness."

"I wanted to enjoy your expression. And also to get it to you before your evening soirees start in earnest next week. I do believe you've scheduled one nearly every night."

He released a deep breath. "Yes. I'm afraid I have." With men coming down from all over the realm to attend the wedding, he'd set himself the goal of meeting and conversing with as many of them as he could—and already was beginning to think it was a task beyond his ability to execute.

The servants had pulled over a step stool, and one climbed it to hammer in a nail and lift the painting into place. He then stepped down and they all stood back to assess it.

"So," Carissa said. "What do you think?"

And standing there in the middle of his new drawing room, with its gleaming parquet floors, fancy wallpaper, fine furnishings, and now this incredible piece of art, Trap was beset with another of those disorienting moments when it felt as if he'd somehow fallen into another man's life. Tailors and secretaries, new suits and feather beds, paintings that belonged in the royal gallery. . . . None of it seemed real.

She was regarding him quizzically. "What?"

He shook his head. "Sometimes I just get overwhelmed with how my life has changed. I know Eidon's promised to reward those who honor him, but seeing it fulfilled like this . . . I guess I never really thought it could happen to me."

"You are living most men's dreams, sir. And you give the rest of us hope that—" she smiled almost sadly, then looked down at her hands—"maybe someday our dreams will be realized, too."

After six months of getting to know her, he understood how much she longed for a husband and children, and also just how dim the prospect of having either looked to her. Oswain Nott held sufficient rank to go with his obvious desire to fill the role, but Carissa continued to keep him at arm's length. Simon Kalladorne, also a duke, was her uncle, and Crown Prince Leyton was too distasteful, even assuming anyone would countenance a second Kiriathan-Chesedhan union. Beyond that there was no one else.

Except himself. When Nott had suggested it last week, he'd laughed it off. But somehow the notion had stayed on at the back of his mind. For he couldn't deny his own interest in her—one birthed and discarded over seventeen years ago when, as a young squire to Prince Raynen, he'd first met her, a fairy princess far out of the reach of a swordmaster's son. . . .

Seeing that the painting was satisfactory, the servants left the two of them staring up at the work. "It reminds me of the tale you and Abramm fought in the Val'Orda that last time," she said presently.

"That's why I like it. Reminds *me* of Eidon's power to deliver."

They stood there a moment more, and then she sighed and sank into one of the chairs. "I wish he'd deliver Abramm from this marriage," she said sourly.

"Well, at least his bride's been acting better this week." In fact, the day after Madeleine left, Briellen had apologized—publicly and very prettily—for her dreadful behavior the night of Katahn's reception and ever after had been excruciatingly sweet and biddable. It seemed not to matter one whit that Abramm wasn't responding. Though to be fair, Abramm had been very attentive and kind to her, not blunt and rude as he was with those closest to him.

"He doesn't love her, Trap," Carissa said.

"They can still make a marriage of it." Trap settled into the chair beside her.

"Not when she knows he's in love with her sister. She may resign herself to it, but she'll never forgive him." Carissa shook her head. "There's something dark in her. It's scary. And she's so emotional—you never know what she'll do. He's a fool if he goes through with this."

Trap frowned, for he'd thought many of the same things.

"Have you *ever* seen him more miserable?" Carissa asked.

"Not since he was a slave . . . though that was such a torment for the body, it left little room for torments of the soul. I thought he was going to die then, though. I don't think he's going to do that now."

"Except on the inside."

He sighed and looked at the painting again. "He has Eidon."

"Does he?" She leaned toward him, drawing his attention back to herself. "Do you really think this is what Eidon would have him do? Because, to me, it seems more like he's trying to punish himself. He seemed almost happy when I told him Briellen hated him. And even he's got to see that the Chesedhans need this alliance much more than we do. *We* should be the angry ones threatening to break it off. Yet he won't even consider asking them to bend on this." She hesitated. "I'd talk to him myself, but since he didn't listen to me the first time, I can't see why he would now."

Her unspoken request hung in the air between them. Trap shifted uncomfortably, the chair squeaking with his movement.

"Isn't that why he made you First Minister?" she prodded when he didn't speak. "So you could tell him things like this?"

She was right. More than that, he was Abramm's closest friend. That standing alone demanded he speak. For while Carissa had no idea why Abramm might be trying to punish himself, Trap did. In fact, she'd just voiced one side of an argument Trap had been having with himself since the night he'd escorted Briellen back to her chambers. He was just afraid to broach the subject. Given the response he'd gotten to his opinion regarding Abramm's crippled arm, he didn't look forward to what would come his way should he challenge Abramm on a matter about which he'd be even more sensitive.

Still, he had to say something.

"I'll try," he told her softly. "But don't expect anything to change."

————

At two o'clock that afternoon, Trap arrived at the palace for the meeting of the king's war council, overtaking Simon Kalladorne as he ascended the east-wing stairway.

"So how is he today?" he asked as he came abreast of the man.

The Duke of Waverlan grimaced. "He went rowing again this morning. Four times around. Already chewed out Haldon and Channon and Mason Crull, I hear."

Which did not bode well for Trap. He shot up another prayer, then shook his head. "I wish I could get him out riding."

Simon snorted. "Not much chance of that. Full rehearsal's tomorrow. Wedding guests pouring in. The final fittings. The service tomorrow night . . ." He paused. "How'd your meeting with the Heartlanders go, by the way?"

"Not bad." He smiled. "I couldn't persuade them to promise they'd try to find out where Gillard's hiding, but at least they have a new and clearer understanding of Abramm's views on governance. And hopefully a new respect for the restraint and generosity he's shown toward those not of like mind."

Most of the other council members were already in the War Room when they arrived, and shortly thereafter Abramm joined them. He had taken to wearing black of late and was growing his beard again. Five days' worth of unshaped honey-colored stubble covered his jaw—despite the fact that Briellen hated beards. But since with her own mouth she'd also very publicly expressed her horror for his "hideous scars," perhaps it didn't matter.

The meeting had barely gotten underway before Abramm was berating a servant for slamming the door and complaining that he didn't have enough weights to hold his maps in place. But finally they got down to business, discussing plans for the expedition to the Gull Islands, the continuing preparations for defense at home, and an update on the search for Gillard, which was turning out to be harder than expected. Trap noted the concerns of his Heart-landers over losing their trained bands in the face of Rennalf's rising bluster, which sparked a lengthy discussion of the potential for a militia army to be co-opted by the Mataio if they settled in the Heartland, as they were talking of doing.

They were wrapping things up, and Abramm was rattling off a series of new instructions to his ministers, when Arik Foxton had the bad sense to ask for a clarification:

"Did you say you wanted that five thousand sovereigns deposited to the Ministry account, sir?"

"I *said* the Military account, Foxton," Abramm said.

"Of course." Foxton shifted uncomfortably. "I was wondering why you would want them put in Ministry."

Abramm skewered him with a disdainful glance. "Yes, I would wonder that, too, Arik." His voice dripped sarcasm. "Why *would* I say such a thing? And why would you even *think* I would?"

"Obviously I was confused, sir."

"Obviously."

Foxton hid his annoyance and glanced at Trap, whom everyone seemed to regard as official keeper of Abramm's mood and tongue. Actually, Abramm *had* said Ministry not Military, but noting that aloud would be in no one's best interest. Abramm continued with his instructions, and shortly the men were filing from the room. All except Trap, who stayed behind, still seated at the table, watching Abramm as he turned his attention to the maps laid out before him.

When after a long moment Trap had still not spoken, the king looked up. "Why are you still here, Duke Eltrap?"

"You are aware, I presume, of just how insufferable you've been lately."

"I'm king. I get to be insufferable if I feel like it." He returned his attention to the topmost map, trailing his finger along the Kiriathan shoreline, then reaching for the straightedge and laying it onto the parchment. After a moment he left off with that and leaned back in the chair, rubbing his temples with thumb and forefinger. "All right. No I don't. And I thank you for pointing it out." He let his hand fall onto the chair's armrest and, after a moment, when Trap still hadn't left, "Was there something else?"

Trap sat with hands folded, rubbing a freckled knuckle with his thumb. Finally he said quietly, "Why are you going through with this, sir? When no one in the realm really wants it and you yourself are so obviously appalled by it? And when . . ." He hesitated to add the rest, then went ahead, as gently as he could, ". . . it's obvious your heart and soul belong to another."

Abramm returned to his maps, shuffling through them now in a display of impassive disinterest that didn't fool Trap for a moment. "Maddie is no longer part of the situation," he said curtly.

But the fact he'd not even bothered to pretend Trap's claim was untrue spoke volumes. "Are you sure?"

Abramm slid a new map to the top and replaced the weights that held it flat. "I can learn to love Briellen," he said. "We're charged to love all those who wear the shield, after all, and she's very pleasant to look at. There is that, at least. She hasn't even been that badly behaved since . . ." But he was unable to finish that thought.

Trap regarded him wordlessly.

"I'll grant she's not what I would have preferred." Abramm laid down the straightedge again. "But our duty doesn't ask us to do only that which we like or prefer."

"I would never argue that," Trap said. "But your duty, first and foremost, is to carry out Eidon's will for your life. As a man as well as a king. I'm not so sure that's what's been guiding you these last few days."

Abramm scowled at him. "Are you presuming to tell me what my duty is, Duke Eltrap?"

"No, sir. But you appointed me First Minister because you wanted someone who would tell you what he thought. And I think I have never seen you more miserable. Worse, you're making everyone around you miserable, too. And none of that is Eidon's will—not for the man nor for the king."

Abramm continued to frown at him, the grizzle bristling on his jaw as he clenched his teeth. "You have no right to judge me in this."

"I'm only suggesting you look at the motives that are driving you. Because I can't believe they're born of the Light."

His words died into a lengthy silence, during which Abramm shifted his gaze to the long row of windows where the trees stood bright in their new spring foliage. His index finger tapped an erratic rhythm atop the map beneath his hand. Finally he let out a long breath and said quietly, "I can't—" His voice died. He tried again, the words coming out harshly with the effort of keeping them even. "I won't let another woman die because of me."

And the look in his eyes set Trap's heart twisting with vicarious pain. Well did he remember that day on the ledge when, shuddering with sporesickness, he'd looked up to see Abramm kneeling in Shettai's blood, as motionless as if he had died himself. Spectators on the bridge had warned of the second veren's approach, and Trap had roused his friend just in time, but he'd never forget the dazed, lost look on Abramm's face. Nor how he'd insisted on carrying Shettai's body to the safety of the tunnel with the veren literally breathing down his neck.

Though he had masked his grief well, everything Abramm had done after that traced back to her—his trip to the SaHal, his efforts to awaken the Heart, his support of her brother, King Shemm. Perhaps even his return to Kiriath could be laid at her feet. Or at least the feet of the guilt Trap now knew Abramm still nursed over her loss.

"Shettai's death was not your doing," he said.

Abramm ran his finger along one of the contour lines on his map. "She wouldn't have been on that ledge at all if it wasn't for me. If I had not taken her that night." He grimaced, swallowed once, and then said very deliberately, "If I had not made love to her that night, in direct violation of the Words' commands . . ."

Trap stared at him, struggling to grasp his meaning, and when finally he did, aghast to think a man could know as much about Eidon as Abramm did, and speak such nonsense. "You believe Eidon took Shettai before her time just to punish *you*?" Trap pushed back from the table, struggling to contain his indignation. "That what Tersius did on that hill outside Xorofin wasn't quite enough, then?"

Abramm looked round at him in protest. "No!"

"Well, it's the same thing." He shook his head. "I'm not condoning what you did that night. But what about the sins you committed today? Do you believe you have to help pay for them, as well? When you upbraided Foxton for no reason and made him look the fool before us all? When you snarled at Cranston for not closing the door quietly enough? When you stalk around the palace in this foul mood, brooding over your misfortune, heedless of the feelings and needs of those around you? Are those somehow less grievous in Eidon's sight, somehow more respectable than coupling with a slave girl out of wedlock the night before you were supposed to die? And that before you even wore his shield?"

Abramm stared at him as if he didn't know what to say.

Trap leaned toward him. "They are all *equally* contemptible as far as he is concerned. Save perhaps for this disgusting hubris that seems to believe *your* particular sin is so great you have to help pay for it. That's probably worse."

Abramm's brows drew down. "That's not it at all."

"No? If you think you have to punish yourself with this marriage, then by default you're saying Tersius didn't do all that was necessary. So which is it? Did he do it all or do you have to help?"

Abramm was not given time to answer, for at that moment a familiar female voice sounded in the hall outside, followed by a servant's lower tones. Then the door swung open and Briellen swept into the room. To her credit, she was just about to speak when she noticed the charged atmosphere. Both men sat straight and rigid as they faced each other. Abramm's face was white behind the crimson scars, his brows knit with indignation. Trap knew himself to look little calmer and felt a mingling of irritation and embarrassment as Briellen's startled gaze passed over him.

Then Abramm drew a deep breath and deliberately relaxed. "What is it, my dear?" he asked very civilly, giving Trap the flick of his fingers that indicated he was dismissed.

Trap wasn't even out of the room before she started in, very sweetly, about that poxed chapel of hers. How that, grateful as she was Abramm had provided it for her, the altar that had been delivered wasn't quite what she had wanted. . . .

As the door closed behind him, Trap felt a pique of frustration. Then he reminded himself that the interruption had not been an accident. He'd said what he needed to say. Abramm would have to take it from here.

26

With sweat dribbling down the sides of his face and chest, Gillard knelt in the Watch's small chapel, a thick pad protecting his fragile knees from the hard stone floor. At least the pain that had earlier cramped his legs had by now given way to numbness, though what he would do when he had to stand again was anyone's guess.

Though he wore only a loincloth, even that was almost too much in this crowded, overheated room. Amicus had assured him the Watch brothers would do whatever was needed to spare his depleted flesh the battle of trying to keep warm during the ceremony, and so they had. Not only did the Holy Flames dance on their brazier atop the altar at the head of the chamber, but candles flickered all round and braziers of glowing coals stood at the four corners of the platform. To this was added the body heat of every member of the highland Watch, all of them crowded in here together. Since many had come directly from working the fields and garden, the overheated air carried a fine, ripe reek that made it hard to breathe.

At least this was almost over.

Gillard kept his head dropped forward as the Mataian who would be his discipler bent over him, one hand pressing into the side of his head as the other slowly drew the razor up from the nape of his neck, shearing away the last few locks of his hair. A few more strokes and the former prince-regent of Kiriath would be completely bald.

He tried not to think of that, preferring to concentrate on the fact that this minor sacrifice would ensure his anonymity when Abramm's men finally arrived. As one of the Watch's thirteen first-year acolytes, Gillard should draw no more than a passing glance. And since all first-year acolytes were required to have their heads shaved monthly during their first year of service—and had, in fact, completed that ritual this very morning—he didn't even have to worry about differences in length of stubble. They'd all be equally bald.

Two more slow pulls of the razor around Gillard's right ear, two more long, soap-sodden locks tossed into the shockingly large pile of white-blond hair in the pan at his knees, and it was done. His discipler's hand lifted off his head and returned with a damp towel to wipe away all traces of soap and stray hairs. Then the man straightened and backed out of Gillard's range of sight. Suddenly even the heated air seemed cool against his naked scalp, and a swirl of nausea danced through his belly.

It will be worth it, he told himself again. *And no one who matters is going to see me anyway. Besides, it will grow back.*

But he felt violated all the same. *Where do these religious freaks come up with such absurd rituals?*

The shearing complete, Master Amicus now rose from his chair beside the altar and launched into a long prayer of gratitude sprinkled with pledges of humility and sincerity to which Gillard added wry and inappropriate mental asides. He found it particularly amusing the way the old Guardian lost nearly all of his northerner brogue when mouthing formal prayers and ceremonial words. Did they train them to do that, he wondered, or did Amicus just get carried away with his own pomposity?

Finally it was Gillard's turn to speak, promising, as he'd been instructed, to work hard, serve humbly, learn well the laws of the Words and Mataian Tradition and observe them with the greatest care.

"So ye have sworn," Amicus declared when he had finished. "Hold true to these vows, and ye shall yourself be pure enough to enter the Holy Keep and touch the FatherFlame. Pass its testing and ye shall be permitted to take your final vows of service."

Which I can assure you, Gillard thought at him, *will never happen.*

Amicus lifted a hand. "Stand before them now."

Awkwardly Gillard slid his splinted right hand under the garments folded up beneath the pan of hair and, balancing both on his right hand as he steadied them with his left, got slowly to his feet. His discipler stood by to catch his elbow and support him, a precaution he definitely needed, for his legs felt as if they had been cut off as surely as his hair.

Amicus began another droning litany, but this time Gillard was completely distracted by the sensations rushing up from his legs. Numbness turned to a jellylike tingling that progressed into outright pain and something very like cramping. By the time it faded, Amicus had finished his recitation and Gillard was standing on his own two feet again, the discipler's hand no longer needed. Perhaps Amicus inserted the long litany for just that purpose. After what he'd said yesterday about serving whether one believed or not, Gillard wouldn't be surprised.

The Guardian Master fell silent, and after a moment the assembled citizens of the Watch broke into a song of praise. Then, at last, Amicus looked directly into Gillard's eyes and launched into the official vow-taking, which Gillard repeated line by line after him:

"I, Galbrath of Two Cities"—they had chosen the most common of Gillard's four names to use here to grant the proceedings credibility—"do swear to serve the Flames with all my heart and soul and strength, to observe the dictates of the brotherhood, and keep myself pure in Eidon's sight.

"I will touch no weapon of warfare." *At least not today.* "His light will be my protection.

"I will abstain from corrupt foods, shunning wine, strong drink, and the meat of animals." *How in torments does anyone get through this without strong drink?* "His Words will be my food, his Light will be my drink.

"I will keep my flesh pure and undefiled from the corruption of women." *This one will definitely be the first to go. . . .* "His Flames will be my only love. . , ."

Barely did Gillard manage to utter those words without laughing. Already he'd been plagued by an intense craving for feminine companionship. If he did not assuage it soon, he'd surely go mad. He'd asked Honarille to see about arranging something last night, but the man had looked at him as if he were out of his mind, seeming appalled Gillard would even consider it. And that had been *before* he'd made these silly vows.

Could they possibly be vows, he wondered, *if you mouthed them with no intent whatever to fulfill them?*

"These things I do swear before these witnesses and the Holy SonFlames of Eidon," said Amicus. "May they strike me with their fury should I violate this troth."

Gillard repeated dutifully, his words fading to silence in the hot, stuffy room.

For a moment Amicus stood with head bowed, eyes closed, muttering to himself. Then he lifted his face and looked at Gillard again. "Thus ye have sworn before these witnesses who have seen and heard and understood."

The gathered Watch congregation lifted their voices in somber unison. "We have seen and heard and understood."

"The time has come, Galbrath. Put off your old self and take on the new."

As he had been instructed earlier, Gillard walked across the slate floor to the edge of the brazier. Gripping the pan of hair with his left hand, he tipped his splinted right and dropped into the Flames the folded breeches, blouses, and underclothing that had been brought with him when he'd been rescued from the Chancellor's Tower—pretty much all he could be said to actually own these days. As the red tongues of fire curled up around them, he dumped his shorn hair after them, awkwardly wiping the pan with the thumb of his splinted hand to be sure every last hair was offered. Then he set the pan beside the brazier and retreated to his spot before the altar.

Amicus was smiling now, the amulet at his throat flickering with a creepy red light. A sudden chill crawled up the back of Gillard's neck, spreading across his barren scalp. For the first time he felt a twinge of uneasiness, a sense that more was going on here than he knew . . . that perhaps things weren't as much in hand as he believed.

"All has now become new," Amicus intoned with that satisfied smile. "What was before is no longer. Ye stand before us newly born, a holy servant of Eidon. Your old name is lost, and your new name . . ." He hesitated, eyes half closing.

Gillard waited, surprised at the level of curiosity he felt about what they had decided to call him. Allegedly no one knew in advance. If the Flames were pleased with the supplicant they would themselves tell his new name to the Master at this time. Gillard scoffed at the idea. Amicus had probably been up all night trying to decide.

The old man's eyes flew open ablaze with a red light matched by that surging in the amulet at his throat and exploding upward from the large brazier behind him. As Gillard flinched back in startlement, Amicus shuddered, his voice sounding lower, laced with an unmistakable amusement. "Makepeace! Your new name is Makepeace."

Makepeace? Despite being genuinely impressed by Amicus's theatrics with the Flames, Gillard felt his brows draw down in displeasure. *What kind of a woolwitted name is that? Is this his revenge for my refusal to believe? He makes me go through this nonsense, then gives me an idiotic name? Makepeace, indeed! The only way I'm making peace is by making Abramm dead!*

The Flames subsided, the amulet darkened, and Amicus's eyes reverted to their normal pale blue watery state. Now he broke into a broad smile, perhaps in welcome, perhaps also in amusement for his prank. "Please, brothers," he said, opening wide his arms, "let us welcome Brother Makepeace into our family."

Eight months, Gillard thought grimly as the others now gathered round him. *That's all I'm staying.* He touched tentative fingers to his shaven scalp, nausea fluttering through him at the smooth, slick feel of it. *Eight months at the very longest. Enough to get my strength back and gain a feel for what all is going on . . . who of my supporters remain alive and free. Then we'll see about making peace. . . .*

Abramm lay on his back in the royal bed, staring at the golden folds of its canopy above him. It was well into the early hours of the morning, and while he'd fallen asleep shortly after going to bed, another unsettling dream had awakened him, and now he couldn't sleep. He couldn't remember the details, only that Maddie was in trouble. It was the second night he'd had it, and that, added to the reports of possible galley sightings off the coast of Blackcliff, troubled him deeply.

In fact, as he lay there he wondered why he'd ever thought to send her by open sea in the first place. Why not upriver to Sterlen, then across the moors to Avramm's Landing? No chance of running into Esurhites that way. But when he'd sent her, there had been no Esurhite sightings off Blackcliff, and the sea route was the quickest way to her final destination. Less chance of her changing her mind and coming back by that route, too. And more chance she'd find a berth on a ship to the Isles. . . .

He closed his eyes to the pain of that thought, a hard weight pressing on his heart. It was pain he'd hoped he was past feeling, or soon would be. Now he wondered if he might never be past it. *If anything happens to her out there . . .*

His eyes flew open, staring at the canopy again so he wouldn't see the images that had welled up in his mind. He'd sent her away so she'd be safe, and now . . .

Trap's accusations had dogged him for the rest of the day, though he'd tried hard to dismiss them. But when that night in Terstmeet Kesrin chose to speak on guilt, Abramm was forced to reconsider. He did not think the two men had conspired together. Kesrin deliberately avoided such things precisely to ensure that his listeners not suspect him of such. *"I want you to know it's not me who's saying it,"* he often told them, *"but the one who's given me the power to speak it in the first place."*

Eidon.

Once Abramm had broken through that barrier, he had become increasingly suspicious of the true nature of his motives. For he could not deny he felt a tremendous shame regarding the sin he'd committed with Shettai. But as Trap said, was that sin any worse than belittling Foxton before all the cabinet? Why pull that one out of so many others—he'd hated Eidon, cursed him, thrown his Star of Life away—to flail himself with. Tersius died for all of them, paying the full penalty Eidon had required of all men. If because of him Abramm was clean in Eidon's sight, how could he not be clean in his own?

To put your own standards above those of the Almighty? Trap's right. It is hubris.

Which meant he had hope. Which meant maybe he wasn't doomed to live out his life in loveless solitude—or worse, a loveless marriage—because of what he'd done. If that was all behind him, the penalty fully paid for . . . then maybe what he felt for Maddie was legitimate. Something to be accepted and embraced instead of denied.

He recalled the moment he had kissed her—a memory never far from his mind—the way the Light had flared between them, the feeling of being knit to her as he'd never been knit to anyone save Eidon himself. As if she were the other half of him, finally come together. He'd always believed Shettai had been that other half, taken from him as punishment for his lust. . . . But he had not even known the Light when he had been with her. Nor had she, for that matter.

So how could he think that was the only relationship for him? Or even, really, the one Eidon had intended for him in the first place? What if there was and always had been another?

Maddie.

Suddenly he saw it all—from the very moment he'd met her on that dock when he'd first returned to Springerlan. She'd looked at him as if he were a hero then, and still did. She'd been the first to pry out his secrets, the one who saw him for the man, even as she saw him for the hero. The balm and buoy of his soul. The light of his life.

She was the one.

It was as if dark bonds were snapping off his soul, chains coming loose, light flowing into darkness. As the guilt let go of him and he opened his eyes to the tremendous wonder of what Eidon wanted to do in his life, he felt a surge of exultation.

Only to feel it die as he realized that, even if she could be persuaded to come back, he was still bound to Briellen. And to back out of it now could well mean the sundering of the alliance Kiriath desperately needed.

Oh, my Lord Eidon, I have made a mess of it all again, haven't I?

He lay there exquisitely aware of his helplessness and failure, but this time there was no guilt in it. Eidon knew what he was. Eidon had known before he was born that he would do this.

Should I break it off and trust you to provide the protection the Chesedhans would have provided? Or continue to go forward on this path I've so foolishly chosen, stick with my word, and trust you to make it into gold? As he had said to Trap earlier, he could learn to love Briellen. Perhaps, in time, she could even learn to love him. And far better that than the lonely, loveless life he had envisioned. *If that is your will for me, I will abide it and count it a miracle in itself. But . . .* He hesitated, the desire welling up in him. But no, he couldn't ask for that.

Why not, my son? Do you think I don't know what you want?

The quiet words settled into his soul, bringing with them the sudden sharp awareness that he was not lying here nattering away unheard in his own head. He felt the heat of embarrassment sweep into his face. *It is too audacious to ask, Lord Eidon.*

Too audacious? Are you not my child and heir? What would be too audacious for you to ask of me?

Again the Shadow within him sought to reassert its guilt-hold on him. He cast it aside, marveling that he could have been blind to it for so long. As the Light rippled through him, he smiled at the canopy overhead.

If you know what I want, Lord Eidon, and you've promised to bless me, why do I need to ask?

Because I want you to. Because I've commanded you to.

Abramm's smile broadened. *Very well, then, I will ask: Deliver me from this dreadful betrothal and bring Maddie back to me.*

He felt his sovereign's laughter deep in his heart. *Is that all, my boy?*

And make her my wife, sir. You know how much I love her. . . .

Ah . . . that will be difficult.

You are jesting with me, Father! I know that nothing is too difficult for you. You've made me king, have you not?

Indeed I have, my son. . . . The laughter rolled over him again, then faded.

There are some things I cannot do, though: I will not violate her freedom to choose.

Abramm's heart fell, the levity subsiding into stillness. *I know that, Lord.*

So if it turns out you cannot have this request of yours?

Then I will abide it with thanksgiving, knowing that whatever you do have for me, it will be what is best.

The best, indeed, my son. I have promised it. But you must rest in that, perhaps for longer than you might wish.

I will rest.

And so he did, falling into a dream wherein he floated on a sea of peace and security, filled with the delicious anticipation of something miraculous about to happen. He was awakened by an annoying pull at his shoulder and Captain Channon's rough brogue intruding into his paradise. "Sire?"

Even half asleep Abramm discerned the tension in the man's voice, and it catapulted him to full wakefulness. "What is it, Captain?"

"It's Princess Briellen, sir."

Abramm pushed himself up onto his elbows, alarm coursing through him. Here he'd worried about Maddie's safety but given no thought to Briellen. Who, he knew with a fair degree of certainty, was already the focus of Belthre'gar's attentions. He didn't much think he would like a solution to his marriage dilemma that involved her being stolen away by the Esurhites. Or, worse . . . "Is she hurt?"

"No, sir. She's . . ." Channon looked incredibly uncomfortable, standing there as rigidly as Abramm had ever seen him, his eyes fixed upon the gilt wallpaper past Abramm's head. "She's been caught, sir."

"Caught?" Abramm sat up fully, noting that Haldon had come into the room and gone immediately to open the wardrobe.

Channon looked as if he might pop with the pressure of the grim tidings he bore, words he obviously did not want to utter. In the end they burst out of him like water through a dam: "In bed, sir. With her lover."

Abramm blinked at him. "Her lover?"

"Aye, sir. Count Blackwell says ye must come and witness it."

"Come and *witness* it?"

"For the trial, sir. He's called Prince Leyton, as well. The law says any man caught in adultery with the queen must be—"

"I know what the law says, Captain." The man executed. The woman cast upon the mercy of the judges. Briellen might not technically be queen yet, but as Abramm's betrothed, the law applied to her as much as—perhaps more than—any wedded queen. It was imperative there be no doubt cast upon the legitimacy of any heirs that might come along after the wedding.

"He says they'll need good and substantial witnesses," Channon went on. "He says ye need t' come, especially, sir. Being her betrothed."

Abramm stared at him grimly. Bad enough Briellen had been caught in this horrid indiscretion, but that he should have to come and witness it? It appalled him. And yet, that, too, was part of the law. The couple caught in such an act would be held in their bed together until the man they had betrayed could be summoned.

Perhaps I am having another nightmare.

Haldon had pulled a blouse from the wardrobe and now stood near the foot of the bed, waiting for Abramm to rise and don it, and Abramm had no choice but to do so.

What happened after that could only be described as surreal. The nightmarish quality of the proceedings never let up, even though it soon became apparent this was no nightmare. At least not the sort you could wake up from and laugh about as meaningless.

Once dressed, Abramm followed Channon through the palace back routes to the far-east wing, up a narrow stair, down a long hallway and into a small sitting chamber, where three armsmen stood guard. Light poured through the open doorway of an adjoining chamber from which the sound of voices carried. At the arrival of their king, all three armsmen came to attention. Their sudden movement caught the notice of the man standing in the lighted doorway, who pushed himself away from the doorjamb with a quiet warning to those within. "He's here."

Teeth clenched with revulsion, Abramm stepped past the armsmen into a shabby bedchamber filled with people, the single lamp on a dressing table in the near corner casting all into a macabre chiaroscuro. The light's low angle threw weird shadows into the corners of the room while describing in unfamiliar highlight the faces of those standing along its perimeter: servants, armsmen, high-court officials, and noblemen. Simon was there, as were Whitethorne, Darnley, Mason Crull, several judges, and Byron Blackwell, looking as if he had eaten something awful. Prince Leyton had apparently arrived shortly before Abramm, for he now stood halfway between the doorway and the foot of the bed, the latter positioned in the middle of the room, headboard against the opposite wall. Leyton's bulk blocked Abramm's sight of the disgraced lovers until announcement of the king's arrival penetrated the Chesedhan's shock and he stepped aside.

The couple lay beneath a rumpled landscape of sheet, coverlet, and discarded clothing, the lamp's angled light casting long shadows away from the bright crests of the fabric's folds. They had pulled themselves up onto the pillows so they could face their accusers half sitting rather than flat on their backs, clutching the sheet to their chests.

After a first quick embarrassed glance that took in the whole scene, Abramm's eyes fixed on the man's face and recognition sent him reeling. *"Foxton?!"*

His Minister of Finance looked completely wretched. He was pale as death and his hands shook where they clenched the sheet. His handsome face was drawn into a wrinkle of misery, and he was quite unable to meet Abramm's gaze, though the king kept his eyes upon the man for some time, willing him to look up. Willing him to offer some excuse, some explanation for this betrayal. He had expected to find a younger man in Briellen's bed. Not someone as seasoned and experienced as Foxton. Not someone who was already married, and certainly not someone who was his friend and a member of his own cabinet.

Briellen, on the other hand, had reverted to her harridan persona the moment Abramm walked into the room, shifting more upright against the pillows to better express her ire. She met his gaze boldly, making no effort to hide her antipathy. "At least now," she spat, "I will not have to endure your crippled hands pawing my flesh!"

"Eidon's mercy, Bree!" Leyton murmured beside him.

Abramm heard him with only a small part of his brain, staring at the woman he was supposed to marry in two days, the shock of what he saw in her eyes reverberating through him with even greater force than what his recognition of Foxton had generated. For with the lamplight shining straight into her face, he could clearly see the thin line of white curd that cupped the base of her blue irises. *Sarotis!*

He'd thought he'd glimpsed it the day she'd arrived when she'd lifted her eyes to his there in the throne room. Being almost immediately distracted by her strong and obvious revulsion to his scars, he'd never been quite sure. When he'd found no sign of it in his subsequent dealings with her, he'd concluded it a trick of the light.

"I thought about waiting until after we were married," she said to him now, spite sharpening her voice. "But in the end I couldn't bear the thought of you being my first. Especially knowing you'd already shared your favors with my sister."

"Hagin's beard, Briellen," Leyton exclaimed. "Don't dig it any deeper."

Flashing another glance at Foxton, Abramm turned and headed for the door, a tremor running through his arms and legs. His heart was beating about as fast as it could beat.

Behind him Whitethorne exclaimed, "Fire and torment, Arik! What were you thinking!"

But Foxton didn't answer.

Abramm stepped into the dimly lit hallway outside, struggling to breathe against the nausea welling within him. Already a gauntlet of spectators lined the hallway, servants and courtiers who had somehow gotten wind of the scandal and come out to see for themselves, most of them still in their night-clothes. They shrank back against the wall, watching him fearfully as he passed. He knew his face must be dead white, which meant the scars would be bright red. Not a pretty picture. But none of this was.

How many, he wondered, would be laughing at him before daybreak?

And why did it have to be Foxton?

27

Though *Starchaser* had lain becalmed in a heavy mist the night after Maddie sighted the mysterious cloud in their wake, nothing untoward had come of it. No dark-tunicked Esurhites had swarmed over the gunwales in the wee hours, no arcane fireballs had materialized, and though the mist did not break until midmorning the next day, it did break and they continued on their way.

The cloud had reappeared in its place on their tail not long afterward, however, and continued to follow them over the next two days. Every now and then someone thought he'd seen something in it, but the sightings were never long enough or clear enough to be anything more than "something." Rocks, unusually thick clots of mist, the occasional bit of flotsam, or even seabirds rising off the water's surface could all account for the claims. Besides that, other similar clouds continually formed and unformed at all points of the compass around them.

If the mysterious cloud *did* hide Esurhite galleys, Windemere asked, why had they hung back for so long? As frail and unreliable as the wind had been, they could easily have captured *Starchaser*. Maddie might have argued that they hadn't done so because they weren't interested in taking a sailing vessel they'd have no use for in a windless realm. She might have suggested other possibilities, as well, but it all took too much effort. And the closer they got to their destination, the less she cared about any of it.

In fact, the morning of the third day after the sighting, the day they expected to reach Avramm's Landing, she awoke beneath a mantle of such debilitating depression that for a while she couldn't move. It pressed upon her like a physical weight. She didn't want to get out of bed, didn't want to eat, and didn't care if they ever reached port. Just getting up and going on deck seemed a monumental effort, and when she considered the tedious, frustrating prospect of finding and booking passage to the west, it over-whelmed her. She wondered what in the world was wrong with her. Had some evil force come in the night and sucked away all of her vitality?

Then she remembered this was the day Abramm was to be married in Springerlan, and she rolled over, clutching the folds of her blanket against her chest as she buried her face in the rough cabin pillow. It was midmorning before she finally forced herself to get up and dress. As she sat for Liza to braid her hair, she stared blindly at the mist-veiled tableau outside the stern cabin's window where the mystery cloud still hovered, closer now than ever. Part of her brain informed her this was a concern, but she watched it numbly, even so. Through the ceiling hatch, she heard the captain and his first mate discussing it, as well, and after a moment Captain Windemere called for the maximum amount of sail to be set.

Maybe it really is Esurhites, she thought. *Maybe they'll take us all away to the southland to be slaves. Then I won't have to worry about booking passage.* And at the moment slavery seemed the more desirable of the two prospects. Surely she couldn't be any more miserable than she already was. . . .

Something flickered in the cloud, drawing her focus. A brief glimpse of something solid. Not a rock, too high for flotsam, and definitely not a seabird. For the first time a spark of discomfit pierced her indifference.

It showed itself again: dark and angular, protruding briefly through the veil of gray and withdrawing—high above the water's surface. "Did you see that?" she asked Liza.

"See what, milady?" the girl murmured absently, fingers tugging at Mad-die's hair as they worked.

"There was something in that cloud."

"Probably a bird."

"I think it's a boat."

"Well, we're nearing Avramm's Landing, so maybe it is."

Maddie pressed her lips to keep from uttering the unkind response that came to mind. "We're not that near. . . ." She kept her eyes on the cloud. "It's never come this close before. Are you almost done?"

"Almost, milady." Liza had reached the end of the long braid and was now looping it up around Maddie's head to fasten it into place.

Once again the dark, angular shape pierced the mist and withdrew. "A dragon's head," Maddie murmured, thinking there was nothing like facing the prospect of real disaster to cut through the self-pity and put one's problems into perspective.

"You think there's a sea dragon in the cloud, ma'am?" Liza's hands stilled on her head, and she knew the girl was looking aft.

"No. I am thinking that Esurhite galleys often have dragon's heads on their prows. . . . Hurry up."

As soon as Liza finished, Maddie snatched her spyglass from its shelf beside the table and joined Captain Windemere and his ship's officers at the taffrail, telescopes trained on the cloud. It had by now halved the distance originally separating it from *Starchaser*. Moments after she arrived, all the angles came together and two narrow-prowed vessels, their sides bristling with oars, glided into view.

She stared at them openmouthed, horror closing her throat. Even with the fact she'd already guessed they were there, she wasn't ready for the reality of seeing them, so close and so big. And so menacing, with those banks of oars flashing up and down in rapid and perfect unison, powering the vessels forward on a course straight up *Starchaser*'s wake.

"In a moment they'll be within range of the stern chaser, sir," said the first mate.

"Fire a ranging shot," Windemere ordered. "Let 'em know we've got working powder."

A series of shouted commands preceded the boom of a single round from the little gun mounted on the quarterdeck along the stern. Maddie watched the dark ball arc over the gray swells and fall only a little short of the two dark ships.

Instead of slowing, however, the galleys glided defiantly forward, leaving their cover of mist entirely.

"Another," Windemere ordered.

The bark of a second round rattled Maddie's teeth and shook her insides. This time the ball barely missed crashing into the deck of the leftmost galley. For answer, the oars' rapid tempo increased.

"What the plague?!" Windemere growled. "Surely they don't intend to ram us from behind."

"I think they mean to board, sir," his first mate said. He gestured at the boats. "D'ye see those groups of men there at the bows? Looks like they've got windlasses."

"Indeed it does, Mr. White," said the captain. "Though I don't see any cables."

"They're probably cloaked," Maddie said, watching the dark-tunicked men frantically cranking the levers of large, heavy-duty windlasses. "They probably attached them the night we lay becalmed outside Blackcliff," she added.

From the corner of her eye she saw Windemere lower his spyglass to stare at her, appalled. "You mean t' say we've been towing them all this way?"

"Most likely, sir. It was misty enough they could do it, and after all the miles they've come, their slaves are probably exhausted."

"But why break cover now? And if they want to take us, why didn't they do it that night at Blackcliff?"

"Because their main mission is probably to attack the fortress at Avramm's Landing, and all they need from us is fresh muscle for their oars. Or they might think we spotted them earlier and didn't want us to give warning. They might just want to twit you, too. Or perhaps do all three."

Windemere began with the first of her suggestions: "Attack the fortress? With only two ships?"

"That's all they sent against Graymeer's."

Windemere frowned and thought for a moment. "That was on the day of Abramm's coronation."

"Yes, sir," Maddie said.

"And today he is getting married. . . ." He glanced again at her. "But why Avramm's Landing? It's hardly central to Kiriath's defenses. And the thirty or so fighting men on those two galleys are not going to be able to take and hold an entire fortress."

"They can if they have a Broho or priest on board, though I doubt they mean to take the fortress. They may want only to infiltrate it, find a place to hide within where they can help from the inside when the main fleet arrives."

Belthre'gar, her brother had said, was supposed to have an obsession with capturing ancient Ophiran fortresses, particularly those whose guardstars were still in place. Avramm's Landing fulfilled both qualifications.

Windemere digested this new information as he watched the approaching galleys. "We've got to find those cables and cut them loose."

"Where would they be likely to attach them?" Maddie asked, peering over the edge of the taffrail.

Windemere glared at her. "Milady, you need to go below."

"If you tell me where to look, Captain," she said, "maybe I can see them.

If I can see them, I can burn away the cloaking so you can cut them free."

He couldn't avoid the logic of her suggestion. And sure enough two cables were found fastened to the middenmast, running flat along the planking to loop around the bollards at either side of the quarterdeck, then out through the aft-most scuppers. But even with the cables released, their pursuers kept right on, their oar-driven speed considerably faster than *Starchaser*, hampered as she was by a faltering breeze.

The men on the windlasses had cut their cables loose the moment they saw themselves disconnected from the big ship, no doubt to avoid fouling the oars. On the galley's decks now, soldiers in helmets and breastplates emerged from a hatch aft of each vessel and congregated at the bows. Many carried grappling hooks and coils of rope, and all were armed. Among the group on the leftward vessel appeared a bald man cloaked in black. Though Maddie had never seen his like before, she knew at once what he was: Broho.

Plagues! We have no chance of escaping. Oh, Father Eidon, we need help!

Around the Broho, the soldiers began to chant and the already feeble wind died. *Starchaser* slowed noticeably as mist congealed around her.

"Sir!" cried the man operating the stern chaser. "The gun won't fire any-more."

Windemere swore softly, then turned to Maddie. "My lady, you must go below." His gaze shifted to his first mate. "Mr. White, take her to the cable tier, and see she's well hidden."

"Cable tier!" Maddie protested. "Absolutely not. I'm staying on deck."

"My lady, if they know you're here—"

"They already know, and I would rather dive into the sea than let myself be found trapped like a rat in the cable tier."

Windemere scowled fiercely. "We've got them far outnumbered, miss. They're not likely to be the ones to find you at all."

"I sincerely hope you're right, Captain, but if you want me in the cable tier you'll have to drag me to it and tie me in there."

The man's scowl couldn't get any darker, but at length he relented. "You are a stubborn one, aren't you? Very well. Go to the foredeck. And stay out of the way."

She gave him a nod and hurried down the companionway to the ship's waist, where she met Liza emerging from the stern cabin. Seeing the terrified girl, she almost panicked herself, for she knew there was no way out. Regard-less of their greater numbers, *Starchaser's* crew would not withstand the Broho's powers. Not if even half of what she'd heard of them was true. The only hope left would be to jump over the side.

"Can you swim?" she asked Liza, shaking her arm to get her attention.

The girl's tear-filled eyes widened further. "No, ma'am."

Plagues! Now what am I to do?

Commanding the girl to come with her, Maddie hurried to the place Windemere had assigned her and was barely hunkered down by the ship's officers' tiny cabins at the bow when the Esurhites swarmed over the stern, screaming like madmen. They had the whole of the ship's crew to face them, nearly every one of the two hundred men armed with something—blade, dagger, awl, even makeshift clubs scavenged from the ship's furnishings. Severely outnumbered, it seemed at first the Esurhites might be pushed back.

But then the dark figure of the Broho climbed over the taffrail and stood overlooking the ship, cloak billowing around him, the amulet on his chest glowing like a purple eye. His bald head gleamed in the gray light, and even with the entire length of the ship between them she felt his eyes upon her and shuddered with the menace they imparted. His mouth opened, his chest expanded . . .

And a great violet plume burst out of him, crashing into the main mast like a pot of burning pitch. Purple fire flew everywhere, igniting canvas, wood, rope, and chaos. In moments, the mainmast was ablaze. Flaming pieces of beams and ratlines and canvas rained down on the men waiting in the waist for their turn to repel the boarders. Smoke quickly obscured Maddie's view of the quarterdeck, stinging her nostrils as Liza clung to her and whimpered. The roar of the flames and the screams and shouts of the men filled her ears.

Then she saw the Broho standing at the quarterdeck railing. The purple amulet flared as his deep voice bellowed through the din and all the flames went out at once. Simultaneously, every man froze and silence descended upon the ship. A dark mist mingled with the paler smoke, coiling round wreckage and men toward the foredeck. Maddie felt its pervasive chill settle around her, felt the pressure of fear start deep in her middle as images of death and torture filled her mind, and the Shadow within her panicked in response.

28

On the morning he was to have married the Chesedhan First Daughter in the ancient Hall of Kings, Abramm was instead seated on the King's Bench in the High Court Chamber at the opposite end of the Mall of Government, presiding over her lover's adultery trial. He had worn Avramm's crown for the occasion, and wished that he had not. Everything he had seen that night in the bedchamber was now amplified. As the evidence was brought forth, the love letters read, the witnesses called, and Foxton's own shaking, miserable confession of guilt heard, Briellen sat defiantly in the defendant's box adjoining his, alternately smirking and glaring at Abramm.

Whether it was a result of his own sight being enhanced by the crown or recent events causing an acceleration of the process, the question of whether Briellen had developed the sarotis was no longer in doubt. Though he wasn't sure whether anyone else could see it, for himself it was a thick line of curd, occluding the bottom half of her irises and creeping down toward her lower lids. Never had the juxtaposition between beauty and horror been so striking.

There was more: the staffid disguised as bracelet that she wore on her arm, the blue flicker of the spore dwelling and active in her flesh, and the hatred in her eyes. Hatred not primarily directed at him, but at Eidon himself, even though she wore his shieldmark over her heart. Hatred shared by the rhu'ema that lurked in the shadows of the great chamber's nooks and corners, come here to watch their plans fulfilled.

That was the worst thing: knowing that both Briellen and Arik Foxton had been manipulated. The fact they had been found at all indicated someone had been watching them and more than likely had even set them up.

They were little more than dupes, and now one of them would have to die.

Still they chose to act as they did. And choices have consequences.

It would have been easier, though, if the choices had been of a different nature. To preside over a trial that would condemn a man to death for doing what Abramm himself had done and been forgiven for . . . was difficult. It roused up all the old guilt again, and he had to remind himself repeatedly that Foxton hadn't just committed adultery, he'd committed treason. The court here wasn't defending Abramm's pride but the authority of his office.

Just as he had arrested High Father Bonafil for his disrespect of that office, so must Foxton be held accountable. And given the act's potential to confuse the line of succession and perhaps one day spark a war that might lead to thousands of deaths . . . execution was not so severe a penalty.

Simon had been adamant in his support of that position. Blackwell had echoed it. As had Hamilton, Whitethorne, Nott, Trap . . . even Kohal Kesrin. And Abramm had received no indication from Eidon that he should offer this man clemency, though he had pled for it. Thus when the trial was concluded, and the judges returned after only an hour's sequestering with their guilty verdict, Abramm said nothing. And when they pronounced their sentences of permanent deportation for the First Daughter and swift execution for Arik Foxton, he did not countermand them.

Far from laughing at him that morning, his people had sympathized, outraged by Briellen's seamy and vicious betrayal. It was only through this that he realized many of his subjects saw his injuries in the same light as Maddie had—as badges of honor. For this Chesedhan vixen to snub him because of them was inexcusable. Not surprisingly, their antipathy toward Briellen had spread to Chesedhans in general, and if they had disliked the proposed alliance before, now they hated it.

Every way Abramm had sought to protect his realm lay in ruins, but even so, he knew Eidon was still at work. The most glaring evidence of that truth lay in the fact that mere hours after making the request, he had been suddenly and completely released from all obligations to marry Briellen. And with that had sprouted a seedling of hope that the remainder of what he had asked might be granted him, as well. . . . *You have only to wait.*

Ironically, it was this very kernel of hope that his inner Shadow used to accuse him of sacrificing Foxton to get Maddie back. Over and over he had to confront the notion, irrational and illogical as it was, and replace it with the truth. Foxton knew the penalty for his actions. He knew that, should he be found out, it would destroy him and his family.

Yet he'd chosen to do as he'd done. The responsibility lay with him. And he knew it, for he hadn't looked Abramm in the eye one time during the entire wretched ordeal.

Neither had Leyton offered a word in his sister's defense. In fact, he'd said very little. His face was hard, masked, and haggard. So far as Abramm knew he had spoken privately with Briellen only once, and her jailers said she'd sent him away with a barrage of words they'd rather not repeat.

Abramm had just exited the building that held the High Court Chamber and was descending the broad stair to his waiting carriage when he heard the distant boom of the guns at Kildar and Graymeer's out at the mouth of the bay. *Noon already?* That was the moment Kesrin was supposed to have declared he and Briellen wed. Instead she was being escorted back to her chambers, where she would await Foxton's execution tomorrow morning. After which she would be required to leave the city.

A second salvo of the guns brought him up short, his gaze turning southward, where a dark cloud bank churned at the mouth of his bay. A mist, he knew at once, that was not natural. Horrified, he watched as three Chesedhan merchantmen came plowing out of it, moving sluggishly as they fled beneath the covering fire of the fort at Graymeer's, the cannon's distant booming sounding with increasing frequency. Since by now the morning land breeze had died, there was no hope of any natural wind driving off that mist and little help for the frigates that were obviously being pursued.

All these thoughts and observations had barely registered when a brilliant purple light streaked out of the fog, heading straight for Springerlan. In barely a heartbeat it had flown the length of the bay, tracking low over the city's roofs to slam into the Hall of Kings at the opposite end of the mall. The impact was followed by a moment of silence. Then a fountain of purple flame erupted from the ancient amphitheater, showering Abramm with pieces of rock and tile even so far away as on the steps of the High Court Chamber.

Those around him exclaimed in horror as purple flame turned to orange and the Hall's great hammerbeam ceiling ignited. Black smoke poured skyward as men rushed out of nearby buildings. Southward on the bay, the Chesedhan vessels were heeling slowly around, their guns flashing as the dark, narrow shapes of far too many Esurhite galleys emerged from their covering veil of mist. Closer to the city, Katahn's galleys were backing out of their docking slips as two naval frigates pulled anchor and set off for the front line, making scant progress in the feeble wind.

Abramm glanced again at the pillar of black smoke and realized with a chill that had the wedding gone as planned, he and Briellen—along with most of his court—would be dead.

As if reading his mind, Channon said, close at his side, "Sir, you need to get to safety."

Abramm turned back toward the High Court Chamber and then, given the accuracy of the Esurhites' aim, decided that might not be the best place to take shelter. Even as he thought it, Simon and Trap emerged from the doorway at the head of a stream of exiting nobles, all of whom stopped to stare at the burning Hall beyond the green.

He heard the clanging of the alarm bells that would call out the bucket brigades and pump wagons, men already beginning to converge upon the flaming Hall. The Hall itself was clearly past saving, but the sparks and flaming debris shooting out of it could easily ignite a secondary blaze among the surrounding sea of wooden roofs. He knew a plan for fighting fires was in place with chain of command already appointed, but he sent Trap down to help nonetheless, even as Simon ran off to direct the shoreline defenses.

Abramm himself joined Admiral Hamilton in his command-post bunker built up against the cliffs east of the city. Leyton Donavan went with him, each of them equipped with a telescope so they could keep an eye on the fire, the shoreline defense preparations, and the battle itself.

The same armada of civilian vessels that had turned out to stop Katahn soon pushed off from their moorings, many of them forming a blockade at the river's broad mouth as others ferried soldiers out to engage the enemy. As with the firefighters, both Simon and Hamilton were carrying out plans Abramm had already set in place—which gave him little to do but watch, a role he found profoundly discomfiting.

Behind the forward line of twelve enemy galleys, two following vessels spewed smoke, obviously the source of the mist. They would be the ones the Kiriathans must attack most vigorously and sink, if possible. The Chesedhan frigates ceased firing now as Katahn's galleys shot by them to ram the enemy ships. As the boats lurched and clung to each other, Katahn's crewmen leaped over the locked gunwales to engage the Esurhites hand to hand. After that, the conflict was slow, virtually soundless, and obscured by shifting veils of shadow and smoke. Often Abramm glimpsed men struggling on the vessels' decks, saw the flash of swords, sometimes a flare of white light or purple. . . . But then another vessel would drift into his line of sight and he'd see no more. At least two of the Esurhite ships were sunk by the ramming maneuver, and finally one galley broke through to attack the smoke ships. A furious firework of white and purple flared in the thickening mists, leaving one smoke-ship adrift and the other sinking. After that the invaders retreated until they had withdrawn from the bay.

By then the column of smoke from the Hall of Kings had been replaced by a pall of gray, and thankfully no more of the city had burned. Abramm was beginning to relax when Hamilton noted that the fog not only remained just at the mouth of the bay but had also reclaimed the two headland fortresses.

"They could be waiting for nightfall to attack," he said worriedly. A concern that made so much sense Abramm took it to heart immediately, certain they were staging another attempt to take Graymeer's.

Perhaps they believed their surprise attack on the Hall of Kings had been successful and Abramm was dead, leaving no one to ruin another corridor, or drive off the mist, or . . . use the guardstar. Suddenly he wondered if the whole conflict in the bay had been nothing more than a distraction from the real target: Graymeer's itself. *I have to drive off that mist. Now.*

He turned to Leyton Donavan. "Didn't you say there are tales claiming my scepter can conjure a wind?"

Leyton frowned at him. His eyes flicked to the burned-out hall at Abramm's back, then returned to meet his gaze. "You think there's any way the regalia survived that fire?"

"If they are what you think they are," said Abramm. "Would you like to come with me and see?"

His carriage brought them around to the bottom of the hill upon which the Hall of Kings had been built, the ride giving them a thorough view of the damage. The Hall, still hot and smoldering, had been gutted. Nearby buildings had also suffered various amounts of damage, most of them saved from complete destruction because they were built with stone. The Jewel House was one of the latter.

Abramm leaped out of the carriage as soon as it pulled to a stop beside it. The house's wooden roof sagged inward, still smoldering despite having been soaked by the bucket brigades. The structure's windows had melted into slag, and even some of the stones in the walls were cracked.

Ducking beneath the charred, half-fallen lintel, Abramm picked his way through the rubble, avoiding the biggest and hottest beam and wondering how he was going to find anything beneath the wet jumble of ash, charred wood, and stone that layered the floor. Part of one wall had tumbled in, and all the furniture and cabinets had been reduced to charred sticks.

It must have been the crown, for he walked straight across the chamber as if he knew where he was going, the heat from the stones and beams searing his face and making the scars burn as if they were newly made. He stopped without knowing why—maybe it seemed like the place he recalled the regalia to have been kept—and bent to pull aside a soot-covered rock, glad he was wearing gloves. Even through them the heat was intense. His men entered behind him now, muttering among themselves.

He kicked away a wooden plank, unmindful of the soot that stained his woolen stockings and the ash that now coated his fine shoes. Before he could remove another, Channon and Will Ames were pulling it away for him—and there at his feet, gleaming white amidst all the black, lay the scepter. The rod showed no sign of char or soot or even tarnish, the great orb at its head flickering with a pale white light.

A slight shifting of the direction of his gaze revealed to him the Orb of Tersius, enfolded in a paper-thin shroud of ash—probably the remains of the velvet drapes that had hung in this room. He stepped toward it, bent, and pulled away the shroud. Behind him came the hissing of Leyton's breath and a murmured exclamation of astonishment. Like the scepter, the orb had weathered the inferno untouched by the heat itself or by the ash and soot in which it lay.

He stepped back and bent to pick up the scepter, Channon's instinctive warning smothered almost as soon as it began. Like the captain of his guard, Abramm expected it to be as hot as the other things he'd touched here and was surprised to find it was no warmer than on the day of his coronation.

"May I bring the orb?" asked Leyton, standing over the object in question.

Abramm gave the man a nod and then, as the latter squatted to pick it up, he pointed out the ring, lying under a fallen stone. "And I think that may be the robe there, under the pile of ash just beyond it."

A creaking from above and a sudden shower of sparks urged him to take Channon's advice to leave, and having found what he'd come for, he did. Commiting the orb and other articles into Fortesque's care, he took the scepter and rode back to the palace to change his clothes and get Warbanner.

An hour later he rode into Graymeer's at the head of a twenty-five-man squadron. Lieutenant Brookes immediately escorted him to the ramparts where Commander Weston was directing the firing of the catapults, which had been placed up there for this very eventuality. The mist was so thick Abramm could not see the top of the seaward observation tower, nor even to the far side of the fortress. Moreover, it was a pale and dry mist, more like smoke than fog, but without the odor.

Weston confirmed Abramm's fear that Esurhites had tried to come up from below. He'd assigned a force to guard the grotto at the bottom, but they'd been pushed upward from their position about an hour earlier. However, they were still holding the newly installed gate at the halfway point. "Though, since the southlanders now have access to all the warrens below us," he said grimly, "they might come up anywhere."

Abramm looked down at the scepter in his gloved hands, thinking he was a fool to have brought it up here with no more idea of what he intended than simply to bring it. Perhaps it was the strange way in which he'd been led to it that had made him think that was all the planning he needed, but clearly it was not enough.

I need a wind, he thought at it. And felt immediately foolish when absolutely nothing happened. He tried releasing a tiny spark of Light into the rod. Which it accepted readily, the orb at its head flickering slightly in acknowledgment.

Did it need more, then?

He tried again, channeling a larger force. The orb flared brightly so long as he kept it up, but faded the moment he stopped. And there was no wind.

He turned to Leyton, who had come up behind him and was watching him closely. For a moment Abramm hesitated, reluctant to appear completely incompetent. His next thought was the wry observation that he was, in fact, exactly that. And this was no time to let pride get in his way. "What am I supposed to do?" he asked the Chesedhan.

Leyton frowned. "The account I read said you must know it."

"Know it. What's that supposed to mean?"

"I have no idea. I got the impression it would be automatic. Perhaps it is a function of one's growth in the Light." He paused. "Would you like me to give it a try?"

NO! Abramm thought. But again that was pride speaking, not sense. And anyway, if the regalia truly were his and only his, Leyton would have little more success than he had. He thrust the implement into the man's hands and told him to go ahead.

And as he'd guessed, although Leyton could also light the orb at the top of the rod, in the end he produced no more than Abramm had. *Well, so much for that*, Abramm thought. *Maybe I can figure out how to light the guardstar with it.*

He took the scepter back and hurried around the wallwalk to the observation tower. Descending its winding stairway he emerged into the Officers' Yard, where the black-striped orb still rested atop its iron struts on the excavated mound. Then he stood there. As Leyton and the others caught up with him, he looked down at the scepter again.

Know it. Well, I certainly don't know it. Not what it's supposed to do, not how it was made, not how it's been used, its history . . . Hadn't Maddie said something about a reference to the regalia in the Words? He'd never followed up on that, too distracted by all the other things. . . .

He thought about the last corridor he'd destroyed here and that odd shifting of his perception that had occurred just before. Was that a form of "knowing"? It had seemed more like knowing his fortress than anything else, though. He didn't recall doing anything specific beyond wanting the corridor gone. Eidon had done the rest. Just as Eidon had been the one to deliver him from the morwhol. He'd had only to trust.

Is that the key here, as well? To simply stand by and trust? But what would he need implements for if he need only stand by and wait?

Lord, what do you want me to do? I see now I've been remiss, occupied with other things when I should have been digging into your Words to find what you have to say about this. Or at the least I should have asked Kesrin. . . .

At that moment a helmeted man in a dark breastplate burst out of the doorway in the observation tower. His dark eyes fell at once upon Abramm and widened in the surprise of recognition, only to narrow with renewed purpose. Shouting a battle cry, he ran at the Kiriathan king as if no one else stood in the yard but the two of them. Leyton and Channon moved simultaneously to cut him off, and he died three yards from his target, Leyton's long sword piercing his throat, Channon's sliding in under his armpit.

His body had not even slid off the two swords when his fellows came pouring into the Officers' Yard on a veil of mist, shouting at the top of their lungs, each of them focused on Abramm alone. Surrounded and severely outnumbered, Abramm found himself swinging the scepter like a club, unwilling to drop it in favor of pulling out his sword for fear of losing it. The Light flowed out of him, flashing and flaring in the orb as it arced through the air, knocking aside heads and blades alike, seeming suddenly much heavier than it had before. It trailed little sparkles of light, and he could feel the wind generated by its passing. . . .

At length he found himself standing shoulder to shoulder with his defenders in a yard littered with bodies, some living, many not. The orb at the scepter's end blazed like a living star, sparks still trailing from it in the wind. The *wind*. He felt it now tugging at his hair and cloak as it whipped around the yard, kicking up dust, flapping the garments of the fallen and driving the invading mist back over the top of the wall as it funneled upward. The moment it did, he heard Weston's bellow to clean the guns and reload them, the echoed shouts of those orders repeated and elaborated, then the trundle of the gun trucks, the hiss and ring of the plungers.

And up above, patches of blue appeared in the rapidly shredding mist.

Abramm's gaze returned to the scepter, already feeling lighter than it had. The flare in its head faded, the fountain of sparks slowed to a few glowing motes, spit forth erratically. He saw Leyton staring at it with eyes so wide the whites showed all around. Slowly now, as if he realized he was staring, he lifted his gaze to meet Abramm's own.

And then, before either of them could speak, one of the armsmen cried, "It lit! The big ball up there, sir. I just saw it flicker. I swear it."

All eyes turned toward the orb on its stanchions and immediately Abramm saw that part of its streaked covering had come loose, a strip of it flapping in the wind.

Handing the scepter to Leyton, he climbed atop the guardstar's platform, then shimmied up one of the struts until he could reach the sphere. The curling, flapping strip peeled away from the orb like the fleshy skin of an orange. He continued to pull off strips until what was left finally came away in one large piece.

The guardstar sat above him on its struts, a smooth, slick orb that looked to be made of highly polished milk glass. But there was no flicker now, nothing beyond the normal reflection of light off any slick surface. And though he struck it with a filament of Light, and felt the Light received, it changed nothing.

He kept trying, even going so far as to lay his bare palm against its surface and let the Light flow out of him, but that had no effect, either. Finally, his arm and legs cramping with the effort of holding himself to the strut, he slid down to rejoin his men on the ground. By then the small wind he'd generated earlier had driven off the remainder of the mist, leaving the fortress clear.

Weston's voice carried down from the ramparts, ordering the reloaded cannon to fire, and moments later the roar of their response rattled Abramm's teeth and shook his innards. As the reload command rang out, he flew up the ramp toward the wallwalk to see how the battle was progressing. Then Weston cried out again: "They're turning away, boys! They're turning tail!

Let's give 'em something to remember us by."

Abramm joined him in time for the last salvo, the long guns bucking as they belched white clouds of smoke and six black balls arced over an ocean turned blue again in the wake of the rapidly retreating mist wall. The balls fell close enough to splash the decks of the five exposed galleys now frantically heeling around to catch up with their departing cover. Abramm leaned against the parapet as the wind rushed around him, flapping his cloak and ruffling his hair. He watched the galleys catch up with the mist, others of their kind doing the same below Kildar, which had also been uncovered. Meanwhile the cloud moved rapidly southeastward and out to sea until he could see it no longer.

"Well," he said finally, pushing back from the stone. "I guess that's over."

"And I guess I was right after all," said Leyton beside him.

"More or less," Abramm agreed. But he still had no real idea what he had done. As with all the other things, it seemed he had done nothing at all.

29

They hanged Arik Foxton at dawn the next day. Abramm made Briellen watch, and she stood under guard in the box across the square from him, waxen faced and unmoving. After the proceedings she was put immediately into a coach and driven away to the city's edge, where all her retinue awaited her. Abramm did not accompany her; instead, the moment Foxton was declared dead, he turned his back on it all and returned to the palace, sickened and depressed.

He couldn't help thinking of the inequity in it—that Briellen, who by her own admission had started it, got off with nothing more than deportation, while Foxton was executed for a crime that would have gone unremarked and unpunished had he committed it with anyone other than the king's betrothed.

Abramm would have been tempted to spend the afternoon brooding about it all had he not so many other things to occupy his thoughts. Changing out of his execution finery, he donned leather tunic, woolen breeches, and boots and went down to the docks with Count Blackwell and Admiral Hamilton to assess the damage his vessels had sustained in yesterday's action. In the afternoon, he attended a meeting of the ship owners who'd hired on in an adjunct military capacity and commended them for their efforts in yesterday's battle. Stressing the vital support their contribution had provided, he warned them that evil days were not yet over. Their services would be required again, possibly soon.

After that speech, many more volunteered their own vessels, thanks in large part to the belief that Abramm had conjured the winds that had driven away the mist yesterday—and could do it again if necessary. Their fears of being becalmed and at the mercy of hostile, oar-driven vessels allayed, they displayed a confidence approaching blind bravado that any conflict with the "vastly inferior" galleys would be swiftly and decisively won.

Needing their support and not even certain they were wrong about what he could do, Abramm said nothing to dissuade them. He was glad, all the same, to leave them for his second meeting of the afternoon, this one back at the Ministry of the Navy. After a comprehensive review of yesterday's action and its results, they turned finally to Abramm's greatest concern: the need to secure the Gull Islands. A few of the officers at the table had already conceded privately the strong possibility the islands had been the staging ground for yesterday's attack, and the fact there'd been no reported galley sighting in the twenty-four hours since they'd fled only made his case stronger.

"I want those islands under our control," Abramm told them. "Whether we must wrest them from the enemy or establish a post on them ourselves, I want it done as soon as possible."

Of course there arose the usual arguments—the treacherous waters surrounding the islands, the mists, the currents, the hidden rocks and capricious winds, all devastating to wind-driven ships. Which was why, he told them, he proposed they send the fleet of galleys he'd received as a coronation gift from Katahn ul Manus. Smaller, more maneuverable, shallower of draft, and not nearly so vulnerable to the vagaries of the wind, they might succeed where the other vessels would not. The only drawback lay in the amount of time and effort required to get them there, and for that, too, Abramm had a solution: "I propose we send a combination of vessels. Use wind-driven ships to carry replacement oarsmen and, if conditions are favorable, even tow the galleys behind them."

The replacement oarsmen he would pull from existing crews, preferably by calling for volunteers who would, for this extraordinary service, receive triple pay and other benefits. If not enough men volunteered—a likely outcome—he proposed to draw the rest by lot, though they'd receive less compensation than would the volunteers.

A spirited discussion of this plan by his naval experts convinced Abramm it would work. At the meeting's end, he gave them two weeks to put it together, then returned to the palace for a hot bath, supper, and the evening's message at Terstmeet.

To his surprise, Prince Leyton was waiting for him in the antechamber of his apartments. The only time they'd spoken since that dreadful night in the bedchamber when Briellen and Foxton were discovered had been their brief interchange regarding the scepter during yesterday's battle. Beyond that, the Chesedhan prince had kept silent, observing all the proceedings of trial and execution without uttering a word. Some of Abramm's advisors suggested he was more embarrassed than scandalized, but whatever the reason, the man who now rose to greet Abramm as he strode through the door was a much-subdued version of the one who'd sat at his coronation banquet last month and shamelessly baited him. His request for a moment of Abramm's time was made in complete humility. That change of attitude, plus the fact they'd not yet had a chance to speak of the scepter's part in driving off the wind, moved Abramm to grant his request.

Thus, the Chesedhan crown prince joined him in his private dining chamber to share a supper of baked codfish, roast quail, boiled leeks and spin-ach, and fine white bread. At first they confined their conversation to banali-ties of weather and yesterday's attack. Then, finally, as the currant duff was served and Leyton still hadn't brought up whatever had moved him to request this audience, Abramm turned to his own concern. "You must know why I agreed to this meeting, Donavan."

"You want to talk to me about the scepter."

"Maddie told me you've done a great deal of research into our regalia."

The Chesedhan shrugged. "Most of it's really just tales."

"But not all."

Leyton concentrated on spooning currant duff from his bowl. "*Did* you conjure that wind, sir?"

"I don't know."

"Well, you certainly did something. Many have taken shieldmarks because of it."

"So I've been told." A number of both the merchants and the officers at the Ministry of the Navy had worn their doublets unbuttoned to reveal the new-made marks that afternoon. "I've also noted they are spreading various tales of what I did, most of which are wrong." He glanced up from his own pudding. "You were there. What do you think I did?"

Leyton's ruddy cheeks reddened further. "I was too busy fighting Esurhites to notice. Certainly there was a wind generated, and it sprang up around you. Since that is what you brought the scepter there to do . . . I wonder why you would question your results now."

"Because I did not consciously move the Light to make that wind."

"Just as you did not generate the Light nor make a wind the day you were crowned."

"Nor the day I cleaned out Graymeer's. Nor even when I slew Beltha'adi. It just . . . happened. That first time it was to be expected, because I was newly marked and knew nothing. But I thought as time went by I was supposed to learn to use the Light, and yet . . ."

"It seems from what you're saying that every time the Light has manifested through you it's been more or less an accident."

"Except for maybe the morwhol." He caught the dubious flicker of Leyton's eyes when he mentioned that incident, but he ignored it. "Though I didn't consciously release it even then. It was more that I . . . rested."

He frowned as he traveled back through that memory—then jerked free of it when he realized how tied up with Maddie it was.

Leyton ran his spoon around his nearly empty pudding bowl, collecting up the remnants. "Well, you certainly didn't appear to be resting yesterday, the way you were swinging the thing around, bashing heads as if it were a war club. I will say I've read nothing about that as a method of unlocking the implement's powers. Though it seemed to work."

"You said yesterday that to use it, I needed to know it. Is that all you remember the account saying?"

"There might have been some elaboration. . . . I've actually brought along a copy of the account. If you'd like I'll send it over."

The man's uncharacteristic openness both surprised Abramm and made him wary, for clearly the Chesedhan was trading for a favor. *Very well, Prince Leyton . . . I'll bite.*

"I'd like that," Abramm said. He left his spoon in his own empty dish and sat back in his chair, eyes upon his guest. "So why have you sought this meeting, Donavan?"

It was astonishing to watch the man shrivel before him, his eyes dropping immediately to his wineglass, which he then picked up and sipped from. Setting it very carefully back into its place, he hesitated, then lifted his face and spoke. "I realize this is brash of me, Your Majesty, but I have to ask . . . do you see any hope at all of repairing this breech that has been opened between us?"

Chesedhans are brash if they are nothing else, Abramm thought, keeping the smile off his face. He let his gaze drop to the hands of the servant removing his empty dish from before him. "My people will never accept Briellen now—even if I were inclined to do so myself, which I am not." He caught Leyton's eyes again. "I will admit, the actions of you and your men in yesterday's fighting have acquitted you to some degree. Were it not for that I'd have sent you away with your sister."

The other man nodded as if he'd expected such an answer. "But that's the limit of your generosity."

"We need your ships, it's true. And I suspect, eventually, it may turn out we'll need much more. . . . Nor do I much like the prospect of having the Shadow controlling my next-door neighbors. Because of that I think we could abide some form of agreement between us. But unless you are willing to accept it without a marriage to bind it, I would have to say no. I see no real hope of true alliance."

"It was only the prospect of seeing you married to a Chesedhan daughter of royal blood that allowed my father's counselors and highest lords to consider agreeing to any alliance at all."

"Well, then, you have found your answer."

Leyton sat staring at his wineglass, running his finger back and forth around the edge of its flattened foot. "There *is* another daughter, sir," he said quietly.

And at those words, a current of Light zinged through Abramm, raising every hair on his body. He stared at the man intently. "A Second Daughter through whom the royal line does not flow. I fail to see how that would solve your problem."

The Chesedhan frowned at his fingers as they stroked the foot of the wineglass a few more times, then he leaned back in his chair, folding his hands at the edge of the linen-draped table, his gaze still turned downward. His voice came low and tight. "Briellen has disgraced us all. She cannot possibly be offered in marriage to anyone now, and Father will certainly disown her once she returns to Chesedh." His gaze lifted to meet Abramm's. "I would be well within my authority to declare her disowned here and now, and make Madeleine First Daughter in her place."

The room lurched at the edges of Abramm's vision. For a moment he could hardly breathe, as a roaring filled his ears. "Maddie would be First Daughter, you say?"

Leyton nodded. "But only if she consents."

Only if she consents . . . Exactly what Eidon had said to him. *I will not violate her freedom to choose.* . . . Abramm felt as if his entire world had taken a cataclysmic shift.

Apparently misreading his shock, Leyton frowned. "I know she is not exactly suitable—"

"She is eminently suitable," Abramm interrupted, his flat tone causing a lift of the Chesedhan's blond brows. "The only question is—"

"Can she be persuaded to undertake a role she has sworn all her life she could never fill and doesn't want to."

Abramm smiled wryly. "There is that, too. But I was thinking more of the logistics. I fear we might not be able to reach her before she leaves for the Western Isles."

"Western Isles? I thought you sent her to investigate the guardstar at Avramm's Landing."

"That was merely the excuse we put to it." And now it was Abramm's turn to contemplate the foot of his wineglass.

After a moment he heard the swift intake of Leyton's breath. "Plagues, man! You mean the rumors about you two were *true*? And you had the gall today to—"

"The rumors were gross exaggerations and lies. Whatever is between us, we did not act upon." *Save that one incident in the library*, his treacherous conscience reminded him. "Or at least, not as the rumors would have it. In truth, it was realizing I had feelings for her that caused me to send her away."

"And are your feelings reciprocated?"

"Without question."

The Chesedhan regarded him narrowly for a moment, an odd, almost surprised expression on his face. "Then you must send word as soon as possible."

"I'll send a pigeon out at dawn. It should arrive by tomorrow afternoon. We can only pray that will be soon enough."

They were rising from the table to leave for Terstmeet when Simon Kalladorne stepped into the room. Donavan started to excuse himself, but Simon stopped him. "You'll need to hear this, too, sir."

But then the old duke said nothing, just stood glancing from one to the other of them.

"Well?" Abramm prodded.

His uncle's gray brows drew down and he looked the king in the eye. "I'm afraid there's bad news from Avramm's Landing, sir." He paused, then said flatly, "*Starchaser*'s been sunk."

"*Starchaser*?" Leyton said. "Wasn't that the vessel my sister—"

Simon nodded. "There was a raid on the fortress there early yesterday, coordinated apparently with the attack here at Springerlan. They believe the Esurhites sank her beforehand off the point of the Widow's Walk. Probably to keep her from warning the fort of their presence. Right now there appears to be no survivors, and seeing as that stretch of the coast is mostly cliffline, I doubt there'll be much wreckage found."

His words faded into silence. Abramm stared at him, his mind blank, his flesh turned cold. *How could this be? To come so close and have it all ripped away. . . ? What are you doing, my Lord?*

Suddenly Leyton whooshed out a deep breath and said, "The Esurhites have a habit of tagging big ships. Sometimes they cable them, then ride behind for a while, using their magic to modulate wind and sea. Eventually they come aboard to take new men to replace the slaves they burnt out on the rowing benches. The rest of the crew they kill before sinking the ship." He paused. "It would make sense they'd do such a thing right before they attacked. They'd need fresh muscle to get in and out again swiftly."

Abramm listened to him without really comprehending what he was saying, merely glad the other was speaking so he didn't have to. Even so, Simon's eyes had not left his own for all the length of Leyton's discourse, and the room seemed to be flashing and spangling around him.

The Chesedhan prince now touched his arm, drawing his eye. "If they found a northern woman aboard, sir, they'd surely take her with them." He risked a small smile. "And knowing Maddie, she'd just as surely find a way of escape."

Abramm realized then that he needed to start breathing again, for he had not since the moment Simon had said his first words. And now that he took in that deep breath, whatever paralysis had locked his mind released it, a thousand thoughts tumbling in.

"They'll have to come by Springerlan," he said grimly, unwilling right now to even consider any possibility other than that she had been captured by Esurhites.

"It would be a tough job to spot 'em if they do," said Simon. "Apparently they can navigate at night. And if it's misty, as it likely would be . . ."

"She'll know they'd protect her if she claims her heritage."

"But they know a Second Daughter is worth nothing," Leyton pointed out.

"Who says she has to claim to be Second Daughter?"

Leyton looked at him hard for a moment. Then one of his bushy brows lifted as if in amusement. "I see you do know her well."

"If I'm right about the Gulls," Abramm went on. "They'll take her there." He fell silent, calculating the number of days it might take a galley to travel from Avramm's Landing to the Gull Islands versus how long it should take his own men to reach them.

He turned to Simon. "Tell Hamilton I'm moving up our departure date by a week. Tell him his people will have to work round the clock, double shifts if need be. We can't afford to let her get there ahead of us." He paused. "Or at least not much ahead of us."

Simon frowned. "Sir, you don't even know for sure that she's—" He broke off, evidently seeing the futility of suggesting anything else. "Yes, sir."

After he left, prince and king stood silently, each lost in his own thoughts. Then Leyton said, "I'd like to add my ships to the attack force."

"Thank you, Prince Leyton, but we have what we need."

"Begging your pardon, sir, but I know that's not true."

"Well, true or not, we have no official alliance. And not really much hope for one, seeing as we have no sure reason to believe she's even alive."

"I think she's alive, and I believe you do, too." He hesitated. "I've heard rumors you two have some sort of mystical connection . . . the sort where you would know if she were dead."

Again Abramm only stared at him, struck by the awful realization that he *had* known. Or at least he'd known something was wrong. In his dreams. The details of which he'd never recalled once he'd awakened. But he couldn't even try to think of them now, lest they cast him into an abyss of hysteria.

"I'm told you mean to pull together a contingent of wind-driven ships and galleys," Leyton said when Abramm did not deny his assertion. "Let my frigates serve as the former. That way you can keep your own big vessels close to home, guarding your shores."

This was an offer Abramm had not expected. A tempting one, for he disliked leaving his shores thinly defended even for the week or two he expected the operation to take. It would also mitigate somewhat his people's hostility toward the Chesedhan alliance, so that, if all worked out and he did get Maddie back, he wouldn't have to fight his own subjects, as well.

"You would be willing to submit yourself to the commander of this mission?"

Leyton frowned. "As the highest-ranking noble, would I not be the commander?"

"If you were the highest-ranking noble."

"Sir?"

And now Abramm gave him a grim smile. "I will be leading this party myself, Donavan. But I will be glad to accept your offer—of ships and men, and of your leadership, as well."

30

Maddie had wrestled down the fear generated by the Broho's magic and freed the Light just before he had appeared on *Starchaser*'s foredeck. As he'd looked into her eyes, she'd felt the strength of his will. Yet she'd also felt his fear, and with the Light running through her, she knew he would not touch her. Nor did he, commanding one of the sailors nearby to bring her and Liza aft. Walking through unspeakable carnage, the images of which she was still trying to forget nearly a week later, she and her maid had been lined up with what remained of the crew. It was then that she declared herself to be the First Daughter of Chesedh and the bride-to-be of Abramm Kalladorne and demanded they treat her as such.

It was a half-baked ploy born of desperation more than sense, so she was gratified to see all the Esurhites within earshot stiffen and look her way— most likely, she thought in retrospect, because they'd recognized Abramm's name. The Broho had not been so impressed, pointing out in his heavily accented Kiriathan that the true First Daughter was being married in Springerlan that very day.

She'd countered with the claim that the wedding was a sham, and that Abramm knew of the plan to attack him and sent her out of danger. Which had set uncertainty into his eyes. She'd showed him her signet ring proving her status as daughter of the Royal House of Donavan. He'd ordered a man to take it off her hand, then snatched it impatiently, glared at it, at her, and finally gestured for her and Liza to be taken to the galleys. Whether that meant he'd believed her, she still didn't know. So far the men had ignored both women, but perhaps it was only because they'd had a mission to complete at the time and even now rowed through dangerous waters.

It had been six days since the Esurhites had torn their captives from the deck of the *Starchaser* and thrown them into this tiny two-bunk cabin on the lead galley's foredeck. Each morning and evening the cabin door was unlocked, the slop bucket emptied, and the empty water jug replaced with a full one. Pieces of salt fish and biscuit were tossed haphazardly onto the lowest bunk, and the door was shut and locked again.

They traveled in perpetual mist, but the fact that in the beginning Maddie had occasionally glimpsed shoreline made her think her narrow window faced east. Since their cabin was on the foredeck, and thus at the front of the ship, she'd deduced they were heading south. And had been for the last six days.

After their capture of the women, the Esurhites had transferred a number of *Starchaser's* crewmen to their vessels to man the oars below. Then they'd sunk the northern ship and rowed on to Avramm's Landing, entering its bay full of anchored ships just after dusk. Gliding brazenly past vessels whose deck lanterns shone like fuzzy stars high above them, they had swung round before reaching the city itself to pull in close to the dark cliff that bordered the bay's southern shore. After mooring there for a bit, the oars were lifted again and they pulled away, heading out into the mist that had rolled in with them. They were well away when the faint clanging of an alarm bell rang out and angry voices echoed across the quiet sea.

They rowed most of the night, stopped sometime before dawn to rest, and continued on hours later, cloaked in a mist that thickened steadily as they went. That they were going south gave her hope, for it meant they would have to pass by Springerlan. When they did, they might encounter Kiriathan vessels—perhaps even Chesedhan vessels—raising the possibility of rescue. . . .

But after six days of travel, the mist was so thick she had not seen the shore in two days and could hardly pick out the form of her galley's sister ship holding position just aft off the port bow. Worse, the seas had grown utterly calm. With conditions as they were, no rescue ship could even get to them, much less find them. Indeed she wondered for a time how the galleys' crews were managing to navigate without stars or sun or moon. Last night she'd noticed a purple glow emanating from somewhere aft of her position, as if a light had been placed in the middle of the galley's deck. Or maybe it was the Broho, manning the helm with his amulet. The other galley had no light, and she doubted the one on her vessel was there simply to illumine the way, since in this deep mist, it would be useless. Perhaps it served as a sort of lodestone, pulling them toward their destination, which, as the days passed, she grew increasingly certain must be the Gull Islands.

On the eighth day she admitted to herself that they had to have passed Springerlan by then and that no rescue had come. Following that came the acknowledgment that soon they would reach their destination, where even if the Broho's commander believed her claim of being First Daughter—highly unlikely—that would only send her to the Supreme Commander's harem. And if he didn't believe it, then she and Liza would certainly be handed over to some subordinate to do with as he pleased.

Neither was a prospect she could consider without inducing deep anxiety, and so she had to cut such speculations off. Better to live one day at a time. Better still, one hour at a time. Better to occupy her mind with thoughts of Eidon's love and goodness. Of his power and his wisdom and the fact that he often let his people get lost so he could find them, let them fall into trouble just so he could deliver them and all could see his power. . . . And that the darker things became, the brighter his Light would shine.

But it was hard to wait with nothing to do but think.

Abramm stood on the quarterdeck of the Chesedhan frigate *Firebrand*, staring at the mist that drifted around the vessel's masts and rigging. The sun, hidden from sight since morning, stood somewhere near the western horizon off the starboard bow, barely visible as a slightly brighter spot in the wool that swirled around them. Sea gulls circled overhead, glimpsed through patches of fog, their sharp squawks echoing over the still water. He frowned up at them, mentally willing them to leave. *If you don't start now, you'll not reach your rookery before dark.*

And finally, almost as if they'd heard him, the birds swirled upward into the mist, their cries fading steadily southward. When he heard them no more, he turned and gave the command to begin. At once the men burst into action, detaching the cabled galleys from the big ships that had pulled them, as the big ships lowered their longboats to the sea and began filling them with the fresh crews of oarsmen that would power the galleys to the islands this night.

Meanwhile Abramm retired to his cabin to darken his face and hair, strap to his bare back the harness and sleeve he'd had made for the scepter, and don his Esurhite uniform over top of it. He reemerged shortly and was ferried over with the last of the crew to the lead galley, *Yverik*.

His expedition had sailed out of Springerlan three days ago, heading east along Kiriath's coast until they came due north of the Gull Islands. During all that time, the retinue of seabirds had accompanied them—spies for the enemy, he had no doubt. Their numbers had increased today as the ships had pushed southward into thickening mist and fading wind. When finally their speed had slowed to a crawl, they'd all dropped anchor under the gulls' watchful eyes and made preparations for the night. Or so Abramm hoped the ones who commanded the gulls would believe.

The plan was mad enough, there was a chance they would.

Their objective was the main island, which the map labeled *Chakos* and which was said to have once been the site of fine Ophiran villas before it was swamped in the Cataclysm and destroyed. The resultant treacherous currents, sandbars, and rocky reefs made it a deathtrap for ships even without the covering of mist it had gained in the last few decades. Most avoided it. With no local source of fresh water and minimal plant life, it now supported only vast populations of gulls, cormorants, and other seabirds. If the Esurhites had established a base in the islands, it would most likely be on Chakos. If they had set up an etherworld corridor, as Abramm feared they had, it, too, would be on Chakos.

Because the mist confused the compass in addition to obscuring the stars, they would have to travel by line of sight alone. Abramm planned to use his extraordinary night sight to follow a reef marked on the old maps, something that seemed doable given the still water and windless conditions—so long as he could see it well enough to keep them from going aground on it or, worse, bashing a hole in the hull. The reef ran south for three leagues, then curved round toward the southwest, leading to a wide and treacherous channel-laced shallows through which lay the route into Chakos Bay.

Admiral Hamilton had been unabashedly opposed to Abramm's plan from the beginning. "Hard enough to navigate those waters in the daylight," he'd protested. "In the dark you'll be dashed to pieces. It's one thing to see down a dark tunnel, quite another to pick out mist-shrouded rocks in time to avoid a collision."

Which was true. Worse, since Abramm alone possessed this dubious ability, the others would have to follow his lead, a feat Hamilton deemed even more unlikely. Nor was his grand admiral the only naysayer. Objections and criticisms had flown freely, some of them offered to Abramm's face at his request, others swirling around him, exchanged by those who did not have his ear, yet definitely had their opinions.

Blackwell had been beside himself with dismay, spouting predictions of death and disaster, and all but demanding Abramm abandon the expedition. The crowning touch came on the eve of their departure, when the count had pressed him to marry one of the Kiriathan noblewomen that very night so he would have a chance to secure an heir in the case of his death. Abramm had stared at his secretary in astonishment, wondering if the man had lost his mind.

"Well, you were set to marry that witch Briellen without loving her," Blackwell pointed out. "Why not one of our own?"

"You're overreacting, Bryon," Abramm had told him.

"Overreacting? You propose to assault the Gull Islands by night with a mere seven galleys to the enemy's thirty? It's madness, my lord."

Actually, it's probably closer to forty, Abramm had thought wryly, but he didn't say that.

"If you don't come back, sir, what will we do? The Mataio is beginning to stir again, Gillard is still out there somewhere, and who knows when the northland's going to explode. . . ."

"Carissa is my heir for now. And Simon will support her." He frowned at his secretary and friend. "Have you so little faith, Bryon? After all we've been through? If not in me, then in Eidon's power to protect me?"

"I fear you put too much stock in what happened at your coronation, sir. Eidon does not suffer fools." He paused. "I can't help but wonder if your motives are entirely pure and adequately thought through." He paused again, longer this time, then added quietly, "Even if she did survive *Starchaser*'s capture . . . how can you think of marrying her after what they've surely done to her?"

Abramm had dismissed his objections as the hysteria of a fragile temperament. Now that he was actually out here, now that he saw how dark it was, how easy it would be to get lost in the night and this smothering blanket of mist, Blackwell's words returned. Like a nest of adder's eggs under a house too hastily built, they had hatched in his bed, infusing their poisonous fears into his heart.

So many things could go wrong. And yet . . . what else could he do? He had to capture the islands or soon he'd have the whole Esurhite navy knocking on his door.

If it was a mad plan, it was also a bold one that hinged upon his unusual abilities. Those were often the plans that worked the best, simply because they were so unexpected.

At length they were ready to go, saying their good-byes and moving slowly south as the darkness gathered steadily around them. Abramm had conceived a system of hooded stern lights by which his little fleet could be guided, one following the other, his own ship in the lead. Katahn would follow him directly, then three more vessels each under the command of the men Katahn had brought, while Trap brought up the rear.

They slid easily through glasslike water, a single lantern hanging under the prow, out of his direct line of sight but enough to illuminate the path ahead. He could see the reef they planned to follow glowing with a pale luminescence beneath the calm waters off the galley's port side. With the water this still, there would be no sounds of waves upon rock, so they would have only sight to warn them. Men lined the gunwale now, peering into the darkness as they listened to the rhythmic trickle and squeak of the oars and the quiet rush of water against the hull.

Abramm stood with the Esurhite helmsman atop his steering box in the stern, making sure all his commands and comments were now uttered in the Tahg. Cloaked and cowled in dark wool, he was the only Kiriathan on deck, but there were others below, soldiers armed and ready to pour out of the hold once it was time for battle. But that would come later. For now he had to keep an eye on the reef beside them, a task that turned out to be far more difficult than he'd expected. Often he lost sight of it altogether and stood tensely as the vessel slid forward blindly, aware of all the things that could subtly alter their course. The compass was now spinning in its case, completely useless, leaving the helmsmen with no means of guidance save to keep his arm steady. Should even one of the oarsmen falter, reducing the power applied on one side of the vessel, they'd begin to veer off course without knowing. Or the reef might suddenly take a jog into their path, or a current catch them, or the tide begin to turn. . . . But it did no good to stand and think of all that might go wrong, so Abramm forced away such thoughts and renewed his concentration on the blackness before his eyes.

They had rowed for about two hours and, from the regular soundings now being taken, looked to be approaching the shallows when Abramm was beset with the sense of something approaching almost ninety degrees to starboard. Stepping to the side to peer into the darkness, he felt the hairs lift on the back of his neck, though there was nothing but dimly lit veils of mist shifting against the dark. As there had been for the last two hours. And yet . . . the sense of cold presence increased. He gripped the rail and stared, and it seemed for a moment he saw a purple flash directly to starboard, low enough to the water that it could be another vessel.

He called for the rowers to cease, told the sternmen to signal the ship behind to do likewise, listening as the oars creaked up in a sudden chorus of dripping water. The sound faded quickly, and they glided along, decelerating slowly in the stark silence that followed. Abramm stared so hard his eyes hurt, and soon others came to stand along the starboard rail, as well.

Then he saw it again: a purple glow, obscured and softened by the mist, and approaching them at a slight angle, so that if Yverik's sweeps were set down and she slowed further, the other might well shoot past without ever seeing her. Abramm gave a quiet order to drop the oars and douse the front light. Then they waited, the helmsman turning the ship with its remaining momentum until the purple was coming up off their stern and well alongside. They stood in darkness, counting down the moments. Finally Abramm heard the distant rhythm of the approaching vessel's oars.

The sound was deceptive, though, still seeming far away when suddenly the other ship loomed out of the darkness, a brilliant purple light blazing from its helmsman. As the boat swept past, Abramm saw him as clearly as if it were full daylight. Dark-skinned, shaven-headed, his angular features fixed in a grimace, hands gripping the wheel as his eyes blazed with the same purple light that flared from his chest. He stared straight ahead, as if he could already see his destination and had only to close the gap between it and himself.

The ship shot by them, and they were just breathing a sigh of relief when a second ship rose up on their tail, passing so close it had to veer sharply away to avoid a collision. As its crewmen shouted imprecations in the Tahg, Abramm gave the order to pull hard aside and up to speed again, then shouted insults back at them, his own crew echoing the sentiments. A few fists were shaken, then the vessel sped off into the darkness.

As Abramm had hoped, Yverik was judged to be one of their own, and even better, now they had a vessel familiar with the waters to follow.

"Bring us up to full speed," he told the shipmaster. "We don't want to lose them."

The other boats were going so much faster, though, and the mist was so thick, that it wasn't long before Abramm did indeed lose sight of them, left with only the green line of phosphorescence that bubbled in their wake. And soon that was so faint, he couldn't be sure he was seeing anything at all. Worse, he'd lost all track of the reef, and the soundings showed the shallows practically upon them. Indeed, moments later off the port railing they glimpsed their first sight of the mats of grass that characterized them. Rooted on sandy ground under the water's surface, the tough, tall grasses would stand fully exposed when the tide was out. They passed the grasses for a long enough time to give Abramm hope, for the soundings were not changing, and he concluded they must be skirting the area.

Up ahead the faintly glowing trail suddenly bent sharply to port, leaving Abramm little time to ponder whether to follow. Hesitation would cause him to lose the tenuous track altogether, which would leave them nothing. And if nothing else, bold plans called for bold decisions.

"Increase the rhythm a half beat," he said quietly, though his heart was suddenly pounding. "Get ready to turn, starboard oars up on my mark." The command was repeated. The rowing tempo increased, the vessel gained speed again. Then, just as the prow obliterated his view of the bend in the phosphorescent wake, he gave the command to raise the starboard sweeps and turn the helm to port. The vessel lurched and stuttered, then heeled after the phosphorescence and was grabbed by a current that hurled them forward double speed. Bristles of grass rose up on either side, beyond which dark, pale-topped shapes glistened here and there in the mist. The stink of guano crept into the air. They continued for nearly an hour, and all that changed was that the guano smell increased. He began to relax, thinking they had surely been led into the channel they had sought.

Then a murmur crept into the stillness, a rushing sound that was soon identified as the crash of waves. The sound grew rapidly louder, ominous in its strength and swift approach, and with this current carrying them, he could no longer discount it all as illusion.

The wake trail had long since vanished, carried away by the current, but now he thought he glimpsed the trailing vessel up ahead, a moment before its oars lifted in unison and it disappeared again, swallowed by the darkness. From the looks on their faces and the way their gazes roved about, he knew none of his crewmen had seen the other galley. Nor, most likely, had any of them perceived the wake he'd been following all this time. What they did see was the forbidding line of massive rocks rising up out of the darkness ahead of them—a wide, crescent-shaped wall crowned and streaked with guano. Water crashed and wreathed whitely about its base, and the current was carrying them on a rapid collision course.

"What should I do, sir?" the helmsman asked.

"Keep her straight and steady."

"Sir?"

Abramm frowned at the rock, certain it was an illusion, yet unable to see the telltale vibration that would confirm his assumption. Still, those vessels had to go somewhere.

"Ease her to port a little," he told the helmsman.

The galley's speed continued to increase.

"The current's gonna take us right into them, sir."

"Yes. We'll ride it through. Just like the others did." He gestured confidently ahead, but already second thoughts assailed him. What if he'd imagined that galley?

"You mean . . . hit the rocks, sir?"

"I don't think we'll hit them, but I want you to aim for them squarely." He turned to the man at the stern. "Signal the others to follow. Repeat the pattern twice."

"Aye, sir."

There was no time for caution. They'd either all crash and sink together, or they'd all get through.

The helmsman's fears were not helped by the scrape of the oars on the rocks through which they now ran. He kept glancing at Abramm, the whites of his eyes visible in the darkness.

"If you lack the nerve, sailor," Abramm said, "give me the helm."

The man tightened his lips as he tightened his hands on the wheel and held his gaze steady. Rocks loomed over the curved prow. Recalling what he thought he'd seen the vessel ahead of them do, Abramm ordered both banks of oars to stand. The sweeps came up sharply, and the boat shot forward faster than ever, the rocks looming before them. On either side, the white foam of breakers flashed in the darkness, their roaring filling his ears.

Then they plunged into the thick, cold-lard sensation of a Shadow-woven illusion and came out still in the channel, but with the mist dramatically thinning. Ahead he saw where grassy shallows gave way to a wide, calm bay beneath a flat ceiling of mist. The two ships they had followed glided ahead, almost out of the channel now as lanterns flared on their decks. More vessels stood out on the bay beyond them, deck lights glowing against the dark hulk of an island, tiny red lights sprinkled along its shoreline.

"Khrell's Fire, sir!" cried the helmsman. "You did it!"

Abramm restrained himself from expressing his intense relief and subsequent flush of triumph. *Thank you, Eidon!* The men needn't know how unsure he'd been all this would work out. Nor how unsure he remained. He merely gave the man a nod, then glanced over their stern in time to see

Katahn's vessel burst out of the mist on their tail.

"What now, sir?"

"Follow after those two that led us in. If Eidon's hand stays with us, maybe we'll find a suitable moorage before they realize we're here."

The oarsmen went back to work, and the bulk of the island soon towered over them. As they drew closer Abramm could pick out lighted arched openings along the bottom of the cliff face, and it was into one of these that their unwitting guides disappeared. The guano smell grew stronger as *Yverik* glided along the wall toward the openings he assumed led to various moorages. A backward glance showed his small fleet had made it through the enchantment intact. Instinct guided him past the first opening, and the second, as well. He chose the third one, so dimly lit as to be barely discernible.

Dark rock walls pressed close about them as a faint light shone ahead. The oars' gurgle-splash took on a hollow quality as the sound bounced off the rock. Then the walls fell away and the boat slid into a large shadow-hung grotto lit with a single lantern and ranked with piers and moorages, all of which looked newly constructed, and all of which stood empty.

The sound of the gulls had alerted Maddie earlier that same afternoon to the fact they were approaching their destination. Their cries echoed in the mist, growing steadily louder, more frequent, and greater in number. Soon she saw the birds themselves, winging alongside the galley, a few coming so close she could see their eyes. The men on deck threw out bits of old biscuit, which they caught in midair before veering away, apparently an amusing shipboard pastime the gulls were as accustomed to as the men.

Then the light faded and the birds winged away. The women received their nightly biscuit and water, and soon darkness had obscured the view. Maddie settled onto her bunk, anxiety simmering in the pit of her stomach. It was nearly impossible now to stop the stream of speculations that flowed into her mind, nor the terror they aroused. And knowing that Eidon often used suffering to make his children stronger did not help in the slightest. Why did she need to be stronger? Hadn't she had enough suffering? Wasn't it sufficient to remove Abramm from her life with no possibility of his ever coming back into it?

Nor did it help that, as the darkness deepened, their mysterious purple guide light became more manifest. She did not think it ever went out, but in the darkness its power magnified into a heavy oppressive evil that increased with every day. It seemed to fuel her fearful speculations, until they became more real than the cabin walls around her. From the gulls and the strong sense of oppression tonight, she feared very soon there would be no need for speculation.

Still, she didn't anticipate it all to come upon her as swiftly as it did. Against all expectation she'd finally drifted off to sleep in what must have been the wee hours of the night, only to be startled awake when the cabin door flew open. Warm light rushed in to blind her as she was yanked from her bunk and shoved out the door. Behind her, Liza screamed as the same was done to her, and she stumbled into Maddie and clung, hysterical with terror.

"It's all right, Liza," Maddie assured her, patting her back. "Eidon will take care of us." But she doubted the girl could even hear her, and anyway, the assurance hadn't sounded nearly as confident as she would have liked. As she blinked around to see where they were, she realized it was not morning, after all. Rather, she stood in a lanternlit grotto filled with moored galleys like the one that had borne her here, now also snugged into its berth. She stared around in shock, for there were at least twenty of them, and maybe more. *This is the Gull Islands,* she thought. *The Esurhites are here. Just as Abramm feared.*

They were escorted off the ship in the wake of the Broho—whose name she'd deduced was Xemai—along with a burly, bare-chested giant who followed after them, pushing a wooden, two-wheeled cart with a canvas bag in it. Sounds echoed confusingly in the great chamber, and the guano stench was now compounded with that of wet wood and rope and rock. As they climbed a moisture-slicked wooden stair, Maddie spied their sister galley gliding out of the entrance tunnel and heading for the last open slip in which to moor. Then the stair gave way to an upward-sloping tunnel and she saw no more.

Small red fires tucked into wall niches lit their way but did nothing to alleviate the damp and cold. She felt the darkness here, a creeping up her spine, a sense of minds not human watching her. Another stairway led into a gallery whose arched openings overlooked a vast, lanternlit chamber filled with uniformed men and the stink of sweat and waste and stale cooking grease. They appeared to be preparing for battle—until a few of them spotted her and Liza. Before long the crowd chattered excitedly, coarse voices rising above the general rumble to hurl what she supposed were vulgar suggestions.

More corridors and stairs led them outside again, where an ancient walled walkway overlooked a dish-shaped valley sloping down to a nearly landlocked cove of water. Red fires lined its shore among ranks of dark-clad soldiers. A column of violet light shot up from the water into the misty ceiling, looking very much like an etherworld corridor, though at least five times wider than the one Maddie had seen Abramm destroy in Graymeer's last fall. Between it and the near shore stood a tall, square-topped platform with a wide wooden ramp sloping into the water, its midpoint passing directly through the violet column. Atop the platform a cluster of robed priests droned in chant, hands uplifted, and she could feel a crackling expectancy in the air.

The walkway curved around a cliff wall to a small circular chamber. Typical of ancient Ophiran villas, its outside wall was a filigree of arched openings that looked out on the valley, while inside it sported a high domed ceiling and three distinctive levels. The lowest and centermost was tiled in blue and white and surrounded a central, recessed basin of coals. Torches on long poles added light to the purple glow that filled the chamber and, as in the valley outside, dark-faced, armored soldiers stood guard. On the middle-level landing, seated on a padded bench directly across from the outer entrance, was an Esurhite wearing a gold-threaded tunic. Several others in plainer tunics attended him, and behind them all hung a series of long, vertical banners, purple with gold edges and bearing the dark orb of the Black Moon.

As Maddie's party entered, the purple light flickered and a puff of air blew in around them, causing the men on the landing to look over sharply, staring not at the newcomers but at the valley behind them. When nothing more happened, however, they went back to their conversation, which seemed to be heated. Finally one of the men hurried off and the leader in the gold-threaded tunic turned his attention toward Maddie's captors. A short, stocky man with powerful chest and shoulders, the Esurhite's broad, swarthy face was scattered with dark moles, and his left cheekbone bore the crescent scar that marked him as a member of the Brogai warrior caste. His dark hair was pulled tightly into the standard warrior's knot, revealing one ear lined with gold honor rings and the other torn half away, the earlobe missing entirely.

He addressed the Broho gruffly. Xemai threw out his chest and rattled off something in the Tahg as he gestured at the canvas in the cart, then at Maddie and her maid. The Brogai lord looked at her in surprise before leaning back to speak to one of his aides, who immediately hurried away.

Having dismissed Maddie for the moment, the leader turned his attention to the cart, indicating the giant should open the canvas bag and remove its contents. But though the strongman's face reddened and his great muscles corded with the effort, he could not lift it from the cart. In the end, two of the soldiers had to help him upend the cart, and even then it teetered out of control to send its canvas-swathed contents crashing to the tile.

The Brogai spoke sharply and the strongman stood hunch-shouldered. Another sharp word spurred the man to continue, and finally he pulled enough of the canvas back to reveal what Maddie knew at once must be the guardstar from Avramm's Landing.

It looked exactly like the one at Graymeer's—the same size, same pebbled, leathery surface, same black streaking. That they had brought it this far seemed to answer the question of whether a guardstar could be taken from its fortress. Although she didn't recall the one at Graymeer's being quite so heavy.

The Brogai lord immediately came to examine it, touching it gently, seeking to push it with his foot. A casual nudge did nothing, of course, and he seemed unwilling to compromise his dignity by trying anything more. One of the guards was told to cut the leathery covering off, but that only produced a dulled sword.

Irritated now, the Esurhite commander turned upon his Broho subordinate, peppering him with questions. Several times during their discourse Maddie heard the word *Avramm*, which seemed to confirm her conclusions as to the orb's origins.

Then another breath of wind gusted through the arched openings from the valley, and out in the cove the purple column flickered erratically. The priest's distant chanting broke off, and no one moved, though Maddie's skin tingled with a sense of anticipation not altogether fearful. . . .

The column soon regained its bright and steady state, and after a moment, the chanting resumed. Plainly discomfited, the men in the chamber returned to their investigation of the orb until, shortly after that, the Brogai's aide returned with a blond man in Kiriathan garb. Maddie thought him at first to be a captive or a slave, but when the commander spoke to him in flawless Kiriathan, she realized he was something else entirely.

"You told us the Chesedhan First Daughter was caught in adultery before the wedding," said the Esurhite. "That Abramm did not marry her, but sent her in disgrace back to her own land. Eastward by a land route, you said."

"That is so, my lord Uumbra," the man continued, though Maddie heard him as from a great distance, stunned by the Esurhite's words. ". . . *caught in adultery . . . didn't marry her. . . ." Oh, my Lord Eidon . . . what have you done?*

"How is it, then, that Xemai has captured her from a Kiriathan vessel just outside of Avramm's Landing?" Uumbra held out the ring that the Broho Xemai had taken from Maddie that first day. "Is this not the signet of Chesedhan royalty?"

The Kiriathan took the object from him, examined it briefly, then turned to look at her, frowning. Finally, though, his face cleared and he handed the ring back. "It is indeed the signet of Chesedh. And she is Chesedhan royalty—just not the First Daughter. The First Daughter is blond and very beautiful. This is the Second Daughter, Madeleine."

The Brogai lord frowned at her. "This one is certainly no beauty. . . . Second Daughter . . . that is the one the royal lineage bypasses, is it not?"

"Yes, my lord."

There followed a sharp rebuke of the Broho, which Maddie could not deny she enjoyed. Xemai's words of defense were irritably cut off, but before the dressing down could really gain momentum, the Kiriathan spy interceded.

"This might actually be a good thing, my lord."

Uumbra turned a scowl on him. "How is that?"

"Everyone in the court knows this is the daughter Abramm really loves. If he knew you had her . . ."

He trailed off suggestively, as Maddie reeled again. *The daughter Abramm really loves? It was true, then. Everything I thought was true. . . .*

Uumbra was now thinking furiously, his dark eyes fixed upon Maddie. Then the frown faded as his lips pulled back in a smile—and another gust of wind rushed through the room. Simultaneously the orb shifted off its cracked landing spot, moving maybe a half turn away from the Brogai lord. Every man who stood near it leaped back as if it were alive.

Another gust whooshed around them, rattling the bushes on the slopes outside and rippling the banners hanging behind the Brogai's bench. Again Maddie felt that sense of something approaching, something the Light within her was responding to.

One of the soldiers raced into the room and uttered a brief statement that clearly infuriated the Brogai lord. A series of commands sent his underlings scurrying away moments before he strode from the room himself, leaving only Xemai to help the giant wrestle the orb back into its cart—and Maddie, for the moment, ignored.

31

Abramm stared in pleased surprise at the empty piers around him. Part of his intent in pretending to drop anchor for the night with Leyton and the frigates was to tempt the Esurhites into making a preemptive attack. That this grotto lay utterly deserted two hours before dawn could well mean his enemies had taken the bait. And in so doing had provided the perfect refuge for him and his fleet. If he'd questioned Eidon's hand in this endeavor before, he did no longer.

They were here, against all odds—safe and apparently undetected. He had only to get some idea of what they were up against, then find a likely spot on the island above and see if the scepter really would start up the winds that would drive the mist away. Which it had better do, for the sake of Leyton's frigates, since, becalmed and with their guns inoperable in the mist, they would be easy targets if an Esurhite fleet did attack. Leyton had refused to return to wind-stirred waters, however, insisting the scepter would work and wanting to be close enough he could move in swiftly when it did. He planned to sail round to a wider, deeper entrance to the bay shown on the old maps to lie southeast of the shallows. There he would bring his guns to bear on the Esurhites' fortress and tip the battle swiftly to the Kiriathans' favor. First, though, Abramm had to remove the Shadow's mist.

The moment *Yverik* touched dock, four Esurhite crewmen jumped ashore, hurrying along the wooden pier and up a short stair to a tunnel opening that looked as if it might lead to the rest of the complex. Being Esurhite and dressed in the right uniform, they hoped to be ignored by any they might encounter. As they disappeared into the tunnel, other men scurried about, seeing the ship snugly moored. By then Katahn's vessel had slipped into the moorage beside *Yverik*, and soon the Gamer stood with Abramm and Channon atop the stair at the tunnel's mouth, watching the other five galleys nose into adjoining slips.

Trap, clad in black with his features darkened like Abramm's, leaped to the dock even before his ship made contact with it, hurrying up the stair to join them. Barely had he done so when one of the four scouts returned to report the tunnel was secured and that two of his fellows had gone on in search of a route to the top of the island.

"I don't know where everyone is," the man said, "but they sure don't seem to be expecting us. There're no guards, and they haven't even locked their gates."

Which was just what Abramm had hoped to hear. Leaving most of his men in the grotto, he took Trap, Katahn, Channon, and Philip, along with a small party of Esurhites, and set off for the island's surface. He had mixed feelings about taking so small a group of men. On the one hand, he didn't want to tip their hand before he could attack the Shadow, since its removal would protect his men from the arcane weapons it enabled his enemies to use: fireballs, fear-spells, the power of Command. On the other hand, destroying it would surely bring down all the men in this fortress upon him, and the dissipation of the mist would not diminish the effectiveness of sword and shield and stone and arrow.

Not long after, they met another of their scouts coming back to report they'd found the way out. The man led them the rest of the way, and even though he'd told Abramm what they'd found in the wide, rock-rimmed valley that formed the top of the island of Chakos, it was still a shock to see it for himself: the fire-rimmed cove with its platform and ramp and massive purple corridor. The question of why the halls had been so deserted was answered, as well, for it seemed that all the men in the fortress had turned out to line the cove alongside the torches.

"Looks like they're bringing something through right now," Trap murmured in the Tahg at his side.

"And as big as that corridor is, with the ramp and the water— Plagues! I'll wager they're bringing whole galleys through."

"That would explain all those rowboats lined up along the side of the cove . . . and why there's so many men out here. It's a sure bet they're not just guards."

Most looked to be unarmed and were facing inward toward the corridor rather than outward in the direction from which a threat would be expected to come. Abramm scanned the valley's rocky, guano-whitened rim, and sure enough the few sentries posted up there were all watching the proceedings below. He drew his men's attention to them, outlined the plan that had just taken form in his mind, and shortly they were heading up to the rim themselves as two from the group headed back to the grotto to bring up the rest of the men.

Impersonating a senior officer, Katahn rebuked the Esurhites for their laxity in guarding the fortress and sent them off in the custody of two of his own. By the time the disciplined pair realized what was going on, it would be far too late. As two of Abramm's men took over the post of the disgraced guards, those on the rim's far side hurriedly turned themselves back to their jobs, leaving Abramm relatively unobserved.

He'd selected the highest ground available, both as the best defensible position and thinking the scepter might work better the more exposure it had. Turning his back to the ceremony, he drew the scepter from its sleeve on his back, gripped the base of the rod with both hands, and swung it back and forth before him, approximating the moves he'd made with it during the battle at Graymeer's.

But he stirred no more air with it than he would've with his sword, and not even the jewel on its top lit this time. Distracted by the crawly feel of the corridor on his back, and the mind-numbing buzz in his ears, he dropped down off the rim line to get it out of sight, stepping out onto the rock-strewn island top to try it again. With similar lack of results.

A third position change sent him stumbling into a mass of the birds that nested on the ground there—birds he'd taken for rocks—knocking them from their hollows, stepping on them and their eggs, and raising a terrible ruckus of squawks and wing flapping that did not go unnoticed.

"All right, enough of this," he muttered, stuffing the scepter back into its sleeve and returning to the rim line. "It's not working," he said to the others. "I can't seem to focus with the corridor right there. Maybe if we take that out first, the scepter will work."

"*Can* we take it out, sir?" Trap asked.

"Well, we've already destroyed two of them . . . so we must be starting to get the hang of it. Which is better than I can say for the scepter."

His men said nothing, but he saw the protest on their faces as they stared down at the cove and the monstrous purple column.

Trap shifted uncomfortably. "Sir, you'll be right out there in the middle of all of it."

"Exactly. We'll be a diversion while our men move into position." He paused, then added before his friend could speak, "And I don't want to hear any suggestions of how I should hide up here with the birds. I came to lead this campaign and I intend to do so. Besides, my presence is part of the plan."

Trap frowned at him.

"They're afraid of the Pretender, remember? If things start to go our way and they suddenly find out that I'm here . . . And yes, I know you don't like it. But I wish you'd have a little more faith, my friend. If not in me, then at least in Eidon." When they only frowned the more, he gave up. "All right, then. Let's get that thing shut down before whatever it is they're bringing through gets here."

Leaving two of their number on the rim, they made their way downslope toward the cove and joined the mass of men waiting for the corridor to deliver its burden. Many had already packed themselves into the rowboats as up on the platform the priests chanted on with increasing rapidity and volume. Abramm and his companions were working their way toward the platform stair when the corridor shivered and a sense of something huge bearing down upon them lifted the hairs up Abramm's spine. A flash to his left drew his eye to the violet column and brought him to a stop. The air grew heavy, difficult to suck into his lungs, pressing upon his chest. His ears ached as the sense of power crawled across his flesh and the priests' cries escalated into screams. Just when it seemed they could not get any louder or higher pitched, the column burst into a light so blinding he had to turn away.

Pressure, sound, and light all dropped away together, and when he could see again, he found the column reduced in both diameter and brightness, a thin vestige of what it had been, but still several times larger than the corridors he had encountered in Graymeer's. The priests lay in a heap on the platform, silent and unmoving, as below them, sliding slowly toward the dark water at ramp's end, loomed the dark bulk of a full-sized Esurhite galley.

After a moment's startled recovery, the men on the shore surged into the water with a collective shout, boats and oars knocking together in their drivers' haste. Abandoning his idea of taking one of the boats for themselves, Abramm hurried around the curving cove to the platform stair, ignored by the Esurhites now that all had their eyes upon the galley, where men in the first of the rowboats were tossing up their grappling hooks, securing their boat to its hull.

With Trap at his side and the others following, Abramm jogged up to the platform where the debilitated priests sprawled unmoving across its railed top, many draped over their fellows. Looking down to pick his way among them, he stared into the glazed eyes of one, the red fire of a rhu'eman indweller flickering deep in the man's dilated pupils. It saw him and knew what he was, but though the red light pulsed in the amulet around his neck, the creature seemed as drained of power as the man it inhabited. Perfect. Maybe Eidon hadn't infused the scepter with his Light because the time wasn't right. . . .

Abramm continued on and came at last to the top of the ramp, where he stopped. The column flared before him now, and he felt its fine vibrations in the scars that ribboned his arm and slashed his face, the sensation hot and crawling. Aversion and fear shivered through him, but he put them aside and started grimly down the ramp, setting his teeth together as the whine increased and the grating started upon his nerves. They were familiar sensations now, and he knew what he had to do.

This thing is evil. It is a danger to my people and an insult to you, my Lord, and I cannot allow it to be as close to my land as this. I want it gone. But you are going to have to do it.

Shouts broke out somewhere below him. Evidently someone had spotted him and decided his actions were not benign. Possibly because of the white glow that had begun to shimmer faintly around him. At his back he heard a few of the priests stirring, calling out drunkenly, felt the force of the rhu'emas' impotent wrath directed at him—and underneath it, their fear. He walked on.

As the white that enfolded him came into contact with the violet of the corridor, the angry buzzing transformed to sibilant voices pronouncing curses. He felt the thoughts and the visions pressing around the edges of his mind, hoping to tempt him away, but he ignored and quenched them. Failing that, they beat at his flesh, stirred up emotions of terror, predictions of being pulled into the corridor to be burned and made crazy like Rhiad. He refused those thoughts as well, focusing on his goal to see this thing destroyed.

All at once the purple fabric tore apart and he was falling, shock and fear overwhelming that sense of purpose. It had taken him! The Light wasn't strong enough.

He tumbled head over heels as if bowled toward shore by a powerful wave, then came suddenly upright and still. Gasping for breath he gazed around in confusion at the red-lit, pillared hall in which he now stood, hundreds of bald, red-robed men lying senseless across the floor. In them flickered the colored lights that were the rhu'ema, trying to strike at him but far too weak. He looked up the hall's vast length, its ceiling lost in darkness. A golden altar stood on a dais between two pots of red flame. Behind and above it loomed the bas relief of a great red dragon clinging to the wall, head and neck curved round over its back to look at him, toothy jaws gaping. Every scale and ripple of muscle was rendered in such exquisite detail he wouldn't have been surprised if it launched itself off the wall and came at him—

The beast's golden eyes flared, and the moment he fixed upon them, he perceived the monstrous scarlet force that burned behind them, a creature both aged and vibrant, whose attention had just riveted upon him, surprised at first to find him standing there, then swiftly filled with rage. The power of its presence seized him like a striking snake, bending his will to its own as it drew him out of his flesh, sucking up his spirit and his soul, as the morwhol had tried to—

Nonsense! he thought at it. *Such a thing is not within your power. You are only trying to deceive me.*

The great vortex pulling at him stopped dead, but the rage only burned the hotter. *Not within my power?* The dragon's head seemed to move, drawing nearer to him. *What do you know of my power, little man? Or of deception. You, who serve the greatest deceiver of them all, one who cannot protect his own followers, who cannot even protect himself. And you wish to challenge me?*

Before Abramm could even think to respond, the creature went on, speaking rapidly now in a stream of sibilant words that birthed a riot of images: a great sea beneath a ceiling of mist, filled from horizon to horizon with a navy of dark narrow galleys, oars flashing in perfect timing as they drove inexorably north; a crowd of people in a great square screaming for Abramm's death; Gillard in Mataian robes, grinning as he shook out a short whip; the palace in flames, Abramm's friends and supporters dead, as the mist flooded into his beloved Springerlan.

His own Shadow rose within him, flooding him with panic and guilt. He captured the feelings and put them down.

Those are only threats. You do not know the future.

I know the plans that are in place for you. I know who your enemies are. I know they will come against you and your god will let them win. Are you sure you want to serve such a one as that?

They will not win. But even if they do . . . I will still serve him.

Laughter echoed in his head as the stone dragon's tail seemed to lash. Its eyes flared again. *Easy for you to say now. Let's see when the time comes.*

Abramm had the sense that it was about to pelt him with more of its awful predictions, but now, finally, he felt the Light move in him, swelling within him to crowd out the evil images with memories of past events—the lighting of the Heart at Hur, his own taking of the Star of Life, the defeat of Beltha'adi, the slaying of the kraggin, the morwhol, his own recent coronation. Before all that this creature was nothing.

And with that realization, the Light burst out of him in a powerful, pulsing wave that obliterated the red chamber and sent him tumbling through space again, but safe this time in the heartbeat of his Lord. He felt the mind sense of Trap and Katahn, Channon and Philip, of men who'd come with him . . . and of one other, not part of his group, yet closer in soul to him than any of them. . . .

Madeleine! He felt her near and strong, felt the sudden fire of her recognition and the response it generated in her—*response*, not hurt-filled reaction. Then it was gone, lost in a cataclysm of whiteness and a growing roar.

He came back to himself in a world gone mad, still standing on the ramp and holding the scepter now, though he had no recollection of pulling it from its sleeve on his back. Yet its headstone blazed and a great wind howled around him, tearing at his hair and tunic, pelting him with pebbles and weeds torn from their moorings. Pieces of wood, cloaks, boots, scarves, even birds struggling to right themselves in the wild currents flew around him in an ever-widening circle. The column was gone, and above where it had stood, a hole had been punched through the roof of mist, revealing a sky turned mauve with the coming dawn. The ramp below it had been blasted in two amidst cove waters that churned and steamed. Huge waves tossed the galley like a toy, the small boats once tied up to it shattering against its sides in the tumult. On the shore, men cowered on the ground, clinging to whatever was at hand.

The whirlwind expanded, driving away the mist to reveal more and more of the sky. He felt the scepter hot against his gloved palm as the light in its jeweled head went out. Gradually the force of the winds lessened around him as on the shore men picked themselves up and looked around dazedly. It wasn't long before all eyes had moved to their precious galley, then to the gap in the ramp where the corridor had been, and finally to Abramm himself standing with the scepter above both.

He could see their collective confusion and bewilderment, for at first glance he looked like one of their own. For a moment they all stood there looking at him, and him at them. Then from a cluster of shaven-headed men standing at the shore's edge, one bellowed, "It's the Pretender! Get him!"

But rather than rally the men to attack, the cry only turned their confusion to panic. They all turned to flee at once, had gone only a few yards when their commanders stopped them in their tracks, ordered them to return and fight. They turned with the jerkiness that betrayed the force of Command upon them, while out in the valley beyond them, Abramm saw the line of his own men readying to strike from behind.

At that moment one of the Broho ashore opened his mouth and bellowed out a purple fireball. It slammed directly into Abramm, almost before he knew it was coming, but his defense was instinctive and instantaneous— white fire flared up to deflect the missile's energy in an explosion that staggered him backward up the ramp.

"Time to retreat!" Trap yelled from atop the platform.

Abramm didn't argue, running up the ramp to join him. But as they started to pick their way around the fallen priests, the Broho launched another fireball, this time at the platform struts. It shattered the wood in a fountain of shards and splinters. A second ball hit beside the first, and the platform began to list. They ran now toward the highest edge, climbing over the priests as they made their way up the smooth wooden planks. Then a final explosion brought the whole thing down in a twisting, shuddering motion attended by a mighty groan.

For Abramm, it was like falling into the corridor again, up turned down and down turned up, struts and wood and people roiling around him. Somehow he managed to land in the water behind the debris rather than under it, coming down sideways so hard the force of his fall drove the air from his lungs. Madly he fought his way back to the surface, where he gasped and choked and sputtered, trying to draw a breath into a chest that would not open. When finally he could breathe again, he realized two things: he was being carried by the water displaced in the platform's fall toward the cove's far shore—which was good—and he'd lost the scepter.

His feet touched bottom, and he drove upright, turning back to the chaos behind him, crestfallen. How would they ever find it now, with the bottom stirred up as it was and all the debris of the platform raining down upon it, as well?

Trap came up beside him, wiping water from his eyes. He looked at Abramm and frowned. "What's wrong?"

"I've lost the scepter."

His friend glanced at the water beside him. "That scepter?"

To Abramm's astonishment, there it was, floating in the water at his elbow. He seized it with a surge of wonder, and they staggered ashore, where the fighting had already fallen off. The hottest conflicts were taking place on the other side of the cove now, as the Esurhites sought to retreat toward the villa.

The hole of sky, light pink with the growing dawn, now overarched the entire valley as the winds continued to push outward, driving back the mist in an ever-widening circle. Around Abramm, however, the gale's ferocity had already dropped off to a light, erratic breeze.

Katahn rose out of the water, Philip at his side, and together they all climbed to a knoll to get a better look at things. Sure enough, the Esurhites were heading rapidly for the villa openings. The commander of this island had probably learned from the gulls that Abramm had six gunships ready to sail in and fire away the moment the mists were lifted. If he didn't start evacuating now, much would soon be lost, a conclusion and action Abramm hoped might give himself and his own men a little breathing room.

What he hadn't dared hope was that Maddie was indeed here. The knowledge thrilled him, even as he knew she would surely be taken as hostage in the Esurhites' retreat. Unless he found her first.

Right after Uumbra had left, Maddie began easing herself and Liza slowly backward from Xemai and the giant as they cursed and struggled to get the orb back onto its canvas wrapper. She was just raising her foot backward onto the first step of the stairway leading out of the chamber when the world inverted itself. The Light flared within her, pulled from her by a powerful hand and guided into a stream alongside that of many others. She glimpsed an oarless galley in a cove of raging waters surrounded by careening rowboats . . . and at the same time sensed the souls of those others from whom the Light was drawn, others who were somewhere nearby, familiar to her . . . especially one of them.

Then it was gone and she stood in the domed chamber again, ears ringing and heart racing. *That was Abramm,* she thought in amazement. *He's here! Light's grace! He's probably just destroyed the corridor.*

She turned back to the guardstar, which was lying once more on the floor amidst the sprawled and senseless forms of the men who'd sought to lift it. Seizing her chance, she ran to get it. "Come on, Liza. Help me roll this into the cart."

Maddie dropped to her knees beside the orb as Liza positioned the cart on its side next to it. Bracing herself for the effort, Maddie placed both hands on the guardstar and shoved with all her might. It rolled away as if it were no heavier than a glass buoy, and she fell forward onto both hands with a grunt. Liza murmured an astonished "Oh my" as Maddie stood and picked the thing up without the slightest strain.

The groan of one of the men startled her, and she ran back up the stair, going out the way she had come in, Liza on her heels. Abramm was on this island somewhere, probably near the cove. She had to find him. But once outside she stopped, chagrinned to find a fierce battle raging on the valley's broad slopes.

"Now what do we do, ma'am?" Liza asked.

"Go back." Whirling as she spoke, Maddie ran right into Xemai, recovered and coming after her. He grabbed her before she'd even come to the end of her rebound and dragged her back into the amphitheater, where the other men were picking themselves off the floor. A moment later, Lord Uumbra and his subordinates burst in upon them. Uumbra stopped abruptly at the sight of Madeleine holding the unwrapped guardstar, looking startled and even a little alarmed at first. He spoke brusquely to Xemai, who answered at some length, and even as he was still speaking, the Brogai's dark eyes flicked to the orb in Maddie's hands again. A calculating look came into his face, and she was reminded of what the Kiriathan spy had said—that it was she whom Abramm truly loved. The same Abramm who was in the process of destroying this man's command.

The Brogai gave a clipped order, and one of his men stepped forward to tear the guardstar from her grasp. Immediately its weight returned, overwhelming his strength and bowing him to the floor as he tried to keep hold of it. Finally he and two others plus the strongman got it back into its wrapping, whereupon Uumbra ordered Maddie to pick it up.

When she refused, Xemai Commanded her, the force of his will wrapping around her like a net, pressing at her back and knees, compelling her forward. But though she did step over to it, she would not bend and pick it up. One of the soldiers struck her a hard, stinging blow with his whip across the back, sending her staggering forward and causing her foot to bump the guardstar, rolling it easily. Just when she was thinking about maybe picking it up and throwing it at someone, Uumbra decided he'd wasted enough time. He ordered the men to put the thing into the cart and for Xemai to bring her along.

But even in that she fought them, refusing to walk, throwing herself about, striking them with her fists, hoping they'd find her too much of a hindrance and let her go. Instead someone cuffed her alongside the head—

When she came to, her head hurt and she was jolting like a sack of wheat over a man's shoulder as he carried her hurriedly down a dark corridor. Her hands were bound at the wrists behind her back, and his shoulder dug painfully into her stomach, pressing up against her lungs so that she could barely breathe. Smoke tainted the air.

The grotto that held the dock area was filled with smoke and shouting. It was difficult to see anything draped as she was with her face to her carrier's back, but glimpses as he moved about showed her that one of the galleys had swung around broadside to become lodged between the walls of the tunnel to the open sea. Helpless to prevent boarding from the enemy outside, it had been set afire, effectively trapping the rest of the nineteen vessels moored here. In the shifting smoke she saw men fighting with swords and clubs on its deck, and in some cases, grappling hand to hand.

At Uumbra's command her party turned and headed back into the fortress. Another dark, stomach-jolting journey ensued, during which she re-acquired enough of her senses to think again and to realize three things: that Abramm must've used the galleys Katahn had brought him to invade this place and prevent the deployment of the enemy's forces; that Uumbra could not be allowed to use her against him, even if she had to throw herself overboard; and that her wrists were bound with a leather thong that she might be able to sever with the Light, a skill she'd heard of others possessing—some said Trap Meridon could do it—but that she herself had never tried.

If she succeeded, the flare would probably startle the man carrying her enough she might elude him. She'd just have to pick her time and place carefully.

Before long they entered a second, much brighter, grotto. The water at the entrance tunnel glowed an intense blue, and the air was much less smoky. As they hurried along the docks, she glimpsed the galleys here moving out through the exit, prow to stern in a close line, oars sweeping in dark silhouette against the bright water. Realizing this could be her last chance for escape, she focused on the leather encircling her wrists and on the Light in her flesh. Her efforts were rewarded by a brief white flash, followed by the man's sudden cry as he flailed back and she fell off his shoulder, her hands coming free not quite quickly enough to shield her from the fall. She landed hard on one shoulder, the breath jolted out of her. Even so, she hurled herself off the dock's edge, stars sparkling across her vision.

The water was shockingly cold, but she ignored it, staying under the surface as she turned and swam under the dock, heading for the deep shadows at its back, and surprised by what a heavy hindrance her skirts suddenly became. Thankfully, she found a piling to cling to and pulled herself up until her head broke through the surface and she could breathe again. By then one of the men had jumped into the water behind her, but he seemed hesitant to let go of the dockside to come after her. Esurhites, she'd heard, were not big swimmers, despite their infamous navy. She watched him treading water at the place where the light melded into shadow as she pulled herself around behind the piling and lifted her dress up around her, willing herself invisible.

He swam back and forth a few times, and then, as she had hoped, time must've run out, for he pulled himself out of the water and she heard thumping on the planks above her.

No sooner had the sound faded than she cursed herself for forgetting about the orb. They still had it. . . .

Frantically she dragged herself back to the light, her skirts more of a weight now than ever. As she pulled herself back onto the dock she saw Uumbra out along one of the slips, already hurrying over the gangplank onto the last galley still moored. He glanced over his shoulder toward the landing where they'd first entered, then shouted at the two men who were still hobbling along the dock with the prodigiously heavy guardstar. At his words, they staggered toward the dock's edge and, to her horror, let their burden go. The whole of it, guardstar and canvas both, plummeted rapidly into the dark depths of the sea and out of sight. As they hurried up the gangplank, the galley was already moving away.

She sagged onto the wet planks, drenched, shivering, and wondering if there'd be any way to get it back. This grotto might not be as deep as open sea and—

She was seized from behind, lifted off her feet and flipped onto someone's shoulder. Struggling and flailing, she soon discovered the man's bald head and knew it was Xemai again, running now along an aisle on the dock, though she had no idea where he was headed. Darkness swallowed them, and the strong odor of axle grease and wet rope suggested they'd entered a storage chamber. A few steps in he stopped and slid her off his shoulder. As soon as her feet touched ground, she swung away from him, but he was ready for that and went with the movement, so that instead of escaping she was slammed hard into a stone wall. Her ears rang and she barely held on to consciousness as he picked her up by the waist and dragged her deeper into the chamber, where he flung her onto the floor and stood over her, fumbling with the fastening on his britches. *He may get you back*, voices suddenly whispered in her ears, *but you'll be damaged goods*. . . .

Desperate, she scrambled away from him, but he Commanded her to stop, and this time the fear the whispered words had generated gave the order the power to take hold. She stared at the ceiling, stunned, thinking this couldn't be happening to her as he dropped to his knees, straddling her, and shoved her sodden skirts up out of the way.

Father Eidon . . .

Barely had she formed the plea when he was yanked off of her. She saw a tall dark form, the flash of a sword, the zing of white as the Light flowed into it, and then only the shadows, lit by the dim torchlight flickering through the opening behind her rescuer.

He was tall, swarthy-faced, and cloaked in black. His hair was dark but short, and the rapier that gleamed in his gloved hand was clearly of Kiriathan make. A kelistar flared to life and she saw the level brows, the fierce blue eyes, the twin scars running the length of his beloved face. As confused familiarity turned to joyful recognition she leaped to her feet and flung herself into his arms. The sword clanged to the stone as he caught her and held her tightly, stroking her hair and kissing her temple and whispering reassurances.

For a time she only clung to him and wept. But after a while the storm receded, and she realized what she was doing, what she was already beginning to feel again, and warned herself to pull away, to keep her distance. Instead she turned her head to lay her cheek against his chest, listening to the powerful beat of his heart and admitting finally that she was never going to be able to stop loving this man. His gloved hand, which had been stroking her hair, came to rest now upon her head, his lips upon her brow, and she felt the current of the Light rise up between them.

"Are you all right?" he asked her finally.

"Yes."

"They didn't—"

"They were saving me for Belthre'gar."

She felt him stiffen, felt his arms tighten around her. Then his breath came out in a long, low sigh. "Oh, Mad," he murmured. "I never should have sent you away . . . it was the stupidest thing I've ever done. And Eidon's mercy alone has brought you back to me. I will never, of my own choosing, let you go again."

Everything in her went still as she recalled again the Kiriathan informant's claim that Briellen had been caught in adultery and sent away in disgrace. Which meant Abramm was free to marry someone else.

Before she could even get her mind around that fact and its many repercussions, however, Trap and two others burst into the chamber. She stepped out of Abramm's arms and saw Xemai slumped glassy-eyed against the wall in a pool of his own blood. Abramm's men looked at the corpse, as well.

Then Trap said, "We've taken this grotto, sir. But almost half of their galleys got out."

Abramm nodded and said something to that, but Trap's words had jolted Maddie's brain back into the here and now. "The guardstar," she cried, stepping back from the king. "They took it from Avramm's Landing and threw it into the harbor."

Abramm frowned at her. "Are you sure it was a guardstar?"

"It looked exactly like the one at Graymeer's. Same pebbled skin, same black streaking . . ."

She hurried back to where the orb had been dropped, the men following after her. "Right here," she said, stopping at the dock's edge. "They dumped it in here, canvas wrapper and all."

As they stood staring down into the water, Trap suggested they'd need a diver, and Abramm agreed, though obviously that would have to wait until the situation was more settled. Then Channon arrived to report that one of the other grottos had been secured, and shortly after that Katahn was hurrying in.

Maddie dropped back to let them work, seating herself on the top of a piling and letting her eyes rove freely over the man she thought she would never see again. He looked much the worse for wear. His clothing was almost as wet as hers, torn and spattered with blood and mud. The dark pigment he'd used on his hair had faded in places, letting the blond come through in an uneven mottling, and the swarthiness on his face was likewise smeared and uneven. She didn't care. If anything it made his eyes bluer.

His men didn't care, either. She could see the awe, the deep respect in which they held him—perhaps greater now than ever. She loved to watch him work with them, for it was obvious he held them in high regard, as well, and did not seem to notice that they worshipped him. This day would birth another legend, another song, which perhaps this time she would be able to write.

The rise of her warm feelings stuttered as she recalled their reunion in the storage chamber, when he'd held her in his arms and promised he would never send her away again. Fear stirred within her. He couldn't marry Briellen now. And since it was possible—even likely—Chesedh had been shamed enough to drop that part of their requirements for the treaty . . . it meant he was free to marry someone else. The fear coalesced into a cold hard lump. Like, maybe . . . herself.

She backed away from that thought with a sudden panicked denial, turning her eyes from him and noting for the first time what bobbed on the water beside the dock.

"Oh!" she cried, sliding off her piling perch. "It's come up on its own. And it seems to have lost its skin."

Abramm, though deep in conversation with his men, was obviously still attuned to her, for the moment she had spoken and moved, he broke off to glance at her. She pointed, and he looked down at the smooth, luminescent gray sphere floating at his feet, almost as if it, too, had come to report itself to him.

For a moment no one said anything. Then Abramm stepped aside as Channon dropped to his knees and grabbed for it. But every time he tried to lift it, it slid back into the water.

"I canna keep hold of it," he said. " 'Tis too slick an' heavy . . . though how it's floatin' I canna say."

Trap looked at Abramm gravely. "Perhaps you should try it yourself, sir."

So the king stripped off his gloves and knelt on the edge of the dock, reaching down to pull out his guardstar as easily as if it were a glass buoy. All were suitably amazed. Especially when he handed it to Channon and it obviously grew heavy again. Not nearly as heavy, Maddie thought, as when the Broho had tried to handle it, but not as light as when she had carried it, either—a fact whose significance now made her spine tingle with a sense of portents.

She caught Abramm looking at her, the blue of his eyes so magnified by the water's light they almost glowed. Or perhaps it wasn't the light, but merely the first time she'd ever looked at him and seen his feelings for her so openly displayed.

And suddenly she could not look him in the eye any longer, stirred by his regard in a way she had never thought to be again, and terrified by the decision she realized she would soon be asked to make. *I don't want to be a queen, my Lord. I can't be. I'm not suited. I'll ruin everything. This cannot be my destiny. It cannot.*

32

Abramm's campaign to take the Gull Islands was a resounding success. Once Leyton arrived with his six ships and full broadsides of cannon, it was only a matter of time before the battle was won. When it ended, they had captured twenty-five galleys—including the one that had just come through the corridor—along with the nearly seven hundred slaves that powered them and over five hundred Esurhite soldiers, many of them injured. By Abramm's figuring, five vessels had been destroyed in the fighting and another ten had escaped either before Leyton arrived or soon after, each of them loaded with escapees, including the Brogai lord, Uumbra.

Though Leyton sent several ships after them, they soon encountered the cloak of mist again and had to turn back. Meanwhile Abramm set about cleaning the island of the dead and establishing his own command post there. Before he left, he gave orders that the cove should be transformed into a series of dry docks where construction of new galleys could begin, leaving behind almost half the slaves, the smallest of the sailing vessels, and a guard of ten of the captured galley ships.

The other fifteen galleys he brought home with him, parading into Kalladorne Bay with the cannon at both fortresses firing and every boat in Springerlan turned out to form the victory gauntlet. Katahn's original galleys led the way, followed by those captured at the islands, the prisoners forced to stand on their decks, bound and stripped down to breeches, as was Kiriathan custom with prisoners of war.

Abramm followed in the flagship of the five Chesedhan frigates that had returned with him, Maddie at his side, Leyton, Trap, and Katahn standing around them. Cheering spectators filled the boats that lined their way, tossing hats into the air and waving aprons and coats and homemade pennants bearing Abramm's dragon-and-shield device. Flags flapped in the breeze as bands played from the decks of the welcoming ships, producing a constant stream of music from one end of the bay to the other. When Abramm reached the midway point, shore-launched rockets screamed into the sky, exploding in blossoms of sparkling color as throughout the city bells rang and all people filled the streets in celebration.

Once ashore the prisoners were marched to Wetherslea and thrown into the deepest dungeon. Many were offered the opportunity of receiving the Star, but few accepted. Meanwhile the slaves who had formerly rowed in the galleys Katahn had given Abramm at his coronation were freed, while the sailors from the Kirithian navy who'd volunteered to row with them were released from the service and paid handsomely. Then after a few days of suffering the hardships of Wetherslea, all the Esurhite soldiers healthy enough were pulled out and chained to the oars in their places.

The stolen guardstar was sent back to Avramm's Landing and set on its platform, unlit but ready should Eidon deign one day to reveal the secrets of how it worked. For now, Abramm had something more important on his mind: Maddie.

Since her return, Maddie had become something of a people's celebrity as the stories of what had befallen her on Chakos and what she had done to save the guardstar circulated ever more widely. Perhaps it was the hideousness of the affair with Briellen, or the fact that many of the common people knew her, thanks to her two years of roaming the inns and byways of the city in her search for information about the Pretender. Or maybe it was the fact that everyone knew by now that their king was madly in love with her and had gone to the Gull Islands himself primarily to rescue her. Like it or not, she had become a part of the legends surrounding him, and people wanted to see them together. Even his privy council voted to accept her as First Daughter and to ratify the treaty between their two countries by a marriage after all. Ironically, the only remaining obstacle to Abramm's dream being fulfilled was Maddie herself.

He knew Leyton had told her of the First Daughter option shortly after they'd taken Chakos. At which point she'd shut herself into the quarters that had been provided for her on the island and avoided Abramm as assiduously as Carissa ever had. Yes, she'd stood dutifully beside him on the deck of the Chesedhan flagship for their homecoming, but she'd spoken to him only as required, and that with cool formality. Once they came ashore in Springerlan she virtually disappeared from public life.

For the first three days, he was busy enough he had no time to think of her and the proposal he had made to her through Leyton. But on the fourth, he awoke restless and uneasy, wondering why she hadn't answered him. Had he hurt her more than he thought? Had she not understood his rationale as much as he supposed? On his morning ride through the green hills and newly leafed-out trees of the royal preserve, he spoke at length to Eidon about it. He'd originally declared that he would stay out of it, giving her the same freedom to decide that his Lord was. Would it now be a violation of that decision to summon her and ask what was going on?

By the end of the ride he had concluded that it would be and was resolved to rein in his impatience and wait it out. Eidon would bring him the answer in his own time, and he would trust in that. Thus he was startled—even shocked—to return to his apartment and have Haldon inform him a young woman was waiting for him in the study. Even then he had the half-cocked notion it would be someone else—Leona, perhaps—and so was schooling himself not to show his disappointment as he walked through the doorway. But it was, indeed, Maddie who stood at the window, her back to the room as she stared out over the valley and bay below.

Seeing her was shock enough, but even more disconcerting was the heat that flared through him. One that sprang not from embarrassment or fear but from sudden and intense desire.

She wore an ivory gown of fine linen, piped in blue and gold, with panels of gold satin slashing the full skirt. The sleeves were short and gathered, with ribbons of gold dangling from them, the neckline scooped low and wide, even in the back. Her hair had been plaited into multiple braids caught up in interwoven loops at the back of her head, tendrils of it dangling fetchingly from her nape.

He crossed the room to stand at her right shoulder, glancing briefly at the view outside before his eyes returned to her, admiring the lovely glow of her skin as he wondered again how he'd ever thought her plain looking.

"So then, my lady," he said softly. "Does this mean you've decided?"

She whirled to face him, her eyes locking on his as a red flush spread over her face and chest, the color setting off the blue in her eyes, which were very wide. Her hands came up to her waist, the fingers interlocking. And then she burst out, "Are you sure about this, Abramm? Because, really, I don't think you understand what you're asking of me. What you'll need of me. And I just . . . I mean . . . You know how unsuited I am to courtly life, and I can't imagine why you would . . . why anyone would . . . I mean, I'm too blunt. I loathe small talk and big parties and getting dressed up. . . . Really, I'm just . . . I'm not . . ." She trailed off helplessly, fingers working back and forth.

He frowned at her. "Are you telling me you don't want to be my wife, Maddie?"

"Oh, plagues, no!" She turned away from him, laying her hands flat on her fiery cheeks, only to drop them and turn back again. "I love you more than I ever thought I could love anyone. The idea of living without you is unthinkable. I *do* want to be your wife! I just . . ." Her face grew pained and her fingers, interlocked once more, worked furiously in her agitation. "I just don't think I can be a queen."

He snorted softly. "I didn't think I could be a king, either, when people first suggested it."

"Yes, but you were obviously made to be one, whereas I'm—"

"Exactly what I want." He smiled. "Exactly what I need."

The color drained from her face. "I don't know. . . . I just . . . I don't see how I can do it."

"Maybe you can't, but Eidon can. If he could make a king of me, he'll have no problem making a queen of you."

"But . . . I . . ."

He slid his hand down her arm and took her hand. "You don't have to do it yourself, Mad," he said. "That's one thing I've definitely learned. He does it while we're not looking. We just have to be willing to let him work." He chuckled. "And I, for one, am absolutely confident you'll be a magnificent queen."

"Oh, Abramm . . . are you *sure*?"

At that he sobered and brought her hand up to lay his lips upon the backs of her trembling fingers, his eyes never leaving hers. "I have never been more sure of anything in all my life."

She caught her lower lip between her teeth. Tears glittered on her eyelashes. She took a deep breath, started to speak, and then gasped, "Oh, heavens!" She took another breath, pressed her fingertips to her lips, and finally nodded as the tears spilled down her cheeks. "Yes. I'll do it. I will be made First Daughter and I will marry you, Abramm Kalladorne. Eidon help us all."

For a moment he could hardly believe she'd said it. Then, nearly whooping aloud, he caught her by the waist and pulled her to him. He brushed the tears from her cheeks, then bent and kissed her as if she were the only woman he had ever kissed. Or ever would. And after a moment her arms came up around his neck, clinging to him with a vigor that belied all her former fear and indecision.

Sometime later Byron Blackwell's startled voice interrupted them.

"Oh. Excuse me, sir. I didn't . . ."

Abramm pulled his mouth free of Maddie's to glance over his shoulder as his secretary reached for the door. "Wait a minute, Byron. I want you to summon the court."

Blackwell turned back to him, his face devoid of expression. "Summon the court, sir?"

"We have an announcement to make."

A moment more Byron stared at him, as if he could not have been more stunned. His eyes flicked down to Maddie, secure in Abramm's arms. Finally understanding registered and a smile broke onto his pasty face. "An announcement, sir. Very good, sir."

———

It was the most surreal thing Maddie had ever done, standing there at the top of the king's gallery stair, her hand in Abramm's as she listened to him announce to the gathered courtiers that she had consented to be his wife. She still couldn't believe she'd said yes. And yet, hard as it had been, the moment she'd done it, she'd known it was the right choice. As much as the prospect terrified her, as impossible as it seemed for her to ever be what Abramm really needed, at the same time she realized this was the reason Eidon had sent her to Kiriath: to marry Abramm, to bear his heirs. To be queen to his people.

It took her breath away and made her legs shake when she thought of it, though that was nothing compared to what she felt when pondering the truth that all she had dreamed and longed for these last months was coming true.

After the announcement they retired to the lower court, where the nobility came to offer their congratulations. Carissa could hardly contain her enthusiasm, and Maddie lost count of how many times she expressed disbelief that her brother had finally done something so imminently sensible. Even Trap and Simon were chuckling, and it was the first time Captain Channon had ever looked at her with anything save a hostile glower.

The other courtiers offered congratulations that ran the gamut from cool propriety to genuine and almost rowdy enthusiasm. Byron Blackwell was one of the former, and his sister Leona went through like a sleepwalker, shaking

Maddie's hand and speaking the proper words without ever making eye contact. She gave Abramm the same treatment but then stood in front of him afterward, looking up at him with a lost and confused expression until Byron finally pulled her away and she fled the hall altogether.

Then suddenly here was Leyton, cutting a swath through the crowd to stop before them, staring first at Abramm, then at her, his blond brows arched above eyes so wide the whites showed. "It's true, then?" he blurted at Abramm. "She's agreed?" But before Abramm could answer him he turned to her. "You said yes?"

She lifted her chin. "I did."

Leyton's brows drew down. "You don't have to, you know. Father will accept the treaty without it."

"I know." She turned to look up at Abramm. "I want to."

"You want to submit to him? Obey him? Give up your freedoms and your independence for him? All those things the Words command a wife that you swore you'd never do?"

She smiled at her betrothed. "Yes, all those things. So far as I am able." *Though really*, she thought, *I don't think it will be that hard. He's already asked me to do the hardest thing he could have asked, and I did it.*

Leyton rocked back on his heels, and for the first time in Maddie's memory, looked thoroughly surprised. "Well." He cleared his throat. "I don't know what to say."

"How about congratulations?" Abramm suggested.

They were married a week later on the wallwalk at Graymeer's because workers had only just begun to rebuild the Hall of Kings and would not be finished for at least a year. Thus it was that she stood before Abramm on the ramparts beneath the bright spring sunlight and joined her life with his, as Kesrin wrapped the traditional binding around their clasped hands. Only this time he used not the silk ribbons that were the norm but the bottom of her bedgown, given to Abramm as her token before he'd faced the morwhol.

Then she looked up into his eyes and said the vows that sealed the binding, meaning them with all of her heart and soul. After that he kissed her and the multitude gathered in the fortress yards and on the wallwalks raised their voices in a thunderous cheer as the bells were rung and the cannon fired. She hardly heard any of it.

They left the fortress in the wedding carriage, the road back to Springerlan lined with well-wishers who cheered and waved and cast handfuls of flower petals over them. And in all that wide blue sky and magical day there was no sign of Shadow and not even the distant silhouette of any dragon. The only disruption occurred when Eudace burst in upon the wedding supper, shrilling out a prophecy that Abramm would be destroyed because he had joined himself with this Chesedhan witch. The holy man was shouted down and dragged off to the prison for his impertinence, and the party continued with hardly a break. The bride and groom barely knew he'd been there, too caught up in one another to trouble themselves with happenings at the other end of the Great Room.

Finally, after the feasting and the singing and the joking and the dancing were completed, the royal couple was brought up to the bridal suite, where Carissa, Peri, Elayne Cooper, and Liza took Maddie into a separate chamber to prepare her. There they stripped off her wedding gown, robed her in fluid, white silk, and unpinned her waistlength hair, all the while offering a steady stream of advice. She hardly heard it, so focused was she on what was to happen next. By the time they delivered her over to her bridegroom, waiting in the adjoining bedchamber, she was shaking with nervous anticipation.

As the door closed and the women's teasing voices faded, she stared at him in wonder. He stood at the room's midst, robed in white, tall and strong and unbearably handsome in the candlelight. Suddenly her heart felt as if it might beat its way out of her chest and she couldn't find her breath. And though she thought surely her legs would give way at any moment, somehow they brought her to stand directly before him.

He looked down at her soberly, his eyes shining dark blue in the shadows of those stern brows. She lifted her hand to touch his face, tracing her fingers along the scars from brow to lip, then continuing down through the narrow beard, along the corded neck, and coming to rest at last upon the shield glittering over his heart. All the while he watched her, unmoving. "Heart of my heart," she murmured, quoting from their marriage vows.

"Bone of my bone," he responded. "Flesh of my flesh. Love of my life."

And now his fingertips brushed her cheek, Light spangling from his touch as he smoothed the hair back from her face. "The impossible *is* possible," he murmured.

By then her feelings had grown so intense they hurt, and she swayed toward him. Surprise flashed across his face. Then his hand slid about her waist, pulling her to him, and she lifted her lips to his, letting the fine sweet fire of his embrace sweep her into her destiny.

Afterward it was said that many took the Star that day, which may have accounted for why, on that very night, the guardstar at Graymeer's blazed to life for the first time in three hundred years.

33

"Makepeace, take this to Master Amicus and his guest." The brother in charge of the kitchen gestured at the tray he had just finished loading with teapot, cups, and plate of shortbread. "You know where they are?"

"In the Master's receiving room," Gillard replied, striving to keep the resentment and irritation from his voice. After two and a half months, he still wasn't used to being ordered around. But he was definitely learning to keep his negative reactions to himself. He'd already been punished too many times for the sin of "pride" to want any more of it. They couldn't cane him as they did the others, for fear of cracking his ribs, so they used a thin, supple switch of the sort one would use on a child. It stung like fire and left more thin marks on his pale flesh than was perhaps normal, but what he hated most was the way it reminded him of his infirmity.

He was still sporting bruises from the last one.

His hand had been unwrapped and freed of its splint a week ago, shocking him by how stiff and useless it had become. He could still hardly bend the fingers, though the brother who'd been treating him assured him it would improve with time and work. Of course, he'd not been able to say how much it would improve, though he'd insisted that even if Gillard might not ever be able to use a pen properly, he would at least be able to write.

Gillard couldn't have cared less about his ability to write. He wanted to be sure of regaining his ability to use a sword, but he knew he couldn't say that. And, of course, he'd had no time to pursue that goal of late, anyway. Despite having had no contact with the outside world, he was almost never alone, and constant hard work, prayer, worship services, memorizing scriptures, and mastering the complex and inscrutable system of mandates to guarantee spiritual purity occupied every waking moment.

Last week he'd been assigned with the other First-years to clean out the garderobes, a task he'd never even realized existed, let alone had to perform. It made sense that if one used the middle of the keep's thick outer walls as a privy, one would eventually have to empty it. But it was a job for the lowest of the low, something not even proper to mention in the presence of a royal prince.

Amicus seemed to enjoy giving him the assignment, and Gillard had nearly refused, despite the prospect of another switching. Only the realization that he'd be singling himself out from the other acolytes by doing so had stopped him. That they'd had visitors that day—a party of wealthy travelers—had only made it all worse. When whispers in the hallways afterward suggested it had been the king himself with his new queen—who was very beautiful—he was more irritated than ever. Bad enough to be hauling excrement out of the keep walls at all, much less be doing it on the day his brother came to visit. The stench was so bad the guests had not stayed long, and in retrospect, Gillard supposed Amicus had chosen that time for the task deliberately so as to shield himself and the keep, and guard the secret of his royal acolyte.

Gillard could hardly blame him. Though he'd escaped the notice of the king's men every time they'd come by in the more than two months since he'd taken his vows, it was largely because they'd barely looked at him—focusing on the older, larger acolytes who had full heads of hair. Abramm, however, knew what to look for.

Still, he'd hated missing the opportunity to at least spy on the visitors. With news of the bigger world deliberately withheld to promote the acolytes' concentration on their calling, he had no idea what was happening with his brother, why he'd come, who he'd married, whether he was strong or weak . . . Apparently his crippling had not restricted him to being carried about in a chair, but it would have been nice to have seen the ugly scars they said he bore.

Now he picked up the tray, one side balanced on his flattened right hand, the other gripped securely by his left, and departed the kitchen. Crossing the yard to the main keep, he went directly to the first-floor receiving room. Voices murmured on the other side of the latched door as he set the tray on the floor so as to free his functional left hand. Depressing the latch as quietly as he could, he eased the door open and the murmuring resolved into actual words.

"... say you might know something about his disappearance," said one that must be the guest. The words themselves were as interest-piquing as the voice, which seemed familiar, so he paused, hoping to hear more. "One man even implied he might be hiding—"

The voice silenced as Gillard realized Amicus, whose desk faced the door, must have seen it open. If Gillard waited another moment he'd be accused of eavesdropping and there'd be another switching. Quickly he squatted again and picked up the tray, using it to push the door open farther before stepping into the Master's austere receiving room.

The visitor sat in a chair facing Amicus's wide, dark desk, a gaunt young man with thick brown hair tied into a queue and a woolly beard upon his face. Homespun tunic and knee breeches, threadbare woolen cloak and well-worn, mud-spattered boots bespoke a commoner status, and a poor one at that, typical of those investigating the possibility of pursuing a life in the religious orders.

"Ah, 'ere's the tea," Amicus said as Gillard drew up beside the visitor's chair. The latter glanced up then, giving Gillard clear sight of his face and he almost dropped the tray with the shock of it. *No wonder the voice sounded familiar!* This was no commoner looking for a better life, this was Ian Matheson, the former Lord of Bryermeade and one of Gillard's oldest and closest friends.

Matheson barely glanced at Gillard as he took the offered teacup and turned back to Master Amicus, while Gillard went around to serve the latter. Did Amicus know who this was? Probably. He seemed to be extremely well informed. And the bit of conversation Gillard had actually heard seemed to indicate—

"Makepeace, ye may leave us now," Amicus said gruffly. "Wait outside the door 'til I call fer ye."

Leaving the tray on the big desk, Gillard hurried out, latching the door behind him before sagging back against it. He was so excited he could hardly contain himself. It shocked him how powerfully he responded to Matheson's presence. Just seeing a familiar face, a friend who was inquiring about him, was wonderful, but even better was knowing that here was someone—unlike that stick Prittleman—who might actually help him do something besides all this religious nonsense. He stood there, grinning madly, then realized the voices had continued their conversation once he'd closed the door. He leaned his head back against the wood, straining to hear the faint words the visitor now spoke:

"Is he here? Please, sir, I have to know."

"Why?" Facing the door, Amicus's voice was much louder and clearer than Matheson's.

"Because if he . . ." Gillard lost the words and turned quickly, pressing his ear full to the wood without a twinge of guilt. ". . . our cause is not lost."

"Yer cause?" Amicus asked.

"To restore the rightful king to his throne," said Matheson, lowering his voice so much that even with his ear to the wood Gillard strained to hear him. And yet, as the words registered, his joy increased tenfold.

When Amicus did not respond, Matheson pressed his point. "Surely you cannot enjoy incidents such as occurred last week. The way he came here as if he owned the place, flaunting that blasphemous shieldmark in your face . . ."

"How would ye know what he did, freeman? Ye were na here."

"Am I wrong?"

Again, Amicus did not respond.

Matheson continued. "I heard that the Flames were dimmed for three days afterward."

"Abramm is our rightful king," said Amicus.

So those rumors were true, Gillard thought. *It was Abramm who came to visit us.*

"He is a pretender!" Matheson spat. "A usurper. A servant of the Shadow."

"Ye're speakin' treason, freeman. And if—"

A voice, loud and close, drowned out the rest of it: "Brother Makepeace, what are you doing?"

Gillard twisted away from the door and stepped forward. Brother Merces stood at the nearby juncture of the corridor and the stairwell, frowning at him.

"Master Amicus told me to wait here, sir," said Gillard.

"To wait, possibly, but not to press your ear to the door." Merces started toward him. "If he'd wanted you to hear his conversation, boy, he'd have bade you stay inside."

"Yes, brother."

Merces slowed as he came even with Gillard, his eyes flicking to the Master's door. Gillard schooled his face to blandness—he was getting better and better at it—and urged the stupid oaf to move on by.

"See you don't do it again," Merces commanded.

"I will, brother." *What a delightfully ambiguous statement.*

The blue eyes narrowed and fixed upon him for a long moment; then the man finally moved on. Gillard counted to thirty after the man had disappeared into the Great Room, and was just about to step back and resume his listening when Amicus's deep voice sounded through the door. "Makepeace!"

Whirling, Gillard pressed the latch and stepped inside again. "Yes, sir."

Both men were now standing as Amicus gestured at his visitor and said, "Bring Freeman Smith t' one of the meditation cubicles an' watch with him there fer as long as he has need."

"Yes, sir."

Though Matheson looked right at him for the second time now, Gillard saw no hint of recognition, nor even any indication he might seem familiar. Disappointed, he turned and led the way out of the receiving room and down the corridor to the stairway, which he climbed with careful concentration. The man he escorted followed wordlessly, and when they arrived at an open cubicle, he stepped past Gillard as if he weren't there.

The room beyond was small, barren, and lit with a single oil lamp on a bronze stand. There was no window and nothing on the wooden floor, though a rolled pad stood beside a three-legged stool in one corner. As his guest surveyed his new environs, Gillard dutifully turned, closed the door, and dropped the bar to secure it from the inside.

When he turned back Matheson was still frowning around at the tiny chamber. "Why is there no chair or bench?"

"We meditate on our knees. The pads there will protect you from the stone. Or you can use the stool if you like."

Frowning, Matheson pulled the stool into the center of the room and sat down.

Gillard watched his old friend closely. He'd expected to be recognized by now, or at least to have piqued the other man's interest, despite the fact that Ian had barely looked at him the entire time they'd been together. Yes, he knew the way aristocrats tended not to *see* those they considered beneath them, and yes, Ian would certainly not think to look for him stubble-headed and cloaked in a Mataian acolyte's tunic. But still . . . *You'd think he'd at least recognize my voice.*

Gillard unrolled the mat that Matheson had ignored and settled onto it, to the right of and slightly behind his friend, the position affording him a clear view of the man's profile. As far as Matheson was concerned, however, he might have been alone. He sat staring at the oil lamp's flame now, right hand propped on the thigh of his dirty breeches, his bearded jaw working as if he were grinding his teeth. Then he glanced at the door, at the flame again, and released a long low breath. After a while he began to bounce his knee up and down, then glanced at the door again, and finally stilled himself and dropped his head forward into both hands.

Gillard decided it was time to speak. "You seem troubled, sir."

Matheson snorted and twisted his head aside to answer him without looking. "Indeed."

"Would you like me to pray for you?" It was hard to get that line out without breaking into laughter.

"No." Matheson twisted his head forward again and rubbed his face with his hands. "But thank you for offering." He was thinner than Gillard remembered him, and his hands were rough and dirty, the nails all but chewed away. Scabs marred the backs of his knuckles.

Should I just blurt out the truth, Gillard wondered, *or continue to play with him for a bit?* It was gratifying to know his disguise was as good as this . . . but at the same time discomfiting, as it reminded him of the other more foundational changes that had been worked in him since Matheson had seen him last. Changes that wouldn't grow back with time or be exchanged like an old robe for something new and different. The old bitter horror flared in him, and for a moment he almost changed his mind about letting Matheson see him.

The other man shifted on the stool and said to his lap, "And just how long does he expect me to wait here?"

"Until you have your answer, I would imagine."

"I wasn't asking you, boy."

"I know. But perhaps you should."

"Like you would know."

"I know more than you credit me."

"Why kind of insolent twit are you, anyway?" As Matheson said this, he turned to glare at Gillard, his eyes fixing squarely upon the acolyte's face. And for the first time he really looked at him. For one instant the frown deepened, then drained away as he stared hard. His eyes tracked over Gillard's face, up to his naked scalp, and down the length of his shrunken body, then back up to the face. Horrified recognition surged across Matheson's countenance as he lurched up and away, stumbling over the stool and falling against the wall, as far from Gillard as he could get in this tiny room. He stood there braced, staring in disbelief. "Eidon's mercy! You're . . . you're *small*."

"Prittleman tells me it was a result of some spell Abramm cast over me, but I prefer to believe it was the morwhol."

Matheson remained backed up against the wall, his face pale, his eyes so wide the whites showed. He blinked, gulped, and then his gaze tracked again over Gillard's body, down and up again to the scalp with its two weeks' worth of pale blond stubble. "So the rumors are true," he murmured. "You *have* taken holy vows."

"A matter of expediency. Nothing more." He frowned. "Come on, man. Are you going to stay slammed up against that wall all day? Whatever's befallen me, it's not catching."

Matheson forced himself to relax and step forward but was unable to stop staring. "Holy vows, my lord?"

"Why do you act so astonished? You must have believed some kernel of those rumors you mentioned, else why would you have come here at all?" *And why has Amicus released word of my vow-taking already, when he told me it would be years?*

"I thought they were hiding you. I thought . . . Everyone said you were as one dead. . . ." His eyes remained on Gillard's bare head, his look of distaste deepening. "I never would have thought you, of all men . . . Eidon's mercy, Gillard. They've made you bald!"

"Yes, and already it has served me well. The king's men hardly give me a look. You yourself didn't even recognize me."

"But not because of the robes and the hair . . ."

"Oh, I think it was very much because of them. You just said it yourself—not even you would have expected me to do this."

Matheson frowned at him, and then a look that almost seemed like sympathy came into his face. "Is it . . . is it because of the shrinking that you . . ." He trailed off, seeming unable to find the word he wanted.

"That I what?"

"Got religious."

"Got relig— Plagues, Ian! Haven't you been listening? This is purely a matter of expediency."

"But how would they—"

"They don't care. I told Amicus I didn't believe a word of his gibberish. He said it wouldn't matter."

"He wants to use you."

"Of course he does. As I want to use him. . . . But enough of me. You're the first person from the outside world I've met since I came here. Tell me what's happened since Seven Peaks. I've heard next to nothing."

And so Matheson obliged him. After the debacle at Seven Peaks, he and a handful of other deposed and wanted supporters had fled north to a remote valley, where they'd lived for several months. Eventually they'd heard the stories that Gillard was being held drugged in Chancellor's Tower. Adopting a false name, Matheson had traveled to Springerlan to investigate. He'd never gotten to see Gillard and, being a wanted man himself, had not stayed long. Returning to Two Cities he'd landed a job at a warehouse, rising through the ranks to become a manager, an accountant, and the boss's sometime personal assistant. He'd recently accompanied him on his trip down to Springerlan to plead with the new Duke of Northille for exemption from the new tax and conscription writ that had just passed.

"Northille?" Gillard interrupted. "That's my property."

"Not anymore, sir."

"Who did Abramm give it to?"

"The former captain of his guard: Trap Meridon."

"He made Meridon a duke? The man's a commoner!"

"Well, now he's one of the highest-ranking men of the peerage. He's also the First Minister."

Gillard's anger erupted as it had not been able to in weeks, spewing forth in a rant on Abramm's monumental stupidity and gall that was exceeded only by that of the peers who allowed him to do such things.

"Well, sir," Matheson said hesitantly when he'd run down, "Abramm *is* working from a strong position these days. What with the regalia manifesting, the business at the Gull Islands, and then the orb at Graymeer's lighting . . . he's won many converts."

Gillard frowned at him. "Regalia? Gull Islands? What are you talking about?"

Matheson was aghast. "You don't even know about *that*?"

"I am an acolyte. No one tells acolytes anything. And before that . . . I was unconscious."

And so Matheson told him of the events of the coronation, and Abramm's victorious campaign to take the Gull Islands, of Briellen's rejection of him because of his scars, his subsequent marriage to Chesedh's Second Daughter, now made First, and the lighting of the guardstar at Graymeer's that same night.

"He is . . . beloved in Springerlan, to hear the talk," he concluded. "Nearly everyone there wears a shield. And he's spent the last two months on progress. He and Queen Madeleine just came up the River Kalladorne, stopping at all the towns and cities, him wearing the crown and bringing the orb for all to see. And leaving more converts in his wake. He's going through the Highlands now to receive the border lords' fealty. Half of them love him, too, on account of his Terstan shield and his turning of their fabled Hasmal'uk stone to gold."

Gillard listened with growing horror. To hear Matheson tell it, the whole world had twisted into some dreadful alternate reality in his absence. How could Abramm be beloved? How could he be so successful? He was a cowardly little runt. How could he have taken Gillard's place so thoroughly and no one even question? "It's not fair," he muttered. "It's not *right*."

"That's why I came," said Matheson. "I had to know if you lived. If there was any hope for those of us who followed you. . . ."

FOURTH

On the late-summer evening before the king was due to return to Whitehill from his months-long progress through the realm, Hazmul stood in the rotunda of the royal gallery, hands clasped behind his back as he stared up at the canvas looming on the green wall before him. It was the centerpiece of the new display set up to celebrate Abramm's return, and he hated it.

Alaric the Bold painted to symbolize Tersius sat astride his great white warhorse, Runjan, depicted in the stylized half-rearing position. The king wore the crown and a white robe and held his broadsword aloft, blazing with the harsh and searing light of Eidon's chosen. And on the ground directly before them cowered a spindly red dragon, about to be trampled by Runjan's raised golden hooves.

It was one of the paintings newly exposed by the crew of Terstans Abramm had assigned to clear away the arcane webbing that had obscured many of the collection's pieces. This one's original images, in fact, had been almost completely obliterated, not only by the webbing but by the dust and oils of time. That their painstaking work had revealed a picture of such contemporary significance—or so they thought—had excited them all, and they were eager that their king should see it upon his return.

Contemporary significance, indeed. Hazmul snorted. It was

an obscene piece of propaganda. An insulting caricature of an imagined reality. And he should know, having seen the incident firsthand. He wanted to burn it right off the wall.

Instead he leaned forward and blew lightly at the canvas, as if there were a dust feather that needed to be dislodged. No one in the room with him would think anything of it, because none of them could see the faint violet light of his breath. . . .

It had been four months since Abramm left Springerlan with his wife to go on progress through his realm. In his absence the people's regard for him had deepened even more than it would have had he stayed. They loved the fairy-tale nature of his courtship and marriage, especially the way Eidon had seemed to anoint the union by lighting the guardstar the night it was consummated. Abramm had been wise to leave right afterward, letting the goodwill solidify without having to worry about the inevitable missteps and irritations a man would make in his day-to-day living.

Hazmul had stayed behind with Meridon and the other counselors to keep the government running smoothly in Abramm's absence, breaking away only for a quick trip up to Skaevik for the border lords' official giving of fealty. He'd been surprised and irritated to see Rennalf of Balmark among the lords who swore allegiance to the king. According to reports, the man had been completely cowed when he'd learned what Abramm had done on the Gull Islands. At Skaevik he'd been docile, polite and respectful in his dealings with the king, but Hazmul had sensed the resentment simmering within him. Which was one of the few things that made the trip worthwhile.

Returning to Springerlan he'd received the summons to a rhu'eman court of inquiry he both expected and had prepared for. The debacle at the Gull Islands could in no way be laid to his account. He had passed on all appropriate information. Surely they should know that the man who had been the White Pretender could be counted on to act daringly in any assault he might bring to bear. Hazmul had passed on his suspicions that the crown imparted some increased ability to see . . . and they all knew of Abramm's history of destroying etherworld corridors.

His defense had been accepted and the commander of the

island operation demoted. Still, he'd not come home without receiving a warning: Madeleine had entered her destiny when she'd been allowed to marry Abramm, and the marriage would be a threat. . . .

But he wasn't worried about that. As with the Light plague, these things happened. Some humans were simply intractable. And anyway, he'd prepared for this.

From Skaevik, Abramm had ridden through the Highlands, visiting the various manors, coming down through Kerrey and Long Valley, where he'd stopped off at Castle Stormcroft to spend the last two weeks of the journey alone with his queen. Or as alone as a king and queen could be with a retinue of nearly one hundred attendants, servants, and armsmen.

They were due back tomorrow around midday.

Already he'd been hearing the reports of how in love they were. How much more relaxed Abramm was, how much more confident Madeleine was. They said Abramm doted on her and that she practically worshipped him in return.

Nauseating. But if the ties between them were half as strong as the reports . . . that could be very useful.

He turned from the painting and strolled about the rotunda, glancing at the other pieces as he exchanged pleasantries with his fellow guests, amusing himself with the thought of how shocked they'd be to know who really dwelt behind Byron Blackwell's annoying spectacles.

Vesprit caught up with him in one of the gallery's shadowed side aisles, Hazmul quenching its kelistars so his underling might approach. Assigned to monitor Abramm's journey north, Vesprit had returned periodically with his reports, the last one being three weeks ago. Now he informed Hazmul that all had gone as planned and the royal couple would arrive as scheduled.

Throughout his report, however, the underwarhast's aura kept shimmering with suppressed excitement, a breach of manners Hazmul found increasingly irritating. He was about to call him on it when Vesprit finally got around to sharing his news:

"He has absolutely devoted himself to her, sir. It's been shocking for a man who once took vows of celibacy. Making up for all the years he lost, I suppose. Do you want to guess how often they—"

"Vesprit, please." Hazmul turned away from him to one of the paintings. *"I have no interest in such prurient details. If you have nothing more to report, you may go."*

The amber aura rippled, blotching momentarily with brown as Vesprit straightened his bronzed shoulders. *"Sorry, sir, there is more. I was merely making note because his efforts have paid off. The queen has conceived. She's not told anyone as yet, though I think her maid suspects."*

Hazmul sat back in his chair. *"And the child?"*

"Male, sir."

"He's sired an heir?" Now, that was unexpected. Thoroughly unexpected and wholly delightful.

"Indeed, he has, sir . . ." Vesprit paused. *"You sound pleased."*

"Oh, Vesprit, I am very pleased. This is a most excellent development."

Silence stretched between them as Hazmul went off on a tangent of possibilities into which Vesprit finally intruded with great wariness:

"Warhast, you have lost me completely. I thought . . . I thought this was something we didn't want to happen. I thought . . . Won't this only strengthen him more?"

"Oh no. Prosperity is one of the most powerful tools we have. Let him have his kingdom and his woman and his children for a time."

"Children, sir?"

"If he can pull it off, I'd love to see more than one. Let him get comfortable with it all. Let him grow to rely upon it, get attached to it. . . . Let him think that with the lighting of the guardstar and the myriad conversions, we have been driven away and defeated. Meanwhile, we will continue to work behind the scenes, nurturing our own family. Gillard is coming along nicely. And Eudace has tremendous potential, particularly now that he's been so unfairly imprisoned."

Hazmul moved on to the next painting, as if he could actually see something in the darkness. *"The more he has to lose, Vesprit, the harder he will fall. And the harder he falls, the more likely he'll never get up. In fact, if all goes as I envision, he won't be able to get up at all, for he will be dead. At the hands of those he loves most."*

EXECUTION
SQUARE

PART FOUR

34

"Papa! Papa, look at me! Can you see me?"

"Aye, Simon, I can see you," Abramm called, grinning at his towheaded young son as the latter clung to the saddle of his gray pony. Philip Meridon, at twenty-five the physical match of his older brother, held the beast's reins just under its chin and led it about the yard, while Jared, taller than Philip now, walked along beside to make sure the little crown prince didn't fall.

Abramm stood with Byron Blackwell in the afternoon shade of the elm trees, holding his other son, Ian, who had one chubby fist fastened tightly to the back of Abramm's doublet as he waved the other in his big brother's direction. " 'Ima! 'Ima!" he said.

"Yes, Ian. That's Simon," Abramm said to him. And Ian jumped up and down in his arm, laughing.

"I'm riding the pony, Papa!" called young Simon. "Do you see me?"

"Aye, and a fine rider you are, too, my little man."

His son's smile was glorious to behold. The boy turned his attention to Philip. "Make him go faster, Lieutenant."

"You must kick him with your heels, Highness," Philip told him.

Simon complied readily, though the kicks could only have registered to the beast as a strange disturbance high on its back, not anything to be heeded and obeyed. But Philip clucked and tugged at the reins and the pony broke into a trot as Simon squealed with delight.

At Abramm's side, Byron Blackwell shook his head and murmured, "Hard to believe he's already four years old. Seems like yesterday he was born."

"It does, indeed. I swear he's a gotten foot taller since I left for Elpis."

Though Abramm had been home from that trip for several days now, he still couldn't get over how much his firstborn had changed in the mere three months he'd been gone.

Byron chuckled. "So much for your fear he'd be small. Frankly I think it's astonishing how much he favors you—in mind and body."

Abramm gave his secretary a doubtful glance. Simon was very blond, and very blue-eyed, but beyond that Abramm could see no similarities between his son's round features and his own scarred, hawkish countenance. If Simon resembled anyone it was Maddie. But everyone was constantly remarking on how the boy was clearly Abramm's progeny. Maybe it gave them comfort to know the heir was truly the heir.

Simon's birthday party was being held on the clipped green at the center of the grove of oaks and elms just north of the East Terrace. The cleared space had been created for ninepins and mallet ball, and for small outdoor parties such as this. Red-striped pavilions lined its perimeter, and multicolored pennants rustled in a languid breeze. It was a fine spring day, with a cloudless, deep blue sky and just enough stirring of the air to keep things from growing too warm.

The festivities had begun at two o'clock with an egg hunt, followed by various games and then the unveiling of the Favor Tree. Afterward there were twistbreads, oranges, sausages, and fruit comfits; and finally Simon had received his gifts, the most exciting being the pony, of course. With the official celebration to be held in conjunction with the Spring Fair and parade tomorrow, only close friends and family had been invited today—Trap, Carissa, and the elder Simon being conspicuous in their absence. The latter was with the army up north, dealing with the border-lord situation now threatening to erupt as the snowmelt opened the passes. Trap and Carissa were merely late.

Movement across the yard beyond Simon and his pony drew Abramm's attention to his wife, now emerging from one of the pavilions. Four of her ladies-in-waiting accompanied her, young noblewomen Maddie had been shocked to discover not only admired her, but genuinely liked her. Even more amazing to her, they actually enjoyed being sent off to old rooms in the University library to hunt up ancient books. Or joining in on some musical composition she might be formulating. And of course all four doted on her sons.

She stopped near the circle in which Philip was leading the pony with its small rider and exclaimed at her son's expertise. He beamed at the praise and started up a lengthy monologue about his "bestest present ever."

Abramm only had eyes for his wife, who all but glowed in the late-afternoon light. Her hair, more softly braided than in the past, shone with red glints, and as always, that endearing tendril dangled alongside her face. Though she fussed about the bit of weight she had put on during her pregnancies, he thought it made her figure finer than ever, thought, in fact, that she was the most beautiful woman in the world. She always laughed at him when he told her so and accused him of saying it only to please and flatter her.

Now, as Simon finished his discourse and turned his attention to the pony, she looked up, meeting Abramm's glance—as if she knew full well he had been watching her. He wondered for not the first time how it was that she had only to look at him to ignite his desire for her all over again. A desire he'd thought was slaked after three nights in her company, yet here he was, wildly impatient at all he had to do before they could be alone again.

Three months was far too long to be away.

As usual, she read him perfectly, smiling and blushing in that way that only stoked his fire and caused her ladies to exchange knowing smiles among themselves.

Ian's small fingers touched his beard, then stole up the doubled white lines of the scars on his face. Abramm looked down to find his younger son staring at him with wide and very serious blue eyes. For a moment they looked at one another. Then the little hand patted Abramm's face. "Papa home," Ian said soberly. With that, he stuck his thumb into his mouth and laid his head on Papa's shoulder, content as Maddie said he'd not been for all the three months Abramm was away.

He'd hated having to be gone, but he hadn't met with King Hadrich face-to-face since the Chesedhan ruler had come to Springerlan four years ago. Given that Abramm had just agreed to send more troops to help fight the Esurhites along the shores of the Strait of Terreo, he wanted to meet with the man to whom he'd entrusted them. He'd also been invited to participate in the planning of a new offensive campaign, which he was especially happy to do since he'd long thought Hadrich's defensive posture was never going to win the war. It was also good to get better acquainted with his sons' grandfather. He'd hoped to talk with Leyton, too, but his brother-in-law had been south, heavily involved in the fighting at Salmanca.

His musing was interrupted then as Master Belmir approached to say his good-byes. "Have to prepare for the ceremony tonight," he said with a rueful smile.

"Tonight? I thought it wasn't for another couple of days."

"That's the official consecration. This is a repentance and purification ritual for those who will be conducting it." For several years the Holy Keep in Springerlan had lain in ruin, abandoned by the High Father, first for the one at Sterlen and then for the new one being built north of the River Snowsong. Recently, though, a partial restoration of the Springerlan Sanctum had been completed and it was to be officially reinstated as a place of worship this week. Which was the reason Belmir was in town.

Now Abramm's old discipler bowed. "Thank you for inviting me, sir. It was a delightful afternoon. Your sons are charming."

"Glad you came, Master Belmir. And I hope your having spent the afternoon with a pack of heretics like ourselves won't bring you too much grief from your associates."

A flicker of uneasiness crossed the old man's face. Then he smiled. "Well, that is what purification ceremonies are for. Besides, they know I have not given up hope of bringing you back to the fold."

"A futile hope, old friend, as I keep telling you."

"Time will tell."

He took his leave, and Abramm couldn't help smiling after him. He thought if anyone was being brought into the fold it was Belmir, who had spent the entire afternoon in conversation with Everitt Kesrin.

"I don't know why you invited him," Blackwell grumbled. "He's an old man. He's not going to change his mind now."

"He's still alive, Byron."

"He's only here to convert you. And now, probably, your sons, as well. He just as much as admitted it."

Abramm only smiled the more. "Perhaps. But it wasn't me or my sons who held the greatest interest for him today."

Blackwell frowned and flicked a glance at Kohal Kesrin, now in conversation with the queen.

Not long after that, Trap finally arrived, without Carissa, Abramm noted unhappily, though he had promised to go to her flat specifically to bring her with him. The moment Simon saw him, he burst into smiles, calling out excitedly, "Look, Uncle Trap. I have a pony."

"You certainly do!" Trap exclaimed, stopping to watch the boy as Philip led the pony around. "And what a fine animal he is, too. What will you name him?"

"Warbanner!"

"Warbanner?"

"Just like Papa."

"Ah." Trap grinned over his shoulder at Abramm. "But . . . if you give your pony the same name as your papa's Warbanner, how will we tell them apart?"

"Because mine is smaller than Papa's, just like *I* am smaller than Uncle Simon. And you can tell us apart, can't you?"

Whereupon Trap laughed and admitted that they could.

"Where's Auntie Crissa?"

"She's not feeling well, Simon. She had to stay home."

"Again?"

"Afraid so, soldier. But she promised she'll make it up to you as soon as she's feeling better." He gestured toward the green. "Now, I want to see you ride that steed around the yard again. Are you sure you can handle him?"

"I'm sure, Uncle. Make him go *fast*, Lieutenant."

And Philip coaxed the newly christened Warbanner into a trot again as Simon hung on to the saddle for dear life, shrieking delightedly with every wild bounce.

Trap drifted over to greet the king.

"So what kind of illness is it this time?" Abramm asked sourly. "The same old sit in the chair and stare out the window illness?"

Trap kept his eyes on the crown prince and his pony, a frown creasing his brow. "She's really not feeling well, sir."

Abramm had thought that once Carissa had taken the Star, her moodiness would end. And for a while it had. She'd been so happy for him and Maddie, and the way everything had worked out. When Simon was born she'd doted on him to the point they'd hardly even needed the nanny. But he'd barely turned one when the darkness returned.

Abramm knew she wanted the kind of relationship he had with Madeleine, knew she wanted children of her own, as well, and that her longings for both sometimes got the best of her. It couldn't help her to see all she so desired playing out before her every day, with no apparent hope of ever seeing it fulfilled in her own life. Though he'd thought for a time she and Trap might get together, whatever romantic relationship was developing between them had died three years ago with her first melancholic episode. And though Abramm thought she was the one who'd pulled away, not Trap, there was no persuading her of that. She'd even remarked to Abramm once that it didn't seem fair Eidon would give *him* everything he'd ever wanted, and reserve for her nothing but disappointment. He'd had no idea how to respond to that, and reminding her that Eidon's plan was marvelous beyond description did not seem to help. So he'd told her what Eidon had told him: that sometimes one had to wait.

Though her moodiness had resurfaced off and on ever since, it had worsened dramatically in the last eight months. Maddie said she'd not visited the palace the entire time Abramm was in Elpis. And the few times Maddie had visited her, Carissa had been so closemouthed and cool it hadn't been easy to stay long. Nor to make the effort to visit again.

Now she'd even skipped her favorite nephew's birthday party. *I'll have to pay her a visit myself and see what's going on,* he thought grimly. Not that he had any idea what he could do about it.

As twilight gathered, a chill crept into the air and the garden torches were lit. The children ran about squealing, playing tag and hide-and-seek, and at seven o'clock, they all moved to the East Terrace, where a small orchestra played and tables of food stood out beside the ranks of chairs and benches arrayed around the platform reserved for the royal family. His hip aching after all the hours of standing, Abramm settled onto one of the two large chairs on that platform, Ian still in his arms. Maddie sat in the one beside him, Simon bobbing between them, his excitement at the prospect of seeing the fireworks almost more than he could bear. Two small chairs had been set up at the couple's feet, but it was unlikely they would be used, Simon being unable to sit at all and Ian unwilling to let go of his papa.

To the west, the sky still glowed a murky russet behind the palace's looming silhouette, but directly ahead of them the stars were one by one coming out to shine over the bay, as out on the western headland the guardstar at Graymeer's shone brightly against the dark sea beyond.

Suddenly, the first rocket shot into the sky and exploded in a burst of golden stars, the boom lagging behind. Ian squealed and buried his face in Abramm's shoulder even as Simon clapped his hands to his ears, shrieking with delight. More rockets screamed up, and soon plumes of red and blue mingled with gold to drift down toward their reflection on the bay. Around him people oohed and aahed, while out on the points of both headlands, the garrisons there launched their own rockets, tiny fountains of light blooming over the dark humps of land.

"There, Simon, see?" Abramm said, bending down to his firstborn. "They're all for you. The whole city telling you happy birthday."

Simon beamed up at him and clapped his hands, then faced forward as another sparkler burst across the sky. It was one of those moments when everything seemed to come together for Abramm into the perfect distillation of pleasure and happiness, and he gave heartfelt thanks for it all, not least that all those rockets could be shot off just for fun.

After the fireworks they trooped down to Terstmeet, where even with taking notes, Abramm found his thoughts drifting off the message and back to his wife. Finally, though, the obligations were met, the sons put to bed, and they returned to the king's bedchamber, where they dismissed all the servants and shut the doors on the world.

"Kesrin was really in a mood tonight, wasn't he?" Maddie exclaimed as she sank into the chair and pulled off her shoes. "All that gloom and doom. It's probably these Mataians in town for the consecration." She said something more, but as Abramm was now enjoying watching her slip off her stockings, he had no idea what it was.

She dropped her skirts around her ankles and said, "You're not listening."

"No." He smiled, then offered his hand to pull her up out of the chair. "And right now the last thing I want to talk about is gloom and doom and Mataians." He grimaced. "Especially not Mataians."

She came up into his arms but laid her hands upon his chest, keeping her distance so she could stare up at him, her eyes dark and deep with emotion. Then she ran her fingers through the short whiskers of his beard. "It is so good to have you back, Abramm. I missed you so. . . ." She caught her lip between her teeth and her eyes teared up. Then she shook her head. "Sometimes I love you so much it scares me. So much I fear Eidon will take you away just so I can learn to love him more."

Abramm regarded her with concern and then dismissed her fear with a chuckle. "Surely you already do love him more," he said, burying his face in the crook between her shoulder and neck to kiss the tender skin there.

"Of course. It's just . . ." Her hands squeezed his arms. "He is not here like you are, strong and handsome and solid. I can't feel his arms around me, and he doesn't do things . . ."

"Like this?" Abramm nibbled on her earlobe.

She giggled. "No. He doesn't do that."

"Or this . . ." He moved his lips to the edge of her jaw, then worked his way down her neck to the base of her throat as she gasped and giggled anew.

"Oh no, he has you to do those things. And a splendid job you do of them, too."

He kissed her full on the mouth then, and her arms slid up around his neck as she pressed her body against his with a practiced intimacy that said he wasn't the only one who had been impatient with the evening's activities. It wasn't long before he picked her up and laid her on the bed, then settled himself beside her to unfasten the long line of buttons that closed the front of her gown. . . .

Later, languorous and profoundly content, he lay staring up at the folds of the canopy over his bed, Maddie nestled under his arm, her cheek upon his chest. Sometimes the gratitude and wonder welled up in him with such power his flesh could hardly contain it. *Blessings . . . beyond anything you can ask or imagine. . . .* Just as Eidon had promised.

Never could he have begun to imagine possessing all the things he possessed: fruitful lands, a prospering realm, relative peace and tranquility, two fine sons, and a wife who adored him, with whom he fell more in love each day.

And yet . . . for all his rejection of gloom and doom, he had to admit Kesrin's words had gotten to him, too: *"'You are about to be cast into prison. . . .'"* the kohal had quoted from the Second Word. *"'They will all desert you, just as they deserted him, and there will be none to help you.'"*

Was it a warning? He had heard those words before, but they had struck him differently tonight, set him thinking about Tersius in a way he hadn't before. For all Tersius's followers had deserted him when the time came to go to that hill outside Xorofin. He had to do it alone—bear the most awful suffering any man had ever born. Alone.

Eidon had also promised Abramm there would be suffering and trials to go with his blessings, and there had been. Things had gone wrong; campaigns had failed; tragedies had occurred. Blackwell's sister Leona had gone mad and flung herself off Razen's Point the day Simon was born; there'd been two Heartlander uprisings in the last two years; the borderlords were growing increasingly antagonistic; assassins still ambushed Abramm regularly; Ian had nearly died of the croup last year; and Carissa was becoming increasingly incapacitated by her melancholic moods. . . . It wasn't like there weren't problems.

"'You are about to be cast into prison. . . .'" That wasn't for everyone . . . so why did his thoughts keep catching on it as if it carried some special portent? *"'They will all desert you . . . as they deserted him.'"*

He could not imagine Trap, for all the prickliness between them of late, deserting him. Nor Simon, nor Kesrin. . . . And yet, to be conformed to

Tersius's likeness there had to be trials. Sometimes fiery trials. Trials you didn't think you would survive.

But surely I've already had my trials. . . .

"You were unmarked when you were sold into slavery. Those trials were just to wake you up." Not to conform him. Not to give him the opportunity—the privilege—of demonstrating his faith. . . .

"You're not sleeping, love," Maddie said.

"I'm thinking."

"About what?"

"How blessed I am." *And how hard it would be to lose it all.*

She pushed up to brace herself on her elbow so she could look at him. Then she frowned. "You're not letting all that talk tonight about fiery trials get to you, are you?"

He smiled up at her. "No more than you, apparently . . . fearing I'll be taken from you, indeed." But though he smiled as he spoke them, the words struck a chill to his heart. Was it coincidence or sheer logic that both of them should have taken the same track of thought after tonight's lesson?

She stayed where she was, that tiny frown between her brows. She knew he wasn't telling her all of it, but she also knew enough to let him keep his thoughts if he did not wish to share them. And so in the end she settled again beside him, the warmth of her body especially nice after the cold of separation.

"Well, whatever happens," she said, "we have Eidon and his Light and each other. We'll face it."

He looked down at the top of her head, lifted his hand to stroke her wavy hair.

"And no matter what else may happen," she said to his chest. *"I will not be deserting you. You can rest on that."*

He smiled again. *That, of all things, seems as impossible to imagine as it would be to bear.* But there were ways to be deserted without a person's will being involved. And he knew what Maddie did not: that despite all that was going so well, evil still simmered beneath the surface. He had many enemies—Bonafil, Gillard, Prittleman, Rennalf—all of whom hated him with deep and self-righteous passion. He knew Oswain Nott was very bitter toward him because he'd appointed Trap First Minister instead of Nott himself, and there was Belthre'gar, too, whose hatred predated all of the others—save possibly Gillard. Many enemies, and now three more ways to attack him: his wife and sons.

And there was that army he'd seen when he was crowned, with the banners bearing his own arms combined with that of the Chesedhan royal line. . . . None of that fulfilled, none of it even making sense. As well the red dragon, whose mark he bore on his own flesh and still did not know why. War still loomed on the horizon, and if they'd had a five-year reprieve, he did himself no favors believing that would last forever.

No, he had the unshakable sense that something dreadful was about to happen, and that perhaps the greatest challenges of his life lay not behind him, but ahead. . . .

His attention was drawn away from those grim thoughts then, for his wife had apparently decided she'd not had enough of him tonight, after all. Indeed, it wasn't long before she'd made it quite impossible for him to think of anything but her.

Trap rode in his carriage from the palace to his own home that night, where he changed his clothes before going out to saddle one of his horses. Then, cloaked and cowled, he rode through streets busy with the preparations for tomorrow's parade and fair, taking a circuitous route to Princess Carissa's prestigious hillside home. There he let himself in through the back door using his own key. Locking the door behind him, he stopped just inside the kitchen and listened carefully, all his arena-trained senses on the alert.

Some of the kitchen staff slept on pallets over by the pantry, their faint breathing and erratic snores the only sound to interrupt the night silence. He peered about the shadowed room, nonetheless, thinking it would be nice to have Abramm's night sight just now. But he saw and sensed nothing and moved through the room into the hall. He patrolled around through the empty front rooms, then climbed the stairs, thinking their creaking was probably a good thing to let go for now. Assuming the intruder he feared would even use the stairs.

But there is no corridor here. We've searched and searched . . . and I don't think he can fly. . . .

On the second floor he nodded to Cooper, who sat in a chair outside Carissa's room, noted there was no light coming from under the door, and went up to his third-floor bedroom where he'd slept every night for the last three months. Ever since Abramm had left.

He conjured a kelistar for the pewter starstick sitting on the desk, then unbuttoned his jacket, wondering how in the world they were going to tell

Abramm. He'd been thinking about it all day, and that conversation at the party had not made any of it easier. Still, they would have to tell him soon, and better he hear it from them than the gossips.

It was just that they both knew how angry he would be when he found out. Angry that they'd kept it from him for so long, and angrier still over the situation itself.

He draped the jacket over the back of the desk chair, then sat to remove his boots, which he placed upright beside the head of the bed, along with his scabbarded sword. Not that he was likely to need the latter. . . .

Finally he stretched out on the bed, staring at the low wooden ceiling above him and asking Eidon for the hundredth time why he had let things come to this.

FIFTH

"YOU SEEM EXCEPTIONALLY full of energy today, my lord," said Hazmul's valet as he ran a comb through his master's graying, shoulder-length locks. "Up before dawn and fidgeting like a man impatient to conquer the world."

"I feel like one, Duffy. Things couldn't be better!" But Hazmul made an effort to quiet his rapidly bobbing knee and stop the fingers of his right hand from drumming impatiently on the arm of the chair. Didn't want to appear too excited or Duffy might talk about it later. Particularly after the way today's events should be unfolding.

Months ago he'd sent off his third successive request for authorization to proceed with his plans, stressing the urgency of his need. When it still hadn't arrived by the time Abramm had returned from Elpis, he'd nearly gone insane with impatience and frustration, even giving thought to proceeding without authorization. The opportunities were coming together so swiftly he feared they would be lost or, worse, that the approval would come too late, leaving him accountable for a failure that could be laid wholly at the feet of those who commanded him.

After last night's message in Terstmeet, he had seen that the moment to act had arrived, yet he was paralyzed for lack of that blasted authorization. Firing off yet another missive to his commanding arkag, he'd infused the rhu'ema who carried it with all the urgency he could muster. Then he'd spent the night pacing and fuming before Vesprit, whom he'd forced to attend him as much out of spite as to prevent himself from launching into another uncontrolled burning spree.

He knew how slow and stupid bureaucratic channels could be, knew, as well, that the Arkag of the Western Regions not only liked to make underlings wait but had a strong tendency to overlook the needs and requests of those stationed outside his immediate sphere of awareness. Which obviously had been the case with Hazmul's earlier requests, despite the fact it must be obvious by now to everyone in the southland what a threat Abramm had become. Especially in light of this new offensive he'd cooked up with the Chesedhans. If Hazmul was not going to be given the freedom he needed to act, at the time he needed to do so . . . he had gotten very close to taking matters into his own hands.

But all his concerns and frustrations were resolved now. The messenger had arrived just hours ago granting him everything he wanted.

Already he'd sent Vesprit off with his orders, and as he submitted now to his valet's ministrations, he marveled at the precision with which he'd brought all these elements to such perfect maturity. Years of effort and careful manipulation had lined them up in an unbroken, inevitable chain of cause and effect, simply waiting for the nudge that would set it all in motion. . . .

And then we'll all see how devoted Abramm is to Eidon and his precious Words. When he finds himself betrayed by the very one he serves and looks his own death in the face, abandoned and alone . . . we'll just see where his loyalties lie. He's been turned once. He can be turned again. . . .

He meant to make that fateful nudge this morning, and he could hardly wait.

"Will you wear it loose or tied back today, sir?" Duffy said, drawing Hazmul's attention back to his morning toilet. His leg was jiggling again, and he made it stop, then inspected his reflection in the mirror. The man had arranged his hair around his shoulders, and it shocked him anew the amount of gray that had come into it lately. The lack of color only seemed to accent the haggard, wrinkled look of the face, reminding him again how fast this body was aging.

"Pull it back," he said, gesturing toward his shoulders. "The gray's not so noticeable that way."

"Yes, sir."

"And I do think I'll have you color it one of these days," he said. There were ways of combating the wrinkles, as well, but that carried a stiffer price, and right now he had other things to do.

Duffy pulled his hair back tightly and fastened it with the standard black ribbon. After making a last bit of adjustment to doublet and cravat, he stepped back, and Hazmul leaped from the chair, snatched up his cloak and folio, and tried to keep his pace even as he left his apartments.

He knew exactly where he had to be and at what time in order to intercept the king. Then he would deliver his message, the perfect catalyst for a man primed to expect betrayal. Again he had to quench his bubbling excitement. *You must be calm and deliberate,* he reminded himself. *Utterly relaxed. Above all, you must not allow this worthless piece of flesh you inhabit to smile while you're telling him. You must be suitably solemn and even a little distraught. But not too distraught. . . .*

He could smile now, though, as he boarded his coach and headed up toward the palace. This was going to be a splendid day. In fact, it should be the first in a series of increasingly splendid days. . . .

35

Abramm started awake with a gasp, already half out of the bed and certain someone had been standing there watching him. He even thought he heard the click of the hidden panel as it closed in the bedchamber wall, and was standing upright on the rug before he remembered the opening had been boarded up. Even so, he crossed the room and pressed it, just to be sure. By then the rationality of increasing wakefulness had superseded the dream-induced certainty of an intruder's presence.

It was only a relic of what had happened in reality three nights ago, right after his return. He'd started awake then, too, shocked to find a small man with long, white-blond hair approaching the bed from Maddie's side, a short blade glinting in his hand. The storm of protective ferocity that had surged through Abramm had taken even him by surprise. In a heartbeat he'd tossed off the cover and leaped over the wide bed to face the man, knocking the blade aside with his bare hand. The intruder had cried out as if he'd been dealt a savage blow, holding that hand to his chest and staggering backward, wide-eyed. At Abramm's back Maddie had awakened and conjured a kelistar, its clear white light flooding around him into a strangely familiar face. Then Abramm had lunged, ready to throttle the life out of whoever he was for daring to come near his wife with a weapon. But the little man had ducked beneath his reach and scrambled around the bed, disappearing into the dark hole that gaped in the wall.

Seeing the open panel, Abramm had raised the alarm and a search had been instituted. It was then he realized why the man had seemed so familiar. The small stature had put him off, but the white-blond hair and pale blue eyes were definitely those of his brother Gillard.

Maddie wasn't so sure. "Do you really think *Gillard* would scramble away like that when all you'd done was knock the blade from his hand?"

"I don't know. He seemed hurt. . . ."

Although how Abramm could have hurt him that badly was another unanswered question. And when the search turned up empty, he wondered if he'd only imagined the similarities. He'd seen the man for less than a heartbeat, after all, his attention focused more on the blade and hands than the face.

In any case, the panel had been boarded back up and remained securely closed. There had been no repeat of that bizarre attack tonight. Only his own jittery nerves, uneasy with the prospect of having his small sons paraded through a crowd in which it was far too easy for his enemies to hide.

Because Maddie was in the room, the doors to the bedchamber were all closed, signaling Haldon and the others that it was not all right to come in. Thus Abramm dressed himself in the riding breeches, shirt, and leather jerkin Haldon had set out last night. He'd just pulled on his boots and was swirling his cloak around his shoulders when Maddie spoke to him from the bed:

"You going out riding?"

"Yes, love."

"And you'll stop by the nursery before?"

"I'm on my way there now." The boys always wakened at the crack of dawn, and if he didn't see them now they would be napping by the time he returned. "I'll tell Pansy to bring them down to the stables once they've eaten. I know Simon will want to try out his new steed before he has to get ready for the parade."

Maddie smiled at him from her nest of pillows and comforters, her fawn-colored hair spread out around her in a most becoming way. "Maybe I'll come down later, then, too."

He stepped to the bed and bent down to give her a lingering kiss, during which he seriously reconsidered his plans for the morning—until she broke it off. Sliding her hand from the back of his neck to the front of his chest, she pushed him away. "Go see your horse and your sons, sir, or we'll be here all day. Then what would people say?"

"I thought we didn't care what people said."

"I'll see you down at the stables later," she replied, turning onto her side and pulling the covers up over her shoulder.

Grinning to think of what had happened the *last* time they'd agreed to meet at the stables later, he picked up his gloves from the sideboard and left.

Byron Blackwell intercepted him on the way to the nursery, already up and energized to face the day. It would be a full one for him with the parade and the other festivities associated with the opening of the Spring Fair. His biggest concern, though, was the Terstans, who in Springerlan outnumbered Mataians two to one and had little toleration for their heretical ways. "The group over in Middlerise is complaining bitterly about it all, especially this consecration ceremony coming up," he said as they walked together down the long west-wing hall. "There's talk of staging a protest."

Abramm sighed resignedly. "Middlerise is Nott's group, isn't it?"

"Yes."

"I guess I'm going to have to talk to him about that. Maybe I can get Carissa to do it . . . he'd take it better from her than me."

"I don't think the princess would be a wise choice for that, sir."

"Why's that?"

Byron looked uncomfortable. "That was another thing I was going to tell you . . . but I'm struggling to find the words, frankly. Plus I know how much you hate gossip."

Abramm frowned at him.

"Forget it, sir. I shouldn't have brought it up."

"Then why did you?"

"The tale's been pervasive, especially after her not showing up yesterday. I thought you ought to know."

"Well, I plan to visit her in the next day or so and find out for myself."

"Of course, sir." He paused, then took off on a new tack. "A dispatch rider came in early this morning from Simon. He's confirmed the reports of those raids and added a new one. At least four settlements have been razed so far, three in Amberton, the fourth at Archer's Vale. That's a small settlement on—"

"On the border of Amberton and Northille. Yes, I'm familiar with the area."

"That's right. You served your Mataian novitiate up there. Anyway, that's the farthest south they've come so far. . . . Simon's out rounding up the perpetrators. He seems to think Rennalf may be personally involved—I guess there were some survivors at Archer's Vale—but if that's true, he could be back in Balmark already. Assuming they're making use of the corridors."

"Just so long as it's not an army yet."

"You might want to go up there before too long, sir."

Abramm frowned, surprised by the degree of aversion he felt to that notion. To have to leave his boys again—and Maddie!—so soon after he'd arrived . . . The thought just about killed him. "Maybe in a couple months," he said. "I know Simon's taken account of the corridors' existence—we discussed it at length before I left for Elpis. And he's got Ethan with him, who's gotten as good at destroying the things as I am. I'll give them the chance to put their plans into action before I go running up there."

"Very good, sir."

"But you'd better let Trap know. It's on his holding, after all."

"I'll see it's done, sir."

They walked in silence for a few steps, slowing as they reached the mouth of the corridor leading to the princes' nursery. There Abramm stopped and turned to his secretary. "Tell me the rumor."

"What?"

"This rumor regarding Carissa you thought I should know about."

Light flashed off Blackwell's spectacles. He seemed startled and, for a moment, strangely pleased. "Well, sir, they're saying she's lying in."

Abramm blinked. "Lying in? You mean . . . like with child?"

"Yes, sir."

And now Abramm snorted. *Why does the gossip always go in that direction? I should have guessed.* "Ridiculous! She's probably just put on a bit of weight. And you know how she keeps having those paranoid, melancholic spells."

"Yes, sir. My thoughts, as well. I just thought you should know the gossip so you wouldn't be too surprised when you heard it. As you're bound to sooner or later."

"Who do they say is the father?"

Byron hesitated, looked down at the folio in his hand. "They're saying it's the Duke of Northille, sir."

"Trap?!" Abramm laughed outright. "Now I know the tale's untrue. If there's one man I can trust, it's Trap."

"Of course, sir."

"I'm going now to spend a few minutes with the boys. Summon the members of my privy council to meet at eight this morning."

"Yes, sir."

Abramm left him then, still chuckling at the absurdity of the idea that Carissa could possibly be pregnant and Trap be the father. . . .

But then, you didn't suspect Arik Foxton, either.

This is different. I know Trap. I didn't know Foxton. At least they're not saying it's Oswain Nott, though in some ways that would be even more impossible to believe.

He definitely had to pay his sister a visit as soon as possible. She probably had no idea what her reclusiveness was breeding.

After sending a messenger to summon Trap, he spent a happy half hour with his sons in their nursery—though he was a little dismayed by Ian's continued clinginess—and was just leaving for the stable when a servant came to tell him that Duke Eltrap was not at his residence and no one knew where he was.

"Some say he's been staying at the Princess Carissa's home, though, sir. Would you like me to try there?"

Abramm scowled. "No. I'll go myself. And put an end to all this. Have Warbanner brought up to the front entrance."

Carissa's house—fenced in iron and brick with a grand circular drive to the front door—stood on a large parcel of wooded land at the upper end of the Middlerise section. The servants saw Abramm coming, and by the time he'd dismounted, the door was already open. As he stepped into the spacious foyer beyond, and the doorman took his cloak and gloves, Trap strode in from the kitchen, dressed in breeches, blouse, and sleeveless jerkin, an apple in his hand. He stopped at the sight of Abramm, his face white beneath its freckles and the trim red beard. For a moment they stood there, staring at one another.

Then Abramm said, "What are you doing here, Trap?"

The Duke of Northille swallowed the bite of apple he had been chewing, handed the half-eaten fruit to one of the servants, and strode forward, indicating Abramm should precede him into the drawing room.

"Have you already eaten, sir? Would you like some tea?"

"I ate with my boys, and I would like some answers right about now."

"Of course." Trap shut the drawing-room doors, having excluded all the servants save Cooper, then turned to Abramm with a grim look. "Rennalf's come back," he said without preamble. "More than once. She asked me to stay the nights here after you left in case he visits again."

Abramm glanced at Felmen Cooper, tall and gray near the door. Cooper nodded.

"Well, I doubt he will," Abramm said. "He's busy leading raids up at Archer's Vale just now. Or at least he was four days ago."

Trap gave a start of surprise. "Archer's Vale?"

"A rider came in early this morning. I sent someone to your place with the news and to summon you to a council meeting, but . . . you weren't there. No wonder the gossip's been what it has."

Trap grimaced and looked at the floor, pallor turned to the flush of embarrassment. "I'm sorry, sir. I should have told you about this when you first returned."

"I presume he's using the corridor again?"

"Yes, but not out of Graymeer's, so far as we can tell. We've searched for three months without success. I suspect it's somewhere closer, probably in the city."

"Well, at least he didn't get her."

But if he expected Trap's expression to soften a bit in agreement, he was disappointed. If anything, the stern look hardened. "Actually, he did get her." He paused, then added in a voice that was no longer steady, "He raped her, Abramm. At least three times, over a period of several years. She doesn't like to speak of it. Even that much was a chore to drag out of her. I didn't find out about any of this until right before you left for Elpis."

His words pummeled Abramm with an almost physical force, shocking him beyond the ability to think, and still they kept coming.

"She made me promise not to tell you. And what could you do? You were all set to leave, the passes would be locked up for months. . . ." He shook his head. "Though believe me I thought many times of trying to find a way up there so I could kill him myself."

Abramm's shock gave way to guilt and dismay for all the evil things he'd thought about her. Who wouldn't have been melancholy after such a visitation? He had no doubt she'd told no one because she'd have been too ashamed. *Ah, Eidon, how could I have failed her so badly?* Too caught up in his own pleasures, reveling in his happy little family while his own sister was being raped by the monster who had once been her husband!

His anger was just beginning to rise when the drawing-room door opened and Carissa stepped in. She wore a dark blue gown of fluid silk whose full skirt draped revealingly over the substantial swelling of her belly. Abramm stared at the bulge numbly, suddenly unable to breathe. Finally he tore his eyes from it and fixed them on her face, where her misery and fear tore at his heart and stoked the anger into a dark, hot current of rage.

"Rennalf did this?" he asked her impassively, surprised at the even tenor of his voice.

She looked at Trap, horrified apparently that he'd already revealed who the father was, though why this should disturb her, Abramm could not guess. Surely she wasn't happy to be carrying the child of the man she'd begged to be divorced from. A man who'd beaten and scorned her when she was his lawful wife, then sought to drag her back to his fortress as if she were a breeding mare when she'd finally fled him. Who, in the end, had resorted to rape to get his way. While she was living in Springerlan, under her brother's care. . . .

He pressed the anger and dismay down deep, knowing he could not afford to indulge either. He must remain clearheaded so he could figure his next move.

Carissa had not answered him, still staring fearfully at Trap, and for one awful moment Abramm's anguish nearly spiraled into the unthinkable. *"They will all betray you. . . ."* But not Trap. Not this way.

"Is the child Rennalf's?" Abramm asked again, and this time the edge in his voice moved her to speak.

"Yes. But he only did this to provoke you, Abramm. He wants you to go up there and take your vengeance face-to-face."

"Well, he's certainly going to get what he wants. Though I would call it something other than vengeance."

"It's a trap, Abramm. He is angry about the stone, and about you granting me my freedom from him. . . . He's planned this for years."

"Then I suppose we'll see how good of a planner he is."

He started past her, then stopped and touched a hand to her face. "It'll be all right."

"Abramm, please don't do this."

"I have to. And this is not your fault. He promised me he would repay me for taking you back from him. I just didn't think he would be this . . . cruel."

The tears that had flooded her eyes now broke at the corners and trailed down her cheeks.

"Go to the palace," he said. "I want you to stay with Maddie."

"Oh, Abramm, I've pushed her away. She won't—"

"She'll understand. And she knows about this." He touched the hard, round surface of her belly. "More than that, she is strong in the Light. She can help you in ways you won't begin to guess. And there are others there, as well. Bring Elayne and Cooper with you, and be up there by dusk tonight."

And when she drew breath to protest, he cut her off, laying his fingers again on her swollen womb. "I don't know why Eidon has allowed this to befall you, but I do know he is just and wise and has good reason, even if we cannot see it now. I also know that whatever else may be claimed, this child is yours. That makes him a Kalladorne. And he will be raised as such."

He glanced back at Trap. "You have your horse here?"

"Yes, sir."

"Then get mounted and meet me out in front. We have work to do."

36

Gillard sat in the morning sun on one of the stone benches lining the porch of the Offices of the Holy Keep. The sun felt good upon his head and shoulders, for the breeze that stirred his long, blond hair was chill. His right hand, bound and splinted once again, throbbed only occasionally now. Enough to remind him it was broken and that he would have to live another six weeks with this splint.

He'd arrived in Springerlan four days ago, coming down for the consecration ceremonies as an aide to Master Amicus. Left here to wait while the man met with High Father Bonafil somewhere inside, he sat alone, the Keep's new gray-stoned buildings looming around the quiet yard before him. Beyond them the city rose in a tumble of tile and slate and wood to the white walls that marked the palace grounds atop the Keharnen Cliffs. The main gate, though shrunken with distance, was just discernible above the new Keep Library's peaked tile roof, its white pennants fluttering above the entry posts.

Anger and bitter disappointment curdled in Gillard's gut. Even now, three days later, he could hardly believe how badly his encounter with Abramm had gone. All he'd done these last five years—all the switchings and rebukings he'd endured, all the nonsense he'd been forced to learn and parrot back, all those long, deep-night hours he'd spent in the Watch's barn working with Matheson to regain his strength and fighting skills—it was all a waste. His hand had been broken in the first move.

It was not at all what he'd expected.

Nausea swirled again in his belly as the horrid memories returned yet again.

When he'd first entered the royal bedchamber, he'd spent some time star-ing at his older brother as he slept, surprised at how big he was and how much he favored their father now—except for the scars, of course. Gillard had taken great pleasure in the way they raked down the left side of Abramm's face, two raised, white lines of scar tissue that could neither be hidden nor ignored. He'd smiled, understanding now why the First Daughter had found him too repellent to marry and enjoying thoughts of the pain her rejection must have caused. . . .

Then Gillard had looked at the woman who *had* married him, and that had been his undoing. He thought in retrospect that his failure could be laid entirely at her feet, for if not for her, he would have kept his focus. She lay on her side, facing her husband, and somehow the contented look on her face combined with the easy, proprietary way her arm was draped across his chest filled Gillard with instant and utter fury. From then on he had been too angry and too eager to have his revenge to think clearly.

Originally he'd planned to confront his brother and force him to engage in a rematch of their last exchange of sword strikes. Once Gillard had proven himself the superior swordsman, he had intended to bind the defeated king—who surely would have been shaking with fear and begging him for mercy by then—and deliver him over to the Mataian leadership who had their own scores to settle with him.

He hadn't expected to find the queen in bed with him, since she had her own chambers, and he could not imagine a woman wanting to spend any more time with Abramm than her duty required. But there she'd been, and even now he was hard-pressed to answer why the sight of her had awakened such a fury in him. A fury that stimulated all sorts of heretofore unconsidered permutations to his plan.

He'd decided to bind her first, lest she hinder him in his match with Abramm. Later, if needed, he could also use her to maintain his control of the situation. So he'd gone to the other side of the bed, moving slowly, con-trolling even his breathing so he'd make no sound.

And somehow had wakened them anyway. He'd been stunned by how fast Abramm reacted, erupting out of the bedclothes like some kind of horror to leap over the entire span of the mattress, knocking Gillard's knife away as he'd landed. That one blow had broken Gillard's hand, and as the pain had rushed through him, hot and shocking, he'd staggered back, overwhelmed again by how big Abramm really was and how ferocious he looked, especially with those scars.

In that moment he had no doubt Abramm would have killed him had he gotten his hands on him. This was the man who'd stood his ground in the arenas of their enemies and survived, the man who'd faced Beltha'adi and survived. Had taken down the kraggin and the morwhol and . . . Gillard himself, when he'd been big and strong and healthy.

Any ideas Gillard had of facing him vanished as he turned and fled through the still-open panel. For a time he'd run wildly through the black passageways with no idea where he was going. Eventually, though, he'd regained his wits and his self-control and made his way back to the meditation cubicle in the Keep, where he'd been observing an all-night vigil.

It was absolutely intolerable. The memory still made his chest seize and his gut squirm. He'd felt like a little rat scrambling around to get away—to get away from *Abramm!* And that would never do. Never.

But what can I do? There is no hope for me, that's what they've all said. I've become a scrawny little runt with porcelain bones, and there's nothing I can do about it.

Unless . . . there really was something to Prittleman's claims that Eidon's Flames could heal him.

He scowled. *You're getting desperate, man. Prittleman's not healed, is he?*

"Brother Makepeace?" Gillard turned at the unfamiliar voice. A young, stubble-headed acolyte stood on the porch beside him. "Master Amicus wants you. If you'll come with me?"

Puzzled and mildly alarmed, Gillard followed the acolyte into the gleaming main hall and all the way to its end, where lay the High Father's new offices. There the boy pulled open the door, and Gillard stepped into the spacious but dimly lit room beyond. Having recently come in from outside, it took his eyes a few moments to adjust. Light filtered through a partially curtained, mullioned window at the room's far end, illuminating the platform and desk just beneath it, as well as a cluster of chairs closer to the door, where sat Father Bonafil, Amicus, Brother Eudace, and two others Gillard did not recognize.

All of them regarded him with a sharpness that increased his alarm, making him think that somehow they had gotten wind of his doings in the palace the other night. But how could they? He knew that both Abramm and his Chesedhan wife had seen him, but only for an instant, and he was sure they hadn't recognized him.

High Father Bonafil was the first to speak. "You've broken your hand, brother."

"Yes, sir."

"Amicus says you took a spill in the hall a couple of nights ago."

The hairs on the back of Gillard's neck stood up. The man hadn't actually asked him a question, so he really needn't say anything. In fact, according to the rules, he shouldn't have said anything in response to the first statement. But he did not like the direction in which this conversation was heading, and now he stood there, his heart hammering against his breastbone as he stared at the floor, hands at his sides.

"Was it a spill? Or did you hit it on something?"

That was a question. He had to answer. "It was hit, sir."

A moment of silence followed, and at the edges of his field of vision Gillard saw the men exchange glances. Then Bonafil said, "I'm glad to see you refrain from lying to me, at least."

Gillard's eyes darted up, not so much in protest as in surprise.

Bonafil smiled. "We know all about your secret meeting with Abramm."

Pox and plagues! He felt the blood rush into his face, shame and embarrassment shaking him like a dog with a doll in its teeth.

Bonafil evidently mistook the reaction for fear. "You think we wouldn't guess? He's the king, Makepeace. Called the alarm at once, set his guards searching the palace and the city. They came here right off, of course, because he still doesn't trust us, and their description of the intruder fit you to a T, right down to the suspicion that you'd been incapacitated by a single blow. And then, of course, your hand turned up broken the very next morning."

He fell silent. Gillard stared at him, his uneasiness rising. The moments crawled by and finally, when Bonafil still did not speak, Gillard burst out, "I *told* Amicus from the beginning I believed none of this. He persuaded me to take the vows merely to protect himself and his Watch."

"Is that what you think this is about?" Bonafil snorted and shook his head. "Your plan was idiotic, young man. To go after *him* with a sword? In your condition? After all these years, do you still refuse to acknowledge who your brother is?"

Gillard studied the carpet, shamed anew and fuming now. "I heard he was injured. That he had lost his skills. That he could not even stand against the Crown Prince of Chesedh."

"And you, of course, could." The tone was withering.

Gillard squirmed inwardly, his fury and frustration swelling almost past the point of containment. This wasn't fair. None of it. And for this pompous, self-righteous fool to be reprimanding him was almost more than he could bear. He wanted to yell and hit things, but his hand throbbed a painful warning and he wrestled down his ire.

"You had your chance, man," Bonafil said sternly, "on the front steps of the Temple of the Dragons in Tuk-Rhaal. When you lost there, you lost everything, and you'll never get any of it back through your own efforts. The sooner you face that, the better."

"I will never face that!" Gillard declared. "My day is far from over."

"You think so?" He gestured to Amicus. "Break his other hand, brother."

Immediately Amicus stepped toward Gillard, smiling so pleasantly one might have thought he offered aid and comfort. The amulet at his throat flickered with scarlet light. "Give me yer hand, Makepeace."

Gillard was too stunned to even react, his mind struggling to get itself around Bonafil's last words. *"Break his hand"? Is that really what he said?* Then to Gillard's astonishment, his left hand come up and placed itself in Amicus's open palm. In horror he watched the man's fingers curl around it, felt the grip tighten and the bones begin to snap. The pain came afterward, sharp and nauseating, and he screamed, trying vainly to jerk his hand free. Amicus continued to grind away until Gillard was on his knees, weeping, begging him to stop.

Finally the holy man released him and stepped back, leaving Gillard hunched over his ruined limb, gasping and sobbing and cursing them all to Torments and back. Eventually he came to the end of his words and fell silent, huddling before them and shuddering with pain.

Only then did Bonafil speak again. "Amicus did not suggest you take holy vows simply to protect his Watch. We want exactly what you want . . . to remove Abramm and put one of our own in his place."

"I would be king at your pleasure, you mean," Gillard grated.

"I would never use so crude a way of phrasing it."

"Elegant or crude, that's what it would be." He looked at them, the room spinning and sparkling around him. "I want no part of it."

Bonafil lifted a brow. "Are you sure?"

"I will be no man's puppet."

At that the five men chuckled and once more exchanged amused glances, and as irritating as that was, it also sent a worm of uncertainty crawling through Gillard's belly.

A moment later Bonafil regained his sober mien. "If you take your final vows now, Makepeace, you can become the true Guardian-King of Kiriath."

"I don't want to be a Guardian-King," Gillard spat. "And anyway, don't I have three years of my novitiate to serve before I can take final vows?"

"The eight-year span is only an advised time. If a man wishes to test the Flames early he will be allowed to do so." He paused. "Because of the difficult times we face, I would give you a special dispensation to do that. A dispensation from Eidon that would not even be the lie you think it would. For in truth, Eidon *does* want you to be king of this land."

Final vows, special dispensations . . . I don't like it. If I'm going to be king, I want to be king . . . not beholden to these self-righteous bloodsuckers. . . . The only problem was, without them he did not see any way he was going to be king at all. And right now his hand was hurting so badly he could hardly think.

"I regret that you don't have much time to make your decision, but the fact is, we are preparing to bring your brother down even now. You can participate in that or be cast aside and a new ruler put upon the throne."

Gillard snorted. "What new ruler? I am the last of the Kalladorne line. No one is going to accept Carissa as ruler in her present mental state."

"Haven't ye been payin' attention, Brother?" Amicus reproved. "Do ye na recall that I told ye Abramm has two sons?"

Gillard stared at him, stunned anew. *No. I do not recall. And surely I would have. I might have gone to the nursery before I went to the royal bedchamber. . . . Two sons?*

"His firstborn, Simon," Bonafil said, "is an impressionable, uncorrupted lad of four." He smiled. "Once removed from the evil influence of his parents and provided with solid teaching in the true ways of Eidon, he will be a willing and able servant on Eidon's behalf."

"If he's only four it's going to take you some time to groom him. You'll have to instate a regency."

"Of course."

"And you have someone who could handle that?"

"Someone on the inside. Someone with a great deal of governing experience, who has worked closely with the king, and who has a heartfelt—if undeclared—reason to oppose him. Someone working even now to bring our plans to fruition."

Gillard stared at them. Pain-induced sweat sheathed his brow, and his hand was a fiery torment, even as the rest of his body had grown chilled and shaky. *I don't want to be their Guardian-King!*

"Everything is now in place. Abramm will leave for Sterlen tonight, all in a fury to gain his vengeance upon Rennalf. . . . Within five hours of his confirmed departure, we will strike. I ask you again, Gillard Kalladorne. Do you want to be part of this, or don't you?"

They stood around him, staring down at him, their eyes flickering with that creepy red light, the same light that flickered in the amulets. He felt them pulling at him to agree, and yet . . . The pain was excruciating. He wanted it to stop, wanted a moment of freedom from agony so he could think, consider his options, see where this path they offered him really led.

"*I can heal your hands, Gillard. . . .*"

A shudder shot through him, for the voice had whispered audibly into his ear, yet no one stood near enough to do so.

"*I can heal your bones, too. So they will no longer break at the slightest touch.*"

Oh, to be free of this pain, to be free of this fragility! Yes! Yes, he wanted that!

Can you make me bigger? he wondered.

"*Only so far as people perceive you . . . but in that, you will be very big indeed.*"

Not quite the answer he'd hoped for.

"*I can give you Abramm, too. To do with as you wish.*" A stream of violent images flooded his mind—all the dreams he'd nursed for years. No more humiliating failures. Abramm would be at his mercy. To beat, to torture, to maim, to kill—whatever he desired.

"I'll do it." The words were out of his mouth before he even realized he'd meant to say them. And he didn't much like the way the others sat back then and smiled.

It happened much faster than he had ever guessed it could. Within an hour the High Father's council had been summoned, all crowded into his spacious office with a traveling brazier of the Holy Flames, which would be used to reseed the new Sanctum at the consecration ceremony. Stripped to his white inner tunic, the splint and bandages removed from his right hand, Gillard stood before the oval brazier as the holy men prayed around him. Their voices droned in a discomfiting harmonic that set the air vibrating and made the room increasingly hot.

Finally Eudace brought forth a black box and from it pulled a Guardian's amulet, except this one's stone was clear instead of red and it had no latch to fasten the two ends together. The praying stopped abruptly when Eudace cast it into the Flames. Then he told Gillard to put both hands in the fire and pull it out.

Gillard thought he must be mad to even consider it, but the lure of gaining his revenge drove him on. Without a moment's hesitation, he plunged his broken hands into the fire and it hurt every bit as badly as he had thought it would. He wanted to scream and jerk them out, but the Masters had told him that doing so would mean the Flames had rejected him, and would likely leave him addled for the rest of his life. So he clenched his teeth and, shaking and jerking as the sweat poured off him now, strove to make his shattered fingers move in search of the amulet. And to his surprise they obeyed. In moments he found the chain and pulled it free, the stone ablaze with the fire from which he'd drawn it. Noting it still had no end latches, he laid it about his neck as if it did. The moment the blazing stone touched his skin he gasped as a new agony shot through him and nearly passed out from the shock of it.

In that moment of disorientation, he felt a coldness spread out from the amulet to enwrap his body, squeezing him ever tighter until he feared he would suffocate. Then, like a snake striking from a bush, a sharp tongue of inhuman presence darted into his soul and took hold. A brief but terrified struggle ensued. Then it was over.

The coldness faded along with the terror. The amulet lay heavy and hot against the base of his throat, its latchless chain having fastened itself around his neck by magic. But he hardly gave it a thought as he held up his hands before him, still thin and spidery, but no longer crushed and broken. He opened and closed the left, then did the same with his right. It too was completely healed.

More than that he felt wonderful. It seemed like years since he had felt this good, this strong, this confident. He looked at the men surrounding him.

Bonafil smiled. "Welcome to the Brotherhood of the Flames, Makepeace. Soon you will have your crown back and we will make good on your holy name."

———

Abramm rode out of Springerlan at midnight, having spent the day involved in the parade, the opening of the fair, the Spring Dance on the green, and the feast that evening. He brought the scepter with him, though he knew little more now than he had when he'd used it to drive the Shadow from the Gull Islands five years ago. With no subsequent need of using it, and the passages in the Words more figurative than practical, the mystery of how it worked remained out of his reach. Kesrin had suggested enlightenment might come along as he grew closer to Eidon. Still, the implement had served him well in the past, and he hoped it would do so now.

He traveled with a troop of seventy-five—all he dared pull out of the standing forces ready to defend Springerlan against surprise attack. He'd not made his commanders happy with that move, though all conceded that with no fog to hide in and no Esurhites sighted in Kiriathan waters since their ill-fated attempt to take the Gull Islands five years ago, the chance of attack was slim.

He'd sent word ahead for more troops to be readied at Briarcreek, which he would pick up on his way north—fifty horsemen and a hundred foot soldiers. With that many men to move, he wanted to be well clear of the royal city before the fair ended, day after tomorrow. Once the celebrants started for home, the roads would be hopelessly clogged.

Trap had surprised him by asking to stay behind, unwilling to leave Carissa alone in her present state, now that all the world knew of it. Besides, he feared Rennalf might still find time to make a visit.

"The child she's carrying is his heir," he'd pointed out. "I have no doubt he'll come by eventually to collect, if he can. And she could deliver any day."

His point was valid, and as much as Abramm regretted not having Trap to fight at his side, there was no one he'd rather leave the care and safety of his loved ones to than "Uncle" Trap.

Even so, leaving was hard. Somehow Ian sensed the change afoot and refused to let go of Abramm when he'd tried to say good-night in the nursery. Screaming desperately, tears streaming down his face, the boy had to be peeled out of his father's arms, a scene as embarrassing as it was heart-wrenching. Little Simon watched the proceedings with wide, startled eyes, and after Ian was carried off to his bed and it was time for his own good-night hug, he wrapped his arms tightly around his father's neck and asked in a tiny voice, "Are you really going away again, Papa?"

"For a little while, Simon. I'll be back soon, though, I promise."

But it wouldn't be soon. Only four months, he hoped, but that was an eternity for a little boy like Simon. He figured it would take him all summer to finish the job. Ian would be almost two then, and there was no telling how tall Simon would have gotten by that time.

"I'll expect you to be riding your Warbanner all by yourself when I get back," he said, attempting a cheerful mien. "And don't forget to look out for your brother. I'm counting on you for that."

Simon nodded soberly. "I will, Papa."

Then Abramm had to stand and turn away lest Simon see the moisture springing up in his eyes. He left the nursery with a lump in his throat.

Saying good-bye to Maddie was the worst. She didn't cry, didn't protest, didn't offer advice, for she had seen and talked with Carissa and knew he had to do what he did. Instead, she put on her brave face and treated it all lightly, teasing him and making jokes about it. But her eyes betrayed the anguish in her soul. And the fear.

She surprised him by bringing out her token—their wedding scarf—for the occasion, winding it about his bare midriff with her own hands before he'd dressed.

"And I don't want any blood on it this time," she'd said sternly as she'd tied it off.

He'd caught her to him and kissed her. "I'll do my best, love."

It gave him comfort to feel it now, snug about his middle, beneath the scepter harness, reminding him of her touch and her eyes and the final kiss she'd given him—long and sensuous and full of passion. Reminding him how desperately he wanted to go home again.

They crossed the Hennepen without incident and reached the Briarcreek Garrison around four in the morning, where they stopped to eat and get a couple hours' sleep before setting off again at seven. By then the troops were already moving out, as Abramm had instructed they do, so at first he and his party rode alongside the great dust-making column of cavalry, footmen, and supply wagons until they reached the head of the line.

It took them a day to reach the Snowsong and another to ford it. From there they traveled easily northward on a wide, smooth road virtually devoid of local traffic. Even the river traffic was unusually sparse. Attributing it to the fact that everyone was in Springerlan—or on the road behind them—he rejoiced in this boon. In the same way he excused the unexpected quietness of the new Holy Keep of the Heartland, thinking that more of the brethren must have gone to Springerlan for the consecration than he'd expected.

But as land and water traffic continued to dwindle, and when that afternoon they came under a high, flat overcast spreading out of the north, he began to have second thoughts. Shadow over the highlands had been an increasing problem over the last few years, one he'd not known how to solve but which had for the most part stayed where it was. Of greater concern was the very real division that had occurred within his realm as those who wore shields migrated southward and those who worshipped the Flames stayed in the Heartland. The new Keep built north of the Snowsong had only encouraged and hastened this division, and despite his insistence that all his subjects have the freedom to choose how they would worship, he had had a hard time enforcing that. The two factions did not get along, and he knew many of the Heartlanders nursed an irrational hatred for him.

It seemed hard to believe that a Terstan king who was just and fair and whose reign had so far seen peace and increasing prosperity, as well as the relighting of two ancient guardstars, could be hated by his subjects and have parts of his realm under Shadow. And yet, the farther north they pressed, the more the clouds thickened. By the next afternoon, a massive thunderhead towered above the rising land ahead, its belly blackest above where Sterlen lay, still out of sight beyond the rolling hills.

He slept poorly that night, beset with doubts and second-guessing—and the increasing fear this was all a setup for a Heartlander ambush. When he finally did doze off, his sleep was plagued by a repeating nightmare in which he ran through the ruins of Hur searching frantically for Ian amidst the invasion of Beltha'adi's forces, the boom of supernatural fireballs echoing around him. Only to find at the end he was not in Hur at all, but in Springerlan.

Finally he woke up gasping, filled with the sense of a light going out and something terrible having happened. For a moment he could hardly move, could hardly breathe, Kesrin's words echoing through his soul: *"They will all be lost. . . ."*

He made himself take a deep breath, forced himself to concentrate on what he knew—that no matter what else, Eidon had not loosed his hand on any of the details of Abramm's life. Abramm had come here because he believed it was where his responsibility lay. . . . But even if he'd made the wrong decision—and he didn't think he had—Eidon was still in control.

Outside, the horses on the picket line stamped and snorted restlessly, drawing his attention to the very real booming that had been sounding in the distance for some time. As he strove to listen more closely, he heard low voices talking outside his tent door, then a rasping rustle as someone pushed back the canvas flap and stepped inside. "Sir?" Channon asked quietly. "Are you awake?"

"What is it, Captain?"

"I think you'll want to see this, sir."

Abramm pulled on boots and cloak and stepped outside into a cold, black night, where Channon stood with a number of the officers and conscripts staring northward toward the massive cloud that had built up yesterday. Multi-colored lights flickered in its belly, the intensity of the powers being unleashed within it sometimes strong enough to illumine the whole of the cloud's towering bulk. A continuous booming, loud enough to shake the ground, accompanied the light show.

Abramm stared in rising horror, for he knew it was no natural storm but a battle between supernatural forces. Though what armies might be involved, he could not begin to guess. Esurhite? Barbarian? How could they possibly have mustered with the winter having locked in the land for these past months? And how could Simon have failed to note and report an enemy presence of that size marching through the realm?

Still, something obviously dire was happening, and he had no doubt Simon was in the midst of it.

He turned to Channon and had just given the order to rouse the men when the flickering in the cloud increased and the booms came so often they overlapped, the ground shaking continuously. Then the cloud lit with a great flash of scarlet . . . and all went dark and still.

Abramm held his breath. No one moved nor spoke around him, all faced toward the cloud, barely visible now in the first dull lightening of the sky as dawn approached. Even the horses stood frozen. Then, into that deathly silence came a low rushing that swiftly escalated to a roar, and a wind swooped down upon them, cold on their faces as it ruffled their beards and tore at their cloaks and tossed the horses' manes yet stirred neither grass nor bush nor any leaf of the trees around them. Then it was gone.

And now, running in its wake, came a host of dark forms, bounding and scurrying and scuttling and leaping, breaking out of the trees, rushing over the grassy hillsides. A sea of creatures running south as from a fire: deer and badgers and squirrels, fox and rabbits and mice . . . They ran past the men and horses as if they did not exist. Then they were gone, too, and an eerie calm descended. Beside them, the great river had become like silver glass, its current having ceased to flow.

Shaken, but determined, Abramm repeated his order to rouse the horsemen. They would move out immediately, leaving the foot soldiers to break camp and follow as fast as they could.

They encountered the first remnants of the defeated army that afternoon—individuals and small groups on foot, bloodied and weaponless and so jumpy, one look at Abramm and his men sent them skittering into the hills. Finally, though, they encountered a party of combined horsemen and foot soldiers that was large enough and ordered enough to hold its ground. It flew no identifying banners, but a look through the spyglass confirmed that one of the men riding point was Simon Kalladorne.

Abramm cantered forward to meet him, and it was a measure of Simon's exhaustion and shock that he only pulled his horse to a stop and waited. He wore no uniform, only a torn and bloodied shirt and filthy breeches. His face was nearly as gray as his untrimmed beard, marred with cuts and blood and a great bruise on one cheekbone.

"I'm afraid you're too late, sir," he said as Abramm reined in before him. "What happened?"

"He took Skaevik, and once he did, it was all over."

Abramm frowned at him. "Who?"

And now Simon frowned back. "Didn't you receive my dispatches?"

"I received dispatches about small raiding parties and the destruction of hill settlements. I thought you had everything in hand. I'm only here now because of Carissa." He explained what Simon obviously knew nothing about, then asked, "So what happened exactly?"

"It was Rennalf, sir. With upwards of five hundred men. They came around the western foothills and were preparing to march on Sterlen when we spotted them. Ethan said we had to keep them out of Skaevik, and for two weeks we did. Yesterday afternoon he broke through our lines. . . . I've been sending urgent requests for the last three weeks—almost daily, sir. Yet you received none of them?"

"Blackwell told me the morning I left that Archer's Vale had been raided and you were out trying to round up the perpetrators."

"There was no raid on Archer's Vale." He grimaced and passed a blood-stained hand through his short gray hair, looking down at his horse. "Once he held Skaevik, he used all those things you told us the Esurhites used: the fearspell, the darkness, the Command. And all sorts of creatures, things that could hardly be killed. We were decimated."

"So he has won," Abramm said grimly, turning his eyes to the north and wondering what in the world he could do that Simon had not even come close to accomplishing.

"No," Simon said. "We were falling back, not quite turned tail to run but close, and suddenly the Mataians took the field. Fifty of the brothers with their pans of flames, and behind them, a phalanx of horse soldiers, maybe a hundred of them—Gadrielites by their uniforms."

"Gadrielites?" Abramm cried. He'd outlawed that order five years ago.

"And with them, a civilian army of foot soldiers. They had a monstrous battle—exploding fireballs, moving walls of darkness or of red light . . . and they won, Abramm. The Mataians and their Gadrielite lackeys won. And once it was clear they had, they turned on us, slaughtering all who wore a shield. They tried to kill me, too. But Ethan used his Light to draw their attention his way, and I escaped. I don't know what happened to him, but we've not seen him since."

Abramm stared at him fixedly, each new incident searing into his soul like a hot iron. A phalanx of Gadrielites and fifty Mataians? No wonder the new Keep had been quiet. They'd known about this. Planned it, even. And kept it all from him.

And then he recalled the sense he had awakened with, the feeling of disaster unfolding back home. The Gadrielites revived . . . the roads deserted . . . the absence of boats on the water even heading north. And all those Mataians in Springerlan for the reconsecration of the Holy Keep. . . .

Oh, my Lord Eidon!

Simon's dispatches had been concealed to keep Abramm from getting up to Sterlen in time to help. And the dispatches had all come through Blackwell, whose sister had committed suicide, it was said, because Abramm hadn't married her. And it was Blackwell who had made a point of telling him about Carissa, and also about a small raid on Trap's land, so he'd learn what Rennalf had done and go up to face him. Pulling him and a sizeable number of his forces out of Springerlan.

He began to feel sick.

"I've got to get back home!" he said.

But even as he did, he feared he would be far too late.

37

Maddie drew the thread tight on the line of stitching she'd just completed to close up the hole in the belly of Simon's precious stuffed horse, then took a number of tiny backstitches to anchor it before tying it off. She cut the thread, then held the toy up for inspection. It looked considerably fatter than it had, more like a pregnant mare than the war stallion Simon had made of it. And she wasn't sure she'd left enough of the buckram in it, for its belly still felt hard and clearly round if one pressed it. Of course, that would be the case regardless, and the point was not to have anyone feel it. The point was to have people ignore it or, in the worst case, cast it aside as a worthless child's toy. Assuming they could get it away from Simon in the first place. . . .

Better not to think of that.

"Here's Horsey, Simon," she said. "Good as new."

Her son, who sat on the carpeted floor of the king's sitting chamber not far away, leaped up and came to her. But he took the stuffed horse doubtfully, his frown reminding her far too much of his father. "He looks fat, Mama."

"He's well fed, Simon. Ready for the long weeks of battle ahead of him." *Oh, Eidon, I hope that wasn't prophetic.*

Byron Blackwell stepped into the room from the antechamber, bringing with him a whiff of smoke, the smell pervasive throughout the palace these days. "Ah, madam. You're here. Good."

Simon was feeling his horse's belly with a frown. "Mama, what kind of stuffing did you—"

"Shush, son." She turned him gently away from her and faced him toward where Ian sat playing—contentedly for the moment—with Pansy's ring of keys. "I used what I had. Be thankful he's whole again, and go play with your brother."

She stood and joined Byron by the windowed double doors looking out on the balcony and beyond. The big oak's new leaves looked dull in the flat light of the overcast sky, coated with the smoke and ash that had been in the air for days. Beyond it lay the city, a blackened char under a layer of smoke, the result of four days' worth of warfare. The river reflected the sky as a dull gray band, devoid of its normal traffic, all but two of its nine bridges blasted into crumbling, gap-holed hulks, useless, or at the very least dangerous for crossing. Bits of flotsam floated on its sluggish current to collect in a wide, ash- and slime-coated dam of debris marking the line where river met the bay. Smoke and fog mingled over the bay and headland so that she could no longer see Graymeer's, only the constant light of its guardstar. The harbor was emptier than it had been even during the time of the kraggin, all the merchants who were able having fled long since.

"Southdock has fallen," Blackwell said quietly. "The Gadrielites will be able to bring all their forces to bear against the palace now. . . ."

She nodded and clamped down on the panic that wailed within her. *"His sovereignty rules over all. . . ."* she quoted silently. *I have no need to fear. As bad as this looks, He* will *deliver us. He has promised. . . .*

It had begun right before dawn, five hours after Abramm had departed Springerlan. Channon had been right to worry about all the Heartlanders that had poured into the city on the pretext of celebrating the crown prince's birthday and the Spring Fair. As it turned out, many of them were members of the revived order of the Gadrielites—lay Mataians sanctified for the purpose of executing Eidon's justice and driving evil from his domain. In addition, a sizable civilian contingent had come out to help, as well as the secret sympathizers who had been systematically put into various positions of authority around the city—magistrates, wardens of the gaol, shipyard authorities, wardens of the river—all of whom were instructed to open gates, release locks, and muster soldiers when called to do so.

In a single coordinated move, they had appeared at the doors of prominent and not so prominent Terstan citizens, bursting in to gather them up and bundle them into the closed coaches they had brought for that purpose. Those who fought back were slain on the spot, as were those regarded as especially dangerous on account of their skill in the Light. Thus it had been three hours before knowledge of what was happening had spread enough that anyone could escape.

A simultaneous attack was mounted on the palace, the aggressors wearing the uniform of the royal guard and claiming they'd been sent by Abramm to protect the queen. Trap had seen through their ruse and called the king's personal guard to arms. A furious battle raged in the Fountain Court, the invaders pressing into the palace's grand entry alcove before being slain or incapacitated. Meanwhile Byron had herded the royal family—Carissa, Maddie, and the two boys—along with their retainers, into the king's apartments and set servants to unboarding the secret panel in the bedchamber wall in case they needed a bolthole.

They hadn't. The palace and its immediate grounds had been secured and held for the last four days. Which was three days longer than they'd expected. All the courtiers and most of the servants had fled, at the queen's insistence. Liza, two of Maddie's ladies-in-waiting, and the princes' nanny had refused to leave. As had Carissa's Peri and the Coopers, Haldon, Jared, and two of the cook staff.

Word had gone out immediately to Abramm and to Briarcreek, by both pigeon and rider, and he should have returned by now with the troops he'd intended to lead to Sterlen.

"Still no word from Abramm?" she asked Blackwell, watching a flock of sea gulls wing toward the bay.

"None at all." He paused, then added, "I believe you must think seriously about fleeing, ma'am."

She frowned at the dead and broken tableau before them and drew a breath to steady herself against the wave of panic his words stimulated.

"I've arranged for a boat," he went on. "If we can hold out until night, we can escape through the bolthole to the docks. From there, it would be a simple matter to row over to the eastern headland beyond their lines and come ashore. Duke Eltrap could meet us there with the horses. It doesn't appear the navy has yet been compromised, so if we are pursued we might expect help from them, as well."

"Or not," Maddie said bitterly. "We have no idea what side they're on."

"Well, they haven't started firing at the palace, and I think that's what they'd do if the Mataians held them."

Maddie flashed him a startled, horrified look. The moment he'd said it she knew it was true. The Mataians had no use and little love for Whitehill, or any of the rest of Springerlan, as was demonstrated by their having burned down half the city in four days. "Maybe I should just surrender." They'd asked for her and the boys right at the start. Surrendering might stop the killing.

Might save the palace from being destroyed.

"Absolutely not," said Trap, coming up close behind them.

They turned to face him, Maddie noting automatically that Pansy and Simon had disappeared, leaving Esmeralda to sit with Ian. Which was why they'd had no notice of Trap's arrival, since Simon made a most excellent herald when it came to his Uncle Trap. The duke looked more like the old captain now, however. Soot stained his plain clothes and smudged his freckled face. Dark half circles cradled his eyes, and his red beard had not been trimmed in days. He met Maddie's gaze soberly.

"Do you have any idea what they'll do with your firstborn?" he murmured, mindful of the boy's sharp ears, keyed to his own name even from another room. "He's only four, he doesn't wear a shield . . . and he's the heir to the throne. If they get their hands on him, he'll be their claim to total legitimacy."

"I heard they've got Gillard as their claim," said Blackwell.

"Simon trumps Gillard for legitimacy," Trap countered.

"But Gillard would be ready to go."

Trap frowned at him. "And what do you think would happen to the boy if that is so? Gillard's already tried to kill his father multiple times. It would be much easier to get rid of a little boy."

"You can't think he'd really murder a child," said Maddie.

"I can and I do. Surrendering is not an option, ma'am."

"So you think we must flee, as well."

"Unless Abramm shows up soon, yes, ma'am. I do."

"He would have been here by now if he were able. We all know that," said Blackwell. "I think we must assume the worst and proceed without expectation of help."

Maddie brought her chin up. "I have no intention of assuming the worst, Count Blackwell," she said sharply.

"Of course not, ma'am."

"But I will admit help does not look like it will come in time."

"I expect they'll attack once it's dark. And they'll have had all day to move their forces into position. We should move out by dusk, if not before."

She frowned, not liking it but not knowing what else to do. She looked at Trap, who appeared no happier with the idea than she. He was concerned, she knew, with the danger and difficulty of moving a party with such a high number of dependents—and especially with Carissa, who could go into labor at any moment.

But he shook his head, defeated. "We don't have enough men to hold them off much longer, ma'am," he said. "With the numbers they'll have freed up from Southdock, we'll be hopelessly outnumbered. And the palace simply isn't secure enough in such a situation."

And so in the end they accepted Blackwell's plan, with the modification that he would be the one to meet them with the horses on the headland, because Trap refused to leave the queen's side. After informing the others of their intentions, they spent the afternoon preparing.

When all had been accomplished, Maddie found herself standing at the sitting-room window again, looking toward Graymeer's and the guardstar's steady light. She knew Graymeer's had been under attack, too, for the Mataians regarded it as a great heresy that must be quenched. Still its defenders held out and gave her hope in a time when all her worst fears seemed to be becoming reality. It was a torment not to have heard from Abramm, and she was daily having more and more trouble believing he was still free and only working on some sort of rescue. But she could not bring herself to consider the possibility he had been killed. Her train of thought might lead her in that direction, but she always veered away before she got there. Even glimmers of such a notion filled her with a terror that sliced into her heart unbearably. She wanted to trust Eidon, to believe he would never be so cruel as to take her beloved from her after only five years of marriage.

But she could not get Kesrin's message out of her mind. . . . *"You are about to be cast into prison. . . . Whatever can be shaken in your life, he will shake. . . ."*

It did no good to dwell on such things, of course, but the fear pressed upon her with a wearying weight, and she found it took all her will and concentration not to let it into her soul.

Ian began to cry inconsolably in the middle of the afternoon. Maddie was the only one who could quiet him at all, and even for her he was fussy. Again, it was as if he knew things were wrong, and she despaired of how they'd keep him quiet when they left. She hoped he'd settle down to sleep, but he was still screaming when Cooper stepped into the room and told her the men were about ready to go.

As Ian continued to cry, she carried him into the servants' wait room, which had been turned into a temporary nursery by their refugee status.

"Stand there at the door, Pansy," she instructed. "If anyone comes, I want you to walk out and shut the door behind you and tell them I am adjusting my small clothes."

"Yes, ma'am."

Once Pansy was at her post, Maddie opened the chest of the children's clothes and bedding, shoved the top things back and drew out the stiff wiry form of the Robe of Light, which she'd taken from the House of Jewels the day Abramm had prepared to leave for the northland. He'd sent her for the scepter, and for some reason she'd been moved to take the other pieces, too—the robe, the orb, the crown, and the ring—in case he might decide to take them, as well. Only the sword she'd left, largely because it wouldn't fit in her valise.

He'd only wanted the scepter, though, and she'd planned to bring the other things back the next morning. But then there was no next morning . . . so she'd hidden them about. The crown lay in her traveling valise, wrapped up in her clothing and tucked between an extra pair of boots.

Now she laid one of Ian's regular blankets on the floor, folded the stiff robe over top of it, and placed another blanket over both. Having seen the way the garment had shivered into suppleness when Abramm had donned it during his coronation, she hoped it would undergo a similar transformation when it enwrapped his son. Of course, Ian was not king nor even crown prince, so she had no real reason to think it would. *But he is Abramm's son, Father Eidon, and surely that counts for something.*

Pansy stepped out of the room and closed the door. Maddie heard her higher tones intermingled with those of a man—Count Blackwell, she thought. Quickly now she took the still-screaming baby from his bed and wrapped him in the blankets, disappointed to note no change in the robe's stiffness. However, it did seem to work a comfort over Ian, as for the first time in hours he fell silent. It was that alone that convinced her to keep things as they were and hope no one noticed the odd fabric tucked between his blankets.

Now the door was opening again. She snatched up Ian, arranging the material around him as best she could, and was just pulling her own cloak around the right side of the bundle when Pansy stuck her head in. "They're ready for you, ma'am."

"Very good, Pansy. I'll be right there." She smiled down at Ian, who was sucking his thumb drowsily, ready to drift off now that they were about to move, an answer to prayers she had offered all afternoon. Pulling the left margin of her cloak over her shoulder and her precious burden, she stepped into the outer room. Carissa stood with Felmen and Elayne Cooper, Jared at her side, the young man holding Simon's hand. The boy was cloaked in heavy wool, the head of his stuffed horse poking out between the garment's front edges, and he fingered the poor thing's straggly yarn mane as he looked around uneasily. Seeing her, he brightened, let go of Jared, and ran to cling to her skirts as he had not in months.

Still holding Ian, she squatted awkwardly to bring herself eye to eye with her son and laid her free hand on his shoulder.

"Master Jared says we're going on a journey, Mama," he said.

"That's right, Simon, we are."

"To meet Papa?"

She hesitated, then smiled. "Yes. An exciting journey that might also be a little scary. You must be brave and strong. Can you do that, Simon?"

He nodded.

"And when we go down the dark stairs pretty soon we must all be very quiet. Especially when we come out in the forest. You must not ask any questions or say anything, no matter what happens. Do you remember what I told you about Father Eidon and the little bunny?"

"When the big wolf comes," Simon said, "the bunny runs right into the bunny hole that Father Eidon has made for him."

"Yes. If a big wolf or anything else scary comes and Jared doesn't have you anymore and no one's there to help, then you look for Father Eidon's bunny hole. Because he will always make one for you, no matter where you go. Do you understand?"

Simon nodded very soberly.

"So what are you going to do, then," Maddie asked, "if things get too scary?"

"Look for the bunny hole."

She smiled at him. "That's right."

"But, Mama, how will I know where to look for it?"

"Eidon will show you, poppet. And Mama—or maybe Papa—will come find you as soon as we can."

"Papa?" Simon's eyes brightened, and he looked around the room. And even though he didn't find what he was looking for, he nodded. "Papa will come," he said.

Trap stepped out of the opened wall panel and started to speak, cut off by Liza, over by the window, exclaiming, "Oh! The guardstar's just gone out."

Everyone looked around at her and then past to the darkness outside, where only red embers glowed in the near ground and nothing beyond. For a moment Maddie thought she might dissolve into tears of despair, holding Ian to her so tightly he began to whimper and squirm. Then Simon slid his small hand into hers and she pulled herself together.

"There was no guardstar when Abramm came here," Trap said grimly. "Yet we survived. We'll survive now. But we *must* go now."

They threaded a series of long, narrow stairways without incident, then put out their kelistars and emerged into the dark underbelly of an abandoned building on the fringes of Portside. Jared swung Simon up into his arms as Trap led them eastward away from the dock, then up through a dark copse of trees and finally to a slender trail that ran along the base of the sheer white cliffs on which the palace perched. It was full dark by then, but they dared not risk using a light to see by, so the journey became abruptly more exciting. The path was dry, narrow, and heart-thumpingly exposed in places where the terrain grew too steep for the trees, swooping sickeningly downward toward a narrow, rocky strand and then sea. Then the trail would reach another fold of land and the forest would shelter them again.

They were almost around the main cliff and had just come onto a flattening out of the landscape when a small light ahead brought them to a stop. Trap stole forward to reconnoiter, then waved them to come on. It was Byron Blackwell. He stood in a clearing bounded by cliff on one side and thick dark forest of small oaks on the other, a shuttered lantern in his hand.

Trap strode to meet him as the others followed after him. "What's wrong?" he said quietly. "Why are you here?"

"There's been a change of plans," said the count. Then he lifted the suddenly unshuttered lantern up between them so that its light shone straight into Trap's night-adjusted eyes and at the same time swung a long, sausage-shaped sandclub with his free hand into the side of Meridon's head, dropping him instantly.

Carissa cried out in horror while Cooper and Ames and the other guards drew their blades even as the men who had been waiting in the woods charged into the clearing to subdue them.

Jared, still holding Simon, dashed through an opening in the scuffle, and was about to win free when he was tackled, knocked forward so that both he and Simon fell rolling across the ground. Horsey was flung from Simon's grasp just as he himself had been flung from Jared's. Simon leaped instantly to his feet, but to Maddie's horror, instead of fleeing he looked round for his toy.

"Never mind Horsey, Simon!" Maddie screamed. "Find the bunny hole!"

But already he had spotted the rotund toy and darted back to snatch it as Jared yelled for him to run and the men closed in. By then Jared had regained his feet enough to tackle one of them, catching the man at the knees and taking him down in a tumble of limbs and cloaks. Simon darted into the darkness, and Maddie started after him.

Only to be caught and yanked around. A tall, dark-haired man in a gray tunic with a tiny red tongue of flame on his breast loomed over her. Grinning, he ripped Ian from her arms, wrappings and all. She screamed and flung herself upon him, trying to get her son back, but he easily knocked her aside and danced back, laughing now, as Ian screamed in earnest, his tiny voice a song of terror. She threw herself after him again, but this time something slammed out of nowhere into her temple, and all the strength left her.

As the forest swooped wildly up around her, she saw the man hurl his screaming bundle into the pale rock wall some five strides away, saw it hit and bounce off in a burst of white and a fluttering of dark blankets. The thin, hysterical wailing silenced abruptly, and with it went all the other sounds, so that Maddie watched in horror as the bundle drifted slowly to the earth, the ends of the blankets moving sinuously after it, then fluttering down over top of it until all had come to still and silent rest.

She lay half on her side, propped up by her left arm, staring at the pile of blankets, dark and light layers intermingled. Her body seemed to have turned to a husk, as if all that was living and vital had drained out of her and she might, if there had been the slightest breeze at all, simply float away. There was no thought, no sound, no feeling . . . Nothing.

Then she lurched up and flung herself toward her child, desperate to get to him, only to be seized again and jerked around to face a slender man with long white hair and narrow, hawkish features that bore an unsettling resemblance to Abramm's. *Gillard*. He grinned at her, and she attacked him like a wild woman, punching and slapping his face in a frenzy until she was pulled off and dragged away to a safe distance, both her arms pulled painfully behind her back.

As she gasped back her breath, she realized the rest of the fighting had ended. Cooper lay motionless on the needle-covered ground, blood blooming darkly across his jerkin. Jared, deathly pale, half lay, half sat on the rock wall under sword point. Trap lay where he'd fallen, just beginning to stir now as one of their captors approached to bind his wrists with a pair of iron manacles. Carissa stood nearby, holding on to Peri, with Liza, Pansy, and Maddie's ladies-in-waiting clustered about them, all under guard. Elayne was nowhere to be seen, and out in the forest, lanterns glowed as the men who searched called out loudly to one another.

She realized then, with a flutter of relief, that it wasn't just Elayne for whom they searched, but Simon, too.

In all her inspection of the situation, however, not once did her gaze even brush over the silent pile of blankets she knew was still lying at the foot of the rock wall.

Gillard stood with his gray-tunicked squadron, smaller than all of them but still imperious. They were Gadrielites, she understood. Blackwell, the traitor who had set the whole thing up, was nowhere to be seen.

She glared at Gillard. "Don't think it will end here," she grated.

"Oh, I'm counting on that, ma'am." He grinned at her from that thin little face of his, then turned to one of his subordinates. "When you find the boy, bring him to the Keep."

"Yes, sir. What about the babe?"

"Isn't he dead?"

"How could he not be, sir."

"Make sure of it. Then leave the body for the birds."

The scream that burst from Maddie was more animal than human, a product of too much grief and fear and fury. She twisted and stomped and kicked her way free of her captors, all emotion now, for thinking had grown as impossible as it was unbearable. She had to act or she would burst apart with the pressure, so she flung herself at Gillard, her momentum carrying him over backward and driving him into the ground.

She must have hit her head again, for the world exploded into scarlet and hurled her into blackness.

38

Broken glass crunched under Abramm's feet, the sound seeming loud, though he knew it wasn't. He followed Seth Tarker into the burned-out first floor of the building, trailed by his uncle Simon, Oswain Nott, and Philip Meridon. Smoke drifted in layers around them, clinging to the charred posts and fallen rafters and rising from the dark mouth of a now freestanding stone hearth. An acrid stink burned his nostrils and the back of his throat, despite the cloth he had tied across his face. Again he pressed on his Adam's apple to keep himself from coughing.

The rubble-strewn streets of this portion of Springerlan reminded him eerily of Hur, save there weren't as many spawn. Yet.

When he and Simon had arrived on the city's outskirts yesterday and found it under heavy guard, they'd corralled their horses in an abandoned barn once used by the Terstan underground, and there happened upon Tarker and his men. Having fled the palace when it had fallen, they'd taken to the old underground routes, as well, hoping to launch some sort of rescue. The meeting had no doubt been Eidon's doing, for the timing couldn't have been better.

From them, Abramm had learned what had happened since he'd left to ride north. How his enemies had risen up before dawn that same day and moved simultaneously on various Terstan strongholds, including Southdock and the palace. They had gone after Kesrin that first night, and no one knew what had become of him—if not dead then surely taken away for rehabilitation. . . .

Terstans had fought a fierce resistance in both Southdock and at the palace. Southdock had fallen first and Whitehill shortly thereafter, the queen and her party apprehended while attempting escape. The little princes had disappeared, but Maddie, Carissa, and Trap had been arrested to be tried tomorrow as servants of the Shadow, four days now after their capture. If they did not renounce their shields and embrace Mataian ways, they would be brought to Execution Square. Or else taken to a remote keep where their captors would seek to change their minds. Abramm had little hope of the latter. Not so long as he was still at large with an army of loyal supporters. They had to be counting on the fact that a public execution would draw him in, frantic to stop the deaths of his loved ones.

What they didn't know was that his army had been disbanded. With the Gadrielite forces that had defeated Rennalf approaching from the north, and the rest of them ensconced in Springerlan to the south, Abramm had re-organized his forces right there on the road back from Sterlen, breaking them into small squadrons under the command of independent officers, each of whom had their own set of orders. Some were camped now in the caves along the River Hennepen, waiting for the dawn, when they would come down to hit the defensive lines along the city's boundaries, providing the diversion Abramm needed for his primary operation to succeed. Others were even now using the old ways of the Terstan Underground to infiltrate the city. By morning most would be secreted along the route down which the prisoners would be taken from the High Court Chamber to the Execution Square tomorrow.

That square was the objective of their current reconnaissance, Tarker now leading them up a charred stairway to a second-floor window overlooking it. Dating back to the reign of Alaric the Bold some six hundred years ago, it was one of the oldest parts of the city. A low stone wall surrounded a square plaza flanked with two opposing sets of stone risers. Buildings surrounded it on three sides, and a busy street ran across its uphill boundary. On the down-hill side, the wall was set with a fence of vertical iron bars, beyond which lay a small second yard where more spectators could gather. At the center of the plaza, between the risers, a stone platform stood holding a wooden block where the condemned would rest his head. Iron staples pounded into the stone around it provided means for securing the prisoners, and a groove cut into both wood and stone served to channel the blood.

It had not been used for centuries, the beheading of condemned criminals having been replaced by hanging. Most public executions now took place to the north of the city at the Riverbend Hanging Tree, leaving this square to the washerwomen. For some reason the Mataians seemed to think executions should be bloody again and had reinstated the beheadings, many of which had been preformed in recent days. None, however, had drawn the crowds that tomorrow's killings would, and Abramm could see the place was scurrying with guards.

In a low voice Tarker noted the potential dangers, obstacles, hiding places, and escape routes in the scene before them.

When he finished, Abramm regarded the square for a moment, then turned away. "It'll be heavily guarded . . . and it's too open. There'll be a crowd, too. . . ." He paused a moment more, then decided. "We'll do it along the route from the Court Chamber. On the third switchback, which is not only the shortest but also the narrowest."

"We won't have much room to work."

"No, but we won't need it. And if we can get a riot going in the square it leads into, it'll be the perfect excuse for the coach to go around by way of Southdock." Where his own men, uniformed as prison guards and having replaced the driver at the outset of the attack, would stop the coach long enough to let its cargo out. Then they'd drive on up to Execution Square, park the empty coach, and if all went as planned, be well away before events settled enough that anyone thought to look inside. By then Maddie and the rest of them should be safely aboard the waiting galley and gliding toward the mouth of Kalladorne Bay. "Meanwhile we'll lead the guards away up the hill."

He was counting on his face and form to do the leading. Once the men realized whom they were chasing, he was pretty sure nothing else would matter.

"I don't know," said Simon. "If we go up the hill, we'll be heading directly into the greatest concentration of troops. It's not going to give us much of an escape route."

"It'll be enough," Abramm said, starting back down the stair.

They went round to the various sites where his small squadrons had set themselves up for tomorrow, and Abramm explained to each of them precisely what he wanted done and when. It was deep into the night when he finally returned to his hiding place in a cellar between the High Court Chamber and the Holy Keep.

"I don't like this plan to reveal yourself, sir," said Simon over a quick meal of smoke-tainted bread and cheese. "I'd be more comfortable knowing you were far away when the action started."

"My face is too valuable an asset not to use."

"It'll set them into a frenzy, though. And you know it won't be common soldiers guarding that street. It'll be Gadrielites, men who see you as Moroq in the flesh."

"Frenzied men are more easily led."

"We'll be outnumbered."

"Aye."

"I don't like it."

"I know, Uncle. I'm not too wild about any of it myself. But we have no other choice." He fingered the crust of bread that remained on his plate. "Have you heard anything about my boys?"

"So far, no. It may be they don't have them. . . ."

"Or else they're keeping them hidden so we don't try to rescue them, as well."

"That's possible, of course." Simon sighed and they fell silent, contemplating the dreadful outcomes of such a situation.

Not long after that, Abramm retired to a side room to try to get some sleep, though it turned out to be an exercise in futility. Without anything else to occupy his mind, it was free to dwell upon the things to come tomorrow— and upon the question of whether what he was doing was right or not. When he'd first seen the forces they faced and contemplated the logistics of trying to get everyone safely away, he'd despaired. Outnumbered, in a city full of people who could not be trusted, with a face as recognizable as his was, he didn't see how he could carry it off.

He believed it was Eidon who had first nudged him in the direction he was now headed. Everything that had happened in the last few days seemed to have been leading him to this inevitable end. How could he have not gone to face Rennalf? And if in hindsight he acknowleged it had not been good to leave with so many Mataians in the city . . . he'd had no reason at the time to think they would do what they did.

No. He was where he was supposed to be. And he knew why.

Those who bore the shield did so because Tersius had been willing to suffer in their place on that hill outside Xorofin. They remained in this world to be made like him, to live as he lived and, if they were ever ready, to suffer as he suffered. *"As men did to him, so they will do to you. . . ."* Kesrin had said in that last lesson. *"Do not be surprised. Be ready."*

No man would ever suffer to the degree that Tersius had, but the same Light that had sustained him through the worst nightmare a man could ever know would sustain Abramm in whatever he would be called to endure.

It was an honor to be entrusted with such a call.

He knew what the rhu'ema—who had brought all this about—would ask of him. And he spent the last hours of that night praying he would have the clarity of mind and strength of will to refuse them.

————————

The next day's drizzle did not keep the crowds from coming out to pack the Mall of Government around the steps of the High Court Chamber in hopes of seeing the queen, the princess, and the Duke of Northille led out in irons after their trial.

Abramm had deliberately placed himself in the third rank back from the front line of the crowd, his position lined up with the face of the stairway Maddie would descend so that, if she happened to look up, she would see him. He hoped that would happen but doubted it would, for the crowd was hostile, and she had surely seen enough hate-filled faces to last a lifetime. His height would make him more noticeable, but that was a double-edged sword, and he knew it. This was probably the riskiest and the most foolish part of his plan. But knowing how things were likely to end, and how much this moment would mean to him in the hours to come, he had to take the risk.

Besides, the plan had plenty of places for error and discovery, so he'd long ago committed it all to Eidon's hand, knowing that if it was going to work, Eidon would have to see that it did.

A black-sided coach with two narrow-barred side windows stood near the foot of the stair, its back door open to receive its passengers. If the three were condemned to die—as expected—it would straightaway bring them down to the square, where the headsman's ax could do its job. The Mataians had intended to bring them down in an open cart, for all to see and mock, but Abramm had made sure that all such carts turned up broken or misplaced. The only ones available were closed coaches. Even if his enemies were to guess it was no accident, he did not think it would matter.

Time dragged as the crowd grew steadily, packing in around him. He stood hunched over and periodically fell into coughing fits that served to maintain a well of space around him. The University clock tolled the half hour, then the hour, then the half again, at which point he had expected the trial to be over. By now he was growing chilled, for the dampness had permeated his cloak and his clothing all the way to his skin.

Finally the double doors opened. A line of armsmen marched out, followed by a cadre of dignitaries and then the prisoners. Trap led the way, hands and feet enchained, Carissa after him, not chained but walking awkwardly, her pregnant belly bigger than ever. Last of all came Madeleine. He lifted his head and looked at her, feeling like a man dying of thirst.

Her hair was braided in the long single plait, but frizzy and mussed, her clothing torn, dirtied, and wrinkled as if she'd been living in it for the last five days. Her face was gray and dead looking, her expression one of such hopeless grief he could hardly bear to look—and could not bear to look away. He thought he would be right in his prediction that she'd never look up, but in the end she did, just as she came up behind Carissa, who was waiting to climb into the coach.

When she met his gaze directly, he knew she had probably recognized him the moment she'd come out the door, refraining thereafter from looking at him so as not to draw attention. And perhaps for other reasons, as well.

Now those wonderful eyes, gray as the clouds and glittering with tears, fixed upon his for a long moment of deep and inarticulate communion. Then she looked away, and he dropped his head, hiding his face in the cowl again. He should leave now, or at least start pulling back, but he didn't. He heard the wooden door shut, heard the key grate in the lock, then looked up one last time. As the coach pulled away, he glimpsed a pale face in the shadows at the narrow barred window, caught the shine of the tears that had spilled down her cheeks, and wondered if in that strange way of hers she'd guessed what he meant to do, when no one else yet had.

Finally the coach turned, and he could see her no longer. It was like a door closing—all the emotion that had welled up in him suddenly shut off. He blinked away the moisture brimming in his eyes, swallowed hard, and stepped back between the people around him who were already surging after the departing coach. He spotted Tarker to his left, heading for an alleyway at the mall's edge. Abramm followed, careful not to hurry, keeping his attention on the coach.

Uniformed guards stood at the alley's entrance, but their focus was into it, not on the doings in the mall. Tarker passed them in a clot of onlookers hurrying down to the next level for another look. Abramm hunched himself over a bit more and followed, carried along by his own clot of citizens. Once past the guards, the two men came together and ducked into another alley, then made their way up a narrow stair, along a balcony, and across several rooftops, their route shared with many others eagerly searching for a place to watch the coach pass by.

Descending to street level again, they threaded the labyrinth of the Guild-man's Sector and finally emerged from an underground tunnel into a house that butted against the back of an inn along the third switchback. The house's attic gave egress to its roof, from which they stepped through one of the inn's third-floor windows left open for them earlier. From there they made their way down to the street and took up the position Abramm had chosen for his own point of attack. The only people with them were those who had exited the surrounding homes and businesses right after the guards had gone through clearing the crowd to make room for the coach and its attending horsemen. Last night the guards had conducted a sweep of the area, searching every structure and questioning closely everyone they found within.

Abramm had feared they might conduct a second such sweep this morning, but they had not, most likely because they lacked the manpower to do so. At this moment the portion of his own troops who'd remained outside the city were seeking to penetrate its defenses. Whether his enemies realized it was a diversion or not, men would be needed to stop it. It had been his hope that that, along with the need for securing the High Court Chamber, the Mall, Execution Square, and all the blocks of street in between, would tax the Gadrielites' resources and allow for a few third-floor windows to be left open here and there.

Now he scanned the flat faces of the buildings across the narrow street, each butting up against the other, some of them actually sharing walls. People hung out of every window and doorway, eager for a view of the infamous prisoners soon to pass by. He noted with satisfaction the lack of a breeze and the continuing drizzle. A wind could disrupt the flight of the arrows, and the drizzle had turned the street's cobbles slick, which would cause the driver to slow and thus give Abramm's bowman plenty of time to aim.

Across the way he saw his men moving into place, cowled and cloaked as he was, their weapons carried close to their legs to conceal them. They made no eye contact with him, as he had instructed, but all had seen him.

He stood at the mouth of the alleyway down which they would escape, ironically only a few strides from the trio of Gadrielite soldiers who guarded it. Soldiers who seemed more interested in the coming of the prisoners than in watching their surroundings for sign of enemy infiltration. He smiled slightly. *Such are the flaws by which battles are so often won or lost . . . people who think their part is irrelevant, yet they can make all the difference.*

He coughed and hunched himself farther. The soldiers glanced at him and edged away.

Finally he heard the first echoing clatter of the approaching cavalcade. Movement and sound rippled along the ranks of bystanders, some of whom leaned into the street to see up the road where the first helmeted horsemen came into view round the tight switchback.

They trotted past two by two, eight of them altogether, breastplates gleaming and gray Gadrielite cloaks spread across their horses' rumps. Riding close to the side of the road, they forced the onlookers' back as the coach finally appeared: a black box on black wheels, led by a team of two black horses. Two helmed and armored men sat on the driving bench—one holding the reins, the other a sword and shield. Four more sat atop the coach itself, all with shields and swords. And of the six, two were not what they seemed.

The coach rumbled by, but Abramm kept his eyes off the railed window, moving his right hand to his sword hilt, belted high up under his left arm. He fingered off the loop of leather that had so far held it lengthwise against his leg and hidden beneath his long cloak. Closing his fingers about the leather-wrapped hilt grip, he tugged the harness gently down to make his draw easier.

The second of the four pair of horsemen trailing the coach passed by him as the vehicle slowed for the turn. With the clatter of the horses' hooves and the rumble of the coach's wheels bouncing and echoing off the hard stone, he never heard the twang of the bows as the arrows were released, never even saw the driver hit. His attention was fixed on the Gadrielites beside him as they stiffened and stepped toward the coach. Straightening from his slouch, Abramm flung back the edge of his cloak, his rapier flashing in the gray daylight. As shouts rang out down the street, he lunged, sliding his blade past the armhole edge of the nearest man's breastplate into his heart and pulling it free to parry the strike of the Gadrielite's companion. Meanwhile Tarker took out the third.

As the escort horsemen drew together behind the halted coach to face their attackers, its back door opened and a dozen more soldiers poured into the street. Exactly as Abramm had hoped. They pelted toward him, and he stepped to meet them, snaring an incoming rapier with his cloak and lunging to score another hit. By then his cowl had fallen all the way back, his hair and face revealed. The bystanders recognized him first, gasping and pointing in their surprise. Once he'd also drawn the attention of the bulk of the Gadrielites, he turned to give them a clear look at his face and was amused to see their eyes widen and their steps falter. Also as he had hoped. In their moment of inaction he called the retreat and raced for the alley, his men running both before and after him in a hedge of protection.

The escape route had been well planned, and he'd already given instructions detailing at what point each group was to peel off on alternate paths. It was designed to look like attempts to confuse the pursuers—his own men believed that was what they were doing—but really it was only to see them safely out of the way. Most of the pursuers ignored the men he sent off to "trick" them, however, so Abramm led the Gadrielites—their number growing with each new street they crossed—on a line directly away from the route the coach should now be taking.

Having gained a bit of a lead and now a good ways from the original point of attack, Abramm led his handful of remaining supporters out the back of a tumbledown stable into a small yard and stopped. A two-story stone building loomed uphill to the left, with smaller structures, also stone, ahead and to the right. Except for a narrow rail-less stone stairway running up the inner side of that tall building, and the small garden area tucked between it and the smaller building ahead, there was no way out.

"Split up," Abramm commanded. "Half of you take the stairs, the other half the garden. Seth, Alex, you know the routes. We'll be taking that tunnel there." He gestured to the age-warped cellar door that lay in the dirt to his left.

The men hesitated, frowning at one another. Finally Tarker said, "But, sir, weren't you—"

"Now!" Abramm ordered sharply.

And they went. All save Simon, Whitethorne, and Philip, who turned back from the parting men to regard him suspiciously.

"What are you waiting for?" he demanded of them. "I told you to go."

Simon was frowning fiercely now. "What are you up to, sir? This was not in your plan."

"It was always in my plan. I simply didn't tell you. Now get out of here before they come."

"There are at least forty of them," his uncle erupted. "You may be good with that blade, but you can't hold off forty all by yourself."

"I don't intend to." He met his uncle's gaze grimly. "I'm sure their orders are to take me alive."

"To take you alive?" Simon gaped at him, understanding at once what he intended. "There is no need for that, sir. Even if you couldn't get away—"

"I can't, Uncle. And neither can the rest of you if I stay with you. They have the city too well guarded. I saw that right from the start." He paused, hearing noises from the stable now as the first of their pursuers entered it, then said quietly, "It's me they want."

"Do you have any idea what they'll do to you as their prisoner?"

He met his uncle's gaze evenly. "This is about far more than you know, Simon. The time for fighting with blades is past. My life is in Eidon's hands now, to take or not as he sees fit. But I have no desire for you to go down with me." He paused as more voices sounded from within the stable. "My sons are out there somewhere. And my wife. And I believe the people of this land will one day want deliverance from this choice they have made. There is much work for you to do, Uncle."

"There is work for *you* to do, sir!" Never had he seen his uncle, the gruff, stoic rock of the family, look so distressed. "I will not leave you, Abramm."

"Not even if I command it?"

"No, sir."

"Very well." And Abramm swung at him hard, smashing the butt end of his swordhilt into the side of his uncle's head. The old man dropped like a stone. Abramm glanced at Whitethorne and Philip. "I trust the two of you can handle him by yourself?"

Whitethorne frowned at him. "Are you *sure* this is what you want? We—"

"Go. Now."

Philip bent to sling the duke's senseless body over his shoulders, and the two of them hurried into the green darkness of the narrow garden, even as the Gadrielites shoved open the wide stable door and poured into the yard. Seeing Abramm standing there alone, they stopped just outside the gate, panting and red-faced from their run, eyes narrow with wariness. A few glanced up at the roofs and bare walls surrounding them, but most kept their gazes fixed on Abramm as more of their fellows poured through the door and gathered alongside them.

Then they just stared at him, seeming reluctant to move. He stared back, marveling that even when they so outnumbered him—and Simon hadn't been far off on his estimate—they feared him.

Finally he sighed and took the lead, stooping to lay his blade on the ground. Then he backed a step away from it and raised his arms, palms open, fixing his mind on Tersius and praying for the courage to endure what would follow.

39

The soldiers closed around him tentatively at first and then, gaining courage, seized him and tore off his cloak, jerkin, and boots. After searching him to be sure he carried no other weapons, they shackled his wrists and ankles and brought him into the stable. There he was shoved and pulled up into the wagon, receiving a steady stream of punches, elbow jabs, and rough jerks, as if each man wanted to be sure he got in his blows while he had the chance. In the bed of the wagon, he was chained round the waist to the driver's bench, forced to stand while the others climbed in around him. They packed together, kneeling with their faces turned out, as if they feared his supporters might return.

They did not know that his men were all on their way out of the city now, each group on its separate course, each with strict orders to stay away from all citizens and a clear understanding of what would happen to them should they be found out. He'd also warned them specifically to be wary of reports that he himself had been captured, telling them it would very likely be used by their enemies as a trap.

By the time any of them learned what had really happened, it would be far too late for them to do anything.

The news spread quickly through the immediate area that he had been captured, and a stunned crowd gathered along the route as the wagon bore him up to the High Court Chamber, where the heresy trials were ongoing. Most would wait weeks to face this tribunal, but the king was granted a special hearing. No doubt they wished to conclude the affair as swiftly as possible, to reduce the chance of him being rescued. Which was just as well, for he, too, wanted it over with quickly.

He was led in through an audience composed of men with familiar faces, men who'd eaten at his banquets, who'd received his largesse, who he'd thought supported him. They stared at him coldly now, their true colors revealed.

The Mataian High Council sat in the raised box at the room's fore: High Father Bonafil in the center flanked by his subordinates, among whom were Abramm's old discipler, Master Belmir, and Bonafil's rising star apprentice, the newly promoted Master Eudace. Darak Prittleman stood in a new and more elaborate Gadrielite uniform to the right of the box, serving as the high court's bailiff. And seated in the king's box to the left of front was Gillard, who, to Abramm's utter astonishment, appeared to have taken Mataian vows. And not just as a novice but as a full Guardian, for he wore the robes of that rank and his white-blond hair was long and caught up into the single braid of the confirmed brother. More than that, he wore the ruby amulet at his throat.

Abramm would not have recognized him had he not seen him in his own bedchamber. Gillard's reduction in size was every bit as dramatic as it had seemed then, but only now did Abramm have the time to appreciate the immensity of what had been done to him. The fire of hatred in his eyes, however, remained unchanged.

Prittleman called the court to order, and following the High Father's lead, everyone sat but Abramm and Prittleman. The charges were read and the evidence presented, beginning with his shirt being cut off him to reveal the shield and dragon—two marks of evil—branded into his flesh, and ending with the testimony of fifty men, each of them determined to outdo the other in the heinousness of their claims. Then the verdict—never in doubt—was read: Guilty as charged of heresy, colluding with evil, obstructing the truth, disrespecting the High Father, and a host of other crimes rendered irrelevant when the penalty for heresy alone was death.

Finally it was time for Bonafil to pronounce the sentence—death, of course—followed by the inevitable offer of mercy. "Given your past, and the fact you were once a dedicated servant of the true Flames," he said ponderously, "if you will renounce your error, allow the mark of evil to be removed from your flesh, and swear to serve the truth forever more, we will let you live."

"I swear only to serve the truth," Abramm said. "And that I do not find here today."

A spark of red flickered in the amulet at the High Father's throat and was echoed faintly in his bulging eyes. He folded his hands very carefully before him, asked, "You are sure?" And to Abramm's astonishment he launched a veil of translucent Shadow through the air to wrap itself around him. Coldness caressed his naked torso, crept into his blood, and sought to ignite the fear that lurked at the edges of his soul, reminding him of what would come after this trial—a trip to the dark den of the torturer, blades and whips and implements of glowing iron applied to his flesh in multifarious, unthinkable ways. The pain would be excruciating, the damage to his body worse than anything the morwhol had done . . .

He turned his thoughts from those fearful speculations and affirmed to himself that whatever Eidon asked him to do, he would give him the power to accomplish. The Light rose in him and the cold pressure vanished.

Lifting his chin, he gave firm answer to Bonafil's question: "I'm sure."

The High Father leaned back in his chair with a grimace. "Well, you give us no choice, then, but to do whatever we must to deliver you from the evil that has captured your soul." He glanced at the bailiff. "Take him to Wetherslea."

Outside the High Court Chamber, the crowd was now openly hostile. People lined the labyrinthine route down to the prison, cursing him and shaking their fists, and he marveled that they could turn so quickly from adoration to hatred.

At the prison, Abramm was marched down a long stair of weathered stone into a nightmare of darkness full of distant screams and dreadful smells. They passed through a series of locked iron gates, then down a long corridor to a dark pillared chamber lit by the flames of a bronze brazier balanced at room center on a waist-high stand. Two men in black tunics waited beside it, and various long-handled iron implements whose purpose Abramm preferred not to consider hung from the upper collar of the stand. Farther out, where the flickering light gave way to shadow, stood a ring of large, freestanding wooden frames—racks to which the torturers' victims were chained so they might do their work.

Wordlessly, Abramm's escort stripped away the remains of his slitted shirt and shackled him into one of the racks, pulling his arms out straight to either side and angled slightly upward, tight enough to put an uncomfortable pressure on his stiffened left arm. His legs were shackled likewise but not spread so far apart they couldn't hold his weight. Throughout this operation not one of them so much as glanced at his face.

When he was secured, the guards took up positions about the room as if they still believed somehow he might escape, while the smaller of the two torturers placed several of the implements into the blaze. Then the other man shook out the small black whip he wore coiled at his waist and, with no more warning than that, came round behind Abramm and started in.

He heard the whip sing through the air half a heartbeat before it struck. The first blow was like fire cutting across the flesh of his back. The second was worse. By the third he was feeling light-headed and queasy. After that he stopped trying to count and concentrated on trying to breathe, for his chest kept wanting to close up, and he found it was hard to think about Tersius anymore, hard to think of anything but the pain which filled up all his senses.

Then it ended and he was left hanging there, gasping and shuddering as his legs trembled beneath him and the dark room spun around him. He hung there for what seemed a very long time, listening as his guards conversed idly with each other and the torturers, and marveling at how pain could so completely command one's thoughts. His left arm had fallen asleep when he heard a distant clang and the men broke off their talk to reassume their formal positions. Approaching footsteps heralded the arrival of more Gadrielites, marching in to intersperse themselves with his original escort. Shortly thereafter, Master Belmir strode into the room, followed by Gillard and Darak Prittleman.

They filed in behind the brazier, standing in a half circle in front of guards, and stared at Abramm with expressions cold, hard, and grim. For a long time no one moved. Then Belmir stepped up to face him.

"You say Eidon has chosen you. Tell me, then, how has it come to pass that you are hanging here, beaten and bloodied? If we are wrong, why has he delivered you into our hands?"

Abramm stared down at him, the old doubts stirring uneasily.

"And why was your army unable to stop the forces of Shadow?" Prittleman added, stepping up behind Belmir. "Where those empowered by Eidon's Holy Flames succeeded?"

"Can't you see how wrong you've been?" Belmir asked. "I told you it would be like this . . . when you said that Eidon himself speaks to you. How could you think he would let such blasphemy go?"

"We promised you would feel his wrath," Prittleman said. "And so you will—"

"Unless," Belmir interrupted, "you repent of this madness and return to the truth!"

"I already have the truth," Abramm said.

Belmir's gaze grew troubled. "Please, Abramm. You know what we have to do if you refuse to bend."

"And this is how your god must gain his followers?" Abramm asked. "By torturing them into submission?"

And Belmir's gaze grew more troubled still.

"Bah!" Prittleman cried, stepping in front of him. "Your god lets you fall into the hands of his enemies and leaves you there, helpless against them." He turned to Belmir. "The Shadow holds him too strongly, Master. We must proceed."

Looking grieved and reluctant, Belmir stepped back and motioned for the torturers to begin. Immediately the smaller one pulled a pair of tongs from the fire, and in it dangled a black, frog-sized, tentacled mass that Abramm recognized at once. As the larger man daubed white hamar onto the side of his ribs, the other lifted the griiswurm, suckered tentacles already groping toward him.

But it hadn't even touched him before it was repelled by a flash of Light he did not consciously generate. Both men staggered backward before it, and the griiswurm wound itself so tightly to the tongs that no amount of prying could unfasten it. Only when it was brought back to the flames did it let go, falling into the safety of its bright nest. Grim-faced, the torturer pulled another from the brazier, as his accomplice picked up a second set of tongs and pulled out another.

This time the men hit with a sudden blast of the fearspell before applying the griiswum, seeming to know that if they could just get a little spawn spore into him, it would give them the leverage they needed to eventually break him. It didn't work, but they kept coming, using griiswurm after griiswurm, as the Light kept driving them off.

Suddenly Gillard strode in among them and bade them stop. "You're wasting our time. Ply the whip again. Or else use those tongs and pokers for what they were intended."

The men looked around at Master Belmir, and Gillard gestured impatiently at the whip dangling from the torturer's belt. "Here. Give me that and I'll do it myself."

The torturer handed the whip over, but as Gillard shook it out and stepped toward Abramm, Belmir stopped him.

"Makepeace," he said sternly, "you have sworn a vow to do no violence."

Gillard looked round at him with arched brows. "Yet I can stand here and direct others to do it at my command?" He snorted. "What's the difference?

I'd rather do it myself anyway. Tell Father Bonafil he can grant me another special dispensation."

And the whip came snapping like fire across Abramm's belly. He grunted with the shock of it and felt his muscles twitch and contract.

"There. See? He can't stop that." The whip sang and snapped again. "Repent!" Gillard snarled. "Give up that stupid mark and yield." But his insincerity was patent.

"Makepeace, that's enough," Belmir commanded. "Give him back the whip!"

Gillard did so, but he then turned to push his face up into Abramm's. "If you are so sure you are right, why hasn't Eidon delivered you, brother dear?" Abramm smelled the incense on his robes and the garlic on his breath. "Why has he let your sons die?"

Abramm stared at him, shaken to the core, and Gillard smiled. "My own man threw your youngest into the side of a cliff." He paused and his smile widened. "Why, it's just as the Words say we are to do to our enemies, isn't it? 'You will dash their little ones against the rocks. . . . ' Remember that passage? Your other boy I chased off the ledge trail under the white wall—same place I nearly pushed you off twenty years ago. . . ." His face twisted into a smirk. "I guess that means for all intents and purposes I've dashed him against the rocks, too."

Abramm hung there, struggling to breathe but determined not to give his brother the satisfaction of knowing how deeply those lies drove into him. For they had to be lies. The alternative was not something he could consider. *Your glory is in your goodness, my Father. And I will trust in that. I do not believe you would take my sons from me in this way.*

"I don't believe you, Gillard," he said tightly. "Or I guess it's Makepeace now, isn't it?" And he smiled a little at that, wondering why in the world they'd given him that name.

Gillard glared at him as if he'd just offered him the gravest insult possible and then attacked like a wild man—slapping, hitting, punching—the blows landing willy-nilly on his face and neck and stomach. . . .

By the time the torturers pulled him off, Abramm's right eye was swelling closed and his nose, which Gillard had already broken once in their youth, felt broken again. His lips were cut and throbbing, and he spat out the blood that filled his mouth.

Gillard wrestled free of the torturers and staggered back, panting and rubbing his hands as if they stung while he grinned ferociously at Abramm.

"You're going down, brother. I will take your place and you will never be king again. In fact, I will see that no one even remembers your name."

And behind him now, Abramm saw another man, who must've entered while Abramm was being pummeled. A man with spectacles and a pasty face and long silver-threaded hair. A man with a telltale tic by his right eye. He was smiling.

Abramm blinked and the man was gone, swallowed back up into the shadows.

"Please, Abramm," Belmir said. "Surely you must see your error. Or if not that, then the futility of resisting. Don't make us go on."

"I'm sorry, old friend. I will not renounce what I know to be true."

"You're being too soft on him, Master Belmir," said a new voice.

Abramm expected Byron Blackwell to appear, but instead it was young Master Eudace who stepped through the circle of Gadrielites to join them. He fixed his luminous blue eyes on Abramm, who was reminded weirdly of the kraggin's great orbs. . . .

"Sentimentality is blinding you, sir," Eudace said, his voice as cool and hard as his eyes. "He is a servant of the Shadow. You will not save him from himself with kindness. Only the agony of great love will do it." The young master smiled up at Abramm. "You will thank us in a day or two."

And then it began in earnest. They used the whip and the hot irons and the griiswurm all together, the pain and shock and constant attempts to infest him with spore along with a steady stream of accusations wearing him down.

"If you are Eidon's chosen, why are you here? Why is this happening? Why does he not rescue you?"

His responses to the griiswurm grew slower. They began to actually touch him, and spore gained a foothold, was burned away, only to gain another. . . .

"Where is your great power now?"

"Why did he let your sons die?"

"Why has he abandoned you?"

He saw the rhu'ema hovering around him in the shadows above, savoring his pain as if it were fine wine, delighting as the Shadow rose up to take him for longer and longer periods of time.

He kept seeing Blackwell now, among the others, his white wrinkled face, his long silver hair, and the tic working rapidly in his excitement. One of the lenses in his spectacles had cracked, but he seemed not to notice. Sometimes he came around behind to whisper alternate accusations into Abramm's ear. . . .

"*You should have protected Carissa. Now she's been defiled with the bastard of your enemy, and it's your doing.*"

Darkness and pain and gasping grunts. His throat was raw. His body felt as if it had been turned inside out, as if all his skin had been stripped away.

"*You did this yourself. Your sin with Shettai, your audacity in going after another. You've ruined Briellen. And Maddie is dead. As are your sons.*"

No . . .

"*They are! See?*" Images flooded his mind, a tiny bundle torn from his wife's arms and hurled against the rocks, falling to the ground, still and silent. A small figure in a child's cloak running in terror along a narrow ledge, clutching a bedraggled stuffed horse to his chest. He looked back, a small white, frightened face, then tripped and fell over the edge. . . .

"NO!"

"*Dead . . . even as your realm lies in ruin, your people betrayed. . . .*"

"Let us cleanse you," Belmir pleaded. "Let us take the mark and we will stop."

"*So many ways you have failed. You think he would ignore it all? Pretend it did not exist? That is why you are here, you know. Because he has had enough of you and your failures.*"

The darkness pressed at him from without and within. Red light reflected off hideous faces, knitted brows, open mouths, and wagging tongues. And on and on it went.

"Let us take the mark, Abramm. Please."

"*Yes, let them take it. You don't deserve to wear it anyway. . . .*"

His sons were dead. His wife taken . . . He had failed them all—family, realm, Eidon. He did not deserve to wear the shield.

Another griiswurm slapped upon him, introducing successive lines of new fire, somehow more excruciating than any of the rest, and he could no longer hold in the screams. As his shrieks echoed off the stone around him, spawn spore raced through his veins, hot and nauseating, flaring blue across his vision as the Shadow took him and held on.

Eventually he ran out of breath and the screams devolved into ragged groans as he hung there, weak and shaking and wanting to die. Surely it would end soon. His body was a bleeding, throbbing agony, his reality a world of darkness and torment into which Belmir now said in a shaking, desperate voice, "Abramm, *please* . . ."

And he heard himself moan, and then his own voice, dry and raspy, said, "Yes. I don't deserve to wear it. Take it and make it stop."

And they did.

———

When he came to again, he was still shackled to the frame, but now Bonafil stood before him with all his High Council, the lot of them staring at him with bright and avid gazes.

The High Father Bonafil smiled condescendingly. "We knew you would come around, son, and we rejoice in having broken the power of evil on your life. See . . . you are no longer bound." He gestured to Abramm's chest.

Abramm looked down at himself, numb and so stupid with pain that it took him a moment to sift through all the welts and slashes cut by the whip, the oozing burn marks, the ugly red bites of the tongs, and the blistering lines of the griiswurm to realize his mark was missing. In its place lay a smooth, pale patch of new skin.

"No." The word came out a half sob. "How could I . . . ?" He closed his eyes, a wave of grief and despair and searing guilt washing through him. How could he have turned? How could he have allowed them to take it? *No. . . !*

"No man shall snatch you from my hands."

The words floated through his mind, stopping the inward wail. And then he recalled the gold shields embossed into the breastbones of the skeletons they'd pulled out of Graymeer's and the pigskin covers some Terstans used to pretend they weren't Terstan. Byron Blackwell had pressed Abramm himself to use one of them more than five years ago, when the Table of Lords wanted to arrest him for wearing a shield. His mark wasn't gone. They'd simply covered it and wanted him to think it was. They'd pressed him and pressed him, and he'd finally said yes. He remembered that now. Guilt welled up in him, sharp, flaying . . . Worse, he had no idea how to remove it and was too ashamed to even seek the one who did, let alone ask.

Which is exactly what they intend.

You knew I would do this.

I did.

He began to weep, overwhelmed by all of it, his pain, his struggle, his failure . . . and the faithfulness extended to him now. *How could you . . . You're still here.*

I am.

Take it off me, Lord. I don't want this. You know that.

If I do, they will order their torturers to continue.

I don't care. I want it off.

He didn't have to ask again. The Light welled up in a terrific burning over his heart, skin, and bone, gathered into a fiery crescendo that exploded out of his heart, and left a cooling tingle in its place.

He opened his eyes. Bonafil was picking the bloody patch of skin off the front of his robe where it had been flung. On Abramm's chest, the mark gleamed bright as ever amidst a patch of newly raw and oozing skin.

Every man in the room stared at him openmouthed. He gazed around at them, his eyes catching on Belmir, who looked as if someone had struck him on the head.

"Well," Eudace huffed, "I see we must begin again." He turned to the torturers. "Wellman, bring more of the Shadow cleaners."

"No," said Bonafil. "He has defied us long enough. Take him to the square."

There ensued an excited discussion regarding the best means of execution, whether it should be burning, beheading, or tearing asunder. Beheading won out because it was quicker and they'd have his head to put on display. Toward the end of the discussion, he saw Gillard standing aside from the main group, nodding speculatively as Blackwell whispered into his ear. Then his brother stepped forward into the silence that had followed their decision and suggested that, since it was already early afternoon, perhaps they should wait until the next morning to carry out the execution. In the meantime they could set Abramm on display so the people could see what had become of their great king and know the inevitable end of all who refused to turn from evil.

There was some concern that Abramm might not survive that long on account of the intensity of his injuries, and even more concern his supporters might find a way to rescue him, but Abramm heard little of the specifics of those arguments. His pain-fogged brain was too busy tussling with the conundrum raised by Gillard's observation that it was only early afternoon. Which made no sense at all. It had been nearly that when the soldiers had first taken him, and surely the nightmare in Wetherslea had lasted longer than a couple of hours. . . .

After much labored cogitation, he realized that it was early afternoon a full day after his arrest—that more than twenty-four hours had passed since he'd been seized in that stable. They were probably right to worry he might not survive the night.

Even so, in the end Bonafil liked the notion of putting the deposed king on display, and that's what they ended up doing.

A framework was set up in Execution Square, where Abramm was shackled anew, half naked, his breeches hanging in tatters about his legs, useless to shield him from the cold. He hung there facing the block he would tomorrow lay his head upon, as the people shuffled by in a never-ending line on the road beyond it, mocking him and pelting him with rotten plums and apples. Gadrielite guards stood in ranks about him, facing both outward and inward, and as a seeming eternity twilight began to gather he spied the colorful ribbons that were the rhu'ema watching avidly from the shadows.

Eventually torches were lit for the people who continued to pass by until, in the deepest hours of the night, a drizzle began to fall. Even then, some curled up under their cloaks on the cobbles, determined to save their place from which to view tomorrow's execution. It was a long and difficult night.

Blackwell came to see him just before dawn, he who had not only betrayed Simon by intercepting his pleas from the battlefield but had also delivered Abramm's family to the Gadrielites. It hadn't taken Abramm long on that desperate ride back to Springlan to figure that out. And more, to realize he wasn't just a man, but a creature in a man's body, whose true name Abramm did not know, but who had been Master Saeral before he was Count Byron Blackwell.

He stood now staring up at Abramm, smiling slightly. "So. You know who I am."

"I think I've known it for a long time." It was hard to speak.

"Yes, I think you have, too. I just wonder why you never acted on it. Perhaps you didn't want to admit you could be so easily deceived. Or perhaps you still want some of what I offer you."

"I don't."

"He's taken everything from you. Why do you still serve him?"

"He gave it all to me in the first place, so if he takes it back, how can I complain? He did not take the shield, though, because that cannot be taken. I belong to him. I always will."

Blackwell snorted and stepped closer. "But why do you want to? If this is all you gain from it."

And when Abramm did not respond, he added, "Surely you don't expect some fantastic manifestation of Light to deliver you now, do you? If that is his plan, why has he waited so long?"

"I don't know what his plan is. I only know it is good."

Blackwell shook his head. "Your sons are dead, Abramm. Killed at your brother's hand. Where is the good in that? Your wife is dead. Your best friend, your sister . . . all lost. You, Eidon's alleged Guardian-King, hang there hurting and humiliated, about to lose your life . . . and you call that good?" He fell silent, the light of the torches reflecting off his broken spectacles, and when Abramm said no more he whispered, "You could've had greatness. You could've been remembered. But now you will be as nothing, for I will blot out all memory of you."

"Where I'm going, it won't matter."

The other man's lips tightened and his brows drew down. Then he expelled a burst of air and stepped back. "Fine, then. Go. I just hope you won't be too disappointed when your expected reward doesn't turn out to be what you think it will."

He left then, and some moments later Abramm sensed another moving in the shadows around him. Brother Belmir stood nearby, the ranks of guards barely visible in the mist. He was close enough to have heard their conversation. For some moments his former discipler stood there looking at him; then he, too, vanished into the darkness, and Abramm was, at last, alone save for the hedge of guards surrounding him.

By now his thirst was intense, his mouth cotton dry, his throat feeling as if it had cracks in it. He was hallucinating about water, the paradise of Eidon filled with it—light flickering off streams and pools and fountains. He had been soaked by a drizzling rain earlier, and now he prayed for it to start again.

He did not think it was possible to hurt as much as he did and still be alive. At least he could think now. Could think about Tersius and what he had done—that it had been more than anything Abramm had suffered here . . . because, while the Shadow had taken him in the end, it had not done so in the way it had taken Tersius, who had never until that moment known its touch. Odd to think that the worst pain Eidon's son had suffered was something Abramm had lived with all his life, something he often had a hard time even identifying, much less experiencing as pain.

But that was because he had only the vaguest grasp of what Tersius had really done. It surprised him now how content he felt, satisfied from knowing he had fought the fight and had finished his course in the Light.

"It won't be long now, my friend."

His requested drizzle began to fall, the moisture falling gently upon his lacerated back. He sagged forward, turning his head so it would run down his cheek into his mouth. Suddenly the stomp and ruckus of a new shift of guards marching up burst into his silence. With them came a Mataian Master with an order from Bonafil that the prisoner be brought over to the Holy Keep so one last attempt might be made to change his mind. *How can they want another attempt?* Abramm thought. *Aren't they tired of this yet?*

The captain approved the request, and the Master and his three cowled Gadrielite helpers approached, hurrying their steps as the rain picked up. When the Mataian stopped before him, Abramm was surprised and a little disappointed to recognize Belmir. The man did not meet Abramm's glance, but kept his gaze focused on fitting his key into the shackle on Abramm's left wrist as the rain fell even harder, smacking the cobbles around them with a crisp, loud crackle. The wind gusted and, along with the torchlight, transformed the falling rain into shifting veils of bronze. The guards hunched over to shield their faces from the pelting drops, and the shackles opened, Abramm's arm falling limply onto the shoulder of the second man as the third stepped close to steady him. Shortly, his right arm was freed, and then the two carried him by shoulders and feet up the hill in Belmir's wake to the waiting wagon.

He was lifted into its bed as the rain came down in earnest now, the men hurrying to get into the wagon and be on their way. They clattered over the cobbles and then turned unexpectedly off the main road into a dark alley and the shelter of an awning. After a moment, hands grasped him gently and maneuvered him into some sort of trough running lengthwise through the wagon's bed—which seemed so bizarre he thought he was hallucinating again, a suspicion intensified when they laid a series of boards overtop of him, as if he lay in wagon with a false bottom. Surely not. How could Master Belmir, after all he had done to break Abramm's faith, be involved in a rescue operation that could see him hanging from a whipping frame himself?

But it was a very vivid and detailed hallucination. Through the rush of rain and wind, he heard and felt the thuds and thumps of cargo loaded atop the boards above him. Shortly after that, the wagon lurched forward, bumping once more down the cobbled street amidst the violent rushing of the rain.

40

Gillard lay on the pallet in his private meditation chamber and wept. Sometimes he cried aloud. Sometimes he howled, and then Amicus would come and tell him to be silent and offer him more of the drink that was supposed to help and did not.

He was ashamed of himself, could hardly believe he was acting like this, for he had always seen himself as a man's man—tough, invincible, and impervious to pain. But never in all his life had he known this kind of agony. Already he'd staggered up and vomited into the chamber pot three times, and the last time nothing but bile had come up. He was cold and sweating and shaking as the pain squeezed him tighter and tighter until he thought it would drive him mad.

It felt as if every bone in his body had been crushed and now throbbed in a symphony of fiery torment. Yet there was no sign of breakage. Nothing swollen or reddened. Every limb working just fine. When one of the brothers had felt the bones in his legs and arms and hands for soundness, Gillard screamed and thrashed in agony while the others held him down. But in the end, nothing was found to be wrong with them. The only possible diagnosis could be a few cracks . . . or maybe more than a few, but they were not hampering his movement or use of anything in the least.

Except for the pain.

Eudace visited him finally, after he'd called for the Mataian at least fifty times. Hearing Gillard's complaints he nodded and allowed that it was possible his bones were cracked. After the abuse he had put them through in beating Abramm, that would not be surprising. The fall he'd taken when

Madeleine rushed him hadn't helped, either.

"You said they wouldn't break," Gillard accused. "That your Flames would make them strong."

"And I was right. Whatever has broken has done so inside, without adverse effects. You can still use everything you have."

"I can hardly even bear to lie here, let alone move."

Eudace's face tightened. "Then you must learn to tolerate the pain."

"For how long?"

"At least a week. Maybe more."

"I cannot."

"Very well—we can give you more hockspur if you like, but it will leave you sluggish and thick-headed for the duration." His tight expression deepened into a frown. "Which would be an inexcusable waste of time and ability, since there's nothing substantially wrong with you."

"Nothing substantially wrong with me?"

"You just need to set your mind to bear it." He turned to go, but Gillard stopped him.

"What of Abramm's execution?"

"It will proceed as scheduled." Eudace flicked a questioning glance at Amicus, seated at Gillard's bedside.

"I heard you'd changed your mind," Gillard pressed. "That now you're going to burn him instead of beheading him."

"We are. Burning signifies judgment. But why do you ask?"

"I want to be there."

Eudace pursed his lips. "Well, then, you're going to have to get yourself out of that bed."

"I'll need something more than the hockspur."

"Very well."

Thus it was that just as the dawn was gilding the clouds over the eastern headland, Abramm Kalladorne, thirty-sixth King of Kiriath, was burned alive in the public square for the crimes of heresy, colluding with evil, and persecuting the true faith of the Flames, and Gillard was there to see it. He had to be carried in a sedan chair, though, and his vision was blurred.

Perhaps that was why, just before the flames licked up around the figure bound to a stake amidst the great pile of burning wood, he experienced a sudden alarm, sure the figure wasn't Abramm after all, but someone else. After a few moments of panic and something approaching terror, he labored through his drug-fogged mental processes to the conclusion that it wasn't possible. He'd have known if Abramm had escaped. He had been far too badly beaten. For him to escape, someone would have had to carry him, and with all the guards on site last night . . .

No. It wasn't possible. Abramm was dead. Finally and for good.

But Gillard was bitterly sorry later that he'd not been able to stand before his brother, look him in the eye, and light the kindling beneath him with his own hand.

———

It was late summer when Abramm finally reached Highmount Holding— the old one, not the new one. The new one, under the rule of Ethan Laramor's son, did not make a habit of welcoming Terstan refugees, though it was certain that many of those who lived there knew the Underground used the old fortress.

He arrived alone and on foot, with nothing but the clothes on his back, his battered rucksack, and a walking stick. He carried no blade, since blades were forbidden to the common folk now—only the Gadrielites could wear them—and he didn't wish to draw attention to himself. Besides, he was pretty good with his stick and with the sling and stones in the pouch at his waist. Good enough he'd not lacked for meat on his hike up here.

The trip had been good for him, the weather generally fine, and his journey without incident. The quiet splendor of the lonely woods through which he walked had been a healing balm to a soul hard-used. As was the increasing sense of freedom that had come with each step farther north he took.

Master Belmir had indeed rescued him, along with Uncle Simon and Philip Meridon. They claimed there was no fourth man, and Abramm could hardly argue with them, given his state at the time. They'd taken him halfway across the city by wagon, then transferred him to a secret room beneath the stable of a prominent inn.

For a couple of days they'd tended him there, enough to get him to the point he could walk on his own. One of his arms had been broken and several of his fingers, as well as nearly all his ribs, but his legs, though bruised and abraded, had been spared.

It was during this time that he learned that his efforts had not been in vain. So far as Simon knew, Maddie, Carissa, and Trap had all escaped cleanly. The prisoner's coach had stopped near the river and they'd been hustled out the unlocked back door to a barge that had taken them to a waiting galley, which had then rowed out of the bay under cover of the rain, heading for Chesedh.

Not the slightest hint had been leaked that Abramm had escaped—though Gillard had been made king upon his "death"—which argued for the fact that no admission would be made with respect to his sons, either. His enemies claimed the princes had been killed when taken from the palace, but Abramm was certain that if it were so, his tormentors would have shown him their small, lifeless bodies in their attempts to break him. And likely would have succeeded.

Thus, he chose to believe the boys still lived and, further, that they would soon be—if they were not already—reunited with their mother. As much as it tore at him not to be with them, and not to know for sure, even this much was a comfort.

When he was strong enough, they had set off again through tunnels and caves long compromised to the authorities, but which they managed to negotiate safely nonetheless, eluding the many guards that patrolled those dark reaches and coming at last to the city's edge. From there they'd traveled by night, on foot, to a place just north of the Hennepen, where a horse and cart awaited them, and once more Abramm was forced to ride in the coffinlike space beneath the cart's false bottom.

Eidon was with them on that busy road, for though they were searched at two different checkpoints, the false bottom passed muster. Which could have been due to the fact that it was carrying manure, an arrangement Abramm wasn't sure he would ever forgive his uncle for.

When they crossed the Snowsong, Belmir had left them, not sure what he was going to do but intending to head back up to his old keep and spend some time in solitude and prayer. When they said good-bye, Abramm had given him a Star of Life to take with him, and he had accepted it. He'd stood there rolling the Star between thumb and forefinger for some time before finally tucking it into his satchel with a snort. "At this rate I might never make it to Haverall's Watch."

"I shall pray that you don't," Abramm said with a smile.

Belmir looked up at him, his gaze suddenly intense and troubled. Finally he said, "What you did that night beneath Wetherslea . . . I thought I had seen Eidon before. Thought that I knew him. But after that night . . ." He trailed off, then shook his head. "It is hard to face the fact that one's entire life has been a waste," he said quietly.

"And yet, so long as you live, it's never too late to start afresh and make it count," Abramm had responded.

They had stood there gaze to gaze for a long silent moment, until finally, wordlessly, his old Master turned away and disappeared into the darkness of the night.

Simon had driven the cart northeast out of the populous Kalladorne River Valley and into the rugged wilderness along the Upper Snowsong to a remote hunting lodge. They'd stayed there three months, hunting, fishing, playing uurka, and spending many a night in long conversations that inevitably took a spiritual turn. To Abramm's surprise, Simon had brought copies of Eidon's Words of Revelation, and though he was not as ready as Belmir, there could be no doubt the things he had seen—the things Abramm had endured for his faith—had worked a mighty change in him. He still had a difficult time accepting the Star Abramm offered him, though.

"If nothing else, it keeps the staffid away," Abramm had told him with a grin. "And may even help protect you from the influence of Command or fearspells."

And so Simon had taken it and slipped it into the pocket of his jerkin.

They had heard by then of the High Father's order that Abramm's name be expunged from all the governmental rolls, all the minutes of the meetings, and even from the histories and the genealogical records. The pictures that had been painted of him and of his wife and sons were burned. Her songs were banned and new ones written ascribing his achievements to others. It was now illegal to utter his name in public, and the punishment for dis-obedience included fines, imprisonment, beatings, and even the cutting out of the perpetrator's tongue.

Simon intended to stay behind and work with those who opposed the new age of tyranny, but they both agreed Abramm's appearance was far too conspicuous to blend in with the general populace. Besides that, he had to find his family.

Thus it was that he had left the hunting lodge on foot in midsummer, traveling cross-country and living off the bounty of the land. And that long, lonely walk had been a time almost sacramental—a communing with Eidon in ways he'd never known before, even as it marked his separation from his old life into a new, utterly unknown phase.

And now he had arrived at Highmount as the leaves were just starting to turn in the highest elevations, the pass through the Aranaak still open, though not for long. A wagonload of fellow refugees had arrived just before him, its passengers bound together by the dangers of their shared journey. He was a stranger among them. One looked at askance and with no small bit of wariness. Though he had been alone now for weeks, he had not really felt it, not really been aware of how little he had until now. His walking stick, his sling, and his battered rucksack with its single cup and pan, its water flask and flint, its thin, rolled blanket and two extra pairs of stockings. No guards, no attendants, no friends—not even a name. With his long, full beard and shaggy hair, and the limping, hunch-shouldered gait he affected when he was in company, few looked at him closely enough to notice the scars. And if they had, it would have not mattered, because as Maddie had often said, people saw what they expected to see. And no one expected to see the former king of Kiriath—dead these last five months of burning in the public square of Springerlan, his name expunged from public life and forbidden to be uttered—wandering on foot through the northern woods.

As he watched the others eating, laughing, and talking together, knowing he dare not join in for fear of bringing harm to them, the sense of loneliness became, for a moment, a crushing, almost unbearable weight.

"They will all desert you. . . . There will be none to help you. . . ."

He had not believed it could happen . . . but it had. Some because of betrayal or cowardice, but others had just been taken from him.

Suddenly the room became suffocating, and he went outside. There, his rucksack hanging over one shoulder, his staff in his hand, he walked a circuit of the yard, then climbed to the wallwalk, where a rising wind tugged at his cloak. Wandering along it for a ways, he stopped finally at a point where he could look south, across rolling waves of forest beneath an overcast sky. None of it was his anymore, and yet somehow it still felt as if it were. . . .

Not having heard anyone approach, he was startled when a voice spoke quietly at his shoulder. "That was quite a journey up from the river, wasn't it?"

Abramm glanced at the man who now stood beside him, also looking south, his face hidden behind the edge of his cowl. "It was," he said finally. Even if the stranger had taken him for someone else, they'd both come up from the river.

"I noticed you came in alone, though," the man said. "And on foot."

"Aye." So he hadn't taken Abramm for part of his group after all.

"Takes a lot of courage to walk this life alone. Though you're hardly the first to do it."

"No, I'm not." *And I'm not alone, either, am I, Lord?* He sighed and leaned his forearms on the stone wall. "I've learned long ago, though, that Eidon sees a picture far bigger than we do. We don't see what he sees, but in the end it is always much better than anything we could've planned."

"That is true."

Abramm let his eyes drift over the hills below, pockets of bright yellow jumping out from the green here and there. "I think I will be back here one day. . . ."

"Yes, I think you will be, too."

He looked around, surprised, and the stranger met his gaze, a pair of dark and friendly eyes looking out of his weathered face. And it almost seemed he knew who Abramm was.

"Hey, up there!" called one of the men from the yard. "They say with the wind that's sprung up we'd best leave soon t' thread the pass before it snows. If ye want t' come, ye'd best get yer baggage gathered up."

"Thanks," Abramm called down to him. "I'll do that."

He turned back to the man who had been beside him, but the stranger was already gone.

POSTLUDE

"HE WAS JUST SPOTTED *at Highmount Holding, sir,*" said Vesprit. *"Came in from the forest, alone."*

Hazmul stared through his apartment window at the lantern-lit Grand Fountain courtyard below him. In the gloomy twilight, fine coaches rolled up to the palace entry one after the other to disgorge their satin- and jewel-bedecked passengers, attendees of the annual Harvest Ball. *"So . . . he does* live."

Behind him Vesprit displayed an admirable improvement in masking the vibrations of his uneasiness but was still not adept enough to escape notice.

"You are concerned he might return," Hazmul observed.

Vesprit's uneasiness spiked and was swiftly veiled. *"He has surprised us many times, sir."*

"Perhaps. But he is alone now, and he's suffered much—a suffering which has not ended even yet. And this time he has no friends to help. I do not think he will return."

In the courtyard below, the coaches continued to roll up and then away, King Makepeace's guests filing up the entryway stair in a near continuous line.

Hazmul snorted. *"Even if he does, what will it matter? In a year, maybe two, no one will even remember his name."* He turned to his underling, smiling. *"We have won, Vesprit. Just as I promised."*